FROM THE PAGES OF *NOSTROMO*

In the time of Spanish rule, and for many years afterwards, the town of Sulaco—the luxuriant beauty of the orange gardens bears witness to its antiquity—had never been commercially anything more important than a coasting port with a fairly large local trade in ox-hides and indigo. (page 19)

"This Nostromo, sir, a man absolutely above reproach, became the terror of all the thieves in the town." (page 26)

Mrs. Gould knew the history of the San Tomé mine. Worked in the early days mostly by means of lashes on the backs of slaves, its yield had been paid for in its own weight of human bones. Whole tribes of Indians had perished in the exploitation; and then the mine was abandoned, since with this primitive method it had ceased to make a profitable return, no matter how many corpses were thrown into its maw. (page 56)

Only in the conduct of our action can we find the sense of mastery over the Fates. (page 67)

"The air of the New World seems favourable to the art of declamation." (page 79)

"A sort of Frenchman—godless—a materialist." (page 167)

It was part of what Decoud would have called his sane materialism that he did not believe in the possibility of friendship existing between man and woman. (page 186)

"The ways of human progress are inscrutable." (page 197)

"The silver might have been indeed put on board the lighter, but it was not conceivable that it should have been taken out to sea."

(page 278)

It was simple. A rule of conduct resting mainly on severe rejections is necessarily simple. Dr. Monygham's view of what it behoved him to do was severe; it was an ideal view, in so much that it was the imaginative exaggeration of a correct feeling. It was also, in its force, influence, and persistency, the view of an eminently loyal nature.

(page 302)

Solicited incessantly by the considerations affecting its fears and desires, the human mind turns naturally away from the marvellous side of events.

(page 339)

After three days of waiting for the sight of some human face, Decoud caught himself entertaining a doubt of his own individuality. It had merged into the world of cloud and water, of natural forces and forms of nature. In our activity alone do we find the sustaining illusion of an independent existence as against the whole scheme of things of which we form a helpless part.

(page 393)

The truth of his nature consisted in his capacity for passion and in the sensitiveness of his temperament. What he lacked was the polished callousness of men of the world, the callousness from which springs an easy tolerance for oneself and others; the tolerance wide as poles asunder from true sympathy and human compassion.

(page 410)

Her word was law. He accepted her denial like an inexplicable fatality affirming the victory of Nostromo's genius over his own. Even before that woman, whom he loved with secret devotion, he had been defeated by the magnificent Capataz de Cargadores, the man who had lived his own life on the assumption of unbroken fidelity, rectitude, and courage!

(page 440)

NOSTROMO

Joseph Conrad

With an Introduction and Notes
by Brent Hayes Edwards

George Stade
Consulting Editorial Director

BARNES & NOBLE CLASSICS
NEW YORK

𝓙𝓑

BARNES & NOBLE CLASSICS
NEW YORK

Published by Barnes & Noble Books
122 Fifth Avenue
New York, NY 10011

www.barnesandnoble.com/classics

Nostromo was first published in 1904. The text for this edition is
based on the 1919 edition.

Published in 2004 by Barnes & Noble Classics with new Introduction,
Notes, Biography, Chronology, Comments & Questions,
and For Further Reading.

Nostromo
ISBN 1-59308-193-6
LC Control Number 2003116603

Produced and published in conjunction with:
Fine Creative Media, Inc.
322 Eighth Avenue
New York, NY 10001
Michael J. Fine, President and Publisher

Printed in the United States of America
QM

1 3 5 7 9 10 8 6 4 2
FIRST PRINTING

JOSEPH CONRAD

Józef Teodor Konrad Korzeniowski was born on December 3, 1857, in a Polish province in the Ukraine to parents ardently opposed to the Russian occupation of eastern Poland. From his father, Apollo, Conrad developed a great love of literature, and he read the works of James Fenimore Cooper, Charles Dickens, William Makepeace Thackeray, and Sir Walter Scott in Polish and French translations. After he lost his parents to tuberculosis in 1865 and 1869, Conrad was cared for by his uncle Tadeusz Bobrowski until 1874, when he left for Marseilles to launch a career at sea that would span some twenty years. He joined the British merchant marine in 1878, climbing the ranks and passing his captain's exam in 1886 — the same year he became a British subject. Conrad's many ocean voyages took him all over the world and provided inspiration for his subsequent writing career, but it was his trip up the Congo River on a steamship that left him disenchanted with humanity and that led him to write his seminal work *Heart of Darkness* (1899). Conrad had begun a decade earlier, at age thirty-one, to compose fiction in English, a language he had not learned until he was a young adult. He published his first novel, *Almayer's Folly*, in 1895 under the pen name Joseph Conrad and, encouraged by the literary critic Edward Garnett, then devoted himself to writing. Although he suffered from physical ailments, such as malaria, as well as psychological problems, Conrad nonetheless produced a substantial body of work, including the great novels *Lord Jim* (1900), *Nostromo* (1904), *The Secret Agent* (1907), and *Under Western Eyes* (1911). He is regarded as one of the premier prose stylists and writers of psychological fiction in the English language. He died of a heart attack on August 3, 1924.

TABLE OF CONTENTS

THE WORLD OF JOSEPH CONRAD

AND *NOSTROMO*

1857 Józef Teodor Konrad Korzeniowski is born in a province in the Russian-occupied Ukraine to Polish parents Ewa (née Bobrowska) and patriot, poet, and translator Apollo Korzeniowski.

1861 Apollo is arrested by the Russian authorities for his nationalist activities.

1862 Apollo is released, and the family is exiled to Vologda, Russia.

1865 Conrad's mother dies of tuberculosis. Conrad first experiences English literature through his father's translations of Shakespeare. (His first two languages are Polish and French.)

1869 Conrad's father dies, also of tuberculosis; Conrad is adopted by his maternal uncle, Tadeusz Bobrowski, who lives in Poland. The completion of the Suez Canal effectively links the Mediterranean and Red Seas.

1874 Conrad sets off for Marseilles to become a seaman in the French merchant marine; his first voyage is to Martinique on the *Mont-Blanc*.

1878 An indebted and lovelorn Conrad attempts suicide by shooting himself in the chest. He subsequently signs on with the British merchant navy. Following Henry Morton Stanley's exploration of the region, King Leopold II of Belgium claims ownership of the Congo, founding the Comité d'Études du Haut-Congo (later the Association Internationale du Congo); Leopold takes this action privately, not on behalf of Belgium.

1881 Conrad sails to the Far East on the *Palestine*, a bark of 425 tons. On this two-year voyage, the *Palestine*'s cargo of coal catches fire and must be abandoned. Conrad is forced to navigate an open boat for more than thirteen hours, until finally landing on an island near Sumatra. Conrad will draw on this experience when he writes the story "Youth."

1883	Conrad ships as second mate on the *Riversdale*, then boards the *Narcissus* at Bombay; he will later translate this experience into the novel *Nigger of the "Narcissus."*

1884	Conrad becomes a first mate.

1886	Conrad becomes a British subject and earns his master's certificate from the Board of Trade.

1889	Conrad begins writing *Almayer's Folly*.

1890	Conrad embarks on a four-month voyage along the Congo River on a steamboat. During this period he keeps a diary, which he will later use when he writes *Heart of Darkness*. He returns to Brussels exhausted, ill with malaria, and profoundly disturbed by what he has experienced in the Congo.

1894	Conrad concludes his sea career and begins writing full time. His uncle dies, leaving him £1,600. Conrad begins socializing with a literary circle that includes the critic Edward Garnett, John Galsworthy, Henry James, and Stephen Crane.

1895	Joseph Conrad formally adopts his pen name, and his first novel, *Almayer's Folly*, is published.

1896	Conrad settles permanently in England and marries twenty-two-year-old Jessie George, with whom he will have two sons. His second novel, *An Outcast of the Islands*, is published.

1897	Conrad's novel *The Nigger of the "Narcissus"* is published.

1898	"Youth" is published in the September issue of *Blackwood's Edinburgh Magazine. Tales of Unrest*, his first volume of short stories, is published. The Conrad family moves to Pent Farm, near the coast of Kent, England. Conrad's son Borys is born.

1899	*Heart of Darkness* is published, as *The Heart of Darkness*, in the February, March, and April issues of *Blackwood's Edinburgh Magazine*.

1900	Conrad's novel *Lord Jim* is published.

1901	Conrad collaborates with Ford Madox Ford; the result is *The Inheritors*.

1902	Edward Garnett favorably reviews *Heart of Darkness* upon its initial publication in book form in *Youth: A Narrative; and Two Other Stories*.

1903	Conrad publishes *Typhoon and Other Stories* and *Romance*, his second collaboration with Ford Madox Ford.

1904 Conrad's novel *Nostromo* is published.

1906 Conrad's son John is born.

1907 Conrad's novel *The Secret Agent* is published.

1911 Conrad publishes the novel *Under Western Eyes*, following a nervous breakdown.

1912 Conrad's memoir *A Personal Record* and *'Twixt Land and Sea*, a short-story collection, are published.

1914 Conrad enjoys popular success for the first time as his novel *Chance* becomes a bestseller. World War I erupts during the Conrads' visit to Poland.

1915 Conrad's novel *Victory* is published.

1917 Conrad's novella *The Shadow-Line* is published.

1920–
1921 Collected editions of Conrad's works are published by Doubleday, Page (in America) and Heinemann (in Britain).

1923 Conrad undertakes a reading tour in the United States.

1924 A rheumatic Conrad refuses an offer of knighthood a few months before he succumbs to a fatal heart attack.

1926 Conrad's volume *Last Essays* is posthumously published.

INTRODUCTION

Joseph Conrad called *Nostromo* his "largest canvas," and since its publication in 1904, it has rightfully been considered one of the first great modernist novels in the English language. He also called it an "achievement in mosaic," and in some ways this is the more precise description: for *Nostromo* is not just a single novel, but a stunning orchestration of many novels at once. It is an adventure story, narrating the extraordinary exploits of the courageous Italian sailor of the title; it is a comedy of errors, offering scene after scene of the entire spectrum of human failings, from unmerited arrogance to the self-destruction of the grandest plans; it is a masterful symbolic architecture, as the silver of the San Tomé mine comes to take on a diabolic significance for every character who comes near it; it is a story of hidden treasure; it is a novel of political intrigue, the double-crossing and scheming behind the scenes of monumental historical events; it is the tale of a particular place and people, recounting the violent origins of the Republic of Sulaco; it is a love story, drawing the reader into the courtship between the strong-willed daughter of the aristocracy, Antonia Avellanos, and the skeptic Martin Decoud, the "idle boulevardier" and disillusioned journalist who is driven to action by his passion; it is a novel of imperialism, a many-layered portrait of the effects of European and U.S. intervention in the affairs of a small country in South America. In his "Author's Note" to the 1917 edition (included here), Conrad explains that for him, *Nostromo* marked "a subtle change in the nature of the inspiration [for his writing]," and the novel is important in his oeuvre not only because it is his most ambitious work, but also because it signals the transition between his two most fruitful periods: from his works dealing with European colonialism in Asia and Africa, especially *Lord Jim* (1900) and *Heart of Darkness* (1899), to what are sometimes termed his political novels, stories of revolutionary unrest set mainly in Europe, including *The Secret Agent* (1907) and

Under Western Eyes (1911). For the first time, Conrad attempted in *Nostromo* a novel more of the land than of the sea ("A Tale of the Seaboard," as the subtitle puts it almost wistfully), and a novel only tangentially based on his personal experience as a sailor.

The novel began as a short story, and expanded in length and scope as Conrad worked on it assiduously from December 1902 until August 1904. From the beginning, it was a traumatic enterprise. Conrad had traveled to South America only once in his life, when in 1876, working as a nineteen-year-old steward on the French ship the *Saint-Antoine*, he sailed to the Caribbean, stopping in St.-Pierre in Martinique, Cartagena in Colombia, Puerto Cabello and La Guaira in Venezuela, St. Thomas, and Haiti. He was ashore only briefly in South America: twelve hours in Puerto Cabello, three days in La Guaira. Not surprisingly, when he attempted to draw on his memories of this experience for *Nostromo*, he was not able to dredge up much. As he began working on the book, Conrad wrote to his lifelong friend R. B. Cunninghame Graham, the famous Scottish aristocrat, radical socialist, and accomplished writer who had lived many years in South America, almost shamefacedly asking for help: "I want to talk to you of the work I am engaged on now. I hardly dare avow my audacity—but I am placing it in Sth America in a Republic I call Costaguana" (May 9, 1903, in *Collected Letters*, vol. 3, p. 34; see "For Further Reading"). Cunninghame Graham provided invaluable information to Conrad, but in July 1903, the latter was still writing to say that he was "dying over that cursed *Nostromo* thing. All my memories of Central America seem to slip away. I just had a glimpse 25 years ago—a short glance. That is not enough *pour bâtir un roman dessus* [to build a novel upon]" (July 8, 1903, in *Collected Letters*, vol. 3, p. 45).

Conrad's correspondence of the period is filled with elaborate descriptions of what he termed the "atrocious misery of writing": In one letter to the novelist H. G. Wells, he wrote that he was "absolutely out of my mind with worry and apprehension of my work. I go on as one would cycle over a precipice along a 14 inch plank. If I falter I am lost" (November–December 1903, in *Collected Letters*, vol. 3, p. 80). In his autobiographical *A Personal Record* (1912), describing the composition of *Nostromo*, Conrad would again figuratively describe the writing process as a kind of extreme nautical distress:

Neglecting the common joys of life that fall to the lot of the humblest on this earth, I had, like the prophet of old [Jacob in the Old Testament], "wrestled with the Lord" for my creation, for the headlands of the coast, for the darkness of the Placid Gulf, the light on the snows, the clouds on the sky, and for the breath of life that had to be blown into the shapes of men and woman, of Latin and Saxon, of Jew and Gentile. These are, perhaps, strong words, but it is difficult to characterise otherwise the intimacy and the strain of a creative effort in which mind and will and conscience are engaged to the full, hour after hour, day after day, away from the world, and to the exclusion of all that makes life really lovable and gentle—something for which a material parallel can only be found in the everlasting sombre stress of the westward winter passage round Cape Horn (pp. 98–99).

By December he was calling it a "disastrous year," and moaning, "if I had written each page with my blood I could not feel more exhausted at the end of this twelvemonth" (Conrad to David Meldrum, December 26, 1903, in *Collected Letters*, vol. 3, p. 100). Conrad had reason to worry, because he had agreed to publish the novel in serial form starting in a few weeks. *Nostromo* appeared in *TP's Weekly* from January 29 until October 7, 1904, and Conrad found the regular demands of this pace nearly impossible to meet. The Conrad family was renting lodgings from the novelist Ford Madox Ford during the spring of 1904, and—having already established a close friendship and an (unsuccessful) series of collaborations (including the novels *The Inheritors* in 1901 and *Romance* in 1903) with the younger writer—Conrad was forced to ask Ford to help him keep up with the installments. Ford composed a small section of *Nostromo*: about sixteen manuscript pages of chapter 5 in the second part of the novel. (Ford would also be integral to the composition of Conrad's *The Mirror of the Sea* [1906], and scholars have suggested that he may have written part of *Heart of Darkness* as well.)

If in *Nostromo*, Martin Decoud succumbs to "solitude," his suffering is parallel to the novelist's. In another letter in the summer of 1903, Conrad lamented that "solitude is taking me over: it is absorbing me. I see nothing, I read nothing. It is like being in a tomb which is at the same time a hell where one must write, write, write"

(Conrad to H. D. Davray, August 22, 1903, in *Collected Letters*, vol. 3, p. 51). Although there is little doubt that *Nostromo* cost Conrad a great deal in stress and strain, it should also be added that the melodrama of Conrad's language about the novel's composition is characteristic. As much as any other twentieth-century writer, Conrad had an almost pathological commitment to the notion that the artist has to sweat and struggle for art. Asked for advice by one young American follower, an aspiring novelist, Conrad shot back an intimidating mandate: "Suffering is an attribute, almost a condition of greatness, of devotion, of an altogether self-forgetful sacrifice to that remorseless fidelity to truth of his own sensations, at whatever cost of pain and contumely, which for me is the whole Credo of the artist" (Conrad to Warrington Dawson, June 20, 1913, in *Collected Letters*, vol. 5, p. 239). But the work on *Nostromo* took its toll, with the result that Conrad was never able to feel entirely content with the completion of his masterwork. After finishing the novel in what he called a "half delirious state," in September 1904, he told one friend: "Personally, I am not satisfied. It is something— but not *the* thing I tried for. There is no exultation, none of that temporary sense of achievement which is so soothing. Even the mere feeling of relief at having done with it is wanting. The strain has been too great, has lasted too long" (Conrad to William Rothenstein, September 3, 1904, in *Collected Letters*, vol. 3, p. 163).

As Conrad writes in his "Author's Note," the germ of the novel was a "vagrant anecdote" about a stolen lighter of silver, a story he had heard while a sailor and then forgotten until he encountered it again in a "shabby volume picked up outside a second-hand bookshop." Conrad was a notorious teller of tall tales about himself, and there is no basis in truth to his claim that the novel was based on the "authoritative" source, the "impartial and eloquent *History of Fifty Years of Misrule*" credited to one of the characters in *Nostromo*, "my venerated friend, the late Don José Avellanos." Frederick Karl, in his excellent biography of Conrad, finds this touch (a novel claiming to be based on a fictional history) worthy of the self-referential works of Borges. There is a playful element in the gesture—it highlights the degree to which *Nostromo* is writing based on reading, on the imaginative extrapolation of facts culled from other sources. At the same time, undermining its own foundation, the novel would seem to throw into question the notion of any "authoritative" source, any fully trustworthy single history of a given set of events.

Critics and biographers such as Norman Sherry and Paul Kirschner have provided exhaustive surveys of the literary sources of *Nostromo*. The anecdote of the silver is found in *On Many Seas: The Life and Exploits of a Yankee Sailor* (1897), a memoir by F. B. Williams (pseudonym of Herbert Elliott Hamblen). Williams worked as a seaman on a schooner captained by a "swarthy, piratical-looking fellow" named Nicolo, who bragged that he once stole a boatload shipment of silver from a former employer, the Pacific Mail Steamship Company. Of course, Nostromo is a very different sort of character, and as Conrad recounts in the "Author's Note," the story began to take shape in his mind when he realized that the silver thief had to be entirely different from the "small cheat" Nicolo: "It was only when it dawned upon me that the purloiner of the treasure need not necessarily be a confirmed rogue, that he could be even a man of character, an actor, and possibly a victim in the changing scenes of a revolution, it was only then that I had the first vision of a twilight country which was to become the province of Sulaco." Conrad found inspiration for the character of Nostromo from a Mediterranean sailor he knew as a young man. In fact, the sailor in question, a Corsican named Dominic Cervoni, had been first mate on the *Saint-Antoine*, and had later been close to Conrad in Marseilles. Cervoni may have provided a partial model for other characters in Conrad's work (Peyrol in *The Rover* and Attilio in *Suspense*), and an entire vivid chapter is devoted to him in *The Mirror of the Sea*. In one passage, Conrad writes that

> there was nothing in the world sudden enough to take Dominic unawares. His thick black moustaches, curled every morning with hot tongs by the barber at the corner of the quay, seemed to hide a perpetual smile. But nobody, I believe, had ever seen the true shape of his lips. From the slow, imperturbable gravity of that broad-chested man you would think he had never smiled in his life. In his eyes lurked a look of perfectly remorseless irony, as though he had been provided with an extremely experienced soul; and the slightest distension of his nostrils would give to his bronzed face a look of extraordinary boldness (pp. 162–163).

Although the main contours of the story of *Nostromo* are wholly original, Conrad dipped into a variety of other sources for "local color," especially with regard to details of South American culture, geography, and history. From G. F. Masterman's *Seven Eventful Years in Paraguay* (1869) he drew names of people (Mitchell, Gould, Barrios, Fidanza) and places, elements of the torture of Dr. Monygham, and information for the depiction of the tyrants Guzman Bento and Pedrito Montero. In E. B. Eastwick's *Venezuela* (1868), there appear other names (Higuerota, Sotillo, Amarilla), as well as a description of Puerto Cabello that seems to have shaped the portrait of the Sulaco port in the novel. Alexandre Dumas's 1860 biography of the Italian nationalist Garibaldi were useful for the character of Giorgio Viola, and contain a scene of torture by strappado, the fate that befalls the hide merchant Hirsch. R. F. Burton's *Letters from the Battle-fields of Paraguay* (1870) describes one Don Juan Decoud, the editor of the newspaper *El Liberal*, who seems to provide a model for Martin Decoud—although Conrad clearly also based Decoud on his own brief (and still murky) adventures running guns to Spanish royalists from Marseilles in 1877, and his own suicide attempt in 1878. Place names were lifted from the entire map of Latin America: There is a Sulaco in Honduras, a Zapiga in Chile, a Punta Mala in Panama, an Esmeraldas in Ecuador. As Conrad wrote in a letter to the critic Edmund Gosse in 1918: "The geographical basis is, as you have seen, mainly Venezuela; but there are bits of Mexico in it, and the aspect presented by the mountains appertains in character more to the Chilean seaboard than to any other. The curtain of clouds hangs always over Iquique. The rest of the meteorology belongs to the Gulf of Panama and, generally, to the Western Coast of Mexico as far as Mazatlan" (June 11, 1918, *Collected Letters*, vol. 6, p. 231). He was aiming for allegorical reach in his depiction of imperialism in the Americas, rather than geographic specificity. As he explained to Cunninghame Graham, "Costaguana is meant for a S. American state in general." At the same time, the setting resonates with other contexts as well: Biographer Gustav Morf has argued convincingly in *The Polish Heritage of Joseph Conrad* that Costaguana may be an imagined version of Conrad's native Poland—which had been overrun and dominated for centuries, and eventually divided up in successive treaties (in 1772, 1793, and 1795) among Prussia, Austria, and Russia (Conrad was born and raised in what was then the Ukraine) as much as any Latin American nation.

That *Nostromo* so explicitly flags its literary sources (even fictional ones) is an indication of one of the major themes of the novel. As the critic Edward Said has described it in *Beginnings: Intention and Method*, the novel concerns "man's overambitious intention to author his own world because the world as he finds it is somehow intolerable" (p. 118). In this sense it is not surprising that throughout we are presented not just with a chorus of voices, but also with a variety of written texts. The director of the San Tomé mine, Charles Gould, is first drawn to the mine in reading about it, while a fourteen-year-old student in England, in agonized letters from his father (who is struggling to make the mine functional and profitable in the midst of political unrest and corruption in Costaguana). Even while in England, "the growing youth attained to as close an intimacy with the San Tomé mine as the old man who wrote these plaintive and enraged letters on the other side of the sea." Reading his father's lengthy complaints about the mine nourishes "another form of enchantment" in Charles, a fascination that might be best described as literary. Charles "grew more and more interested in that thing which could provoke such a tumult of words and passion" (p. 61), and his reading is at the root of his self-appointed mission to return to Sulaco and "rehabilitate" the mine that had defeated the efforts of his father. At the urging of the venerated former diplomat, Don José Avellanos, the talented if blasé Martin Decoud becomes a journalist, editing a newspaper called the *Porvenir* intended to "voice the aspirations of the province" (p. 136). Some of the key descriptions of the revolt in Costaguana are found in the letters he writes to his sister in Paris, which are quoted at length in chapter 7 of the second section of the novel. In that passage, the narrative points at this broader theme in *Nostromo*, the compulsion to shape one's own world. Even "in the most sceptical heart," especially in periods of mortal danger or social transformation, "there lurks . . . a desire to leave a correct impression of the feelings, like a light by which the action may be seen when personality is gone, gone where no light of investigation can ever reach the truth which every death takes out of the world" (p. 191).

As the story of a province determined to secede from the Republic of Costaguana in the midst of a civil war, *Nostromo* can also be read as a record of Sulaco's own attempt to author its own narrative, to determine its own destiny. In the very first paragraph of the novel, we are told that the Golfo Placido (Placid Gulf) provides Sulaco an "inviolable sanctuary from the temptations of a trading world," and visitors are continually shocked at how "isolated" life seems in the small port, sheltered by the ocean and by the mountain ranges that surround it. The broad strokes of the story have to do with the intrusion of outside forces—commerce, technology, foreign influence and "interests," grand plans of colonization and extraction—into Sulaco, and the endeavors of a variety of local actors to manage, derail, or appropriate that intrusion. *Nostromo* is a novel about the messiness of modernity, in other words. What in the twentieth century would be called nonalignment or disengagement is not an option in Sulaco, but there is a deadly struggle over the terms of the province's relations with the world around it.

As with the explosives in *Under Western Eyes*, technology in *Nostromo* plays an ambiguous role in Sulaco's negotiation of modernity. Its deliverers lurk at the edges of the novel, spinning plans to link the province to the world (and thereby to increase the speed and efficiency with which its wealth can be extracted). Sir John, the chairman of the railway board who is visiting from London, promises Mrs. Gould that "you shall have more steamers, a railway, a telegraph-cable—a future in the great world" (p. 44). And on the one hand, technology does seem to have a positive impact: For example, the telegraph plays a crucial role in warning the Sulaco elite of the overthrow of Ribiera, and of the incoming invasion from Cayta. Later, the Ribierist defeat of Sotillo's army is possible in part because of the advanced rifles that Decoud has helped to smuggle into Sulaco. On the other hand, though, technology is always also a sign of the loss of autonomy: Modernity extends into the province as something alien, portending enormous upheaval and even a sort of domination. As the fighting begins to break out, "the sparse row of telegraph poles strode obliquely clear of the town, bearing a single, almost invisible wire far into the great *campo* [countryside]—like a slender, vibrating feeler of that progress waiting outside for a moment of peace to enter and twine itself about the weary heart of the land" (pp. 142–143).

This ambiguity is most vividly articulated in the character of Holroyd, the financier from San Francisco who funds the technological modernization of the San Tomé mine. Although he remains in the shadows of the main action of *Nostromo*, Holroyd is one of Conrad's more memorable creations, and one of the most incisive satirical portraits of a capitalist in modern literature. Holroyd, better than any other figure, captures the moment when American robber baron mercantilism first extended its gaze beyond the borders of the United States, insinuating its influence (and increasing its profit margins) in the regions formerly dominated by the European colonial powers. To him, the mine is "a great man's caprice" (p. 78); he has such enormous wealth, and such widely spread holdings, that the far-off San Tomé is "a matter of no great consequence, one way or another" (p. 76). It is a hobby, and yet one which Holroyd approaches with what the chief engineer of the railway terms a nearly "missionary" air (p. 259), finding in it not just spectacular profit but also an "imaginative satisfaction which other minds would get from drama, from art, or from a risky and fascinating sport" (p. 305). At the same time, he is deadly serious about his money, and expects Gould to succeed—and to succeed handsomely. His long speech—it is more of a declamation, as Charles Gould says later to his wife—is one of the more breathtaking passages in the novel. From the view of Holroyd's San Francisco offices, American imperialism is not an ambition, but an impending fact. "Now, what is Costaguana?" he brusquely asks, and answers his own question:

"It is the bottomless pit of ten-per-cent loans and other fool investments. European capital has been flung into it with both hands for years. Not ours, though. . . . Of course, some day we shall step in. We are bound to. But there's no hurry. Time itself has got to wait on the greatest country in the whole of God's Universe. We shall be giving the word for everything: industry, trade, law, journalism, art, politics, and religion, from Cape Horn clear over to Smith's Sound, and beyond, too, if anything worth taking hold of turns up at the North Pole. And then we shall have the leisure to take in hand the outlying islands and continents of the earth. We shall run the world's business whether the world likes it or not. The world can't help it—and neither can we, I guess" (p. 75).

Even as it strives toward independence, Sulaco is being shaped—being "given the word"—in the form of Holroyd's investment in the silver mine, an outside influence that is irresistible in more than one sense.

Time and again, *Nostromo* has been characterized as a particularly challenging novel. In a 1918 essay on Conrad, Virginia Woolf declares curtly that "it is a difficult book to read through" (p. 227). One Conrad biographer, Jacques Berthoud, writes only half-jokingly in *Joseph Conrad: The Major Phase* that the book has gained "some notoriety as a novel that one cannot read unless one has read it before." Without a doubt, *Nostromo* rewards multiple readings: One begins to catch new symbolic connections, new levels of depth and resonance. Part of the issue has to do with what the critic Cedric Watts, in *A Preface to Conrad*, has termed the "problematic mobility" of time and perspective in the novel. *Nostromo* is reminiscent of Tolstoy's *War and Peace* in its historical sweep, but its exposition seems more like works of Faulkner and Joyce written decades later: It is "jumpy, pouncy, twisting" rather than linear and chronological (p. 150). We are faced with a wide cast of characters, many of them multilingual expatriates, and even though the main action of the story (the flight of Nostromo and Decoud with the load of silver, the Montero revolt) takes place in the space of little more than a week, our sense of the events is filled in only gradually, with hindsight, as we get pieces of the tale in the voices of various players, at various times, not just during but also long before and after the main events.

Even the title would seem to be misleading, as Nostromo himself can by no measure be considered the main character of the novel. Nostromo (or to use his given name, Giovanni Battista Fidanza) passes through the narrative—alluded to in Captain Mitchell's self-serving pontifications on the history of Sulaco (an "invaluable fellow," Mitchell says of "his" Capataz: "a man absolutely above reproach"), or stopping briefly by the inn of Giorgio Viola—but he only takes center stage at the end of each of the novel's three parts. Even his name is not his own: *Nostromo* means "boatswain" in Italian (which is the job that brings him to Sulaco, where he eventually decides to stay and take a position as Capataz of the cargo workers of the English shipping company in the port), but it is also

Mitchell's mispronunciation of the Italian *nostro uomo* ("our man"), as Mitchell takes credit for having hired this "prodigy of efficiency in his own sphere of life" (p. 50). The English residents of Sulaco call him Nostromo, but the innkeeper's Italian wife, Teresa Viola (who calls him Gian' Battista), scoffs at the way he accepts "a name that is properly no word from them" (p. 34). Conrad commented in one letter to R. B. Cunninghame Graham that "truly Nostromo is nothing at all,—a fiction, embodied vanity of the sailor kind,—a romantic mouthpiece of the 'people' which (I mean 'the people') frequently experience the very feelings to which he gives utterance. I do not defend him as a creation" (October 31, 1904, *Collected Letters*, vol. 3, p. 175). In 1923 Conrad would remark further that "Nostromo has never been intended for the hero of the Tale of the Seaboard. Silver is the pivot of the moral and material events, affecting the lives of everybody in the tale" (quoted in Norman Sherry, "Introduction," p. viii). Ultimately, the novel is not a tale of heroism revolving around Nostromo's individual exploits, but instead an investigation of the corrupting influence of material wealth both in his life and in Sulaco as a whole.

There has been a great deal of disagreement about the politics of *Nostromo*. Some have characterized it as one of the great anti-imperialist novels, while others have found it lacking in its portrait of the intricacies of international capitalism. Of course, Conrad's work is famous for provoking just these kinds of divisions among its readership. One thinks immediately of *Heart of Darkness*, a fiction that some consider the single most damning critique of European colonialism, while others (most notably the Nigerian novelist Chinua Achebe) castigate it for the overly broad strokes of its portrait of the African "native." *Nostromo* amplifies these questions by offering a much wider tableau of political positions, scattered among a dizzying range of personalities. Nostromo himself is uninterested in the sphere of politics, obsessed instead with the state of his "impeccable" reputation as a Man of the People. This is not to say that he is blind to the forces around him; but his politics seem to go not much further than his endless cynicism. As he lays mortally wounded in the final pages of the book, Emilia Gould tells him that she, too, hates the silver that has placed a wall between her and her husband, and Nostromo erupts sarcastically, "Marvellous!—that one of you should hate the wealth that you know so well how to take from the hands of the poor" (p. 440). But shortly thereafter, this outburst is counterbalanced by a brief and curious scene in which an unnamed character, apparently a leftist radical, visits Nostromo after Mrs. Gould has left. The man, a "pale photographer, small, frail, bloodthirsty, the hater of capitalists," asks the dying Capataz whether he has "any dispositions to make"—any funds to donate to the cause. "Do not forget," he says, "that we want money for our work. The rich must be fought with their own weapons" (p. 441). But Nostromo does not even grace the man's entreaty with an answer. The novel recapitulates this cynicism at every level of its structure. It has no patience with the cruelty and exploitation that inundate the world it describes, but it dismisses any organized solution, much less any revolutionary politics, as inherently debased and equally tainted in the end.

Does *Nostromo* demonstrate any sympathy for the inhabitants of Costaguana? If it is difficult to gauge the attitude toward the Africans in *Heart of Darkness*, then it may be even more perplexing to read *Nostromo*, where the prevailing narrative perspective seems at times to be even more dismissive of everyone except the expatriate elite of Sulaco. Captain Mitchell, exhibiting his scars from the violent uprising after the overthrow of Ribiera, tells a visitor that he had been fighting the "worst kind of nigger out there" (p. 26). Like his fellow Sulaco aristocrats, Don Pepe habitually refers to the "Negro liberal" politicians running the Republic of Costaguana as no more than "thieves, swindlers, and sanguinary *macaques* [monkeys]" (p. 100). The lightermen of the Oceanic Steam Navigation Company are described as "an outcast lot of very mixed blood, mainly Negroes, everlastingly at feud with the other customers of low grog shops in the town" (p. 27). Similarly, the *cargadores* (dockers) commanded by Nostromo are described as "an unruly brotherhood of all sorts of scum" (p. 88), and elsewhere, as "a turbulent body of men, quite apt to raise a tumult" (p. 166). One engineer who temporarily "borrows" Nostromo from the Company to lead a team of workers says admiringly that the Capataz "seems to know how to rule all these muleteers and peons. We had not the slightest trouble with our people" (p. 49).

The innkeeper Giorgio Viola has been a committed nationalist elsewhere (having fought with Garibaldi in Uruguay and in Italy), but has not the slightest sympathy for the masses in Costaguana. "These were not a people striving for justice," he is convinced, "but thieves. Even to defend his life against them was a sort of degradation for a man who had been one of Garibaldi's immortal thousand in the conquest of Sicily. He had an immense scorn for this outbreak of scoundrels and *leperos* [rabble], who did not know the meaning of the word 'liberty' " (p. 32). Aside from the occasional passing policeman on the beat, no Costaguana "native" is allowed to set foot in Viola's inn, which caters to English engineers from the mine and Basque or Italian engine drivers and foremen from the railroad. In the Viola household, his wife spends her time scolding "the squat, thick-legged China girls handling linen, plucking fowls, pounding corn in wooden mortars" (p. 29).

The English family of Charles Gould, although based in Costaguana for three generations, "always went to England for their education and for their wives" (p. 51). The oxymoronic Costaguana Goulds, we learn, are "pure-bred Englishmen, but all born in the country" (p. 77). Because his uncle was put to death ("martyred in the cause of aristocracy") under the vicious former dictator Guzman Bento, Charles Gould is able to draw on key support for the mine from the "first families" of Sulaco, who call themselves Oligarchs or Blancos (that is, the "Whites"), as "families of pure Spanish descent" (p. 52).

As for the mine itself, we are informed matter-of-factly that before the independence of Costaguana, "its yield has been paid for in its own weight of human bones. Whole tribes of Indians had perished in the exploitation; and then the mine was abandoned, since with this primitive method it had ceased to make a profitable return, no matter how many corpses were thrown into its maw" (p. 56). Charles Gould brings technological expertise and modern methods (and, most indispensably, the American finance capital of Holroyd) to the mine, but takes advantage of the same cheap labor pool. To Gould's wife, having come to Sulaco to join her husband in his effort to "rehabilitate" the country by reviving the mine, the Indian workers' "flat, joyless faces . . . looked all alike, as if run into the same ancestral mould of suffering and patience" (p. 92). Emilia Gould considers the stream of revolutions and coups in Costaguana, the "constant 'saving of the country,'" to be no more than "a puerile and bloodthirsty game of murder and rapine played with terrible earnestness by depraved children. In the early days of her Costaguana life, the little lady used to clench her hands with exasperation at not being able to take the public affairs of the country as seriously as the incidental atrocity of methods deserved. She saw in them a comedy of naïve pretences, but hardly anything genuine except her own appalled indignation" (p. 54). As she accommodates herself to life in Sulaco, Mrs. Gould "heroically conceal[s] her dismay at the appearance of men and events so remote from her racial conventions, dismay too deep to be uttered in words even to her husband" (pp. 141–142).

And yet, close attention to the nuances of Conrad's prose reveals that these derogatory generalizations may be more complicated than they seem. When voiced in the narrative itself—that is, when they do not simply capture the prejudices of a particular character (as with Captain Mitchell or Emilia Gould)—they are always carefully tempered. One example is a scene in the second chapter of part Three, set in the Custom House of the Sulaco port. While interrogating Captain Mitchell in hopes of seizing the shipment of silver for the Montero revolution, the rebel leader Sotillo becomes fascinated with Mitchell's watch, a "sixty-guinea gold half-chronometer." Sotillo "became so interested that for an instant he forgot his precious prisoner." Then the narrative extrapolates this fact into a generalization: "There is always something childish in the rapacity of the passionate, clear-minded, Southern races, wanting in the misty idealism of the Northerners, who at the smallest encouragement dream of nothing less than the conquest of the earth" (p. 271). But from what perspective is this observation offered? The sentence is carefully balanced, clearly disparaging of the petty materialism of the South American colonel, yet equally uncharitable to the self-aggrandizing imperialist habits of Europeans such as Mitchell.

Nostromo forces us to look for these subtle modulations of tone. Sometimes they are signaled with no more than a single word, a particular verb tense, a parenthetical digression. Take the passage in chapter 8 of the first part of the novel, describing the positive influence of the San Tomé mine. We are told that on feast days, the impoverished natives had taken up the habit of wearing better quality clothes, bought from the mine storehouse, especially in the traditional colors of the province (green and white). The passage continues with a comment:

> A peaceable *cholo* [Indian] wearing these colours (unusual in Costaguana) was somehow very seldom beaten to within an inch of his life on a charge of disrespect to the town police; neither ran he much risk of being suddenly lassoed on the road by a recruiting party of *lanceros* [government soldiers armed with lances]—a method of voluntary enlistment looked upon as almost legal in the Republic (p. 90).

There is a critique in the sentence, but it is muted, nearly buried. It is only legible behind the basic message—against the grain of the language, as it were. That an Indian dressed this way was "somehow very seldom beaten to within an inch of his life" means, of course, that it had been—and perhaps still is—habitual for Indians to receive such treatment. The word "somehow" is so thoroughly laced with sarcasm that it threatens to slip by unnoticed. One could say the same thing about the words "voluntary" and "almost" at the end of the sentence, in a description of what is clearly forced conscription of the most blatant sort. A few chapters later, there is a similar description of the new soldiers going off to fight under General Barrios against the Montero revolution: "Those *Indios*, only caught the other day, had gone swinging past in double-quick time, like *bersaglieri* [Italian soldiers in the rifle regiment]; they looked well fed, too, and had whole uniforms" (p. 143). There is no explicit protest against forced conscription here, only the tone of feigned surprise that newly enlisted ("only caught the other day") native troops would be so organized and well-outfitted. The sentence demonstrates its contempt for the normal state of things only by marveling at the ways this moment departs from it.

This is to say that *Nostromo* is a special sort of novel about European imperialism, not just because of its setting and date of composition, but also because of its tone. It is Conrad's most sustained investigation of the paradoxes and ramifications of the colonial enterprise, and thus an elaboration of Marlow's well-known statement in *Heart of Darkness* that "the conquest of the earth, which mostly

means the taking it away from those who have a different complexion or slightly flatter noses than ourselves, is not a pretty thing when
you look into it too much. What redeems it is the idea only." But
this observation is given new layers of complexity and depth when
situated in an imaginary Latin America, rather than in the Congo.
Nostromo keeps reminding us of these layers: The Sulaco elite
come to refer to the San Tomé mine with the phrase *imperium in
imperio* (an empire within an empire).

It is important to note that, although there are numerous "proj-
ects" for the "systematic colonization" of the province (p. 106), there
is no single foreign power in the country. The story takes place in
the turbulent years *after* the war of independence (fought against
Spain) that led to the founding of the Republic of Costaguana. *Nostromo* is arguably the first postcolonial novel, in other words. Yet its
main message is that the word postcolonial never means the end of
colonialism. Instead, there are always empires within empires, new
imperial forces slipping into the confusion left by the defeat of the
old, a jumble of colonization schemes that overlap and compete,
even in—especially in, one might say more accurately—countries
that have recently achieved independence. It is worth recalling that
the Goulds, exemplars of the new material interests, live in an "old
Spanish house." The novel seems thus to offer not a narrative of historical progression, but a palimpsest, informed by Emilia Gould's
insight that life "must contain the care of the past and of the future
in every passing moment of the present" (p. 410). "What redeems it
is the idea only," perhaps, but in *Nostromo* there are many "ideas" of
conquest, of effective action in the world, and the novel puts them
into tense juxtaposition. In Sulaco, the various imperial ideas trans-
form, inhibit, or complement each other as they are carried out.

Nostromo is also unusual in that it focuses, like almost all of Conrad's fiction, on a particular class of actors: Neither politician nor ple-
beian, neither socialist nor monarchist, but people in a given
historical situation who don't quite fit with their times, and who thus
best indicate the ways that society is being transformed. We are introduced to outcasts, exiles, expatriates, fallen heroes, old soldiers, former diplomats, midlevel functionaries, inspired dilettantes, inveterate
skeptics. There is a reason, in other words, that this novel is not titled something like *Costaguana* (as Conrad's friend Cunninghame

Graham argued it should have been called), or *The Gould Conces-sion*, or even *Imperium in Imperio*. Above all else, Conrad is inter-ested in the unique human characters who are forged in what he calls (in his "Author's Note") "the changing scenes of a revolution" in a "twilight country." Interestingly, Conrad singles out "Antonia the Aristocrat and Nostromo the Man of the People" as what he terms "the artisans of the New Era, the true creators of the New State." Nostromo is the "universal factotum," the infallible man tal-ented and bold enough to carry out any mission, the sole force working for the "material interests" who can control the more com-bustible elements of the labor pool—at every turn, he is the indis-pensable lubricant of the wheels of modernity in the Sulaco province. Nostromo is both a harbinger and a facilitator of radical change; Decoud calls him the "active usher-in of the material im-plements for our progress" (pp. 161–162).

Cedric Watts has noted the irony of Nostromo's given name, Giovanni Battista (that is, "John the Baptist"): "John the Baptist prepared the way for Jesus Christ and was thus the inaugurator of the Christian era; Nostromo prepares the way for the control of Su-laco by the economic imperialists and is thus an inaugurator of its capitalistic era" (Watts, *A Preface to Conrad*, p. 195). Antonia Avel-lanos, on the other hand, is an aristocrat, and yet she stands out from the rest of the Sulaco elite, with her burning patriotism, her English education, her stubborn intelligence, her "unfeminine" self-assertiveness, her grave manner, her precocious maturity. Only she is able to inspire the "trifler" Decoud out of his indolence and skepticism. With both of these "artisans," *Nostromo* draws our at-tention to the edges of society, to its interstices rather than its center.

The novel does not consider figures such as Nostromo and Anto-nia in isolation. It charts their participation in the "changing scenes" of the Montero uprising and the Sulaco counterrevolution. Disturbingly, the narrative gives us the sensation of watching the events unfold from the "wrong" side, as it were: not from the per-spective of the Monterists (a popular uprising against the oppres-sion of the "President-Dictator" Ribiera), but from the vantage of the threatened elite desperate to keep Ribiera in power. The calcu-lating and single-minded Charles Gould, having helped to install Ribiera in the hope of ensuring the stability of the country (so that nothing will disrupt the accelerated production of the San Tomé mine), uses the "weapon" of the mine's wealth to support the President-Dictator's cause, while Don José Avellanos and the rest of the Sulaco elite complain loudly about the Montero movement's "Negro Liberalism" and its "atrocious calumnies" against Ribiera and the Blancos (p. 137). On the other side, Montero has "declared the national honour sold to foreigners," charging that Ribiera, "by his weak compliance with the demands of the European powers—for the settlement of long outstanding money claims—had showed himself unfit to rule" (p. 126).

In chapter 5 of the second part of *Nostromo*, there occurs one of the most extraordinary passages in the novel, as Martin Decoud and Antonia Avellanos seduce each other in conversation and debate, her independent-mindedness and national pride wrestling his skepticism and disillusionment—in cautious struggle, in carefully restrained passion—into a peculiar alliance. Without "patriotic illusions" but with the "supreme illusion of a lover," as he puts it (p. 160), Decoud begins to formulate his plans for Sulacan independence under Antonia's influence. Delicately, Conrad sets this conversation in whispers, at the edge of an informal party the Goulds are hosting for the Sulaco elite. Antonia opens and shuts her fan as she and Martin lean close together on the balcony of the *sala*, their growing intimacy emphasized by their "comparative isolation" from the animated discussion of the rest of the group. The brilliance of the scene resides in part in the contrast between their dialogue, intermittently reported in the narrative, and the "political tide" among the rest of the guests. In attendance are not only the Sulaco aristocracy, such as the priest Corbelán and Antonia's father Don José, but also a motley crew of would-be colonizers: the representatives of what Decoud acidly refers to as "our friends, the speculators" (p. 149). They include the English chief engineer of the railroad, as well as a Dane, a couple of Frenchmen, and some Germans, among them the hide merchant Hirsch (who three chapters later, somewhat surprisingly, will provide some comic if pitiful relief in the pivotal scene with the silver). These men are advance scouts for European finance capital. Gould's home is the center of Sulaco for these men, "paying their court" to the "King of Sulaco" (as the inhabitants have come to call Gould), because he is for them the "visible sign of the stability that could be achieved on the shifting ground of revolutions" (p. 163). In other words, the Monterist rebels are not exactly mistaken about the influence of foreigners; and indeed, it is precisely Gould's mine that has opened the country to the ambitions of a host of other "material interests." Even as Antonia and Martin touch elbows, in partial seclusion, discussing the future of Sulaco and winning each other's hearts, the bright, loud room next to them is bustling with the excitement of another sort of conquest. The layout of the scene repeats in miniature the symbolic geography of the country: a small, quiet passion, poised at the threshold of the "great gust" that would overwhelm and crush it.

Charles Gould says to his wife that he doesn't know whether Holroyd's pronouncements about the coming U.S. domination of the globe are "the voice of destiny or simply a bit of clap-trap eloquence" (p. 79). But *Nostromo* gives a partial answer in its closing pages, when a naval demonstration in the harbor by the U.S. cruiser, *Powhattan,* is in fact the show of force that brings an end to the Costaguana-Sulaco War (p. 385). As Captain Mitchell reports boastfully, the United States is "the first great power to recognize the Occidental Republic" of Sulaco (p. 384). This scene gives us a clue to the other main historical reference point for *Nostromo.* The book echoes not just the history of South America in the last decades of the nineteenth century (the period in which it is set), but also the moment in which Conrad is writing the novel. Until 1903 Panama was a part of Colombia, separated from the rest of the country by a mountain range. The United States, along with its European allies, incited separatist movements in what was then called Colombia's "Occidental Province"—the first stirrings of what eventually became the independent republic of Panama (which declared its independence on November 3, 1903). Of course, the ultimate goal of the United States was the expansion of trade through the construction of the Panama Canal, which was finally completed under U.S. direction in 1914. Conrad was certainly aware of these developments. On December 26, 1903, he wrote a letter to Cunninghame Graham mocking American imperialist pretensions in the region: "And à propos what do you think of the Yankee Conquistadores in Panamá? Pretty, isn't it?" (*Collected Letters,* vol. 3, p. 102).

Conrad must have relished the irony of a "Western" independence struggle set in the shadow of an emerging Western domination (recall that the provincials of Sulaco refer to themselves pridefully as "Occidentals"). His choice of a name for his imaginary South American country may hold some of the same irony. In "Costa-guana," some scholars have identified a hint of geographic specificity: The action of the book, for instance, is basically set in the region (covering the countries of Panama, Colombia, and Venezuela) between the nations of *Costa* Rica on one side and British *Guiana* (now Guyana) on the other. Others have considered the name to be a reference to *guano*; Cedric Watts notes that *guano* is an indigenous term for a palm tree, and suggests that Costaguana might be most accurately translated as "Palm Coast" (he reminds us that the national flag of Costaguana is "diagonal red and yellow, with two green palm trees in the middle" [p. 109]; see Watts, *A Preface to Conrad*, p. 107). Still others have drawn a connection to a more common meaning of *guano*: the manure of seabirds that is found in large quantities on the Pacific coast of South America. One might then render the name of the country as "Guano Coast."

There are reasons to pause over the term *guano*. In *Lord Jim* (the novel Conrad published before *Nostromo*), Marlow encounters a West Australian sailor named Chester (based on a well-known historical figure of Conrad's time) who "had discovered—so he said—a guano island somewhere," and who hopes to hire Jim to oversee the laborers he plans to hire to extract it. "As good as a gold-mine," Chester exclaims. Guano is unusual excrement, that is, in that in the nineteenth century it was widely used as a fertilizer due to its rich concentration of nitrogen and phosphate. The major importer of guano was the United States, where it in fact became the first commercial fertilizer. By 1860, more than 400,000 tons per year were being brought in from South America, especially from islands off the coast of Peru. Newspapers of the period described the "guano mania" that had infected American farmers; the fertilizer was called "a blessing to the nation" and extolled as a substance more valuable than all the gold in California. There were even popular rumors that guano possessed "magical" powers to stimulate growth and regeneration. Some historians have given the guano craze especial importance in the emergence of U.S. imperial ambitions, since it provoked legislation such as the Guano Islands Act (1856), which gave American entrepreneurs the right to claim any guano-covered island "in the name of the United States."

The best-known literary response to these developments may be Herman Melville's remarkable anti-imperialist story "The Encantadas," but we might hear in Conrad's "Costaguana" another, more oblique reference to the history of guano in the expansion of commerce. Guano itself plays no direct role in *Nostromo*. Indeed, we are informed that "the sea-birds of the gulf shun the Isabels," the three small islands where the silver is hidden, and prefer to nest on the "stony levels and chasms" of the Azuera peninsula (p. 392). But we should recall that the novel opens with a legend set on the Azuera, which the common people believe holds a "cursed" treasure of its own, "heaps of shining gold" that once trapped two wandering sailors (white foreigners: "*gringos* of some sort"). They are said to haunt the Azuera's crevices and precipices, unable to find their way out, "under the fatal spell of their success" (p. 20); in other words, the novel begins by linking seabirds, treasure, and malediction. The Azuera resounds with the birds' "wild and tumultuous clamour as if they were for ever quarrelling over the legendary treasure" (p. 393).

If in the name "Costaguana" we hear the echo of guano, it serves to remind us of the ways that in *Nostromo*, wealth is also waste. That the treasure in the novel is silver rather than guano actually serves to accentuate this point, since as a raw material, silver does not even possess the agricultural usefulness of guano. One might say that it is less than bird droppings. But when conjured with value and coveted by the "material interests" of human beings, silver becomes a terrible force that obsesses and drags down all who put their hands on it. "There is something accursed in wealth," as Nostromo succinctly phrases it (p. 440). That is, as "incorruptible" as the metal may be, its metaphorical stench and stain are unavoidable: As even Charles Gould realizes, it is impossible to "disentangle one's activity from its debasing contacts," to keep the mining operations outside the "close-meshed net of crime and corruption" in the whole country (p. 291). In Costaguana, a treasure is always a curse.

If so, we might be tempted to ask just how deep Conrad's pessimism runs. Does *Nostromo* provide any possibility of hope, any vision of a future beyond degradation and oppression? In fact, this is one of the central questions asked by the novel itself. How is hope justified? On what basis can one imagine a different future, radical change? Does one's idea of a better future (of justice, of equality, of retribution, of peace) justify one's action in the world, or is an attempt to realize an idea always necessarily a perversion or a debasement of that inspiration? This theme is introduced most powerfully in one of the last letters Charles Gould receives from his father, in which the elder Gould despairs about Latin America that "God looked wrathfully at these countries, or else He would let some ray of hope fall through a rift in the appalling darkness of intrigue, bloodshed, and crime that hung over the Queen of Continents" (p. 80). Gould's answer is the mine itself: He finds hope in the pursuit of "material interests," as he announces to his wife in one of the most famous passages in the novel:

> "What is wanted here is law, good faith, order, security. Anyone can declaim about these things, but I pin my faith to material interests. Only let the material interests once get a firm footing, and they are bound to impose the conditions on which alone they can continue to exist. That's how your money-making is justified here in the face of lawlessness and disorder. It is justified because the security which it demands must be shared with an oppressed people. A better justice will come afterwards. That's your ray of hope" (p. 80).

The San Tomé mine, Gould continues, will become "that little rift in the darkness which poor Father despaired of ever seeing."

In a sense, all of *Nostromo* is designed to put this proposition to the test. It is one of the reasons that the novel is so relevant to us today: With astounding prescience, it questions one of the key assertions behind a great deal of present-day action in the sphere of international affairs, particularly by those capitalists who claim to intervene in other countries in order to bring the "universal" values of democracy. Can the pursuit of material wealth, especially in countries emerging from colonial domination, lead to a "ray of hope," to the propagation of law, good faith, order, security? Is the pressure of market capitalism—the endless demand for a higher rate of return—itself enough to "impose the conditions" of a "better justice"?

In an important 1951 essay on the novel, Robert Penn Warren contends memorably that there is indeed grounds for measured hope: "There has been a civil war but the forces of 'progress'—i.e., the San Tomé mine and the capitalistic order—have won. And we must admit that the society at the end of the book is preferable to that at the beginning" (p. xxix). It seems hard, though, to discover the justification of such a "preference" in the novel itself. Instead, at length, in excruciating detail, *Nostromo* refutes Charles Gould's argument, showing at every turn the perverse impact of material interests (symbolized in the increasingly fetishized silver) on every segment of Sulaco society. The most articulate riposte is given by Monygham, the damaged, embittered, universally mistrusted doctor who in the end plays a crucial, even heroic, role in deceiving Sotillo as he searches for the treasure. Monygham says to Emilia Gould:

> "There is no peace and no rest in the development of material interests. They have their law, and their justice. But it is founded on expediency, and is inhuman; it is without rectitude, without the continuity and force that can be found only in a moral principle. Mrs. Gould, the time approaches when all that the Gould Concession stands for shall weigh as heavily upon the people as the barbarism, cruelty, and misrule of a few years back" (p. 403).

Echoing this counterargument, Mrs. Gould comes to the realization at the end of the same chapter that "there was something inherent in the necessities of successful action which carried with it the moral degradation of the idea. She saw the San Tomé mountain hanging over the Campo, over the whole land, feared, hated, wealthy; more soulless than any tyrant, more pitiless and autocratic than the worst Government; ready to crush innumerable lives in the expansion of its greatness" (p. 411). Even Charles Gould himself, holding onto his idealist notion of using the "weapon" of the mine "in the defence of the commonest decencies of organized society," comes to recognize the fallibility of that "weapon of wealth, double-edged with the cupidity and misery of mankind, steeped in all the vices of self-indulgence as in a concoction of poisonous roots, tainting the very cause for which it is drawn, always ready to turn

awkwardly in the hand" (p. 294). None of these counterarguments
is triumphant, however. Indeed, part of what is excruciating in *Nostromo* is its drawn-out investigation of the irreversible effects of material interests on the marriage of the Goulds. These effects are
irreversible, Emilia realizes: She has lost her husband to San Tomé,
to the "energetic concentration of a will haunted by a fixed idea."
And the narrative allows no redress, no release from his obsession:
"A man haunted by a fixed idea is insane. He is dangerous even if
that idea is an idea of justice" (p. 305). In other words, the attempt
to link market capitalism, in the form of the "material interests" that
coalesce around the silver, to the achievement of a "better justice"
is treacherous, a fixation that threatens to have precisely the opposite effect.

The difficulty is that *Nostromo* is resolute and unsentimental in
its refusal to provide the grounds of a "ray of hope." It gives no inti-
mation of a better or proper solution, even through what Monygham
calls "a moral principle." This has led some to charge that the novel
is, as the biographer Jocelyn Baines has put it, "a monument to futility," in a phrase that alludes to Decoud's declaration in the book that
"there is a curse of futility upon our character" (p. 146). Throughout
the novel, it would seem, human endeavors are destined to fail. As
we are told, "action is consolatory. It is the enemy of thought and the
friend of flattering illusions. Only in the conduct of our action can
we find the sense of mastery over the Fates" (p. 67). But in the words
of Mrs. Gould, "there was something inherent in the necessities of
successful action which carried with it the moral degradation of the
idea." One finds this point repeated in the destinies of all the main
characters. Nostromo, held in bondage by the silver that he has secretly kept for himself, is killed by Viola in a stupid case of mistaken
identity. At the same time—given that he is dressed in his old Capataz uniform, and mistaken for his bold, young protégé, Ramirez
(who has replaced him as Capataz, and who like Nostromo has designs on Viola's daughter)—one might say conversely that Nostromo
is killed because he is misrecognized as himself. Always a man for
others, cultivating the image others have of him at the expense of
any devotion to sentiment or principle, Nostromo dies when he is
taken for his own image. With a different irony but the same futility,

Martin Decoud—a "man with a passion, but without a mission," as he tells his sister (p. 203)—commits suicide, abandoned alone with the silver at the very moment when his own idea (an independent Sulaco) is coming to fruition in the port. He dies in despair, out of "solitude and want of faith in himself and others" (p. 392), in the one situation where his gifts cannot help him survive, where what he needs is the one thing—faith—he does not have: "Both his intelligence and his passion were swallowed up easily in this great unbroken solitude of waiting without faith" (p. 394). Even Mrs. Gould, the "good fairy" of *Nostromo*, the empathetic and virtuous woman who some have considered the only redeemed character in the novel, ends up "weary with a long career of well-doing, touched by the withering suspicion of the uselessness of her labours, the powerlessness of her magic" (p. 410).

Conrad's most extended statement on action and futility is found in a letter that precedes the composition of *Nostromo* by a few years. Writing in January 1898, he argues that

> Into the noblest cause men manage to put something of their baseness. . . . Every cause is tainted: and you reject this one, espouse that other one as if one were evil and the other good while the same evil you hate is in both, but disguised in different words. . . . Alas! What you want to reform are not institutions—it is human nature. Your faith will never move that mountain. Not that I think mankind intrinsically bad. It is only silly and cowardly. Now *You* know that in cowardice is every evil—especially that cruelty so characteristic of our civilization. But without it, mankind would vanish. No great matter truly. . . . I belong to the wretched gang. We all belong to it. We are born initiated, and succeeding generations clutch the inheritance of fear and brutality without a thought, without a doubt, without compunction—in the name of God (Conrad to R. B. Cunninghame Graham, January 23, 1898, in *Collected Letters*, vol. 2, p. 25).

A pessimistic vision, surely, and yet Conrad seems to pitch it more as a kind of realistic refusal of boundless optimism, a cold-eyed understanding of "human nature" that still never becomes paralyzing. In a later essay titled "Books," he considers the role of the artist,

particularly in terms of modern fiction: "What one feels so hopelessly barren in declared pessimism is just its arrogance. It seems as
if the discovery made by many men at various times that there is
much evil in the world were a source of proud and unholy joy unto
some of the modern writers. That frame of mind is not the proper
one in which to approach seriously the art of fiction" (p. 8). Conrad's conclusion in the essay is perhaps his most telling statement
on the subject: "To be hopeful in an artistic sense it is not necessary
to think that the world is good. It is enough to believe that there is
no impossibility of its being made so" (p. 9).

Nostromo thus leaves us in a "great land of plain and mountain
and people, suffering and mute, waiting for the future in a pathetic
immobility of patience" (p. 83). We are not granted a road map (or
a sea chart) of that future, but neither are we denied its arrival, end-
lessly deferred into the *Porvenir* (the unknowable shape of what is
"to come"), in the title of Decoud's newspaper. In the celebrated
preface to *The Nigger of the "Narcissus"* (1897), Conrad argues that
the task of fiction is, "by the power of the written word to make you
hear, to make you feel—it is, before all, to make you *see*. That—
and no more, and it is everything." Yet *Nostromo*, in embodying this
dictum, also transforms it. This novel makes its appeal to our temperament by aiming instead to make us *hear*: by striving for what
Conrad in the same preface calls "the magic suggestiveness of music—which is the art of arts." If the book is panoramic in its description of Sulaco, it is just as strikingly polyphonic, straining to
capture the range of sounds that seem best to record the "changing
scenes" of a turbulent time: the birds' clamor on the Azuera; the
"explosive noise" of the railway; the parrot in the Gould reception
room crying *Viva Costaguana!*; the clattering of the silver ore tumbling down the mine shoots; Nostromo's silver whistle, with which
he calls his *cargadores*; the sound of the church bell in the town
square; the hiss and rustle of Sotillo's steamer as it creeps into the
gulf; the "ironical and senseless buzzing" that drives Decoud to despair on the Great Isabel; and most memorably, the "great cry" of
Linda Viola when she learns of Nostromo's death, that "true cry of
undying passion that seemed to ring aloud from Punta Mala to
Azuera and away to the bright line of the horizon" (p. 444). In the

words of Decoud, marveling at the thunder of a passing train, in *Nostromo* it is sound, above all, that "puts a new edge on a very old truth" (p. 148).

Brent Hayes Edwards is Associate Professor in the Department of English at Rutgers University. He is the author of *The Practice of Diaspora: Literature, Translation, and the Rise of Black Internationalism* (Harvard University Press, 2003) and of numerous articles on twentieth-century African-American literature, contemporary poetry, Francophone Caribbean literature, surrealism, and jazz. He is coeditor of the anthology *Uptown Conversation: The New Jazz Studies* (Columbia University Press, 2004). He is an accomplished translator; his versions of works by Jacques Derrida, Jean Baudrillard, Edouard Glissant, Monchoachi, and Sony Labou Tansi have been published widely. He is coeditor of the journal *Social Text* and serves on the editorial boards of *Transition* and *Callaloo*.

NOSTROMO

To
John Galsworthy

"So foul a sky
clears not
without a storm"
—WILLIAM SHAKESPEARE

CONTENTS

AUTHOR'S NOTE

NOSTROMO IS THE MOST anxiously meditated of the longer novels which belong to the period following upon the publication of the *Typhoon* volume of short stories.

I don't mean to say that I became then conscious of any impending change in my mentality and in my attitude toward the tasks of my writing life. And perhaps there was never any change, except in that mysterious, extraneous thing which has nothing to do with the theories of art; a subtle change in the nature of the inspiration; a phenomenon for which I can not in any way be held responsible. What, however, did cause me some concern was that after finishing the last story of the *Typhoon* volume it seemed somehow that there was nothing more in the world to write about.

This so strangely negative but disturbing mood lasted some little time; and then, as with many of my longer stories, the first hint for *Nostromo* came to me in the shape of a vagrant anecdote completely destitute of valuable details.

As a matter of fact in 1875 or '76, when very young, in the West Indies or rather in the Gulf of Mexico, for my contacts with land were short, few, and fleeting, I heard the story of some man who was supposed to have stolen single-handed a whole lighterful of silver, somewhere on the Tierra Firme seaboard during the troubles of a revolution.

On the face of it this was something of a feat. But I heard no details, and having no particular interest in crime *qua* crime I was not likely to keep that one in mind. And I forgot it till twenty-six or -seven years afterwards I came upon the very thing in a shabby volume picked up outside a secondhand bookshop. It was the life story of an American seaman written by himself with the assistance of a journalist. In the course of his wanderings that American sailor worked for some months on board a schooner, the master and owner of which was the thief of whom I had heard in my very young days.

9

I have no doubt of that because there could hardly have been two exploits of that peculiar kind in the same part of the world and both connected with a South American revolution.

The fellow had actually managed to steal a lighter with silver, and this, it seems, only because he was implicitly trusted by his employers, who must have been singularly poor judges of character. In the sailor's story he is represented as an unmitigated rascal, a small cheat, stupidly ferocious, morose, of mean appearance, and altogether unworthy of the greatness this opportunity had thrust upon him. What was interesting was that he would boast of it openly.

He used to say: "People think I make a lot of money in this schooner of mine. But that is nothing. I don't care for that. Now and then I go away quietly and lift a bar of silver. I must get rich slowly— you understand."

There was also another curious point about the man. Once in the course of some quarrel the sailor threatened him: "What's to prevent me reporting ashore what you have told me about that silver?"

The cynical ruffian was not alarmed in the least. He actually laughed. "You fool, if you dare talk like that on shore about me you will get a knife stuck in your back. Every man, woman, and child in that port is my friend. And who's to prove the lighter wasn't sunk? I didn't show you where the silver is hidden. Did I? So you know nothing. And suppose I lied? Eh?"

Ultimately the sailor, disgusted with the sordid meanness of that impenitent thief, deserted from the schooner. The whole episode takes about three pages of his autobiography. Nothing to speak of; but as I looked them over, the curious confirmation of the few casual words heard in my early youth evoked the memories of that distant time when everything was so fresh, so surprising, so venturesome, so interesting; bits of strange coasts under the stars, shadows of hills in the sunshine, men's passions in the dusk, gossip half-forgotten, faces grown dim. . . . Perhaps, perhaps, there still was in the world something to write about. Yet I did not see anything at first in the mere story. A rascal steals a large parcel of a valuable commodity—so people say. It's either true or untrue; and in any case it has no value in itself. To invent a circumstantial account of the robbery did not appeal to me, because my talents not running that way I did not think that the game was worth the candle. It was only when it dawned upon me that the purloiner of the treasure need not necessarily be a confirmed rogue, that he could be even a man of character, an actor, and possibly a victim in the changing scenes of a revolution, it was only then that I had the first vision of a twilight country which was to become the province of Sulaco, with its high shadowy Sierra and its misty Campo for mute witnesses of events flowing from the passions of men short-sighted in good and evil.

Such are in very truth the obscure origins of *Nostromo*—the book. From that moment, I suppose, it had to be. Yet even then I hesitated, as if warned by the instinct of self-preservation from venturing on a distant and toilsome journey into a land full of intrigues and revolutions. But it had to be done.

It took the best part of the years 1903–4 to do; with many intervals of renewed hesitation, lest I should lose myself in the ever-enlarging vistas opening before me as I progressed deeper in my knowledge of the country. Often, also, when I had thought myself to a standstill over the tangled-up affairs of the Republic, I would, figuratively speaking, pack my bag, rush away from Sulaco for a change of air, and write a few pages of *The Mirror of the Sea*. But generally, as I've said before, my sojourn on the continent of Latin America, famed for its hospitality, lasted for about two years. On my return I found (speaking somewhat in the style of Captain Gulliver) my family all well, my wife heartily glad to learn that the fuss was all over, and our small boy considerably grown during my absence.

My principal authority for the history of Costaguana is, of course, my venerated friend, the late Don José Avellanos, Minister to the Courts of England and Spain, etc., etc., in his impartial and eloquent *History of Fifty Years of Misrule*. That work was never published—the reader will discover why—and I am in fact the only person in the world possessed of its contents. I have mastered them in not a few hours of earnest meditation, and I hope that my accuracy will be trusted. In justice to myself, and to allay the fears of prospective readers, I beg to point out that the few historical allusions are never dragged in for the sake of parading my unique erudition, but that each of them is closely related to actuality; either throwing a light on the nature of current events or affecting directly the fortunes of the people of whom I speak.

As to their own histories I have tried to set them down, Aristocracy and People, men and women, Latin and Anglo-Saxon, bandit and politician, with as cool a hand as was possible in the heat and clash of my own conflicting emotions. And after all this is also the story of their conflicts. It is for the reader to say how far they are deserving of interest in their actions and in the secret purposes of their hearts revealed in the bitter necessities of the time. I confess that, for me, that time is the time of firm friendships and unforgotten hospitalities. And in my gratitude I must mention here Mrs. Gould, "the first lady of Sulaco," whom we may safely leave to the secret devotion of Dr. Monygham, and Charles Gould, the Idealist-creator of Material Interests whom we must leave to his Mine—from which there is no escape in this world.

About Nostromo, the second of the two racially and socially contrasted men, both captured by the silver of the San Tomé Mine, I feel bound to say something more.

I did not hesitate to make that central figure an Italian. First of all the thing is perfectly credible: Italians were swarming into the Occidental Province at the time, as anybody who will read further can see; and secondly, there was no one who could stand so well by the side of Giorgio Viola, the Garibaldino, the Idealist of the old, humanitarian revolutions. For myself I needed there a man of the People as free as possible from his class-conventions and all settled modes of thinking. This is not a side-snarl at conventions. My reasons were not moral but artistic. Had he been an Anglo-Saxon he would have tried to get into local politics. But Nostromo does not aspire to be a leader in a personal game. He does not want to raise himself above the mass. He is content to feel himself a power—within the People.

But mainly Nostromo is what he is because I received the inspiration for him in my early days from a Mediterranean sailor. Those who have read certain pages of mine will see at once what I mean when I say that Dominic, the *padrone* of the *Tremolino*, might under given circumstances have been a Nostromo. At any rate Dominic would have understood the younger man perfectly—if scornfully. He and I were engaged together in a rather absurd adventure, but the absurdity does not matter. It is a real satisfaction to think that in my very young days there must, after all, have been something in me worthy to command that man's half-bitter fidelity, his half-ironic devotion. Many of Nostromo's speeches I have heard first in Dominic's voice. His hand on the tiller and his fearless eyes roaming the horizon from within the monkish hood shadowing his face, he would utter the usual exordium of his remorseless wisdom: "*Vous autres gentilhommes!*" in a caustic tone that hangs on my ear yet. Like Nostromo! "You *hombres finos!*" Very much like Nostromo. But Dominic the Corsican nursed a certain pride of ancestry from which my Nostromo is free; for Nostromo's lineage had to be more ancient still. He is a man with the weight of countless generations behind him and no parentage to boast of. . . . Like the People.

In his firm grip on the earth he inherits, in his improvidence and generosity, in his lavishness with his gifts, in his manly vanity, in the obscure sense of his greatness, and in his faithful devotion with something despairing as well as desperate in its impulses, he is a Man of the People, their very own unenvious force, disdaining to lead but ruling from within. Years afterwards, grown older as the famous Captain Fidanza, with a stake in the country, going about his many affairs followed by respectful glances in the modernized streets of Sulaco, calling on the widow of the *cargador*, attending the Lodge, listening in unmoved silence to anarchist speeches at the meeting, the enigmatical patron of the new revolutionary agitation, the trusted, the wealthy comrade Fidanza with the knowledge of his moral ruin locked up in his breast, he remains essentially a Man of the People. In his mingled love and scorn of life and in the bewildered conviction of having been betrayed, of dying betrayed he hardly knows by what or by whom, he is still of the People, their undoubted Great Man—with a private history of his own.

One more figure of those stirring times I would like to mention: and that is Antonia Avellanos—the "beautiful Antonia." Whether she is a possible variation of Latin-American girlhood I wouldn't dare to affirm. But, for me, she *is*. Always a little in the background by the side of her father (my venerated friend) I hope she has yet relief enough to make intelligible what I am going to say. Of all the people who had seen with me the birth of the Occidental Republic, she is the only one who has kept in my memory the aspect of continued life. Antonia the Aristocrat and Nostromo the Man of the People are the artisans of the New Era, the true creators of the New State; he by his legendary and daring feat, she, like a woman, simply by the force of what she is: the only being capable of inspiring a sincere passion in the heart of a trifler.

If anything could induce me to revisit Sulaco (I should hate to see all these changes) it would be Antonia. And the true reason for that—why not be frank about it?—the true reason is that I have modeled her on my first love. How we, a band of tallish schoolboys, the chums of her two brothers, how we used to look up to that girl just out of the schoolroom herself, as the standard-bearer of a faith to which we all were born but which she alone knew how to hold aloft with an unflinching hope! She had perhaps more glow and less serenity in her soul than Antonia, but she was an uncompromising Puritan of patriotism with no taint of the slightest worldliness in her thoughts. I was not the only one in love with her; but it was I who had to hear oftenest her scathing criticism of my levities—very much like poor Decoud—or stand the brunt of her austere, unanswerable invective. She did not quite understand—but never mind. That afternoon when I came in, a shrinking yet defiant sinner, to say the final good-bye I received a hand-squeeze that made my heart leap and saw a tear that took my breath away. She was softened at the last as though she had suddenly perceived (we were such children still!) that I was really going away for good, going very far away—even as far as Sulaco, lying unknown, hidden from our eyes in the darkness of the Placid Gulf.

That's why I long sometimes for another glimpse of the "beautiful Antonia" (or can it be the Other?) moving in the dimness of the great cathedral, saying a short prayer at the tomb of the first and last Cardinal-Archbishop of Sulaco, standing absorbed in filial devotion before the monument of Don José Avellanos, and, with a lingering, tender, faithful glance at the medallion-memorial to Martin Decoud, going out serenely into the sunshine of the Plaza with her upright carriage and her white head; a relic of the past disregarded by men awaiting impatiently the Dawns of other New Eras, the coming of more Revolutions.

But this is the idlest of dreams; for I did understand perfectly well at the time that the moment the breath left the body of the Magnificent Capataz, the Man of the People, freed at last from the toils of love and wealth, there was nothing more for me to do in Sulaco.

October 1917   J.C.

PART ONE

The Silver of the Mine

CHAPTER 1

IN THE TIME OF Spanish rule, and for many years afterwards, the town of Sulaco—the luxuriant beauty of the orange gardens bears witness to its antiquity—had never been commercially anything more important than a coasting port with a fairly large local trade in oxhides and indigo. The clumsy deep-sea galleons of the conquerors that, needing a brisk gale to move at all, would lie becalmed, where your modern ship built on clipper lines forges ahead by the mere flapping of her sails, had been barred out of Sulaco by the prevailing calms of its vast gulf. Some harbours of the earth are made difficult of access by the treachery of sunken rocks and the tempests of their shores. Sulaco had found an inviolable sanctuary from the temptations of a trading world in the solemn hush of the deep Golfo Placido as if within an enormous semi-circular and unroofed temple open to the ocean, with its walls of lofty mountains hung with the mourning draperies of cloud.

On one side of this broad curve in the straight seaboard of the Republic of Costaguana, the last spur of the coast range forms an insignificant cape whose name is Punta Mala.* From the middle of the gulf the point of the land itself is not visible at all; but the shoulder of a steep hill at the back can be made out faintly like a shadow on the sky.

On the other side, what seems to be an isolated patch of blue mist floats lightly on the glare of the horizon. This is the peninsula of Azuera, a wild chaos of sharp rocks and stony levels cut about by vertical ravines. It lies far out to sea like a rough head of stone stretched from a green-clad coast at the end of a slender neck of sand covered with thickets of thorny scrub. Utterly waterless, for the rainfall runs off at once on all sides into the sea, it has not soil

---

*Bad Point (Spanish)—that is, treacherous to passing ships. (Henceforth, translations are from Spanish unless otherwise noted.)

enough—it is said—to grow a single blade of grass, as if it were blighted by a curse. The poor, associating by an obscure instinct of consolation the ideas of evil and wealth, will tell you that it is deadly because of its forbidden treasures. The common folk of the neighborhood, peons of the *estancias*,* *vaqueros*† of the seaboard plains, tame Indians coming miles to market with a bundle of sugar-cane or a basket of maize worth about three-pence, are well aware that heaps of shining gold lie in the gloom of the deep precipices cleaving the stony levels of Azuera. Tradition has it that many adventurers of olden time had perished in the search. The story goes also that within men's memory two wandering sailors—*Americanos*, perhaps, but *gringos*‡ of some sort for certain—talked over a gambling, good-for-nothing *mozo*,§ and the three stole a donkey to carry for them a bundle of dry sticks, a water-skin, and provisions enough to last a few days. Thus accompanied, and with revolvers at their belts, they had started to chop their way with machetes through the thorny scrub on the neck of the peninsula.

On the second evening an upright spiral of smoke (it could only have been from their camp-fire) was seen for the first time within memory of man standing up faintly upon the sky above a razor-backed ridge on the stony head. The crew of a coasting schooner, lying becalmed three miles off the shore, stared at it with amazement till dark. A Negro fisherman, living in a lonely hut in a little bay near by, had seen the start and was on the lookout for some sign. He called to his wife just as the sun was about to set. They had watched the strange portent with envy, incredulity, and awe.

The impious adventurers gave no other sign. The sailors, the Indian, and the stolen *burro* were never seen again. As to the *mozo*, a Sulaco man—his wife paid for some Masses, and the poor four-footed beast, being without sin, had been probably permitted to die; but the two *gringos*, spectral and alive, are believed to be dwelling to this day amongst the rocks, under the fatal spell of their success. Their souls cannot tear themselves away from their bodies

---

*Farms, country estates.
†Cowboys, herdsmen.
‡Foreigners, especially English or American.
§Young man, fellow.

mounting guard over the discovered treasure. They are now rich and hungry and thirsty—a strange theory of tenacious *gringo* ghosts suffering in their starved and parched flesh of defiant heretics, where a Christian would have renounced and been released.

These, then, are the legendary inhabitants of Azuera guarding its forbidden wealth; and the shadow on the sky on one side, with the round patch of blue haze blurring the bright skirt of the horizon on the other, mark the two outermost points of the bend which bears the name of Golfo Placido, because never a strong wind had been known to blow upon its waters.

On crossing the imaginary line drawn from Punta Mala to Azuera the ships from Europe bound to Sulaco lose at once the strong breezes of the ocean. They become the prey of capricious airs that play with them for thirty hours at a stretch sometimes. Before them the head of the calm gulf is filled on most days of the year by a great body of motionless and opaque clouds. On the rare clear mornings another shadow is cast upon the sweep of the gulf. The dawn breaks high behind the towering and serrated wall of the Cordillera,* a clear-cut vision of dark peaks rearing their steep slopes on a lofty pedestal of forest rising from the very edge of the shore. Amongst them the white head of Higuerota rises majestically upon the blue. Bare clusters of enormous rocks sprinkle with tiny black dots the smooth dome of snow.

Then, as the midday sun withdraws from the gulf the shadow of the mountains, the clouds begin to roll out of the lower valleys. They swathe in sombre tatters the naked crags of precipices above the wooded slopes, hide the peaks, smoke in stormy trails across the snows of Higuerota. The Cordillera is gone from you as if it had dissolved itself into great piles of grey and black vapours that travel out slowly to seaward and vanish into thin air all along the front before the blazing heat of the day. The wasting edge of the cloud-bank always strives for, but seldom wins, the middle of the gulf. The sun— as the sailors say—is eating it up. Unless perchance a sombre thunder-head breaks away from the main body to career all over the gulf till it escapes into the offing beyond Azuera, where it bursts

---

*Mountain range.

suddenly into flame and crashes like a sinister pirate-ship of the air, hove-to above the horizon, engaging the sea.

At night the body of clouds advancing higher up the sky smothers the whole quiet gulf below with an impenetrable darkness, in which the sound of the falling showers can be heard beginning and ceasing abruptly—now here, now there. Indeed, these cloudy nights are proverbial with the seamen along the whole west coast of a great continent. Sky, land, and sea disappear together out of the world when the Placido—as the saying is—goes to sleep under its black poncho.* The few stars left below the seaward frown of the vault shine feebly as into the mouth of a black cavern. In its vastness your ship floats unseen under your feet, her sails flutter invisible above your head. The eye of God Himself—they add with grim profanity—could not find out what work a man's hand is doing in there; and you would be free to call the devil to your aid with impunity if even his malice were not defeated by such a blind darkness.

The shores on the gulf are steep-to all round; three uninhabited islets basking in the sunshine just outside the cloud veil, and opposite the entrance to the harbour of Sulaco, bear the name of "The Isabels."

There is the Great Isabel; the Little Isabel, which is round; and Hermosa, which is the smallest.

That last is no more than a foot high, and about seven paces across, a mere flat top of a grey rock which smokes like a hot cinder after a shower, and where no man would care to venture a naked sole before sunset. On the Little Isabel an old ragged palm with a thick bulging trunk rough with spines, a very witch amongst palm trees, rustles a dismal bunch of dead leaves above the coarse sand. The Great Isabel has a spring of fresh water issuing from the overgrown side of a ravine. Resembling an emerald green wedge of land a mile long, and laid flat upon the sea, it bears two forest trees standing close together, with a wide spread of shade at the foot of their smooth trunks. A ravine extending the whole length of the island is full of bushes; and presenting a deep tangled cleft on the

---

*Blanket-like cloak worn in South America, with a hole in the middle for the head.

high side spreads itself out on the other into a shallow depression abutting on a small strip of sandy shore.

From that low end of the Great Isabel the eye plunges through an opening two miles away, as abrupt as if chopped with an axe out of the regular sweep of the coast, right into the harbour of Sulaco. It is an oblong, lake-like piece of water. On one side the short wooded spurs and valleys of the Cordillera come down at right angles to the very strand; on the other the open view of the great Sulaco plain passes into the opal mystery of great distances overhung by dry haze. The town of Sulaco itself—tops of walls, a great cupola, gleams of white miradors in a vast grove of orange trees—lies between the mountains and the plain, at some little distance from its harbour and out of the direct line of sight from the sea.

CHAPTER 2

THE ONLY SIGN OF commercial activity within the harbour, visible from the beach of the Great Isabel, is the square blunt end of the wooden jetty which the Oceanic Steam Navigation Company (the O.S.N. of familiar speech) had thrown over the shallow part of the bay soon after they had resolved to make of Sulaco one of their ports of call for the Republic of Costaguana. The State possesses several harbours on its long seaboard, but except Cayta, an important place, all are either small and inconvenient inlets in an iron-bound coast—like Esmeralda, for instance, sixty miles to the south—or else mere open roadsteads exposed to the winds and fretted by the surf.

Perhaps the very atmospheric conditions which had kept away the merchant fleets of bygone ages induced the O.S.N. Company to violate the sanctuary of peace sheltering the calm existence of Sulaco. The variable airs sporting lightly with the vast semicircle of waters within the head of Azuera could not baffle the steam power of their excellent fleet. Year after year the black hulls of their ships had gone up and down the coast, in and out, past Azuera, past the Isabels, past Punta Mala—disregarding everything but the tyranny of time. Their names, the names of all mythology, became the household words of a coast that had never been ruled by the gods of Olympus. The *Juno* was known only for her comfortable cabins amidships, the *Saturn* for the geniality of her captain and the painted and gilt luxuriousness of her saloon, whereas the *Ganymede* was fitted out mainly for cattle transport, and to be avoided by coastwise passengers. The humblest Indian in the obscurest village on the coast was familiar with the *Cerberus*, a little black puffer without charm or living accommodation to speak of, whose mission was to creep inshore along the wooded beaches close to mighty ugly rocks, stopping obligingly before every cluster of huts to collect produce, down to three-pound parcels of india-rubber bound in a wrapper of dry grass.

And as they seldom failed to account for the smallest package, rarely lost a bullock, and had never drowned a single passenger, the name of the O.S.N. stood very high for trustworthiness. People declared that under the Company's care their lives and property were safer on the water than in their own houses on shore.

The O.S.N.'s superintendent in Sulaco for the whole Costaguana section of the service was very proud of his Company's standing. He resumed it in a saying which was very often on his lips, "We never make mistakes." To the Company's officers it took the form of a severe injunction, "We must make no mistakes. I'll have no mistakes here, no matter what Smith may do at his end."

Smith, on whom he had never set eyes in his life, was the other superintendent of the service, quartered some fifteen hundred miles away from Sulaco. "Don't talk to me of your Smith."

Then, calming down suddenly, he would dismiss the subject with studied negligence.

"Smith knows no more of this continent than a baby."

"Our excellent Señor Mitchell" for the business and official world of Sulaco; "Fussy Joe" for the commanders of the Company's ships, Captain Joseph Mitchell prided himself on his profound knowledge of men and things in the country—*cosas de Costaguana*. Amongst these last he accounted as most unfavourable to the orderly working of his Company the frequent changes of government brought about by revolutions of the military type.

The political atmosphere of the Republic was generally stormy in these days. The fugitive patriots of the defeated party had the knack of turning up again on the coast with half a steamer's load of small arms and ammunition. Such resourcefulness Captain Mitchell considered as perfectly wonderful in view of their utter destitution at the time of the flight. He had observed that "they never seemed to have enough change about them to pay for their passage ticket out of the country." And he could speak with knowledge; for on a memorable occasion he had been called upon to save the life of a dictator, together with the lives of a few Sulaco officials—the political chief, the director of the customs, and the head of police—belonging to an overturned government. Poor Señor Ribiera (such was the dictator's name) had come pelting eighty miles over mountain tracks after the lost battle of Socorro, in the hope of out-distancing the fatal news—which, of course, he could not manage to do on a lame mule. The animal, moreover, expired under him at the end of the Alameda, where the military band plays sometimes in the evenings between the revolutions. "Sir," Captain Mitchell would pursue with portentous gravity, "the ill-timed end of that mule attracted attention to the unfortunate rider. His features were recognized by several deserters from the Dictatorial army amongst the rascally mob already engaged in smashing the windows of the Intendencia."*

Early on the morning of that day the local authorities of Sulaco had fled for refuge to the O.S.N. Company's offices, a strong building near the shore end of the jetty, leaving the town to the mercies of a revolutionary rabble; and as the Dictator was execrated by the populace on account of the severe recruitment law his necessities had compelled him to enforce during the struggle, he stood a good chance of being torn to pieces. Providentially, Nostromo—invaluable fellow—with some Italian workmen, imported to work upon the National Central Railway, was at hand, and managed to snatch him away—for the time at least. Ultimately, Captain Mitchell succeeded in taking everybody off in his own gig† to one of the Company's steamers—it was the *Minerva*—just then, as luck would have it, entering the harbour.

He had to lower these gentlemen at the end of a rope out of a hole in the wall at the back, while the mob which, pouring out of

---

*Office of the *intendente* (provincial governor).
†Long, light ship's boat designed for speed.

the town, had spread itself all along the shore, howled and foamed at the foot of the building in front. He had to hurry them then the whole length of the jetty; it had been a desperate dash, neck or nothing—and again it was Nostromo, a fellow in a thousand, who, at the head, this time, of the Company's body of lightermen,* held the jetty against the rushes of the rabble, thus giving the fugitives time to reach the gig lying ready for them at the other end with the Company's flag at the stern. Sticks, stones, shots flew; knives, too, were thrown. Captain Mitchell exhibited willingly the long cicatrice of a cut over his left ear and temple, made by a razor-blade fastened to a stick—a weapon, he explained, very much in favour with the "worst kind of nigger out here."

Captain Mitchell was a thick, elderly man, wearing high, pointed collars and short side-whiskers, partial to white waistcoats, and really very communicative under his air of pompous reserve.

"These gentlemen," he would say, staring with great solemnity, "had to run like rabbits, sir. I ran like a rabbit myself. Certain forms of death are—er—distasteful to a—a—er respectable man. They would have pounded me to death, too. A crazy mob, sir, does not discriminate. Under providence we owed our preservation to my Capataz de Cargadores,† as they called him in the town, a man who, when I discovered his value, sir, was just the bos'n of an Italian ship, a big Genoese ship, one of the few European ships that ever came to Sulaco with a general cargo before the building of the National Central. He left her on account of some very respectable friends he made here, his own countrymen, but also, I suppose, to better himself. Sir, I am a pretty good judge of character. I engaged him to be the foreman of our lightermen, and caretaker of our jetty. That's all that he was. But without him Señor Ribiera would have been a dead man. This Nostromo, sir, a man absolutely above reproach, became the terror of all the thieves in the town. We were infested, infested, overrun, sir, here at that time by *ladrones* and *matreros*,‡ thieves and murderers from the whole province. On this occasion they had been flocking into Sulaco for a week past. They had scented the end, sir.

---

*Operators of lighters (flat-bottomed barges used to load and unload at port).
†Foreman of the dockers.
‡Thieves and fugitives.

Fifty per cent of that murdering mob were professional bandits from the Campo, sir, but there wasn't one that hadn't heard of Nostromo. As to the town *leperos*,* sir, the sight of his black whiskers and white teeth was enough for them. They quailed before him, sir. That's what the force of character will do for you."

It could very well be said that it was Nostromo alone who saved the lives of these gentlemen. Captain Mitchell, on his part, never left them till he had seen them collapse, panting, terrified, and exasperated, but safe, on the luxurious velvet sofas in the first class saloon of the *Minerva*. To the very last he had been careful to address the ex-Dictator as "Your Excellency."

"Sir, I could do no other. The man was down—ghastly, livid, one mass of scratches."

The *Minerva* never let go her anchor that call. The superintendent ordered her out of the harbour at once. No cargo could be landed, of course, and the passengers for Sulaco naturally refused to go ashore. They could hear the firing and see plainly the fight going on at the edge of the water. The repulsed mob devoted its energies to an attack upon the Custom House, a dreary, unfinished-looking structure with many windows two hundred yards away from the O.S.N. Offices, and the only other building near the harbour. Captain Mitchell, after directing the commander of the *Minerva* to land "these gentlemen" in the first port of call outside Costaguana, went back in his gig to see what could be done for the protection of the Company's property. That and the property of the railway were preserved by the European residents; that is, by Captain Mitchell himself and the staff of engineers building the road, aided by the Italian and Basque workmen who rallied faithfully round their English chiefs. The Company's lightermen, too, natives of the Republic, behaved very well under their Capataz. An outcast lot of very mixed blood, mainly Negroes, everlastingly at feud with the other customers of low grog shops in the town, they embraced with delight this opportunity to settle their personal scores under such favourable auspices. There was not one of them that had not, at some time or other, looked with terror at Nostromo's revolver poked very close at

---

*Impoverished inhabitants, rabble.

his face, or been otherwise daunted by Nostromo's resolution. He was "much of a man," their Capataz was, they said, too scornful in his temper ever to utter abuse, a tireless taskmaster, and the more to be feared because of his aloofness. And behold! there he was that day, at their head, condescending to make jocular remarks to this man or the other.

Such leadership was inspiriting, and in truth all the harm the mob managed to achieve was to set fire to one—only one—stack of railway-sleepers, which, being creosoted, burned well. The main attack on the railway yards, on the O.S.N. Offices, and especially on the Custom House, whose strong-room, it was well known, contained a large treasure in silver ingots, failed completely. Even the little hotel kept by old Giorgio, standing alone half-way between the harbour and the town, escaped looting and destruction, not by a miracle, but because with the safes in view they had neglected it at first, and afterwards found no leisure to stop. Nostromo, with his *cargadores*, was pressing them too hard then.

CHAPTER 3

IT MIGHT HAVE BEEN said that there he was only protecting his own. From the first he had been admitted to live in the intimacy of the family of the hotel-keeper who was a countryman of his. Old Giorgio Viola, a Genoese with a shaggy white leonine head—often called simply "the Garibaldino" (as Mohammedans are called after their prophet)—was, to use Captain Mitchell's own words, the "respectable married friend" by whose advice Nostromo had left his ship to try for a run of shore luck in Costaguana.

The old man, full of scorn for the populace, as your austere republican so often is, had disregarded the preliminary sounds of trouble. He went on that day as usual pottering about the *casa* in his slippers, muttering angrily to himself his contempt of the non-political nature of the riot, and shrugging his shoulders. In the end he was taken unawares by the out-rush of the rabble. It was too late then to remove his family, and, indeed, where could he have run to with the portly Signora Teresa and two little girls on that great plain? So, barricading every opening, the old man sat down sternly in the middle of the darkened café with an old shot-gun on his knees. His wife sat on another chair by his side, muttering pious invocations to all the saints of the calendar.

The old republican did not believe in saints, or in prayers, or in what he called "priests' religion." Liberty and Garibaldi were his divinities; but he tolerated "superstition" in women, preserving in these matters a lofty and silent attitude.

His two girls, the eldest fourteen, and the other two years younger, crouched on the sanded floor, on each side of the Signora Teresa, with their heads on their mother's lap, both scared, but each in her own way, the dark-haired Linda indignant and angry, the fair Giselle, the younger, bewildered and resigned. The Padrona* removed her arms, which embraced her daughters, for a moment to cross herself and wring her hands hurriedly. She moaned a little louder.

"Oh! Gian' Battista, why art thou not here? Oh! why art thou not here?"

She was not then invoking the saint himself, but calling upon Nostromo, whose patron he was. And Giorgio, motionless on the chair by her side, would be provoked by these reproachful and distracted appeals.

"Peace, woman! Where's the sense of it? There's his duty," he murmured in the dark; and she would retort, panting:

"Eh! I have no patience. Duty! What of the woman who has been like a mother to him? I bent my knee to him this morning; don't you go out, Gian' Battista—stop in the house, Battistino—look at those two little innocent children!"

Mrs. Viola was an Italian, too, a native of Spezzia, and though considerably younger than her husband, already middle-aged. She had a handsome face, whose complexion had turned yellow because the climate of Sulaco did not suit her at all. Her voice was a rich contralto. When, with her arms folded tight under her ample bosom, she scolded the squat, thick-legged China girls handling linen, plucking fowls, pounding corn in wooden mortars amongst the mud

---

*Lady of the house, mistress (Italian; henceforth, It.).

outbuildings at the back of the house, she could bring out such an impassioned, vibrating, sepulchral note that the chained watch-dog bolted into his kennel with a great rattle. Luis, a cinnamon-coloured mulatto with a sprouting moustache and thick, dark lips, would stop sweeping the café with a broom of palm-leaves to let a gentle shudder run down his spine. His languishing almond eyes would remain closed for a long time.

This was the staff of the Casa Viola, but all these people had fled early that morning at the first sounds of the riot, preferring to hide on the plain rather than trust themselves in the house; a preference for which they were in no way to blame, since, whether true or not, it was generally believed in the town that the Garibaldino had some money buried under the clay floor of the kitchen. The dog, an irritable, shaggy brute, barked violently and whined plaintively in turns at the back, running in and out of his kennels as rage or fear prompted him.

Bursts of great shouting rose and died away, like wild gusts of wind on the plain round the barricaded house; the fitful popping of shots grew louder above the yelling. Sometimes there were intervals of unaccountable stillness outside, and nothing could have been more gaily peaceful than the narrow bright lines of sunlight from the cracks in the shutters, ruled straight across the café over the disarranged chairs and tables to the wall opposite. Old Giorgio had chosen that bare, whitewashed room for a retreat. It had only one window, and its only door swung out upon the track of thick dust fenced by aloe hedges between the harbour and the town, where clumsy carts used to creak along behind slow yokes of oxen guided by boys on horseback.

In a pause of stillness Giorgio cocked his gun. The ominous sound wrung a low moan from the rigid figure of the woman sitting by his side. A sudden outbreak of defiant yelling quite near the house sank all at once to a confused murmur of growls. Somebody ran along; the loud catching of his breath was heard for an instant passing the door; there were hoarse mutters and footsteps near the wall; a shoulder rubbed against the shutter, effacing the bright lines of sunshine pencilled across the whole breadth of the room. Signora Teresa's arms thrown about the kneeling forms of her daughters embraced them closer with a convulsive pressure.

The mob, driven away from the Custom House, had broken up into several bands, retreating across the plain in the direction of the town. The subdued crash of irregular volleys fired in the distance was answered by faint yells far away. In the intervals the single shots rang feebly, and the low, long, white building blinded in every window seemed to be the centre of a turmoil widening in a great circle about its closed-up silence. But the cautious movements and whispers of a routed party seeking a momentary shelter behind the wall made the darkness of the room, striped by threads of quiet sunlight, alight with evil stealthy sounds. The Violas had them in their ears as though invisible ghosts hovering about their chairs had consulted in mutters as to the advisability of setting fire to this foreigner's *casa*.*

It was trying to the nerves. Old Viola had risen slowly, gun in hand, irresolute, for he did not see how he could prevent them. Already voices could be heard talking at the back. Signora Teresa was beside herself with terror.

"Ah! the traitor! the traitor!" she mumbled, almost inaudibly. "Now we are going to be burnt; and I bent my knee to him. No! he must run at the heels of his English."

She seemed to think that Nostromo's mere presence in the house would have made it perfectly safe. So far, she, too, was under the spell of that reputation the Capataz de Cargadores had made for himself by the waterside, along the railway line, with the English, and with the populace of Sulaco. To his face, and even against her husband, she invariably affected to laugh it to scorn, sometimes good-naturedly, more often with a curious bitterness. But then women are unreasonable in their opinions, as Giorgio used to remark calmly on fitting occasions. On this occasion, with his gun held at ready before him, he stooped down to his wife's head, and, keeping his eyes steadfastly on the barricaded door, he breathed out into her ear that Nostromo would have been powerless to help. What could two men shut up in a house do against twenty or more bent upon setting fire to the roof? Gian' Battista was thinking of the *casa* all the time, he was sure.

---

*House.

"He think of the *casa*! He!" gasped Signora Viola, crazily. She struck her breast with her open hands. "I know him. He thinks of nobody but himself."

A discharge of firearms nearby made her throw her head back and close her eyes. Old Giorgio set his teeth hard under his white moustache, and his eyes began to roll fiercely. Several bullets struck the end of the wall together; pieces of plaster could be heard falling outside; a voice screamed "Here they come!" and after a moment of uneasy silence there was a rush of running feet along the front.

Then the tension of old Giorgio's attitude relaxed, and a smile of contemptuous relief came upon his lips of an old fighter with a leonine face. These were not a people striving for justice, but thieves. Even to defend his life against them was a sort of degradation for a man who had been one of Garibaldi's immortal thousand in the conquest of Sicily. He had an immense scorn for this outbreak of scoundrels and *leperos*, who did not know the meaning of the word "liberty."

He grounded his old gun, and, turning his head, glanced at the coloured lithograph of Garibaldi in a black frame on the white wall; a thread of strong sunshine cut it perpendicularly. His eyes, accustomed to the luminous twilight, made out the high colouring of the face, the red of the shirt, the outlines of the square shoulders, the black patch of the Bersagliere* hat with cock's feathers curling over the crown. An immortal hero! This was your liberty; it gave you not only life, but immortality as well!

For that one man his fanaticism had suffered no diminution. In the moment of relief from the apprehension of the greatest danger, perhaps, his family had been exposed to in all their wanderings, he had turned to the picture of his old chief, first and only, then laid his hand on his wife's shoulder.

The children kneeling on the floor had not moved. Signora Teresa opened her eyes a little, as though he had awakened her from a very deep and dreamless slumber. Before he had time in his deliberate way to say a reassuring word she jumped up, with the children clinging to her, one on each side, gasped for breath, and let out a hoarse shriek.

---

*Italian soldier in the rifle regiment (It.).

It was simultaneous with the bang of a violent blow struck on the outside of the shutter. They could hear suddenly the snorting of a horse, the restive tramping of hoofs on the narrow, hard path in front of the house; the toe of a boot struck at the shutter again; a spur jingled at every blow, and an excited voice shouted, "Hola!* hola, in there!"

CHAPTER 4

ALL THE MORNING NOSTROMO had kept his eye from afar on the Casa Viola, even in the thick of the hottest scrimmage near the Custom House. "If I see smoke rising over there," he thought to himself, "they are lost." Directly the mob had broken he pressed with a small band of Italian workmen in that direction, which, indeed, was the shortest line towards the town. That part of the rabble he was pursuing seemed to think of making a stand under the house; a volley fired by his followers from behind an aloe hedge made the rascals fly. In a gap chopped out for the rails of the harbour branchline Nostromo appeared, mounted on his silver-grey mare. He shouted, sent after them one shot from his revolver, and galloped up to the café window. He had an idea that old Giorgio would choose that part of the house for a refuge.

His voice had penetrated to them, sounding breathlessly hurried: "*Hola! Vecchio!*† *O, vecchio!* Is it all well with you in there?"

"You see—" murmured old Viola to his wife.

Signora Teresa was silent now. Outside Nostromo laughed.

"I can hear the *padrona* is not dead."

"You have done your best to kill me with fear," cried Signora Teresa. She wanted to say something more, but her voice failed her.

Linda raised her eyes to her face for a moment, but old Giorgio shouted apologetically:

"She is a little upset."

---

*Hello!
†Old man (It.).

Outside Nostromo shouted back with another laugh:

"She cannot upset me."

Signora Teresa found her voice.

"It is what I say. You have no heart—and you have no conscience, Gian' Battista—"

They heard him wheel his horse away from the shutters. The party he led were babbling excitedly in Italian and Spanish, inciting each other to the pursuit. He put himself at their head, crying, "*Avanti!*"*

"He has not stopped very long with us. There is no praise from strangers to be got here," Signora Teresa said, tragically. "*Avanti!* Yes! That is all he cares for. To be first somewhere—somehow—to be first with these English. They will be showing him to everybody. 'This is our Nostromo!'" She laughed ominously. "What a name! What is that? Nostromo? He would take a name that is properly no word from them."

Meantime Giorgio, with tranquil movements, had been unfastening the door; the flood of light fell on Signora Teresa, with her two girls gathered to her side, a picturesque woman in a pose of maternal exaltation. Behind her the wall was dazzlingly white, and the crude colours of the Garibaldi lithograph paled in the sunshine.

Old Viola, at the door, moved his arm upwards as if referring all his quick, fleeting thoughts to the picture of his old chief on the wall. Even when he was cooking for the "*signori inglesi*"†—the engineers (he was a famous cook, though the kitchen was a dark place)—he was, as it were, under the eye of the great man who had led him in a glorious struggle where, under the walls of Gaeta, tyranny would have expired for ever had it not been for that accursed Piedmontese race of kings and ministers. When sometimes a frying-pan caught fire during a delicate operation with some shredded onions, and the old man was seen backing out of the doorway, swearing and coughing violently in an acrid cloud of smoke, the name of Cavour—the arch intriguer sold to kings and tyrants—could be heard involved in

---

*Go on! (It.).
†English gentlemen (It.).

imprecations against the China girls, cooking in general, and the brute of a country where he was reduced to live for the love of liberty that traitor had strangled.[1]

Then Signora Teresa, all in black, issuing from another door, advanced, portly and anxious, inclining her fine, black-browed head, opening her arms, and crying in a profound tone—

"Giorgio! thou passionate man! *Misericordia divina!*[*] In the sun like this! He will make himself ill."

At her feet the hens made off in all directions, with immense strides; if there were any engineers from up the line staying in Sulaco, a young English face or two would appear at the billiard-room occupying one end of the house; but at the other end, in the café, Luis, the mulatto, took good care not to show himself. The Indian girls, with hair like flowing black manes, and dressed only in a shift and short petticoat, stared dully from under the square-cut fringes on their foreheads; the noisy frizzling of fat had stopped, the fumes floated upwards in sunshine, a strong smell of burnt onions hung in the drowsy heat, enveloping the house; and the eye lost itself in a vast flat expanse of grass to the west, as if the plain between the Sierra overtopping Sulaco and the coast range away there towards Esmeralda had been as big as half the world.

Signora Teresa, after an impressive pause, remonstrated:

"Eh, Giorgio! Leave Cavour alone and take care of yourself now we are lost in this country all alone with the two children, because you cannot live under a king."

And while she looked at him she would sometimes put her hand hastily to her side with a short twitch of her fine lips and a knitting of her black, straight eyebrows like a flicker of angry pain or an angry thought on her handsome, regular features.

It was pain; she suppressed the twinge. It had come to her first a few years after they had left Italy to emigrate to America and settle at last in Sulaco after wandering from town to town, trying shopkeeping in a small way here and there; and once an organized enterprise of fishing—in Maldonado—for Giorgio, like the great Garibaldi, had been a sailor in his time.

---

[*]Divine Mercy!

Sometimes she had no patience with pain. For years its gnawing had been part of the landscape embracing the glitter of the harbour under the wooded spurs of the range; and the sunshine itself was heavy and dull—heavy with pain—not like the sunshine of her girlhood, in which middle-aged Giorgio had wooed her gravely and passionately on the shores of the gulf of Spezzia.

"You go in at once, Giorgio," she directed. "One would think you do not wish to have any pity on me—with four Signori Inglesi staying in the house."

"*Va bene,** va bene*," Giorgio would mutter.

He obeyed. The Signori Inglesi would require their midday meal presently. He had been one of the immortal and invincible band of liberators who had made the mercenaries of tyranny fly like chaff before a hurricane, "*un uragano terribile.*"[†] But that was before he was married and had children; and before tyranny had reared its head again amongst the traitors who had imprisoned Garibaldi, his hero.

There were three doors in the front of the house, and each afternoon the Garibaldino could be seen at one or another of them with his big bush of white hair, his arms folded, his legs crossed, leaning back his leonine head against the lintel, and looking up the wooded slopes of the foothills at the snowy dome of Higuerota. The front of his house threw off a black long rectangle of shade, broadening slowly over the soft ox-cart track. Through the gaps, chopped out in the oleander hedges, the harbour branch railway, laid out temporarily on the level of the plain, curved away its shining parallel ribbons on a belt of scorched and withered grass within sixty yards of the end of the house. In the evening the empty material trains of flat cars circled round the dark green grove of Sulaco, and ran, undulating slightly with white jets of steam, over the plain towards the Casa Viola, on their way to the railway yards by the harbour. The Italian drivers saluted him from the footplate with raised hand, while the Negro brakesmen sat carelessly on the brakes, looking straight forward, with the rims of their big hats flapping in the wind. In return Giorgio would give a slight sideways jerk of the head, without unfolding his arms.

---

*Very well (It.).
†A terrible hurricane (It.).

On this memorable day of the riot his arms were not folded on his chest. His hand grasped the barrel of the gun grounded on the threshold; he did not look up once at the white dome of Higuerota, whose cool purity seemed to hold itself aloof from a hot earth. His eyes examined the plain curiously. Tall trails of dust subsided here and there. In a speckless sky the sun hung clear and blinding. Knots of men ran headlong; others made a stand; and the irregular rattle of firearms came rippling to his ears in the fiery, still air. Single figures on foot raced desperately. Horsemen galloped towards each other, wheeled round together, separated at speed. Giorgio saw one fall, rider and horse disappearing as if they had galloped into a chasm, and the movements of the animated scene were like the passages of a violent game played upon the plain by dwarfs mounted and on foot, yelling with tiny throats, under the mountain that seemed a colossal embodiment of silence. Never before had Giorgio seen this bit of plain so full of active life; his gaze could not take in all its details at once; he shaded his eyes with his hand, till suddenly the thundering of many hoofs near by startled him.

A troop of horses had broken out of the fenced paddock of the Railway Company. They came on like a whirlwind, and dashed over the line snorting, kicking, squealing in a compact, piebald, tossing mob of bay, brown, grey backs, eyes staring, necks extended, nostrils red, long tails streaming. As soon as they had leaped upon the road the thick dust flew upwards from under their hoofs, and within six yards of Giorgio only a brown cloud with vague forms of necks and cruppers rolled by, making the soil tremble on its passage.

Viola coughed, turning his face away from the dust, and shaking his head slightly.

"There will be some horse-catching to be done before tonight," he muttered.

In the square of sunlight falling through the door Signora Teresa, kneeling before the chair, had bowed her head, heavy with a twisted mass of ebony hair streaked with silver, into the palm of her hands. The black lace shawl she used to drape about her face dropped to the ground by her side. The two girls had got up, hand-in-hand, in short skirts, their loose hair falling in disorder. The younger had thrown her arm across her eyes, as if afraid to face the light. Linda, with her hand on the other's shoulder, stared fearlessly. Viola looked at his children.

The sun brought out the deep lines on his face, and, energetic in expression, it had the immobility of a carving. It was impossible to discover what he thought. Bushy grey eyebrows shaded his dark glance.

"Well! And do you not pray like your mother?"

Linda pouted, advancing her red lips, which were almost too red; but she had admirable eyes, brown, with a sparkle of gold in the irises, full of intelligence and meaning, and so clear that they seemed to throw a glow upon her thin, colourless face. There were bronze glints in the sombre clusters of her hair, and the eyelashes, long and coal black, made her complexion appear still more pale.

"Mother is going to offer up a lot of candles in the church. She always does when Nostromo has been away fighting. I shall have some to carry up to the Chapel of the Madonna in the Cathedral."

She said all this quickly, with great assurance, in an animated, penetrating voice. Then, giving her sister's shoulder a slight shake, she added:

"And she will be made to carry one, too!"

"Why made?" inquired Giorgio, gravely. "Does she not want to?"

"She is timid," said Linda, with a little burst of laughter. "People notice her fair hair as she goes along with us. They call out after her, 'Look at the *rubia*!* Look at the *rubiacita*!' They call out in the streets. She is timid."

"And you? You are not timid—eh?" the father pronounced, slowly.

She tossed back all her dark hair.

"Nobody calls out after me."

Old Giorgio contemplated his children thoughtfully. There was two years difference between them. They had been born to him late, years after the boy had died. Had he lived he would have been nearly as old as Gian' Battista—he whom the English called Nostromo; but as to his daughters, the severity of his temper, his advancing age, his absorption in his memories, had prevented his taking much notice of them. He loved his children, but girls belong more to the mother, and much of his affection had been expended in the worship and service of liberty.

---

*Blond girl.

When quite a youth he had deserted from a ship trading to La Plata, to enlist in the navy of Montevideo, then under the command of Garibaldi.[2] Afterwards, in the Italian legion of the Republic struggling against the encroaching tyranny of Rosas, he had taken part, on great plains, on the banks of immense rivers, in the fiercest fighting perhaps the world had ever known. He had lived amongst men who had declaimed about liberty, suffered for liberty, died for liberty, with a desperate exaltation, and with their eyes turned towards an oppressed Italy. His own enthusiasm had been fed on scenes of carnage, on the examples of lofty devotion, on the din of armed struggle, on the inflamed language of proclamations. He had never parted from the chief of his choice — the fiery apostle of independence — keeping by his side in America and in Italy till after the fatal day of Aspromonte,[3] when the treachery of kings, emperors, and ministers had been revealed to the world in the wounding and imprisonment of his hero — a catastrophe that had instilled into him a gloomy doubt of ever being able to understand the ways of divine justice.

He did not deny it, however. It required patience, he would say. Though he disliked priests, and would not put his foot inside a church for anything, he believed in God. Were not the proclamations against tyrants addressed to the peoples in the name of God and liberty? "God for men — religions for women," he muttered sometimes. In Sicily, an Englishman who had turned up in Palermo after its evacuation by the army of the king, had given him a Bible in Italian — the publication of the British and Foreign Bible Society, bound in a dark leather cover. In periods of political adversity, in the pauses of silence when the revolutionists issued no proclamations, Giorgio earned his living with the first work that came to hand — as sailor, as dock labourer on the quays of Genoa, once as a hand on a farm in the hills above Spezzia — and in his spare time he studied the thick volume. He carried it with him into battles. Now it was his only reading, and in order not to be deprived of it (the print was small) he had consented to accept the present of a pair of silver-mounted spectacles from Señora Emilia Gould, the wife of the Englishman who managed the silver mine in the mountains three leagues from the town. She was the only Englishwoman in Sulaco.

Giorgio Viola had a great consideration for the English. This feeling, born on the battlefields of Uruguay, was forty years old at the very least. Several of them had poured their blood for the cause of freedom in America, and the first he had ever known he remembered by the name of Samuel; he commanded a Negro company under Garibaldi, during the famous siege of Montevideo, and died heroically with his Negroes at the fording of the Boyana.[4] He, Giorgio, had reached the rank of ensign — *alferez* — and cooked for the general. Later, in Italy, he, with the rank of lieutenant, rode with the staff and still cooked for the general. He had cooked for him in Lombardy through the whole campaign; on the march to Rome he had lassoed his beef in the Campagna after the American manner; he had been wounded in the defence of the Roman Republic; he was one of the four fugitives who, with the general, carried out of the woods the inanimate body of the general's wife into the farmhouse where she died, exhausted by the hardships of that terrible retreat. He had survived that disastrous time to attend his general in Palermo when the Neapolitan shells from the castle crashed upon the town. He had cooked for him on the field of Volturno after fighting all day. And everywhere he had seen Englishmen in the front rank of the army of freedom. He respected their nation because they loved Garibaldi. Their very countesses and princesses had kissed the general's hands in London, it was said. He could well believe it; for the nation was noble, and the man was a saint. It was enough to look once at his face to see the divine force of faith in him and his great pity for all that was poor, suffering, and oppressed in this world.

The spirit of self-forgetfulness, the simple devotion to a vast humanitarian idea which inspired the thought and stress of that revolutionary time, had left its mark upon Giorgio in a sort of austere contempt for all personal advantage. This man, whom the lowest class in Sulaco suspected of having a buried hoard in his kitchen, had all his life despised money. The leaders of his youth had lived poor, had died poor. It had been a habit of his mind to disregard tomorrow. It was engendered partly by an existence of excitement, adventure, and wild warfare. But mostly it was a matter of principle. It did not resemble the carelessness of a *condottiere*,* it was a puritanism of religion.

---

*Soldier of fortune, mercenary (It.).

This stern devotion to a cause had cast a gloom upon Giorgio's old age. It cast a gloom because the cause seemed lost. Too many kings and emperors flourished yet in the world which God had meant for the people. He was sad because of his simplicity. Though always ready to help his countrymen, and greatly respected by the Italian emigrants wherever he lived (in his exile he called it), he could not conceal from himself that they cared nothing for the wrongs of down-trodden nations. They listened to his tales of war readily, but seemed to ask themselves what he had got out of it after all. There was nothing that they could see. "We wanted nothing, we suffered for the love of all humanity!" he cried out furiously sometimes, and the powerful voice, the blazing eyes, the shaking of the white mane, the brown, sinewy hand pointing upwards as if to call heaven to witness, impressed his hearers. After the old man had broken off abruptly with a jerk of the head and a movement of the arm, meaning clearly, "But what's the good of talking to you?" they nudged each other. There was in old Giorgio an energy of feeling, a personal quality of conviction, something they called "*terribilita*"* — "an old lion," they used to say of him. Some slight incident, a chance word, would set him off talking on the beach to the Italian fishermen of Maldonado; in the little shop he kept afterwards (in Valparaiso) to his countrymen customers; of an evening, suddenly, in the café at one end of the Casa Viola (the other was reserved for the English engineers) to the select clientele of engine-drivers and foremen of the railway shops.

With their handsome, bronzed, lean faces, shiny black ringlets, glistening eyes, broad-chested, bearded, sometimes a tiny gold ring in the lobe of the ear, the aristocracy of the railway works listened to him, turning away from their cards or dominoes. Here and there a fair-haired Basque studied his hand meantime, waiting without protest. No native of Costaguana intruded there. This was the Italian stronghold. Even the Sulaco policemen on a night patrol let their horses pace softly by, bending low in the saddle to glance through the window at the heads in a fog of smoke; and the drone of old Giorgio's declamatory narrative seemed to sink behind them into the plain. Only now and then the assistant of the chief of police,

---

*Awesomeness, terribleness (idiomatic It.).

some broad-faced, brown little gentleman, with a great deal of Indian in him, would put in an appearance. Leaving his man outside with the horses he advanced with a confident, sly smile, and without a word up to the long trestle table. He pointed to one of the bottles on the shelf; Giorgio, thrusting his pipe into his mouth abruptly, served him in person. Nothing would be heard but the slight jingle of the spurs. His glass emptied, he would take a leisurely, scrutinizing look all round the room, go out, and ride away slowly, circling towards the town.

CHAPTER 5

IN THIS WAY ONLY was the power of the local authorities vindicated amongst the great body of strong-limbed foreigners who dug the earth, blasted the rocks, drove the engines for the "progressive and patriotic undertaking." In these very words eighteen months before the Excellentissimo Señor don Vincente Ribiera, the Dictator of Costaguana, had described the National Central Railway in his great speech at the turning of the first sod.

He had come on purpose to Sulaco, and there was a one-o'clock dinner-party, a *convité** offered by the O.S.N. Company on board the *Juno* after the function on shore. Captain Mitchell had himself steered the cargo lighter, all draped with flags, which, in tow of the *Juno's* steam launch, took the Excellentissimo from the jetty to the ship. Everybody of note in Sulaco had been invited—the one or two foreign merchants, all the representatives of the old Spanish families then in town, the great owners of estates on the plain, grave, courteous, simple men, *caballeros†* of pure descent, with small hands and feet, conservative, hospitable, and kind. The Occidental Province was their stronghold; their Blanco party had triumphed now; it was their President-Dictator, a Blanco of the Blancos, who sat smiling

---

*Invitation to a ceremony (French; henceforth, Fr.).
†Gentlemen.

urbanely between the representatives of two friendly foreign powers. They had come with him from Sta. Marta to countenance by their presence the enterprise in which the capital of their countries was engaged.

The only lady of that company was Mrs. Gould, the wife of Don Carlos, the administrator of the San Tomé silver mine. The ladies of Sulaco were not advanced enough to take part in the public life to that extent. They had come out strongly at the great ball at the Intendencia the evening before, but Mrs. Gould alone had appeared, a bright spot in the group of black coats behind the President-Dictator, on the crimson cloth-covered stage erected under a shady tree on the shore of the harbour, where the ceremony of turning the first sod had taken place. She had come off in the cargo lighter, full of notabilities, sitting under the flutter of gay flags, in the place of honour by the side of Captain Mitchell, who steered, and her clear dress gave the only truly festive note to the sombre gathering in the long, gorgeous saloon of the *Juno*.

The head of the chairman of the railway board (from London), handsome and pale in a silvery mist of white hair and clipped beard, hovered near her shoulder attentive, smiling, and fatigued. The journey from London to Sta. Marta in mail boats and the special carriages of the Sta. Marta coast-line (the only railway so far) had been tolerable—even pleasant—quite tolerable. But the trip over the mountains to Sulaco was another sort of experience, in an old *diligencia** over impassable roads skirting awful precipices.

"We have been upset twice in one day on the brink of very deep ravines," he was telling Mrs. Gould in an undertone. "And when we arrived here at last I don't know what we should have done without your hospitality. What an out-of-the-way place Sulaco is!—and for a harbour, too! Astonishing!"

"Ah, but we are very proud of it. It used to be historically important. The highest ecclesiastical court, for two viceroyalties, sat here in the olden time," she instructed him with animation.

"I am impressed. I didn't mean to be disparaging. You seem very patriotic."

---

*Stagecoach.

"The place is lovable, if only by its situation. Perhaps you don't know what an old resident I am."

"How old, I wonder," he murmured, looking at her with a slight smile. Mrs. Gould's appearance was made youthful by the mobile intelligence of her face. "We can't give you your ecclesiastical court back again; but you shall have more steamers, a railway, a telegraph-cable—a future in the great world which is worth infinitely more than any amount of ecclesiastical past. You shall be brought in touch with something greater than two viceroyalties. But I had no notion that a place on a sea-coast could remain so isolated from the world. If it had been a thousand miles inland now—most remarkable! Has anything ever happened here for a hundred years before today?"

While he talked in a slow, humorous tone, she kept her little smile. Agreeing ironically, she assured him that certainly not—nothing ever happened in Sulaco. Even the revolutions, of which there had been two in her time, had respected the repose of the place. Their course ran in the more populous southern parts of the Republic, and in the great valley of Sta. Marta, which was like one great battlefield of the parties, with the possession of the capital for a prize and an outlet to another ocean. They were more advanced over there. Here in Sulaco they heard only the echoes of these great questions, and, of course, their official world changed each time, coming to them over their rampart of mountains which he himself had traversed in an old *diligencia*, with such a risk to life and limb.

The chairman of the railway had been enjoying her hospitality for several days, and he was really grateful for it. It was only since he had left Sta. Marta that he had utterly lost touch with the feeling of European life on the background of his exotic surroundings. In the capital he had been the guest of the Legation, and had been kept busy negotiating with the members of Don Vincente's Government—cultured men, men to whom the conditions of civilized business were not unknown.

What concerned him most at the time was the acquisition of land for the railway. In the Sta. Marta Valley, where there was already one line in existence, the people were tractable, and it was only a matter of price. A commission had been nominated to fix the values, and the difficulty resolved itself into the judicious influencing of the

Commissioners. But in Sulaco—the Occidental Province for whose very development the railway was intended—there had been trouble. It had been lying for ages ensconced behind its natural barriers, repelling modern enterprise by the precipices of its mountain range, by its shallow harbour opening into the everlasting calms of a gulf full of clouds, by the benighted state of mind of the owners of its fertile territory—all these aristocratic old Spanish families, all these Don Ambrosios this and Don Fernandos that, who seemed actually to dislike and distrust the coming of the railway over their lands. It had happened that some of the surveying parties scattered all over the province had been warned off with threats of violence. In other cases outrageous pretensions as to price had been raised. But the man of railways prided himself on being equal to every emergency. Since he was met by the inimical sentiment of blind conservatism in Sulaco he would meet it by sentiment, too, before taking his stand on his right alone. The Government was bound to carry out its part of the contract with the board of the new railway company, even if it had to use force for the purpose. But he desired nothing less than an armed disturbance in the smooth working of his plans. They were much too vast and far reaching, and too promising to leave a stone unturned; and so he imagined to get the President-Dictator over there on a tour of ceremonies and speeches, culminating in a great function at the turning of the first sod by the harbour shore. After all he was their own creature—that Don Vincente. He was the embodied triumph of the best elements in the State. These were facts, and, unless facts meant nothing, Sir John argued to himself, such a man's influence must be real, and his personal action would produce the conciliatory effect he required. He had succeeded in arranging the trip with the help of a very clever advocate, who was known in Sta. Marta as the agent of the Gould silver mine, the biggest thing in Sulaco, and even in the whole Republic. It was indeed a fabulously rich mine. Its so-called agent, evidently a man of culture and ability, seemed, without official position, to possess an extraordinary influence in the highest Government spheres. He was able to assure Sir John that the President-Dictator would make the journey. He regretted, however, in the course of the same conversation, that General Montero insisted upon going, too.

General Montero, whom the beginning of the struggle had found an obscure army captain employed on the wild eastern frontier of the State, had thrown in his lot with the Ribiera party at a moment when special circumstances had given that small adhesion a fortuitous importance. The fortunes of war served him marvelously, and the victory of Río Seco (after a day of desperate fighting) put a seal to his success. At the end he emerged General, Minister of War, and the military head of the Blanco party, although there was nothing aristocratic in his descent. Indeed, it was said that he and his brother, orphans, had been brought up by the munificence of a famous European traveller, in whose service their father had lost his life. Another story was that their father had been nothing but a charcoal burner in the woods, and their mother a baptized Indian woman from the far interior.

However that might be, the Costaguana Press was in the habit of styling Montero's forest march from his commandancia to join the Blanco forces at the beginning of the troubles, the "most heroic military exploit of modern times." About the same time, too, his brother had turned up from Europe, where he had gone apparently as secretary to a consul. Having, however, collected a small band of outlaws, he showed some talent as guerrilla chief and had been rewarded at the pacification by the post of Military Commandant of the capital.

The Minister of War, then, accompanied the Dictator. The board of the O.S.N. Company, working hand-in-hand with the railway people for the good of the Republic, had on this important occasion instructed Captain Mitchell to put the mailboat *Juno* at the disposal of the distinguished party. Don Vincente, journeying south from Sta. Marta, had embarked at Cayta, the principal port of Costaguana, and came to Sulaco by sea. But the chairman of the railway company had courageously crossed the mountains in a ramshackle *diligencia*, mainly for the purpose of meeting his engineer-in-chief engaged in the final survey of the road.

For all the indifference of a man of affairs to nature, whose hostility can always be overcome by the resources of finance, he could not help being impressed by his surroundings during his halt at the surveying camp established at the highest point his railway was to reach. He spent the night there, arriving just too late to see the last dying glow of sunlight upon the snowy flank of Higuerota. Pillared masses of black basalt framed like an open portal a portion of the white field lying aslant against the west. In the transparent air of the high altitudes everything seemed very near, steeped in a clear stillness as in an imponderable liquid; and with his ear ready to catch the first sound of the expected *diligencia* the engineer-in-chief, at the door of a hut of rough stones, had contemplated the changing hues on the enormous side of the mountain, thinking that in this sight, as in a piece of inspired music, there could be found together the utmost delicacy of shaded expression and a stupendous magnificence of effect.

Sir John arrived too late to hear the magnificent and inaudible strain sung by the sunset amongst the high peaks of the Sierra. It had sung itself out into the breathless pause of deep dusk before, climbing down the fore wheel of the *diligencia* with stiff limbs, he shook hands with the engineer.

They gave him his dinner in a stone hut like a cubical boulder, with no door or windows in its two openings; a bright fire of sticks (brought on muleback from the first valley below) burning outside sent in a wavering glare; and two candles in tin candlesticks lighted, it was explained to him, in his honour—stood on a sort of rough camp table, at which he sat on the right hand of the chief. He knew how to be amiable; and the young men of the engineering staff, for whom the surveying of the railway track had the glamour of the first steps on the path of life, sat there, too, listening modestly, with their smooth faces tanned by the weather, and very pleased to witness so much affability in so great a man.

Afterwards, late at night, pacing to and fro outside, he had a long talk with his chief engineer. He knew him well of old. This was not the first undertaking in which their gifts, as elementally different as fire and water, had worked in conjunction. From the contact of these two personalities, who had not the same vision of the world, there was generated a power for the world's service—a subtle force that could set in motion mighty machines, men's muscles, and awaken also in human breasts an unbounded devotion to the task. Of the young fellows at the table, to whom the survey of the track was like the tracing of the path of life, more than one would be called to meet death before the work was done. But the work would be done: the force would be almost as strong as a faith. Not quite, however. In the silence of the sleeping camp upon the moonlit plateau forming the top of the pass like the floor of a vast arena surrounded by the basalt walls of precipices, two strolling figures in thick ulsters stood still, and the voice of the engineer pronounced distinctly the words:

"We can't move mountains!"

Sir John, raising his head to follow the pointing gesture, felt the full force of the words. The white Higuerota soared out of the shadows of rock and earth like a frozen bubble under the moon. All was still, till near by, behind the wall of a corral for the camp animals, built roughly of loose stones in the form of a circle, a pack mule stamped his forefoot and blew heavily twice.

The engineer-in-chief had used the phrase in answer to the chairman's tentative suggestion that the tracing of the line could, perhaps, be altered in deference to the prejudices of the Sulaco landowners. The chief engineer believed that the obstinacy of men was the lesser obstacle. Moreover, to combat that they had the great influence of Charles Gould, whereas tunnelling under Higuerota would have been a colossal undertaking.

"Ah, yes! Gould. What sort of a man is he?"

Sir John had heard much of Charles Gould in Sta. Marta, and wanted to know more. The engineer-in-chief assured him that the administrator of the San Tomé silver mine had an immense influence over all these Spanish Dons. He had also one of the best houses in Sulaco, and the Gould hospitality was beyond all praise.

"They received me as if they had known me for years," he said. "The little lady is kindness personified. I stayed with them for a month. He helped me to organize the surveying parties. His practical ownership of the San Tomé silver mine gives him a special position. He seems to have the ear of every provincial authority apparently, and, as I said, he can wind all the *hidalgos** of the province round his little finger. If you follow his advice the difficulties will fall away, because he wants the railway. Of course, you must be careful in what you say. He's English, and besides he must be immensely wealthy. The Holroyd house is in with him in that mine, so you may imagine—"

---

*Noblemen.

He interrupted himself as, from before one of the little fires burning outside the low wall of the corral, arose the figure of a man wrapped in a poncho up to the neck. The saddle which he had been using for a pillow made a dark patch on the ground against the red glow of embers.

"I shall see Holroyd himself on my way back through the States," said Sir John. "I've ascertained that he, too, wants the railway."

The man who, perhaps disturbed by the proximity of the voices, had arisen from the ground, struck a match to light a cigarette. The flame showed a bronzed, black-whiskered face, a pair of eyes gazing straight; then, rearranging his wrappings, he sank full length and laid his head again on the saddle.

"That's our camp-master, whom I must send back to Sulaco now we are going to carry our survey into the Sta. Marta Valley," said the engineer. "A most useful fellow, lent me by Captain Mitchell of the O.S.N. Company. It was very good of Mitchell. Charles Gould told me I couldn't do better than take advantage of the offer. He seems to know how to rule all these muleteers and peons. We had not the slightest trouble with our people. He shall escort your *diligencia* right into Sulaco with some of our railway peons. The road is bad. To have him at hand may save you an upset or two. He promised me to take care of your person all the way down as if you were his father."

This camp-master was the Italian sailor whom all the Europeans in Sulaco, following Captain Mitchell's mispronunciation, were in the habit of calling Nostromo. And indeed, taciturn and ready, he did take excellent care of his charge at the bad parts of the road, as Sir John himself acknowledged to Mrs. Gould afterwards.

CHAPTER 6

AT THAT TIME NOSTROMO had been already long enough in the country to raise to the highest pitch Captain Mitchell's opinion of the extraordinary value of his discovery. Clearly he was one of those invaluable subordinates whom to possess is a legitimate cause of boasting. Captain Mitchell plumed himself upon his eye for men—but he was not selfish—and in the innocence of his pride was already developing that mania for "lending you my Capataz de Cargadores" which was to bring Nostromo into personal contact, sooner or later, with every European in Sulaco, as a sort of universal factotum—a prodigy of efficiency in his own sphere of life.

"The fellow is devoted to me, body and soul!" Captain Mitchell was given to affirm; and though nobody, perhaps, could have explained why it should be so, it was impossible on a survey of their relation to throw doubt on that statement, unless, indeed, one were a bitter, eccentric character like Dr. Monygham—for instance— whose short, hopeless laugh expressed somehow an immense mistrust of mankind. Not that Dr. Monygham was a prodigal either of laughter or of words. He was bitterly taciturn when at his best. At his worst people feared the open scornfulness of his tongue. Only Mrs. Gould could keep his unbelief in men's motives within due bounds; but even to her (on an occasion not connected with Nostromo, and in a tone which for him was gentle), even to her, he had said once, "Really, it is most unreasonable to demand that a man should think of other people so much better than he is able to think of himself."

And Mrs. Gould had hastened to drop the subject. There were strange rumors of the English doctor. Years ago, in the time of Guzman Bento, he had been mixed up, it was whispered, in a conspiracy which was betrayed and, as people expressed it, drowned in blood. His hair had turned grey, his hairless, seamed face was of a brick-dust colour; the large check pattern of his flannel shirt and his old stained Panama hat were an established defiance to the conventionalities of Sulaco. Had it not been for the immaculate cleanliness of his apparel he might have been taken for one of those shiftless Europeans that are a moral eyesore to the respectability of a foreign colony in almost every exotic part of the world. The young ladies of Sulaco, adorning with clusters of pretty faces the balconies along the Street of the Constitution, when they saw him pass, with his limping gait and bowed head, a short linen jacket drawn on carelessly over the flannel check shirt, would remark to each other, "Here is the Señor Doctor going to call on Doña Emilia. He has got his little coat on." The inference was true. Its deeper meaning was hidden from their simple intelligence. Moreover, they expended no store of thought on the doctor. He was old, ugly, learned—and a little *loco** — mad, if not a bit of a sorcerer, as the common people suspected him of being. The little white jacket was in reality a concession to Mrs. Gould's humanizing influence. The doctor, with his habit of skeptical, bitter speech, had no other means of showing his profound respect for the character of the woman who was known in the country as the English Señora. He presented this tribute very seriously indeed; it was no trifle for a man of his habits. Mrs. Gould felt that, too, perfectly. She would never have thought of imposing upon him this marked show of deference.

She kept her old Spanish house (one of the finest specimens in Sulaco) open for the dispensation of the small graces of existence. She dispensed them with simplicity and charm because she was guided by an alert perception of values. She was highly gifted in the art of human intercourse which consists in delicate shades of self-forgetfulness and in the suggestion of universal comprehension. Charles Gould (the Gould family, established in Costaguana for three generations, always went to England for their education and for their wives) imagined that he had fallen in love with a girl's sound common sense like any other man, but these were not exactly the reasons why, for instance, the whole surveying camp, from the youngest of the young men to their mature chief, should have found occasion to allude to Mrs. Gould's house so frequently amongst the high peaks of the Sierra. She would have protested that she had done nothing for them, with a low laugh and a surprised widening of her grey eyes, had anybody told her how convincingly she was remembered on the edge of the snow-line above Sulaco. But directly, with a little capable air of setting her wits to work, she would have found an explanation. "Of course, it was such a surprise for these boys to find any sort of welcome here. And I suppose they are homesick. I suppose everybody must be always just a little homesick."

She was always sorry for homesick people.

Born in the country, as his father before him, spare and tall, with a flaming moustache, a neat chin, clear blue eyes, auburn hair, and a thin, fresh, red face, Charles Gould looked like a new arrival from over the sea. His grandfather had fought in the cause of

---

*Crazy, eccentric.

independence under Bolívar, in that famous English legion which on the battlefield of Carabobo had been saluted by the great Liberator as Saviours of his country.[5] One of Charles Gould's uncles had been the elected President of that very province of Sulaco (then called a State) in the days of Federation, and afterwards had been put up against the wall of a church and shot by the order of the barbarous Unionist general, Guzman Bento. It was the same Guzman Bento who, becoming later Perpetual President, famed for his ruthless and cruel tyranny, reached his apotheosis in the popular legend of a sanguinary land-haunting spectre whose body had been carried off by the devil in person from the brick mausoleum in the nave of the Church of Assumption in Sta. Marta. Thus, at least, the priests explained its disappearance to the barefooted multitude that streamed in, awestruck, to gaze at the hole in the side of the ugly box of bricks before the great altar.

Guzman Bento of cruel memory had put to death great numbers of people besides Charles Gould's uncle; but with a relative martyred in the cause of aristocracy, the Sulaco Oligarchs (this was the phraseology of Guzman Bento's time; now they were called Blancos,* and had given up the federal idea), which meant the families of pure Spanish descent, considered Charles as one of themselves. With such a family record, no one could be more of a Costaguanero than Don Carlos Gould; but his aspect was so characteristic that in the talk of common people he was just the Inglés — the Englishman of Sulaco. He looked more English than a casual tourist, a sort of heretic pilgrim, however, quite unknown in Sulaco. He looked more English than the last arrived batch of young railway engineers, than anybody out of the hunting-field pictures in the numbers of *Punch* reaching his wife's drawing-room two months or so after date. It astonished you to hear him talk Spanish (Castillan, as the natives say) or the Indian dialect of the country-people so naturally. His accent had never been English; but there was something so indelible in all these ancestral Goulds — liberators, explorers, coffee planters, merchants, revolutionists — of Costaguana, that he, the only representative of the third generation in a continent possessing

---

*Whites.

its own style of horsemanship, went on looking thoroughly English even on horseback. This is not said of him in the mocking spirit of the *llaneros**—men of the great plains—who think that no one in the world knows how to sit a horse but themselves. Charles Gould, to use the suitably lofty phrase, rode like a centaur. Riding for him was not a special form of exercise; it was a natural faculty, as walking straight is to all men sound of mind and limb; but, all the same, when cantering beside the rutty ox-cart track to the mine he looked in his English clothes and with his imported saddlery as though he had come this moment to Costaguana at his easy swift *pasotrote,*† straight out of some green meadow at the other side of the world.

His way would lie along the old Spanish road—the Camino Real of popular speech—the only remaining vestige of a fact and name left by that royalty old Giorgio Viola hated, and whose very shadow had departed from the land; for the big equestrian statue of Charles IV‡ at the entrance of the alameda, towering white against the trees, was only known to the folk from the country and to the beggars of the town that slept on the steps around the pedestal, as the Horse of Stone. The other Carlos, turning off to the left with a rapid clatter of hoofs on the disjointed pavement—Don Carlos Gould, in his English clothes, looked as incongruous, but much more at home than the kingly cavalier reining in his steed on the pedestal above the sleeping *leperos*, with his marble arm raised towards the marble rim of a plumed hat.

The weather-stained effigy of the mounted king, with its vague suggestion of a saluting gesture, seemed to present an inscrutable breast to the political changes which had robbed it of its very name; but neither did the other horseman, well known to the people, keen and alive on his well-shaped, slate-coloured beast with a white eye, wear his heart on the sleeve of his English coat. His mind preserved its steady poise as if sheltered in the passionless stability of private and public decencies at home in Europe. He accepted with a like calm the shocking manner in which the Sulaco ladies smothered their faces with pearl powder till they looked like white plaster casts

---

*Plainsmen, cowboys.
†Short trot.
‡King of Spain from 1788 to 1808.

with beautiful living eyes, the peculiar gossip of the town, and the continuous political changes, the constant "saving of the country," which to his wife seemed a puerile and bloodthirsty game of murder and rapine played with terrible earnestness by depraved children. In the early days of her Costaguana life, the little lady used to clench her hands with exasperation at not being able to take the public affairs of the country as seriously as the incidental atrocity of methods deserved. She saw in them a comedy of naïve pretences, but hardly anything genuine except her own appalled indignation. Charles, very quiet and twisting his long moustaches, would decline to discuss them at all. Once, however, he observed to her gently:

"My dear, you seem to forget that I was born here."

These few words made her pause as if they had been a sudden revelation. Perhaps the mere fact of being born in the country did make a difference. She had a great confidence in her husband; it had always been very great. He had struck her imagination from the first by his unsentimentalism, by that very quietude of mind which she had erected in her thought for a sign of perfect competency in the business of living. Don José Avellanos, their neighbor across the street, a statesman, a poet, a man of culture, who had represented his country at several European Courts (and had suffered untold indignities as a state prisoner in the time of the tyrant Guzman Bento), used to declare in Doña Emilia's drawing-room that Carlos had all the English qualities of character with a truly patriotic heart.

Mrs. Gould, raising her eyes to her husband's thin, red and tan face, could not detect the slightest quiver of a feature at what he must have heard said of his patriotism. Perhaps he had just dismounted on his return from the mine; he was English enough to disregard the hottest hours of the day. Basilio, in a livery of white linen and a red sash, had squatted for a moment behind his heels to unstrap the heavy, blunt spurs in the patio; and then the Señor Administrator would go up the staircase into the gallery. Rows of plants in pots, ranged on the balustrade between the pilasters of the arches, screened the *corredor** with their leaves and flowers from the quadrangle below, whose paved space is the true hearthstone of a South

---

*Gallery, balcony.

American house, where the quiet hours of domestic life are marked by the shifting of light and shadow on the flagstones.

Señor Avellanos was in the habit of crossing the patio at five o'clock almost every day. Don José chose to come over at teatime because the English rite at Doña Emilia's house reminded him of the time when he lived in London as Minister Plenipotentiary to the Court of St. James. He did not like tea; and, usually, rocking his American chair, his neat little shiny boots crossed on the footrest, he would talk on and on with a sort of complacent virtuosity wonderful in a man of his age, while he held the cup in his hands for a long time. His close-cropped head was perfectly white; his eyes coal-black.

On seeing Charles Gould step into the *sala** he would nod provisionally and go on to the end of the oratorial period. Only then he would say:

"Carlos, my friend, you have ridden from San Tomé in the heat of the day. Always the true English activity. No? What?"

He drank up all the tea at once in one draught. This performance was invariably followed by a slight shudder and a low, involuntary "br-r-r-r," which was not covered by the hasty exclamation, "Excellent!"

Then giving up the empty cup into his young friend's hand, extended with a smile, he continued to expatiate upon the patriotic nature of the San Tomé mine for the simple pleasure of talking fluently, it seemed, while his reclining body jerked backwards and forwards in a rocking-chair of the sort exported from the United States. The ceiling of the largest drawing-room of the Casa Gould extended its white level far above his head. The loftiness dwarfed the mixture of heavy, straight-backed Spanish chairs of brown wood with leathern seats, and European furniture, low, and cushioned all over, like squat little monsters gorged to bursting with steel springs and horsehair. There were knick-knacks on little tables, mirrors let into the wall above marble consoles, square spaces of carpet under the two groups of armchairs, each presided over by a deep sofa; smaller rugs scattered all over the floor of red tiles; three windows from ceiling down to the ground, opening on a balcony, and flanked by the perpendicular

---

*Drawing room.

folds of the dark hangings. The stateliness of ancient days lingered between the four high, smooth walls, tinted a delicate primrose-colour; and Mrs. Gould, with her little head and shining coils of hair, sitting in a cloud of muslin and lace before a slender mahogany table, resembled a fairy posed lightly before dainty philtres dispensed out of vessels of silver and porcelain.

Mrs. Gould knew the history of the San Tomé mine. Worked in the early days mostly by means of lashes on the backs of slaves, its yield had been paid for in its own weight of human bones. Whole tribes of Indians had perished in the exploitation; and then the mine was abandoned, since with this primitive method it had ceased to make a profitable return, no matter how many corpses were thrown into its maw. Then it became forgotten. It was rediscovered after the War of Independence. An English company obtained the right to work it, and found so rich a vein that neither the exactions of successive governments, nor the periodical raids of recruiting officers upon the population of paid miners they had created, could discourage their perseverance. But in the end, during the long turmoil of *pronunciamientos** that followed the death of the famous Guzman Bento, the native miners, incited to revolt by the emissaries sent out from the capital, had risen upon their English chiefs and murdered them to a man. The decree of confiscation which appeared immediately afterwards in the *Diario Oficial*, published in Sta. Marta, began with the words:

Justly incensed at the grinding oppression of foreigners, actuated by sordid motives of gain rather than by love for a country where they come impoverished to seek their fortunes, the mining population of San Tomé, etc. . . .

and ended with the declaration:

The chief of the State has resolved to exercise to the full his power of clemency. The mine, which by every law, international, human, and divine, reverts now to the Government as national property, shall

---

*Military revolts or uprisings.

remain closed till the sword drawn for the sacred defence of liberal principles has accomplished its mission of securing the happiness of our beloved country.

And for many years this was the last of the San Tomé mine. What advantage that Government had expected from the spoliation, it is impossible to tell now. Costaguana was made with difficulty to pay a beggarly money compensation to the families of the victims, and then the matter dropped out of diplomatic dispatches. But afterwards another Government bethought itself of that valuable asset. It was an ordinary Costaguana Government—the fourth in six years—but it judged of its opportunities sanely. It remembered the San Tomé mine with a secret conviction of its worthlessness in their own hands, but with an ingenious insight into the various uses a silver mine can be put to, apart from the sordid process of extracting the metal from under the ground. The father of Charles Gould, for a long time one of the most wealthy merchants of Costaguana, had already lost a considerable part of his fortune in forced loans to the successive Governments. He was a man of calm judgement, who never dreamed of pressing his claims; and when, suddenly, the perpetual concession of the San Tomé mine was offered to him in full settlement, his alarm became extreme. He was versed in the ways of Governments. Indeed, the intention of this affair, though no doubt deeply meditated in the closet, lay open on the surface of the document presented urgently for his signature. The third and most important clause stipulated that the concession-holder should pay at once to the Government five years' royalties on the estimated output of the mine.

Mr. Gould, senior, defended himself from this fatal favour with many arguments and entreaties, but without success. He knew nothing of mining; he had no means to put his concession on the European market; the mine as a working concern did not exist. The buildings had been burnt down, the mining plant had been destroyed, the mining population had disappeared from the neighborhood years and years ago; the very road had vanished under a flood of tropical vegetation as effectually as if swallowed by the sea; and the main gallery had fallen in within a hundred yards from the entrance. It was no longer an abandoned mine; it was a wild, inaccessible, and rocky gorge of the Sierra, where vestiges of charred timber, some heaps of smashed bricks, and a few shapeless pieces of rusty iron could have been found under the matted mass of thorny creepers covering the ground. Mr. Gould, senior, did not desire the perpetual possession of that desolate locality; in fact, the mere vision of it arising before his mind in the still watches of the night had the power to exasperate him into hours of hot and agitated insomnia.

It so happened, however, that the Finance Minister of the time was a man to whom, in years gone by, Mr. Gould had, unfortunately, declined to grant some small pecuniary assistance, basing his refusal on the ground that the applicant was a notorious gambler and cheat, besides being more than half suspected of a robbery with violence on a wealthy *ranchero** in a remote country district, where he was actually exercising the function of a judge. Now, after reaching his exalted position, that politician had proclaimed his intention to repay evil with good to Señor Gould—the poor man. He affirmed and reaffirmed this resolution in the drawing-rooms of Sta. Marta, in a soft and implacable voice, and with such malicious glances that Mr. Gould's best friends advised him earnestly to attempt no bribery to get the matter dropped. It would have been useless. Indeed, it would not have been a very safe proceeding. Such was also the opinion of a stout, loud-voiced lady of French extraction, the daughter, she said, of an officer of high rank *(officier supérieur de l'armée)*, who was accommodated with lodgings within the walls of a secularized convent next door to the Ministry of Finance. That florid person, when approached on behalf of Mr. Gould in a proper manner, and with a suitable present, shook her head despondently. She was good-natured, and her despondency was genuine. She imagined she could not take money in consideration of something she could not accomplish. The friend of Mr. Gould, charged with the delicate mission, used to say afterwards that she was the only honest person closely or remotely connected with the Government he had ever met. "No go," she had said with a cavalier, husky intonation which was natural to her, and using turns of expression more suitable to a child of parents unknown than to the orphaned daughter

---

*Rancher.

of a general officer. "No; it's no go. *Pas moyen, mon garçon. C'est dommage, tout de même. Ah! zut! Je ne vole pas mon monde. Je ne suis pas ministre—moi! Vous pouvez emporter votre petit sac."**

For a moment, biting her carmine lip, she deplored inwardly the tyranny of the rigid principles governing the sale of her influence in high places. Then, significantly, and with a touch of impatience, "*Allez,*" she added, "*et dites bien à votre bonhomme—entendezvous?— qu'il faut avaler la pilule."*†

After such a warning there was nothing for it but to sign and pay. Mr. Gould had swallowed the pill, and it was as though it had been compounded of some subtle poison that acted directly on his brain. He became at once mine-ridden, and as he was well read in light literature it took to his mind the form of the Old Man of the Sea fastened upon his shoulders.[6] He also began to dream of vampires. Mr. Gould exaggerated to himself the disadvantages of his new position, because he viewed it emotionally. His position in Costaguana was no worse than before. But man is a desperately conservative creature, and the extravagant novelty of this outrage upon his purse distressed his sensibilities. Everybody around him was being robbed by the grotesque and murderous bands that played their game of governments and revolutions after the death of Guzman Bento. His experience had taught him that, however short the plunder might fall of their legitimate expectations, no gang in possession of the Presidential Palace would be so incompetent as to suffer itself to be baffled by the want of a pretext. The first casual colonel of the barefooted army of scarecrows that came along was able to expose with force and precision to any mere civilian his titles to a sum of ten thousand dollars; the while his hope would be immutably fixed upon a gratuity, at any rate, of no less than a thousand. Mr. Gould knew that very well, and, armed with resignation, had waited for better times. But to be robbed under the forms of legality and business was intolerable to his imagination. Mr. Gould, the father, had one fault in his sagacious and honourable character: he attached

---

*"It can't be done, my boy. It's a shame, all the same. Ah! Darn! I don't steal my world. I'm not a minister. You can take your little bag away" (Fr.).

†"Go and say to your good man—do you understand?—that he'll have to swallow the bitter pill" (Fr.).

too much importance to form. It is a failing common to mankind, whose views are tinged by prejudices. There was for him in that affair a malignancy of perverted justice which, by means of a moral shock, attacked his vigorous physique. "It will end by killing me," he used to affirm many times a day. And, in fact, since that time he began to suffer from fever, from liver pains, and mostly from a worrying inability to think of anything else. The Finance Minister could have formed no conception of the profound subtlety of his revenge. Even Mr. Gould's letters to his fourteen-year-old boy Charles, then away in England for his education, came at last to talk of practically nothing but the mine. He groaned over the injustice, the persecution, the outrage of that mine; he occupied whole pages in the exposition of the fatal consequences attaching to the possession of that mine from every point of view, with every dismal inference, with words of horror at the apparently eternal character of that curse. For the Concession had been granted to him and his descendants for ever. He implored his son never to return to Costaguana, never to claim any part of his inheritance there, because it was tainted by the infamous Concession; never to touch it, never to approach it, to forget that America existed, and pursue a mercantile career in Europe. And each letter ended with bitter self-reproaches for having stayed too long in that cavern of thieves, intriguers, and brigands.

To be told repeatedly that one's future is blighted because of the possession of a silver mine is not, at the age of fourteen, a matter of prime importance as to its main statement; but in its form it is calculated to excite a certain amount of wonder and attention. In course of time the boy, at first only puzzled by the angry jeremiads, but rather sorry for his dad, began to turn the matter over in his mind in such moments as he could spare from play and study. In about a year he had evolved from the lecture of the letters a definite conviction that there was a silver mine in the Sulaco province of the Republic of Costaguana, where poor Uncle Harry had been shot by soldiers a great many years before. There was also connected closely with that mine a thing called the "iniquitous Gould Concession," apparently written on a paper which his father desired ardently to "tear and fling into the faces" of presidents, members of judicature, and ministers of State. And this desire persisted, though the names of these people, he noticed, seldom remained the same for a whole year together.

This desire (since the thing was iniquitous) seemed quite natural to the boy, though why the affair was iniquitous he did not know. Afterwards, with advancing wisdom, he managed to clear the plain truth of the business from the fantastic intrusions of the Old Man of the Sea, vampires, and ghouls, which had lent to his father's correspondence the flavour of a gruesome Arabian Nights tale. In the end, the growing youth attained to as close an intimacy with the San Tomé mine as the old man who wrote these plaintive and enraged letters on the other side of the sea. He had been made several times already to pay heavy fines for neglecting to work the mine, he reported, besides other sums extracted from him on account of future royalties, on the ground that a man with such a valuable concession in his pocket could not refuse his financial assistance to the Government of the Republic. The last of his fortune was passing away from him against worthless receipts, he wrote, in a rage, whilst he was being pointed out as an individual who had known how to secure enormous advantages from the necessities of his country. And the young man in Europe grew more and more interested in that thing which could provoke such a tumult of words and passion.

He thought of it every day; but he thought of it without bitterness. It might have been an unfortunate affair for his poor dad, and the whole story threw a queer light upon the social and political life of Costaguana. The view he took of it was sympathetic to his father, yet calm and reflective. His personal feelings had not been outraged, and it is difficult to resent with proper and durable indignation the physical or mental anguish of another organism, even if that other organism is one's own father. By the time he was twenty Charles Gould had, in his turn, fallen under the spell of the San Tomé mine. But it was another form of enchantment, more suitable to his youth, into whose magic formula there entered hope, vigour, and self-confidence, instead of weary indignation and despair. Left after he was twenty to his own guidance (except for the severe injunction not to return to Costaguana), he had pursued his studies in Belgium and France with the idea of qualifying for a mining engineer. But this scientific aspect of his labours remained vague and imperfect in his mind. Mines had acquired for him a dramatic interest. He studied their peculiarities from a personal point of view, too, as one would study the varied characters of men. He visited them as one goes with curiosity to call upon remarkable persons. He visited mines in Germany, in Spain, in Cornwall. Abandoned workings had for him strong fascination. Their desolation appealed to him like the sight of human misery, whose causes are varied and profound. They might have been worthless, but also they might have been misunderstood. His future wife was the first, and perhaps the only person to detect this secret mood which governed the profoundly sensible, almost voiceless attitude of this man towards the world of material things. And at once her delight in him, lingering with half-open wings like those birds that cannot rise easily from a flat level, found a pinnacle from which to soar up into the skies.

They had become acquainted in Italy, where the future Mrs. Gould was staying with an old and pale aunt who, years before, had married a middle-aged, impoverished Italian marquis. She now mourned that man, who had known how to give up his life to the independence and unity of his country, who had known how to be as enthusiastic in his generosity as the youngest of those who fell for that very cause of which old Giorgio Viola was a drifting relic, as a broken spar is suffered to float away disregarded after a naval victory. The Marchesa* led a still, whispering existence, nun-like in her black robes and a white band over the forehead, in a corner of the first floor of an ancient and ruinous palace, whose big, empty halls downstairs sheltered under their painted ceilings the harvests, the fowls, and even the cattle, together with the whole family of the tenant farmer.

The two young people had met in Lucca. After that meeting Charles Gould visited no mines, though they went together in a carriage, once, to see some marble quarries, where the work resembled mining in so far that it also was the tearing of the raw material of treasure from the earth. Charles Gould did not open his heart to her in any set speeches. He simply went on acting and thinking in her sight. This is the true method of sincerity. One of his frequent remarks was, "I think sometimes that poor father takes a wrong view of that San Tomé business." And they discussed that opinion long and earnestly, as if they could influence a mind across half the globe; but in reality they discussed it because the sentiment of love can enter

---

*Marchioness, Italian noblewoman.

into any subject and live ardently in remote phrases. For this natural reason these discussions were precious to Mrs. Gould in her engaged state. Charles feared that Mr. Gould, senior, was wasting his strength and making himself ill by his efforts to get rid of the Concession. "I fancy that this is not the kind of handling it requires," he mused aloud, as if to himself. And when she wondered frankly that a man of character should devote his energies to plotting and intrigues, Charles would remark, with a gentle concern that understood her wonder, "You must not forget that he was born there."

She would set her quick mind to work upon that, and then make the inconsequent retort, which he accepted as perfectly sagacious, because, in fact, it was so—

"Well, and you? You were born there, too."

He knew his answer.

"That's different. I've been away ten years. Dad never had such a long spell; and it was more than thirty years ago."

She was the first person to whom he opened his lips after receiving the news of his father's death.

"It has killed him!" he said.

He had walked straight out of town with the news, straight out before him in the noonday sun on the white road, and his feet had brought him face to face with her in the hall of the ruined *palazzo*,[*] a room magnificent and naked, with here and there a long strip of damask, black with damp and age, hanging down on a bare panel of the wall. It was furnished with exactly one gilt armchair, with a broken back, and an octagon columnar stand bearing a heavy marble vase ornamented with sculptured masks and garlands of flowers, and cracked from top to bottom. Charles Gould was dusty with the white dust of the road lying on his boots, on his shoulders, on his cap with two peaks. Water dripped from under it all over his face, and he grasped a thick oaken cudgel in his bare right hand.

She went very pale under the roses of her big straw hat, gloved, swinging a clear sunshade, caught just as she was going out to meet him at the bottom of the hill, where three poplars stand near the wall of a vineyard.

---

[*]Palace (It.).

"It has killed him!" he repeated. "He ought to have had many years yet. We are a long-lived family."

She was too startled to say anything; he was contemplating with a penetrating and motionless stare the cracked marble urn as though he had resolved to fix its shape for ever in his memory. It was only when, turning suddenly to her, he blurted out twice, "I've come to you—I've come straight to you—," without being able to finish his phrase, that the great pitifulness of that lonely and tormented death in Costaguana came to her with the full force of its misery. He caught hold of her hand, raised it to his lips, and at that she dropped her parasol to pat him on the cheek, murmured "Poor boy," and began to dry her eyes under the downward curve of her hat-brim, very small in her simple, white frock, almost like a lost child crying in the degraded grandeur of the noble hall, while he stood by her, again perfectly motionless in the contemplation of the marble urn.

Afterwards they went out for a long walk, which was silent till he exclaimed suddenly:

"Yes. But if he had only grappled with it in a proper way!"

And then they stopped. Everywhere there were long shadows lying on the hills, on the roads, on the enclosed fields of olive trees; the shadows of poplars, of wide chestnuts, of farm buildings, of stone walls; and in mid-air the sound of a bell, thin and alert, was like the throbbing pulse of the sunset glow. Her lips were slightly parted as though in surprise that he should not be looking at her with his usual expression. His usual expression was unconditionally approving and attentive. He was in his talks with her the most anxious and deferential of dictators, an attitude that pleased her immensely. It affirmed her power without detracting from his dignity. That slight girl, with her little feet, little hands, little face attractively overweighted by great coils of hair; with a rather large mouth, whose mere parting seemed to breathe upon you the fragrance of frankness and generosity, had the fastidious soul of an experienced woman. She was, before all things and all flatteries, careful of her pride in the object of her choice. But now he was actually not looking at her at all; and his expression was tense and irrational, as is natural in a man who elects to stare at nothing past a young girl's head.

"Well, yes. It was iniquitous. They corrupted him thoroughly, the poor old boy. Oh! why wouldn't he let me go back to him? But now I shall know how to grapple with this."

After pronouncing these words with immense assurance, he glanced down at her, and at once fell a prey to distress, incertitude, and fear.

The only thing he wanted to know now, he said, was whether she did love him enough—whether she would have the courage to go with him so far away? He put these questions to her in a voice that trembled with anxiety—for he was a determined man.

She did. She would. And immediately the future hostess of all the Europeans in Sulaco had the physical experience of the earth falling away from under her. It vanished completely, even to the very sound of the bell. When her feet touched the ground again, the bell was still ringing in the valley; she put her hands up to her hair, breathing quickly, and glanced up and down the stony lane. It was reassuringly empty. Meantime, Charles, stepping with one foot into a dry and dusty ditch, picked up the open parasol, which had bounded away from them with a martial sound of drum taps. He handed it to her soberly, a little crestfallen.

They turned back, and after she had slipped her hand on his arm, the first words he pronounced were:

"It's lucky that we shall be able to settle in a coast town. You've heard its name. It is Sulaco. I am so glad poor Father did get that house. He bought a big house there years ago, in order that there should always be a Casa Gould in the principal town of what used to be called the Occidental Province. I lived there once, as a small boy, with my dear mother, for a whole year, while poor Father was away in the United States on business. You shall be the new mistress of the Casa Gould."

And later, in the inhabited corner of the *palazzo* above the vineyards, the marble hills, the pines and olives of Lucca, he also said:

"The name of Gould has been always highly respected in Sulaco. My uncle Harry was chief of the State for some time, and has left a great name amongst the first families. By this I mean the pure Creole families, who take no part in the miserable farce of governments. Uncle Harry was no adventurer. In Costaguana we Goulds are no adventurers. He was of the country, and he loved it, but he remained essentially an Englishman in his ideas. He made use of the political cry of his time. It was Federation. But he was no politician. He simply stood up for social order out of pure love for rational liberty and from his hate of oppression. There was no nonsense about him. He went to work in his own way because it seemed right, just as I feel I must lay hold of that mine."

In such words he talked to her because his memory was very full of the country of his childhood, his heart of his life with that girl, and his mind of the San Tomé Concession. He added that he would have to leave her for a few days to find an American, a man from San Francisco, who was still somewhere in Europe. A few months before he had made his acquaintance in an old historic German town, situated in a mining district. The American had his womankind with him, but seemed lonely while they were sketching all day long the old doorways and the turreted corners of the medieval houses. Charles Gould had with him the inseparable companionship of the mine. The other man was interested in mining enterprises, knew something of Costaguana, and was no stranger to the name of Gould. They had talked together with some intimacy which was made possible by the difference of their ages. Charles wanted now to find that capitalist of shrewd mind and accessible character. His father's fortune in Costaguana, which he had supposed to be still considerable, seemed to have melted in the rascally crucible of revolutions. Apart from some ten thousand pounds deposited in England, there appeared to be nothing left except the house in Sulaco, a vague right of forest exploitation in a remote and savage district, and the San Tomé Concession, which had attended his poor father to the very brink of the grave.

He explained those things. It was late when they parted. She had never before given him such a fascinating vision of herself. All the eagerness of youth for a strange life, for great distances, for a future in which there was an air of adventure, of combat—a subtle thought of redress and conquest—had filled her with an intense excitement, which she returned to the giver with a more open and exquisite display of tenderness.

He left her to walk down the hill, and directly he found himself alone he became sober. That irreparable change a death makes in the course of our daily thoughts can be felt in a vague and poignant discomfort of mind. It hurt Charles Gould to feel that never more, by no effort of will, would he be able to think of his father in the same way he used to think of him when the poor man was alive. His breathing image was no longer in his power. This consideration, closely affecting his own identity, filled his breast with a mournful and angry desire for action. In this his instinct was unerring. Action is consolatory. It is the enemy of thought and the friend of flattering illusions. Only in the conduct of our action can we find the sense of mastery over the Fates. For his action, the mine was obviously the only field. It was imperative sometimes to know how to disobey the solemn wishes of the dead. He resolved firmly to make his disobedience as thorough (by way of atonement) as it well could be. The mine had been the cause of an absurd moral disaster; its working must be made a serious and moral success. He owed it to the dead man's memory. Such were the—properly speaking—emotions of Charles Gould. His thoughts ran upon the means of raising a large amount of capital in San Francisco or elsewhere; and incidentally there occurred to him also the general reflection that the counsel of the departed must be an unsound guide. Not one of them could be aware beforehand what enormous changes the death of any given individual may produce in the very aspect of the world.

The latest phase in the history of the mine Mrs. Gould knew from personal experience. It was in essence the history of her married life. The mantle of the Goulds' hereditary position in Sulaco had descended amply upon her little person; but she would not allow the peculiarities of the strange garment to weigh down the vivacity of her character, which was the sign of no mere mechanical sprightliness, but of an eager intelligence. It must not be supposed that Mrs. Gould's mind was masculine. A woman with a masculine mind is not a being of superior efficiency; she is simply a phenomenon of imperfect differentiation—interestingly barren and without importance. Doña Emilia's intelligence being feminine led her to achieve the conquest of Sulaco, simply by lighting the way for her unselfishness and sympathy. She could converse charmingly, but she was not talkative. The wisdom of the heart having no concern with the erection or demolition of theories any more than with the defence of prejudices, has no random words at its command. The words it pronounces have the value of acts of integrity, tolerance, and compassion. A woman's true tenderness, like the true virility of man, is expressed in action of a conquering kind. The ladies of Sulaco adored Mrs. Gould. "They still look upon me as something of a monster," Mrs. Gould had said pleasantly to one of the three gentlemen from San Francisco she had to entertain in her new Sulaco house just about a year after her marriage.

They were her first visitors from abroad, and they had come to look at the San Tomé mine. She jested most agreeably, they thought; and Charles Gould, besides knowing thoroughly what he was about, had shown himself a real hustler. These facts caused them to be well disposed towards his wife. An unmistakable enthusiasm, pointed by a slight flavour of irony, made her talk of the mine absolutely fascinating to her visitors, and provoked them to grave and indulgent smiles in which there was a good deal of deference. Perhaps had they known how much she was inspired by an idealistic view of success they would have been amazed at the state of her mind as the Spanish-American ladies had been amazed at the tireless activity of her body. She would—in her own words—have been for them "something of a monster." However, the Goulds were in essentials a reticent couple, and their guests departed without the suspicion of any other purpose but simple profit in the working of a silver mine. Mrs. Gould had out her own carriage, with two white mules, to drive them down to the harbour, whence the *Ceres* was to carry them off into the Olympus of plutocrats. Captain Mitchell had snatched at the occasion of leave-taking to remark to Mrs. Gould, in a low, confidential mutter, "This marks an epoch."

Mrs. Gould loved the patio of her Spanish house. A broad flight of stone steps was overlooked silently from a niche in the wall by a Madonna in blue robes with the crowned child sitting on her arm. Subdued voices ascended in the early mornings from the paved well of the quadrangle, with the stamping of horses and mules led out in pairs to drink at the cistern. A tangle of slender bamboo stems drooped its narrow, blade-like leaves over the square pool of water, and the fat coachman sat muffled up on the edge, holding lazily the ends of halters in his hand. Bare-footed servants passed to and fro, issuing from dark, low doorways below; two laundry girls with baskets of washed linen; the baker with the tray of bread made for the day; Leonarda—her own *camerista**—bearing high up, swung from her hand raised above her raven black head, a bunch of starched underskirts dazzlingly white in the slant of sunshine. Then the old porter would hobble in, sweeping the flagstones, and the house was ready for the day. All the lofty rooms on three sides of the quadrangle opened into each other and into the *corredor*, with its wrought-iron railings and a border of flowers, whence, like the lady of the medieval castle, she could witness from above all the departures and arrivals of the Casa, to which the sonorous arched gateway lent an air of stately importance.

She had watched her carriage roll away with the three guests from the north. She smiled. Their three arms went up simultaneously to their three hats. Captain Mitchell, the fourth, in attendance, had already begun a pompous discourse. Then she lingered. She lingered, approaching her face to the clusters of flowers here and there as if to give time to her thoughts to catch up with her slow footsteps along the straight vista of the corridor.

A fringed Indian hammock from Aroa, gay with coloured feather-work, had been swung judiciously in a corner that caught the early sun; for the mornings are cool in Sulaco. The cluster of *flor de noche buena* blazed in great masses before the open glass doors of the reception-rooms. A big green parrot, brilliant like an emerald in a cage that flashed like gold, screamed out ferociously, *"Viva Costaguana!"* then called twice mellifluously, *"Leonarda! Leonarda!"* in imitation of Mrs. Gould's voice, and suddenly took refuge in immobility and silence. Mrs. Gould reached the end of the gallery and put her head through the door of her husband's room.

Charles Gould, with one foot on a low wooden stool, was already strapping his spurs. He wanted to hurry back to the mine. Mrs. Gould, without coming in, glanced about the room. One tall, broad bookcase, with glass doors, was full of books; but in the other, without shelves, and lined with red baize, were arranged firearms: Winchester carbines, revolvers, a couple of shot-guns, and even two pairs of double-barrelled holster pistols. Between them, by itself, upon a strip of scarlet velvet, hung an old cavalry saber, once the property

---

*Maid.

of Don Enrique Gould, the hero of the Occidental Province, presented by Don José Avellanos, the hereditary friend of the family.

Otherwise, the plastered white walls were completely bare, except for a water-colour sketch of the San Tomé mountain—the work of Doña Emilia herself. In the middle of the red-tiled floor stood two long tables littered with plans and papers, a few chairs, and a glass show-case containing specimens of ore from the mine. Mrs. Gould, looking at all these things in turn, wondered aloud why the talk of these wealthy and enterprising men discussing the prospects, the working, and the safety of the mine rendered her so impatient and uneasy, whereas she could talk of the mine by the hour with her husband with unwearied interest and satisfaction.

And dropping her eyelids expressively, she added:

"What do *you* feel about it, Charley?"

Then, surprised at her husband's silence, she raised her eyes, opened wide, as pretty as pale flowers. He had done with the spurs, and, twisting his moustache with both hands, horizontally, he contemplated her from the height of his long legs with a visible appreciation of her appearance. The consciousness of being thus contemplated pleased Mrs. Gould.

"They are considerable men," he said.

"I know. But have you listened to their conversation? They don't seem to have understood anything they have seen here."

"They have seen the mine. They have understood that to some purpose," Charles Gould interjected, in defence of the visitors; and then his wife mentioned the name of the most considerable of the three. He was considerable in finance and in industry. His name was familiar to many millions of people. He was so considerable that he would never have travelled so far away from the centre of his activity if the doctors had not insisted, with veiled menaces, on his taking a long holiday.

"Mr. Holroyd's sense of religion," Mrs. Gould pursued, "was shocked and disgusted at the tawdriness of the dressed-up saints in the cathedral—the worship, he called it, of wood and tinsel. But it seemed to me that he looked upon his own God as a sort of influential partner, who gets his share of profits in the endowment of churches. That's a sort of idolatry. He told me he endowed churches every year, Charley."

"No end of them," said Mr. Gould, marvelling inwardly at the mobility of her physiognomy. "All over the country. He's famous for that sort of munificence."

"Oh, he didn't boast," Mrs. Gould declared, scrupulously. "I believe he's really a good man, but so stupid! A poor Cholo* who offers a little silver arm or leg to thank his god for a cure is as rational and more touching."

"He's at the head of immense silver and iron interests," Charles Gould observed.

"Ah, yes! The religion of silver and iron. He's a very civil man, though he looked awfully solemn when he first saw the Madonna on the staircase, who's only wood and paint; but he said nothing to me. My dear Charley, I heard those men talk among themselves. Can it be that they really wish to become, for an immense consideration, drawers of water and hewers of wood to all the countries and nations of the earth?"

"A man must work to some end," Charles Gould said, vaguely.

Mrs. Gould, frowning, surveyed him from head to foot. With his riding-breeches, leather leggings (an article of apparel never before seen in Costaguana), a Norfolk coat of grey flannel, and those great flaming moustaches, he suggested an officer of cavalry turned gentleman farmer. This combination was gratifying to Mrs. Gould's tastes. "How thin the poor boy is!" she thought. "He overworks himself." But there was no denying that his fine-drawn, keen red face, and his whole, long-limbed, lank person had an air of breeding and distinction. And Mrs. Gould relented.

"I only wondered what you felt," she murmured, gently.

During the last few days, as it happened, Charles Gould had been kept too busy thinking twice before he spoke to have paid much attention to the state of his feelings. But theirs was a successful match, and he had no difficulty in finding his answer.

"The best of my feelings are in your keeping, my dear," he said lightly; and there was so much truth in that obscure phrase that he experienced towards her at the moment a great increase of gratitude and tenderness.

---

*Indian; person of mixed heritage.

Mrs. Gould, however, did not seem to find this answer in the least obscure. She brightened up delicately; already he had changed his tone.

"But there are facts. The worth of the mine—as a mine—is beyond doubt. It shall make us very wealthy. The mere working of it is a matter of technical knowledge, which I have—which ten thousand other men in the world have. But its safety, its continued existence as an enterprise, giving a return to men—to strangers, comparative strangers—who invest money in it, is left altogether in my hands. I have inspired confidence in a man of wealth and position. You seem to think this perfectly natural—do you? Well, I don't know. I don't know why I have; but it is a fact. This fact makes everything possible, because without it I would never have thought of disregarding my father's wishes. I would never have disposed of the Concession as a speculator disposes of a valuable right to a company—for cash and shares, to grow rich eventually if possible, but at any rate to put some money at once in his pocket. No. Even if it had been feasible—which I doubt—I would not have done so. Poor Father did not understand. He was afraid I would hang on to the ruinous thing, waiting for just some such chance, and waste my life miserably. That was the true sense of his prohibition, which we have deliberately set aside."

They were walking up and down the corridor. Her head just reached to his shoulder. His arm, extended downwards, was about her waist. His spurs jingled slightly.

"He had not seen me for ten years. He did not know me. He parted from me for my sake, and he would never let me come back. He was always talking in his letters of leaving Costaguana, of abandoning everything and making his escape. But he was too valuable a prey. They would have thrown him into one of their prisons at the first suspicion."

His spurred feet clinked slowly. He was bending over his wife as they walked. The big parrot, turning its head askew, followed their pacing figures with a round, unblinking eye.

"He was a lonely man. Ever since I was ten years old he used to talk to me as if I had been grown up. When I was in Europe he wrote to me every month. Ten, twelve pages every month of my life for ten years. And, after all, he did not know me! Just think of it—ten whole years away; the years I was growing up into a man. He could not know me. Do you think he could?"

Mrs. Gould shook her head negatively; which was just what her husband had expected from the strength of the argument. But she shook her head negatively only because she thought that no one could know her Charles—really know him for what he was but herself. The thing was obvious. It could be felt. It required no argument. And poor Mr. Gould, senior, who had died too soon to ever hear of their engagement, remained too shadowy a figure for her to be credited with knowledge of any sort whatever.

"No, he did not understand. In my view this mine could never have been a thing to sell. Never! After all his misery I simply could not have touched it for money alone," Charles Gould pursued: and she pressed her head to his shoulder approvingly.

These two young people remembered the life which had ended wretchedly just when their own lives had come together in that splendour of hopeful love, which to the most sensible minds appears like a triumph of good over all the evils of the earth. A vague idea of rehabilitation had entered the plan of their life. That it was so vague as to elude the support of argument made it only the stronger. It had presented itself to them at the instant when the woman's instinct of devotion and the man's instinct of activity receive from the strongest of illusions their most powerful impulse. The very prohibition imposed the necessity of success. It was as if they had been morally bound to make good their vigorous view of life against the unnatural error of weariness and despair. If the idea of wealth was present to them it was only so far as it was bound with that other success. Mrs. Gould, an orphan from early childhood and without fortune, brought up in an atmosphere of intellectual interests, had never considered the aspects of great wealth. They were too remote, and she had not learned that they were desirable. On the other hand, she had not known anything of absolute want. Even the very poverty of her aunt, the Marchesa, had nothing intolerable to a refined mind; it seemed in accord with a great grief; it had the austerity of a sacrifice offered to a noble ideal. Thus even the most legitimate touch of materialism was wanting in Mrs. Gould's character. The dead man of whom she thought with tenderness (because he was Charley's father), and with some impatience (because he had been weak), must be put completely in the wrong. Nothing else would do to keep their prosperity without a stain on its only real, on its immaterial side!

Charles Gould, on his part, had been obliged to keep the idea of wealth well to the fore; but he brought it forward as a means, not as an end. Unless the mine was good business it could not be touched. He had to insist on that aspect of the enterprise. It was his lever to move men who had capital. And Charles Gould believed in the mine. He knew everything that could be known of it. His faith in the mine was contagious, though it was not served by a great eloquence; but businessmen are frequently as sanguine and imaginative as lovers. They are affected by a personality much oftener than people would suppose; and Charles Gould, in his unshaken assurance, was absolutely convincing. Besides, it was a matter of common knowledge to the men to whom he addressed himself that mining in Costaguana was a game that could be made considerably more than worth the candle. The men of affairs knew that very well. The real difficulty in touching it was elsewhere. Against that there was an implication of calm and implacable resolution in Charles Gould's very voice. Men of affairs venture sometimes on acts that the common judgement of the world would pronounce absurd; they make their decisions on apparently impulsive and human grounds. "Very well," had said the considerable personage to whom Charles Gould on his way out through San Francisco had lucidly exposed his point of view. "Let us suppose that the mining affairs of Sulaco are taken in hand. There would then be in it: first, the house of Holroyd, which is all right; then, Mr. Charles Gould, a citizen of Costaguana, who is also all right; and, lastly, the Government of the Republic. So far this resembles the first start of the Atacama nitrate fields, where there was a financing house, a gentleman of the name of Edwards, and—a Government; or, rather, two Governments—two South American Governments. And you know what came of it. War came of it;[7] devastating and prolonged war came of it, Mr. Gould. However, here we possess the advantage of having only one South American Government hanging around for plunder out of the deal. It is an advantage; but then there are degrees of badness, and that Government is the Costaguana Government."

Thus spoke the considerable personage, the millionaire endower of churches on a scale befitting the greatness of his native land—the same to whom the doctors used the language of horrid and veiled

menaces. He was a big-limbed, deliberate man, whose quiet burliness
lent to an ample silk-faced frock-coat a superfine dignity. His hair was
iron grey, his eyebrows were still black, and his massive profile was the
profile of a Caesar's head on an old Roman coin. But his parentage
was German and Scotch and English, with remote strains of Danish
and French blood, giving him the temperament of a Puritan and an
insatiable imagination of conquest. He was completely unbending to
his visitor, because of the warm introduction the visitor had brought
from Europe, and because of an irrational liking for earnestness and
determination wherever met, to whatever end directed.

"The Costaguana Government shall play its hand for all it's
worth—and don't you forget it, Mr. Gould. Now, what is
Costaguana? It is the bottomless pit of ten-per-cent loans and other
fool investments. European capital has been flung into it with both
hands for years. Not ours, though. We in this country know just
about enough to keep indoors when it rains. We can sit and watch.
Of course, some day we shall step in. We are bound to. But there's
no hurry. Time itself has got to wait on the greatest country in the
whole of God's Universe. We shall be giving the word for everything:
industry, trade, law, journalism, art, politics, and religion, from Cape
Horn clear over to Smith's Sound, and beyond, too, if anything
worth taking hold of turns up at the North Pole. And then we shall
have the leisure to take in hand the outlying islands and continents
of the earth. We shall run the world's business whether the world
likes it or not. The world can't help it—and neither can we, I guess."

By this he meant to express his faith in destiny in words suitable to
his intelligence, which was unskilled in the presentation of general
ideas. His intelligence was nourished on facts; and Charles Gould,
whose imagination had been permanently affected by the one great
fact of a silver mine, had no objection to this theory of the world's future. If it had seemed distasteful for a moment it was because the sudden statement of such vast eventualities dwarfed almost to
nothingness the actual matter in hand. He and his plans and all the
mineral wealth of the Occidental Province appeared suddenly
robbed of every vestige of magnitude. The sensation was disagreeable; but Charles Gould was not dull. Already he felt that he was pro-
ducing a favourable impression; the consciousness of that flattering
fact helped him to a vague smile, which his big interlocutor took for

a smile of discreet and admiring assent. He smiled quietly, too; and immediately Charles Gould, with that mental agility mankind will display in defence of a cherished hope, reflected that the very apparent insignificance of his aim would help him to success. His personality and his mine would be taken up because it was a matter of no great consequence, one way or another, to a man who referred his action to such a prodigious destiny. And Charles Gould was not humiliated by this consideration, because the thing remained as big as ever for him. Nobody else's vast conceptions of destiny could diminish the aspect of his desire for the redemption of the San Tomé mine. In comparison to the correctness of his aim, definite in space and absolutely attainable within a limited time, the other man appeared for an instant as a dreamy idealist of no importance.

The great man, massive and benignant, had been looking at him thoughtfully; when he broke the short silence it was to remark that concessions flew about thick in the air of Costaguana. Any simple soul that just yearned to be taken in could bring down a concession at the first shot.

"Our consuls get their mouths stopped with them," he continued, with a twinkle of genial scorn in his eyes. But in a moment he became grave. "A conscientious, upright man, that cares nothing for boodle, and keeps clear of their intrigues, conspiracies, and factions, soon gets his passports. See that, Mr. Gould? *Persona non grata.* That's the reason our Government is never properly informed. On the other hand, Europe must be kept out of this continent, and for proper interference on our part the time is not yet ripe, I dare say. But we here—we are not this country's Government, neither are we simple souls. Your affair is all right. The main question for us is whether the second partner, and that's you, is the sort to hold his own against the third and unwelcome partner, which is one or another of the high and mighty robber gangs that run the Costaguana Government. What do you think, Mr. Gould, eh?"

He bent forward to look steadily into the unflinching eyes of Charles Gould, who, remembering the large box full of his father's letters, put the accumulated scorn and bitterness of many years into the tone of his answer:

"As far as the knowledge of these men and their methods and their politics is concerned, I can answer for myself. I have been fed on that sort of knowledge since I was a boy. I am not likely to fall into mistakes from excess of optimism."

"Not likely, eh? That's all right. Tact and a stiff upper lip is what you'll want; and you could bluff a little on the strength of your backing. Not too much, though. We will go with you as long as the thing runs straight. But we won't be drawn into any large trouble. This is the experiment which I am willing to make. There is some risk, and we will take it; but if you can't keep up your end, we will stand our loss, of course, and then—we'll let the thing go. This mine can wait; it has been shut up before, you know. You must understand that under no circumstances will we consent to throw good money after bad."

Thus the great personage had spoken then, in his own private office, in a great city where other men (very considerable in the eyes of a vain populace) waited with alacrity upon a wave of his hand. And rather more than a year later, during his unexpected appearance in Sulaco, he had emphasized his uncompromising attitude with a freedom of sincerity permitted to his wealth and influence. He did this with the less reserve, perhaps, because the inspection of what had been done, and more still the way in which successive steps had been taken, had impressed him with the conviction that Charles Gould was perfectly capable of keeping up his end.

"This young fellow," he thought to himself, "may yet become a power in the land."

This thought flattered him, for hitherto the only account of this young man he could give to his intimates was:

"My brother-in-law met him in one of these one-horse old German towns, near some mines, and sent him on to me with a letter. He's one of the Costaguana Goulds, pure-bred Englishmen, but all born in the country. His uncle went into politics, was the last Provincial President of Sulaco, and got shot after a battle. His father was a prominent businessman in Sta. Marta, tried to keep clear of their politics, and died ruined after a lot of revolutions. And that's your Costaguana in a nutshell."

Of course, he was too great a man to be questioned as to his motives, even by his intimates. The outside world was at liberty to wonder respectfully at the hidden meaning of his actions. He was so great a man that his lavish patronage of the "purer forms of Christianity" (which in its naïve form of church-building amused Mrs. Gould) was looked upon by his fellow-citizens as the manifestation of a pious and humble spirit. But in his own circles of the financial world the taking up of such a thing as the San Tomé mine was regarded with respect, indeed, but rather as a subject for discreet jocularity. It was a great man's caprice. In the great Holroyd building (an enormous pile of iron, glass, and blocks of stone at the corner of two streets, cobwebbed aloft by the radiation of telegraph wires) the heads of principal departments exchanged humorous glances, which meant that they were not let into the secrets of the San Tomé business. The Costaguana mail (it was never large—one fairly heavy envelope) was taken unopened straight into the great man's room, and no instructions dealing with it had ever been issued thence. The office whispered that he answered personally—and not by dictation either, but actually writing in his own hand, with pen and ink, and, it was to be supposed, taking a copy in his own private press copybook, inaccessible to profane eyes. Some scornful young men, insignificant pieces of minor machinery in that eleven-storey-high workshop of great affairs, expressed frankly their private opinion that the great chief had done at last something silly, and was ashamed of his folly; others, elderly and insignificant, but full of romantic reverence for the business that had devoured their best years, used to mutter darkly and knowingly that this was a portentous sign; that the Holroyd connection meant by-and-by to get hold of the whole Republic of Costaguana, lock, stock, and barrel. But, in fact, the hobby theory was the right one. It interested the great man to attend personally to the San Tomé mine; it interested him so much that he allowed this hobby to give a direction to the first complete holiday he had taken for quite a startling number of years. He was not running a great enterprise there; no mere railway board or individual corporation. He was running a man! A success would have pleased him very much on refreshingly novel grounds; but, on the other side of the same feeling, it was incumbent upon him to cast it off utterly at the first sign of failure. A man may be thrown off. The papers had unfortunately trumpeted all over the land his journey to Costaguana. If he was pleased at the way Charles Gould was going on, he infused an added grimness into his assurances of support. Even at the very last interview, half an hour or so before he rolled out of the patio, hat in hand, behind Mrs. Gould's white mules, he had said in Charles's room:

"You go ahead in your own way, and I shall know how to help you as long as you hold your own. But you may rest assured that in a given case we shall know how to drop you in time."

To this Charles Gould's only answer had been: "You may begin sending out the machinery as soon as you like."

And the great man had liked this imperturbable assurance. The secret of it was that to Charles Gould's mind these uncompromising terms were agreeable. Like this the mine preserved its identity, with which he had endowed it as a boy; and it remained dependent on himself alone. It was a serious affair, and he, too, took it grimly.

"Of course," he said to his wife, alluding to this last conversation with the departed guest, while they walked slowly up and down the corridor, followed by the irritated eye of the parrot—"of course, a man of that sort can take up a thing or drop it when he likes. He will suffer from no sense of defeat. He may have to give in, or he may have to die tomorrow, but the great silver and iron interests shall survive, and some day shall get hold of Costaguana along with the rest of the world."

They had stopped near the cage. The parrot, catching the sound of a word belonging to his vocabulary, was moved to interfere. Parrots are very human.

"*Viva Costaguana!*" he shrieked, with intense self-assertion, and, instantly ruffling up his feathers, assumed an air of puffed-up somnolence behind the glittering wires.

"And do you believe that, Charley?" Mrs. Gould asked. "This seems to me most awful materialism, and—"

"My dear, it's nothing to me," interrupted her husband, in a reasonable tone. "I make use of what I see. What's it to me whether his talk is the voice of destiny or simply a bit of clap-trap eloquence? There's a good deal of eloquence of one sort or another produced in both Americas. The air of the New World seems favourable to the art of declamation. Have you forgotten how dear Avellanos can hold forth for hours here—?"

"Oh, but that's different," protested Mrs. Gould, almost shocked. The allusion was not to the point. Don José was a dear good man, who talked very well, and was enthusiastic about the greatness of the San Tomé mine. "How can you compare them, Charles?" she exclaimed, reproachfully. "He has suffered—and yet he hopes."

The working competence of men—which she never questioned—was very surprising to Mrs. Gould, because upon so many obvious issues they showed themselves strangely muddle-headed.

Charles Gould, with a careworn calmness which secured for him at once his wife's anxious sympathy, assured her that he was not comparing. He was an American himself, after all, and perhaps he could understand both kinds of eloquence—"if it were worth while to try," he added, grimly. But he had breathed the air of England longer than any of his people had done for three generations, and really he begged to be excused. His poor father could be eloquent, too. And he asked his wife whether she remembered a passage in one of his father's last letters where Mr. Gould had expressed the conviction that "God looked wrathfully at these countries, or else He would let some ray of hope fall through a rift in the appalling darkness of intrigue, bloodshed, and crime that hung over the Queen of Continents."

Mrs. Gould had not forgotten. "You read it to me, Charley," she murmured. "It was a striking pronouncement. How deeply your father must have felt its terrible sadness!"

"He did not like to be robbed. It exasperated him," said Charles Gould. "But the image will serve well enough. What is wanted here is law, good faith, order, security. Anyone can declaim about these things, but I pin my faith to material interests. Only let the material interests once get a firm footing, and they are bound to impose the conditions on which alone they can continue to exist. That's how your money-making is justified here in the face of lawlessness and disorder. It is justified because the security which it demands must be shared with an oppressed people. A better justice will come afterwards. That's your ray of hope." His arm pressed her slight form closer to his side for a moment. "And who knows whether in that sense even the San Tomé mine may not become that little rift in the darkness which poor Father despaired of ever seeing?"

She glanced up at him with admiration. He was competent; he had given a vast shape to the vagueness of her unselfish ambitions.

"Charley," she said, "you are splendidly disobedient."

He left her suddenly in the *corredor* to go and get his hat, a soft, grey sombrero, an article of national costume which combined unexpectedly well with his English get-up. He came back, a riding-whip under his arm, buttoning up a dogskin glove; his face reflected the resolute nature of his thoughts. His wife had waited for him at the head of the stairs, and before he gave her the parting kiss he finished the conversation:

"What should be perfectly clear to us," he said, "is the fact that there is no going back. Where could we begin life afresh? We are in now for all that there is in us."

He bent over her upturned face very tenderly and a little remorsefully. Charles Gould was competent because he had no illusions. The Gould Concession had to fight for life with such weapons as could be found at once in the mire of corruption that was so universal as to almost lose its significance. He was prepared to stoop for his weapons. For a moment he felt as if the silver mine, which had killed his father, had decoyed him further than he meant to go; and with the roundabout logic of emotions, he felt that the worthiness of his life was bound up with success. There was no going back.

CHAPTER 7

Mrs. Gould was too intelligently sympathetic not to share that feeling. It made life exciting, and she was too much of a woman not to like excitement. But it frightened her, too, a little; and when Don José Avellanos, rocking in the American chair, would go so far as to say, "Even, my dear Carlos, if you had failed; even if some untowards event were yet to destroy your work—which God forbid!— you would have deserved well of your country," Mrs. Gould would look up from the tea-table profoundly at her unmoved husband stirring the spoon in the cup as though he had not heard a word.

Not that Don José anticipated anything of the sort. He could not praise enough dear Carlos's tact and courage. His English, rock-like quality of character was his best safeguard, Don José affirmed; and, turning to Mrs. Gould, "As to you, Emilia, my soul"—he would address her with the familiarity of his age and old friendship—"you are as true a patriot as though you had been born in our midst."

This might have been less or more than the truth. Mrs. Gould, accompanying her husband all over the province in the search for labour, had seen the land with a deeper glance than a trueborn Costaguana could have done. In her travel-worn riding habit, her face powdered white like a plaster cast, with a further protection of a small silk mask during the heat of the day, she rode on a well-shaped, light-footed pony in the centre of a little cavalcade. Two *mozos de campo*,* picturesque in great hats, with spurred bare heels, in white embroidered *calzoneras*,† leather jackets, and striped ponchos, rode ahead with carbines across their shoulders, swaying in unison to the pace of the horses. A *tropilla*‡ of pack mules brought up the rear in charge of a thin brown muleteer, sitting his long-eared beast very near the tail, legs thrust far forward, the wide brim of his hat set far back, making a sort of halo for his head. An old Costaguana officer, a retired senior major of humble origins, but patronized by the first families on account of his Blanco opinions, had been recommended by Don José for commissary and organizer of that expedition. The points of his grey moustache hung far below his chin, and, riding on Mrs. Gould's left hand, he looked about with kindly eyes, pointing out the features of the country, telling the names of the little *pueblos*§ and of the estates, of the smooth-walled *haciendas*‖ like long fortresses crowning the knolls above the level of the Sulaco Valley. It unrolled itself, with green young crops, plains, woodland, and gleams of water, park-like, from the blue vapour of the distant sierra to an immense quivering horizon of grass and sky, where big white clouds seemed to fall slowly into the darkness of their own shadows.

Men ploughed with wooden ploughs and yoked oxen, small on a boundless expanse, as if attacking immensity itself. The mounted figures of *vaqueros* galloped in the distance, and the great herds fed with all their horned heads one way, in one single wavering line as far as eye could reach across the broad *potreros*.# A spreading cotton-wool tree shaded a thatched *rancho*** by the road; the trudging files

---

*Escorts.
†Pants buttoned down the side seams.
‡Group.
§Villages, settlements.
‖Ranches, estates, farms.
#Pastures.
**Hut.

of burdened Indians, taking off their hats, would lift sad, mute eyes to the cavalcade raising the dust of the crumbling *camino real** made by the hands of their enslaved forefathers. And Mrs. Gould, with each day's journey, seemed to come nearer to the soul of the land in the tremendous disclosure of this interior unaffected by the slight European veneer of the coast towns, a great land of plain and mountain and people, suffering and mute, waiting for the future in a pathetic immobility of patience.

She knew its sights and its hospitality, dispensed with a sort of slumbrous dignity in those great houses presenting long, blind walls and heavy portals to the windswept pastures. She was given the head of the tables, where masters and dependants sat in a simple and patriarchal state. The ladies of the house would talk softly in the moonlight under the orange trees of the courtyards, impressing upon her the sweetness of their voices and the something mysterious in the quietude of their lives. In the morning the gentlemen, well mounted in braided sombreros and embroidered riding-suits, with much silver on the trappings of their horses, would ride forth to escort the departing guests before committing them, with grave good-byes, to the care of God at the boundary pillars of their estates. In all these households she could hear stories of political outrage; friends, relatives, ruined, imprisoned, killed in the battles of senseless civil wars, barbarously executed in ferocious proscriptions, as though the government of the country had been a struggle of lust between bands of absurd devils let loose upon the land with sabres and uniforms and grandiloquent phrases. And on all the lips she found a weary desire for peace, the dread of officialdom with its nightmarish parody of administration without law, without security, and without justice.

She bore a whole two months of wandering very well; she had that power of resistance to fatigue which one discovers here and there in some quite frail-looking women with surprise — like a state of possession by a remarkably stubborn spirit. Don Pepe — the old Costaguana major — after much display of solicitude for the delicate lady, had ended by conferring upon her the name of the "Never-tired Señora."

---

*Royal highway.

Mrs. Gould was indeed becoming a Costaguanera. Having acquired in southern Europe a knowledge of true peasantry, she was able to appreciate the great worth of the people. She saw the man under the silent, sad-eyed beast of burden. She saw them on the road carrying loads, lonely figures upon the plain, toiling under great straw hats, with their white clothing flapping about their limbs in the wind; she remembered the villages by some group of Indian women at the fountain impressed upon her memory, by the face of some young Indian girl with a melancholy and sensual profile, raising an earthenware vessel of cool water at the door of a dark hut with a wooden porch cumbered with great brown jars. The solid wooden wheels of an ox-cart, halted with its shafts in the dust, showed the strokes of the axe; and a party of charcoal carriers, with each man's load resting above his head on the top of the low mud wall, slept stretched in a row within the strip of shade.

The heavy stonework of bridges and churches left by the conquerors proclaimed the disregard of human labour, the tribute-labour of vanished nations. The power of king and church was gone, but at the sight of some heavy ruinous pile overtopping from a knoll the low mud walls of a village, Don Pepe would interrupt the tale of his campaigns to exclaim:

"Poor Costaguana! Before, it was everything for the padres, nothing for the people; and now it is everything for these great *políticos**** in Sta. Marta, for Negroes and thieves."

Charles talked with the *alcades*, with the *fiscales*,[†] with the principal people in towns, and with the *caballeros* on the estates. The *comandantes*[‡] of the districts offered him escorts—for he could show an authorization from the Sulaco political chief of the day. How much the document had cost him in gold twenty-dollar pieces was a secret between himself, a great man in the United States (who condescended to answer the Sulaco mail with his own hand), and a great man of another sort, with a dark olive complexion and shifty eyes, inhabiting then the Palace of the Intendencia in Sulaco, and who piqued himself on his culture and Europeanism generally in a

---

*Politicians.

†*Alcades* are magistrates; *fiscales* are district attorneys.

‡Commanders.

rather French style because he had lived in Europe for some years—in exile, he said. However, it was pretty well known that just before this exile he had incautiously gambled away all the cash in the Custom House of a small port where a friend in power had procured for him the post of subcollector. That youthful indiscretion had, amongst other inconveniences, obliged him to earn his living for a time as a café waiter in Madrid; but his talents must have been great, after all, since they had enabled him to retrieve his political fortunes so splendidly. Charles Gould, exposing his business with an imperturbable steadiness, called him Excellency.

The provincial Excellency assumed a weary superiority, tilting his chair far back near an open window in the true Costaguana manner. The military band happened to be braying operatic selections on the *plaza* just then, and twice he raised his hand imperatively for silence in order to listen to a favourite passage.

"Exquisite, delicious!" he murmured; while Charles Gould waited, standing by with inscrutable patience. "Lucia, Lucia di Lammermoor![8] I am passionate for music. It transports me. Ha! the divine—ha!—Mozart. *Sí!* divine . . . What is it you were saying?"

Of course, rumours had reached him already of the newcomer's intentions. Besides, he had received an official warning from Sta. Marta. His manner was intended simply to conceal his curiosity and impress his visitor. But after he had locked up something valuable in the drawer of a large writing-desk in a distant part of the room, he became very affable, and walked back to his chair smartly.

"If you intend to build villages and assemble a population near the mine, you shall require a decree of the Minister of the Interior for that," he suggested in a businesslike manner.

"I have already sent a memorial," said Charles Gould, steadily, "and I reckon now confidently upon your Excellency's favourable conclusions."

The Excellency was a man of many moods. With the receipt of the money a great mellowness had descended upon his simple soul. Unexpectedly he fetched a deep sigh.

"Ah, Don Carlos! What we want is advanced men like you in the province. The lethargy—the lethargy of these aristocrats! The want of public spirit! The absence of all enterprise! I, with my profound studies in Europe, you understand—"

With one hand thrust into his swelling bosom, he rose and fell on his toes, and for ten minutes, almost without drawing breath, went on hurling himself intellectually to the assault of Charles Gould's polite silence; and when, stopping abruptly, he fell back into his chair, it was as though he had been beaten off from a fortress. To save his dignity he hastened to dismiss this silent man with a solemn inclination of the head and the words, pronounced with moody, fatigued condescension:

"You may depend upon my enlightened goodwill as long as your conduct as a good citizen deserves it."

He took up a paper fan and began to cool himself with a consequential air, while Charles Gould bowed and withdrew. Then he dropped the fan at once, and stared with an appearance of wonder and perplexity at the closed door for quite a long time. At last he shrugged his shoulders as if to assure himself of his disdain. Cold, dull. No intellectuality. Red hair. A true Englishman. He despised him.

His face darkened. What meant this unimpressed and frigid behaviour? He was the first of the successive politicians sent out from the capital to rule the Occidental Province whom the manner of Charles Gould in official intercourse was to strike as offensively independent.

Charles Gould assumed that if the appearance of listening to deplorable balderdash must form part of the price he had to pay for being left unmolested, the obligation of uttering balderdash personally was by no means included in the bargain. He drew the line there. To these provincial autocrats, before whom the peaceable population of all classes had been accustomed to tremble, the reserve of that English-looking engineer caused an uneasiness which swung to and fro between cringing and truculence. Gradually all of them discovered that, no matter what party was in power, that man remained in most effective touch with the higher authorities in Sta. Marta.

This was a fact, and it accounted perfectly for the Goulds being by no means so wealthy as the engineer-in-chief on the new railway could legitimately suppose. Following the advice of Don José Avellanos, who was a man of good counsel (though rendered timid by his horrible experiences of Guzman Bento's time), Charles Gould had kept clear of the capital; but in the current gossip of the foreign residents there he was known (with a good deal of seriousness underlying the irony) by the nickname of "King of Sulaco." An advocate of the Costaguana Bar, a man of reputed ability and good character, member of the distinguished Moraga family possessing extensive estates in the Sulaco Valley, was pointed out to strangers, with a shade of mystery and respect, as the agent of the San Tomé mine— "political, you know." He was tall, black-whiskered, and discreet. It was known that he had easy access to ministers, and that the numerous Costaguana generals were always anxious to dine at his house. Presidents granted him audience with facility. He corresponded actively with his maternal uncle, Don José Avellanos; but his letters— unless those expressing formally his dutiful affection—were seldom entrusted to the Costaguana post office. There the envelopes are opened, indiscriminately, with the frankness of a brazen and childish impudence characteristic of some Spanish-American Governments. But it must be noted that at about the time of the reopening of the San Tomé mine the muleteer who had been employed by Charles Gould in his preliminary travels on the Campo added his small train of animals to the thin stream of traffic carried over the mountain passes between the Sta. Marta upland and the Valley of Sulaco. There are no travellers by that arduous and unsafe route unless under very exceptional circumstances, and the state of inland trade did not visibly require additional transport facilities; but the man seemed to find his account in it. A few packages were always found for him whenever he took the road. Very brown and wooden, in goatskin breeches with the hair outside, he sat near the tail of his own smart mule, his great hat turned against the sun, an expression of blissful vacancy on his long face, humming day after day a love-song in a plaintive key, or, without a change of expression, letting out a yell at his small *tropilla* in front. A round little guitar hung high up on his back; and there was a place scooped out artistically in the wood of one of his pack-saddles where a tightly rolled piece of paper could be slipped in, the wooden plug replaced, and the coarse canvas nailed on again. When in Sulaco it was his practice to smoke and doze all day long (as though he had no care in the world) on a stone bench outside the doorway of the Casa Gould and facing the windows of the Avellanos house. Years and years ago his mother had been chief laundry-woman in that family—very accomplished in the matter of clear-starching. He himself had been born on one of their *haciendas*. His name was

Bonifacio, and Don José, crossing the street about five o'clock to call on Doña Emilia, always acknowledged his humble salute by some movement of hand or head. The porters of both houses conversed lazily with him in tones of grave intimacy. His evenings he devoted to gambling and to calls in a spirit of generous festivity upon the *peyne d'oro* girls* in the more remote side-streets of the town. But he, too, was a discreet man.

CHAPTER 8

THOSE OF US WHOM business or curiosity took to Sulaco in these years before the first advent of the railway can remember the steadying effect of the San Tomé mine upon the life of that remote province. The outward appearances had not changed then as they have changed since, as I am told, with cable cars running along the streets of the Constitution, and carriage roads far into the country, to Rincón and other villages, where the foreign merchants and the *ricos*† generally have their modern villas, and a vast railway goods-yard by the harbour, which has a quayside, a long range of ware-houses, and quite serious, organized labour troubles of its own.

Nobody had ever heard of labour troubles then. The Cargadores of the port formed, indeed, an unruly brotherhood of all sorts of scum, with a patron saint of their own. They went on strike regularly (every bullfight day), a form of trouble that even Nostromo at the height of his prestige could never cope with efficiently; but the morning after each fiesta, before the Indian market-women had opened their mat parasols on the *plaza*, when the snows of Higuerota gleamed pale over the town on a yet black sky, the appearance of a phantom-like horseman mounted on a silver-grey mare solved the problem of labour without fail. His steed paced the lanes of the slums and the weed-grown enclosures within the old ramparts, between the black, lightless cluster of huts, like cow-byres, like dog-kennels. The

---

*Prostitutes (*peine d'oro* means, literally, "golden comb").
†Wealthy.

horseman hammered with the butt of a heavy revolver at the doors of low *pulperías*,* of obscene lean-to sheds sloping against the tumble-down piece of a noble wall, at the wooden sides of dwellings so flimsy that the sound of snores and sleepy mutters within could be heard in the pauses of the thundering clatter of his blows. He called out men's names menacingly from the saddle, once, twice. The drowsy answers—grumpy, conciliating, savage, jocular, or deprecating—came out into the silent darkness in which the horseman sat still, and presently a dark figure would flit out coughing in the still air. Some-times a low-toned woman cried through the window-hole softly, "He's coming directly, *señor*," and the horseman waited silent on a motionless horse. But if perchance he had to dismount, then, after a while, from the door of that hovel or of that *pulpería*, with a ferocious scuffle and stifled imprecations, a *cargador* would fly out head first and hands abroad, to sprawl under the forelegs of the silver-grey mare, who only pricked forward her sharp little ears. She was used to that work; and the man, picking himself up, would walk away hastily from Nostromo's revolver, reeling a little along the street and snarling low curses. At sunrise Captain Mitchell, coming out anxiously in his night attire on to the wooden balcony running the whole length of the O.S.N. Company's lonely building by the shore, would see the lighters already under way, figures moving busily about the cargo cranes, perhaps hear the invaluable Nostromo, now dismounted and in the checked shirt and red sash of a Mediterranean sailor, bawling orders from the end of the jetty in a stentorian voice. A fellow in a thousand!

The material apparatus of perfected civilization which obliterates the individuality of old towns under the stereotyped conveniences of modern life had not intruded as yet; but over the worn-out antiquity of Sulaco, so characteristic with its stuccoed houses and barred win-dows, with the great yellow-white walls of abandoned convents be-hind the rows of sombre green cypresses, that fact—very modern in its spirit—the San Tomé mine had already thrown its subtle influence. It had altered, too, the outward character of the crowds on feast days on the *plaza* before the open portal of the cathedral, by the

---

*General stores.

number of white ponchos with a green stripe affected as holiday
wear by the San Tomé miners. They had also adopted white hats
with green cord and braid—articles of good quality, which could be
obtained in the storehouse of the administration for very little
money. A peaceable *cholo* wearing these colours (unusual in
Costaguana) was somehow very seldom beaten to within an inch of
his life on a charge of disrespect to the town police; neither ran he
much risk of being suddenly lassoed on the road by a recruiting
party of *lanceros**—a method of voluntary enlistment looked upon
as almost legal in the Republic. Whole villages were known to have
volunteered for the army in that way; but, as Don Pepe would say
with a hopeless shrug to Mrs. Gould, "What would you! Poor people! *Pobrecitos!*† *Pobrecitos!* But the State must have its soldiers."

Thus professionally spoke Don Pepe, the fighter, with pendent
moustaches, a nut-brown, lean face, and a clean run of a cast-iron
jaw, suggesting the type of a cattle-herd horseman from the great
Llanos of the South. "If you will listen to an old officer of Paez,
señores,"‡ was the exordium§ of all his speeches in the Aristocratic
Club of Sulaco, where he was admitted on account of his past services to the extinct cause of Federation. The club, dating from the
days of the proclamation of Costaguana's independence, boasted
many names of liberators amongst its first founders. Suppressed arbi-
trarily innumerable times by various Governments, with memories of
proscriptions and of at least one wholesale massacre of its members,
sadly assembled for a banquet by the order of a zealous military *comandante* (their bodies were afterwards stripped naked and flung into
the *plaza* out of the windows by the lowest scum of the populace), it
was again flourishing, at that period, peacefully. It extended to
strangers the large hospitality of the cool, big rooms of its historic
quarters in the front part of a house, once the residence of a high official of the Holy Office. The two wings, shut up, crumbled behind the
nailed doors, and what may be described as a grove of young orange
trees grown in the unpaved *patio* concealed the utter ruin of the back

---

*Government soldiers armed with lances.
†Poor ones!
‡Gentlemen.
§Opening passage of a speech.

part facing the gate. You turned in from the street, as if entering a secluded orchard, where you came upon the foot of a disjointed staircase, guarded by a moss-stained effigy of some saintly bishop, mitred
and staffed, and bearing the indignity of a broken nose meekly, with
his fine stone hands crossed on his breast. The chocolate-coloured
faces of servants with mops of black hair peeped at you from above;
the click of billiard balls came to your ears, and ascending the steps,
you would perhaps see in the first *sala*, very stiff upon a straight-
backed chair, in a good light, Don Pepe moving his long moustaches
as he spelt his way, at arm's length, through an old Sta. Marta newspaper. His horse—a stony-hearted but persevering black brute with a
hammer head—you would have seen in the street dozing motionless
under an immense saddle, with its nose almost touching the kerb-
stone of the sidewalk.

Don Pepe, when "down from the mountain," as the phrase, often
heard in Sulaco, went, could also be seen in the drawing-room of the
Casa Gould. He sat with modest assurance at some distance from the
tea-table. With his knees close together, and a kindly twinkle of
drollery in his deep-set eyes, he would throw his small and ironic
pleasantries into the current of conversation. There was in that man a
sort of sane, humorous shrewdness, and a vein of genuine humanity
so often found in simple old soldiers of proved courage who have
seen much desperate service. Of course he knew nothing whatever of
mining, but his employment was of a special kind. He was in charge
of the whole population in the territory of the mine, which extended
from the head of the gorge to where the cart-track from the foot of the
mountain enters the plain, crossing a stream over a little wooden
bridge painted green—green, the colour of hope, being also the
colour of the mine.

It was reported in Sulaco that up there "at the mountain" Don
Pepe walked about precipitous paths, girt with a great sword and in
a shabby uniform with tarnished bullion epaulettes* of a senior major. Most miners being Indians, with big wild eyes, addressed him
as "Taita" (father), as these barefooted people of Costaguana will
address anybody who wears shoes; but it was Basilio, Mr. Gould's

---

*Metal-knobbed shoulder ornaments.

own *mozo* and the head servant of the Casa, who, in all good faith and from a sense of propriety, announced him once in the solemn words, "El Señor Gobernador has arrived."

Don José Avellanos, then in the drawing-room, was delighted beyond measure at the aptness of the title, with which he greeted the old major banteringly as soon as the latter's soldierly figure appeared in the doorway. Don Pepe only smiled in his long moustaches, as much as to say, "You might have found a worse name for an old soldier."

And "El Señor Gobernador" he had remained, with his small jokes upon his function and upon his domain, where he affirmed with humorous exaggeration to Mrs. Gould:

"No two stones could come together anywhere without the Gobernador hearing the click, *señora*."

And he would tap his ear with the tip of his forefinger knowingly. Even when the number of the miners alone rose to over six hundred he seemed to know each of them individually, all the innumerable Josés, Manuels, Ignacios, from the villages *primero—segundo—*or *tercero* (there were three mining villages) under his government. He could distinguish them not only by their flat, joyless faces, which to Mrs. Gould looked all alike, as if run into the same ancestral mould of suffering and patience, but apparently also by the infinitely graduated shades of reddish-brown, of blackish-brown, of coppery-brown backs, as the two shifts, stripped to linen drawers and leather skull-caps, mingled together with a confusion of naked limbs, of shouldered picks, swinging lamps, in a great shuffle of sandalled feet on the open plateau before the entrance of the main tunnel. It was a time of pause. The Indian boys leaned idly against the long line of little cradle wagons standing empty; the screeners and ore-breakers squatted on their heels smoking long cigars; the great wooden shoots* slanting over the edge of the tunnel plateau were silent; and only the ceaseless, violent rush of water in the open flumes† could be heard, murmuring fiercely, with the splash and rumble of revolving turbine-wheels, and the thudding march of the

---

*Conduits through which the ore travels.
†Channels.

stamps* pounding to powder the treasure rock on the plateau below. The heads of gangs, distinguished by brass medals hanging on their bare breasts, marshalled their squads; and at last the mountain would swallow one half of the silent crowd, while the other half would move off in long files down the zigzag paths leading to the bottom of the gorge. It was deep; and, far below, a thread of vegetation winding between the blazing rock faces resembled a slender green cord, in which three lumpy knots of banana patches, palm-leaf roots, and shady trees marked the Village One, Village Two, Village Three, housing the miners of the Gould Concession.

Whole families had been moving from the first towards the spot in the Higuerota range, whence the rumour of work and safety had spread over the pastoral Campo, forcing its way also, even as the waters of a high flood, into the nooks and crannies of the distant blue walls of the Sierras. Father first, in a pointed straw hat, then the mother with the bigger children, generally also a diminutive donkey, all under burdens, except the leader himself, or perhaps some grown girl, the pride of the family, stepping barefooted and straight as an arrow, with braids of raven hair, a thick, haughty profile, and no load to carry but the small guitar of the country and a pair of soft leather sandals tied together on her back. At the sight of such parties strung out on the cross trails between the pastures, or camped by the side of the royal road, travellers on horseback would remark to each other:

"More people going to the San Tomé mine. We shall see others tomorrow."

And spurring on in the dusk they would discuss the great news of the province, the news of San Tomé mine. A rich Englishman was going to work it—and perhaps not an Englishman, *Quién sabe!*[†] A foreigner with much money. Oh, yes, it had begun. A party of men who had been to Sulaco with a herd of black bulls for the next *corrida*[‡] had reported that from the porch of the *posada*[§] in Rincón, only a short league from the town, the lights on the mountain were

---

*Iron pestles used at a mill to crush the silver ore.
†Who knows?
‡Bullfight.
§Lodging house.

visible, twinkling above the trees. And there was a woman seen riding a horse sideways, not in the chair seat, but upon a sort of saddle, and a man's hat on her head. She walked about, too, on foot up the mountain paths. A woman engineer, it seemed she was.

"What an absurdity! Impossible, *señor!*"

"*Sí! Sí! Una americana del Norte.*"*

"Ah, well! if your worship is informed. *Una Americana*; it need be something of that sort."

And they would laugh a little with astonishment and scorn, keeping a wary eye on the shadows of the road, for one is liable to meet bad men when travelling late on the Campo.

And it was not only the men that Don Pepe knew so well, but he seemed able, with one attentive, thoughtful glance, to classify each woman, girl, or growing youth of his domain. It was only the small fry that puzzled him sometimes. He and the padre could be seen frequently side by side, meditative and gazing across the street of a village at a lot of sedate brown children, trying to sort them out, as it were, in low, consulting tones, or else they would together put searching questions as to the parentage of some small, staid urchin met wandering, naked and grave, along the road with a cigar in his baby mouth, and perhaps his mother's rosary, purloined for purposes of ornamentation, hanging in a loop of beads low down on his rotund little stomach. The spiritual and temporal pastors of the mine flock were very good friends. With Dr. Monygham, the medical pastor, who had accepted the charge from Mrs. Gould, and lived in the hospital building, they were on not so intimate terms. But no one could be on intimate terms with El Señor Doctor, who, with his twisted shoulders, drooping head, sardonic mouth, and side-long bitter glance, was mysterious and uncanny. The other two authorities worked in harmony. Father Román, dried-up, small, alert, wrinkled, with big round eyes, a sharp chin, and a great snuff-taker, was an old campaigner, too; he had shriven many simple souls on the battlefields of the Republic, kneeling by the dying on hillsides, in the long grass, in the gloom of the forests, to hear the last confession with the smell of gunpowder smoke in his nostrils, the rattle of muskets,

---

*Yes! Yes! A North American woman.

the hum and spatter of bullets in his ears. And where was the harm if, at the presbytery, they had a game with a pack of greasy cards in the early evening, before Don Pepe went his last rounds to see that all the watchmen of the mine—a body organized by himself—were at their posts? For that last duty before he slept Don Pepe did actually gird his old sword on the veranda of an unmistakable American white frame-house, which Father Román called the presbytery. Near by, a long, low, dark building, steeple-roofed, like a vast barn with a wooden cross over the gable, was the miners' chapel. There Father Román said Mass every day before a sombre altarpiece representing the Resurrection, the grey slab of the tombstone balanced on one corner, a figure soaring upwards, long-limbed and vivid, in an oval of pallid light, and a helmeted brown legionary smitten down, right across the bituminous foreground. "This picture, my children, *muy linda e maravillosa*"* Father Román would say to some of his flock, "which you behold here through the munificence of the wife of our Señor Administrator, has been painted in Europe, a country of saints and miracles, and much greater than our Costaguana." And he would take a pinch of snuff with unction. But when once an inquisitive spirit desired to know in what direction this Europe was situated, whether up or down the coast, Father Román, to conceal his perplexity, became very reserved and severe. "No doubt it is extremely far away. But ignorant sinners like you of the San Tomé mine should think earnestly of everlasting punishment instead of inquiring into the magnitude of the earth, with its countries and populations altogether beyond your understanding."

With a "Good night Padre"; "Good night, Don Pepe," the Gobernador would go off, holding up his sabre against his side, his body bent forward, with a long, plodding stride in the dark. The jocularity proper to an innocent card game for a few cigars or a bundle of yerba† was replaced at once by the stern duty mood of an officer setting out to visit the outposts of an encamped army. One loud blast of the whistle that hung from his neck provoked instantly a great shrilling of responding whistles, mingled with the barking of

---

*Very beautiful and wonderful.
†Herbs, used to make yerba maté, a bitter herbal tealike beverage drunk in South America.

dogs, that would calm down slowly at last, away up at the head of the gorge; and in the stillness two *serenos*,* on guard by the bridge, would appear walking noiselessly towards him. On one side of the road a long frame-building—the store—would be closed and barricaded from end to end; facing it another white frame-house, still longer, and with a veranda—the hospital—would have lights in the two windows of Dr. Monygham's quarters. Even the delicate foliage of a clump of pepper trees did not stir, so breathless would be the darkness warmed by the radiation of the overheated rocks. Don Pepe would stand still for a moment with the two motionless *serenos* before him, and, abruptly, high up on the sheer face of the mountain, dotted with single torches, like drops of fire fallen from the two great blazing clusters of lights above, the ore shoots would begin to rattle. The great clattering, shuffling noise, gathering speed and weight, would be caught up by the walls of the gorge, and sent upon the plain in a growl of thunder. The *posadero*† in Rincón swore that on calm nights, by listening intently, he could catch the sound in his doorway as of a storm in the mountains.

To Charles Gould's fancy it seemed that the sound must reach the uttermost limits of the province. Riding at night towards the mine, it would meet him at the edge of a little wood just beyond Rincón. There was no mistaking the growling mutter of the mountain pouring its stream of treasure under the stamps; and it came to his heart with the peculiar force of a proclamation thundered forth over the land and the marvellousness of an accomplished fact fulfilling an audacious desire. He had heard this desire. He had heard this very sound in his imagination on that far-off evening when his wife and himself, after a tortuous ride through a strip of forest, had reined in their horses near the stream, and had gazed for the first time upon the jungle-grown solitude of the gorge. The head of a palm rose here and there. In a high ravine round the corner of the San Tomé mountain (which is square like a blockhouse) the thread of a slender waterfall flashed bright and glassy through the dark green of the heavy fronds of tree-ferns. Don Pepe, in attendance,

---

*Night-watchmen.
†Innkeeper.

rode up, and, stretching his arm up the gorge, had declared with mock solemnity, "Behold the very paradise of snakes, *señora*."

And then they had wheeled their horses and ridden back to sleep that night at Rincón. The *alcalde*—an old, skinny Moreno, a sergeant of Guzman Bento's time—had cleared respectfully out of his house with his three pretty daughters, to make room for the foreign *señora* and their worships the *caballeros*. All he asked Charles Gould (whom he took for a mysterious and official person) to do for him was to remind the supreme Government—*el Gobierno supremo*—of a pension (amounting to about a dollar a month) to which he believed himself entitled. It had been promised to him, he affirmed, straightening his bent back martially, "many years ago, for my valour in the wars with the wild *indios* when a young man, *señor*."

The waterfall existed no longer. The tree-ferns that had luxuriated in its spray had dried around the dried-up pool, and the high ravine was only a big trench half filled up with the refuse of excavations and tailings. The torrent, dammed up above, sent its water rushing along the open flumes of scooped tree trunks striding on trestle-legs to the turbines working the stamps on the lower plateau—the *mesa grande** of the San Tomé mountain. Only the memory of the waterfall, with its amazing fernery, like a hanging garden above the rocks of the gorge, was preserved in Mrs. Gould's watercolour sketch; she had made it hastily one day from a cleared patch in the bushes, sitting in the shade of a roof of straw erected for her on three rough poles under Don Pepe's direction.

Mrs. Gould had seen it all from the beginning: the clearing of the wilderness, the making of the road, the cutting of new paths up the cliff face of San Tomé. For weeks together she had lived on the spot with her husband; and she was so little in Sulaco during that year that the appearance of the Gould carriage on the Alameda would cause social excitement. From the heavy family coaches full of stately *señoras* and black-eyed *señoritas* rolling solemnly in the shaded alley white hands were waved towards her with animation in a flutter of greetings. Doña Emilia was "down from the mountain."

---

*Great plateau.

But not for long. Doña Emilia would be gone "up to the mountain" in a day or two, and her sleek carriage mules would have an easy time of it for another spell. She had watched the erection of the first frame-house put up on the lower *mesa* for an office and Don Pepe's quarters; she heard with a thrill of thankful emotion the first wagon-load of ore rattle down the then only shoot; she had stood by her husband's side perfectly silent, and gone cold all over with excitement at the instant when the first battery of only fifteen stamps was put in motion for the first time. On the occasion when the fires under the first set of retorts in their shed had glowed far into the night she did not retire to rest on the rough cadre set up for her in the as yet bare frame-house till she had seen the first spongy lump of silver yielded to the hazards of the world by the dark depths of the Gould Concession; she had laid her unmercenary hands, with an eagerness that made them tremble, upon the first silver ingot turned out still warm from the mould; and by her imaginative estimate of its power she endowed that lump of metal with a justificative conception, as though it were not a mere fact, but something far-reaching and impalpable, like the true expression of an emotion or the emergence of a principle.

Don Pepe, extremely interested, too, looked over her shoulder with a smile that, making longitudinal folds on his face, caused it to resemble a leathern mask with a benignantly diabolic expression.

"Would not the *muchachos** of Hernandez like to get hold of this insignificant object, that looks, *por Dios*, very much like a piece of tin?" he remarked, jocularly.

Hernandez, the robber, had been an inoffensive, small *ranchero*, kidnapped in circumstances of peculiar atrocity from his home during one of the civil wars, and forced to serve in the army. There his conduct as soldier was exemplary, till, watching his chance, he killed his colonel, and managed to get clear away. With a band of deserters, who chose him for their chief, he had taken refuge beyond the wild and waterless Bolson de Tonoro. The *haciendas* paid him blackmail in cattle and horses; extraordinary stories were told of his powers and of his wonderful escapes from capture. He used to ride, single-handed, into the villages and the little towns on the Campo, driving a

---

*Boys, lads.

pack mule before him, with two revolvers in his belt, go straight to the shop or store, select what he wanted, and ride away unopposed because of the terror his exploits and his audacity inspired. Poor country people he usually left alone; the upper class were often stopped on the roads and robbed; but any unlucky official that fell into his hands was sure to get a severe flogging. The army officers did not like his name to be mentioned in their presence. His followers, mounted on stolen horses, laughed at the pursuit of the regular cavalry sent to hunt them down, and whom they took pleasure to ambush most scientifically in the broken ground of their own fastness. Expeditions had been fitted out; a price had been put upon his head; even attempts had been made, treacherously of course, to open negotiations with him, without in the slightest way affecting the even tenor of his career. At last, in true Costaguana fashion, the Fiscal of Tonoro, who was ambitious of the glory of having reduced the famous Hernandez, offered him a sum of money and a safe conduct out of the country for the betrayal of his band. But Hernandez evidently was not of the stuff of which the distinguished military politicians and conspirators of Costaguana are made. This clever but common device (which frequently works like a charm in putting down revolutions) failed with the chief of vulgar Salteadores.* It promised well for the Fiscal at first, but ended very badly for the squadron of *lanceros* posted (by the Fiscal's directions) in a fold of the ground into which Hernandez had promised to lead his unsuspecting followers. They came, indeed, at the appointed time, but creeping on their hands and knees through the bush, and only let their presence be known by a general discharge of firearms, which emptied many saddles. The troopers who escaped came riding very hard into Tonoro. It is said that their commanding officer (who, being better mounted, rode far ahead of the rest) afterwards got into a state of despairing intoxication and beat the ambitious Fiscal severely with the flat of his sabre in the presence of his wife and daughters, for bringing this disgrace upon the National Army. The highest civil official of Tonoro, falling to the ground in a swoon, was further kicked all over the body and rowelled† with sharp spurs about the neck and face

---

*Highwaymen.

†That is, he was scratched and cut with a rowel (revolving disk at the end of a spur edged with sharp points).

because of the great sensitiveness of his military colleague. This gossip of the inland Campo, so characteristic of the rulers of the country and its story of oppression, inefficiency, fatuous methods, treachery, and savage brutality, was perfectly known to Mrs. Gould. That it should be accepted with no indignant comment by people of intelligence, refinement, and character as something inherent in the nature of things was one of the symptoms of degradation that had the power to exasperate her almost to the verge of despair. Still looking at the ingot of silver, she shook her head at Don Pepe's remark:

"If it had not been for the lawless tyranny of your Government, Don Pepe, many an outlaw now with Hernandez would be living peaceably and happy by the honest work of his hands."

"*Señora*," cried Don Pepe, with enthusiasm, "it is true! It is as if God had given you the power to look into the very breasts of people. You have seen them working round you, Doña Emilia—meek as lambs, patient like their own *burros*, brave like lions. I have led them to the very muzzles of guns—I, who stand here before you, *señora*— in the time of Paez, who was full of generosity, and in courage only approached by the uncle of Don Carlos here, as far as I know. No wonder there are bandits in the Campo when there are none but thieves, swindlers, and sanguinary *macaques** to rule us in Sta. Marta. However, all the same, a bandit is a bandit, and we shall have a dozen good straight Winchesters to ride with the silver down to Sulaco."

Mrs. Gould's ride with the first silver escort to Sulaco was the closing episode of what she called "my camp life" before she had settled in her town-house permanently, as was proper and even necessary for the wife of the administrator of such an important institution as the San Tomé mine. For the San Tomé mine was to become an institution, a rallying-point for everything in the province that needed order and stability to live. Security seemed to flow upon this land from the mountain-gorge. The authorities of Sulaco had learned that the San Tomé mine could make it worth their while to leave things and people alone. This was the nearest approach to the rule of common sense and justice Charles Gould felt it possible to secure at first. In fact, the mine, with its organization, its population

---

*Meaning scum, or hoodlums (a macaque is a breed of monkey).

growing fiercely attached to their position of privileged safety, with its armoury, with its Don Pepe, with its armed body of *serenos* (where, it was said, many an outlaw and deserter—and even some members of Hernandez's band—had found a place), the mine was a power in the land. As a certain prominent man in Sta. Marta had exclaimed with a hollow laugh, once, when discussing the line of action taken by the Sulaco authorities at a time of political crisis:

"You call these men Government officials? They? Never! They are officials of the mine—officials of the Concession—I tell you."

The prominent man (who was then a person in power, with a lemon-coloured face and a very short and curly, not to say woolly, head of hair) went so far in his temporary discontent as to shake his yellow fist under the nose of his interlocutor, and shriek:

"Yes! All! Silence! All! I tell you! The political *jefe*, the chief of the police, the chief of the customs, the general, all, all are the officials of that Gould."

Thereupon an intrepid but low and argumentative murmur would flow on for a space in the ministerial cabinet, and the prominent man's passion would end in a cynical shrug of the shoulders. After all, he seemed to say, what did it matter as long as the minister himself was not forgotten during his brief day of authority? But all the same, the unofficial agent of the San Tomé mine, working for a good cause, had his moments of anxiety, which were reflected in his letters to Don José Avellanos, his maternal uncle.

"No sanguinary *macaque* from Sta. Marta shall set foot on that part of Costaguana which lies beyond the San Tomé bridge," Don Pepe used to assure Mrs. Gould. "Except, of course, as an honoured guest—for our Señor Administrador is a deep *político*." But to Charles Gould, in his own room, the old Major would remark with a grim and soldierly cheeriness, "We are all playing our heads at this game."

Don José Avellanos would mutter "*Imperium in imperio** Emilia, my soul," with an air of profound self-satisfaction which, somehow, in a curious way, seemed to contain a queer admixture of bodily discomfort. But that, perhaps, could only be visible to the initiated.

---

*An empire within an empire (Latin).

And for the initiated it was a wonderful place, this drawing-room of the Casa Gould, with its momentary glimpses of the master—El Señor Administrador—older, harder, mysteriously silent, with the lines deepened on his English, ruddy, out-of-doors complexion; flitting on his thin cavalryman's legs across the doorways, either just "back from the mountain" or with jingling spurs and riding-whip under his arm, on the point of starting "for the mountain." Then Don Pepe, modestly martial in his chair, the *llanero* who seemed somehow to have found his martial jocularity, his knowledge of the world, and his manner perfect for his station, in the midst of savage armed contests with his kind; Avellanos, polished and familiar, the diplomatist with his loquacity covering much caution and wisdom in delicate advice, with his manuscript of a historical work on Costaguana, entitled *Fifty Years of Misrule*, which, at present, he thought it was not prudent (even if it were possible) "to give to the world"; these three, and also Doña Emilia amongst them, gracious, small, and fairylike, before the glittering tea-set, with one common master-thought in their heads, with one common feeling of a tense situation, with one ever-present aim to preserve the inviolable character of the mine at every cost. And there was also to be seen Captain Mitchell, a little apart, near one of the long windows, with an air of old-fashioned neat old bachelorhood about him, slightly pompous, in a white waistcoat, a little disregarded and unconscious of it; utterly in the dark, and imagining himself to be in the thick of things. The good man, having spent a clear thirty years of his life on the high seas before getting what he called a "shore billet," was astonished at the importance of transactions (other than relating to shipping) which take place on dry land. Almost every event out of the usual daily course "marked an epoch" for him or else was "history"; unless with his pomposity struggling with a discomfited droop of his rubicund, rather handsome face, set off by snow-white close hair and short whiskers, he would mutter:

"Ah, that! That, sir, was a mistake."

The reception of the first consignment of San Tomé silver for shipment to San Francisco in one of O.S.N. Company's mailboats had, of course, "marked an epoch" for Captain Mitchell. The ingots packed in boxes of stiff ox-hide with plaited handles, small enough to be carried easily by two men, were brought down by the *serenos* of the mine walking in careful couples down the half mile or so of steep, zigzag paths to the foot of the mountain. There they would be loaded into a string of two-wheeled carts, resembling roomy coffers with a door at the back, and harnessed tandem with two mules each, waiting under the guard of armed and mounted *serenos*. Don Pepe padlocked each door in succession, and at the signal of his whistle the string of carts would move off, closely surrounded by the clank of spur and carabine, with jolts and cracking of whips, with a sudden deep rumble over the boundary bridge ("into the land of thieves and sanguinary *macaques*," Don Pepe defined that crossing); hats bobbing in the first light of the dawn, on the heads of cloaked figures; Winchesters on hip; bridle hands protruding lean and brown from under the falling folds of the ponchos. The convoy, skirting a little wood, along the mine trail, between the mud huts and low walls of Rincón, increased its pace on the *camino real*, mules urged to speed, escort galloping, Don Carlos riding alone ahead of a dust storm affording a vague vision of long ears of mules, of fluttering little green and white flags stuck upon each cart; of raised arms in a mob of sombreros with the white gleam of ranging eyes; and Don Pepe, hardly visible in the rear of that rattling dust trail, with a stiff seat and impassive face, rising and falling rhythmically on a ewe-necked silver-bitted black brute with a hammer head.

The sleepy people in the little clusters of huts, in the small *ranchos* near the road, recognized by the headlong sound the charge of the San Tomé silver escort towards the crumbling wall of the city on the Campo side. They came to the doors to see it dash by over ruts and stones, with a clatter and clank and cracking of whips, with the reckless rush and precise driving of a field battery hurrying into action, and the solitary English figure of the Señor Administrador riding far ahead in the lead.

In the fenced roadside paddocks loose horses galloped wildly for a while; the heavy cattle stood up breast deep in the grass, lowing mutteringly at the flying noise; a meek Indian villager would glance back once and hasten to shove his loaded little donkey bodily against a wall, out of the way of the San Tomé silver escort going to the sea; a small knot of chilly *leperos* under the Stone Horse of the Alameda would mutter: "*Caramba!*"* on seeing it take a wide curve at a gallop

---

*Good gracious!

and dart into the empty street of the Constitution; for it was considered the correct thing, the only proper style by the mule-drivers of the San Tomé mine to go through the waking town from end to end without a check in the speed as if chased by a devil.

The early sunshine glowed on the delicate primrose, pale pink, pale blue fronts of the big houses with all their gates shut yet, and no face behind the iron bars of the windows. In the whole sunlit range of empty balconies along the street only one white figure would be visible high up above the clear pavement—the wife of the Señor Administrador—leaning over to see the escort go by to the harbour, a mass of heavy, fair hair twisted up negligently on her little head, and a lot of lace about the neck of her muslin wrapper. With a smile to her husband's single, quick, upward glance, she would watch the whole thing stream past below her feet with an orderly uproar, till she answered by a friendly sign the salute of the galloping Don Pepe, the stiff, deferential inclination with a sweep of the hat below the knee.

The string of padlocked carts lengthened, the size of the escort grew bigger as the years went on. Every three months an increasing stream of treasure swept through the streets of Sulaco on its way to the strong room in the O.S.N. Company's building by the harbour, there to await shipment for the north. Increasing in volume, and of immense value also; for, as Charles Gould told his wife once with some exultation, there had never been seen anything in the world to approach the vein of the Gould Concession. For them both, each passing of the escort under the balconies of the Casa Gould was like another victory gained in the conquest of peace for Sulaco.

No doubt the initial action of Charles Gould had been helped at the beginning by a period of comparative peace which occurred just about that time; and also by the general softening of manners as compared with the epoch of civil wars whence had emerged the iron tyranny of Guzman Bento of fearful memory. In the contests that broke out at the end of his rule (which had kept peace in the country for a whole fifteen years) there was more fatuous imbecility, plenty of cruelty and suffering still, but much less of the old-time fierce and blindly ferocious political fanaticism. It was all more vile, more base, more contemptible, and infinitely more manageable in the very outspoken cynicism of motives. It was more clearly a brazen-faced scramble for a constantly diminishing quantity of booty; since all enterprise had been stupidly killed in the land. Thus it came to pass that the province of Sulaco, once the field of cruel party vengeances, had become in a way one of the considerable prizes of political career. The great of the earth (in Sta. Marta) reserved the posts in the old Occidental State to those nearest and dearest to them; nephews, brothers, husbands of favourite sisters, bosom friends, trusty supporters—or prominent supporters of whom perhaps they were afraid. It was the blessed province of great opportunities and of largest salaries; for the San Tomé mine had its own unofficial pay list, whose items and amounts, fixed in consultation by Charles Gould and Señor Avellanos, were known to a prominent businessman in the United States, who for twenty minutes or so in every month gave his undivided attention to Sulaco affairs. At the same time the material interests of all sorts, backed up by the influence of the San Tomé mine, were quietly gathering substance in that part of the Republic. If, for instance, the Sulaco Collectorship was generally understood, in the political world of the capital, to open the way to the Ministry of Finance, and so on for every official post, then, on the other hand, the despondent business circles of the Republic had come to consider the Occidental Province as the promised land of safety, especially if a man managed to get on good terms with the administration of the mine. "Charles Gould; excellent fellow! Absolutely necessary to make sure of him before taking a single step. Get an introduction to him from Moraga if you can—the agent of the King of Sulaco, don't you know."

No wonder, then, that Sir John, coming from Europe to smooth the path for his railway, had been meeting the name (and even the nickname) of Charles Gould at every turn in Costaguana. The agent of San Tomé Administration in Sta. Marta (a polished, well-informed gentleman, Sir John thought him) had certainly helped so greatly in bringing about the presidential tour that he began to think that there was something in the faint whispers hinting at the immense occult influence of the Gould Concession. What was currently whispered was this—that the San Tomé Administration had, in part, at least, financed the last revolution, which had brought into a five-year dictatorship Don Vincente Ribiera, a man of culture and of unblemished character, invested with a mandate of reform by the best elements of the State. Serious, well-informed men seemed to believe the fact, to hope for better things, for the establishment of legality, of good faith and order in public life. So much the better, then, thought Sir John. He worked always on a great scale; there was a loan to the State, and a project for systematic colonization of the Occidental Province, involved in one vast scheme with the construction of the National Central Railway. Good faith, order, honesty, peace, were badly wanted for this great development of material interests. Anybody on the side of these things, and especially if able to help, had an importance in Sir John's eyes. He had not been disappointed in the "king of Sulaco." The local difficulties had fallen away, as the engineer-in-chief had foretold they would, before Charles Gould's mediation. Sir John had been extremely fêted in Sulaco, next to the President-Dictator, a fact which might have accounted for the evident ill-humour General Montero displayed at lunch given on board the Juno just before she was to sail, taking away from Sulaco the President-Dictator and the distinguished foreign guests in his train.

The Excellentissimo ("the hope of honest men," as Don José had addressed him in a public speech delivered in the name of the Provincial Assembly of Sulaco) sat at the head of the long table; Captain Mitchell, positively stony-eyed and purple in the face with the solemnity of this "historical event," occupied the foot as the representative of the O.S.N. Company in Sulaco, the hosts of that informal function, with the captain of the ship and some minor officials from the shore around him. Those cheery, swarthy little gentlemen cast jovial side-glances at the bottles of champagne beginning to pop behind the guests' backs in the hands of the ship's stewards. The amber wine creamed up to the rims of the glasses.

Charles Gould had his place next to a foreign envoy, who, in a listless undertone, had been talking to him fitfully of hunting and shooting. The well-nourished, pale face, with an eye-glass and drooping yellow moustache, made the Señor Administrador appear by contrast twice as sunbaked, more flaming red, a hundred times more intensely and silently alive. Don José Avellanos touched elbows with the other foreign diplomat, a dark man with a quiet, watchful, self-confident demeanour, and a touch of reserve. All etiquette being laid aside on the occasion, General Montero was the only one there in full uniform, so stiff with embroideries in front that his broad chest seemed protected by a cuirass* of gold. Sir John at the beginning had got away from high places for the sake of sitting near Mrs. Gould.

The great financier was trying to express to her his grateful sense of her hospitality and of his obligation to her husband's "enormous influence in this part of the country," when she interrupted him by a low "Hush!" The President was going to make an informal pronouncement.

The Excellentissimo was on his legs. He said only a few words, evidently deeply felt, and meant perhaps mostly for Avellanos—his old friend—as to the necessity of unremitting effort to secure the lasting welfare of the country emerging after this last struggle, he hoped, into a period of peace and material prosperity.

Mrs. Gould, listening to the mellow, slightly mournful voice, looking at this rotund, dark, spectacled face, at the short body, obese to the point of infirmity, thought that this man of delicate and melancholy mind, physically almost a cripple, coming out of his retirement into a dangerous strife at the call of his fellows, had the right to speak with the authority of his self-sacrifice. And yet she was made uneasy. He was more pathetic than promising, this first civilian Chief of the State Costaguana had ever known, pronouncing, glass in hand, his simple watchwords of honesty, peace, respect for law, political good faith abroad and at home—the safeguards of national honour.

He sat down. During the respectful, appreciative buzz of voices that followed the speech, General Montero raised a pair of heavy, drooping eyelids and rolled his eyes with a sort of uneasy dullness from face to face. The military backwoods hero of the party, though secretly impressed by the sudden novelties and splendours of his position (he had never been on board a ship before, and had hardly ever seen the sea except from a distance), understood by a sort of instinct the advantage his surly, unpolished attitude of a savage fighter gave him amongst all these refined Blanco aristocrats. But why was it that nobody was looking at him? he wondered to himself angrily. He was able to spell out the print of newspapers, and knew that he had performed the "greatest military exploit of modern times."

---

*Piece of armor covering the body from neck to waist.

"My husband wanted the railway," Mrs. Gould said to Sir John in the general murmur of resumed conversations. "All this brings nearer the sort of future we desire for the country, which has waited for it in sorrow long enough, God knows. But I will confess that the other day, during my afternoon drive when I suddenly saw an Indian boy ride out of a wood with the red flag of a surveying party in his hand, I felt something of a shock. The future means change — an utter change. And yet even here there are simple and picturesque things that one would like to preserve."

Sir John listened, smiling. But it was his turn now to hush Mrs. Gould.

"General Montero is going to speak," he whispered, and almost immediately added, in comic alarm, "Heavens! he's going to propose my own health, I believe."

General Montero had risen with a jingle of steel scabbard and a ripple of glitter on his gold-embroidered breast; a heavy sword-hilt appeared at his side above the edge of the table. In this gorgeous uniform, with his bull neck, his hooked nose flattened on the tip upon a blue-black, dyed moustache, he looked like a disguised and sinister *vaquero*. The drone of his voice had a strangely rasping, soulless ring. He floundered, lowering, through a few vague sentences; then suddenly raising his big head and his voice together, burst out harshly:

"The honour of the country is in the hands of the army. I assure you I shall be faithful to it." He hesitated till his roaming eyes met Sir John's face, upon which he fixed a lurid, sleepy glance; and the figure of the lately negotiated loan came into his mind. He lifted his glass. "I drink to the health of the man who brings us a million and a half of pounds."

He tossed off his champagne, and sat down heavily with a half-surprised, half-bullying look all round the faces in the profound, as if appalled, silence which succeeded the felicitous toast. Sir John did not move.

"I don't think I am called upon to rise," he murmured to Mrs. Gould. "That sort of thing speaks for itself." But Don José Avellanos came to the rescue with a short oration, in which he alluded pointedly to England's goodwill towards Costaguana — "a goodwill," he continued significantly, "of which I, having been in my time accredited to the Court of St. James, am able to speak with some knowledge."

Only then Sir John thought fit to respond, which he did gracefully in bad French, punctuated by bursts of applause and the "Hear! Hears!" of Captain Mitchell, who was able to understand a word now and then. Directly he had done, the financier of railways turned to Mrs. Gould:

"You were good enough to say that you intended to ask me for something," he reminded her, gallantly. "What is it? Be assured that any request from you would be considered in the light of a favour to myself."

She thanked him by a gracious smile. Everybody was rising from the table.

"Let us go on deck," she proposed, "where I'll be able to point out to you the very object of my request."

An enormous national flag of Costaguana, diagonal red and yellow, with two green palm trees in the middle, floated lazily at the mainmast head of the *Juno*. A multitude of fireworks being let off in their thousands at the water's edge in honour of the President kept up a mysterious crepitating noise half round the harbour. Now and then a lot of rockets, swishing upwards invisibly, detonated overhead with only a puff of smoke in the bright sky. Crowds of people could be seen between the town gate and the harbour, under the bunches of multicoloured flags fluttering on tall poles. Faint bursts of military music would be heard suddenly, and the remote sound of shouting. A knot of ragged Negroes at the end of the wharf kept on loading and firing a small iron cannon time after time. A greyish haze of dust hung thin and motionless against the sun.

Don Vincente Ribiera made a few steps under the deck-awning, leaning on the arm of Señor Avellanos; a wide circle was formed round him, where the mirthless smile of his dark lips and the sightless glitter of his spectacles could be seen turning amiably from side to side. The informal function arranged on purpose on board the *Juno* to give the President-Dictator an opportunity to meet intimately some of his most notable adherents in Sulaco was drawing to an end. On one side, General Montero, his bald head covered now by a plumed cocked hat, remained motionless on a skylight seat, a pair of big gauntleted hands folded on the hilt of the sabre standing upright between his legs. The white plume, the coppery tint of his broad face, the blue-black of the moustaches under the curved beak, the mass of gold on sleeves and breast, the high shining boots with enormous spurs, the working nostrils, the imbecile and domineering stare of the glorious victor of Río Seco had in them something ominous and incredible; the exaggeration of a cruel caricature, the fatuity of solemn masquerading, the atrocious grotesqueness of some military idol of Aztec conception and European bedecking, awaiting the homage of worshippers. Don José approached diplomatically this weird and inscrutable portent, and Mrs. Gould turned her fascinated eyes away at last.

Charles, coming up to take leave of Sir John, heard him say, as he bent over his wife's hand, "Certainly. Of course, my dear Mrs. Gould, for a protégé of yours! Not the slightest difficulty. Consider it done."

Going ashore in the same boat with the Goulds, Don José Avellanos was very silent. Even in the Gould carriage he did not open his lips for a long time. The mules trotted slowly away from the wharf between the extended hands of the beggars, who for that day seemed to have abandoned in a body the portals of churches. Charles Gould sat on the back seat and looked away upon the plain. A multitude of booths made of green boughs, of rushes, of odd pieces of plank eked out with bits of canvas had been erected all over it for the sale of cana,* of dulces,† of fruit, of cigars. Over little heaps of glowing charcoal Indian women, squatting on mats, cooked food in black earthen pots, and boiled the water for the maté‡ gourds, which they offered in soft, caressing voices to the country people. A racecourse had been staked out for the *vaqueros*; and away to the left, from where the crowd was massed thickly about a huge temporary erection, like a circus tent of wood with a conical grass roof, came the resonant twanging of harp strings, the sharp ping of guitars, with the grave drumming throb of an Indian gombo§ pulsating steadily through the shrill choruses of the dancers.

Charles Gould said presently:

---

*Kind of rum.

†Sweets.

‡That is, yerba maté (*maté* can refer both to the drink itself and to the small gourd in which it is drunk).

§Indigenous South American drum.

"All this piece of land belongs now to the Railway Company. There will be no more popular feasts held here."

Mrs. Gould was rather sorry to think so. She took this opportunity to mention how she had just obtained from Sir John the promise that the house occupied by Giorgio Viola should not be interfered with. She declared she could never understand why the survey engineers ever talked of demolishing that old building. It was not in the way of the projected harbour branch of the line in the least.

She stopped the carriage before the door to reassure at once the old Genoese, who came out bare-headed and stood by the carriage step. She talked to him in Italian, of course, and he thanked her with calm dignity. An old Garibaldino was grateful to her from the bottom of his heart for keeping the roof over the heads of his wife and children. He was too old to wander any more.

"And is it for ever, *signora*?" he asked.

"For as long as you like."

"*Bene.** Then the place must be named. It was not worth while before."

He smiled ruggedly, with a running together of wrinkles at the corners of his eyes. "I shall set about the painting of the name tomorrow."

"And what is it going to be, Giorgio?"

"Albergo d'Italia Una,"† said the old Garibaldino, looking away for a moment. "More in memory of those who have died," he added, "than for the country stolen from us soldiers of liberty by the craft of that accursed Piedmontese race of kings and ministers."

Mrs. Gould smiled slightly, and, bending over a little, began to inquire about his wife and children. He had sent them into town on that day. The *padrona* was better in health; many thanks to the *signora* for inquiring.

People were passing in twos and threes, in whole parties of men and women attended by trotting children. A horseman mounted on a silver-grey mare drew rein quietly in the shade of the house after taking off his hat to the party in the carriage, who returned smiles

---

*Good (It.).

†Inn of the United Italy (It.).

and familiar nods. Old Viola, evidently very pleased with the news he had just heard, interrupted himself for a moment to tell him rapidly that the house was secured, by the kindness of the English *signora*, for as long as he liked to keep it. The other listened attentively, but made no response.

When the carriage moved on he took off his hat again, a grey sombrero with a silver cord and tassels. The bright colours of a Mexican serape twisted on the cantle, the enormous silver buttons on the embroidered leather jacket, the row of tiny silver buttons down the seam of the trousers, the snowy linen, a silk sash with embroidered ends, the silver plates on headstall and saddle, proclaimed the unapproachable style of the famous Capataz de Cargadores—a Mediterranean sailor—got up with more finished splendour than any well-to-do young *ranchero* of the Campo had ever displayed on a high holiday.

"It is a great thing for me," murmured old Giorgio, still thinking of the house, for now he had grown weary of change. "The *signora* just said a word to the Englishman."

"The old Englishman who has enough money to pay for a railway? He is going off in an hour," remarked Nostromo, carelessly. "*Buon viaggio*,* then. I've guarded his bones all the way from the Entrada pass down to the plain and into Sulaco, as though he had been my own father."

Old Giorgio only moved his head sideways absently. Nostromo pointed after the Goulds' carriage, nearing the grass-grown gate in the old town wall that was like a wall of matted jungle.

"And I have sat alone at night with my revolver in the Company's warehouse time and again by the side of that other Englishman's heap of silver, guarding it as though it had been my own."

Viola seemed lost in thought. "It is a great thing for me," he repeated again, as if to himself.

"It is," agreed the magnificent Capataz de Cargadores, calmly. "Listen, *vecchio*—go in and bring me out a cigar, but don't look for it in my room. There's nothing there."

Viola stepped into the café and came out directly, still absorbed in this idea, and tendered him a cigar, mumbling thoughtfully in

*Have a good trip (It.).

his moustache. "Children growing up—and girls, too! Girls!" He sighed and fell silent.

"What, only one?" remarked Nostromo, looking down with a sort of comic inquisitiveness at the unconscious old man. "No matter," he added, with lofty negligence; "one is enough till another is wanted."

He lit and let the match drop from his passive fingers. Giorgio Viola looked up, and said abruptly:

"My son would have been just such a fine young man as you, Gian' Battista, if he had lived."

"What? Your son? But you are right, *padrone*. If he had been like me he would have been a man."

He turned his horse slowly, and paced on between the booths, checking the mare almost to a standstill now and then for children, for the groups of people from the distant Campo, who stared after him with admiration. The Company's lightermen saluted him from afar; and the greatly envied Capataz de Cargadores advanced, amongst murmurs of recognition and obsequious greetings, towards the huge circus-like erection. The throng thickened; the guitars tinkled louder; other horsemen sat motionless, smoking calmly above the heads of the crowd; it eddied and pushed before the doors of the high-roofed building, whence issued a shuffle and thumping of feet in time to the dance music vibrating and shrieking with a racking rhythm, overhung by the tremendous, sustained, hollow roar of the gombo. The barbarous and imposing noise of the big drum, that can madden a crowd, and that even Europeans cannot hear without a strange emotion, seemed to draw Nostromo on to its source, while a man, wrapped up in a faded, torn poncho, walked by his stirrup, and, buffeted right and left, begged "his worship" insistently for employment on the wharf. He whined, offering the Señor Capataz half his daily pay for the privilege of being admitted to the swaggering fraternity of *cargadores*; the other half would be enough for him, he protested. But Captain Mitchell's right-hand man— "invaluable for our work—a perfectly incorruptible fellow"—after looking down critically at the ragged *mozo*, shook his head without a word in the uproar going on around.

The man fell back; and a little farther on Nostromo had to pull up. From the doors of the dance-hall men and women emerged tottering, streaming with sweat, trembling in every limb, to lean, panting, with staring eyes and parted lips, against the wall of the structure, where the harps and guitars played on with mad speed in an incessant roll of thunder. Hundreds of hands clapped in there; voices shrieked, and then all at once would sink low, chanting in unison the refrain of a love song, with a dying fall. A red flower, flung with a good aim from somewhere in the crowd, struck the resplendent Capataz on the cheek.

He caught it as it fell, neatly, but for some time did not turn his head. When at last he condescended to look round, the throng near him had parted to make way for a pretty Morenita,* her hair held up by a small golden comb, who was walking towards him in the open space.

Her arms and neck emerged plump and bare from a snowy chemisette; the blue woollen skirt, with all the fullness gathered in front, scanty on the hips and tight across the back, disclosed the provoking action of her walk. She came straight on and laid her hand on the mare's neck with a timid, coquettish look upwards out of the corner of her eyes.

"*Querido*"† she murmured, caressingly, "why do you pretend not to see me when I pass?"

"Because I don't love thee any more," said Nostromo, deliberately, after a moment of reflective silence.

The hand on the mare's neck trembled suddenly. She dropped her head before all the eyes in the wide circle formed round the generous, the terrible, the inconstant Capataz de Cargadores, and his Morenita.

Nostromo, looking down, saw tears beginning to fall down her face.

"Has it come true, then, ever beloved of my heart?" she whispered. "Is it true?"

"No," said Nostromo, looking away carelessly. "It was a lie. I love thee as much as ever."

"Is that true?" she cooed, joyously, her cheeks still wet with tears. "It is true."

---

*Little dark-haired or brown-skinned girl.
†Darling.

"True on the life?"

"As true as that; but thou must not ask me to swear it on the Madonna that stands in thy room." And the Capataz laughed a little in response to the grins of the crowd.

She pouted—very pretty—a little uneasy.

"No, I will not ask for that. I can see love in your eyes." She laid her hand on his knee. "Why are you trembling like this? From love?" she continued, while the cavernous thundering of the gombo went on without a pause. "But if you love her as much as that, you must give your Paquita a gold-mounted rosary of beads for the neck of her Madonna."

"No," said Nostromo, looking into her uplifted, begging eyes, which suddenly turned stony with surprise.

"No? Then what else will your worship give me on the day of the fiesta?" she asked, angrily; "so as not to shame me before all these people."

"There is no shame for thee in getting nothing from thy lover for once."

"True! The shame is your worship's—my poor lover's," she flared up, sarcastically.

Laughs were heard at her anger, at her retort. What an audacious spitfire she was! The people aware of this scene were calling out urgently to others in the crowd. The circle round the silver-grey mare narrowed slowly.

The girl went off a pace or two, confronting the mocking curiosity of the eyes, then flung back to the stirrup, tiptoeing, her enraged face turned up to Nostromo with a pair of blazing eyes. He bent low to her in the saddle.

"Juan," she hissed, "I could stab thee to the heart!"

The dreaded Capataz de Cargadores, magnificent and carelessly public in his amours, flung his arm round her neck and kissed her spluttering lips. A murmur went round.

"A knife!" he demanded at large, holding her firmly by the shoulder.

Twenty blades flashed out together in the circle. A young man in holiday attire, bounding in, thrust one in Nostromo's hand and bounded back into the ranks, very proud of himself. Nostromo had not even looked at him.

"Stand on my foot," he commanded the girl, who, suddenly subdued, rose lightly, and when he had her up, encircling her waist, her face near to his, he pressed the knife into her little hand.

"No, Morenita! You shall not put me to shame," he said. "You shall have your present; and so that everyone should know who is your lover today, you may cut all the silver buttons off my coat."

There were shouts of laughter and applause at this witty freak, while the girl passed the keen blade, and the impassive rider jingled in his palm the increasing hoard of silver buttons. He eased her to the ground with both her hands full. After whispering for a while with a very strenuous face, she walked away, staring haughtily, and vanished into the crowd.

The circle had broken up, and the lordly Capataz de Cargadores, the indispensable man, the tried and trusty Nostromo, the Mediterranean sailor come ashore casually to try his luck in Costaguana, rode slowly towards the harbour. The *Juno* was just then swinging round; and even as Nostromo reined up again to look on, a flag ran up on the improvised flagstaff erected in an ancient and dismantled little fort at the harbour entrance. Half a battery of field guns had been hurried over there from the Sulaco barracks for the purpose of firing the regulation salutes for the President-Dictator and the War Minister. As the mail-boat headed through the pass, the badly timed reports announced the end of Don Vincente Ribiera's first official visit to Sulaco, and for Captain Mitchell the end of another "historic occasion." Next time when the "Hope of honest men" was to come that way, a year and a half later, it was unofficially, over the mountain tracks, fleeing after a defeat on a lame mule, to be only just saved by Nostromo from an ignominious death at the hands of a mob. It was a very different event, of which Captain Mitchell used to say:

"It was history—history, sir! And that fellow of mine, Nostromo, you know, was right in it. Absolutely making history, sir."

But this event, creditable to Nostromo, was to lead immediately to another, which could not be classed either as "history" or as "a mistake" in Captain Mitchell's phraseology. He had another word for it.

"Sir," he used to say afterwards, "that was no mistake. It was a fatality. A misfortune, pure and simple, sir. And that poor fellow of mine was right in it—right in the middle of it! A fatality, if ever there was one—and to my mind he has never been the same man since."

PART TWO

The Isabels

CHAPTER 1

THROUGH GOOD AND EVIL report in the varying fortune of that struggle which Don José had characterized in the phrase, "the fate of national honesty trembles in the balance," the Gould Concession, "*Imperium in Imperio*," had gone on working; the square mountain had gone on pouring its treasure down the wooden shoots to the unresting batteries of stamps; the lights of San Tomé had twinkled night after night upon the great, limitless shadow of the Campo; every three months the silver escort had gone down to the sea as if neither the war nor its consequences could ever affect the ancient Occidental State secluded beyond its high barrier of the Cordillera. All the fighting took place on the other side of that mighty wall of serrated peaks lorded over by the white dome of Higuerota and as yet breached by the railway, of which only the first part, the easy Campo part from Sulaco to the Ivie Valley at the foot of the pass, had been laid. Neither did the telegraph line cross the mountains yet; its poles, like slender beacons on the plain, penetrated into the forest fringe of the foothills cut by the deep avenue of the track; and its wire ended abruptly in the construction camp at a white deal table supporting a Morse apparatus, in a long hut of planks with a corrugated-iron roof overshadowed by gigantic cedar trees—the quarters of the engineer in charge of the advance section.

The harbour was busy, too, with the traffic in railway material, and with the movements of troops along the coast. The O.S.N. Company had found much occupation for its fleet. Costaguana had no navy, and, apart from a few coastguard cutters, there were no national ships except a couple of old merchant steamers used as transports.

Captain Mitchell, feeling more and more in the thick of history, found time for an hour or so during an afternoon in the drawing-room of the Casa Gould, where, with a strange ignorance of the real forces at work around him, he professed himself delighted to get away from the strain of affairs. He did not know what he would have done without his invaluable Nostromo, he declared. Those confounded Costaguana politics gave him more work—he confided to Mrs. Gould—than he had bargained for.

Don José Avellanos had displayed in the service of the endangered Ribiera Government an organizing activity and an eloquence of which the echoes reached even Europe. For, after the new loan to the Ribiera Government, Europe had become interested in Costaguana. The Sala of the Provincial Assembly (in the Municipal Buildings of Sulaco), with its portraits of the Liberators on the walls and an old flag of Cortés[9] preserved in a glass case above the President's chair, had heard all these speeches—the early one containing the impassioned declaration "Militarism is the enemy," the famous one of the "trembling balance" delivered on the occasion of the vote for the raising of a second Sulaco regiment in the defence of the reforming Government; and when the provinces again displayed their old flags (proscribed in Guzman Bento's time) there was another of those great orations, when Don José greeted these old emblems of the war of Independence, brought out again in the name of new Ideals. The old idea of Federalism had disappeared. For his part he did not wish to revive old political doctrines. They were perishable. They died. But the doctrine of political rectitude was immortal. The second Sulaco regiment, to whom he was presenting this flag, was going to show its valour in a contest for order, peace, progress; for the establishment of national self-respect without which—he declared with energy—"we are a reproach and a byword amongst the powers of the world."

Don José Avellanos loved his country. He had served it lavishly with his fortune during his diplomatic career, and the later story of his captivity and barbarous ill-usage under Guzman Bento was well known to his listeners. It was a wonder that he had not been a victim of the ferocious and summary executions which marked the course of that tyranny; for Guzman had ruled the country with the sombre imbecility of political fanaticism. The power of Supreme Government had become in his dull mind an object of strange worship, as if it were some sort of cruel deity. It was incarnated in himself, and his adversaries, the Federalists, were the supreme sinners, objects of hate, abhorrence, and fear, as heretics would be to a convinced Inquisitor.

For years he had carried about at the tail of the Army of Pacification, all over the country, a captive band of such atrocious criminals, who considered themselves most unfortunate at not having been summarily executed. It was a diminishing company of nearly naked skeletons, loaded with irons, covered with dirt, with vermin, with raw wounds, all men of positions, of education, of wealth, who had learned to fight amongst themselves for scraps of rotten beef thrown to them by soldiers, or to beg a Negro cook for a drink of muddy water in pitiful accents. Don José Avellanos, clanking his chains amongst the others, seemed only to exist in order to prove how much hunger, pain, degradation, and cruel torture a human body can stand without parting with the last spark of life. Sometimes interrogatories, backed by some primitive method of torture, were administered to them by a commission of officers hastily assembled in a hut of sticks and branches, and made pitiless by the fear for their own lives. A lucky one or two of that spectral company of prisoners would perhaps be led tottering behind a bush to be shot by a file of soldiers. Always an army chaplain—some unshaven, dirty man, girt with a sword and with a tiny cross embroidered in white cotton on the left breast of a lieutenant's uniform—would follow, cigarette in the corner of the mouth, wooden stool in hand, to hear the confession and give absolution; for the Citizen Saviour of the Country (Guzman Bento was called thus officially in petitions) was not averse from the exercise of rational clemency. The irregular report of the firing squad would be heard, followed sometimes by a single finishing shot; a little bluish cloud of smoke would float up above the green bushes, and the Army of Pacification would move on over the savannas, through the forests, crossing rivers, invading rural *pueblos*, devastating the *haciendas* of the horrid aristocrats, occupying the inlaid towns in the fulfillment of its patriotic mission, and leaving behind a united land wherein the evil taint of Federalism could no longer be detected in the smoke of burning houses and the smell of spilt blood.

Don José Avellanos had survived that time.

Perhaps, when contemptuously signifying to him his release, the Citizen Saviour of the Country might have thought this benighted aristocrat too broken in health and spirit and fortune to be any longer dangerous. Or, perhaps, it may have been a simple caprice. Guzman Bento, usually full of fanciful fears and brooding suspicions, had sudden accesses of unreasonable self-confidence when he perceived himself elevated on a pinnacle of power and safety beyond the reach of mere mortal plotters. At such times he would impulsively command the celebration of a solemn Mass of thanksgiving which would be sung in great pomp in the cathedral of Sta. Marta by the trembling, subservient Archbishop of his creation. He heard it sitting in a gilt armchair placed before the high altar, surrounded by the civil and military heads of his Government. The unofficial world of Sta. Marta would crowd into the cathedral, for it was not quite safe for anybody of mark to stay away from these manifestations of presidential piety. Having thus acknowledged the only power he was at all disposed to recognize as above himself, he would scatter acts of political grace in a sardonic wantonness of clemency. There was no other way left now to enjoy his power but by seeing his crushed adversaries crawl impotently into the light of day out of the dark, noisome cells of the Collegio. Their harmlessness fed his insatiable vanity, and they could always be got hold of again. It was the rule for all the women of their families to present thanks afterwards in a special audience. The incarnation of that strange god, El Gobierno Supremo, received them standing, cocked hat on head, and exhorted them in a menacing mutter to show their gratitude by bringing up their children in fidelity to the democratic form of government, "which I have established for the happiness of our country." His front teeth having been knocked out in some accident of his former herdsman's life, his utterance was spluttering and indistinct. He had been working for Costaguana alone in the midst of treachery and opposition. Let it cease now lest he should become weary of forgiving!

Don José Avellanos had known this forgiveness.

He was broken in health and fortune deplorably enough to present a truly gratifying spectacle to the supreme chief of democratic institutions. He retired to Sulaco. His wife had an estate in that province, and she nursed him back to life out of the house of death and captivity. When she died, their daughter, an only child, was old enough to devote herself to "poor papa."

Miss Avellanos, born in Europe and educated partly in England, was a tall, grave girl, with a self-possessed manner, a wide, white forehead, a wealth of rich brown hair, and blue eyes.

The other young ladies of Sulaco stood in awe of her character and accomplishments. She was reputed to be terribly learned and serious. As to pride, it was well known that all the Corbeláns were proud, and her mother was a Corbelán. Don José Avellanos depended very much upon the devotion of his beloved Antonia. He accepted it in the benighted way of men, who, though made in God's image, are like stone idols without sense before the smoke of certain burnt offerings. He was ruined in every way, but a man possessed of passion is not a bankrupt in life. Don José Avellanos desired passionately for his country: peace, prosperity, and (as the end of the preface to *Fifty Years of Misrule* has it) "an honourable place in the comity of civilized nations." In this last phrase the Minister Plenipotentiary, cruelly humiliated by the bad faith of his Government towards the foreign bondholders, stands disclosed in the patriot.

The fatuous turmoil of greedy factions succeeding the tyranny of Guzman Bento seemed to bring his desire to the very door of opportunity. He was too old to descend personally into the centre of the arena at Sta. Marta. But the men who acted there sought his advice at every step. He himself thought that he could be most useful at a distance, in Sulaco. His name, his connections, his former position, his experience commanded the respect of his class. The discovery that this man, living in dignified poverty in the Corbelán town residence (opposite the Casa Gould), could dispose of material means towards the support of the cause increased his influence. It was his open letter of appeal that decided the candidature of Don Vincente Ribiera for the Presidency. Another of these informal State papers drawn up by Don José (this time in the shape of an address from the Province) induced that scrupulous constitutionalist to accept the extraordinary powers conferred upon him for five years by an overwhelming vote of congress in Sta. Marta. It was a specific mandate to establish the prosperity of the people on the basis of firm peace at home, and to redeem the national credit by the satisfaction of all just claims abroad.

In the afternoon the news of that vote had reached Sulaco by the usual roundabout postal way through Cayta, and up the coast by steamer. Don José, who had been waiting for the mail in the Goulds' drawing-room, got out of the rocking-chair, letting his hat fall off his knees. He rubbed his silvery, short hair with both hands, speechless with the excess of joy.

"Emilia, my soul," he had burst out, "let me embrace you! Let me—"

Captain Mitchell, had he been there, would no doubt have made an apt remark about the dawn of a new era; but if Don José thought something of the kind, his eloquence failed him on this occasion. The inspirer of that revival of the Blanco party tottered where he stood. Mrs. Gould moved forward quickly and, as she offered her cheek with a smile to her old friend, managed very cleverly to give him the support of her arm he really needed.

Don José had recovered himself at once, but for a time he could do no more than murmur, "Oh, you two patriots! Oh, you two patriots!"—looking from one to the other. Vague plans of another historical work, wherein all the devotions to the regeneration of the country he loved would be enshrined for the reverent worship of posterity, flitted through his mind. The historian who had enough elevation of soul to write of Guzman Bento: "Yet this monster, imbrued in the blood of his countrymen, must not be held unreservedly to the execration of future years. It appears to be true that he, too, loved his country. He had given it twelve years of peace; and, absolute master of lives and fortunes as he was, he died poor. His worst fault, perhaps, was not his ferocity, but his ignorance"; the man who could write thus of a cruel persecutor (the passage occurs in his *History of Misrule*) felt at the foreshadowing of success an almost boundless affection for his two helpers, for these two young people from over the sea.

Just as years ago, calmly, from the conviction of practical necessity, stronger than any abstract political doctrine, Henry Gould had drawn the sword, so now, the times being changed, Charles Gould had flung the silver of the San Tomé into the fray. The Inglés of Sulaco, the "Costaguana Englishman" of the third generation, was as far from being a political intriguer as his uncle from a revolutionary swashbuckler. Springing from the instinctive uprightness of their natures their action was reasoned. They saw an opportunity and used the weapon to hand.

Charles Gould's position—a commanding position in the background of that attempt to retrieve the peace and the credit of the

Republic—was very clear. At the beginning he had had to accommodate himself to existing circumstances of corruption so naïvely brazen as to disarm the hatred of a man courageous enough not to be afraid of its irresponsible potency to ruin everything it touched. It seemed to him too contemptible for hot anger even. He made use of it with a cold, fearless scorn, manifested rather than concealed by the forms of stony courtesy which did away with much of the ignominy of the situation. At bottom, perhaps, he suffered from it, for he was not a man of cowardly illusions, but he refused to discuss the ethical view with his wife. He trusted that, though a little disenchanted, she would be intelligent enough to understand that his character safeguarded the enterprise of their lives as much as or more than his policy. The extraordinary development of the mine had put a great power into his hands. To feel that prosperity always at the mercy of unintelligent greed had grown irksome to him. To Mrs. Gould it was humiliating. At any rate, it was dangerous. In the confidential communications passing between Charles Gould, the King of Sulaco, and the head of the silver and steel interests far away in California, the conviction was growing that any attempt made by men of education and integrity ought to be discreetly supported. "You may tell your friend Avellanos that I think so," Mr. Holroyd had written at the proper moment from his inviolable sanctuary within the eleven-storey-high factory of great affairs. And shortly afterwards, with a credit opened by the Third Southern Bank (located next door but one to the Holroyd Building), the Ribierist party in Costaguana took a practical shape under the eye of the administrator of the San Tomé mine. And Don José, the hereditary friend of the Gould family, could say: "Perhaps, my dear Carlos, I shall not have believed in vain."

CHAPTER 2

AFTER ANOTHER ARMED STRUGGLE, decided by Montero's victory of Río Seco, had been added to the tale of civil wars, the "honest men," as Don José called them, could breathe freely for the first time in half a century. The Five-Year-Mandate law became the basis of that regeneration, the passionate desire and hope for which had been like the elixir of everlasting youth for Don José Avellanos.

And when it was suddenly—and not quite unexpectedly—endangered by that "brute Montero," it was a passionate indignation that gave him a new lease of life, as it were. Already, at the time of the President-Dictator's visit to Sulaco, Moraga had sounded a note of warning from Sta. Marta about the War Minister. Montero and his brother made the subject of an earnest talk between the Dictator-President and the Nestor-inspirer[10] of the party. But Don Vincente, a doctor of philosophy from the Cordova University, seemed to have an exaggerated respect for military ability, whose mysteriousness—since it appeared to be altogether independent of intellect—imposed upon his imagination. The Victor of Río Seco was a popular hero. His services were so recent that the President-Dictator quailed before the obvious charge of political ingratitude. Great regenerating transactions were being initiated—the fresh loan, a new railway line, a vast colonization scheme. Anything that could unsettle the public opinion in the capital was to be avoided. Don José bowed to these arguments and tried to dismiss from his mind the gold-laced portent in boots, and with a sabre, made meaningless now at last, he hoped, in the new order of things.

Less than six months after the President-Dictator's visit, Sulaco learned with stupefaction of the military revolt in the name of national honour. The Minister of War, in a barrack-square allocution to the officers of the artillery regiment he had been inspecting, had declared the national honour sold to foreigners. The Dictator, by his weak compliance with the demands of the European powers—for the settlement of long outstanding money claims—had showed himself unfit to rule. A letter from Moraga explained afterwards that the initiative, and even the very text, of the incendiary allocution came, in reality, from the other Montero, the ex-*guerrillero*,* the Commandante de Plaza. The energetic treatment of Dr. Monygham, sent for in haste "to the mountain," who came galloping three leagues in the dark, saved Don José from a dangerous attack of jaundice.

---

*Former guerrilla.

After getting over the shock, Don José refused to let himself be prostrated. Indeed, better news succeeded at first. The revolt in the capital had been suppressed after a night of fighting in the streets. Unfortunately, both the Monteros had been able to make their escape south, to their native province of Entre-Montes. The hero of the forest march, the victor of Río Seco, had been received with frenzied acclamations in Nicoya, the provincial capital. The troops in garrison there had gone to him in a body. The brothers were organizing an army, gathering malcontents, sending emissaries primed with patriotic lies to the people, and with promises of plunder to the wild *llaneros*. Even a Monterist press had come into existence, speaking oracularly of the secret promises of support given by "our great sister Republic of the North" against the sinister land-grabbing designs of European powers, cursing in every issue the "miserable Ribiera," who had plotted to deliver his country, bound hand and foot, for a prey to foreign speculators.

Sulaco, pastoral and sleepy, with its opulent Campo and the rich silver mine, heard the din of arms fitfully in its fortunate isolation. It was nevertheless in the very forefront of the defence with men and money; but the very rumours reached it circuitously—from abroad even, so much was it cut off from the rest of the Republic, not only by natural obstacles, but also by the vicissitudes of the war. The Monteristos were besieging Cayta, an important postal link. The overland couriers ceased to come across the mountains, and no muleteer would consent to risk the journey at last; even Bonifacio on one occasion failed to return from Sta. Marta, either not daring to start, or perhaps captured by the parties of the enemy raiding the country between the Cordillera and the capital. Monterist publications, however, found their way into the province, mysteriously enough; and also Monterist emissaries preaching death to aristocrats in the villages and towns of the Campo. Very early, at the beginning of the trouble, Hernandez, the bandit, had proposed (through the agency of an old priest of a village in the wilds) to deliver two of them to the Ribierist authorities in Tonoro. They had come to offer him a free pardon and the rank of colonel from General Montero in consideration of joining the rebel army with his mounted band. No notice was taken at the time of the proposal. It was joined, as an evidence of good faith, to a petition praying the

Sulaco Assembly for permission to enlist, with all his followers, in the forces being then raised in Sulaco for the defence of the Five-Year-Mandate of its regeneration. The petition, like everything else, had found its way into Don José's hands. He had showed to Mrs. Gould these pages of dirty-greyish rough paper (perhaps looted in some village store), covered with the crabbed, illiterate handwriting of the old padre, carried off from his hut by the side of a mud-walled church to be the secretary of the dreaded *Salteador*. They had both bent in the lamplight of the Gould drawing-room over the document containing the fierce and yet humble appeal of the man against the blind and stupid barbarity turning an honest *ranchero* into a bandit. A postscript of the priest stated that, but for being deprived of his liberty for ten days, he had been treated with humanity and the respect due to his sacred calling. He had been, it appears, confessing and absolving the chief and most of the band, and he guaranteed the sincerity of their good disposition. He had distributed heavy penances, no doubt in the way of litanies and fasts; but he argued shrewdly that it would be difficult for them to make their peace with God durably till they made peace with men.

Never before, perhaps, had Hernandez's head been in less jeopardy than when he petitioned humbly for permission to buy a pardon for himself and his gang of deserters by armed service. He could range afar from the waste lands protecting his fastness, unchecked, because there were no troops left in the whole province. The usual garrison of Sulaco had gone south to the war, with its brass band playing the "Bolívar March" on the bridge of one of the O.S.N. Company's steamers. The great family coaches drawn up along the shore of the harbour were made to rock on the high leathern springs by the enthusiasm of the *señoras* and the *señoritas* standing up to wave their lace handkerchiefs, as lighter after lighter packed full of troops left the end of the jetty.

Nostromo directed the embarkation, under the superintendence of Captain Mitchell, red-faced in the sun, conspicuous in a white waistcoat, representing the allied and anxious goodwill of all the material interests of civilization. General Barrios, who commanded the troops, assured Don José on parting that in three weeks he would have Montero in a wooden cage drawn by three pair of oxen ready for a tour through all the towns of the Republic.

"And then, *señora*," he continued, baring his curly iron-grey head to Mrs. Gould in her landau* — "and then, *señora*, we shall convert our swords into plowshares and grow rich. Even I, myself, as soon as this little business is settled, shall open a *fundación*† on some land I have on the *llanos*‡ and try to make a little money in peace and quietness. *Señora*, you know, all Costaguana knows — what do I say? — this whole South American continent knows, that Pablo Barrios has had his fill of military glory."

Charles Gould was not present at the anxious and patriotic send-off. It was not his part to see the soldiers embark. It was neither his part, nor his inclination, nor his policy. His part, his inclination, and his policy were united in one endeavour to keep unchecked the flow of treasure he had started single-handed from the reopened scar in the flank of the mountain. As the mine developed he had trained for himself some native help. There were foremen, artificers, and clerks, with Don Pepe for the *gobernador* of the mining population. For the rest his shoulders alone sustained the whole weight of the "*Imperium in Imperio*," the great Gould Concession whose mere shadow had been enough to crush the life out of his father.

Mrs. Gould had no silver mine to look after. In the general life of the Gould Concession she was represented by her two lieutenants, the doctor and the priest, but she fed her woman's love for excitement on events whose significance was purified to her by the fire of her imaginative purpose. On that day she had brought the Avellanos, father and daughter, down to the harbour with her.

Amongst his other activities of that stirring time, Don José had become the chairman of a Patriotic Committee which had armed a great proportion of troops in the Sulaco command with an improved model of a military rifle. It had been just discarded for something still more deadly by one of the great European powers. How much of the market-price for secondhand weapons was covered by the voluntary contributions of the principal families, and how much came from those funds Don José was understood to command abroad, remained a secret which he alone could have disclosed; but

---

*Four-wheel carriage with a removable top.
†Establishment.
‡Plains.

the *ricos*, as the populace called them, had contributed under the pressure of their Nestor's eloquence. Some of the more enthusiastic ladies had been moved to bring offerings of jewels into the hands of the man who was the life and soul of the party.

There were moments when both his life and his soul seemed overtaxed by so many years of undiscouraged belief in regeneration. He appeared almost inanimate, sitting rigidly by the side of Mrs. Gould in the landau, with his fine, old, clean-shaven face of a uniform tint as if modelled in yellow wax, shaded by a soft felt hat, the dark eyes looking out fixedly. Antonia, the beautiful Antonia, as Miss Avellanos was called in Sulaco, leaned back, facing them; and her full figure, the grave oval of her face with full red lips, made her look more mature than Mrs. Gould, with her mobile expression and small, erect person under a slightly swaying sunshade.

Whenever possible Antonia attended her father; her recognized devotion weakened the shocking effect of her scorn for the rigid conventions, regulating the life of Spanish-American girlhood. And, in truth, she was no longer girlish. It was said that she often wrote State papers from her father's dictation, and was allowed to read all the books in his library. At the receptions—where the situation was saved by the presence of a very decrepit old lady (a relation of the Corbeláns), quite deaf and motionless in an armchair—Antonia could hold her own in a discussion with two or three men at a time. Obviously she was not the girl to be content with peeping through a barred window at a cloaked figure of a lover ensconced in a doorway opposite—which is the correct form of Costaguana courtship. It was generally believed that with her foreign upbringing and foreign ideas the learned and proud Antonia would never marry— unless, indeed, she married a foreigner from Europe or North America, now that Sulaco seemed on the point of being invaded by all the world.

CHAPTER 3

WHEN GENERAL BARRIOS STOPPED to address Mrs. Gould, Antonia raised negligently her hand holding an open fan, as if to shade from the sun her head, wrapped in a light lace shawl. The clear gleam of her blue eyes gliding behind the black fringe of eyelashes paused for a moment upon her father, then travelled farther to the figure of a young man of thirty at most, of medium height, rather thick-set, wearing a light overcoat. Bearing down with the open palm of his hand upon the knob of a flexible cane, he had been looking on from a distance; but directly he saw himself noticed, he approached quietly and put his elbow over the door of the landau.

The shirt collar, cut low in the neck, the big bow of his cravat, the style of his clothing, from the round hat to the varnished shoes, suggested an idea of French elegance; but otherwise he was the very type of a fair Spanish creole. The fluffy moustache and the short, curly, golden beard did not conceal his lips, rosy, fresh, almost pouting in expression. His full, round face was of that warm, healthy creole white which is never tanned by its native sunshine. Martin Decoud was seldom exposed to the Costaguana sun under which he was born. His people had been long settled in Paris, where he had studied law, had dabbled in literature, had hoped now and then in moments of exaltation to become a poet like that other foreigner of Spanish blood, José Maria Heredia.[11] In other moments he had, to pass the time, condescended to write articles on European affairs for the *Semenario*, the principal newspaper in Sta. Marta, which printed them under the heading "From our special correspondent," though the authorship was an open secret. Everybody in Costaguana, where the tale of compatriots in Europe is jealously kept, knew that it was "the son Decoud," a talented young man, supposed to be moving in the higher spheres of Society. As a matter of fact, he was an idle boulevardier, in touch with some smart journalists, made free of a few newspaper offices, and welcomed in the pleasure-haunts of pressmen. This life, whose dreary superficiality is covered by the glitter of universal *blague*,* like the stupid clowning of a harlequin by the spangles of a motley costume, induced in him a Frenchified—but most un-French—cosmopolitanism, in reality a mere barren indifferentism posing as intellectual superiority. Of his own country he used to say to his French associates: "Imagine an atmosphere of *opéra bouffe*† in which all the comic business of stage statesmen, brigands, etc., etc., all their farcical stealing, intriguing, and stabbing is done in dead earnest. It is screamingly funny, the blood flows all the time, and the actors believe themselves to be influencing the fate of the universe. Of course, government in general, any government anywhere, is a thing of exquisite comicality to a discerning mind; but really we Spanish–Americans do overstep the bounds. No man of ordinary intelligence can take part in the intrigues of *une farce macabre*.‡ However, these Ribierists, of whom we hear so much just now, are really trying in their own comical way to make the country habitable, and even to pay some of its debts. My friends, you had better write up Señor Ribiera all you can in kindness to your own bondholders. Really, if what I am told in my letters is true, there is some chance for them at last."

And he would explain with railing verve what Don Vincente Ribiera stood for—a mournful little man oppressed by his own good intentions, the significance of battles won, who Montero was (*un grotesque vaniteux et féroce*),§ and the manner of the new loan connected with railway development, and the colonization of vast tracts of land in one great financial scheme.

And his French friends would remark that evidently this little fellow Decoud *connaissait la question à fond.*‖ An important Parisian review asked him for an article on the situation. It was composed in a serious tone and in a spirit of levity. Afterwards he asked one of his intimates:

---

*Buffoonery (Fr.).
†Comic opera (Fr.).
‡A macabre joke.
§A vain and ferocious grotesque (Fr.).
‖Understood the question thoroughly (Fr.).

"Have you read my thing about the regeneration of Costaguana—
une bonne blague, hein?"[*]

He imagined himself Parisian to the tips of his fingers. But far
from being that he was in danger of remaining a sort of nondescript
dilettante all his life. He had pushed the habit of universal raillery
to a point where it blinded him to the genuine impulses of his own
nature. To be suddenly selected for the executive member of the
patriotic small-arms committee of Sulaco seemed to him the height
of the unexpected, one of those fantastic moves of which only his
"dear countrymen" were capable.

"It's like a tile falling on my head. I—I—executive member! It's
the first I hear of it! What do I know of military rifles? *C'est funambu-
lesque!*"[†] he had exclaimed to his favourite sister; for the Decoud
family—except the old father and mother—used the French language amongst themselves. "And you should see the explanatory and
confidential letter! Eight pages of it—no less!"

This letter, in Antonia's handwriting, was signed by Don José, who
appealed to the "young and gifted Costaguanero" on public grounds,
and privately opened his heart to his talented godson, a man of
wealth and leisure, with wide relations, and by his parentage and
bringing-up worthy of all confidence.

"Which means," Martin commented, cynically, to his sister, "that
I am not likely to misappropriate the funds, or go blabbing to our
Chargé d'Affaires here."

The whole thing was being carried out behind the back of the
War Minister, Montero, a mistrusted member of the Ribiera Government, but difficult to get rid of at once. He was not to know anything of it till the troops under Barrios's command had the new rifle
in their hands. The President-Dictator, whose position was very difficult, was alone in the secret.

"How funny!" commented Martin's sister and confidant; to
which the brother, with an air of best Parisian *blague*, had retorted:

"It's immense! The idea of that Chief of the State engaged,
with the help of private citizens, in digging a mine under his own

---

[*]A good joke, eh? (Fr.).
[†]It's bizarre! (Fr.).

indispensable War Minister. No! We are unapproachable!" And he
laughed immoderately.

Afterwards his sister was surprised at the earnestness and ability
he displayed in carrying out his mission, which circumstances made
delicate, and his want of special knowledge rendered difficult. She
had never seen Martin take so much trouble about anything in his
whole life.

"It amuses me," he had explained, briefly. "I am beset by a lot of
swindlers trying to sell all sorts of gaspipe weapons. They are charming; they invite me to expensive luncheons; I keep up their hopes; it's
extremely entertaining. Meanwhile, the real affair is being carried
through in quite another quarter."

When the business was concluded he declared suddenly his intention of seeing the precious consignment delivered safely in Sulaco. The whole burlesque business, he thought, was worth following
up to the end. He mumbled his excuses, tugging at his golden beard,
before the acute young lady who (after the first wide stare of astonishment) looked at him with narrowed eyes, and pronounced slowly:

"I believe you want to see Antonia."

"What Antonia?" asked the Costaguana boulevardier, in a vexed
and disdainful tone. He shrugged his shoulders, and spun round on
his heel. His sister called out after him joyously:

"The Antonia you used to know when she wore her hair in two
plaits down her back."

He had known her some eight years since, shortly before the
Avellanos had left Europe for good, as a tall girl of sixteen, youth-
fully austere, and of a character already so formed that she ventured
to treat slightingly his pose of disabused wisdom. On one occasion,
as though she had lost all patience, she flew out at him about the
aimlessness of his life and the levity of his opinions. He was twenty
then, an only son, spoiled by his adoring family. This attack disconcerted him so greatly that he had faltered in his affection of amused
superiority before that insignificant chit of a schoolgirl. But the impression left was so strong that ever since all the girl friends of his
sisters recalled to him Antonia Avellanos by some faint resemblance,
or by the great force of contrast. It was, he told himself, like a ridiculous fatality. And, of course, in the news the Decouds received regularly from Costaguana, the name of their friends, the Avellanos,

cropped up frequently—the arrest and the abominable treatment of the ex-Minister, the dangers and hardships endured by the family, its withdrawal in poverty to Sulaco, the death of the mother.

The Monterist *pronunciamiento* had taken place before Martin Decoud reached Costaguana. He came out in a roundabout way, through Magellan's Straits by the main line and the West Coast Service of the O.S.N. Company. His precious consignment arrived just in time to convert the first feelings of consternation into a mood of hope and resolution. Publicly he was made much of by the *familias principales.** Privately Don José, still shaken and weak, embraced him with tears in his eyes.

"You have come out yourself! No less could be expected from a Decoud. Alas! our worst fears have been realized," he moaned, affectionately. And again he hugged his godson. This was indeed the time for men of intellect and conscience to rally round the endangered cause.

It was then that Martin Decoud, the adopted child of Western Europe, felt the absolute change of atmosphere. He submitted to being embraced and talked to without a word. He was moved in spite of himself by that note of passion and sorrow unknown on the more refined stage of European politics. But when the tall Antonia, advancing with her light step in the dimness of the big bare *sala* of the Avellanos house, offered him her hand (in her emancipated way), and murmured, "I am glad to see you here, Don Martin," he felt how impossible it would be to tell these two people that he had intended to go away by the next month's packet. Don José, meantime, continued his praises. Every accession added to public confidence, and, besides, what an example to the young men at home from the brilliant defender of the country's regeneration, the worthy expounder of the party's political faith before the world! Everybody had read the magnificent article in the famous *Parisian Review*. The world was now informed: and the author's appearance at this moment was like a public act of faith. Young Decoud felt overcome by a feeling of impatient confusion. His plan had been to return by way of the United States through California, visit Yellowstone Park,

---

*Leading families.

see Chicago, Niagara, have a look at Canada, perhaps make a short stay in New York, a longer one in Newport, use his letters of introduction. The pressure of Antonia's hand was so frank, the tone of her voice was so unexpectedly unchanged in its approving warmth, that all he found to say after his low bow was:

"I am inexpressibly grateful for your welcome; but why need a man be thanked for returning to his native country? I am sure Doña Antonia does not think so."

"Certainly not, *señor*," she said, with that perfectly calm openness of manner which characterized all her utterances. "But when he returns, as you return, one may be glad—for the sake of both."

Martin Decoud said nothing of his plans. He not only never breathed a word of them to anyone, but only a fortnight later asked the mistress of the Casa Gould (where he had of course obtained admission at once), leaning forward in his chair with an air of well-bred familiarity, whether she could not detect in him that day a marked change—an air, he explained, of more excellent gravity. At this Mrs. Gould turned her face full towards him with the silent inquiry of slightly widened eyes and the merest ghost of a smile, a habitual movement with her, which was very fascinating to men by something subtly devoted, finely self-forgetful in its lively readiness of attention. Because, Decoud continued imperturbably, he felt no longer an idle cumberer of the earth. She was, he assured her, actually beholding at that moment the Journalist of Sulaco. At once Mrs. Gould glanced towards Antonia, posed upright in the corner of a high, straightbacked Spanish sofa, a large black fan waving slowly against the curves of her fine figure, the tips of crossed feet peeping from under the hem of the black skirt. Decoud's eyes also remained fixed there, while in an undertone he added that Miss Avellanos was quite aware of his new and unexpected vocation, which in Costaguana was generally the speciality of half-educated Negroes and wholly penniless lawyers. Then, confronting with a sort of urbane effrontery Mrs. Gould's gaze, now turned sympathetically upon himself, he breathed out the words, "*Pro patria!*"

What had happened was that he had all at once yielded to Don José's pressing entreaties to take the direction of a newspaper that would "voice the aspirations of the province." It had been Don José's old and cherished idea. The necessary plant (on a modest scale) and a large consignment of paper had been received from America some time before; the right man alone was wanted. Even Señor Moraga in Sta. Marta had not been able to find one, and the matter was now becoming pressing; some organ was absolutely needed to counteract the effect of the lies disseminated by the Monterist Press: the atrocious calumnies, the appeals of the people calling upon them to rise with their knives in their hands and put an end once for all to the Blancos, to these Gothic remnants, to these sinister mummies, these impotent *paralíticos*,* who plotted with foreigners for the surrender of the lands and the slavery of the people.

The clamour of this "Negro Liberalism" frightened Señor Avellanos. A newspaper was the only remedy. And now that the right man had been found in Decoud, great black letters appeared painted between the windows above the arcaded ground floor of a house on the Plaza. It was next to Anzani's great emporium of boots, silks, ironware, muslins, wooden toys, tiny silver arms, legs, heads, hearts (for ex-voto offerings), rosaries, champagne, women's hats, patent medicines, even a few dusty books in paper covers and mostly in the French language. The big black letters formed the words, "Offices of the *Porvenir.*" From these offices a single folded sheet of Martin's journalism issued three times a week; and the sleek yellow Anzani prowling in a suit of ample black and carpet slippers, before the many doors of his establishment, greeted by a deep, sidelong inclination of his body the Journalist of Sulaco going to and fro on the business of his august calling.

CHAPTER 4

PERHAPS IT WAS IN the exercise of his calling that he had come to see the troops depart. The *Porvenir* of the day after next would no doubt relate the event, but its editor, leaning his side against the landau, seemed to look at nothing. The front rank of the company of

---

*Paralytics—here meaning men incapable of action.

infantry drawn up three deep across the shore-end of the jetty when pressed too close would bring their bayonets to the charge ferociously, with an awful rattle; and then the crowd of spectators swayed back bodily, even under the noses of the big white mules. Notwithstanding the great multitude there was only a low, muttering noise; the dust hung in a brown haze, in which the horsemen, wedged in the throng here and there, towered from the hips upwards, gazing all one way over the heads. Almost every one of them had mounted a friend, who steadied himself with both hands grasping his shoulders from behind; and the rims of their hats touching, made like one disc sustaining the cones of two pointed crowns with a double face underneath. A hoarse *mozo* would bawl out something to an acquaintance in the ranks, or a woman would shriek suddenly the word *Adiós!* followed by the Christian name of a man.

General Barrios, in a shabby blue tunic and white peg-top trousers falling upon strange red boots, kept his head uncovered and stooped slightly, propping himself up with a thick stick. No! He had earned enough military glory to satiate any man, he insisted to Mrs. Gould, trying at the same time to put an air of gallantry into his attitude. A few jetty hairs hung sparsely from his upper lip, he had a salient nose, a thin, long jaw, and a black silk patch over one eye. His other eye, small and deep-set, twinkled erratically in all directions, aimlessly affable. The few European spectators, all men, who had naturally drifted into the neighbourhood of the Gould carriage, betrayed by the solemnity of their faces their impression that the general must have had too much punch (Swedish punch, imported in bottles by Anzani) at the Amarilla Club before he had started with his Staff on a furious ride to the harbour. But Mrs. Gould bent forward, self-possessed, and declared her conviction that still more glory awaited the general in the near future.

"*Señora!*" he remonstrated, with great feeling, "in the name of God, reflect! How can there be any glory for a man like me in overcoming that bald-headed *embustero** with the dyed moustaches?"

Pablo Ignacio Barrios, son of a village *alcalde*, general of division, commanding in chief the Occidental Military district, did not

---

*Liar.

frequent the higher society of the town. He preferred the unceremonious gatherings of men where he could tell jaguar-hunt stories, boast of his powers with the lasso, with which he could perform extremely difficult feats of the sort "no married man should attempt," as the saying goes amongst the *llaneros*; relate tales of extraordinary night rides, encounters with wild bulls, struggles with crocodiles, adventures in the great forests, crossings of swollen rivers. And it was not mere boastfulness that prompted the general's reminiscences, but a genuine love of that wild life which he had led in his young days before he turned his back for ever on the thatched roof of the parental *toldería** in the woods. Wandering away as far as Mexico he had fought against the French by the side (as he said) of Juarez,[12] and was the only military man of Costaguana who had ever encountered European troops in the field. That fact shed a great lustre upon his name till it became eclipsed by the rising star of Montero. All his life he had been an inveterate gambler. He alluded himself quite openly to the current story how once, during some campaign (when in command of a brigade), he had gambled away his horses, pistols, and accoutrements, to the very epaulettes, playing *monte*† with his colonels the night before the battle. Finally, he had sent under escort his sword (a presentation sword, with a gold hilt) to the town in the rear of his position to be immediately pledged for five hundred pesetas with a sleepy and frightened shopkeeper. By daybreak he had lost the last of that money, too, when his only remark, as he rose calmly, was, "Now let us go and fight to the death." From that time he had become aware that a general could lead his troops into battle very well with a simple stick in his hand. "It has been my custom ever since," he would say.

He was always overwhelmed with debts; even during the periods of splendour in his varied fortunes of a Costaguana general, when he held high military commands, his gold-laced uniforms were almost always in pawn with some tradesman. And at last, to avoid the incessant difficulties of costume caused by the anxious lenders, he had assumed a disdain of military trappings, an eccentric fashion of

---

*Indian encampment or village.
†Card game played with a deck of forty-five cards.

shabby old tunics, which had become like a second nature. But the faction Barrios joined needed to fear no political betrayal. He was too much of a real soldier for the ignoble traffic of buying and selling victories. A member of the foreign diplomatic body in Sta. Marta had once passed a judgement upon him: "Barrios is a man of perfect honesty and even of some talent for war, *mais il manque de tenue.*"* After the triumph of the Ribierists he had obtained the reputedly lucrative Occidental command, mainly through the exertions of his creditors (the Sta. Marta shopkeepers, all great politicians), who moved heaven and earth in his interest publicly, and privately besieged Señor Moraga, the influential agent of the San Tomé mine, with the exaggerated lamentations that if the general were passed over, "we shall all be ruined." An incidental but favourable mention of his name in Mr. Gould senior's long correspondence with his son had something to do with his appointment, too; but most of all undoubtedly his established political honesty. No one questioned the personal bravery of the Tiger-killer, as the populace called him. He was, however, said to be unlucky in the field—but this was to be the beginning of an era of peace. The soldiers liked him for his humane temper, which was like a strange and precious flower unexpectedly blooming on the hotbed of corrupt revolutions; and when he rode slowly through the streets during some military display, the contemptuous good humour of his solitary eye roaming over the crowds extorted the acclamations of the populace. The women of that class especially seemed positively fascinated by the long drooping nose, the peaked chin, the heavy lower lip, the black silk eye-patch and band slanting rakishly over the forehead. His high rank always procured an audience of *caballeros* for his sporting stories, which he detailed very well with a simple, grave enjoyment. As to the society of ladies, it was irksome by the restraints it imposed without any equivalent, as far as he could see. He had not, perhaps, spoken three times on the whole to Mrs. Gould since he had taken up his high command; but he had observed her frequently riding with the Señor Administrator, and had pronounced that there was more sense in her little bridle-hand than in all the

---

*But he lacks decorum (Fr.).

female heads in Sulaco. His impulse had been to be very civil on parting to a woman who did not wobble in the saddle, and happened to be the wife of a personality very important to a man always short of money. He even pushed his attentions so far as to desire the aide-de-camp at his side (a thick-set, short captain with a Tartar physiognomy) to bring along a corporal with a file of men in front of the carriage, lest the crowd in its backward surges would "incommode the mules of the *señora.*" Then, turning to the small knot of silent Europeans looking on within earshot, he raised his voice protectingly:

"*Señores,* have no apprehension. Go on quietly making your Ferro Carril—your railways, your telegraphs. Your— There's enough wealth in Costaguana to pay for everything—or else you would not be here. Ha! ha! Don't mind this little *picardía* of my friend Montero. In a little while you shall behold his dyed moustaches through the bars of a strong wooden cage. *Sí, señores!* Fear nothing, develop the country, work, work!"

The little group of engineers received this exhortation without a word, and after waving his hand at them loftily, he addressed himself again to Mrs. Gould:

"That is what Don José says we must do. Be enterprising! Work! Grow rich! To put Montero in a cage is my work; and when that insignificant piece of business is done, then, as Don José wishes us, we shall grow rich, one and all, like so many Englishmen, because it is money that saves a country, and—"

But a young officer in a very new uniform, hurrying up from the direction of the jetty, interrupted his interpretation of Señor Avellanos's ideals. The general made a movement of impatience; the other went on talking to him insistently, with an air of respect. The horses of the Staff had been embarked, the steamer's gig was awaiting the general at the boat steps; and Barrios, after a fierce stare of his one eye, began to take leave. Don José roused himself for an appropriate phrase pronounced mechanically. The terrible strain of hope and fear was telling on him, and he seemed to husband the last sparks of his fire for those oratorical efforts of which even the distant Europe was to hear. Antonia, her red lips firmly closed, averted her head behind the raised fan; and young Decoud, though he felt the girl's eyes upon him, gazed away persistently, hooked on his elbow, with a scornful and complete detachment. Mrs. Gould heroically concealed her dismay at the appearance of men and events so remote from her racial conventions, dismay too deep to be uttered in words even to her husband. She understood his voiceless reserve better now. Their confidential intercourse fell, not in moments of privacy, but precisely in public, when the quick meeting of their glances would comment upon some fresh turn of events. She had gone to his school of un-compromising silence, the only one possible, since so much that seemed shocking, weird, and grotesque in the working out of their purposes had to be accepted as normal in this country. Decidedly, the stately Antonia looked more mature and infinitely calm; but she would never have known how to reconcile the sudden sinkings of her heart with an amiable mobility of expression.

Mrs. Gould smiled a good-bye at Barrios, nodded round to the Europeans (who raised their hats simultaneously) with an engaging invitation, "I hope to see you all presently, at home"; then said ner-vously to Decoud, "Get in, Don Martin," and heard him mutter to himself in French, as he opened the carriage door, "*Le sort en est jeté.*"* She heard him with a sort of exasperation. Nobody ought to have known better than himself that the first cast of dice had been already thrown long ago in a most desperate game. Distant accla-mations, words of command yelled out, and a roll of drums on the jetty greeted the departing general. Something like a slight faint-ness came over her, and she looked blankly at Antonia's face, won-dering what would happen to Charley if that absurd man failed. "A *la casa, Ignacio,*"† she cried at the motionless broad back of the coachman, who gathered the reins without haste, mumbling to himself under his breath, "*Sí, la, casa. Sí, sí, niña.*"‡

The carriage rolled noiselessly on the soft track, the shadows fell long on the dusty little plain interspersed with dark bushes, mounds of turned-up earth, low wooden buildings with iron roofs of the Railway Company; the sparse row of telegraph poles strode obliquely clear of the town, bearing a single, almost invisible wire far into the great *campo*§—like a slender, vibrating feeler of that progress

---

*The die is cast (Fr.).
†To the house, Ignacio.
‡Yes, the house. Yes, yes, my girl.
§Countryside.

waiting outside for a moment of peace to enter and twine itself about the weary heart of the land.

The café window of the Albergo d'Italia Una was full of sun-burnt, whiskered faces of railway men. But at the other end of the house, the end of the Signori Inglesi, old Giorgio, at the door with one of his girls on each side, bared his bushy head, as white as the snows of Higuerota. Mrs. Gould stopped the carriage. She seldom failed to speak to the protégé; moreover, the excitement, the heat, and the dust had made her thirsty. She asked for a glass of water. Giorgio sent the children indoors for it, and approached with pleasure expressed in his whole rugged countenance. It was not often that he had occasion to see his benefactress, who was also an Englishwoman—another title to his regard. He offered some ex-cuses for his wife. It was a bad day with her; her oppressions—he tapped his own broad chest. She could not move from her chair that day.

Decoud, ensconced in the corner of his seat, observed gloomily Mrs. Gould's old revolutionist, then, offhand:

"Well, and what do you think of it all, Garibaldino?"

Old Giorgio, looking at him with some curiosity, said civilly that the troops had marched very well. One-eyed Barrios and his officers had done wonders with the recruits in a short time. Those *Indios*, only caught the other day, had gone swinging past in double-quick time, like *bersaglieri*;* they looked well fed, too, and had whole uniforms. "Uniforms!" he repeated with a half-smile of pity. A look of grim retrospect stole over his piercing, steady eyes. It had been oth-erwise in his time when men fought against tyranny, in the forests of Brazil, or on the plains of Uruguay, starving on half-raw beef with-out salt, half naked, with often only a knife tied to a stick for a weapon. "And yet we used to prevail against the oppressor," he con-cluded, proudly.

His animation fell; the slight gesture of his hand expressed dis-couragement; but he added that he had asked one of the sergeants to show him the new rifle. There was no such weapon in his fight-ing days; and if Barrios could not—

---

*Italian soldiers in the rifle regiment (It.).

"Yes, yes," broke in Don José, almost trembling with eagerness. "We are safe. The good Señor Viola is a man of experience. Extremely deadly—is it not so? You have accomplished your mission admirably, my dear Martin."

Decoud, lolling back moodily, contemplated old Viola.

"Ah! Yes. A man of experience. But who are you for, really, in your heart?"

Mrs. Gould leaned over to the children. Linda had brought out a glass of water on a tray, with extreme care; Giselle presented her with a bunch of flowers gathered hastily.

"For the people," declared old Viola, sternly.

"We are all for the people—in the end."

"Yes," muttered old Viola, savagely. "And meantime they fight for you. Blind. *Esclavos!*"*

At that moment young Scarfe of the railway staff emerged from the door of the part reserved for the Signori Inglesi. He had come down to headquarters from somewhere up the line on a light engine, and had had just time to get a bath and change his clothes. He was a nice boy, and Mrs. Gould welcomed him.

"It's a delightful surprise to see you, Mrs. Gould. I've just come down. Usual luck. Missed everything, of course. This show is just over, and I hear there has been a great dance at Don Juste Lopez's last night. Is it true?"

"The young patricians," Decoud began suddenly in his precise English, "have indeed been dancing before they started off to the war with the Great Pompey."

Young Scarfe stared, astounded. "You haven't met before," Mrs. Gould intervened. "Mr. Decoud—Mr. Scarfe."

"Ah! But we are not going to Pharsalia,"† protested Don José, with nervous haste, also in English. "You should not jest like this, Martin."

Antonia's breast rose and fell with a deeper breath. The young engineer was utterly in the dark. "Great what?" he muttered, vaguely.

"Luckily, Montero is not a Caesar," Decoud continued. "Not the two Monteros put together would make a decent parody of a Caesar."

---

*Slaves.

†Or Pharsalus; ancient city of Greece, site of Julius Caesar's defeat of the Roman general Pompey in 48 B.C.

He crossed his arms on his breast, looking at Señor Avellanos, who had returned to his immobility. "It is only you, Don José, who are a genuine old Roman—*vir Romanus*—eloquent and inflexible."

Since he had heard the name of Montero pronounced, young Scarfe had been eager to express his simple feelings. In a loud and youthful tone he hoped that this Montero was going to be licked once for all and done with. There was no saying what would happen to the railway if the revolution got the upper hand. Perhaps it would have to be abandoned. It would not be the first railway gone to pot in Costaguana. "You know, it's one of their so-called national things," he ran on, wrinkling up his nose as if the world had a suspicious flavor to his profound experience of South American affairs. And, of course, he chatted with animation, it had been such an immense piece of luck for him at his age to get appointed on the staff "of a big thing like that—don't you know." It would give him the pull over a lot of chaps all through life, he asserted. "Therefore— down with Montero! Mrs. Gould." His artless grin disappeared slowly before the unanimous gravity of the faces turned upon him from the carriage; only that "old chap," Don José, presenting a motionless, waxy profile, stared straight on as if deaf. Scarfe did not know the Avellanos very well. They did not give balls, and Antonia never appeared at a ground-floor window, as some other young ladies used to do attended by elder women, to chat with the *caballeros* on horseback in the *calle*. The stares of these creoles did not matter much; but what on earth had come to Mrs. Gould? She said, "Go on, Ignacio," and gave him a slow inclination of the head. He heard a short laugh from that round-faced, Frenchified fellow. He coloured up to the eyes, and stared at Giorgio Viola, who had fallen back with the children, hat in hand.

"I shall want a horse presently," he said with some asperity to the old man.

"*Si, señor*. There are plenty of horses," murmured the Garibaldino, smoothing absently, with his brown hands, the two heads, one dark with bronze glints, the other fair with a coppery ripple, of the two girls by his side. The returning stream of sightseers raised a great dust on the road. Horsemen noticed the group. "Go to your mother," he said. "They are growing up as I am growing older, and there is nobody—"

He looked at the young engineer and stopped, as if awakened from a dream; then, folding his arms on his breast, took up his usual position, leaning back in the doorway with an upward glance fastened on the white shoulder of Higuerota far away.

In the carriage Martin Decoud, shifting his position as though he could not make himself comfortable, muttered as he swayed towards Antonia, "I suppose you hate me." Then in a loud voice he began to congratulate Don José upon all the engineers being convinced Ribierists. The interest of all those foreigners was gratifying. "You have heard this one. He is an enlightened well-wisher. It is pleasant to think that the prosperity of Costaguana is of some use to the world."

"He is very young," Mrs. Gould remarked, quietly.

"And so very wise for his age," retorted Decoud. "But here we have the naked truth from the mouth of that child. You are right, Don José. The natural treasures of Costaguana are of importance to the progressive Europe represented by this youth, just as three hundred years ago the wealth of our Spanish fathers was a serious object to the rest of Europe—as represented by the bold buccaneers. There is a curse of futility upon our character: Don Quixote and Sancho Panza, chivalry and materialism, high-sounding sentiments and a supine morality, violent efforts for an idea and a sullen acquiescence in every form of corruption. We convulsed a continent for our independence only to become the passive prey of a democratic parody, the helpless victims of scoundrels and cut-throats, our institutions a mockery, our laws a farce—a Guzman Bento our master! And we have sunk so low that when a man like you has awakened our conscience, a stupid barbarian of a Montero—Great Heavens! a Montero!—becomes a deadly danger, and an ignorant, boastful *indio*, like Barrios, is our defender."

But Don José, disregarding the general indictment as though he had not heard a word of it, took up the defence of Barrios. The man was competent enough for his special task in the plan of campaign. It consisted in an offensive movement, with Cayta as base, upon the flank of the revolutionist forces advancing from the south against Sta. Marta, which was covered by another army with the President-Dictator in its midst. Don José became quite animated with a great flow of speech, bending forward anxiously under the steady eyes of his daughter. Decoud, as if silenced by so much ardour, did not make a sound. The bells of the city were striking the hour of *Oración** when the carriage rolled under the old gateway facing the harbour like a shapeless monument of leaves and stones. The rumble of wheels under the sonorous arch was traversed by a strange, piercing shriek, and Decoud, from his back seat, had a view of the people behind the carriage trudging along the road outside, all turning their heads, in sombreros and rebozos, to look at a locomotive which rolled quickly out of sight behind Giorgio Viola's house, under a white trail of steam that seemed to vanish in the breathless, hysterically prolonged scream of warlike triumph. And it was all like a fleeting vision, the shrieking ghost of a railway engine fleeing across the frame of the archway, behind the startled movement of the people streaming back from a military spectacle with silent footsteps on the dust of the road. It was a material train returning from the Campo to the palisaded yards. The empty cars rolled lightly on the single track; there was no rumble of wheels, no tremor on the ground. The engine-driver, running past the Casa Viola with the salute of an uplifted arm, checked his speed smartly before entering the yard; and when the ear-splitting screech of the steam-whistle for the brakes had stopped, a series of hard, battering shocks, mingled with the clanking of chain-couplings, made a tumult of blows and shaken fetters under the vault of the gate.

CHAPTER 5

THE GOULD CARRIAGE WAS the first to return from the harbour to the empty town. On the ancient pavement, laid out in patterns, sunk into ruts and holes, the portly Ignacio, mindful of the springs of the Parisian-built landau, had pulled up to a walk, and Decoud in his corner contemplated moodily the inner aspect of the gate. The squat turreted sides held up between them a mass of masonry with bunches of grass growing at the top, and a grey, heavily

---

*Prayer.

scrolled armorial shield of stone above the apex of the arch with the arms of Spain nearly smoothed out as if in readiness for some new device typical of the impending progress.

The explosive noise of the railway trucks seemed to augment Decoud's irritation. He muttered something to himself, then began to talk aloud in curt, angry phrases thrown at the silence of the two women. They did not look at him at all; while Don José, with his semi-translucent, waxy complexion, overshadowed by the soft grey hat, swayed a little to the jolts of the carriage by the side of Mrs. Gould.

"This sound puts a new edge on a very old truth."

Decoud spoke in French, perhaps because of Ignacio on the box above him; the old coachman, with his broad back filling a short, silver-braided jacket, had a big pair of ears, whose thick rims stood well away from his cropped head.

"Yes, the noise outside the city wall is new, but the principle is old."

He ruminated his discontent for a while, then began afresh with a sidelong glance at Antonia:

"No, but just imagine our forefathers in morions* and corselets† drawn up outside this gate, and a band of adventurers just landed from their ships in the harbour there. Thieves, of course. Speculators, too. Their expeditions, each one, were the speculations of grave and reverend persons in England. That is history, as that absurd sailor Mitchell is always saying."

"Mitchell's arrangements for the embarkation of the troops were excellent!" exclaimed Don José.

"That!—that! oh, that's really the work of that Genoese seaman! But to return to my noises; there used to be in the old days the sound of trumpets outside that gate. War trumpets! I'm sure they were trumpets. I have read somewhere that Drake, who was the greatest of these men, used to dine alone in his cabin on board ship to the sound of trumpets. In those days this town was full of wealth. Those men came to take it. Now the whole land is like a treasure-house, and all these

---

*Crested helmets worn by sixteenth- and seventeenth-century Spanish infantry-men.

†Pieces of armor covering the trunk but usually not the legs.

people are breaking into it, whilst we are cutting each other's throats. The only thing that keeps them out is mutual jealousy. But they'll come to an agreement some day—and by the time we've settled our quarrels and become decent and honourable, there'll be nothing left for us. It has always been the same. We are a wonderful people, but it has always been our fate to be"—he did not say "robbed," but added, after a pause—"exploited!"

Mrs. Gould said, "Oh, this is unjust!" And Antonia interjected, "Don't answer him, Emilia. He is attacking me."

"You surely do not think I was attacking Don Carlos!" Decoud answered.

And then the carriage stopped before the door of the Casa Gould. The young man offered his hand to the ladies. They went in first together; Don José walked by the side of Decoud, and the gouty old porter tottered after them with some light wraps on his arm.

Don José slipped his hand under the arm of the journalist of Sulaco.

"The *Porvenir* must have a long and confident article upon Barrios and the irresistibleness of his army of Cayta! The moral effect should be kept up in the country. We must cable encouraging extracts to Europe and the United States to maintain a favourable impression abroad."

Decoud muttered, "Oh, yes, we must comfort our friends, the speculators."

The long open gallery was in shadow, with its screen of plants in vases along the balustrade, holding out motionless blossoms, and all the glass doors of the reception-rooms thrown open. A jingle of spurs died out at the farther end.

Basilio, standing aside against the wall, said in a soft tone to the passing ladies, "The Señor Administrador is just back from the mountain."

In the great *sala*, with its groups of ancient Spanish and modern European furniture making as if different centres under the high white spread of the ceiling, the silver and porcelain of the tea-service gleamed among a cluster of dwarf chairs, like a bit of a lady's boudoir, putting in a note of feminine and intimate delicacy.

Don José in his rocking-chair placed his hat on his lap, and Decoud walked up and down the whole length of the room, passing between tables loaded with knickknacks and almost disappearing behind the high backs of leathern sofas. He was thinking of the angry face of Antonia; he was confident that he would make his peace with her. He had not stayed in Sulaco to quarrel with Antonia.

Martin Decoud was angry with himself. All he saw and heard going on around him exasperated the preconceived views of his European civilization. To contemplate revolutions from the distance of the Parisian Boulevards was quite another matter. Here on the spot it was not possible to dismiss their tragic comedy with the expression, *"Quelle farce!"**

The reality of the political action, such as it was, seemed closer, and acquired poignancy by Antonia's belief in the cause. Its crudeness hurt his feelings. He was surprised at his own sensitiveness.

"I suppose I am more of a Costaguanero than I would have believed possible," he thought to himself.

His disdain grew like a reaction of his scepticism against the action into which he was forced by his infatuation for Antonia. He soothed himself by saying he was not a patriot, but a lover.

The ladies came in bareheaded, and Mrs. Gould sank low before the little tea-table. Antonia took up her usual place at the reception hour—the corner of a leathern couch, with a rigid grace in her pose and a fan in her hand. Decoud, swerving from the straight line of his march, came to lean over the high back of her seat.

For a long time he talked into her ear from behind, softly, with a half smile and an air of apologetic familiarity. Her fan lay half grasped on her knees. She never looked at him. His rapid utterance grew more, and more insistent and caressing. At last he ventured a slight laugh.

"No, really. You must forgive me. One must be serious sometimes." He paused. She turned her head a little; her blue eyes glided slowly towards him, slightly upwards, mollified and questioning.

"You can't think I am serious when I call Montero a *gran' bestia*†† every second day in the *Porvenir?* That is not a serious occupation.

No occupation is serious, not even when a bullet through the heart is the penalty of failure!"

Her hand closed firmly on her fan.

"Some reason, you understand, I mean some sense, may creep into thinking; some glimpse of truth. I mean some effective truth, for which there is no room in politics or journalism. I happen to have said what I thought. And you are angry! If you do me the kindness to think a little you will see that I spoke like a patriot."

She opened her red lips for the first time, not unkindly.

"Yes, but you never see the aim. Men must be used as they are. I suppose nobody is really disinterested, unless, perhaps, you, Don Martin."

"God forbid! It's the last thing I should like you to believe of me." He spoke lightly, and paused.

She began to fan herself with a slow movement without raising her hand. After a time he whispered passionately:

"Antonia!"

She smiled, and extended her hand after the English manner towards Charles Gould, who was bowing before her; while Decoud, with his elbows spread on the back of the sofa, dropped his eyes and murmured, *"Bonjour."*

The Señor Administrador of the San Tomé mine bent over his wife for a moment. They exchanged a few words, of which only the phrase, "The greatest enthusiasm," pronounced by Mrs. Gould, could be heard.

"Yes," Decoud began in a murmur. "Even he!"

"This is sheer calumny," said Antonia, not very severely.

"You just ask him to throw his mine into the melting-pot for the great cause," Decoud whispered.

Don José had raised his voice. He rubbed his hands cheerily. The excellent aspect of the troops and the great quantity of new deadly rifles on the shoulders of those brave men seemed to fill him with an ecstatic confidence.

Charles Gould, very tall and thin before his chair, listened, but nothing could be discovered in his face except a kind and deferential attention.

Meantime, Antonia had risen, and, crossing the room, stood looking out of one of the three long windows giving on the street.

Decoud followed her. The window was thrown open, and he leaned
against the thickness of the wall. The long folds of the damask curtain, falling straight from the broad brass cornice, hid him partly
from the room. He folded his arms on his breast, and looked
steadily at Antonia's profile.

The people returning from the harbour filled the pavements;
the shuffle of sandals and a low murmur of voices ascended to the
window. Now and then a coach rolled slowly along the disjointed
roadway of the Calle de la Constitución. There were not many private carriages in Sulaco; at the most crowded hour on the Alameda
they could be counted with one glance of the eye. The great family arks swayed on high leathern springs, full of pretty powdered
faces in which the eyes looked intensely alive and black. And first
Don Juste Lopez, the President of the Provincial Assembly, passed
with his three lovely daughters, solemn in a black frock-coat and
stiff white tie, as when directing a debate from a high tribune.
Though they all raised their eyes, Antonia did not make the usual
greeting gesture of a fluttered hand, and they affected not to see
the two young people, Costaguaneros with European manners,
whose eccentricities were discussed behind the barred windows of
the first families in Sulaco. And then the widowed Señora Gavilaso
de Valdes rolled by, handsome and dignified, in a great machine in
which she used to travel to and from her country house, surrounded
by an armed retinue in leather suits and big sombreros, with carbines at the bows of their saddles. She was a woman of most distinguished family, proud, rich, and kind-hearted. Her second son,
Jaime, had just gone off on the Staff of Barrios. The eldest, a
worthless fellow of a moody disposition, filled Sulaco with the
noise of his dissipations, and gambled heavily at the club. The two
youngest boys, with yellow Ribierist cockades in their caps, sat on
the front seat. She, too, affected not to see the Señor Decoud talking publicly with Antonia in defiance of every convention. And he
not even her *novio** as far as the world knew! Though, even in that
case, it would have been scandal enough. But the dignified old
lady, respected and admired by the first families, would have been

---

*Fiancé, or boyfriend.

still more shocked if she could have heard the words they were exchanging.

"Did you say I lost sight of the aim? I have only one aim in the world."

She made an almost imperceptible negative movement of her head, still staring across the street at the Avellanos's house, grey, marked with decay, and with iron bars like a prison.

"And it would be so easy of attainment," he continued, "this aim which, whether knowingly or not, I have always had in my heart— ever since the day when you snubbed me so horribly once in Paris, you remember."

A slight smile seemed to move the corner of the lip that was on his side.

"You know you were a very terrible person, a sort of Charlotte Corday in a schoolgirl's dress; a ferocious patriot. I suppose you would have stuck a knife into Guzman Bento?"[13]

She interrupted him. "You do me too much honour."

"At any rate," he said, changing suddenly to a tone of bitter levity, "you would have sent me to stab him without compunction."

"Ah, *par exemple!*"* she murmured in a shocked tone.

"Well," he argued, mockingly, "you do keep me here writing deadly nonsense. Deadly to me! It has already killed my self-respect. And you may imagine," he continued, his tone passing into light banter, "that Montero, should he be successful, would get even with me in the only way such a brute can get even with a man of intelligence who condescends to call him a *gran' bestia* three times a week. It's a sort of intellectual death; but there is the other one in the background for a journalist of my ability."

"If he is successful!" said Antonia, thoughtfully.

"You seem satisfied to see my life hang on a thread," Decoud replied, with a broad smile. "And the other Montero, the 'my trusted brother' of the proclamations, the *guerrillero*—haven't I written that he was taking the guests' overcoats and changing plates in Paris at our Legation in the intervals of spying on our refugees there, in the time of Rojas? He will wash out that sacred truth in blood. In my

---

*For example (Fr.).

blood! Why do you look annoyed? This is simply a bit of the biography of one of our great men. What do you think he will do to me? There is a certain convent wall round the corner of the Plaza, opposite the door of the Bull Ring. You know? Opposite the door with the inscription, 'Intrada de la Sombra.'[14] Appropriate, perhaps! That's where the uncle of our host gave up his Anglo-South-American soul. And, note, he might have run away. A man who has fought with weapons may run away. You might have let me go with Barrios if you had cared for me. I would have carried one of those rifles, in which Don José believes, with the greatest satisfaction, in the ranks of poor peons and *indios*, that know nothing either of reason or politics. The most forlorn hope in the most forlorn army on earth would have been safer than that for which you made me stay here. When you make war you may retreat, but not when you spend your time in inciting poor ignorant fools to kill and to die."

His tone remained light, and as if unaware of his presence she stood motionless, her hands clasped lightly, the fan hanging down from her interlaced fingers. He waited for a while, and then:

"I shall go to the wall," he said, with a sort of jocular desperation.

Even that declaration did not make her look at him. Her head remained still, her eyes fixed upon the house of the Avellanos, whose chipped pilasters,* broken cornices, the whole degradation of dignity was hidden now by the gathering dusk of the street. In her whole figure her lips alone moved, forming the words:

"Martin, you will make me cry."

He remained silent for a minute, startled, as if overwhelmed by a sort of awed happiness, with the lines of the mocking smile still stiffened about his mouth, and incredulous surprise in his eyes. The value of a sentence is in the personality which utters it, for nothing new can be said by man or woman; and those were the last words, it seemed to him, that could ever have been spoken by Antonia. He had never made it up with her so completely in all their intercourse of small encounters; but even before she had time to turn towards him, which she did slowly with a rigid grace, he had begun to plead:

---

*Columns projected from a wall.

"My sister is only waiting to embrace you. My father is transported with joy. I won't say anything of my mother! Our mothers were like sisters. There is the mail-boat for the south next week—let us go. That Morago is a fool! A man like Montero is bribed. It's the practice of the country. It's tradition—it's politics. Read *Fifty Years of Misrule*."

"Leave poor papa alone, Don Martin. He believes—"

"I have the greatest tenderness for your father," he began, hurriedly. "But I love you, Antonia! And Moraga has miserably mismanaged this business. Perhaps your father did, too; I don't know. Montero was bribable. Why, I suppose he only wanted his share of this famous loan for national development. Why didn't the stupid Sta. Marta people give him a mission to Europe, or something? He would have taken five years' salary in advance, and gone on loafing in Paris, this stupid, ferocious *indio*!"

"The man," she said, thoughtfully, and very calm before this outburst, "was intoxicated with vanity. We had all the information, not from Morago only; from others, too. There was his brother intriguing, too."

"Oh, yes!" he said. "Of course you know. You know everything. You read all the correspondence, you write all the papers—all those State papers that are inspired here, in this room, in blind deference to a theory of political purity. Hadn't you Charles Gould before your eyes? 'Rey de Sulaco!' He and his mine are the practical demonstration of what could have been done. Do you think he succeeded by his fidelity to a theory of virtue? And all those railway people, with their honest work! Of course, their work is honest! But what if you cannot work honestly till the thieves are satisfied? Could he not, a gentleman, have told this Sir John what's-his-name that Montero had to be bought off—he and all his Negro liberals hanging on to his gold-laced sleeve? He ought to have been bought off with his own stupid weight of gold—his weight of gold, I tell you, boots, sabre, spurs, cocked hat, and all."

She shook her head slightly. "It was impossible," she murmured.

"He wanted the whole lot? What?"

She was facing him now in the deep recess of the window, very close and motionless. Her lips moved rapidly. Decoud, leaning his back against the wall, listened with crossed arms and lowered eyelids. He drank the tones of her even voice, and watched the agitated life of her throat, as if waves of emotion had run from her heart to pass out into the air in her reasonable words. He also had his aspirations, he aspired to carry her away out of these deadly futilities of *pronunciamientos* and reforms. All this was wrong—utterly wrong; but she fascinated him, and sometimes the sheer sagacity of a phrase would break the charm, replace the fascination by a sudden unwilling thrill of interest. Some women hovered, as it were, on the threshold of genius, he reflected. They did not want to know, or think, or understand. Passion stood for all that, and he was ready to believe that some startlingly profound remark, some appreciation of character, or a judgement upon an event, bordered on the miraculous. In the mature Antonia he could see with an extraordinary vividness the austere schoolgirl of the earlier days. She seduced his attention; sometimes he could not restrain a murmur of assent; now and then he advanced an objection quite seriously. Gradually they began to argue; the curtain half hid them from the people in the *sala*.

Outside it had grown dark. From the deep trench of shadow between the houses, lit up vaguely by the glimmer of street lamps, ascended the evening silence of Sulaco; the silence of a town with a few carriages, of unshod horses, and a softly sandalled population. The windows of the Casa Gould flung their shining parallelograms upon the house of Avellanos. Now and then a shuffle of feet passed below with the pulsating red glow of a cigarette at the foot of the walls; and the night air, as if cooled by the snows of Higuerota, refreshed their faces.

"We Occidentals," said Martin Decoud, using the usual term the provincials of Sulaco applied to themselves, "have been always distinct and separated. As long as we hold Cayta nothing can reach us. In all our troubles no army has marched over those mountains. A revolution in the central provinces isolates us at once. Look how complete it is now! The news of Barrios's movement will be cabled to the United States, and only in that way will it reach Sta. Marta by the cable from the other seaboard. We have the greatest riches, the greatest fertility, the purest blood in our great families, the most labourious population. The Occidental Province should stand alone. The early Federalism was not bad for us. Then came this union which Don Henrique Gould resisted. It opened the road to tyranny; and, ever since, the rest of Costaguana hangs like a millstone round our necks.

The Occidental territory is large enough to make any man's country. Look at the mountains! Nature itself seems to cry to us 'Separate!'"

She made an energetic gesture of negation. A silence fell.

"Oh, yes, I know it's contrary to the doctrine laid down in the *History of Fifty Years' Misrule*. I am only trying to be sensible. But my sense seems always to give you cause for offense. Have I startled you very much with this perfectly reasonable aspiration?"

She shook her head. No, she was not startled, but the idea shocked her early convictions. Her patriotism was larger. She had never considered that possibility.

"It may yet be the means of saving some of your convictions," he said, prophetically.

She did not answer. She seemed tired. They leaned side by side on the rail of the little balcony, very friendly, having exhausted politics, giving themselves up to the silent feeling of their nearness, in one of those profound pauses that fall upon the rhythm of passion. Towards the *plaza* end of the street the glowing coals in the *brazeros** of the market women cooking their evening meal gleamed red along the edge of the pavement. A man appeared without a sound in the light of a street lamp, showing the coloured inverted triangle of his bordered poncho, square on his shoulders, hanging to a point below his knees. From the harbour end of the *calle†* a horseman walked his soft-stepping mount, gleaming silver-grey abreast each lamp under the dark shape of the rider.

"Behold the illustrious Capataz de Cargadores," said Decoud, gently, "coming in all his splendour after his work is done. The next great man of Sulaco after Don Carlos Gould. But he is good-natured, and let me make friends with him."

"Ah, indeed!" said Antonia. "How did you make friends?"

"A journalist ought to have his finger on the popular pulse, and this man is one of the leaders of the populace. A journalist ought to know remarkable men—and this man is remarkable in his way."

"Ah, yes!" said Antonia, thoughtfully. "It is known that this Italian has a great influence."

---

*Braziers; pans for holding burning coals.
†Street.

The horseman had passed below them, with a gleam of dim light on the shining broad quarters of the grey mare, on a bright heavy stirrup, on a long silver spur; but the short flick of yellowish flame in the dusk was powerless against the muffled-up mysteriousness of the dark figure with an invisible face concealed by a great sombrero.

Decoud and Antonia remained leaning over the balcony, side by side, touching elbows, with their heads overhanging the darkness of the street, and the brilliantly lighted *sala* at their backs. This was a *tête-à-tête* of extreme impropriety; something of which in the whole extent of the Republic only the extraordinary Antonia could be capable—the poor, motherless girl, never accompanied, with a careless father, who had thought only of making her learned. Even Decoud himself seemed to feel that this was as much as he could expect of having her to himself till—till the revolution was over and he could carry her off to Europe, away from the endlessness of civil strife, whose folly seemed even harder to bear than its ignominy. After one Montero there would be another, the lawlessness of a populace of all colours and races, barbarism, irremediable tyranny. As the great Liberator Bolívar had said in the bitterness of his spirit, "America is ungovernable. Those who worked for her independence have ploughed the sea." He did not care, he declared boldly; he seized every opportunity to tell her that though she had managed to make a Blanco journalist of him, he was no patriot. First of all, the word had no sense for cultured minds, to whom the narrowness of every belief is odious; and secondly, in connection with the everlasting troubles of this unhappy country it was hopelessly besmirched; it had been the cry of dark barbarism, the cloak of lawlessness, of crimes, of rapacity, of simple thieving.

He was surprised at the warmth of his own utterance. He had no need to drop his voice; it had been low all the time, a mere murmur in the silence of dark houses with their shutters closed early against the night air, as is the custom of Sulaco. Only the *sala* of the Casa Gould flung out defiantly the blaze of its four windows, the bright appeal of light in the whole dumb obscurity of the street. And the murmur on the little balcony went on after a short pause.

"But we are labouring to change all that," Antonia protested. "It is exactly what we desire. It is our object. It is the great cause. And the word you despise has stood also for sacrifice, for courage, for constancy, for suffering. Papa, who—"

"Ploughing the sea," interrupted Decoud, looking down.

There was below the sound of hasty and ponderous footsteps.

"Your uncle, the Grand Vicar of the cathedral, has just turned under the gate," observed Decoud. "He said Mass for the troops in the Plaza this morning. They had built for him an altar of drums, you know. And they brought outside all the painted blocks to take the air. All the wooden saints stood militarily in a row at the top of the great flight of steps. They looked like a gorgeous escort attending the Vicar-General. I saw the great function from the windows of the *Porvenir*. He is amazing, your uncle, the last of the Corbeláns. He glittered exceedingly in his vestments with a great crimson velvet cross down his back. And all the time our saviour Barrios sat in the Amarilla Club drinking punch at an open window. *Espirit fort*[*] — our Barrios. I expected every moment your uncle to launch an excommunication there and then at the black eye-patch in the window across the Plaza. But not at all. Ultimately the troops marched off. Later Barrios came down with some of the officers, and stood with his uniform all unbuttoned, discoursing at the edge of the pavement. Suddenly your uncle appeared, no longer glittering, but all black, at the cathedral door with that threatening aspect he has— you know, like a sort of avenging spirit. He gives one look, strides over straight at the group of uniforms, and leads away the general by the elbow. He walked him for a quarter of an hour in the shade of a wall. Never let go his elbow for a moment, talking all the time with exaltation, and gesticulating with a long black arm. It was a curious scene. The officers seemed struck with astonishment. Remarkable man, your missionary uncle. He hates an infidel much less than a heretic, and prefers a heathen many times to an infidel. He condescends graciously to call me a heathen, sometimes, you know."

Antonia listened with her hands over the balustrade, opening and shutting the fan gently; and Decoud talked a little nervously, as if afraid that she would leave him at the first pause. Their comparative isolation, the precious sense of intimacy, the slight contact of

---

[*]Or *esprit fort*; strong spirit (Fr.).

their arms, affected him softly; for now and then a tender inflection crept into the flow of his ironic murmurs.

"Any slight sign of favour from a relative of yours is welcome, Antonia. And perhaps he understands me, after all! But I know him, too, our Padre Corbelán. The idea of political honour, justice, and honesty for him consists in the restitution of the confiscated Church property. Nothing else could have drawn that fierce converter of savage Indians out of the wilds to work for the Ribierist cause! Nothing else but that wild hope! He would make a *pronunciamiento* himself for such an object against any Government if he could only get followers! What does Don Carlos Gould think of that? But, of course, with his English impenetrability, nobody can tell what he thinks. Probably he thinks of nothing apart from his mine; of his '*Imperium in Imperio.*' As to Mrs. Gould, she thinks of her schools, of her hospitals, of the mothers with the young babies, of every sick old man in the three villages. If you were to turn your head now you would see her extracting a report from that sinister doctor in a check shirt—what's his name? Monygham—or else catechizing Don Pepe or perhaps listening to Padre Román. They are all down here today—all her ministers of state. Well, she is a sensible woman, and perhaps Don Carlos is a sensible man. It's a part of solid English sense not to think too much; to see only what may be of practical use at the moment. These people are not like ourselves. We have no political reason; we have political passions—sometimes. What is a conviction? A particular view of our personal advantage either practical or emotional. No one is a patriot for nothing. The word serves us well. But I am clear-sighted, and I shall not use that word to you, Antonia! I have no patriotic illusions. I have only the supreme illusion of a lover."

He paused, then muttered almost inaudibly, "That can lead one very far, though."

Behind their backs the political tide that once in every twenty-four hours set with a strong flood through the Gould drawing-room could be heard, rising higher in a hum of voices. Men had been dropping in singly, or in twos and threes: the higher officials of the province, engineers of the railway, sunburnt and in tweeds, with the frosted head of their chief smiling with slow, humorous indulgence amongst the young eager faces. Scarfe, the lover of fandangos, had already slipped out in search of some dance, no matter where, on the out-skirts of the town. Don Juste Lopez, after taking his daughters home, had entered solemnly, in a black creased coat buttoned up under his spreading brown beard. The few members of the Provin-cial Assembly present clustered at once around their President to discuss the news of the war and the last proclamation of the rebel Montero, the miserable Montero, calling in the name of "a justly incensed democracy" upon all the Provincial Assemblies of the Re-public to suspend their sittings till his sword had made peace and the will of the people could be consulted. It was practically an invi-tation to dissolve: an unheard-of audacity of that evil madman.

The indignation ran high in the knot of deputies behind José Avellanos. Don José, lifting up his voice, cried out to them over the high back of his chair, "Sulaco has answered by sending today an army upon his flank. If all the other provinces show only half as much patriotism as we, Occidentals—"

A great outburst of acclamations covered the vibrating treble of the life and soul of the party. Yes! Yes! This was true! A great truth! Sulaco was in the forefront as ever! It was a boastful tumult, the hopefulness inspired by the event of the day breaking out amongst those *caballeros* of the Campo thinking of their herds, of their lands, of the safety of their families. Everything was at stake. . . . No! It was impossible that Montero should succeed! This criminal, this shameless *indio*! The clamour continued for some time, everybody else in the room looking towards the group where Don Juste had put on his air of impartial solemnity as if presiding at a sitting of the Provincial Assembly. Decoud had turned round at the noise, and, leaning his back on the balustrade, shouted into the room with all the strength of his lungs, "*Gran' bestia!*"

This unexpected cry had the effect of stilling the noise. All the eyes were directed to the window with an approving expectation; but Decoud had already turned his back upon the room, and was again leaning out over the quiet street.

"This is the quintessence of my journalism; this is the supreme ar-gument," he said to Antonia. "I have invented this definition, this last word on a great question. But I am no patriot. I am no more of a pa-triot than the Capataz of the Sulaco Cargadores, this Genoese who has done such great things for this harbour—this active usher-in of the material implements for our progress. You have heard Captain Mitchell confess over and over again that till he got this man he could never tell how long it would take to unload a ship. That is bad for progress. You have seen him pass by after his labours on his famous horse to dazzle the girls in some ballroom with an earthen floor. He is a fortunate fellow! His work is an exercise of personal powers; his leisure is spent in receiving the marks of extraordinary adulation. And he likes it, too. Can anybody be more fortunate? To be feared and admired is—"

"And are these your highest aspirations, Don Martin?" interrupted Antonia.

"I was speaking of a man of that sort," said Decoud, curtly. "The heroes of the world have been feared and admired. What more could he want?"

Decoud had often felt his familiar habit of ironic thought fall shattered against Antonia's gravity. She irritated him as if she, too, had suffered from that inexplicable feminine obtuseness which stands so often between a man and a woman of the more ordinary sort. But he overcame his vexation at once. He was very far from thinking Antonia ordinary, whatever verdict his scepticism might have pronounced upon himself. With a touch of penetrating tenderness in his voice he assured her that his only aspiration was to a felicity so high that it seemed almost unrealizable on this earth.

She coloured invisibly, with a warmth against which the breeze from the sierra seemed to have lost its cooling power in the sudden melting of the snows. His whisper could not have carried so far, though there was enough ardour in his tone to melt a heart of ice. Antonia turned away abruptly, as if to carry his whispered assurance into the room behind, full of light, noisy with voices.

The tide of political speculation was beating high within the four walls of the great *sala*, as if driven beyond the marks by a great gust of hope. Don Juste's fanshaped beard was still the centre of loud and animated discussions. There was a self-confident ring in all the voices. Even the few Europeans around Charles Gould—a Dane, a couple of Frenchmen, a discreet fat German, smiling, with down-cast eyes, the representatives of those material interests that had got a footing in Sulaco under the protecting might of the San Tomé mine—had infused a lot of good humour into their deference.

Charles Gould, to whom they were paying their court, was the visible sign of the stability that could be achieved on the shifting ground of revolutions. They felt hopeful about their various undertakings. One of the two Frenchmen, small, black, with glittering eyes lost in an immense growth of bushy beard, waved his tiny brown hands and delicate wrists. He had been traveling in the interior of the province for a syndicate of European capitalists. His forcible *"Monsieur l'Administrateur"* returning every minute shrilled above the steady hum of conversations. He was relating his discoveries. He was ecstatic. Charles Gould glanced down at him courteously.

At a given moment of these necessary receptions it was Mrs. Gould's habit to withdraw quietly into a little drawing-room, especially her own, next to the great *sala*. She had risen, and, waiting for Antonia, listened with a slightly worried graciousness to the engineer-in-chief of the railway, who stooped over her, relating slowly, without the slightest gesture, something apparently amusing, for his eyes had a humorous twinkle. Antonia, before she advanced into the room to join Mrs. Gould, turned her head over her shoulder towards Decoud, only for a moment.

"Why should any one of us think his aspirations unrealizable?" she said, rapidly.

"I am going to cling to mine to the end, Antonia," he answered, through clenched teeth, then bowed very low, a little distantly.

The engineer-in-chief had not finished telling his amusing story. The humours of railway building in South America appealed to his keen appreciation of the absurd, and he told his instances of ignorant prejudice and as ignorant cunning very well. Now, Mrs. Gould gave him all her attention as he walked by her side escorting the ladies out of the room. Finally all three passed unnoticed through the glass doors in the gallery. Only a tall priest stalking silently in the noise of the *sala* checked himself to look after them. Father Corbelán, whom Decoud had seen from the balcony turning into the gateway of the Casa Gould, had addressed no one since coming in. The long, skimpy soutane accentuated the tallness of his stature; he carried his powerful torso thrown forward; and the straight, black bar of his joined eyebrows, the pugnacious outline of the bony face, the white spot of a scar on the bluish shaven cheeks (a testimonial to his apostolic zeal from a party of unconverted Indians), suggested something unlawful behind his priesthood, the idea of a chaplain of bandits.

He separated his bony knotted hands clasped behind his back, to shake his finger at Martin.

Decoud had stepped into the room after Antonia. But he did not go far. He had remained just within, against the curtain, with an expression of not quite genuine gravity, like a grown-up person taking part in a game of children. He gazed quietly at the threatening finger.

"I have watched your reverence converting General Barrios by a special sermon on the Plaza," he said, without making the slightest movement.

"What miserable nonsense!" Father Corbelán's deep voice resounded all over the room, making all the heads turn on the shoulders. "The man is a drunkard. *Señores*, the God of your General is a bottle!"

His contemptuous, arbitrary voice caused an uneasy suspension of every sound, as if the self-confidence of the gathering had been staggered by a blow. But nobody took up Father Corbelán's declaration.

It was known that Father Corbelán had come out of the wilds to advocate the sacred rights of the Church with the same fanatical fearlessness with which he had gone preaching to bloodthirsty savages, devoid of human compassion or worship of any kind. Rumours of legendary proportions told of his successes as a missionary beyond the eye of Christian men. He had baptized whole nations of Indians, living with them like a savage himself. It was related that the padre used to ride with his Indians for days, half naked, carrying a bullock-hide shield, and, no doubt, a long lance, too—who knows? That he had wandered clothed in skins, seeking for proselytes somewhere near the snow line of the Cordillera. Of these exploits Padre Corbelán himself was never known to talk. But he made no secret of his opinion that the politicians of Sta. Marta had harder hearts and more corrupt minds than the heathen to whom he had carried the word of God. His injudicious zeal for the temporal welfare of the Church was damaging the Ribierist cause. It was common knowledge that he had refused to be made titular bishop of the Occidental diocese till justice was done to a despoiled

Church. The political *jefe** of Sulaco (the same dignitary whom Captain Mitchell saved from the mob afterwards) hinted with naïve cynicism that doubtless their Excellencies the Ministers sent the padre over the mountains to Sulaco in the worst season of the year in the hope that he would be frozen to death by the icy blasts of the high *páramos*.† Every year a few hardy muleteers—men inured to exposure—were known to perish in that way. But what would you have? Their Excellencies possibly had not realized what a tough priest he was. Meantime, the ignorant were beginning to murmur that the Ribierist reforms meant simply the taking away of the land from the people. Some of it was to be given to foreigners who made the railway; the greater part was to go to the padres.

These were the results of the Grand Vicar's zeal. Even from the short allocution to the troops on the Plaza (which only the first ranks could have heard) he had not been able to keep out his fixed idea of an outraged Church waiting for reparation from a penitent country. The political *jefe* had been exasperated. But he could not very well throw the brother-in-law of Don José into the prison of the Cabildo. The chief magistrate, an easy-going and popular official, visited the Casa Gould, walking over after sunset from the Intendencia, unattended, acknowledging with dignified courtesy the salutations of high and low alike. That evening he had walked up straight to Charles Gould and had hissed out to him that he would have liked to deport the Grand Vicar out of Sulaco, anywhere, to some desert island, to the Isabels, for instance. "The one without water preferably—eh, Don Carlos?" he had added in a tone between jest and earnest. This uncontrollable priest, who had rejected his offer of the episcopal palace for a residence and preferred to hang his shabby hammock amongst the rubble and spiders of the sequestrated Dominican Convent, had taken into his head to advocate an unconditional pardon for Hernandez the Robber! And this was not enough; he seemed to have entered into communication with the most audacious criminal the country had known for years. The Sulaco police knew, of course, what was going on. Padre Corbelán

---

*Chief, boss.
†Bleak plateaus.

had got hold of that reckless Italian, the Capataz de Cargadores, the only man fit for such an errand, and had sent a message through him. Father Corbelan had studied in Rome, and could speak Italian. The Capataz was known to visit the old Dominican Convent at night. An old woman who served the Grand Vicar had heard the name of Hernandez pronounced; and only last Saturday afternoon the Capataz had been observed galloping out of town. He did not return for two days. The police would have laid the Italian by the heels if it had not been for fear of the *cargadores*, a turbulent body of men, quite apt to raise a tumult. Nowadays it was not so easy to govern Sulaco. Bad characters flocked into it, attracted by the money in the pockets of the railway workmen. The populace was made restless by Father Corbelán's discourses. And the first magistrate explained to Charles Gould that now the province was stripped of troops any outbreak of lawlessness would find the authorities with their boots off, as it were.

Then he went away moodily to sit in an armchair, smoking a long, thin cigar, not very far from Don José, with whom, bending over sideways, he exchanged a few words from time to time. He ignored the entrance of the priest, and whenever Father Corbelán's voice was raised behind him, he shrugged his shoulders impatiently.

Father Corbelán had remained quite motionless for a time with that something vengeful in his immobility which seemed to characterize all his attitudes. A lurid glow of strong convictions gave its peculiar aspect to the black figure. But its fierceness became softened as the padre, fixing his eyes upon Decoud, raised his long, black arm slowly, impressively:

"And you—you are a perfect heathen," he said, in a subdued, deep voice.

He made a step nearer, pointing a forefinger at the young man's breast. Decoud, very calm, felt the wall behind the curtain with the back of his head. Then, with his chin tilted well up, he smiled.

"Very well," he agreed with the slightly weary nonchalance of a man well used to these passages. "But is it perhaps that you have not discovered yet what is the God of my worship? It was an easier task with our Barrios."

The priest suppressed a gesture of discouragement. "You believe neither in stick nor stone," he said.

"Nor bottle," added Decoud without stirring. "Neither does the other of your reverence's confidants. I mean the Capataz of the Cargadores. He does not drink. Your reading of my character does honour to your perspicacity. But why call me a heathen?"

"True," retorted the priest. "You are ten times worse. A miracle could not convert you."

"I certainly do not believe in miracles," said Decoud, quietly. Father Corbelán shrugged his high, broad shoulders doubtfully.

"A sort of Frenchman—godless—a materialist," he pronounced slowly, as if weighing the terms of a careful analysis. "Neither the son of his own country nor of any other," he continued thoughtfully.

"Scarcely human, in fact," Decoud commented under his breath, his head at rest against the wall, his eyes gazing up at the ceiling.

"The victim of his faithless age," Father Corbelán resumed in a deep but subdued voice.

"But of some use as a journalist." Decoud changed his pose and spoke in a more animated tone. "Has your worship neglected to read the last number of the *Porvenir*? I assure you it is just like the others. On the general policy it continues to call Montero a *gran' bestia*, and stigmatize his brother, the *guerrillero*, for a combination of lacquey and spy. What could be more effective? In local affairs it urges the Provincial Government to enlist bodily into the national army the band of Hernandez the Robber—who is apparently the protégé of the Church—or at least of the Great Vicar. Nothing could be more sound."

The priest nodded and turned on the heels of his square-toed shoes with big steel buckles. Again, with his hands clasped behind his back, he paced to and fro, planting his feet firmly. When he swung about, the skirt of his soutane* was inflated slightly by the brusqueness of his movements.

The great *sala* had been emptying itself slowly. When the Jefe Politico rose to go, most of those still remaining stood up suddenly in sign of respect, and Don José Avellanos stopped the rocking of the chair. But the good-natured First Official made a deprecatory

---

*Cassock.

gesture, waved his hand to Charles Gould, and went out discreetly.

In the comparative peace of the room the screaming "*Monsieur l'Administrateur*" of the frail, hairy Frenchman seemed to acquire a preternatural shrillness. The explorer of the Capitalist syndicate was still enthusiastic. "Ten million dollars' worth of copper practically in sight, *Monsieur l'Administrateur*. Ten millions in sight! And a railway coming—a railway! They will never believe my report. *C'est trop beau.*"* He fell a prey to a screaming ecstasy, in the midst of sagely nodding heads, before Charles Gould's imperturbable calm.

And only the priest continued his pacing, flinging round the skirt of his soutane at each end of his beat. Decoud murmured to him ironically: "Those gentlemen talk about their gods."

Father Corbelán stopped short, looked at the journalist of Sulaco fixedly for a moment, shrugged his shoulders slightly, and resumed his plodding walk of an obstinate traveller.

And now the Europeans were dropping off from the group around Charles Gould till the Administrator of the Great Silver Mine could be seen in his whole lank length, from head to foot, left stranded by the ebbing tide of his guests on the great square of carpet, as it were a multi-coloured shoal of flowers and arabesques under his brown boots. Father Corbelán approached the rocking-chair of Don José Avellanos.

"Come, brother," he said, with kindly brusqueness and a touch of relieved impatience a man may feel at the end of a perfectly useless ceremony. "*A la Casa! A la Casa!* This has been all talk. Let us now go and think and pray for guidance from Heaven."

He rolled his black eyes upwards. By the side of the frail diplomatist—the life and soul of the party—he seemed gigantic, with a gleam of fanaticism in the glance. But the voice of the party, or, rather, its mouthpiece, the "son Decoud" from Paris, turned journalist for the sake of Antonia's eyes, knew very well that it was not so, that he was only a strenuous priest with one idea, feared by the women and execrated by the men of the people. Martin Decoud, the dilettante in life, imagined himself to derive an artistic pleasure from watching the picturesque extreme of wrong-headedness into

---

*It's too beautiful (Fr.).

which an honest, almost sacred, conviction may drive a man. "It is like madness. It must be—because it's self-destructive," Decoud had said to himself often. It seemed to him that every conviction, as soon as it became effective, turned into that form of dementia the gods send upon those they wish to destroy. But he enjoyed the bitter flavor of that example with the zest of a connoisseur in the art of his choice. Those two men got on well together, as if each had felt respectively that a masterful conviction, as well as utter scepticism, may lead a man very far on the by-paths of political action.

Don José obeyed the touch of the big hairy hand. Decoud followed out the brothers-in-law. And there remained only one visitor in the vast empty *sala*, bluishly hazy with tobacco smoke, a heavy-eyed, round-cheeked man, with a drooping moustache, a hide merchant from Esmeralda, who had come overland to Sulaco, riding with a few peons across the coast range. He was very full of his journey, undertaken mostly for the purpose of seeing the Señor Administrador of San Tomé in relation to some assistance he required in his hide-exporting business. He hoped to enlarge it greatly now that the country was going to be settled. It was going to be settled, he repeated several times, degrading by a strange, anxious whine the sonority of the Spanish language, which he pattered rapidly, like some sort of cringing jargon. A plain man could carry on his little business now in the country, and even think of enlarging it—with safety. Was it not so? He seemed to beg Charles Gould for a confirmatory word, a grunt of assent, a simple nod even.

He could get nothing. His alarm increased, and in the pauses he would dart his eyes here and there; then, loth to give up, he would branch off into feeling allusion to the dangers of his journey. The audacious Hernandez, leaving his usual haunts, had crossed the Campo of Sulaco, and was known to be lurking in the ravines of the coast range. Yesterday, when distant only a few hours from Sulaco, the hide merchant and his servants had seen three men on the road arrested suspiciously, with their horses' heads together. Two of these rode off at once and disappeared in a shallow *quebrada** to the left. "We stopped," continued the man from Esmeralda, "and I tried to

---

*Gorge.

hide behind a small bush. But none of my *mozos* would go forward to find out what it meant, and the third horseman seemed to be waiting for us to come up. It was no use. We had been seen. So we rode slowly on, trembling. He let us pass—a man on a grey horse with his hat down on his eyes—without a word of greeting; but by-and-by we heard him galloping after us. We faced about, but that did not seem to intimidate him. He rode up at speed, and touching my foot with the toe of his boot, asked me for a cigar, with a blood-curdling laugh. He did not seem armed, but when he put his hand back to reach for the matches I saw an enormous revolver strapped to his waist. I shuddered. He had very fierce whiskers, Don Carlos, and as he did not offer to go on we dared not move. At last, blowing the smoke of my cigar into the air through his nostrils, he said, 'Señor, it would be perhaps better for you if I rode behind your party. You are not very far from Sulaco now. Go you with God.' What would you? We went on. There was no resisting him. He might have been Hernandez himself; though my servant, who has been many times to Sulaco by sea, assured me that he had recognized him very well for the Capataz of the Steamship Company's *cargadores*. Later, that same evening, I saw that very man at the corner of the Plaza talking to a girl, a Morenita, who stood by the stirrup with her hand on the grey horse's mane."

"I assure you, Señor Hirsch," murmured Charles Gould, "that you ran no risk on this occasion."

"That may be, *señor*, though I tremble yet. A most fierce man—to look at. And what does it mean? A person employed by the Steamship Company talking with *salteadores*—no less, *señor*; the other horsemen were *salteadores*—in a lonely place, and behaving like a robber himself! A cigar is nothing, but what was there to prevent him asking me for my purse?"

"No, no, Señor Hirsch," Charles Gould murmured, letting his glance stray away a little vacantly from the round face, with its hooked beak upturned towards him in an almost childlike appeal. "If it was the Capataz de Cargadores you met—and there is no doubt, is there?—you were perfectly safe."

"Thank you. You are very good. A very fierce-looking man, Don Carlos. He asked me for a cigar in a most familiar manner. What would have happened if I had not had a cigar? I shudder yet. What business had he to be talking with robbers in a lonely place?"

But Charles Gould, openly preoccupied now, gave not a sign, made no sound. The impenetrability of the embodied Gould Concession had its surface shades. To be dumb is merely a fatal affliction; but the King of Sulaco had words enough to give him all the mysterious weight of a taciturn force. His silences, backed by the power of speech, had as many shades of significance as uttered words in the way of assent, of doubt, of negation—even of simple comment. Some seemed to say plainly, "Think it over"; others meant clearly "Go ahead," a simple, low "I see," with an affirmative nod, at the end of a patient listening half-hour was the equivalent of a verbal contract, which men had learned to trust implicitly, since behind it all there was the great San Tomé mine, the head and front of the material interests, so strong that it depended on no man's goodwill in the whole length and breadth of the Occidental Province—that is, on no goodwill which it could not buy ten times over. But to the little hook-nosed man from Esmeralda, anxious about the export of hides, the silence of Charles Gould portended a failure. Evidently this was no time for extending a modest man's business. He enveloped in a swift mental malediction the whole country, with all its inhabitants, partisans of Ribiera and Montero alike; and there were incipient tears in his mute anger at the thought of the innumerable ox-hides going to waste upon the dreamy expanse of the Campo, with its single palms rising like ships at sea within the perfect circle of the horizon, its clumps of heavy timber motionless like solid islands of leaves above the running waves of grass. There were hides there, rotting, with no profit to anybody— rotting where they had been dropped by men called away to attend the urgent necessities of political revolutions. The practical, mercantile soul of Señor Hirsch rebelled against all that foolishness, while he was taking a respectful but disconcerted leave of the might and majesty of the San Tomé mine in the person of Charles Gould. He could not restrain a heart-broken murmur, wrung out of his very aching heart, as it were.

"It is a great, great foolishness, Don Carlos, all this. The price of hides in Hamburg is gone way up—up. Of course the Ribierist

Government will do away with all that—when it gets established firmly. Meantime—"

He sighed.

"Yes, meantime," repeated Charles Gould, inscrutably.

The other shrugged his shoulders. But he was not ready to go yet. There was a little matter he would like to mention very much if permitted. It appeared he had some good friends in Hamburg (he murmured the name of the firm) who were very anxious to do business, in dynamite, he explained. A contract for dynamite with the San Tomé mine, and then, perhaps, later on, other mines, which were sure to— The little man from Esmeralda was ready to enlarge, but Charles interrupted him. It seemed as though the patience of the Señor Administrador was giving way at last.

"Señor Hirsch," he said, "I have enough dynamite stored up at the mountain to send it down crashing into the valley"—his voice rose a little—"to send half Sulaco into the air if I liked."

Charles Gould smiled at the round, startled eyes of the dealer in hides, who was murmuring hastily, "Just so. Just so." And now he was going. It was impossible to do business in explosives with an Administrador so well provided and so discouraging. He had suffered agonies in the saddle and had exposed himself to the atrocities of the bandit Hernandez for nothing at all. Neither hides nor dynamite— and the very shoulders of the enterprising Israelite expressed dejection. At the door he bowed low to the engineer-in-chief. But at the bottom of the stairs in the patio he stopped short, with his podgy hand over his lips in attitude of meditative astonishment.

"What does he want to keep so much dynamite for?" he muttered. "And why does he talk like this to me?"

The engineer-in-chief, looking in at the door of the empty *sala*, whence the political tide had ebbed out to the last insignificant drop, nodded familiarly to the master of the house, standing motionless like a tall beacon amongst the deserted shoals of furniture.

"Good night, I am going. Got my bike downstairs. The railway will know where to go for dynamite should we get short at any time. We have done cutting and chopping for a while now. We shall begin soon to blast our way through."

"Don't come to me," said Charles Gould, with perfect serenity. "I shan't have an ounce to spare for anybody. Not an ounce. Not for my own brother, if I had a brother, and he were the engineer-in-chief of the most promising railway in the world."

"What's that?" asked the engineer-in-chief, with equanimity. "Unkindness?"

"No," said Charles Gould, stolidly. "Policy."

"Radical, I should think," the engineer-in-chief observed from the doorway.

"Is that the right name?" Charles Gould said, from the middle of the room.

"I mean, going to the roots, you know," the engineer explained, with an air of enjoyment.

"Why, yes," Charles pronounced, slowly. "The Gould Concession has struck such deep roots in this country, in this province, in that gorge of the mountains, that nothing but dynamite shall be allowed to dislodge it from there. It's my choice. It's my last card to play."

The engineer-in-chief whistled low. "A pretty game," he said, with a shade of discretion. "And have you told Holroyd of that extraordinary trump card you hold in your hand?"

"Card only when it's played; when it falls at the end of the game. Till then you may call it a—a—"

"Weapon," suggested the railway man.

"No. You may call it rather an argument," corrected Charles Gould, gently. "And that's how I've presented it to Mr. Holroyd."

"And what did he say to it?" asked the engineer, with undisguised interest.

"He"—Charles Gould spoke after a slight pause—"he said something about holding on like grim death and putting our trust in God. I should imagine he must have been rather startled. But then"—pursued the Administrador of the San Tomé mine—"but then, he is very far away, you know, and, as they say in this country, God is very high above."

The engineer's appreciative laugh died away down the stairs, where the Madonna with the Child on her arm seemed to look after his shaking broad back from her shallow niche.

CHAPTER 6

A PROFOUND STILLNESS REIGNED in the Casa Gould. The master of the house, walking along the corridor, opened the door of his room, and saw his wife sitting in a big armchair—his own smoking armchair—thoughtful, contemplating her little shoes. And she did not raise her eyes when he walked in.

"Tired?" asked Charles Gould.

"A little," said Mrs. Gould. Still without looking up, she added with feeling, "There is an awful sense of unreality about all this."

Charles Gould, before the long table strewn with papers, on which lay a hunting crop and a pair of spurs, stood looking at his wife: "The heat and dust must have been awful this afternoon by the waterside," he murmured, sympathetically. "The glare on the water must have been simply terrible."

"One could close one's eyes to the glare," said Mrs. Gould. "But, my dear Charley, it is impossible for me to close my eyes to our position; to this awful. . . ."

She raised her eyes and looked at her husband's face, from which all sign of sympathy or any other feeling had disappeared. "Why don't you tell me something?" she almost wailed.

"I thought you had understood me perfectly from the first," Charles Gould said, slowly. "I thought we had said all there was to say a long time ago. There is nothing to say now. There were things to be done. We have done them; we have gone on doing them. There is no going back now. I don't suppose that, even from the first, there was really any possible way back. And, what's more, we can't even afford to stand still."

"Ah, if one only knew how far you mean to go," said his wife, inwardly trembling, but in an almost playful tone.

"Any distance, any length, of course," was the answer, in a matter-of-fact tone, which caused Mrs. Gould to make another effort to repress a shudder.

She stood up, smiling graciously, and her little figure seemed to be diminished still more by the heavy mass of her hair and the long train of her gown.

"But always to success," she said, persuasively.

Charles Gould, enveloping her in the steely blue glance of his attentive eyes, answered without hesitation:

"Oh, there is no alternative."

He put an immense assurance into his tone. As to the words, this was all that his conscience would allow him to say.

Mrs. Gould's smile remained a shade too long upon her lips. She murmured:

"I will leave you; I've a slight headache. The heat, the dust, were indeed—I suppose you are going back to the mine before the morning?"

"At midnight," said Charles Gould. "We are bringing down the silver tomorrow. Then I shall take three whole days off in town with you."

"Ah, you are going to meet the escort. I shall be on the balcony at five o'clock to see you pass. Till then, good-bye."

Charles Gould walked rapidly round the table, and, seizing her hands, bent down, pressing them both to his lips. Before he straightened himself up again to his full height she had disengaged one to smooth his cheek with a light touch, as if he were a little boy.

"Try to get some rest for a couple of hours," she murmured, with a glance at a hammock stretched in a distant part of the room. Her long train swished softly after her on the red tiles. At the door she looked back.

Two big lamps with unpolished glass globes bathed in a soft and abundant light the four white walls of the room, with a glass case of arms, the brass hilt of Henry Gould's cavalry sabre on its square of velvet, and the water-colour sketch of the San Tomé gorge. And Mrs. Gould, gazing at the last in its black wooden frame, sighed out:

"Ah, if we had left it alone, Charley!"

"No," Charles Gould said, moodily; "it was impossible to leave it alone."

"Perhaps it was impossible," Mrs. Gould admitted, slowly. Her lips quivered a little, but she smiled with an air of dainty bravado. "We have disturbed a good many snakes in that Paradise, Charley, haven't we?"

"Yes, I remember," said Charles Gould, "it was Don Pepe who called the gorge the Paradise of snakes. No doubt we have disturbed a great many. But remember, my dear, that it is not now as it was when you made that sketch." He waved his hand towards the small water-colour hanging alone upon the great bare wall. "It is no longer a Paradise of snakes. We have brought mankind into it, and we cannot turn our backs upon them to go and begin a new life elsewhere."

He confronted his wife with a firm, concentrated gaze, which Mrs. Gould returned with a brave assumption of fearlessness before she went out, closing the door gently after her.

In contrast with the white glaring room the dimly lit corridor had the restful mysteriousness of a forest glade, suggested by the stems and the leaves of the plants ranged along the balustrade of the open side. In the streaks of light falling through the open doors of the reception-rooms, the blossoms, white and red and pale lilac, came out vivid with the brilliance of flowers in a stream of sunshine; and Mrs. Gould, passing on, had the vividness of a figure seen in the clear patches of sun that chequer the gloom of open glades in the woods. The stones in the rings upon her hand pressed to her forehead glittered in the lamplight abreast of the door of the *sala*.

"Who's there?" she asked, in a startled voice. "Is that you, Basilio?" She looked in, and saw Martin Decoud walking about, with an air of having lost something, amongst the chairs and tables.

"Antonia has forgotten her fan in here," said Decoud, with a strange air of distraction; "so I entered to see."

But, even as he said this, he had obviously given up his search, and walked straight towards Mrs. Gould, who looked at him with doubtful surprise.

"Señora," he began, in a low voice.

"What is it, Don Martin?" asked Mrs. Gould. And then she added, with a slight laugh, "I am so nervous today," as if to explain the eagerness of the question.

"Nothing immediately dangerous," said Decoud, who now could not conceal his agitation. "Pray don't distress yourself. No, really, you must not distress yourself."

Mrs. Gould, with her candid eyes very wide open, her lips composed into a smile, was steadying herself in the doorway with a little bejewelled hand.

"Perhaps you don't know how alarming you are, appearing like this unexpectedly—"

"I! Alarming!" he protested, sincerely vexed and surprised. "I assure you that I am not in the least alarmed myself. A fan is lost; well, it will be found again. But I don't think it is here. It is a fan I am looking for. I cannot understand how Antonia could—Well! Have you found it, *amigo*?"

"No, *señor*," said behind Mrs. Gould the soft voice of Basilio, the head servant of the Casa. "I don't think the *señorita* could have left it in this house at all."

"Go and look for it in the patio again. Go now, my friend; look for it on the steps, under the gate; examine every flagstone; search for it till I come down again. . . . That fellow"—he addressed himself in English to Mrs. Gould—"is always stealing up behind one's back on his bare feet. I set him to look for that fan directly I came in to justify my reappearance, my sudden return."

He paused and Mrs. Gould said, amiably, "You are always welcome." She paused for a second, too. "But I am waiting to learn the cause of your return."

Decoud affected suddenly the utmost nonchalance.

"I can't bear to be spied upon. Oh, the cause? Yes, there is a cause; there is something else that is lost besides Antonia's favourite fan. As I was walking home after seeing Don José and Antonia to their house, the Capataz de Cargadores, riding down the street, spoke to me."

"Has anything happened to the Violas?" inquired Mrs. Gould.

"The Violas? You mean the old Garibaldino who keeps the hotel where the engineers live? Nothing happened there. The Capataz said nothing of them; he only told me that the telegraphist of the Cable Company was walking on the Plaza, bareheaded, looking out for me. This is news from the interior, Mrs. Gould. I should rather say rumours of news."

"Good news?" said Mrs. Gould in a low voice.

"Worthless, I should think. But if I must define them, I would say bad. They are to the effect that a two days' battle has been fought near Sta. Marta, and that the Ribierists are defeated. It must have happened a few days ago—perhaps a week. The rumour has just reached Cayta, and the man in charge of the cable station there has telegraphed the news to his colleague here. We might just as well have kept Barrios in Sulaco."

"What's to be done now?" murmured Mrs. Gould.

"Nothing. He's at sea with the troops. He will get to Cayta in a couple of days' time and learn the news there. What he will do then, who can say? Hold Cayta? Offer his submission to Montero? Disband his army—this last most likely, and go himself in one of the O.S.N. Company's steamers, north or south—to Valparaiso or to San Francisco, no matter where. Our Barrios has a great practice in exiles and repatriations; which mark the points in the political game."

Decoud, exchanging a steady stare with Mrs. Gould, added, tentatively, as it were, "And yet, if we had Barrios with his two thousand improved rifles here, something could have been done."

"Montero victorious, completely victorious!" Mrs. Gould breathed out in a tone of unbelief.

"A canard, probably. That sort of a bird is hatched in great numbers in such times as these. And even if it were true? Well, let us put things at their worst, let us say it is true."

"Then everything is lost," said Mrs. Gould, with the calmness of despair.

Suddenly she seemed to divine, she seemed to see Decoud's tremendous excitement under its cloak of studied carelessness. It was, indeed, becoming visible in his audacious and watchful stare, in the curve, half-reckless, half-contemptuous, of his lips. And a French phrase came upon them as if, for this Costaguanero of the Boulevard, that had been the only forcible language:

"*Non, Madame. Rien n'est perdu.*"*

It electrified Mrs. Gould out of her benumbed attitude, and she said, vivaciously:

"What would you think of doing?"

But already there was something of mockery in Decoud's suppressed excitement.

"What would you expect a true Costaguanero to do? Another revolution, of course. On my word of honour, Mrs. Gould, I believe I

---

*No, Madam. Nothing is lost (Fr.).

am a true *hijo del pais,* a true son of the country, whatever Father Corbelán may say. And I'm not so much of an unbeliever as not to have faith in my own ideas, in my own remedies, in my own desires."

"Yes," said Mrs. Gould, doubtfully.

"You don't seem convinced," Decoud went on again in French. "Say, then, in my passions."

Mrs. Gould received this addition unflinchingly. To understand it thoroughly she did not require to hear his muttered assurance:

"There is nothing I would not do for the sake of Antonia. There is nothing I am not prepared to undertake. There is no risk I am not ready to run."

Decoud seemed to find a fresh audacity in this voicing of his thoughts. "You would not believe me if I were to say that it is the love of the country which—"

She made a sort of discouraged protest with her arm, as if to express that she had given up expecting that motive from anyone.

"A Sulaco revolution," Decoud pursued in a forcible undertone. "The Great Cause may be served here, on the very spot of its inception, in the place of its birth, Mrs. Gould."

Frowning, and biting her lower lip thoughtfully, she made a step away from the door.

"You are not going to speak to your husband?" Decoud arrested her anxiously.

"But you will need his help?"

"No doubt," Decoud admitted without hesitation. "Everything turns upon the San Tomé mine, but I would rather he didn't know anything as yet of my—my hopes."

A puzzled look came upon Mrs. Gould's face, and Decoud, approaching, explained confidentially:

"Don't you see, he's such an idealist."

Mrs. Gould flushed pink, and her eyes grew darker at the same time.

"Charley an idealist!" she said, as if to herself, wonderingly. "What on earth do you mean?"

"Yes," conceded Decoud, "it's a wonderful thing to say with the sight of the San Tomé mine, the greatest fact in the whole of South America, perhaps, before our very eyes. But look even at that, he has idealized this fact to a point—" He paused. "Mrs. Gould, are you aware to what point he has idealized the existence, the worth, the meaning of the San Tomé mine? Are you aware of it?"

He must have known what he was talking about.

The effect he expected was produced. Mrs. Gould, ready to take fire, gave it up suddenly with a low little sound that resembled a moan.

"What do you know?" she asked in a feeble voice.

"Nothing," answered Decoud, firmly. "But, then, don't you see, he's an Englishman?"

"Well, what of that?" asked Mrs. Gould.

"Simply that he cannot act or exist without idealizing every simple feeling, desire, or achievement. He could not believe his own motives if he did not make them first a part of some fairy tale. The earth is not quite good enough for him, I fear. Do you excuse my frankness? Besides, whether you excuse it or not, it is part of the truth of things which hurts the—what do you call them?—the Anglo-Saxon's susceptibilities, and at the present moment I don't feel as if I could treat seriously either his conception of things or— if you allow me to say so—or yet yours."

Mrs. Gould gave no sign of being offended. "I suppose Antonia understands you thoroughly?"

"Understands? Well, yes. But I am not sure that she approves. That, however, makes no difference. I am honest enough to tell you that, Mrs. Gould."

"Your idea, of course, is separation," she said.

"Separation, of course," declared Martin. "Yes; separation of the whole Occidental Province from the rest of the unquiet body. But my true idea, the only one I care for, is not to be separated from Antonia."

"And that is all?" asked Mrs. Gould, without severity.

"Absolutely. I am not deceiving myself about my motives. She won't leave Sulaco for my sake, therefore Sulaco must leave the rest of the Republic to its fate. Nothing could be clearer than that. I like a clearly defined situation. I cannot part with Antonia, therefore the one and indivisible Republic of Costaguana must be made to part with its western province. Fortunately it happens to be also a sound policy. The richest, the most fertile part of this land may be saved from anarchy. Personally, I care little, very little; but it's a fact that the establishment of Montero in power would mean death to me. In all the proclamations of general pardon which I have seen, my name, with a few others, is specially excepted. The brothers hate me, as you know very well, Mrs. Gould; and behold, here is the rumour of them having won a battle. You say that supposing it is true, I have plenty of time to run away."

The slight, protesting murmur on the part of Mrs. Gould made him pause for a moment, while he looked at her with a sombre and resolute glance.

"Oh, but I would, Mrs. Gould. I would run away if it served that which at present is my only desire. I am courageous enough to say that, and to do it, too. But women, even our women, are idealists. It is Antonia that won't run away. A novel sort of vanity."

"You call it vanity," said Mrs. Gould, in a shocked voice.

"Say pride, then, which, Father Corbelán would tell you, is a mortal sin. But I am not proud. I am simply too much in love to run away. At the same time I want to live. There is no love for a dead man. Therefore it is necessary that Sulaco should not recognize the victorious Montero."

"And you think my husband will give you his support?"

"I think he can be drawn into it, like all idealists, when he once sees a sentimental basis for his action. But I wouldn't talk to him. Mere clear facts won't appeal to his sentiment. It is much better for him to convince himself in his own way. And, frankly, I could not, perhaps, just now pay sufficient respect to either his motives or even, perhaps, to yours, Mrs. Gould."

It was evident that Mrs. Gould was very determined not to be offended. She smiled vaguely, while she seemed to think the matter over. As far as she could judge from the girl's half-confidences, Antonia understood that young man. Obviously there was promise of safety in his plan, or rather in his idea. Moreover, right or wrong, the idea could do no harm. And it was quite possible, also, that the rumour was false.

"You have some sort of a plan," she said.

"Simplicity itself. Barrios has started, let him go on then; he will hold Cayta, which is the door of the sea route to Sulaco. They cannot send a sufficient force over the mountains. No; not even to cope with the band of Hernandez. Meantime we shall organize our resistance here. And for that, this very Hernandez will be useful. He has defeated troops as a bandit; he will no doubt accomplish the same thing if he is made a colonel or even a general. You know the country well enough not to be shocked by what I say, Mrs. Gould. I have heard you assert that this poor bandit was the living, breathing example of cruelty, injustice, stupidity, and oppression, that ruin men's souls as well as their fortunes in this country. Well, there would be some poetical retribution in that man arising to crush the evils which had driven an honest *ranchero* into a life of crime. A fine idea of retribution in that, isn't there?"

Decoud had dropped easily into English, which he spoke with precision, very correctly, but with too many *z* sounds.

"Think also of your hospitals, of your schools, of your ailing mothers and feeble old men, of all that population which you and your husband have brought into the rocky gorge of San Tomé. Are you not responsible to your conscience for all these people? Is it not worth while to make another effort, which is not at all so desperate as it looks, rather than—"

Decoud finished his thought with an upward toss of the arm, suggesting annihilation; and Mrs. Gould turned away her head with a look of horror.

"Why don't you say all this to my husband?" she asked, without looking at Decoud, who stood watching the effect of his words.

"Ah! But Don Carlos is so English," he began. Mrs. Gould interrupted:

"Leave that alone, Don Martin. He's as much a Costaguanero— No! He's more of a Costaguanero than yourself."

"Sentimentalist, sentimentalist," Decoud almost cooed, in a tone of gentle and soothing deference. "Sentimentalist, after the amazing manner of your people. I have been watching El Rey de Sulaco since I came here on a fool's errand, and perhaps impelled by some treason of fate lurking behind the unaccountable turns of a man's life. But I don't matter, I am not a sentimentalist, I cannot endow my personal desires with a shining robe of silk and jewels. Life is not for me a moral romance derived from the tradition of a pretty fairy tale. No, Mrs. Gould; I am practical. I am not afraid of my motives. But, pardon me, I have been rather carried away. What I wish to say is that I have been observing. I won't tell you what I have discovered—"

"No. That is unnecessary," whispered Mrs. Gould, once more averting her head.

"It is. Except one little fact, that your husband does not like me. It's a small matter, which, in the circumstances, seems to acquire a perfectly ridiculous importance. Ridiculous and immense; for, clearly, money is required for my plan," he reflected; then added, meaningly, "and we have two sentimentalists to deal with."

"I don't know that I understand you, Don Martin," said Mrs. Gould, coldly, preserving the low key of their conversation. "But, speaking as if I did, who is the other?"

"The great Holroyd in San Francisco, of course," Decoud whispered, lightly. "I think you understand me very well. Women are idealists; but then they are so perspicacious."

But whatever was the reason of that remark, disparaging and complimentary at the same time, Mrs. Gould seemed not to pay attention to it. The name of Holroyd had given a new tone to her anxiety.

"The silver escort is coming down to the harbour tomorrow; a whole six months' working, Don Martin!" she cried in dismay.

"Let it come down, then," breathed out Decoud, earnestly, almost into her ear.

"But if the rumour should get about, and especially if it turned out true, troubles might break out in the town," objected Mrs. Gould.

Decoud admitted that it was possible. He knew well the town children of the Sulaco Campo: sullen, thievish, vindictive, and bloodthirsty, whatever great qualities their brothers of the plain might have had. But then there was that other sentimentalist, who attached a strangely idealistic meaning to concrete facts. This stream of silver must be kept flowing north to return in the form of financial backing from the great house of Holroyd. Up at the mountain in the strong-room of the mine the silver bars were worth less for his purpose than so much lead, from which at least bullets may be run. Let it come down to the harbour, ready for shipment.

The next north-going steamer would carry it off for the very salvation of the San Tomé mine, which has produced so much treasure. And, moreover, the rumour was probably false, he remarked, with much conviction in his hurried tone.

"Besides, *señora*," concluded Decoud, "we may suppress it for many days. I have been talking with the telegraphist in the middle of the Plaza Mayor; thus I am certain that we could not have been overheard. There was not even a bird in the air near us. And also let me tell you something more. I have been making friends with this man called Nostromo, the Capataz. We had a conversation this very evening, I walking by the side of his horse as he rode slowly out of the town just now. He promised me that if a riot took place for any reason—even for the most political of reasons, you understand—his *cargadores*, an important part of the populace, you will admit, should be found on the side of the Europeans."

"He has promised you that?" Mrs. Gould inquired, with interest. "What made him make that promise to you?"

"Upon my word, I don't know," declared Decoud, in a slightly surprised tone. "He certainly promised me that, but now you ask me why I certainly could not tell you his reasons. He talked with his usual carelessness, which, if he had been anything else but a common sailor, I would call a pose or an affectation."

Decoud, interrupting himself, looked at Mrs. Gould curiously.

"Upon the whole," he continued, "I suppose he expects something to his advantage from it. You mustn't forget that he does not exercise his extraordinary power over the lower classes without a certain amount of personal risk and without a great profusion in spending his money. One must pay in some way or other for such a solid thing as individual prestige. He told me after we made friends at a dance, in a *posada* kept by a Mexican just outside the walls, that he had come here to make his fortune. I suppose he looks upon his prestige as a sort of investment."

"Perhaps he prizes it for its own sake," Mrs. Gould said in a tone as if she were repelling an undeserved aspersion. "Viola, the Garibaldino, with whom he has lived for some years, calls him the Incorruptible."

"Ah! he belongs to the group of your protégés out there towards the harbour, Mrs. Gould. *Muy bien.** And Captain Mitchell calls him wonderful. I have heard no end of tales of his strength, his audacity, his fidelity. No end of fine things. H'm! incorruptible! It is indeed a name of honour for the Capataz of the Cargadores of Sulaco.

---

*Very well.

Incorruptible! Fine, but vague. However, I suppose he's sensible, too. And I talked to him upon that sane and practical assumption."

"I prefer to think him disinterested, and therefore trustworthy," Mrs. Gould said, with the nearest approach to curtness it was in her nature to assume.

"Well, if so, then the silver will be still more safe. Let it come down, *señora*. Let it come down, so that it may go north and return to us in the shape of credit."

Mrs. Gould glanced along the corridor towards the door of her husband's room. Decoud, watching her as if she had his fate in her hands, detected an almost imperceptible nod of assent. He bowed with a smile, and, putting his hand into the breast pocket of his coat, pulled out a fan of light feathers set upon painted leaves of sandal-wood. "I had it in my pocket," he murmured, triumphantly, "for a plausible pretext." He bowed again. "Good night, *señora*."

Mrs. Gould continued along the corridor away from her husband's room. The fate of the San Tomé mine was lying heavy upon her heart. It was a long time now since she had begun to fear it. It had been an idea. She had watched it with misgivings turning into a fetish, and now the fetish had grown into a monstrous and crushing weight. It was as if the inspiration of their early years had left her heart to turn into a wall of silverbricks, erected by the silent work of evil spirits, between her and her husband. He seemed to dwell alone within a circumvallation* of precious metal, leaving her outside with her school, her hospital, the sick mothers, and the feeble old men, mere insignificant vestiges of the initial inspiration. "Those poor people!" she murmured to herself.

Below she heard the voice of Martin Decoud in the patio speaking loudly:

"I have found Doña Antonia's fan, Basilio. Look, here it is!"

---

*Entrenchment.

CHAPTER 7

IT WAS PART OF what Decoud would have called his sane materialism that he did not believe in the possibility of friendship between man and woman.

The one exception he allowed confirmed, he maintained, that absolute rule. Friendship was possible between brother and sister, meaning by friendship the frank unreserve, as before another human being, of thoughts and sensations; all the objectless and necessary sincerity of one's innermost life trying to react upon the profound sympathies of another existence.

His favourite sister, the handsome, slightly arbitrary, and resolute angel, ruling the father and mother Decoud in the first-floor apartments of a very fine Parisian house, was the recipient of Martin Decoud's confidences as to his thoughts, actions, purposes, doubts, and even failures. . . .

Prepare our little circle in Paris for the birth of another South American Republic. One more or less, what does it matter? They may come into the world like evil flowers on a hotbed of rotten institutions; but the seed of this one has germinated in your brother's brain, and that will be enough for your devoted assent. I am writing this to you by the light of a single candle, in a sort of inn, near the harbour, kept by an Italian called Viola, a protégé of Mrs. Gould. The whole building, which, for all I know, may have been contrived by a Conquistador farmer of the pearl fishery three hundred years ago, is perfectly silent. So is the plain between the town and the harbour; silent, but not so dark as the house, because the pickets of Italian workmen guarding the railway have lighted little fires all along the line. It was not so quiet around here yesterday. We had an awful riot—a sudden outbreak of the populace, which was not suppressed till late today. Its object, no doubt, was loot, and that was defeated, as you must have learned already from the cablegram sent via San

Francisco and New York last night, when the cables were still open. You have read already there that the energetic action of the Europeans of the railway has saved the town from destruction, and you may believe that. I wrote out the cable myself. We have no Reuter's agency man here. I have also fired at the mob from the windows of the club, in company with some other young men of position. Our object was to keep the Calle de la Constitución clear for the exodus of the ladies and children, who have taken refuge on board a couple of cargo ships now in the harbour here. That was yesterday. You should also have learned from the cable that the missing President, Ribiera, who had disappeared after the battle of Sta. Marta, has turned up here in Sulaco by one of those strange coincidences that are almost incredible, riding on a lame mule into the very midst of the street fighting. It appears that he had fled, in company with a muleteer called Bonifacio, across the mountains from the threats of Montero into the arms of an enraged mob.

The Capataz of Cargadores, that Italian sailor of whom I have written to you before, has saved him from an ignoble death. That man seems to have a particular talent for being on the spot whenever there is something picturesque to be done.

He was with me at four o'clock in the morning at the offices of the *Porvenir*, where he had turned up so early in order to warn me of the coming trouble, and also to assure me that he would keep his *cargadores* on the side of order. When the full daylight came we were looking together at the crowd on foot and on horseback, demonstrating on the Plaza and shying stones at the windows of the Intendencia. Nostromo (that is the name they call him by here) was pointing out to me his *cargadores* interspersed in the mob.

The sun shines late upon Sulaco, for it has first to climb above the mountains. In that clear morning light, brighter than twilight, Nostromo saw right across the vast Plaza, at the end of the street beyond the cathedral, a mounted man apparently in difficulties with a yelling knot of *leperos*. At once he said to me, "That's a stranger. What is it they are doing to him?" Then he took out the silver whistle he is in the habit of using on the wharf (this man seems to disdain the use of any metal less precious than silver) and blew into it twice, evidently a preconcerted signal for his *cargadores*. He ran out immediately, and they rallied round him. I ran out, too, but was too late to follow them and help in the rescue of the stranger, whose animal had fallen. I was set upon at once as a hated aristocrat, and was only too glad to get to the club, where Don Jaime Berges (you may remember him visiting at our house in Paris some three years ago) thrust a sporting gun into my hands. They were already firing from the windows. There were little heaps of cartridges lying about on the open card-tables. I remember a couple of overturned chairs, some bottles rolling on the floor amongst the packs of cards scattered suddenly as the *caballeros* rose from their game to open fire upon the mob. Most of the young men had spent the night at the club in the expectation of some such disturbance. In two of the candelabra, on the consoles, the candles were burning down in their sockets. A large iron nut, probably stolen from the railway workshops, flew in from the street as I entered, and broke one of the large mirrors set in the wall. I noticed also one of the club servants tied up hand and foot with the cords of the curtain and flung in a corner. I have a vague recollection of Don Jaime assuring me hastily that the fellow had been detected putting poison into the dishes at supper. But I remember distinctly he was shrieking for mercy, without stopping at all, continuously, and so absolutely disregarded that nobody even took the trouble to gag him. The noise he made was so disagreeable that I had half a mind to do it myself. But there was no time to waste on such trifles. I took my place at one of the windows and began firing.

I didn't learn till later in the afternoon whom it was that Nostromo, with his *cargadores* and some Italian workmen as well, had managed to save from those drunken rascals. That man has a peculiar talent when anything striking to the imagination has to be done. I made that remark to him afterwards when we met after some sort of order had been restored in the town, and the answer he made rather surprised me. He said quite moodily, "And how much do I get for that, *señor?*" Then it dawned upon me that perhaps this man's vanity has been satiated by the adulation of the common people and the confidences of his superiors!

Decoud paused to light a cigarette, then, with his head still over his writing, he blew a cloud of smoke, which seemed to rebound from the paper. He took up the pencil again.

That was yesterday evening on the Plaza, while he sat on the steps of the cathedral, his hands between his knees, holding the bridle of his famous silver-grey mare. He had led his body of *cargadores* splendidly all day long. He looked fatigued. I don't know how I looked. Very dirty, I suppose. But I suppose I also looked pleased. From the time the fugitive President had been got off to the s.s. *Minerva*, the tide of success had turned against the mob. They had been driven off the harbour, and out of the better streets of the town, into their own maze of ruins and *tolderías*. You must understand that this riot, whose primary object was undoubtedly the getting hold of the San Tomé silver stored in the lower rooms of the Custom House (besides the general looting of the *ricos*), had acquired a political colouring from the fact of two Deputies to the Provincial Assembly, Señores Gamacho and Fuentes, both from Bolson, putting themselves at the head of it—late in the afternoon, it is true, when the mob, disappointed in their hopes of loot, made a stand in the narrow streets to the cries of "*Viva la libertad!* Down with Feudalism!" (I wonder what they imagine feudalism to be?) "Down with the Goths and Paralytics." I suppose the Señores Gamacho and Fuentes knew what they were doing. They are prudent gentlemen. In the Assembly they called themselves Moderates, and opposed every energetic measure with philanthropic pensiveness. At the first rumours of Montero's victory, they began to show a subtle change of the pensive temper, and began to defy poor Don Juste Lopez in his Presidential tribune with an effrontery to which the poor man could only respond by a dazed smoothing of his beard and ringing of the Presidential bell. Then, when the downfall of the Ribierist cause became confirmed beyond the shadow of a doubt, they have blossomed into convinced Liberals, acting together as if they were Siamese twins, and ultimately taking charge, as it were, of the riot in the name of Monterist principles.

Their last move of eight o'clock last night was to organize themselves into a Monterist Committee which sits, as far as I know, in a *posada* kept by a retired Mexican bull-fighter, a great politician, too, whose name I have forgotten. Thence they have issued a communication to us, the Goths and Paralytics of the Amarilla Club (who have our own committee), inviting us to come to some provisional understanding for a truce, in order, they have the impudence

to say, that the noble cause of Liberty "should not be stained by the
criminal excesses of Conservative selfishness"! As I came out to sit
with Nostromo on the cathedral steps the club was busy considering
a proper reply in the principal room, littered with exploded cartridges, with a lot of broken glass, blood smears, candlesticks, and
all sorts of wreckage on the floor. But all this is nonsense. Nobody
in the town has any real power except the railway engineers, whose
men occupy the dismantled houses acquired by the Company for
their town station on one side of the Plaza, and Nostromo, whose
cargadores were sleeping under the arcades along the front of Anzani's shops. A fire of broken furniture out of the Intendencia sa-
loons, mostly gilt, was burning on the Plaza, in a high flame
swaying right upon the statue of Charles IV. The dead body of a
man was lying on the steps of the pedestal, his arms thrown
wide open, and his sombrero covering his face—the attention of
some friend, perhaps. The light of the flame touched the foliage of
the first trees on the Alameda, and played on the end of a side-street
near by, blocked up by a jumble of ox-carts and dead bullocks. Sitting on one of the carcases, a *lepero*, muffled up, smoked a cigarette. It was a truce, you understand. The only other living being on
the Plaza besides ourselves was a *cargador* walking to and fro, with
a long, bare knife in his hand, like a sentry before the Arcades,
where his friends were sleeping. And the only other spot of light in
the dark town were the lighted windows of the club, at the corner of
the Calle.

After having written so far, Don Martin Decoud, the exotic dandy
of the Parisian boulevard, got up and walked across the sanded floor
of the café at one end of the Albergo of United Italy, kept by Giorgio Viola, the old companion of Garibaldi. The highly coloured
lithograph of the Faithful Hero seemed to look dimly, in the light of
one candle, at the man with no faith in anything except the truth of
his own sensations. Looking out of the window, Decoud was met by
a darkness so impenetrable that he could see neither the mountains
nor the town, nor yet the buildings near the harbour; and there was
not a sound, as if the tremendous obscurity of the Placid Gulf,
spreading from the waters over the land, had made it dumb as well
as blind. Presently Decoud felt a light tremor of the floor and a

distant clank of iron. A bright white light appeared, deep in the darkness, growing bigger with a thundering noise. The rolling stock usually kept on the sidings in Rincón was being run back to the yards for safe keeping. Like a mysterious stirring of the darkness behind the headlight of the engine, the train passed in a gust of hollow uproar, by the end of the house, which seemed to vibrate all over in response. And nothing was clearly visible but, on the end of the last car, a Negro, in white trousers and naked to the waist, swinging a blazing torch basket incessantly with a circular movement of his bare arm. Decoud did not stir.

Behind him, on the back of the chair from which he had risen, hung his elegant Parisian overcoat, with a pearl-grey silk lining. But when he turned back to come to the table the candlelight fell upon a face that was grimy and scratched. His rosy lips were blackened with heat, the smoke of gun-powder. Dirt and rust tarnished the lustre of his short beard. His shirt collar and cuffs were crumpled; the blue silken tie hung down his breast like a rag; a greasy smudge crossed his white brow. He had not taken off his clothing nor used water, except to snatch a hasty drink greedily, for some forty hours. An awful restlessness had made him its own, had marked him with all the signs of desperate strife, and put a dry, sleepless stare into his eyes. He murmured to himself in a hoarse voice. "I wonder if there's any bread here," looked vaguely about him, then dropped into the chair and took the pencil up again. He became aware he had not eaten anything for many hours.

It occurred to him that no one could understand him so well as his sister. In the most sceptical heart there lurks at such moments, when the chances of existence are involved, a desire to leave a correct impression of the feelings, like a light by which the action may be seen when personality is gone, gone where no light of investigation can ever reach the truth which every death takes out of the world. Therefore, instead of looking for something to eat, or trying to snatch an hour or so of sleep, Decoud was filling the pages of a large pocket-book with a letter to his sister.

In the intimacy of that intercourse he could not keep out his weariness, his great fatigue, the close touch of his bodily sensations. He began again as if he were talking to her. With almost an illusion of her presence, he wrote the phrase, "I am very hungry."

I have the feeling of a great solitude around me [he continued]. Is it, perhaps, because I am the only man with a definite idea in his head, in the complete collapse of every resolve, intention, and hope about me? But the solitude is also very real. All the engineers are out, and have been for two days, looking after the property of the National Central Railway, of that great Costaguana undertaking which is to put money into the pockets of Englishmen, Frenchmen, Americans, Germans, and God knows who else. The silence about me is ominous. There is above the middle part of this house a sort of first floor, with narrow openings like loopholes for windows, probably used in old times for the better defence against the savages, when the persistent barbarism of our native continent did not wear the black coats of politicians, but went about yelling, half-naked, with bows and arrows in its hands. The woman of the house is dying up there, I believe, all alone with her old husband. There is a narrow staircase, the sort of staircase one man could easily defend against a mob, leading up there, and I have just heard, through the thickness of the wall, the old fellow going down into their kitchen for something or other. It was a sort of noise a mouse might make behind the plaster of a wall. All the servants they had ran away yesterday and have not returned yet, if ever they do. For the rest, there are only two children here, two girls. The father has sent them downstairs, and they have crept into this café, perhaps because I am here. They huddle together in a corner, in each other's arms; I just noticed them a few minutes ago, and I feel more lonely than ever.

Decoud turned half round in his chair, and asked, "Is there any bread here?"

Linda's dark head was shaken negatively in response, above the fair head of her sister nestling on her breast.

"You couldn't get me some bread?" insisted Decoud. The child did not move; he saw her large eyes stare at him very dark from the corner. "You're not afraid of me?" he said.

"No," said Linda, "we are not afraid of you. You came here with Gian' Battista."

"You mean Nostromo?" said Decoud.

"The English call him so, but that is no name either for man or beast," said the girl, passing her hand gently over her sister's hair.

"But he lets people call him so," remarked Decoud.

"Not in this house," retorted the child.

"Ah! well, I shall call him the Capataz then."

Decoud gave up the point, and after writing steadily for a while turned round again.

"When do you expect him back?" he asked.

"After he brought you here he rode off to fetch the Señor Doctor from the town for mother. He will be back soon."

"He stands a good chance of getting shot somewhere on the road," Decoud murmured to himself audibly; and Linda declared in her high-pitched voice:

"Nobody would dare to fire a shot at Gian' Battista."

"You believe that," asked Decoud, "do you?"

"I know it," said the child, with conviction. "There is no one in this place brave enough to attack Gian' Battista."

"It doesn't require much bravery to pull a trigger behind a bush," muttered Decoud to himself. "Fortunately, the night is dark, or there would be but little chance of saving the silver of the mine."

He turned again to his pocket-book, glanced back through the pages, and again started his pencil.

That was the position yesterday, after the *Minerva* with the fugitive President had gone out of harbour, and the rioters had been driven back into the side-lanes of the town. I sat on the steps of the cathedral with Nostromo, after sending out the cable message for the information of a more or less attentive world. Strangely enough, though the offices of the Cable Company are in the same building as the *Porvenir*, the mob, which has thrown my presses out of the window and scattered the type all over the Plaza, has been kept from interfering with the instruments on the other side of the courtyard. As I sat talking with Nostromo, Bernhardt, the telegraphist, came out from under the Arcades with a piece of paper in his hand. The little man had tied himself up to an enormous sword and was hung all over with revolvers. He is ridiculous, but the bravest German of his size that ever tapped the key of a Morse transmitter. He had received the message from Cayta reporting the transports with Barrios's army just entering the port, and ending with the words, "The greatest enthusiasm prevails." I walked off to drink some water at the fountain, and I was shot at from the Alameda by somebody hiding behind a tree. But I drank, and didn't care; with Barrios in Cayta and the great Cordillera between us and Montero's victorious army I seemed, notwithstanding Messrs. Gamacho and Fuentes, to hold my new State in the hollow of my hand. I was ready to sleep, but when I got as far as the Casa Gould I found the patio full of wounded laid out on straw. Lights were burning, and in that enclosed courtyard on that hot night a faint odour of chloroform and blood hung about. At one end Dr. Monygham, the doctor of the mine, was dressing the wounds; at the other, near the stairs, Father Corbelán, kneeling, listened to the confession of a dying *cargador*. Mrs. Gould was walking about through these shambles with a large bottle in one hand and a lot of cotton wool in the other. She just looked at me and never even winked. Her *camerista* was following her, also holding a bottle, and sobbing gently to herself.

I busied myself for some time in fetching water from the cistern for the wounded. Afterwards I wandered upstairs, meeting some of the first ladies of Sulaco, paler than I had ever seen them before, with bandages over their arms. Not all of them had fled to the ships. A good man had taken refuge for the day in the Casa Gould. On the landing a girl, with her hair half down, was kneeling against the wall under the niche where stands a Madonna in blue robes and a gilt crown on her head. I think it was the eldest Miss Lopez; I couldn't see her face, but I remember looking at the high French heel of her little shoe. She did not make a sound, she did not stir, she was not sobbing; she remained there, perfectly still, all black against the white wall, a silent figure of passionate piety. I am sure she was no more frightened than the other white-faced ladies I met carrying bandages. One was sitting on the top step tearing a piece of linen hastily into strips—the young wife of an elderly man of fortune here. She interrupted herself to wave her hand to my bow, as though she were in her carriage on the Alameda. The women of our country are worth looking at during a revolution. The rouge and pearl powder fall off, together with that passive attitude towards the outer world which education, tradition, custom impose upon them from the earliest infancy. I thought of your face, which from your infancy had the stamp of intelligence instead of that patient and resigned cast which appears when some political commotion tears down the veil of cosmetics and usage.

In the great *sala* upstairs a sort of Junta of Notables was sitting, the remnant of the vanished Provincial Assembly. Don Juste Lopez had had half his beard singed off at the muzzle of a *trabuco* loaded with slugs, of which every one missed him, providentially. And as he turned his head from side to side it was exactly as if there had been two men inside his frock-coat, one nobly whiskered and solemn, the other untidy and scared.

They raised a cry of "Decoud! Don Martin!" at my entrance. I asked them, "What are you deliberating upon, gentlemen?" There did not seem to be any president, though Don José Avellanos sat at the head of the table. They all answered together, "On the preservation of life and property." "Till the new officials arrive," Don Juste explained to me, with the solemn side of his face offered to my view. It was as if a stream of water had been poured upon my glowing idea of a new State. There was a hissing sound in my ears, and the room grew dim, as if suddenly filled with vapour.

I walked up to the table blindly, as though I had been drunk. "You are deliberating upon surrender," I said. They all sat still, with their noses over the sheet of paper each had before him, God only knows why. Only Don José hid his face in his hands, muttering, "Never, never!" But as I looked at him, it seemed to me that I could have blown him away with my breath, he looked so frail, so weak, so worn out. Whatever happens, he will not survive. The deception is too great for a man of his age; and hasn't he seen the sheets of *Fifty Years of Misrule*, which we have begun printing on the presses of the *Porvenir*, littering the Plaza, floating in the gutters fired out as wads for trabucos* loaded with handfuls of type, blown in the wind, trampled in the mud? I have seen pages floating upon the very waters of the harbour. It would be unreasonable to expect him to survive. It would be cruel.

"Do you know," I cried, "what surrender means to you, to your women, to your children, to your property?"

I declaimed for five minutes without drawing breath, it seems to me, harping on our best chances, on the ferocity of Montero, whom I made out to be as great a beast as I have no doubt he would like to

---

*Blunderbusses.

be if he had intelligence enough to conceive a systematic reign of terror. And then for another five minutes or more I poured out an impassioned appeal to their courage and manliness, with all the passion of my love for Antonia. For if ever man spoke well, it would be from a personal feeling, denouncing an enemy, defending himself, or pleading for what really may be dearer than life. My dear girl, I absolutely thundered at them. It seemed as if my voice would burst the walls asunder, and when I stopped I saw all their scared eyes looking at me dubiously. And that was all the effect I had produced! Only Don José's head had sunk lower and lower on his breast. I bent my ear to his withered lips, and made out his whisper, something like, "In God's name, then, Martin, my son!" I don't know exactly. There was the name of God in it, I am certain. It seems to me I have caught his last breath—the breath of his departing soul on his lips.

He lives yet, it is true. I have seen him since; but it was only a senile body, lying on its back, covered to the chin, with open eyes, and so still that you might have said it was breathing no longer. I left him thus, with Antonia kneeling by the side of the bed, just before I came to this Italian's *posada*, where the ubiquitous death is also waiting. But I know that Don José has really died there, in the Casa Gould, with that whisper urging me to attempt what no doubt his soul, wrapped up in the sanctity of diplomatic treaties and solemn declarations, must have abhorred. I had exclaimed very loud, "There is never any God in a country where men will not help themselves."

Meanwhile, Don Juste had begun a pondered oration whose solemn effect was spoiled by the ridiculous disaster to his beard. I did not wait to make it out. He seemed to argue that Montero's (he called him The General) intentions were probably not evil, though, he went on, "that distinguished man" (only a week ago we used to call him a *gran' bestia*) "was perhaps mistaken as to the true means." As you may imagine, I didn't stay to hear the rest. I know the intentions of Montero's brother, Pedrito, the *guerrillero*, whom I exposed in Paris, some years ago, in a café frequented by South American students, where he tried to pass himself off for a Secretary of Legation. He used to come in and talk for hours, twisting his felt hat in his hairy paws, and his ambition seemed to be to become a sort of Duc de Morny to a sort of Napoleon.[15] Already, then, he used to talk of his brother in inflated terms. He seemed fairly safe from being found out, because the students, all of the Blanco families, did not, as you may imagine, frequent the Legation. It was only Decoud, a man without faith and principles, as they used to say, that went in there sometimes for the sake of the fun, as it were to an assembly of trained monkeys. I know his intentions. I have seen him change the plates at table. Whoever is allowed to live on in terror, I must die the death.

No, I didn't stay to the end to hear Don Juste Lopez trying to persuade himself in a grave oration of the clemency and justice, and honesty, and purity of the brothers Montero. I went out abruptly to seek Antonia. I saw her in the gallery. As I opened the door, she extended to me her clasped hands.

"What are they doing in there?" she asked.

"Talking," I said, with my eyes looking into hers.

"Yes, yes, but—"

"Empty speeches," I interrupted her. "Hiding their fears behind imbecile hopes. They are all great Parliamentarians there—on the English model, as you know." I was so furious that I could hardly speak. She made a gesture of despair.

Through the door I held a little ajar behind me, we heard Don Juste's measured mouthing monotone go on from phrase to phrase, like a sort of awful and solemn madness.

"After all, the Democratic aspirations have, perhaps, their legitimacy. The ways of human progress are inscrutable, and if the fate of the country is in the hand of Montero, we ought—"

I crashed the door to on that; it was enough; it was too much. There was never a beautiful face expressing more horror and despair than the face of Antonia. I couldn't bear it; I seized her wrists.

"Have they killed my father in there?" she asked.

Her eyes blazed with indignation, but as I looked on, fascinated, the light in them went out.

"It is a surrender," I said. And I remember I was shaking her wrists I held apart in my hands. "But it's more than talk. Your father told me to go on in God's name."

My dear girl, there is that in Antonia which would make me believe in the feasibility of anything. One look at her face is enough to set my brain on fire. And yet I love her as any other man would—with the heart, and with that alone. She is more to me than his

Church to Father Corbelán (the Grand Vicar disappeared last night from the town; perhaps gone to join the band of Hernandez). She is more to me than his precious mine to that sentimental Englishman. I won't speak of his wife. She may have been sentimental once. The San Tomé mine stands now between those two people. "Your father himself, Antonia," I repeated; "your father, do you understand? has told me to go on."

She averted her face, and in a pained voice—

"He has?" she cried. "Then, indeed, I fear he will never speak again."

She freed her wrists from my clutch and began to cry in her handkerchief. I disregarded her sorrow; I would rather see her miserable than not see her at all, never any more; for whether I escaped or stayed to die, there was for us no coming together, no future. And that being so, I had no pity to waste upon the passing moments of her sorrow. I sent her off in tears to fetch Doña Emilia and Don Carlos, too. Their sentiment was necessary to the very life of my plan; the sentimentalism of the people that will never do anything for the sake of their passionate desire, unless it comes to them clothed in the fair robes of an idea.

Late at night we formed a small junta of four—the two women, Don Carlos, and myself—in Mrs. Gould's blue-and-white boudoir.

El Rey de Sulaco thinks himself, no doubt, a very honest man. And so he is, if one could look behind his taciturnity. Perhaps he thinks that this alone makes his honesty unstained. Those Englishmen live on illusions which somehow or other help them to get a firm hold of the substance. When he speaks it is by a rare "yes" or "no" that seems as impersonal as the words of an oracle. But he could not impose on me by his dumb reserve. I knew what he had in his head; he has his mine in his head; and his wife had nothing in her head but his precious person, which he has bound up with the Gould Concession and tied to that little woman's neck. No matter. The thing was to make him present the affair to Holroyd (the Steel and Silver King) in such a manner as to secure his financial support. At that time last night, just twenty-four hours ago, we thought the silver of the mine safe in the Custom House vaults till the northbound steamer came to take it away. And as long as the treasure flowed north, without a break, that utter sentimentalist, Holroyd, would not drop his idea of introducing, not only justice, industry, peace, to the benighted continents, but also that pet dream of his of a purer form of Christianity. Later on, the principal European really in Sulaco, the engineer-in-chief of the railway, came riding up the *calle*, from the harbour, and was admitted to our conclave. Meantime, the Junta of the Notables in the great *sala* was still deliberating; only, one of them had run out in the corridor to ask the servant whether something to eat couldn't be sent in. The first words the engineer-in-chief said as he came into the boudoir were, "What is your house, dear Mrs. Gould? A war hospital below, and apparently a restaurant above. I saw them carrying trays full of good things into the *sala*."

"And here, in this boudoir," I said, "you behold the inner cabinet of the Occidental Republic that is to be."

He was so preoccupied that he didn't smile at that, he didn't even look surprised.

He told us that he was attending to the general dispositions for the defence of the railway property at the railway yards when he was sent for to go into the railway telegraph office. The engineer of the railhead, at the foot of the mountains, wanted to talk to him from his end of the wire. There was nobody in the office but himself and the operator of the railway telegraph, who read off the clicks aloud as the tape coiled its length upon the floor. And the purport of that talk, clicked nervously from a wooden shed in the depths of the forests, had informed the chief that President Ribiera had been, or was being, pursued. This was news, indeed, to all of us in Sulaco. Ribiera himself, when rescued, revived, and soothed by us, had been inclined to think that he had not been pursued.

Ribiera had yielded to the urgent solicitations of his friends, and had left the headquarters of his discomfited army alone, under the guidance of Bonifacio, the muleteer, who had been willing to take the responsibility with the risk. He had departed at daybreak of the third day. His remaining forces had melted away during the night. Bonifacio and he rode hard on horses towards the Cordillera; then they obtained mules, entered the passes, and crossed the Paramo of Ivie just before a freezing blast swept over that stony plateau, burying in a drift of snow the little shelter-hut of stones in which they had spent the night. Afterwards poor Ribiera had many adventures, got separated from his guide, lost his mount, struggled down to the Campo on foot, and if he had not thrown himself on the mercy of a *ranchero* would have perished a long way from Sulaco. That man, who, as a matter of fact, recognized him at once, let him have a fresh mule, which the fugitive, heavy and unskilful, had ridden to death. And it was true he had been pursued by a party commanded by no less a person than Pedro Montero, the brother of the general. The cold wind of the Paramo luckily caught the pursuers on the top of the pass. Some few men, and all the animals, perished in the icy blast. The stragglers died, but the main body kept on. They found poor Bonifacio lying half-dead at the foot of a snow slope, and bayoneted him promptly in the true Civil War style. They would have had Ribiera, too, if they had not, for some reason or other, turned off the track of the old *camino real*, only to lose their way in the forests at the foot of the lower slopes. And there they were at last, having stumbled in unexpectedly upon the construction camp. The engineer at the railhead told his chief by wire that he had Pedro Montero absolutely there, in the very office, listening to the clicks. He was going to take possession of Sulaco in the name of the Democracy. He was very overbearing. His men slaughtered some of the Railway Company's cattle without asking leave, and went to work broiling the meat on the embers. Pedrito made many pointed inquiries as to the silver mine, and what had become of the product of the last six months' working. He had said peremptorily, "Ask your chief up there by wire, he ought to know; tell him that Don Pedro Montero, Chief of the Campo and Minister of the Interior of the new Government, desires to be correctly informed."

He had his feet wrapped up in blood-stained rags, a lean, haggard face, ragged beard and hair, and had walked in limping, with a crooked branch of a tree for a staff. His followers were, perhaps, in a worse plight, but apparently they had not thrown away their arms, and, at any rate, not all their ammunition. Their lean faces filled the door and the windows of the telegraph hut. As it was at the same time the bedroom of the engineer-in-charge there, Montero had thrown himself on his clean blankets and lay there shivering and dictating requisitions to be transmitted by wire to Sulaco. He demanded a train of cars to be sent down at once to transport his men up.

"To this I answered from my end," the engineer-in-chief related to us, "that I dared not risk the rolling-stock in the interior, as there had been attempts to wreck trains all along the line several times. I did that for your sake, Gould," said the chief engineer. "The answer to this was, in the words of my subordinate, 'The filthy brute on my bed said, "Suppose I were to have you shot?" ' To which my subordinate, who, it appears, was himself operating, remarked that it would not bring the cars up. Upon that, the other, yawning, said, 'Never mind, there is no lack of horses on the Campo.' And, turning over, went to sleep on Harris's bed."

This is why, my dear girl, I am a fugitive tonight. The last wire from the railhead says that Pedro Montero and his men left at daybreak, after feeding on *asado** beef all night. They took all the horses; they will find more on the road; they'll be here in less than thirty hours, and thus Sulaco is no place either for me or the great store of silver belonging to the Gould Concession.

But that is not the worst. The garrison of Esmeralda has gone over to the victorious party. We have heard this by means of the telegraphist of the Cable Company, who came to the Casa Gould in the early morning with the news. In fact, it was so early that the day had not yet quite broken over Sulaco. His colleague in Esmeralda had called him up to say that the Garrison, after shooting some of their officers, had taken possession of a Government steamer laid up in the harbour. It is really a heavy blow for me. I thought I could depend on every man in this province. It was a mistake. It was a Monterist Revolution in Esmeralda, just such as was attempted in Sulaco, only that *that* one came off. The telegraphist was signalling to Bernhardt all the time, and his last transmitted words were, "They are bursting in the door, and taking possession of the cable office. You are cut off. Can do no more."

But, as a matter of fact, he managed somehow to escape the vigilance of his captors, who had tried to stop the communication with the outer world. He did manage it. How it was done I don't know, but a few hours afterwards he called up Sulaco again, and what he said was, "The insurgent army has taken possession of the Government transport in the bay and are filling her with troops, with the intention of going round the coast to Sulaco. Therefore look out for

---

*Grilled or roasted.

yourselves. They will be ready to start in a few hours, and may be upon you before daybreak."

This is all he could say. They drove him away from his instrument this time for good, because Bernhardt has been calling up Esmeralda ever since without getting an answer.

After setting these words down in the pocket-book which he was filling up for the benefit of his sister, Decoud lifted his head to listen. But there were no sounds, neither in the room nor in the house, except the drip of the water from the filter into the vast earthenware jar under the wooden stand. And outside the house there was a great silence. Decoud lowered his head again over the pocket-book.

I am not running away, you understand [he wrote on]. I am simply going away with that great treasure of silver which must be saved at all costs. Pedro Montero from the Campo and the revolted garrison of Esmeralda from the sea are converging upon it. That it is there lying ready for them is only an accident. The real object is the San Tomé mine itself, as you may well imagine; otherwise the Occidental Province would have been, no doubt, left alone for many weeks, to be gathered at leisure into the arms of the victorious party. Don Carlos Gould will have enough to do to save his mine, with its organization and its people; this *"Imperium in Imperio,"* this wealth-producing thing, to which his sentimentalism attaches a strange idea of justice. He holds to it as some men hold to the idea of love or revenge. Unless I am much mistaken in the man, it must remain inviolate or perish by an act of his will alone. A passion has crept into his cold and idealistic life. A passion which I can only comprehend intellectually. A passion that is not like the passions we know, we men of another blood. But it is as dangerous as any of ours.

His wife has understood it, too. That is why she is such a good ally of mine. She seizes upon all my suggestions with a sure instinct that in the end they make for the safety of the Gould Concession. And he defers to her because he trusts her perhaps, but I fancy more rather as if he wished to make up for some subtle wrong, for that sentimental unfaithfulness which surrenders her happiness, her life, to the seduction of an idea. The little woman has discovered that he lives for the mine rather than for her. But let them be. To each his fate, shaped by passion or sentiment. The principal thing is that she has backed up my advice to get the silver out of the town, out of the country, at once, at any cost, at any risk. Don Carlos's mission is to preserve unstained the fair name of his mine; Mrs. Gould's mission is to save him from the effects of that cold and overmastering passion, which she dreads more than if it were an infatuation for another woman. Nostromo's mission is to save the silver. The plan is to load it into the largest of the Company's lighters, and send it across the gulf to a small port out of Costaguana territory just on the other side of the Azuera, where the first northbound steamer will get orders to pick it up. The waters here are calm. We shall slip away into the darkness of the gulf before the Esmeralda rebels arrive; and by the time the day breaks over the ocean we shall be out of sight, invisible, hidden by Azuera, which itself looks from the Sulaco shore like a faint blue cloud on the horizon.

The incorruptible Capataz de Cargadores is the man for that work; and I, the man with a passion, but without a mission, I go with him to return—to play my part in the farce to the end, and, if successful, to receive my reward, which no one but Antonia can give me.

I shall not see her again now before I depart. I left her, as I have said, by Don José's bedside. The street was dark, the houses shut up, and I walked out of the town in the night. Not a single street-lamp had been lit for two days, and the archway of the gate was only a mass of darkness in the vague form of a tower, in which I heard low, dismal groans that seemed to answer the murmurs of a man's voice.

I recognized something impassive and careless in the tone, characteristic of that Genoese sailor who, like me, has come casually here to be drawn into the events for which his scepticism as well as mine seems to entertain a sort of passive contempt. The only thing he seems to care for, as far as I have been able to discover, is to be well spoken of. An ambition fit for noble souls, but also a profitable one for an exceptionally intelligent scoundrel. Yes. His very words, "To be well spoken of. *Sí señor.*" He does not seem to make any difference between speaking and thinking. Is it sheer naïveness or the practical point of view, I wonder? Exceptional individualities always interest me, because they are true to the general formula expressing the moral state of humanity.

He joined me on the harbour road after I had passed them under the dark archway without stopping. It was a woman in trouble he had been talking to. Through discretion I kept silent while he walked by my side. After a time he began to talk himself. It was not what I expected. It was only an old woman, an old lace-maker, in search of her son, one of the street-sweepers employed by the municipality. Friends had come the day before at daybreak to the door of their hovel calling him out. He had gone with them, and she had not seen him since; so she had left the food she had been preparing half-cooked on the extinct embers and had crawled out as far as the harbour, where she had heard that some town *mozos* had been killed on the morning of the riot. One of the *cargadores* guarding the Custom House had brought out a lantern, and had helped her to look at the few dead left lying about there. Now she was creeping back, having failed in her search. So she sat down on the stone seat under the arch, moaning, because she was very tired. The Capataz had questioned her, and after hearing her broken and groaning tale had advised her to go and look amongst the wounded in the patio of the Casa Gould. He had also given her a quarter dollar, he mentioned carelessly.

"Why did you do that?" I asked. "Do you know her?"

"No, *señor*. I don't suppose I have ever seen her before. How should I? She has not probably been out in the streets for years. She is one of those old women that you find in this country at the back of huts, crouching over fireplaces, with a stick on the ground by their side, and almost too feeble to drive away the stray dogs from their cooking-pots. *Caramba!* I could tell by her voice that death had forgotten her. But, old or young, they like money, and will speak well of the man who gives it to them." He laughed a little. "*Señor*, you should have felt the clutch of her paw as I put the piece in her palm." He paused. "My last, too," he added.

I made no comment. He's known for his liberality, and his bad luck at the game of *monte*, which keeps him as poor as when he first came here.

"I suppose, Don Martin," he began, in a thoughtful, speculative tone, "that the Señor Administrador of San Tomé will reward me some day if I save his silver?"

I said that it could not be otherwise, surely. He walked on, muttering to himself. "*Sí, sí*, without doubt, without doubt; and, look you, *Señor* Martin, what it is to be well spoken of! There is not another man that could have been even thought of for such a thing. I shall get something great for it some day. And let it come soon," he mumbled. "Time passes in this country as quick as anywhere else."

This, *sœur chérie*,* is my companion in the great escape for the sake of the great cause. He is more naïve than shrewd, more masterful than crafty, more generous with his personality than the people who make use of him are with their money. At least, that is what he thinks himself with more pride than sentiment. I am glad I have made friends with him. As a companion he acquires more importance than he ever had as a sort of minor genius in his way—as an original Italian sailor whom I allowed to come in in the small hours and talk familiarly to the editor of the *Porvenir* while the paper was going through the press. And it is curious to have met a man for whom the value of life seems to consist in personal prestige.

I am waiting for him here now. On arriving at the *posada* kept by Viola we found the children alone down below, and the old Genoese shouted to his countryman to go and fetch the doctor. Otherwise we would have gone on to the wharf, where it appears Captain Mitchell with some volunteer Europeans and a few picked *cargadores* are loading the lighter with the silver that must be saved from Montero's clutches in order to be used for Montero's defeat. Nostromo galloped furiously back towards the town. He has been long gone already. This delay gives me time to talk to you. By the time this pocket-book reaches your hands much will have happened. But now it is a pause under the hovering wing of death in that silent house buried in the black night, with this dying woman, the two children crouching without a sound, and that old man whom I can hear through the thickness of the wall passing up and down with a light rubbing noise no louder than a mouse. And I, the only other with them, don't really know whether to count myself with the living or with the dead. "*Quién sabe?*" as the people here are prone to say in answer to every question. But no! feeling for you is certainly not dead, and the whole thing, the house, the dark night, the silent children in this dim room, my very presence here—all this is life, must be life, since it is so much like a dream.

---

*Dear sister (Fr.).

With the writing of the last line there came upon Decoud a moment of sudden and complete oblivion. He swayed over the table as if struck by a bullet. The next moment he sat up, confused, with the idea that he had heard his pencil roll on the floor. The low door of the café, wide open, was filled with the glare of a torch in which was visible half of a horse, switching its tail against the leg of a rider with a long iron spur strapped to the naked heel. The two girls were gone, and Nostromo, standing in the middle of the room, looked at him from under the round brim of the sombrero low down over his brow.

"I have brought that sour-faced English doctor in Señora Gould's carriage," said Nostromo. "I doubt if, with all his wisdom, he can save the Padrona this time. They have sent for the children. A bad sign that."

He sat down on the end of a bench. "She wants to give them her blessing, I suppose."

Dazedly Decoud observed that he must have fallen sound asleep, and Nostromo said, with a vague smile, that he had looked in at the window and had seen him lying still across the table with his head on his arms. The English *señora* had also come in the carriage, and went upstairs at once with the doctor. She had told him not to wake up Don Martin yet; but when they sent for the children he had come into the café.

The half of the horse with its half of the rider swung round outside the door; the torch of tow and resin in her iron basket which was carried on a stick at the saddle-bow flared right into the room for a moment, and Mrs. Gould entered hastily with a very white, tired face. The hood of her dark, blue cloak had fallen back. Both men rose.

"Teresa wants to see you, Nostromo," she said.

The Capataz did not move. Decoud, with his back to the table, began to button up his coat.

"The silver, Mrs. Gould, the silver," he murmured in English. "Don't forget that the Esmeralda garrison have got a steamer. They may appear at any moment at the harbour entrance."

"The doctor says there is no hope," Mrs. Gould spoke rapidly, also in English. "I shall take you down to the wharf in my carriage and then come back to fetch away the girls." She changed swiftly into Spanish to address Nostromo. "Why are you wasting time? Old Giorgio's wife wishes to see you."

"I am going to her, *señora*," muttered the Capataz.

Dr. Monygham now showed himself, bringing back the children. To Mrs. Gould's inquiring glance he only shook his head and went outside at once, followed by Nostromo.

The horse of the torch-bearer, motionless, hung his head low, and the rider had dropped the reins to light a cigarette. The glare of the torch played on the front of the house crossed by the big black letters of its inscription in which only the word ITALIA was lighted fully. The patch of wavering glare reached as far as Mrs. Gould's carriage waiting on the road, with the yellow-faced, portly Ignacio apparently dozing on the box. By his side Basilio, dark and skinny, held a Winchester carbine in front of him, with both hands, and peered fearfully into the darkness. Nostromo touched lightly the doctor's shoulder.

"Is she really dying, Señor Doctor?"

"Yes," said the doctor, with a strange twitch of his scarred cheek. "And why she wants to see you I cannot imagine."

"She has been like that before," suggested Nostromo, looking away.

"Well, Capataz, I can assure you she will never be like that again," snarled Dr. Monygham. "You may go to her or stay away. There is very little to be got from talking to the dying. But she told Doña Emilia in my hearing that she has been like a mother to you ever since you first set foot ashore here."

"*Sí!* And she never had a good word to say for me to anybody. It is more as if she could not forgive me for being alive, and such a man, too, as she would have liked her son to be."

"Maybe!" exclaimed a mournful deep voice near them. "Women have their own ways of tormenting themselves." Giorgio Viola had come out of the house. He threw a heavy black shadow in the torch-light, and the glare fell on his big face, on the great bushy head of white hair. He motioned the Capataz indoors with his extended arm.

Dr. Monygham, after busying himself with a little medicament box of polished wood on the seat of the landau, turned to old Giorgio and thrust into his big, trembling hand one of the glass-stoppered bottles out of the case.

"Give her a spoonful of this now and then, in water," he said. "It will make her easier."

"And there is nothing more for her?" asked the old man patiently.

"No. Not on earth," said the doctor, with his back to him, clicking the lock of the medicine case.

Nostromo slowly crossed the large kitchen, all dark but for the glow of a heap of charcoal under the heavy mantel of the cooking-range, where water was boiling in an iron pot with a loud bubbling sound. Between the two walls of a narrow staircase a bright light streamed from the sick-room above; and the magnificent Capataz de Cargadores stepping noiselessly in soft leather sandals, bushy whiskered, his muscular neck and bronzed chest bare in the open check shirt, resembled a Mediterranean sailor just come ashore from some wine- or fruit-laden felucca.* At the top he paused, broad shouldered, narrow hipped, and supple, looking at the large bed, like a white couch of state, with a profusion of snowy linen, amongst which the Padrona sat unpropped and bowed, her handsome, black-browed face bent over her chest. A mass of raven hair with only a few white threads in it covered her shoulders; one thick strand fallen forward half veiled her cheek. Perfectly motionless in that pose, expressing physical anxiety and unrest, she turned her eyes alone towards Nostromo.

The Capataz had a red sash wound many times round his waist, and a heavy silver ring on the forefinger of the hand he raised to give a twist to his moustache.

"Their revolutions, their revolutions," gasped Señora Teresa. "Look, Gian' Battista, it has killed me at last!"

Nostromo said nothing, and the sick woman with an upward glance insisted. "Look, this one has killed me, while you were away fighting for what did not concern you, foolish man."

"Why talk like this?" mumbled the Capataz between his teeth. "Will you never believe in my good sense? It concerns me to keep on being what I am: every day alike."

"You never change, indeed," she said, bitterly. "Always thinking

---

*Narrow, fast-sailing ship.

of yourself and taking your pay out in fine words from those who care nothing for you."

There was between them an intimacy of antagonism as close in its way as the intimacy of accord and affection. He had not walked along the way of Teresa's expectations. It was she who had encouraged him to leave his ship, in the hope of securing a friend and defender for the girls. The wife of old Giorgio was aware of her precarious health, and was haunted by the fear of her aged husband's loneliness and the unprotected state of the children. She had wanted to annex that apparently quiet and steady young man, affectionate and pliable, an orphan from his tenderest age, as he had told her, with no ties in Italy except an uncle, owner and master of a felucca, from whose ill-usage he had run away before he was fourteen. He had seemed to her courageous, a hard worker, determined to make his way in the world. From gratitude and the ties of habit he would become like a son to herself and Giorgio; and then, who knows, when Linda had grown up. . . . Ten years' difference between husband and wife was not so much. Her own great man was nearly twenty years older than herself. Gian' Battista was an attractive young fellow, besides; attractive to men, women, and children, just by that profound quietness of personality which, like a serene twilight, rendered more seductive the promise of his vigourous form and the resolution of his conduct.

Old Giorgio, in profound ignorance of his wife's views and hopes, had a great regard for his young countryman. "A man ought not to be tame," he used to tell her, quoting the Spanish proverb in defence of the splendid Capataz. She was growing jealous of his success. He was escaping from her, she feared. She was practical, and he seemed to her to be an absurd spendthrift of these qualities which made him so valuable. He got too little for them. He scattered them with both hands amongst too many people, she thought. He laid no money by. She railed at his poverty, his exploits, his adventures, his loves, and his reputation; but in her heart she had never given him up, as though, indeed, he had been her son.

Even now, ill as she was, ill enough to feel the chill, black breath of the approaching end, she had wished to see him. It was like putting out her benumbed hand to regain her hold. But she had presumed too much on her strength. She could not command her thoughts; they had become dim, like her vision. The words faltered on her lips, and only the paramount anxiety and desire of her life seemed to be too strong for death.

The Capataz said, "I have heard these things many times. You are unjust, but it does not hurt me. Only now you do not seem to have much strength to talk, and I have but little time to listen. I am engaged in a work of very great moment."

She made an effort to ask him whether it was true that he had found time to go and fetch a doctor for her. Nostromo nodded affirmatively.

She was pleased: it relieved her sufferings to know that the man had condescended to do so much for those who really wanted his help. It was a proof of his friendship. Her voice became stronger.

"I want a priest more than a doctor," she said, pathetically. She did not move her head; only her eyes ran into the corners to watch the Capataz standing by the side of her bed. "Would you go to fetch a priest for me now? Think! A dying woman asks you!"

Nostromo shook his head resolutely. He did not believe in priests in their sacerdotal character. A doctor was an efficacious person; but a priest, as priest, was nothing, incapable of doing either good or harm. Nostromo did not even dislike the sight of them as old Giorgio did. The utter uselessness of the errand was what struck him most.

"Padrona," he said, "you have been like this before, and got better after a few days. I have given you already the very last moments I can spare. Ask Señora Gould to send you one."

He was feeling uneasy at the impiety of this refusal. The Padrona believed in priests, and confessed herself to them. But all women did that. It could not be of much consequence. And yet his heart felt oppressed for a moment—at the thought of what absolution would mean to her if she believed in it only ever so little. No matter. It was quite true that he had given her already the very last moment he could spare.

"You refuse to go?" she gasped. "Ah! you are always yourself, indeed."

"Listen to reason, Padrona," he said. "I am needed to save the silver of the mine. Do you hear? A greater treasure than the one which they say is guarded by ghosts and devils in Azuera. It is true. I am resolved to make this the most desperate affair I was ever engaged on in my whole life."

She felt a despairing indignation. The supreme test had failed. Standing above her, Nostromo did not see the distorted features of her face, distorted by a paroxysm of pain and anger. Only she began to tremble all over. Her bowed head shook. The broad shoulders quivered.

"Then God, perhaps, will have some mercy upon me! But do you look to it, man, that you get something for yourself out of it, besides the remorse that shall overtake you some day."

She laughed feebly. "Get riches at least for once, you indispensable, admired Gian' Battista, to whom the peace of a dying woman is less than the praise of people who have given you a silly name — and nothing besides — in exchange for your soul and body."

The Captain de Cargadores swore to himself under his breath.

"Leave my soul alone, Padrona, and I shall know how to take care of my body. Where is the harm of people having need of me? What are you envying me that I have robbed you and the children of? Those very people you are throwing in my teeth have done more for old Giorgio than they ever thought of doing for me."

He struck his breast with his open palm; his voice had remained low though he had spoken in a forcible tone. He twisted his moustaches one after another, and his eyes wandered a little about the room.

"Is it my fault that I am the only man for their purposes? What angry nonsense are you talking, mother? Would you rather have me timid and foolish, selling water-melons on the market-place or rowing a boat for passengers along the harbour, like a soft Neapolitan without courage or reputation? Would you have a young man live like a monk? I do not believe it. Would you want a monk for your eldest girl? Let her grow. What are you afraid of? You have been angry with me for everything I did for years; ever since you first spoke to me, in secret from old Giorgio, about your Linda. Husband to one and brother to the other, did you say? Well, why not! I like the little ones, and a man must marry some time. But ever since that time you have been making little of me to everyone. Why? Did you think you could put a collar and chain on me as if I were one of the watchdogs they keep over there in the railway yards? Look here, Padrona, I am the same man who came ashore one evening and sat down in the thatched *rancho* you lived in at that time on the other side of the town and told you all about himself. You were not unjust to me then. What has happened since? I am no longer an insignificant youth. A good name, Giorgio says, is a treasure, Padrona."

"They have turned your head with their praises," gasped the sick woman. "They have been paying you with words. Your folly shall betray you into poverty, misery, starvation. The very *leperos* shall laugh at you—the great Capataz."

Nostromo stood for a time as if struck dumb. She never looked at him. A self-confident, mirthless smile passed quickly from his lips, and then he backed away. His disregarded figure sank down beyond the doorway. He descended the stairs backwards, with the usual sense of having been somehow baffled by this woman's disparagement of this reputation he had obtained and desired to keep.

Downstairs in the big kitchen a candle was burning, surrounded by the shadows of the walls, of the ceiling, but no ruddy glare filled the open square of the outer door. The carriage with Mrs. Gould and Don Martin, preceded by the horseman bearing the torch, had gone on to the jetty. Dr. Monygham, who had remained, sat on the corner of a hard wood table near the candlestick, his seamed, shaved face inclined sideways, his arms crossed on his breast, his lips pursed up, and his prominent eyes glaring stonily upon the floor of black earth. Near the overhanging mantel of the fireplace, where the pot of water was still boiling violently, old Giorgio held his chin in his hand, one foot advanced, as if arrested by a sudden thought.

"*Adios, viejo,*"* said Nostromo, feeling the handle of his revolver in the belt and loosening his knife in its sheath. He picked up a blue poncho lined with red from the table, and put it over his head. "*Adios,* look after my things in my sleeping-room, and if you hear from me no more, give up the box to Paquita. There is not much of value there, except my new serape from Mexico, and a few silver buttons on my best jacket. No matter! The things will look well

---

*Good-bye, old man.

enough on the next lover she gets, and the man need not be afraid I shall linger on earth after I am dead, like those *gringos* that haunt the Azuera."

Dr. Monygham twisted his lips into a bitter smile. After old Giorgio, with an almost imperceptible nod and without a word, had gone up the narrow stairs, he said:

"Why, Capataz! I thought you could never fail in anything."

Nostromo, glancing contemptuously at the doctor, lingered in the doorway rolling a cigarette, then struck a match, and, after lighting it, held the burning piece of wood above his head till the flame nearly touched his fingers.

"No wind!" he muttered to himself. "Look here, *señor*—do you know the nature of my undertaking?"

Dr. Monygham nodded sourly.

"It is as if I were taking up a curse upon me, Señor Doctor. A man with a treasure on this coast will have every knife raised against him in every place upon the shore. You see that, Señor Doctor? I shall float along with a spell upon my life till I meet somewhere the north-bound steamer of the Company, and then indeed they will talk about the Capataz of the Sulaco Cargadores from one end of America to another."

Dr. Monygham laughed his short, throaty laugh. Nostromo turned round in the doorway.

"But if your worship can find any other man ready and fit for such business I will stand back. I am not exactly tired of my life, though I am so poor that I can carry all I have with myself on my horse's back."

"You gamble too much, and never say 'no' to a pretty face, Capataz," said Dr. Monygham, with sly simplicity. "That's not the way to make a fortune. But nobody that I know ever suspected you of being poor. I hope you have made a good bargain in case you come back safe from this adventure."

"What bargain would your worship have made?" asked Nostromo, blowing the smoke out of his lips through the doorway.

Dr. Monygham listened up the staircase for a moment before he answered, with another of his short, abrupt laughs:

"Illustrious Capataz, for taking the curse of death upon my back, as you call it, nothing else but the whole treasure would do."

Nostromo vanished out of the doorway with a grunt of discontent at his jeering answer. Dr. Monygham heard him gallop away. Nostromo rode furiously in the dark. There were lights in the buildings of the O.S.N. Company near the wharf, but before he got there he met the Gould carriage. The horseman preceded it with the torch, whose light showed the white mules trotting, the portly Ignacio driving, and Basilio with the carbine on the box. From the dark body of the landau Mrs. Gould's voice cried, "They are waiting for you, Capataz!" She was returning, chilly and excited, with Decoud's pocket-book still held in her hand. He had confided it to her to send to his sister. "Perhaps my last words to her," he had said, pressing Mrs. Gould's hand.

The Capataz never checked his speed. At the head of the wharf vague figures with rifles leapt to the head of his horse; others closed upon him—*cargadores* of the company posted by Captain Mitchell on the watch. At a word from him they fell back with subservient murmurs, recognizing his voice. At the other end of the jetty, near a cargo crane, in a dark group with glowing cigars, his name was pronounced in a tone of relief. Most of the Europeans in Sulaco were there, rallied round Charles Gould, as if the silver of the mine had been the emblem of a common cause, the symbol of the supreme importance of material interests. They had loaded it into the lighter with their own hands. Nostromo recognized Don Carlos Gould, a thin, tall shape, standing a little apart and silent, to whom another tall shape, the engineer-in-chief, said aloud, "If it must be lost, it is a million times better that it should go to the bottom of the sea."

Martin Decoud called out from the lighter, "*Au revoir, messieurs,* till we clasp hands again over the newborn Occidental Republic." Only a subdued murmur responded to his clear ringing tones; and then it seemed to him that the wharf was floating away into the night; but it was Nostromo, who was already pushing against a pile with one of the heavy sweeps.* Decoud did not move; the effect was that of being launched into space. After a splash or two there was not a sound but the thud of Nostromo's feet leaping about the boat. He hoisted the big sail; a breath of wind fanned Decoud's cheek. Everything had vanished but the light of the lantern Captain Mitchell had

---

*Large oars.

hoisted upon the post at the end of the jetty to guide Nostromo out of the harbour.

The two men, unable to see each other, kept silent till the lighter, slipping before the fitful breeze, passed out between almost invisible headlands into the still deeper darkness of the gulf. For a time the lantern on the jetty shone after them. The wind failed, then fanned up again, but so faintly that the big, half-decked boat slipped along with no more noise than if she had been suspended in the air.

"We are out in the gulf now," said the calm voice of Nostromo. A moment after he added, "Señor Mitchell has lowered the light."

"Yes," said Decoud; "nobody can find us now."

A great recrudescence of obscurity embraced the boat. The sea in the gulf was as black as the clouds above. Nostromo, after striking a couple of matches to get a glimpse of the boat-compass he had with him in the lighter, steered by the feel of the wind on his cheek.

It was a new experience for Decoud, this mysteriousness of the great waters spread out strangely smooth, as if their restlessness had been crushed by the weight of that dense night. The Placido was sleeping profoundly under its black poncho.

The main thing now for success was to get away from the coast and gain the middle of the gulf before day broke. The Isabels were somewhere at hand. "On your left as you look forward, *señor*," said Nostromo, suddenly. When his voice ceased, the enormous stillness, without light or sound, seemed to affect Decoud's senses like a powerful drug. He didn't even know at times whether he were asleep or awake. Like a man lost in slumber, he heard nothing, he saw nothing. Even his hand held before his face did not exist for his eyes. The change from the agitation, the passions and the dangers, from the sights and sounds of the shore, was so complete that it would have resembled death had it not been for the survival of his thoughts. In this foretaste of eternal peace they floated vivid and light, like unearthly clear dreams of earthly things that may haunt the souls freed by death from the misty atmosphere of regrets and hopes. Decoud shook himself, shuddered a bit, though the air that drifted past him was warm. He had the strangest sensation of his soul having just returned into his body from the circumambient darkness in which land, sea, sky, the mountains, and the rocks were as if they had not been.

Nostromo's voice was speaking, though he, at the tiller, was also as if he were not. "Have you been asleep, Don Martin? *Caramba!* If it were possible I would think that I, too, have dozed off. I have a strange notion somehow of having dreamt that there was a sound of blubbering, a sound a sorrowing man could make, somewhere near this boat. Something between a sigh and a sob."

"Strange!" muttered Decoud, stretched upon the pile of treasure boxes covered by many tarpaulins. "Could it be that there is another boat near us in the gulf? We could not see it, you know."

Nostromo laughed a little at the absurdity of the idea. They dismissed it from their minds. The solitude could almost be felt. And when the breeze ceased, the blackness seemed to weigh upon Decoud like a stone.

"This is overpowering," he muttered. "Do we move at all, Capataz?"

"Not so fast as a crawling beetle tangled in the grass," answered Nostromo, and his voice seemed deadened by the thick veil of obscurity that felt warm and hopeless all about them. There were long periods when he made no sound, invisible and inaudible as if he had mysteriously stepped out of the lighter.

In the featureless night Nostromo was not even certain which way the lighter headed after the wind had completely died out. He peered for the islands. There was not a hint of them to be seen, as if they had sunk to the bottom of the gulf. He threw himself down by the side of Decoud at last, and whispered into his ear that if daylight caught them near the Sulaco shore through want of wind, it would be possible to sweep the lighter behind the cliff at the high end of the Great Isabel, where she would lie concealed. Decoud was surprised at the grimness of his anxiety. To him the removal of the treasure was a political move. It was necessary for several reasons that it should not fall into the hands of Montero, but here was a man who took another view of this enterprise. The *caballeros* over there did not seem to have the slightest idea of what they had given him to do. Nostromo, as if affected by the gloom around, seemed nervously resentful. Decoud was surprised. The Capataz, indifferent to those dangers that seemed obvious to his companion, allowed himself to become scornfully exasperated by the deadly nature of the trust put, as a matter of course, into his hands. It was more dangerous,

Nostromo said, with a laugh and a curse, than sending a man to get the treasure that people said was guarded by devils and ghosts in the deep ravines of Azuera. "*Señor,*" he said, "we must catch the steamer at sea. We must keep out in the open looking for her till we have eaten and drunk all that has been put on board here. And if we miss her by some mischance, we must keep away from the land till we grow weak, and perhaps mad, and die, and drift dead, until one or another of the steamers of the Compania comes upon the boat with the two dead men who have saved the treasure. That, *señor,* is the only way to save it; for, don't you see? for us to come to the land anywhere in a hundred miles along this coast with this silver in our possession is to run the naked breast against the point of a knife. This thing has been given to me like a deadly disease. If men discover it I am dead, and you, too, *señor,* since you would come with me. There is enough silver to make a whole province rich, let alone a seaboard *pueblo* inhabited by thieves and vagabonds. *Señor,* they would think that heaven itself sent these riches into their hands, and would cut our throats without hesitation. I would trust no fair words from the best man around the shores of this gulf. Reflect that, even by giving up the treasure at the first demand, we would not be able to save our lives. Do you understand this, or must I explain?"

"No, you needn't explain," said Decoud, a little listlessly. "I can see it well enough myself, that the possession of this treasure is very much like a deadly disease for men situated as we are. But it had to be removed from Sulaco, and you were the man for the task."

"I was; but I cannot believe," said Nostromo, "that its loss would have impoverished Don Carlos Gould very much. There is more wealth in the mountain. I have heard it rolling down the shoots on quiet nights when I used to ride to Rincón to see a certain girl, after my work at the harbour was done. For years the rich rocks have been pouring down with a noise like thunder, and the miners say that there is enough at the heart of the mountain to thunder on for years and years to come. And yet, since the day before yesterday, we have been fighting to save it from the mob, and tonight I am sent out with it into this darkness, where there is no wind to get away with; as if it were the last lot of silver on earth to get bread for the hungry with. Ha! ha! Well, I am going to make it the most famous and desperate affair of my life—wind or no wind. It shall be talked about when the little children are grown up and the grown men are old. Aha! the Monterists must not get hold of it, I am told, whatever happens to Nostromo the Capataz; and they shall not have it, I tell you, since it has been tied for safety round Nostromo's neck."

"I see it," murmured Decoud. He saw, indeed, that his companion had his own peculiar view of this enterprise.

Nostromo interrupted his reflections upon the way men's qualities are made use of, without any fundamental knowledge of their nature, by the proposal that they should slip the long oars out and sweep the lighter in the direction of the Isabels. It wouldn't do for daylight to reveal the treasure floating within a mile or so of the harbour entrance. The denser the darkness generally, the smarter were the puffs of wind on which he had reckoned to make his way; but tonight the gulf, under its poncho of clouds, remained breathless, as if dead rather than asleep.

Don Martin's soft hands suffered cruelly, tugging at the thick handle of the enormous oar. He stuck to it manfully, setting his teeth. He, too, was in the toils of an imaginative existence, and that strange work of pulling a lighter seemed to belong naturally to the inception of a new state, and acquired an ideal meaning from his love for Antonia. For all their efforts, the heavily laden lighter hardly moved. Nostromo could be heard swearing to himself between the regular splashes of the sweeps. "We are making a crooked path," he muttered to himself. "I wish I could see the islands."

In his unskilfulness Don Martin over-exerted himself. Now and then a sort of muscular faintness would run from the tips of his aching fingers through every fibre of his body, and pass off in a flush of heat. He had fought, talked, suffered mentally and physically, exerting his mind and body for the last forty-eight hours without intermission. He had had no rest, very little food, no pause in the stress of his thoughts and his feelings. Even his love for Antonia, whence he drew his strength and his inspiration, had reached the point of tragic tension during their hurried interview by Don José's bedside. And now, suddenly, he was thrown out of all this into a dark gulf, whose very gloom, silence, and breathless peace added a torment to the necessity for physical exertion. He imagined the lighter sinking to the bottom with an extraordinary shudder of delight. "I am on the verge of delirium," he thought. He mastered the trembling of all his limbs, of his breast, the inward trembling of all his body exhausted of its nervous force.

"Shall we rest, Capataz?" he proposed in a careless tone. "There are many hours of night yet before us."

"True. It is but a mile or so, I suppose. Rest your arms, *señor*, if that is what you mean. You will find no other sort of rest, I can promise you, since you let yourself be bound to this treasure whose loss would make no poor man poorer. No, *señor*; there is no rest till we find a northbound steamer, or else some ship finds us drifting about stretched out dead upon the Englishman's silver. Or rather— no; *por Dios!* I shall cut down the gunwale with the axe right to the water's edge before thirst and hunger rob me of my strength. By all the saints and devils I shall let the sea have the treasure rather than give it up to any stranger. Since it was the good pleasure of the *caballeros* to send me off on such an errand, they shall learn I am just the man they take me for."

Decoud lay on the silver boxes panting. All his active sensations and feelings from as far back as he could remember seemed to him the maddest of dreams. Even his passionate devotion to Antonia into which he had worked himself up out of the depths of his scepticism had lost all appearance of reality. For a moment he was the prey of an extremely languid but not unpleasant indifference.

"I am sure they didn't mean you to take such a desperate view of this affair," he said.

"What was it, then? A joke?" snarled the man, who on the paysheets of the O.S.N. Company's establishment in Sulaco was described as "Foreman of the wharf" against the figure of his wages. "Was it for a joke they woke me up from my sleep after two days of street fighting to make me stake my life upon a bad card? Everybody knows, too, that I am not a lucky gambler."

"Yes, everybody knows of your good luck with women, Capataz," Decoud propitiated his companion in a weary drawl.

"Look here, *señor*," Nostromo went on. "I never even remonstrated about this affair. Directly I heard what was wanted I saw what a desperate affair it must be, and I made up my mind to see it out. Every minute was of importance. I had to wait for you first. Then, when we arrived at the Italia Una, old Giorgio shouted to me to go for the English doctor. Later on, that poor dying woman wanted to see me, as you know. *Señor*, I was reluctant to go. I felt already this cursed silver growing heavy upon my back, and I was afraid that, knowing herself to be dying, she would ask me to ride off again for a priest. Father Corbelán, who is fearless, would have come at a word; but Father Corbelán is far away, safe with the band of Hernandez, and the populace, that would have liked to tear him to pieces, are much incensed against the priests. Not a single fat padre would have consented to put his head out of his hiding-place tonight to save a Christian soul, except, perhaps, under my protection. That was in her mind. I pretended I did not believe she was going to die. *Señor*, I refused to fetch a priest for a dying woman. . . ."

Decoud was heard to stir.

"You did, Capataz!" he exclaimed. His tone changed. "Well, you know—it was rather fine."

"You do not believe in priests, Don Martin? Neither do I. What was the use of wasting time? But she—she believes in them. The thing sticks in my throat. She may be dead already, and here we are floating helpless with no wind at all. Curse on all superstition. She died thinking I deprived her of Paradise, I suppose. It shall be the most desperate affair of my life."

Decoud remained lost in reflection. He tried to analyse the sensations awakened by what he had been told. The voice of the Capataz was heard again:

"Now, Don Martin, let us take up the sweeps and try to find the Isabels. It is either that or sinking the lighter if the day overtakes us. We must not forget that the steamer from Esmeralda with the soldiers may be coming along. We will pull straight on now. I have discovered a bit of a candle here, and we must take the risk of a small light to make a course by the boat compass. There is not enough wind to blow it out—may the curse of Heaven fall upon this blind gulf!"

A small flame appeared burning quite straight. It showed fragmentarily the stout ribs and planking in the hollow, empty part of the lighter. Decoud could see Nostromo standing up to pull. He saw him as high as the red sash on his waist, with a gleam of white-handled revolver and the wooden haft of a long knife protruding on his left side. Decoud nerved himself for the effort of rowing. Certainly there was not enough wind to blow the candle out, but its flame swayed a little to the slow movement of the heavy boat. It was so big that with their utmost efforts they could not move it quicker than about a mile an hour. This was sufficient, however, to sweep them amongst the Isabels long before daylight came. There was a good six hours of darkness before them, and the distance from the harbour to the Great Isabel did not exceed two miles. Decoud put this heavy toil to the account of the Capataz's impatience. Sometimes they paused, and then strained their ears to hear the boat from Esmeralda. In this perfect quietness a steamer moving would have been heard from far off. As to seeing anything it was out of the question. They could not see each other. Even the lighter's sail, which remained set, was invisible. Very often they rested.

"*Caramba!*" said Nostromo, suddenly, during one of those intervals when they lolled idly against the heavy handles of the sweeps. "What is it? Are you distressed, Don Martin?"

Decoud assured him that he was not distressed in the least. Nostromo for a time kept perfectly still, and then in a whisper invited Martin to come aft.

With lips touching Decoud's ear he declared his belief that there was somebody else besides themselves upon the lighter. Twice now he had heard the sound of stifled sobbing.

"*Señor,*" he whispered with awed wonder, "I am certain that there is somebody weeping in this lighter."

Decoud had heard nothing. He expressed his incredulity. However, it was easy to ascertain the truth of the matter.

"It is most amazing," muttered Nostromo. "Could anybody have concealed himself on board while the lighter was lying alongside the wharf?"

"And you say it was like sobbing?" asked Decoud, lowering his voice, too. "If he is weeping, whoever he is he cannot be very dangerous."

Clambering over the precious pile in the middle, they crouched low on the foreside of the mast and groped under the half-deck. Right forward, in the narrowest part, their hands came upon the limbs of a man, who remained as silent as death. Too startled themselves to make a sound, they dragged him aft by one arm and the collar of his coat. He was limp—lifeless.

The light of the bit of candle fell upon a round, hook-nosed face with black moustaches and little sidewhiskers. He was extremely dirty. A greasy growth of beard was sprouting on the shaven parts of the cheeks. The thick lips were slightly parted, but the eyes remained closed. Decoud, to his immense astonishment, recognized Señor Hirsch, the hide merchant from Esmeralda. Nostromo, too, had recognized him. And they gazed at each other across the body, lying with its naked feet higher than its head, in an absurd pretense of sleep, faintness, or death.

CHAPTER 8

FOR A MOMENT, BEFORE this extraordinary find, they forgot their own concerns and sensations. Señor Hirsch's sensations as he lay there must have been those of extreme terror. For a long time he refused to give a sign of life, till at last Decoud's objurgations,* and, perhaps more, Nostromo's impatient suggestion that he should be thrown overboard, as he seemed to be dead, induced him to raise one eyelid first, and then the other.

It appeared that he had never found a safe opportunity to leave Sulaco. He lodged with Anzani, the universal storekeeper, on the Plaza Mayor. But when the riot broke out he had made his escape from his host's house before daylight, and in such a hurry that he had forgotten to put on his shoes. He had run out impulsively in his socks, and with his hat in his hand, into the garden of Anzani's house. Fear gave him the necessary agility to climb over several low walls, and afterwards he blundered into the overgrown cloisters of the ruined Franciscan convent in one of the by-streets. He forced himself into the midst of matted bushes with the recklessness of desperation, and this accounted for his scratched body and his torn clothing. He lay hidden there all day, his tongue cleaving to the roof of his mouth with all the intensity of thirst engendered by heat and fear. Three times different bands of men invaded the place with shouts and imprecations, looking for Father Corbelán; but

---

*Scoldings, denouncements.

towards the evening, still lying on his face in the bushes, he thought he would die from the fear of silence. He was not very clear as to what had induced him to leave the place, but evidently he had got out and slunk successfully out of town along the deserted back lanes. He wandered in the darkness near the railway, so maddened by apprehension that he dared not even approach the fires of the pickets of Italian workmen guarding the line. He had a vague idea evidently of finding refuge in the railway yards, but the dogs rushed upon him, barking; men began to shout; a shot was fired at random. He fled away from the gates. By the merest accident, as it happened, he took the direction of the O.S.N. Company's offices. Twice he stumbled upon the bodies of men killed during the day. But everything living frightened him much more. He crouched, crept, crawled, made dashes, guided by a sort of animal instinct, keeping away from every light and from every sound of voices. His idea was to throw himself at the feet of Captain Mitchell and beg for shelter in the Company's offices. It was all dark there as he approached on his hands and knees, but suddenly someone on guard challenged loudly, *"Quién vive?"** There were more dead men lying about, and he flattened himself down at once by the side of a cold corpse. He heard a voice saying, "Here is one of those wounded rascals crawling about. Shall I go and finish him?" And another voice objected that it was not safe to go out without a lantern upon such an errand; perhaps it was only some Negro liberal looking for a chance to stick a knife into the stomach of an honest man. Hirsch didn't stay to hear any more, but crawling away to the end of the wharf, hid himself amongst a lot of empty casks. After a while some people came along, talking, and with glowing cigarettes. He did not stop to ask himself whether they would be likely to do him any harm, but bolted incontinently along the jetty, saw a lighter lying moored at the end, and threw himself into it. In his desire to find cover he crept right forward under the half-deck, and he had remained there more dead than alive, suffering agonies of hunger and thirst, and almost fainting with terror, when he heard numerous footsteps and the voices of the Europeans who came in a body escorting the

---

*Who goes there?

wagon-load of treasure, pushed along the rails by a squad of *car-gadores*. He understood perfectly what was being done from the talk, but did not disclose his presence from the fear that he would not be allowed to remain. His only idea at the time, overpowering and masterful, was to get away from this terrible Sulaco. And now he regretted it very much. He had heard Nostromo talk to Decoud, and wished himself back on shore. He did not desire to be involved in any desperate affair—in a situation where one could not run away. The involuntary groans of his anguished spirit had betrayed him to the sharp ears of the Capataz.

They had propped him up in a sitting posture against the side of the lighter, and he went on with the moaning account of his adventures till his voice broke, and his head fell forward. "Water," he whispered, with difficulty. Decoud held one of the cans to his lips. He revived after an extraordinarily short time, and scrambled up to his feet wildly. Nostromo, in an angry and threatening voice, ordered him forward. Hirsch was one of those men whom fear lashed like a whip, and he must have had an appalling idea of the Capataz's ferocity. He displayed an extraordinary agility in disappearing forward into the darkness. They heard him getting over the tarpaulin; then there was the sound of a heavy fall, followed by a weary sigh. Afterwards all was still in the fore-part of the lighter, as though he had killed himself in his headlong tumble. Nostromo shouted in a menacing voice:

"Lie still there! Do not move a limb. If I hear as much as a loud breath from you I shall come over there and put a bullet through your head."

The mere presence of a coward, however passive, brings an element of treachery into a dangerous situation. Nostromo's nervous impatience passed into gloomy thoughtfulness. Decoud, in an undertone, as if speaking to himself, remarked that, after all, this bizarre event made no great difference. He could not conceive what harm the man could do. At most he would be in the way, like an inanimate and useless object—like a block of wood, for instance.

"I would think twice before getting rid of a piece of wood," said Nostromo, calmly. "Something may happen unexpectedly where you could make use of it. But in an affair like ours a man like this ought to be thrown overboard. Even if he were as brave as a lion we would not want him here. We are not running away for our lives. *Señor*, there is no harm in a brave man trying to save himself with ingenuity and courage; but you have heard his tale, Don Martin. His being here is a miracle of fear—" Nostromo paused. "There is no room for fear in this lighter," he added through his teeth.

Decoud had no answer to make. It was not a position for argument, for a display of scruples or feelings. There were a thousand ways in which a panic-stricken man could make himself dangerous. It was evident that Hirsch could not be spoken to, reasoned with, or persuaded into a rational line of conduct. The story of his own escape demonstrated that clearly enough. Decoud thought that it was a thousand pities the wretch had not died of fright. Nature, who had made him what he was, seemed to have calculated cruelly how much he could bear in the way of atrocious anguish without actually expiring. Some compassion was due to so much terror. Decoud, though imaginative enough for sympathy, resolved not to interfere with any action that Nostromo would take. But Nostromo did nothing. And the fate of Señor Hirsch remained suspended in the darkness of the gulf at the mercy of events which could not be foreseen.

The Capataz, extending his hand, put out the candle suddenly. It was to Decoud as if his companion had destroyed, by a single touch, the world of affairs, of loves, of revolution, where his complacent superiority analyzed fearlessly all motives and all passions, including his own.

He gasped a little. Decoud was affected by the novelty of his position. Intellectually self-confident, he suffered from being deprived of the only weapon he could use with effect. No intelligence could penetrate the darkness of the Placid Gulf. There remained only one thing he was certain of, and that was the overweening vanity of his companion. It was direct, uncomplicated, naïve, and effectual. Decoud, who had been making use of him, had tried to understand his man thoroughly. He had discovered a complete singleness of motive behind the varied manifestations of a consistent character. This was why the man remained so astonishingly simple in the jealous greatness of his conceit. And now there was a complication. It was evident that he resented having been given a task in which there were so many chances of failure. "I wonder," thought De-coud, "how he would behave if I were not here."

He heard Nostromo mutter again, "No! there is no room for fear on this lighter. Courage itself does not seem good enough. I have a good eye and a steady hand; no man can say he ever saw me tired or uncertain what to do; but *por Dios*,* Don Martin, I have been sent out into this black calm on a business where neither a good eye, nor a steady hand, nor judgement are any use. . . ." He swore a string of oaths in Spanish and Italian under his breath. "Nothing but sheer desperation will do for this affair."

These words were in strange contrast to the prevailing peace—to this almost stolid stillness of the gulf. A shower fell with an abrupt whispering sound all round the boat, and Decoud took off his hat, and, letting his head get wet, felt greatly refreshed. Presently a steady little draught of air caressed his cheek. The lighter began to move, but the shower distanced it. The drops ceased to fall upon his head and hands, the whispering died out in the distance. Nostromo emitted a grunt of satisfaction, and grasping the tiller, chirruped softly, as sailors do, to encourage the wind. Never for the last three days had Decoud felt less the need for what the Capataz would call desperation.

"I fancy I hear another shower on the water," he observed in a tone of quiet content. "I hope it will catch us up."

Nostromo ceased chirruping at once. "You hear another shower?" he said, doubtfully. A sort of thinning of the darkness seemed to have taken place, and Decoud could see now the outline of his companion's figure, and even the sail came out of the night like a square block of dense snow.

The sound which Decoud had detected came along the water harshly. Nostromo recognized that noise partaking of a hiss and a rustle which spreads out on all sides of a steamer making her way through a smooth water on a quiet night. It could be nothing else but the captured transport with troops from Esmeralda. She carried no lights. The noise of her steaming, growing louder every minute,

---

*For heaven's sake.

would stop at times altogether, and then begin again abruptly, and sound startlingly nearer, as if that invisible vessel, whose position could not be precisely guessed, were making straight for the lighter. Meantime, that last kept on sailing slowly and noiselessly before a breeze so faint that it was only by leaning over the side and feeling the water slip through his fingers that Decoud convinced himself they were moving at all. His drowsy feeling had departed. He was glad to know that the lighter was moving. After so much stillness the noise of the steamer seemed uproarious and distracting. There was a weirdness in not being able to see her. Suddenly all was still. She had stopped, but so close to them that the steam, blowing off, sent its rumbling vibration right over their heads.

"They are trying to make out where they are," said Decoud in a whisper. Again he leaned over and put his fingers into the water. "We are moving quite smartly," he informed Nostromo.

"We seem to be crossing her bows," said the Capataz in a cautious tone. "But this is a blind game with death. Moving on is of no use. We mustn't be seen or heard."

His whisper was hoarse with excitement. Of all his face there was nothing visible but a gleam of white eyeballs. His fingers gripped Decoud's shoulder. "That is the only way to save the treasure from this steamer full of soldiers. Any other would have carried lights. But you observe there is not a gleam to show us where she is."

Decoud stood as if paralysed; only his thoughts were wildly active. In the space of a second he remembered the desolate glance of Antonia as he left her at the bedside of her father in the gloomy house of Avellanos, with shuttered windows, but all the doors standing open, and deserted by all the servants except an old Negro at the gate. He remembered the Casa Gould on his last visit, the arguments, the tones of his voice, the impenetrable attitude of Charles, Mrs. Gould's face so blanched with anxiety and fatigue that her eyes seemed to have changed colour, appearing nearly black by contrast. Even whole sentences of the proclamation which he meant to make Barrios issue from his headquarters at Cayta as soon as he got there passed through his mind; the very germ of the new State, the Separatist proclamation which he had tried before he left to read hurriedly to Don José, stretched out on his bed under the fixed gaze of his daughter. God knows whether the old statesman had understood it; he was unable to speak, but he had certainly lifted his arm off the coverlet; his hand had moved as if to make the sign of the cross in the air, a gesture of blessing, of consent. Decoud had that very draught in his pocket, written in pencil on several loose sheets of paper, with the heavily printed heading, "Administration of the San Tomé Silver Mine. Sulaco. Republic of Costaguana." He had written it furiously, snatching page after page on Charles Gould's table. Mrs. Gould had looked several times over his shoulder as he wrote; but the Señor Administrador, standing straddle-legged, would not even glance at it when it was finished. He had waved it away firmly. It must have been scorn, and not caution, since he never made a remark about the use of the Administration's paper for such a compromising document. And that showed his disdain, the true English disdain of common prudence, as if everything outside the range of their own thoughts and feelings were unworthy of serious recognition. Decoud had the time in a second or two to become furiously angry with Charles Gould, and even resentful against Mrs. Gould, in whose care, tacitly it is true, he had left the safety of Antonia. Better perish a thousand times than owe your preservation to such people, he exclaimed mentally. The grip of Nostromo's fingers never removed from his shoulder, tightening fiercely, recalled him to himself.

"The darkness is our friend," the Capataz murmured into his ear. "I am going to lower the sail, and trust our escape to this black gulf. No eyes could make us out lying silent with a naked mast. I will do it now, before this steamer closes still more upon us. The faint creak of a block would betray us and the San Tomé treasure into the hands of those thieves."

He moved about as warily as a cat. Decoud heard no sound; and it was only by the disappearance of the square blotch of darkness that he knew the yard had come down, lowered as carefully as if it had been made of glass. Next moment he heard Nostromo's quiet breathing by his side.

"You had better not move at all from where you are, Don Martin," advised the Capataz, earnestly. "You might stumble or displace something which would make a noise. The sweeps and the punting poles are lying about. Move not for your life. *Por Dios*, Don Martin," he went on in a keen but friendly whisper, "I am so desperate that if I didn't know your worship to be a man of courage, capable of standing stock still whatever happens, I would drive my knife into your heart."

A deathlike stillness surrounded the lighter. It was difficult to believe that there was near a steamer full of men with many pairs of eyes peering from her bridge for some hint of land in the night. Her steam had ceased blowing off, and she remained stopped too far off apparently for any other sound to reach the lighter.

"Perhaps you would, Capataz," Decoud began in a whisper. "However, you need not trouble. There are other things than the fear of your knife to keep my heart steady. It shall not betray you. Only, have you forgotten—"

"I spoke to you openly as to a man as desperate as myself," explained the Capataz. "The silver must be saved from the Monterists. I told Captain Mitchell three times that I preferred to go alone. I told Don Carlos Gould, too. It was in the Casa Gould. They had sent for me. The ladies were there; and when I tried to explain why I did not wish to have you with me, they promised me, both of them, great rewards for your safety. A strange way to talk to a man you are sending out to an almost certain death. Those gentlefolk do not seem to have sense enough to understand what they are giving one to do. I told them I could do nothing for you. You would have been safer with the bandit Hernandez. It would have been possible to ride out of the town with no greater risk than a chance shot sent after you in the dark. But it was as if they had been deaf. I had to promise I would wait for you under the harbour gate. I did wait. And now because you are a brave man you are as safe as the silver. Neither more nor less."

At that moment, as if by way of comment upon Nostromo's words, the invisible steamer went ahead at half speed only, as could be judged by the leisurely beat of her propeller. The sound shifted its place markedly, but without coming nearer. It even grew a little more distant right abeam of the lighter, and then ceased again.

"They are trying for a sight of the Isabels," muttered Nostromo, "in order to make for the harbour in a straight line and seize the Custom House with the treasure in it. Have you ever seen the Commandant of Esmeralda, Sotillo? A handsome fellow, with a soft voice. When I first came here I used to see him in the Calle talking to the *señoritas* at the windows of the houses, and showing his white teeth all the time. But one of my *cargadores*, who had been a soldier, told me that he had once ordered a man to be flayed alive in the remote Campo, where he was sent recruiting amongst the people of the *estancias*. It has never entered his head that the *compañía* had a man capable of baffling his game."

The murmuring loquacity of the Capataz disturbed Decoud like a hint of weakness. And yet, talkative resolution may be as genuine as grim silence.

"Sotillo is not baffled so far," he said. "Have you forgotten that crazy man forward?"

Nostromo had not forgotten Señor Hirsch. He reproached himself bitterly for not having visited the lighter carefully before leaving the wharf. He reproached himself for not having stabbed and flung Hirsch overboard at the very moment of discovery without even looking at his face. That would have been consistent with the desperate character of the affair. Whatever happened, Sotillo *was* already baffled. Even if that wretch, now as silent as death, did anything to betray the nearness of the lighter, Sotillo—if Sotillo it was in command of the troops on board—would be still baffled of his plunder.

"I have an axe in my hand," Nostromo whispered, wrathfully, "that in three strokes would cut through the side down to the water's edge. Moreover, each lighter has a plug in the stern, and I know exactly where it is. I feel it under the sole of my foot."

Decoud recognized the ring of genuine determination in the nervous murmurs, the vindictive excitement of the famous Capataz. Before the steamer, guided by a shriek or two (for there could be no more than that, Nostromo said, gnashing his teeth audibly), could find the lighter there would be plenty of time to sink this treasure tied up round his neck.

The last words he hissed into Decoud's ear. Decoud said nothing. He was perfectly convinced. The usual characteristic quietness of the man was gone. It was not equal to the situation as he conceived it. Something deeper, something unsuspected by everyone, had come to the surface. Decoud, with careful movements, slipped off his overcoat and divested himself of his boots; he did not consider himself bound in honour to sink with the treasure. His object was to get down to Barrios, in Cayta, as the Capataz knew very well; and he, too, meant, in his own way, to put into that attempt all the desperation of which he was capable. Nostromo muttered, "True, true! You are a politician, *señor*. Rejoin the army, and start another revolution." He pointed out, however, that there was a little boat belonging to every lighter fit to carry two men, if not more. Theirs was towing behind.

Of that Decoud had not been aware. Of course, it was too dark to see, and it was only when Nostromo put his hand upon its painter* fastened to a cleat in the stern that he experienced a full measure of relief. The prospect of finding himself in the water and swimming, overwhelmed by ignorance and darkness, probably in a circle, till he sank from exhaustion, was revolting. The barren and cruel futility of such an end intimidated his affectation of careless pessimism. In comparison to it, the chance of being left floating in a boat, exposed to thirst, hunger, discovery, imprisonment, execution, presented itself with an aspect of amenity worth securing even at the cost of some set self-contempt. He did not accept Nostromo's proposal that he should get into the boat at once. "Something sudden may overwhelm us, *señor*," the Capataz remarked promising faithfully, at the same time, to let go the painter at the moment when the necessity became manifest.

But Decoud assured him lightly that he did not mean to take to the boat till the very last moment, and that then he meant the Capataz to come along, too. The darkness of the gulf was no longer for him the end of all things. It was part of a living world since, pervading it, failure and death could be felt at your elbow. And at the same time it was a shelter. He exulted in its impenetrable obscurity. "Like a wall, like a wall," he muttered to himself.

The only thing which checked his confidence was the thought of Señor Hirsch. Not to have bound and gagged him seemed to Decoud now the height of improvident folly. As long as the miserable creature had the power to raise a yell he was a constant danger. His abject terror was mute now, but there was no saying from what cause it might suddenly find vent in shrieks.

This very madness of fear which both Decoud and Nostromo had seen in the wild and irrational glances, and in the continuous

---

*Line used to secure or tow a boat.

twitchings of his mouth, protected Señor Hirsch from the cruel necessities of this desperate affair. The moment of silencing him for
ever had passed. As Nostromo remarked, in answer to Decoud's regrets, it was too late! It could not be done without noise, especially
in the ignorance of the man's exact position. Wherever he had
elected to crouch and tremble, it was too hazardous to go near him.
He would begin probably to yell for mercy. It was much better to
leave him quite alone since he was keeping so still. But to trust to
his silence became every moment a greater strain upon Decoud's
composure.

"I wish, Capataz, you had not let the right moment pass," he
murmured.

"What! To silence him for ever! I thought it good to hear first
how he came to be here. It was too strange. Who could imagine
that it was all an accident? Afterwards, *señor*, when I saw you giving
him water to drink, I could not do it. Not after I had seen you holding up the can to his lips as though he were your brother. *Señor*,
that sort of necessity must not be thought of too long. And yet it
would have been no cruelty to take away from him his wretched
life. It is nothing but fear. Your compassion saved him then, Don
Martin, and now it is too late. It couldn't be done without noise."

In the steamer they were keeping a perfect silence, and the stillness was so profound that Decoud felt as if the slightest sound conceivable must travel unchecked and audible to the end of the world.
What if Hirsch coughed or sneezed? To feel himself at the mercy of
such an idiotic contingency was too exasperating to be looked upon
with irony. Nostromo, too, seemed to be getting restless. Was it possible, he asked himself, that the steamer, finding the night too dark
altogether, intended to remain stopped where she was till daylight?
He began to think that this, after all, was the real danger. He was
afraid that the darkness, which was his protection, would, in the
end, cause his undoing.

Sotillo, as Nostromo had surmised, was in command on board
the transport. The events of the last forty-eight hours in Sulaco
were not known to him; neither was he aware that the telegraphist
in Esmeralda had managed to warn his colleague in Sulaco. Like
a good many officers of the troops garrisoning the province,
Sotillo had been influenced in his adoption of the Ribierist cause

by the belief that it had the enormous wealth of the Gould Concession on its side. He had been one of the frequenters of the Casa Gould, where he had aired his Blanco convictions and his ardour for reform before Don José Avellanos, casting frank, honest glances towards Mrs. Gould and Antonia the while. He was known to belong to a good family persecuted and impoverished during the tyranny of Guzman Bento. The opinions he expressed appeared eminently natural and proper in a man of his parentage and antecedents. And he was not a deceiver; it was perfectly natural for him to express elevated sentiments while his whole faculties were taken up with what seemed then a solid and practical notion—the notion that the husband of Antonia Avellanos would be, naturally, the intimate friend of the Gould Concession. He even pointed this out to Anzani once, when negotiating the sixth or seventh small loan in the gloomy, damp apartment with enormous iron bars, behind the principal shop in the whole row under the Arcades. He hinted to the universal shopkeeper at the excellent terms he was on with the emancipated *señorita*, who was like a sister to the Englishwoman. He would advance one leg and put his arms akimbo, posing for Anzani's inspection, and fixing him with a haughty stare.

"Look, miserable shopkeeper! How can a man like me fail with any woman, let alone an emancipated girl living in scandalous freedom?" he seemed to say.

His manner in the Casa Gould was, of course, very different—devoid of all truculence, and even slightly mournful. Like most of his countrymen, he was carried away by the sound of fine words, especially if uttered by himself. He had no convictions of any sort upon anything except as to the irresistible power of his personal advantages. But that was so firm that even Decoud's appearance in Sulaco, and his intimacy with the Goulds and the Avellanos, did not disquiet him. On the contrary, he tried to make friends with that rich Costaguanero from Europe in the hope of borrowing a large sum by-and-by. The only guiding motive of his life was to get money for the satisfaction of his expensive tastes, which he indulged recklessly, having no self-control. He imagined himself a master of intrigue, but his corruption was as simple as an animal instinct. At times, in solitude, he had his moments of ferocity, and also on such occasions as, for instance, when alone in a room with Anzani trying to get a loan.

He had talked himself into the command of the Esmeralda garrison. That small seaport had its importance as the station of the main submarine cable connecting the Occidental Provinces with the outer world, and the junction with it of the Sulaco branch. Don José Avellanos proposed him, and Barrios, with a rude and jeering guffaw, had said, "Oh, let Sotillo go. He is a very good man to keep guard over the cable, and the ladies of Esmeralda ought to have their turn." Barrios, an indubitably brave man, had no great opinion of Sotillo.

It was through the Esmeralda cable alone that the San Tomé mine could be kept in constant touch with the great financier, whose tacit approval made the strength of the Ribierist movement. This movement had its adversaries even there. Sotillo governed Esmeralda with repressive severity till the adverse course of events upon the distant theatre of civil war forced upon him the reflection that, after all, the great silver mine was fated to become the spoil of the victors. But caution was necessary. He began by assuming a dark and mysterious attitude towards the faithful Ribierist municipality of Esmeralda. Later on, the information that the commandant was holding assemblies of officers in the dead of night (which had leaked out somehow) caused those gentlemen to neglect their civil duties altogether, and remain shut up in their houses. Suddenly one day all the letters from Sulaco by the overland courier were carried off by a file of soldiers from the post office to the Comandancia, without disguise, concealment, or apology. Sotillo had heard through Cayta of the final defeat of Ribiera.

This was the first open sign of the change in his convictions. Presently notorious democrats, who had been living till then in constant fear of arrest, leg irons, and even floggings, could be observed going in and out at the great door of the Comandancia, where the horses of the orderlies doze under their heavy saddles, while the men, in ragged uniforms and pointed straw hats, lounge on a bench, with their naked feet stuck out beyond the strip of shade; and a sentry, in a red baize coat with holes at the elbows, stands at the top of the steps glaring haughtily at the common people, who uncover their heads to him as they pass.

Sotillo's ideas did not soar above the care for his personal safety and the chance of plundering the town in his charge, but he feared that such a late adhesion would earn but scant gratitude from the victors. He had believed just a little too long in the power of the San Tomé mine. The seized correspondence had confirmed his previous information of a large amount of silver ingots lying in the Sulaco Custom House. To gain possession of it would be a clear Monterist move; a sort of service that would have to be rewarded. With the silver in his hands he could make terms for himself and his soldiers. He was aware neither of the riots, nor of the President's escape to Sulaco and the close pursuit led by Montero's brother, the *guerrillero*. The game seemed in his own hands. The initial moves were the seizure of the cable telegraph office and the securing of the Government steamer lying in the narrow creek which is the harbour of Esmeralda. The last was effected without difficulty by a company of soldiers swarming with a rush over the gangways as she lay alongside the quay; but the lieutenant charged with the duty of arresting the telegraphist halted on the way before the only café in Esmeralda, where he distributed some brandy to his men, and refreshed himself at the expense of the owner, a known Ribierist. The whole party became intoxicated, and proceeded on their mission up the street yelling and firing random shots at the windows. This little festivity, which might have turned out dangerous to the telegraphist's life, enabled him in the end to send his warning to Sulaco. The lieutenant, staggering upstairs with a drawn sabre, was before long kissing him on both cheeks in one of those swift changes of mood peculiar to a state of drunkenness. He clasped the telegraphist close round the neck, assuring him that all the officers of the Esmeralda garrison were going to be made colonels, while tears of happiness streamed down his sodden face. Thus it came about that the town major, coming along later, found the whole party sleeping on the stairs and in passages, and the telegraphist (who scorned this chance of escape) very busy clicking the key of the transmitter. The major led him away bareheaded, with his hands tied behind his back, but concealed the truth from Sotillo, who remained in ignorance of the warning dispatched to Sulaco.

The colonel was not the man to let any sort of darkness stand in the way of the planned surprise. It appeared to him a dead certainty;

his heart was set upon his object with an ungovernable, childlike impatience. Ever since the steamer had rounded Punta Mala, to enter the deeper shadow of the gulf, he had remained on the bridge in a group of officers as excited as himself. Distracted between the coaxings and menaces of Sotillo and his Staff, the miserable commander of the steamer kept her moving with as much prudence as they would let him exercise. Some of them had been drinking heavily, no doubt; but the prospect of laying hands on so much wealth made them absurdly foolhardy, and, at the same time, extremely anxious. The old major of the battalion, a stupid, suspicious man, who had never been afloat in his life, distinguished himself by putting out suddenly the binnacle light,* the only one allowed on board for the necessities of navigation. He could not understand of what use it could be for finding the way. To the vehement protestations of the ship's captain, he stamped his foot and tapped the handle of his sword. "Aha! I have unmasked you," he cried, triumphantly. "You are tearing your hair from despair at my acuteness. Am I a child to believe that a light in that brass box can show you where the harbour is? I am an old soldier, I am. I can smell a traitor a league off. You wanted the gleam to betray our approach to your friend the Englishman. A thing like that show you the way! What a miserable lie! *Que picardía!*† You Sulaco people are all in the pay of those foreigners. You deserve to be run through the body with my sword." Other officers, crowding round, tried to calm his indignation, repeating persuasively, "No, no! This is an appliance of the mariners, major. This is no treachery." The captain of the transport flung himself face downwards on the bridge, and refused to rise. "Put an end to me at once," he repeated in a stifled voice. Sotillo had to interfere.

The uproar and confusion on the bridge became so great that the helmsman fled from the wheel. He took refuge in the engine-room, and alarmed the engineers, who, disregarding the threats of the soldiers set on guard over them, stopped the engines, protesting that they would rather be shot than run the risk of being drowned down below.

---

*Boxed light that illuminates the compass.
†What trickery!

This was the first time Nostromo and Decoud heard the steamer stop. After order had been restored, and the binnacle lamp re-lighted, she went ahead again, passing wide of the lighter in her search for the Isabels. The group could not be made out, and, at the pitiful entreaties of the captain, Sotillo allowed the engines to be stopped again to wait for one of those periodical lightenings of darkness caused by the shifting of the cloud canopy spread above the waters of the gulf.

Sotillo, on the bridge, muttered from time to time angrily to the captain. The other, in an apologetic and cringing tone, begged *su merced** the colonel to take into consideration the limitations put upon human faculties by the darkness of the night. Sotillo swelled with rage and impatience. It was the chance of a lifetime.

"If your eyes are of no more use to you than this, I shall have them put out," he burst out.

The captain of the steamer made no answer, for just then the mass of the Great Isabel loomed up darkly after a passing shower, then vanished, as if swept away by a wave of greater obscurity pre-ceding another downpour. This was enough for him. In the voice of a man come back to life again, he informed Sotillo that in an hour he would be alongside the Sulaco wharf. The ship was put then full speed on the course, and a great bustle of preparation for landing arose among the soldiers on her deck.

It was heard distinctly by Decoud and Nostromo. The Capataz understood its meaning. They had made out the Isabels, and were going on now in a straight line for Sulaco. He judged that they would pass close; but believed that lying still like this, with the sail lowered, the lighter could not be seen. "No, not even if they rubbed sides with us," he muttered.

The rain began to fall again; first like a wet mist, then with a heav-ier touch, thickening into a smart, perpendicular downpour; and the hiss and thump of the approaching steamer was coming extremely near. Decoud, with his eyes full of water, and lowered head, asked himself how long it would be before she drew past, when unexpect-edly he felt a lurch. An inrush of foam broke swishing over the stern,

---

*Your grace.

simultaneously with a crack of timbers and a staggering shock. He had the impression of an angry hand laying hold of the lighter and dragging it along to destruction. The shock, of course, had knocked him down, and he found himself rolling in a lot of water at the bottom of the lighter. A violent churning went on alongside; a strange and amazed voice cried out something above him in the night. He heard a piercing shriek for help from Señor Hirsch. He kept his teeth hard set all the time. It was a collision!

The steamer had struck the lighter obliquely, heeling her over till she was half swamped, starting some of her timbers, and swinging her head parallel to her own course with the force of the blow. The shock of it on board of her was hardly perceptible. All the violence of that collision was, as usual, felt only on board the smaller craft. Even Nostromo himself thought that this was perhaps the end of his desperate adventure. He, too, had been flung away from the long tiller, which took charge of the lurch. Next moment the steamer would have passed on, leaving the lighter to sink or swim after having shouldered her thus out of her way, and without ever getting a glimpse of her form, had it not been that, being deeply laden with stores and the great number of people on board, her anchor was low enough to hook itself into one of the wire shrouds of the lighter's mast. For the space of two or three gasping breaths that new rope held against the sudden strain. It was this that gave Decoud the sensation of the snatching pull, dragging the lighter away to destruction. The cause of it, of course, was inexplicable to him. The whole thing was so sudden that he had no time to think. But all his sensations were perfectly clear; he had kept complete possession of himself; in fact, he was even pleasantly aware of that calmness at the very moment of being pitched head first over the transom, to struggle on his back in a lot of water. Señor Hirsch's shriek he had heard and recognized while he was regaining his feet, always with that mysterious sensation of being dragged headlong through the darkness. Not a word, not a cry escaped him; he had no time to see anything; and following upon the despairing screams for help, the dragging motion ceased so suddenly that he staggered forward with open arms and fell against the pile of the treasure boxes. He clung to them instinctively, in the vague apprehension of being flung about again; and immediately he heard another lot of shrieks for help, prolonged and despairing, not near him at all, but unaccountably in the distance, away from the lighter altogether, as if some spirit in the night were mocking at Señor Hirsch's terror and despair.

Then all was still—as still as when you wake up in your bed in a dark room from a bizarre and agitated dream. The lighter rocked slightly; the rain was still falling. Two groping hands took hold of his bruised sides from behind, and the Capataz's voice whispered, in his ear, "Silence, for your life! Silence! The steamer has stopped."

Decoud listened. The gulf was dumb. He felt the water nearly up to his knees. "Are we sinking?" he asked in a faint breath.

"I don't know," Nostromo breathed back to him. "*Señor*, make not the slightest sound."

Hirsch, when ordered forward by Nostromo, had not returned into his first hiding-place. He had fallen near the mast, and had no strength to rise; moreover, he feared to move. He had given himself up for dead, but not on any rational grounds. It was simply a cruel and terrifying feeling. Whenever he tried to think what would become of him his teeth would start chattering violently. He was too absorbed in the utter misery of his fear to take notice of anything.

Though he was stifling under the lighter's sail which Nostromo had unwittingly lowered on top of him, he did not even dare to put out his head till the very moment of the steamer striking. Then, indeed, he leaped right out, spurred on to new miracles of bodily vigour by this new shape of danger. The inrush of water when the lighter heeled over unsealed his lips. His shriek, "Save me!" was the first distinct warning of the collision for the people on board the steamer. Next moment the wire shroud parted, and the released anchor swept over the lighter's forecastle. It came against the breast of Señor Hirsch, who simply seized hold of it, without in the least knowing what it was, but curling his arms and legs upon the part above the fluke with an invincible, unreasonable tenacity. The lighter yawed off wide, and the steamer, moving on, carried him away, clinging hard, and shouting for help. It was some time, however, after the steamer had stopped that his position was discovered. His sustained yelping for help seemed to come from somebody swimming in the water. At last a couple of men went over the bows and hauled him on board. He was carried straight off to Sotillo on the bridge. His examination confirmed the impression that some craft had been run over and sunk, but it was impracticable on such a dark night to look for the positive proof of floating wreckage. Sotillo was more anxious than ever now to enter the harbour without loss of time; the idea that he had destroyed the principal object of his expedition was too intolerable to be accepted. This feeling made the story he had heard appear the more incredible. Señor Hirsch, after being beaten a little for telling lies, was thrust into the chartroom. But he was beaten only a little. His tale had taken the heart out of Sotillo's Staff, though they all repeated round their chief, "Impossible! impossible!" with the exception of the old major, who triumphed gloomily.

"I told you; I told you," he mumbled. "I could smell some treachery, some *diablería* a league off."

Meantime, the steamer had kept on her way towards Sulaco, where only the truth of that matter could be ascertained. Decoud and Nostromo heard the loud churning of her propeller diminish and die out; and then, with no useless words, busied themselves in making for the Isabels. The last shower had brought with it a gentle but steady breeze. The danger was not over yet, and there was no time for talk. The lighter was leaking like a sieve. They splashed in the water at every step. The Capataz put into Decoud's hands the handle of the pump which was fitted at the side aft, and at once, without question or remark, Decoud began to pump in utter forgetfulness of every desire but that of keeping the treasure afloat. Nostromo hoisted the sail, flew back to the tiller, pulled at the sheet like mad. The short flare of a match (they had been kept dry in a tight tin box, though the man himself was completely wet), the vivid flare of a match, disclosed to the toiling Decoud the eagerness of his face, bent low over the box of the compass, and the attentive stare of his eyes. He knew now where he was, and he hoped to run the sinking lighter ashore in the shallow cove where the high, cliff-like end of the Great Isabel is divided in two equal parts by a deep and overgrown ravine.

Decoud pumped without intermission. Nostromo steered without relaxing for a second the intense, peering effort of his stare. Each of them was as if utterly alone with his task. It did not occur to them to speak. There was nothing in common between them but the knowledge that the damaged lighter must be slowly but surely sinking. In that knowledge, which was like the crucial test of their desires, they seemed to have become completely estranged, as if they had discovered in the very shock of the collision that the loss of the lighter would not mean the same thing to them both. This common danger brought their differences in aim, in view, in character, and in position, into absolute prominence in the private vision of each. There was no bond of conviction, of common idea; they were merely two adventurers pursuing each his own adventure, involved in the same imminence of deadly peril. Therefore they had nothing to say to each other. But this peril, this only incontrovertible truth in which they shared, seemed to act as an inspiration to their mental and bodily powers.

There was certainly something almost miraculous in the way the Capataz made the cove with nothing but the shadowy hint of the island's shape and the vague gleam of a small sandy strip for a guide. Where the ravine opens between the cliffs, and a slender, shallow rivulet meanders out of the bushes to lose itself in the sea, the lighter was run ashore; and the two men, with a taciturn, undaunted energy, began to discharge her precious freight, carrying each ox-hide box up the bed of the rivulet beyond the bushes to a hollow place which the caving in of the soil had made below the roots of a large tree. Its big smooth trunk leaned like a falling column far over the trickle of water running amongst the loose stones.

A couple of years before Nostromo had spent a whole Sunday, all alone, exploring the island. He explained this to Decoud after their task was done, and they sat, weary in every limb, with their legs hanging down the low bank, and their backs against the tree, like a pair of blind men aware of each other and their surroundings by some indefinable sixth sense.

"Yes," Nostromo repeated, "I never forget a place I have carefully looked at once." He spoke slowly, almost lazily, as if there had been a whole leisurely life before him, instead of the scanty two hours before daylight. The existence of the treasure, barely concealed in this improbable spot, laid a burden of secrecy upon every contemplated step, upon every intention and plan of future conduct. He felt the partial failure of this desperate affair entrusted to the great reputation he had known how to make for himself. However, it was also a partial success. His vanity was half appeased. His nervous irritation had subsided.

"You never know what may be of use," he pursued with his usual quietness of tone and manner. "I spent a whole miserable Sunday in exploring this crumb of land."

"A misanthropic sort of occupation," muttered Decoud, viciously. "You had no money, I suppose, to gamble with, and to fling about amongst the girls in your usual haunts, Capataz."

"*È vero!*"* exclaimed the Capataz, surprised into the use of his native tongue by so much perspicacity. "I had not! Therefore I did not want to go amongst those beggarly people accustomed to my generosity. It is looked for from the Capataz of the Cargadores, who are the rich men, and, as it were, the *caballeros* amongst the common people. I don't care for cards but as a pastime; and as to those girls that boast of having opened their doors to my knock, you know I wouldn't look at any one of them twice except for what the people would say. They are queer, the good people of Sulaco, and I have got much useful information simply by listening patiently to the talk of the women that everybody believed I was in love with. Poor Teresa could never understand that. On that particular Sunday, *señor*, she scolded so that I went out of the house swearing that I would never darken their door again unless to fetch away my hammock and my chest of clothes. *Señor*, there is nothing more exasperating than to hear a woman you respect rail against your good reputation when you have not a single brass coin in your pocket. I untied one of the small boats and pulled myself out of the harbour with nothing but three cigars in my pocket to help me spend the day on this island. But the water of this rivulet you hear under your feet is cool and sweet and good, *señor*, both before and after a smoke." He was silent for a while, then added reflectively, "That was the first Sunday after I brought the white-whiskered English *rico* all the way down the mountains from the Paramo on the top of the Entrada Pass—and in the coach, too! No coach had gone up or down that mountain road within the memory of man, *señor*, till I brought this one down in charge of fifty peons working like one

---

*It's true (It.).

man with ropes, pick-axes, and poles under my direction. That was the rich Englishman who, as people say, pays for the making of this railway. He was very pleased with me. But my wages were not due till the end of the month."

He slid down the bank suddenly. Decoud heard the splash of his feet in the brook and followed his footsteps down the ravine. His form was lost among the bushes till he had reached the strip of sand under the cliff. As often happens in the gulf when the showers during the first part of the night had been frequent and heavy, the darkness had thinned considerably towards the morning though there were no signs of daylight as yet.

The cargo-lighter, relieved of its precious burden, rocked feebly, half-afloat, with her fore-foot on the sand. A long rope stretched away like a black cotton thread across the strip of white beach to the grapnel* Nostromo had carried ashore and hooked to the stem of a tree-like shrub in the very opening of the ravine.

There was nothing for Decoud but to remain on the island. He received from Nostromo's hands whatever food the foresight of Captain Mitchell had put on board the lighter and deposited it temporarily in the little dinghy which on their arrival they had hauled up out of sight amongst the bushes. It was to be left with him. The island was to be a hiding-place, not a prison; he could pull out to a passing ship. The O.S.N. Company's mail boats passed close to the islands when going into Sulaco from the north. But the *Minerva*, carrying off the ex-president, had taken the news up north of the disturbances in Sulaco. It was possible that the next steamer down would get instructions to miss the port altogether since the town, as far as the *Minerva's* officers knew, was for the time being in the hands of the rabble. This would mean that there would be no steamer for a month, as far as the mail service went; but Decoud had to take his chance of that. The island was his only shelter from the proscription hanging over his head. The Capataz was, of course, going back. The unloaded lighter leaked much less, and he thought that she would keep afloat as far as the harbour.

---

*Small anchor with four or five flukes or claws.

He passed to Decoud, standing knee-deep alongside, one of the two spades which belonged to the equipment of each lighter for use when ballasting ships. By working with it carefully as soon as there was daylight enough to see, Decoud could loosen a mass of earth and stones overhanging the cavity in which they had deposited the treasure, so that it would look as if it had fallen naturally. It would cover up not only the cavity, but even all traces of their work, the footsteps, the displaced stones, and even the broken bushes.

"Besides, who would think of looking either for you or the treasure here?" Nostromo continued, as if he could not tear himself away from the spot. "Nobody is ever likely to come here. What could any man want with this piece of earth as long as there is room for his feet on the mainland! The people in this country are not curious. There are even no fishermen here to intrude upon your worship. All the fishing that is done in the gulf goes on near Zapiga, over there. *Señor*, if you are forced to leave this island before anything can be arranged for you, do not try to make for Zapiga. It is a settlement of thieves and *matreros*, where they would cut your throat promptly for the sake of your gold watch and chain. And, *señor*, think twice before confiding in anyone whatever; even in the officers of the Company's steamers, if you ever get on board one. Honesty alone is not enough for security. You must look to discretion and prudence in a man. And always re-member, *señor*, before you open your lips for a confidence, that this treasure may be left safely here for hundreds of years. Time is on its side, *señor*. And silver is an incorruptible metal that can be trusted to keep its value for ever. . . . An incorruptible metal," he repeated, as if the idea had given him a profound pleasure.

"As some men are said to be," Decoud pronounced, inscrutably, while the Capataz, who busied himself in baling out the lighter with a wooden bucket, went on throwing the water over the side with a regular splash. Decoud, incorrigible in his scepticism, reflected, not cynically, but with general satisfaction, that this man was made incorruptible by his enormous vanity, that finest form of egoism which can take on the aspect of every virtue.

Nostromo ceased baling, and, as if struck with a sudden thought, dropped the bucket with a clatter into the lighter.

"Have you any message?" he asked in a lowered voice. "Remember, I shall be asked questions."

"You must find the hopeful words that ought to be spoken to the people in town. I trust for that your intelligence and your experience, Capataz. You understand?"

"*Sí, señor.* . . . For the ladies."

"Yes, yes," said Decoud, hastily. "Your wonderful reputation will make them attach great value to your words; therefore be careful what you say. I am looking forward," he continued, feeling the fatal touch of contempt for himself to which his complex nature was subject, "I am looking forward to a glorious and successful ending to my mission. Do you hear, Capataz? Use the words glorious and successful when you speak to the *señorita.* Your own mission is accomplished gloriously and successfully. You have indubitably saved the silver of the mine. Not only this silver, but probably all the silver that shall ever come out of it."

Nostromo detected the ironic tone. "I dare say, Señor Don Martin," he said, moodily. "There are very few things that I am not equal to. Ask the foreign *signori.* I, a man of the people, who cannot always understand what you mean. But as to this lot which I must leave here, let me tell you that I would believe it in greater safety if you had not been with me at all."

An exclamation escaped Decoud, and a short pause followed. "Shall I go back with you to Sulaco?" he asked in an angry tone.

"Shall I strike you dead with my knife where you stand?" retorted Nostromo, contemptuously. "It would be the same thing as taking you to Sulaco. Come, *señor.* Your reputation is in your politics, and mine is bound up with the fate of this silver. Do you wonder I wish there had been no other man to share my knowledge? I wanted no one with me, *señor.*"

"You could not have kept the lighter afloat without me," Decoud almost shouted. "You would have gone to the bottom with her."

"Yes," uttered Nostromo, slowly; "alone."

Here was a man, Decoud reflected, that seemed as though he would have preferred to die rather than deface the perfect form of his egoism. Such a man was safe. In silence he helped the Capataz to get the grapnel on board. Nostromo cleared the shelving shore with one push of the heavy oar, and Decoud found himself solitary on the beach like a man in a dream. A sudden desire to hear a human voice once more seized upon his heart. The lighter was hardly distinguishable from the black water upon which she floated.

"What do you think has become of Hirsch?" he shouted.

"Knocked overboard and drowned," cried Nostromo's voice confidently out of the black wastes of sky and sea around the islet. "Keep close in the ravine, *señor*. I shall try to come out to you in a night or two."

A slight swishing rustle showed that Nostromo was setting the sail. It filled all at once with a sound as of a single loud drum-tap. Decoud went back to the ravine. Nostromo, at the tiller, looked back from time to time at the vanishing mass of the Great Isabel, which, little by little, merged into the uniform texture of the night. At last, when he turned his head again, he saw nothing but a smooth darkness, like a solid wall.

Then he, too, experienced that feeling of solitude which had weighed heavily on Decoud after the lighter had slipped off the shore. But while the man on the island was oppressed by a bizarre sense of unreality affecting the very ground upon which he walked, the mind of the Capataz of the Cargadores turned alertly to the problem of future conduct. Nostromo's faculties, working on parallel lines, enabled him to steer straight, to keep a look-out for Hermosa, near which he had to pass, and to try to imagine what would happen tomorrow in Sulaco. Tomorrow, or, as a matter of fact, today, since the dawn was not very far, Sotillo would find out in what way the treasure had gone. A gang of *cargadores* had been employed in loading it into a railway truck from the Custom House store-rooms, and running the truck on to the wharf. There would be arrests made, and certainly before noon Sotillo would know in what manner the silver had left Sulaco, and who it was that took it out.

Nostromo's intention had been to sail right into the harbour; but at this thought by a sudden touch of the tiller he threw the lighter into the wind and checked her rapid way. His reappearance with the very boat would raise suspicions, would cause surmises, would absolutely put Sotillo on the track. He himself would be arrested; and once in the *calabozo** there was no saying what they would do

---

*Dungeon.

to him to make him speak. He trusted himself, but he stood up to look round. Near by, Hermosa showed low its white surface as flat as a table, with the slight run of the sea raised by the breeze washing over its edges noisily. The lighter must be sunk at once.

He allowed her to drift with her sail aback. There was already a good deal of water in her. He allowed her to drift towards the harbour entrance, and, letting the tiller swing about, squatted down and busied himself in loosening the plug. With that out she would fill very quickly, and every lighter carried a little iron ballast— enough to make her go down when full of water. When he stood up again the noisy wash about the Hermosa sounded far away, almost inaudible; and already he could make out the shape of land about the harbour entrance. This was a desperate affair, and he was a good swimmer. A mile was nothing to him, and he knew of an easy place for landing just below the earthworks of the old abandoned fort. It occurred to him with a peculiar fascination that this fort was a good place in which to sleep the day through after so many sleepless nights.

With one blow of the tiller he unshipped for the purpose, he knocked the plug out, but did not take the trouble to lower the sail. He felt the water welling up heavily about his legs before he leaped on to the taffrail.* There, upright and motionless, in his shirt and trousers only, he stood waiting. When he had felt her settle he sprang far away with a mighty splash.

At once he turned his head. The gloomy, clouded dawn from behind the mountains showed him on the smooth waters the upper corner of the sail, a dark wet triangle of canvas waving slightly to and fro. He saw it vanish, as if jerked under, and then struck out for the shore.

---

*Rail around the stern of a ship.

PART THREE

The Lighthouse

CHAPTER 1

DIRECTLY THE CARGO BOAT had slipped away from the wharf and got lost in the darkness of the harbour the Europeans of Sulaco separated, to prepare for the coming of the Monterist régime, which was approaching Sulaco from the mountains, as well as from the sea.

This bit of manual work in loading the silver was their last concerted action. It ended the three days of danger, during which, according to the newspaper press of Europe, their energy had preserved the town from the calamities of popular disorder. At the shore end of the jetty, Captain Mitchell said good night and turned back. His intention was to walk the planks of the wharf till the steamer from Esmeralda turned up. The engineers of the railway staff, collecting their Basque and Italian workmen, marched them away to the railway yards, leaving the Custom House, so well defended on the first day of the riot, standing open to the four winds of heaven. Their men had conducted themselves bravely and faithfully during the famous "three days" of Sulaco. In a great part this faithfulness and that courage had been exercised in self-defence rather than in the cause of those material interests to which Charles Gould had pinned his faith. Amongst the cries of the mob not the least loud had been the cry of death to foreigners. It was, indeed, a lucky circumstance for Sulaco that the relations of those imported workmen with the people of the country had been uniformly bad from the first.

Dr. Monygham, going to the door of Viola's kitchen, observed this retreat marking the end of the foreign interference, this withdrawal of the army of material progress from the field of Costaguana revolutions.

Algarroba torches* carried on the outskirts of the moving body sent their penetrating aroma into his nostrils. Their light, sweeping

---

*Torches made of wood from carob trees.

along the front of the house, made the letters of the inscription, "Albergo d'Italia Una," leap out black from end to end of the long wall. His eyes blinked in the clear blaze. Several young men, mostly fair and tall, shepherding this mob of dark bronzed heads, surmounted by the glint of slanting rifle barrels, nodded to him familiarly as they went by. The doctor was a well-known character. Some of them wondered what he was doing there. Then, on the flank of their workmen they tramped on, following the line of rails.

"Withdrawing your people from the harbour?" said the doctor, addressing himself to the chief engineer of the railway, who had accompanied Charles Gould so far on his way to the town, walking by the side of the horse, with his hand on the saddlebow. They had stopped just outside the open door to let the workmen cross the road.

"As quick as I can. We are not a political faction," answered the engineer, meaningly. "And we are not going to give our new rulers a handle against the railway. You approve me, Gould?"

"Absolutely," said Charles Gould's impassive voice, high up and outside the dim parallelogram of light falling on the road through the open door.

With Sotillo expected from one side, and Pedro Montero from the other, the engineer-in-chief's only anxiety now was to avoid a collision with either. Sulaco, for him, was a railway station, a terminus, workshops, a great accumulation of stores. As against the mob the railway defended its property, but politically the railway was neutral. He was a brave man; and in that spirit of neutrality he had carried proposals of truce to the self-appointed chiefs of the popular party, the deputies Fuentes and Gamacho. Bullets were still flying about when he had crossed the Plaza on that mission, waving above his head a white napkin belonging to the table linen of the Amarilla Club.

He was rather proud of this exploit; and reflecting that the doctor, busy all day with the wounded in the *patio* of the Casa Gould, had not had time to hear the news, he began a succinct narrative. He had communicated to them the intelligence from the Construction Camp as to Pedro Montero. The brother of the victorious general, he had assured them, could be expected at Sulaco at any time now. This news (as he anticipated), when shouted out of the window by Señor Gamacho, induced a rush of the mob along the Campo Road towards Rincón. The two deputies also, after shaking hands with him effusively, mounted and galloped off to meet the great man. "I have misled them a little as to the time," the chief engineer confessed. "However hard he rides, he can scarcely get here before the morning. But my object is attained. I've secured several hours' peace for the losing party. But I did not tell them anything about Sotillo, for fear they would take it into their heads to try to get hold of the harbour again, either to oppose him or welcome him—there's no saying which. There was Gould's silver, on which rests the remnant of our hopes. Decoud's retreat had to be thought of, too. I think the railway had done pretty well by its friends without compromising itself hopelessly. Now the parties must be left to themselves."

"Costaguana for the Costaguaneros," interjected the doctor, sardonically. "It is a fine country, and they have raised a fine crop of hates, vengeance, murder, and rapine—those sons of the country."

"Well, I am one of them," Charles Gould's voice sounded, calmly, "and I must be going to see to my own crop of trouble. My wife has driven straight on, doctor?"

"Yes. All was quiet on this side. Mrs. Gould has taken the two girls with her."

Charles Gould rode on, and the engineer-in-chief followed the doctor indoors.

"That man is calmness personified," he said, appreciatively, dropping on a bench, and stretching his well-shaped legs in cycling stockings nearly across the doorway. "He must be extremely sure of himself."

"If that's all he is sure of, then he is sure of nothing," said the doctor. He had perched himself again on the end of the table. He nursed his cheek in the palm of one hand, while the other sustained the elbow. "It is the last thing a man ought to be sure of." The candle, half-consumed and burning dimly with a long wick, lighted up from below his inclined face, whose expression, affected by the drawn-in cicatrices in the cheeks, had something vaguely unnatural, an exaggerated remorseful bitterness. As he sat there he had the air of meditating upon sinister things. The engineer-in-chief gazed at him for a time before he protested.

"I really don't see that. For me there seems to be nothing else. However—"

He was a wise man, but he could not quite conceal his contempt for that sort of paradox; in fact, Dr. Monygham was not liked by the Europeans of Sulaco. His outward aspect of an outcast, which he preserved even in Mrs. Gould's drawing-room, provoked unfavourable criticism. There could be no doubt of his intelligence; and as he had lived for over twenty years in the country, the pessimism of his outlook could not be altogether ignored. But instinctively, in self-defence of their activities and hopes, his hearers put it to the account of some hidden imperfection in the man's character. It was known that many years before, when quite young, he had been made by Guzman Bento chief medical officer of the army. Not one of the Europeans then in the service of Costaguana had been so much liked and trusted by the fierce old Dictator.

Afterwards his story was not so clear. It lost itself amongst the innumerable tales of conspiracies and plots against the tyrant as a stream is lost in an arid belt of sandy country before it emerges, diminished and troubled, perhaps, on the other side. The doctor made no secret of it that he had lived for years in the wildest parts of the Republic, wandering with almost unknown Indian tribes in the great forests of the far interior where the great rivers have their sources. But it was mere aimless wandering; he had written nothing, collected nothing, brought nothing for science out of the twilight of the forests, which seemed to cling to his battered personality limping about Sulaco, where it had drifted in casually, only to get stranded on the shores of the sea.

It was also known that he had lived in a state of destitution till the arrival of the Goulds from Europe. Don Carlos and Doña Emilia had taken up the mad English doctor, when it became apparent that for all his savage independence he could be tamed by kindness. Perhaps it was only hunger that had tamed him. In years gone by he had certainly been acquainted with Charles Gould's father in Sta. Marta; and now, no matter what were the dark passages of his history, as the medical officer of the San Tomé mine he became a recognized personality. He was recognized, but not unreservedly accepted. So much defiant eccentricity and such an outspoken scorn for mankind seemed to point to mere recklessness of judgement, the bravado of guilt. Besides, since he had become again of some account, vague whispers had been heard that years ago, when fallen into disgrace and thrown into prison by Guzman Bento at the time of the so-called Great Conspiracy, he had betrayed some of his best friends amongst the conspirators. Nobody pretended to believe that whisper; the whole story of the Great Conspiracy was hopelessly involved and obscure; it is admitted in Costaguana that there never had been a conspiracy except in the diseased imagination of the Tyrant; and, therefore, nothing and no one to betray; though the most distinguished Costaguaneros had been imprisoned and executed upon that accusation. The procedure had dragged on for years, decimating the better class like a pestilence. The mere expression of sorrow for the fate of executed kinsmen had been punished with death. Don José Avellanos was perhaps the only one living who knew the whole story of those unspeakable cruelties. He had suffered from them himself, and he, with a shrug of the shoulders and a nervous, jerky gesture of the arm, was wont to put away from him, as it were, every allusion to it. But whatever the reason, Dr. Monygham, a personage in the administration of the Gould Concession, treated with reverent awe by the miners, and indulged in his peculiarities by Mrs. Gould, remained somehow outside the pale.

It was not from any liking for the doctor that the engineer-in-chief had lingered in the inn upon the plain. He liked old Viola much better. He had come to look upon the Albergo d'Italia Una as a dependence of the railway. Many of his subordinates had their quarters there. Mrs. Gould's interest in the family conferred upon it a sort of distinction. The engineer-in-chief, with an army of workers under his orders, appreciated the moral influence of the old Garibaldino upon his countrymen. His austere, old-world Republicanism had a severe, soldier-like standard of faithfulness and duty, as if the world were a battlefield where men had to fight for the sake of universal love and brotherhood, instead of a more or less large share of booty.

"Poor old chap!" he said, after he had heard the doctor's account of Teresa. "He'll never be able to keep the place going by himself. I shall be sorry."

"He's quite alone up there," grunted Dr. Monygham, with a toss of his heavy head towards the narrow staircase. "Every living soul has cleared out, and Mrs. Gould took the girls away just now. It might not be over-safe for them out here before very long. Of course, as a doctor, I can do nothing more here; but she has asked me to stay with old Viola, and as I have no horse to get back to the mine, where I ought to be, I made no difficulty to stay. They can do without me in the town."

"I have a good mind to remain with you, doctor, till we see whether anything happens tonight at the harbour," declared the engineer-in-chief. "He must not be molested by Sotillo's soldiery, who may push on as far as this at once. Sotillo used to be very cordial to me at the Goulds' and at the club. How that man'll ever dare to look any of his friends here in the face I can't imagine."

"He'll no doubt begin by shooting some of them to get over the first awkwardness," said the doctor. "Nothing in this country serves better your military man who has changed sides than a few summary executions." He spoke with a gloomy positiveness that left no room for protest. The engineer-in-chief did not attempt any. He simply nodded several times regretfully, then said:

"I think we shall be able to mount you in the morning, doctor. Our peons have recovered some of our stampeded horses. By riding hard and taking a wide circuit by Los Hatos and along the edge of the forest, clear of Rincón altogether, you may hope to reach the San Tomé bridge without being interfered with. The mine is just now, to my mind, the safest place for anybody at all compromised. I only wish the railway was as difficult to touch."

"Am I compromised?" Dr. Monygham brought out slowly after a short silence.

"The whole Gould Concession is compromised. I could not have remained for ever outside the political life of the country—if those convulsions may be called life. The thing is—can it be touched? The moment was bound to come when neutrality would become impossible, and Charles Gould understood this well. I believe he is prepared for every extremity. A man of his sort has never contemplated remaining indefinitely at the mercy of ignorance and corruption. It was like being a prisoner in a cavern of *banditti** with

---

*Bandits (It.).

the price of your ransom in your pocket, and buying your life from day to day. Your mere safety, not your liberty, mind, doctor. I know what I am talking about. The image at which you shrug your shoulders is perfectly correct, especially if you conceive such a prisoner endowed with the power of replenishing his pocket by means as remote from the faculties of his captors as if they were magic. You must have understood that as well as I do, doctor. He was in the position of the goose with the golden eggs. I broached this matter to him as far back as Sir John's visit here. The prisoner of stupid and greedy *banditti* is always at the mercy of the first imbecile ruffian, who may blow out his brains in a fit of temper or for some prospect of an immediate big haul. The tale of killing the goose with the golden eggs has not been evolved for nothing out of the wisdom of mankind. It is a story that will never grow old. That is why Charles Gould in his deep, dumb way has countenanced the Ribierist Mandate, the first public act that promised him safety on other than venal grounds. Ribierism has failed, as everything merely rational fails in this country. But Gould remains logical in wishing to save this big lot of silver. Decoud's plan of a counter-revolution may be practicable or not, it may have a chance, or it may not have a chance. With all my experience of this revolutionary continent, I can hardly yet look at their methods seriously. Decoud has been reading to us his draught of a proclamation, and talking very well for two hours about his plan of action. He had arguments which should have appeared solid enough if we, members of old, stable political and national organizations, were not startled by the mere idea of a new State evolved like this out of the head of a scoffing young man fleeing for his life, with a proclamation in his pocket, to a rough, jeering, half-bred swash-buckler, who in this part of the world is called a general. It sounds like a comic fairy tale—and behold, it may come off; because it is true to the very spirit of the country."

"Is the silver gone off, then?" asked the doctor, moodily.

The chief engineer pulled out his watch. "By Captain Mitchell's reckoning—and he ought to know—it has been gone long enough now to be some three or four miles outside the harbour; and, as Mitchell says, Nostromo is the sort of seaman to make the best of his opportunities." Here the doctor grunted so heavily that the other changed his tone.

"You have a poor opinion of that move, doctor? But why? Charles Gould has got to play his game out, though he is not the man to formulate his conduct even to himself, perhaps, let alone to others. It may be that the game has been partly suggested to him by Holroyd; but it accords with his character, too; and that is why it has been so successful. Haven't they come to calling him 'El Rey de Sulaco'* in Sta. Marta? A nickname may be the best record of a success. That's what I call putting the face of a joke upon the body of a truth. My dear sir, when I first arrived in Sta. Marta I was struck by the way all those journalists, demagogues, members of Congress, and all those generals and judges cringed before a sleepy-eyed advocate without practice simply because he was the plenipotentiary of the Gould Concession. Sir John when he came out was impressed, too."

"A new State, with that plump dandy, Decoud, for the first President," mused Dr. Monygham, nursing his cheek and swinging his legs all the time.

"Upon my word, and why not?" the chief engineer retorted in an unexpectedly earnest and confidential voice. It was as if something subtle in the air of Costaguana had inoculated him with the local faith in *pronunciamientos*. All at once he began to talk, like an expert revolutionist, of the instrument ready to hand in the intact army at Cayta, which could be brought back in a few days to Sulaco if only Decoud managed to make his way at once down the coast. For the military chief there was Barrios, who had nothing but a bullet to expect from Montero, his former professional rival and bitter enemy. Barrios's concurrence was assured. As to his army, it had nothing to expect from Montero either; not even a month's pay. From that point of view the existence of the treasure was of enormous importance. The mere knowledge that it had been saved from the Monterists would be a strong inducement for the Cayta troops to embrace the cause of the new State.

The doctor turned round and contemplated his companion for some time.

"This Decoud, I see, is a persuasive young beggar," he remarked at last. "And pray is it for this, then, that Charles Gould

---

*The King of Sulaco.

has let the whole lot of ingots go out to sea in charge of that Nostromo?"

"Charles Gould," said the engineer-in-chief, "has said no more about his motive than usual. You know, he doesn't talk. But we all here know his motive, and he has only one—the safety of the San Tomé mine with the preservation of the Gould Concession in the spirit of his compact with Holroyd. Holroyd is another uncommon man. They understand each other's imaginative side. One is thirty, the other nearly sixty, and they have been made for each other. To be a millionaire, and such a millionaire as Holroyd, is like being eternally young. The audacity of youth reckons upon what it fancies an unlimited time at its disposal; but a millionaire has unlimited means in his hand—which is better. One's time on earth is an uncertain quantity, but about the long reach of millions there is no doubt. The introduction of a pure form of Christianity into this continent is a dream for a youthful enthusiast, and I have been trying to explain to you why Holroyd at fifty-eight is like a man on the threshold of life, and better, too. He's not a missionary, but the San Tomé mine holds just that for him. I assure you, in sober truth, that he could not manage to keep this out of a strictly business conference upon the finances of Costaguana he had with Sir John a couple of years ago. Sir John mentioned it with amazement in a letter he wrote to me here, from San Francisco, when on his way home. Upon my word, doctor, things seem to be worth nothing by what they are in themselves. I begin to believe that the only solid thing about them is the spiritual value which everyone discovers in his own form of activity—"

"Bah!" interrupted the doctor, without stopping for an instant the idle swinging movement of his legs. "Self-flattery. Food for that vanity which makes the world go round. Meantime, what do you think is going to happen to the treasure floating about the gulf with the great Capataz and the great politician?"

"Why are you uneasy about it, doctor?"

"I uneasy! And what the devil is it to me? I put no spiritual value into my desires, or my opinions, or my actions. They have not enough vastness to give me room for self-flattery. Look, for instance, I should certainly have liked to ease the last moments of that poor woman. And I can't. It's impossible. Have you met the impossible face to face—or have you, the Napoleon of railways, no such word in your dictionary?"

"Is she bound to have a very bad time of it?" asked the chief engineer, with humane concern.

Slow, heavy footsteps moved across the planks above the heavy hard wood beams of the kitchen. Then down the narrow opening of the staircase made in the thickness of the wall, and narrow enough to be defended by one man against twenty enemies, came the murmur of two voices, one faint and broken, the other deep and gentle answering it, and in its graver tone covering the weaker sound.

The two men remained still and silent till the murmurs ceased, then the doctor shrugged his shoulders and muttered:

"Yes, she's bound to. And I could do nothing if I went up now."

A long period of silence above and below ensued.

"I fancy," began the engineer, in a subdued voice, "that you mistrust Captain Mitchell's Capataz."

"Mistrust him!" muttered the doctor through his teeth. "I believe him capable of anything—even of the most absurd fidelity. I am the last person he spoke to before he left the wharf, you know. The poor woman up there wanted to see him, and I let him go up to her. The dying must not be contradicted, you know. She seemed then fairly calm and resigned, but the scoundrel in those ten minutes or so has done or said something which seems to have driven her into despair. You know," went on the doctor, hesitatingly, "women are so very unaccountable in every position, and at all times of life, that I thought sometimes she was in a way, don't you see? in love with him—the Capataz. The rascal has his own charm indubitably, or he would not have made the conquest of all the populace of the town. No, no, I am not absurd. I may have given a wrong name to some strong sentiment for him on her part, to an unreasonable and simple attitude a woman is apt to take up emotionally towards a man. She used to abuse him to me frequently, which, of course, is not inconsistent with my idea. Not at all. It looked to me as if she were always thinking of him. He was something important in her life. You know, I have seen a lot of those people. Whenever I came down from the mine Mrs. Gould used to ask me to keep my eye on them. She likes Italians; she has lived a long time in Italy, I believe, and she took a special fancy to that old Garibaldino. A remarkable chap enough. A rugged and dreamy character, living in the republicanism of his young days as if in a cloud. He has encouraged much of the Capataz's confounded nonsense—the high-strung, exalted old beggar!"

"What sort of nonsense?" wondered the chief engineer. "I found the Capataz always a very shrewd and sensible fellow, absolutely fearless, and remarkably useful. A perfect handyman. Sir John was greatly impressed by his resourcefulness and attention when he made that overland journey from Sta. Marta. Later on, as you might have heard, he rendered us a service by disclosing to the then chief of police the presence in the town of some professional thieves, who came from a distance to wreck and rob our monthly pay train. He has certainly organized the lighterage service of the harbour for the O.S.N. Company with great ability. He knows how to make himself obeyed, foreigner though he is. It is true that the *cargadores* are strangers here, too, for the most part—immigrants, *isleños.*'*

"His prestige is his fortune," muttered the doctor, sourly.

"The man has proved his trustworthiness up to the hilt on innumerable occasions and in all sorts of ways," argued the engineer. "When this question of the silver arose, Captain Mitchell naturally was very warmly of the opinion that his Capataz was the only man fit for the trust. As a sailor, of course, I suppose so. But as a man, don't you know, Gould, Decoud, and myself judged that it didn't matter in the least who went. Any boatman would have done just as well. Pray, what could a thief do with such a lot of ingots? If he ran off with them he would have in the end to land somewhere, and how could he conceal his cargo from the knowledge of the people ashore? We dismissed that consideration from our minds. Moreover, Decoud was going. There have been occasions when the Capataz has been more implicitly trusted."

"He took a slightly different view," the doctor said. "I heard him declare in this very room that it would be the most desperate affair of his life. He made a sort of verbal will here in my hearing, appointing old Viola his executor; and, by Jove! do you know, he—he's not grown rich by his fidelity to you good people of the railway and

---

*Islanders.

the harbour. I suppose he obtains some—how do you say that?—some spiritual value for his labours, or else I don't know why the devil he should be faithful to you, Gould, Mitchell, or anybody else. He knows this country well. He knows, for instance, that Gamacho, the Deputy from Javira, has been nothing else but a *tramposo** of the commonest sort, a petty pedlar of the Campo, till he managed to get enough goods on credit from Anzani to open a little store in the wilds, and got himself elected by the drunken *mozos* that hang about the *estancias* and the poorest sort of *rancheros* who were in his debt. And Gamacho, who tomorrow will be probably one of our high officials, is a stranger, too—an *isleño*. He might have been a *cargador* on the O.S.N. wharf had he not (the *posadero* of Rincón is ready to swear it) murdered a pedlar in the woods and stolen his pack to begin life on. And do you think that Gamacho, then, would have ever become a hero with the democracy of this place, like our Capataz? Of course not. He isn't half the man. No; decidedly, I think that Nostromo is a fool."

The doctor's talk was distasteful to the builder of railways. "It is impossible to argue that point," he said, philosophically. "Each man has his gifts. You should have heard Gamacho haranguing his friends in the street. He has a howling voice, and he shouted like mad, lifting his clenched fist right above his head, and throwing his body half out of the window. At every pause the rabble below yelled, 'Down with the Oligarchs! *Viva la libertad!*' Fuentes inside looked extremely miserable. You know, he is the brother of Jorge Fuentes, who has been Minister of the Interior for six months or so, some few years back. Of course, he has no conscience; but he is a man of birth and education—at one time the director of the Customs of Cayta. That idiot-brute Gamacho fastened himself upon him with his following of the lowest rabble. His sickly fear of that ruffian was the most rejoicing sight imaginable."

He got up and went to the door to look out towards the harbour. "All quiet," he said; "I wonder if Sotillo really means to turn up here?"

---

*Swindler.

CHAPTER 2

CAPTAIN MITCHELL, PACING THE wharf, was asking himself the same question. There was always the doubt whether the warning of the Esmeralda telegraphist—a fragmentary and interrupted message—had been properly understood. However, the good man had made up his mind not to go to bed till daylight, if even then. He imagined himself to have rendered an enormous service to Charles Gould. When he thought of the saved silver he rubbed his hands together with satisfaction. In his simple way he was proud at being a party to this extremely clever expedient. It was he who had given it a practical shape by suggesting the possibility of intercepting at sea the northbound steamer. And it was advantageous to his Company, too, which would have lost a valuable freight if the treasure had been left ashore to be confiscated. The pleasure of disappointing the Monterists was also very great. Authoritative by temperament and the long habit of command, Captain Mitchell was no democrat. He even went so far as to profess a contempt for parliamentarism itself. "His Excellency Don Vincente Ribiera," he used to say, "whom I and that fellow of mine, Nostromo, had the honour, sir, and the pleasure of saving from a cruel death, deferred too much to his Congress. It was a mistake—a distinct mistake, sir."

The guileless old seaman superintending the O.S.N. service imagined that the last three days had exhausted every startling surprise the political life of Costaguana could offer. He used to confess afterwards that the events which followed surpassed his imagination. To begin with, Sulaco (because of the seizure of the cables and the disorganization of the steam service) remained for a whole fortnight cut off from the rest of the world like a besieged city.

"One would not have believed it possible; but so it was, sir. A full fortnight."

The account of the extraordinary things that happened during that time, and the powerful emotions he experienced, acquired a

263

comic impressiveness from the pompous manner of his personal narrative. He opened it always by assuring his hearer that he was "in the thick of things from first to last." Then he would begin by describing the getting away of the silver, and his natural anxiety lest "his fellow" in charge of the lighter should make some mistake. Apart from the loss of so much precious metal, the life of Señor Martin Decoud, an agreeable, wealthy, and well-informed young gentleman, would have been jeopardized through his falling into the hands of his political enemies. Captain Mitchell also admitted that in his solitary vigil on the wharf he had felt a certain measure of concern for the future of the whole country.

"A feeling, sir," he exclaimed, "perfectly comprehensible in a man properly grateful for the many kindnesses received from the best families of merchants and other native gentlemen of independent means, who, barely saved by us from the excesses of the mob, seemed, to my mind's eye, destined to become the prey in person and fortune of the native soldiery, which, as is well known, behave with regrettable barbarity to the inhabitants during their civil commotions. And then, sir, there were the Goulds, for both of whom, man and wife, I could not but entertain the warmest feelings deserved by their hospitality and kindness. I felt, too, the dangers of the gentlemen of the Amarilla Club, who had made me honourary member, and had treated me with uniform regard and civility, both in my capacity of Consular Agent and as Superintendent of an important Steam Service. Miss Antonia Avellanos, the most beautiful and accomplished young lady whom it had ever been my privilege to speak to, was not a little in my mind, I confess. How the interests of my Company would be affected by the impending change of officials claimed a large share of my attention, too. In short, sir, I was extremely anxious and very tired, as you may suppose, by the exciting and memorable events in which I had taken my little part. The Company's building containing my residence was within five minutes' walk, with the attraction of some supper and of my hammock (I always take my nightly rest in a hammock, as the most suitable to the climate); but somehow, sir, though evidently I could do nothing for anyone by remaining about, I could not tear myself away from that wharf, where the fatigue made me stumble painfully at times. The night was excessively dark—the darkest I remember in my life;

so that I began to think that the arrival of the transport from Esmeralda could not possibly take place before daylight, owing to the difficulty of navigating the gulf. The mosquitoes bit like fury. We have been infested here with mosquitoes before the late improvements; a peculiar harbour brand, sir, renowned for its ferocity. They were like a cloud about my head, and I shouldn't wonder that but for their attacks I would have dozed off as I walked up and down, and got a heavy fall. I kept on smoking cigar after cigar, more to protect myself from being eaten up alive than from any real relish for the weed. Then, sir, when perhaps for the twentieth time I was approaching my watch to the lighted end in order to see the time, and observing with surprise that it wanted yet ten minutes to midnight, I heard the splash of a ship's propeller—an unmistakable sound to a sailor's ear on such a calm night. It was faint indeed, because they were advancing with precaution and dead slow, both on account of the darkness and from their desire of not revealing too soon their presence: a very unnecessary care, because, I verily believe, in all the enormous extent of this harbour I was the only living soul about. Even the usual staff of watchmen and others had been absent from their posts for several nights owing to the disturbances. I stood still, after dropping and stamping out my cigar—a circumstance highly agreeable, I should think, to the mosquitoes, if I may judge from the state of my face next morning. But that was a trifling inconvenience in comparison with the brutal proceedings I became victim of on the part of Sotillo. Something utterly inconceivable, sir; more like the proceedings of a maniac than the action of a sane man, however lost to all sense of honour and decency. But Sotillo was furious at the failure of his thievish scheme."

In this Captain Mitchell was right. Sotillo was indeed infuriated. Captain Mitchell, however, had not been arrested at once; a vivid curiosity induced him to remain on the wharf (which is nearly four hundred feet long) to see, or rather hear, the whole process of disembarkation. Concealed by the railway truck used for the silver, which had been run back afterwards to the shore end of the jetty, Captain Mitchell saw the small detachment thrown forward, pass by, taking different directions upon the plain. Meantime, the troops were being landed and formed into a column, whose head crept up gradually so close to him that he made it out, barring nearly the whole width of the wharf, only a very few yards from him. Then the low, shuffling, murmuring, clinking sounds ceased, and the whole mass remained for about an hour motionless and silent, awaiting the return of the scouts. On land nothing was to be heard except the deep baying of the mastiffs at the railway yards, answered by the faint barking of the curs infesting the outer limits of the town. A detached knot of dark shapes stood in front of the head of the column.

Presently the picket at the end of the wharf began to challenge in undertones single figures approaching from the plain. Those messengers sent back from the scouting parties flung to their comrades brief sentences and passed on rapidly, becoming lost in the great motionless mass, to make their report to the Staff. It occurred to Captain Mitchell that his position could become disagreeable and perhaps dangerous, when suddenly, at the head of the jetty, there was a shout of command, a bugle call, followed by a stir and a rattling of arms, and a murmuring noise that ran right up the column. Near by a loud voice directed hurriedly, "Push that railway car out of the way!" At the rush of bare feet to execute the order Captain Mitchell skipped back a pace or two; the car, suddenly impelled by many hands, flew away from him along the rails, and before he knew what had happened he found himself surrounded and seized by his arms and the collar of his coat.

"We have caught a man hiding here, *mi teniente!*"* cried one of his captors.

"Hold him on one side till the rearguard comes along," answered the voice. The whole column streamed past Captain Mitchell at a run, the thundering noise of their feet dying away suddenly on the shore. His captors held him tightly, disregarding his declaration that he was an Englishman and his loud demands to be taken at once before their commanding officer. Finally he lapsed into dignified silence. With a hollow rumble of wheels on the planks a couple of field guns, dragged by hand, rolled by. Then, after a small body of men had marched past escorting four or five figures which walked in advance, with a jingle of steel scabbards, he felt a tug at his arms, and was ordered to come along. During the passage from the wharf

_____

*My lieutenant.

to the Custom House it is to be feared that Captain Mitchell was subjected to certain indignities at the hands of the soldiers—such as jerks, thumps on the neck, forcible application of the butt of a rifle to the small of his back. Their ideas of speed were not in accord with his notion of his dignity. He became flustered, flushed, and helpless. It was as if the world were coming to an end.

The long building was surrounded by troops, which were already piling arms by companies and preparing to pass the night lying on the ground in their ponchos with their sacks under their heads. Corporals moved with swinging lanterns posting sentries all round the walls wherever there was a door or an opening. Sotillo was taking his measures to protect his conquest as if it had indeed contained the treasure. His desire to make his fortune at one audacious stroke of genius had overmastered his reasoning faculties. He would not believe in the possibility of failure; the mere hint of such a thing made his brain reel with rage. Every circumstance pointing to it appeared incredible. The statement of Hirsch, which was so absolutely fatal to his hopes, could by no means be admitted. It is true, too, that Hirsch's story had been told so incoherently, with such excessive signs of distraction, that it really looked improbable. It was extremely difficult, as the saying is, to make head or tail of it. On the bridge of the steamer, directly after his rescue, Sotillo and his officers, in their impatience and excitement, would not give the wretched man time to collect such few wits as remained to him. He ought to have been quieted, soothed, and reassured, whereas he had been roughly handled, cuffed, shaken, and addressed in menacing tones. His struggles, his wriggles, his attempts to get down on his knees, followed by the most violent efforts to break away, as if he meant incontinently to jump overboard, his shrieks and shrinkings and cowering wild glances had filled them first with amazement, then with a doubt of his genuineness, as men are wont to suspect the sincerity of every great passion. His Spanish, too, became so mixed up with German that the better half of his statements remained incomprehensible. He tried to propitiate them by calling them *hochwohlgeborene Herren*,* which in itself sounded suspicious.

---

*Honorable lords (German).

When admonished sternly not to trifle he repeated his entreaties and protestations of loyalty and innocence again in German, obstinately, because he was not aware in what language he was speaking. His identity, of course, was perfectly known as an inhabitant of Esmeralda, but this made the matter no clearer. As he kept on forgetting Decoud's name, mixing him up with several other people he had seen in the Casa Gould, it looked as if they all had been in the lighter together; and for a moment Sotillo thought that he had drowned every prominent Ribierist of Sulaco. The improbability of such a thing threw a doubt upon the whole statement. Hirsch was either mad or playing a part—pretending fear and distraction on the spur of the moment to cover the truth. Sotillo's rapacity, excited to the highest pitch by the prospect of an immense booty, could believe in nothing adverse. This Jew might have been very much frightened by the accident, but he knew where the silver was concealed, and had invented this story, with his Jewish cunning, to put him entirely off the track as to what had been done.

Sotillo had taken up his quarters on the upper floor in a vast apartment with heavy black beams. But there was no ceiling, and the eye lost itself in the darkness under the high pitch of the roof. The thick shutters stood open. On a long table could be seen a large inkstand, some stumpy, inky quill pens, and two square wooden boxes, each holding half a hundredweight of sand. Sheets of grey coarse official paper bestrewed the floor. It must have been a room occupied by some higher official of the Customs, because a large leathern armchair stood behind the table, with other highbacked chairs scattered about. A net hammock was swung under one of the beams—for the official's afternoon siesta, no doubt. A couple of candles stuck into tall iron candlesticks gave a dim reddish light. The colonel's hat, sword, and revolver lay between them, and a couple of his more trusty officers lounged gloomily against the table. The colonel threw himself into the armchair, and a big Negro with a sergeant's stripes on his ragged sleeve, kneeling down, pulled off his boots. Sotillo's ebony moustache contrasted violently with the livid colouring of his cheeks. His eyes were sombre and as if sunk very far into his head. He seemed exhausted by his perplexities, languid with disappointment; but when the sentry on the landing thrust his head in to announce the arrival of a prisoner, he revived at once.

"Let him be brought in," he shouted, fiercely.

The door flew open, and Captain Mitchell, bareheaded, his waist-coat open, the bow of his tie under his ear, was hustled into the room.

Sotillo recognized him at once. He could not have hoped for a more precious capture; here was a man who could tell him, if he chose, everything he wished to know—and directly the problem of how to make him talk to the point presented itself to his mind. The resentment of a foreign nation had no terrors for Sotillo. The might of the whole armed Europe would not have protected Captain Mitchell from insults and ill-usage, so well as the quick reflection of Sotillo that this was an Englishman who would most likely turn ob-stinate under bad treatment, and become quite unmanageable. At all events, the colonel smoothed the scowl on his brow.

"What! The excellent Señor Mitchell!" he cried, in affected dis-may. The pretended anger of his swift advance and of his shout, "Release the *caballero* at once," was so effective that the astounded soldiers positively sprang away from their prisoner. Thus suddenly deprived of forcible support, Captain Mitchell reeled as though about to fall. Sotillo took him familiarly under the arm, led him to a chair, waved his hand at the room. "Go out, all of you," he com-manded.

When they had been left alone he stood looking down, irresolute and silent, watching till Captain Mitchell had recovered his power of speech.

Here in his very grasp was one of the men concerned in the re-moval of the silver. Sotillo's temperament was of that sort that he experienced an ardent desire to beat him; just as formerly when ne-gotiating with difficulty a loan from the cautious Anzani, his fingers always itched to take the shopkeeper by the throat. As to Captain Mitchell, the suddenness, unexpectedness, and general inconceiv-ableness of this experience had confused his thoughts. Moreover, he was physically out of breath.

"I've been knocked down three times between this and the wharf," he gasped out at last. "Somebody shall be made to pay for this." He had certainly stumbled more than once, and had been dragged along for some distance before he could regain his stride. With his recovered breath his indignation seemed to madden him. He jumped up, crimson, all his white hair bristling, his eyes glaring vengefully, and shook violently the flaps of his ruined waistcoat before the disconcerted Sotillo. "Look! Those uniformed thieves of yours downstairs have robbed me of my watch."

The old sailor's aspect was very threatening. Sotillo saw himself cut off from the table on which his sabre and revolver were lying.

"I demand restitution and apologies," Mitchell thundered at him, quite beside himself. "From you! Yes, from you!"

For the space of a second or so the colonel stood with a perfectly stony expression of face; then, as Captain Mitchell flung out an arm towards the table as if to snatch up the revolver, Sotillo, with a yell of alarm, bounded to the door and was gone in a flash, slamming it after him. Surprise calmed Captain Mitchell's fury. Behind the closed door Sotillo shouted on the landing, and there was a great tumult of feet on the wooden staircase.

"Disarm him! Bind him!" the colonel could be heard vociferating.

Captain Mitchell had just the time to glance once at the windows, with three perpendicular bars of iron each and some twenty feet from the ground, as he well knew, before the door flew open and the rush upon him took place. In an incredibly short time he found himself bound with many turns of a hide rope to a high-backed chair, so that his head alone remained free. Not till then did Sotillo, who had been leaning in the doorway trembling visibly, venture again within. The soldiers, picking up from the floor the rifles they had dropped to grapple with the prisoner, filed out of the room. The officers remained leaning on their swords and looking on.

"The watch! the watch!" raved the colonel, pacing to and fro like a tiger in a cage. "Give me that man's watch."

It was true, that when searched for arms in the hall downstairs, before being taken into Sotillo's presence, Captain Mitchell had been relieved of his watch and chain; but at the colonel's clamour it was produced quickly enough, a corporal bringing it up, carried carefully in the palms of his joined hands. Sotillo snatched it, and pushed the clenched fist from which it dangled close to Captain Mitchell's face.

"Now then! You arrogant Englishman! You dare to call the soldiers of the army thieves! Behold your watch."

He flourished his fist as if aiming blows at the prisoner's nose. Captain Mitchell, helpless as a swathed infant, looked anxiously at the sixty-guinea gold half-chronometer, presented to him years ago by a Committee of Underwriters for saving a ship from total loss by fire. Sotillo, too, seemed to perceive its valuable appearance. He became silent suddenly, stepped aside to the table, and began a careful examination in the light of the candles. He had never seen anything so fine. His officers closed in and craned their necks behind his back.

He became so interested that for an instant he forgot his precious prisoner. There is always something childish in the rapacity of the passionate, clear-minded, Southern races, wanting in the misty idealism of the Northerners, who at the smallest encouragement dream of nothing less than the conquest of the earth. Sotillo was fond of jewels, gold trinkets, of personal adornment. After a moment he turned about, and with a commanding gesture made all his officers fall back. He laid down the watch on the table, then, negligently, pushed his hat over it.

"Ha!" he began, going up very close to the chair. "You dare call my valiant soldiers of the Esmeralda regiment, thieves. You dare! What impudence! You foreigners come here to rob our country of its wealth. You never have enough! Your audacity knows no bounds."

He looked towards the officers, among whom there was an approving murmur. The older major was moved to declare:

"*Sí, mi coronel.* They are all traitors."

"I shall say nothing," continued Sotillo, fixing the motionless and powerless Mitchell with an angry but uneasy stare. "I shall say nothing of your treacherous attempt to get possession of my revolver to shoot me while I was trying to treat you with consideration you did not deserve. You have forfeited your life. Your only hope is in my clemency."

He watched for the effect of his words, but there was no obvious sign of fear on Captain Mitchell's face. His white hair was full of dust, which covered also the rest of his helpless person. As if he had heard nothing, he twitched an eyebrow to get rid of a bit of straw which hung amongst the hairs.

Sotillo advanced one leg and put his arms akimbo. "It is you, Mitchell," he said, emphatically, "who are the thief, not my soldiers!" He pointed at his prisoner a forefinger with a long, almond-shaped nail. "Where is the silver of the San Tomé mine? I ask you, Mitchell, where is the silver that was deposited in this Custom House? Answer me that! You stole it. You were a party to stealing it. It was stolen from the Government. Aha! you think I do not know what I say; but I am up to your foreign tricks. It is gone, the silver! No? Gone in one of your *lanchas*,* you miserable man! How dared you?"

This time he produced his effect. "How on earth could Sotillo know that?" thought Mitchell. His head, the only part of his body that could move, betrayed his surprise by a sudden jerk.

"Ha! you tremble," Sotillo shouted, suddenly. "It is a conspiracy. It is a crime against the State. Did you not know that the silver belongs to the Republic till the Government claims are satisfied? Where is it? Where have you hidden it, you miserable thief?"

At this question Captain Mitchell's sinking spirits revived. In whatever incomprehensible manner Sotillo had already got his information about the lighter, he had not captured it. That was clear. In his outraged heart, Captain Mitchell had resolved that nothing would induce him to say a word while he remained so disgracefully bound, but his desire to help the escape of the silver made him depart from this resolution. His wits were very much at work. He detected in Sotillo a certain air of doubt, of irresolution.

"That man," he said to himself, "is not certain of what he advances." For all his pomposity in social intercourse, Captain Mitchell could meet the realities of life in a resolute and ready spirit. Now he had got over the first shock of the abominable treatment he was cool and collected enough. The immense contempt he felt for Sotillo steadied him, and he said oracularly, "No doubt it is well concealed by this time."

Sotillo, too, had had time to cool down. "*Muy bien*, Mitchell," he said in a cold and threatening manner. "But can you produce the Government receipt for the royalty and the Custom House permit of embarkation, hey? Can you? No. Then the silver has been removed illegally, and the guilty shall be made to suffer, unless it is produced within five days from this." He gave orders for the prisoner to be unbound and locked up in one of the smaller rooms

---

*Boats or launches.

downstairs. He walked about the room, moody and silent, till Captain Mitchell, with each of his arms held by a couple of men, stood up, shook himself, and stamped his feet.

"How did you like to be tied up, Mitchell?" he asked, derisively.

"It is the most incredible, abominable use of power!" Captain Mitchell declared in a loud voice. "And whatever your purpose, you shall gain nothing from it, I can promise you."

The tall colonel, livid, with his coal-black ringlets and moustache, crouched, as it were, to look into the eyes of the short, thickset, red-faced prisoner with rumpled white hair.

"That we shall see. You shall know my power a little better when I tie you up to a *potalón**** outside in the sun for a whole day." He drew himself up haughtily, and made a sign for Captain Mitchell to be led away.

"What about my watch?" cried Captain Mitchell, hanging back from the efforts of the men pulling him towards the door.

Sotillo turned to his officers. "No! But only listed to this *pícaro*,† *caballeros*," he pronounced with affected scorn, and was answered by a chorus of derisive laughter. "He demands his watch!" . . . He ran up again to Captain Mitchell, for the desire to relieve his feelings by inflicting blows and pain upon this Englishman was very strong within him. "Your watch! You are a prisoner in war time, Mitchell! In war time! You have no rights and no property! *Caramba!* The very breath in your body belongs to me. Remember that."

"Bosh!" said Captain Mitchell, concealing a disagreeable impression.

Down below, in a great hall, with the earthen floor and with a tall mound thrown up by white ants in a corner, the soldiers had kindled a small fire with broken chairs and tables near the arched gateway, through which the faint murmur of the harbour waters on the beach could be heard. While Captain Mitchell was being led down the staircase, an officer passed him, running up to report to Sotillo the capture of more prisoners. A lot of smoke hung about in the vast gloomy place, the fire crackled, and, as if through a haze,

---

*Anchor.
†Rascal, knave.

Captain Mitchell made out, surrounded by short soldiers with fixed bayonets, the heads of three tall prisoners—the doctor, the engineer-in-chief, and the white leonine mane of old Viola, who stood half-turned away from the others with his chin on his breast and his arms crossed. Mitchell's astonishment knew no bounds. He cried out; the other two exclaimed also. But he hurried, on, diagonally, across the big cavern-like hall. Lots of thoughts, surmises, hints of caution, and so on, crowded his head to distraction.

"Is he actually keeping you?" shouted the chief engineer, whose single eyeglass glittered in the firelight.

An officer from the top of the stairs was shouting urgently. "Bring them all up—all three."

In the clamour of voices and the rattle of arms, Captain Mitchell made himself heard imperfectly: "By heavens! the fellow has stolen my watch."

The engineer-in-chief on the staircase resisted the pressure long enough to shout, "What? What did you say?"

"My chronometer!" Captain Mitchell yelled violently at the very moment of being thrust head foremost through a small door into a sort of cell, perfectly black, and so narrow that he fetched up against the opposite wall. The door had been instantly slammed. He knew where they had put him. This was the strong-room of the Custom House, whence the silver had been removed only a few hours earlier. It was almost as narrow as a corridor, with a small square aperture, barred by a heavy grating, at the distant end. Captain Mitchell staggered for a few steps, then sat down on the earthen floor with his back to the wall. Nothing, not even a gleam of light from anywhere, interfered with Captain Mitchell's meditation. He did some hard but not very extensive thinking. It was not of a gloomy cast. The old sailor, with all his small weaknesses and absurdities, was constitutionally incapable of entertaining for any length of time a fear of his personal safety. It was not so much firmness of soul as the lack of a certain kind of imagination—the kind whose undue development caused intense suffering to Señor Hirsch; that sort of imagination which adds the blind terror of bodily suffering and of death, envisaged as an accident to the body alone, strictly—to all the other apprehensions on which the sense of one's existence is based. Unfortunately, Captain Mitchell had not much penetration of any kind; characteristic, illuminating trifles of expression, action, or movement, escaped him completely. He was too pompously and innocently aware of his own existence to observe that of others. For instance, he could not believe that Sotillo had been really afraid of him, and this simply because it would never have entered into his head to shoot anyone except in the most pressing case of self-defence. Anybody could see he was not a murdering kind of man, he reflected quite gravely. Then why this preposterous and insulting charge? he asked himself. But his thoughts mainly clung around the astounding and unanswerable question: How the devil had the fellow got to know that the silver had gone off in the lighter? It was obvious that he had not captured it. And, obviously, he could not have captured it! In this last conclusion Captain Mitchell was misled by the assumption drawn from his observation of the weather during his long vigil on the wharf. He thought that there had been much more wind than usual that night in the gulf; whereas, as a matter of fact, the reverse was the case.

"How in the name of all that's marvellous did that confounded fellow get wind of the affair?" was the first question he asked directly after the bang, clatter, and flash of the open door (which was closed again almost before he could lift his dropped head) informed him that he had a companion of captivity. Dr. Monygham's voice stopped muttering curses in English and Spanish.

"Is that you, Mitchell?" he made answer, surlily. "I struck my forehead against this confounded wall with enough force to fell an ox. Where are you?"

Captain Mitchell, accustomed to the darkness, could make out the doctor stretching out his hands blindly.

"I am sitting here on the floor. Don't fall over my legs," Captain Mitchell's voice announced with great dignity of tone. The doctor, entreated not to walk about in the dark, sank down to the ground, too. The two prisoners of Sotillo, with their heads nearly touching, began to exchange confidences.

"Yes," the doctor related in a low tone to Captain Mitchell's vehement curiosity, "we have been nabbed in old Viola's place. It seems that one of their pickets, commanded by an officer, pushed as far as the town gate. They had orders not to enter, but to bring along every soul they could find on the plain. We had been talking in there with the door open, and no doubt they saw the glimmer of our light. They must have been making their approaches for some time. The engineer laid himself on a bench in a recess by the fire-place, and I went upstairs to have a look. I hadn't heard any sound from there for a long time. Old Viola, as soon as he saw me come up, lifted his arm for silence. I stole in on tiptoe. By Jove, his wife was lying down and had gone to sleep. The woman had actually dropped off to sleep! 'Señor Doctor,' Viola whispers to me, 'it looks as if her oppression was going to get better.' 'Yes,' I said, very much surprised; 'your wife is a wonderful woman, Giorgio.' Just then a shot was fired in the kitchen, which made us jump and cower as if at a thunder-clap. It seems that the party of soldiers had stolen quite close up, and one of them had crept up to the door. He looked in, thought there was no one there, and, holding his rifle ready, entered quietly. The chief told me that he had just closed his eyes for a mo-ment. When he opened them, he saw the man already in the mid-dle of the room peering into the dark corners. The chief was so startled that, without thinking, he made one leap from the recess right out in front of the fireplace. The soldier, no less startled, ups with his rifle and pulls the trigger, deafening and singeing the engi-neer, but in his flurry missing him completely. But, look what hap-pens! At the noise of the report the sleeping woman sat up, as if moved by a spring, with a shriek, 'The children, Gian' Battista! Save the children!' I have it in my ears now. It was the truest cry of distress I ever heard. I stood as if paralysed, but the old husband ran across to the bedside, stretching out his hands. She clung to them! I could see her eyes go glazed; the old fellow lowered her down on the pillows and then looked round at me. She was dead! All this took less than five minutes, and then I ran down to see what was the matter. It was no use thinking of any resistance. Nothing we two could say availed with the officer, so I volunteered to go up with a couple of soldiers and fetch down old Viola. He was sitting at the foot of the bed, looking at his wife's face, and did not seem to hear what I said; but after I had pulled the sheet over her head, he got up and followed us downstairs quietly, in a sort of thoughtful way. They marched us off along the road, leaving the door open and the can-dle burning. The chief engineer strode on without a word, but I looked back once or twice at the feeble gleam. After we had gone some considerable distance, the Garibaldino, who was walking by my side, suddenly said, 'I have buried many men on battlefields on this continent. The priests talk of consecrated ground! Bah! All the earth made by God is holy; but the sea, which knows nothing of kings and priests and tyrants, is the holiest of all. Doctor! I should like to bury her in the sea. No mummeries, candles, incense, no holy water mumbled over by priests. The spirit of liberty is upon the waters.' . . . Amazing old man. He was saying all this in an undertone as if talking to himself."

"Yes, yes," interrupted Captain Mitchell, impatiently. "Poor old chap! But have you any idea how that ruffian Sotillo obtained his information? He did not get hold of any of our *cargadores* who helped with the truck, did he? But no, it is impossible! These were picked men we've had in our boats for these five years, and I paid them myself specially for the job, with instructions to keep out of the way for twenty-four hours at least. I saw them with my own eyes march on with the Italians to the railway yards. The chief promised to give them rations as long as they wanted to remain there."

"Well," said the doctor, slowly, "I can tell you that you may say good-bye for ever to your best lighter, and to the Capataz of Cargadores."

At this, Captain Mitchell scrambled up to his feet in the excess of his excitement. The doctor, without giving him time to exclaim, stated briefly the part played by Hirsch during the night.

Captain Mitchell was overcome. "Drowned!" he muttered, in a bewildered and appalled whisper. "Drowned!" Afterwards he kept still, apparently listening, but too absorbed in the news of the catastrophe to follow the doctor's narrative with attention.

The doctor had taken up an attitude of perfect ignorance, till at last Sotillo was induced to have Hirsch brought in to repeat the whole story, which was got out of him again with the greatest difficulty, because every moment he would break out into lamentations. At last, Hirsch was led away, looking more dead than alive, and shut up in one of the upstairs rooms to be close at hand. Then the doctor, keeping up his character of a man not admitted to the inner councils of the San Tomé Administration, remarked that the story sounded incredible. Of course, he said, he couldn't tell what had been the action of the Europeans, as he had been exclusively occupied with his own work in looking after the wounded, and also in attending Don José Avellanos. He had succeeded in assuming so well a tone of impartial indifference that Sotillo seemed to be completely deceived. Till then a show of regular inquiry had been kept up; one of the officers sitting at the table wrote down the questions and the answers, the others, lounging about the room, listened attentively, puffing at their long cigars and keeping their eyes on the doctor. But at that point Sotillo ordered everybody out.

CHAPTER 3

DIRECTLY THEY WERE ALONE, the colonel's severe official manner changed. He rose and approached the doctor. His eyes shone with rapacity and hope; he became confidential. "The silver might have been indeed put on board the lighter, but it was not conceivable that it should have been taken out to sea." The doctor, watching every word, nodded slightly, smoking with apparent relish the cigar which Sotillo had offered him as a sign of his friendly intentions. The doctor's manner of cold detachment from the rest of the Europeans led Sotillo on, till, from conjecture to conjecture, he arrived at hinting that in his opinion this was a put-up job on the part of Charles Gould, in order to get hold of that immense treasure all to himself. The doctor, observant and self-possessed, muttered, "He is very capable of that."

Here Captain Mitchell exclaimed with amazement, amusement, and indignation, "You said that of Charles Gould!" Disgust, and even some suspicion, crept into his tone, for to him, too, as to other Europeans, there appeared to be something dubious about the doctor's personality.

"What on earth made you say that to this watch-stealing scoundrel?" he asked. "What's the object of an infernal lie of that sort? That confounded pickpocket was quite capable of believing you."

He snorted. For a time the doctor remained silent in the dark.

"Yes, that is exactly what I did say," he uttered at last, in a tone which would have made it clear enough to a third party that the pause was not of a reluctant but of a reflective character. Captain Mitchell thought that he had never heard anything so brazenly impudent in his life.

"Well, well!" he muttered to himself, but he had not the heart to voice his thoughts. They were swept away by others full of astonishment and regret. A heavy sense of discomfiture crushed him: the loss of the silver, the death of Nostromo, which was really quite a blow to his sensibilities, because he had become attached to his Capataz as people get attached to their inferiors from love of ease and almost unconscious gratitude. And when he thought of Decoud being drowned, too, his sensibility was almost overcome by this miserable end. What a heavy blow for that poor young woman! Captain Mitchell did not belong to the species of crabbed old bachelors; on the contrary, he liked to see young men paying attentions to young women. It seemed to him a natural and proper thing. Proper especially. As to sailors, it was different; it was not their place to marry, he maintained, but it was on moral grounds as a matter of self-denial, for, he explained, life on board ship is not fit for a woman even at best, and if you leave her on shore, first of all it is not fair, and next she either suffers from it or doesn't care a bit, which, in both cases, is bad. He couldn't have told what upset him most—Charles Gould's immense material loss, the death of Nostromo, which was a heavy loss to himself, or the idea of that beautiful and accomplished young woman being plunged into mourning.

"Yes," the doctor, who had been apparently reflecting some more, began again, "he believed me right enough. I thought he would have hugged me. '*Sí, sí*,' he said, 'he will write to that partner of his, the rich *americano* in San Francisco, that it is all lost. Why not? There is enough to share with many people.'"

"But this is perfectly imbecile!" cried Captain Mitchell.

The doctor remarked that Sotillo *was* imbecile, and that his imbecility was ingenious enough to lead him completely astray. He had helped him only but a little way.

"I mentioned," the doctor said, "in a sort of casual way, that treasure is generally buried in the earth rather than being set afloat upon the sea. At this my Sotillo slapped his forehead. '*Por Dios*, yes,' he said; 'they must have buried it on the shores of this harbour somewhere before they sailed out.'"

"Heavens and earth!" muttered Captain Mitchell, "I should not have believed that anybody could be ass enough—" He paused, then went on mournfully: "But what's the good of all this? It would have been a clever enough lie if the lighter had been still afloat. It would have kept that inconceivable idiot perhaps from sending out the steamer to cruise in the gulf. That was the danger that worried me no end." Captain Mitchell sighed profoundly.

"I had an object," the doctor pronounced, slowly.

"Had you?" muttered Captain Mitchell. "Well, that's lucky, or else I would have thought that you went on fooling him for the fun of the thing. And perhaps that was your object. Well, I must say I personally wouldn't condescend to that sort of thing. It is not to my taste. No, no. Blackening a friend's character is not my idea of fun, if it were to fool the greatest blackguard on earth."

Had it not been for Captain Mitchell's depression, caused by the fatal news, his disgust of Dr. Monygham would have taken a more outspoken shape; but he thought to himself that now it really did not matter what that man, whom he had never liked, would say and do.

"I wonder," he grumbled, "why they have shut us up together, or why Sotillo should have shut you up at all, since it seems to me you have been fairly chummy up there?"

"Yes, I wonder?" said the doctor, grimly.

Captain Mitchell's heart was so heavy that he would have preferred for the time being a complete solitude to the best of company. But any company would have been preferable to the doctor's, at whom he had always looked askance as a sort of beachcomber of superior intelligence partly reclaimed from his abased state. That feeling led him to ask:

"What has that ruffian done with the other two?"

"The chief engineer he wouldn't have let go in any case," said the doctor. "He would like to have a quarrel with the railway upon his hands. Not just yet, at any rate. I don't think, Captain Mitchell, that you understand exactly what Sotillo's position is—"

"I don't see why I should bother my head about it," snarled Captain Mitchell.

"No," assented the doctor, with the same grim composure. "I don't see why you should. It wouldn't help a single human being in the world if you thought ever so hard upon any subject whatever."

"No," said Captain Mitchell, simply, and with evident depression. "A man locked up in a confounded dark hole is not much use to anybody."

"As to old Viola," the doctor continued, as though he had not heard, "Sotillo released him for the same reason he is presently going to release you."

"Eh? What?" exclaimed Captain Mitchell, staring like an owl in the darkness. "What is there in common between me and old Viola? More likely because the old chap has no watch and chain for the pickpocket to steal. And I tell you what, Dr. Monygham," he went on with rising choler. "He will find it more difficult than he thinks to get rid of me. He will burn his fingers over that job yet, I can tell you. To begin with, I won't go without my watch, and as to the rest—we shall see. I dare say it is no great matter for you to be locked up. But Joe Mitchell is a different kind of man, sir. I don't mean to submit tamely to insult and robbery. I am a public character, sir."

And then Captain Mitchell became aware that the bars of the opening had become visible, a black grating upon a square of grey. The coming of the day silenced Captain Mitchell as if by the reflection that now in all the future days he would be deprived of the invaluable services of his Capataz. He leaned against the wall with his arms folded on his breast, and the doctor walked up and down the whole length of the place with his peculiar hobbling gait, as if slinking about on damaged feet. At the end farthest from the grating he would be lost altogether in the darkness. Only the slight limping shuffle could be heard. There was an air of moody detachment in that painful prowl kept up without a pause. When the door of the prison was suddenly flung open and his name shouted out he showed no surprise. He swerved sharply in his walk, and passed out at once, as though much depended upon his speed; but Captain Mitchell remained for some time with his shoulders against the wall, quite undecided in the bitterness of his spirit whether it wouldn't be better to refuse to stir a limb in the way of protest. He had half a mind to get himself carried out, but after the officer at the door had shouted three or four times in tones of remonstrance and surprise he condescended to walk out.

Sotillo's manner had changed. The colonel's offhand civility was slightly irresolute, as though he were in doubt if civility were

the proper course in this case. He observed Captain Mitche
tively before he spoke from the big armchair behind the tab\
condescending voice:

"I have concluded not to detain you, Señor Mitchell. I am o\
forgiving disposition. I make allowances. Let this be a lesson to you,
however."

The peculiar dawn of Sulaco, which seems to break far away to
the westward and creep back into the shade of the mountains, mingled with the reddish light of the candles. Captain Mitchell, in sign
of contempt and indifference, let his eyes roam all over the room,
and he gave a hard stare to the doctor, perched already on the casement of one of the windows, with his eyelids lowered, careless and
thoughtful—or perhaps ashamed.

Sotillo, ensconced in the vast armchair, remarked, "I should
have thought that the feelings of a *caballero* would have dictated to
you an appropriate reply."

He waited for it, but Captain Mitchell remaining mute, more
from extreme resentment than from reasoned intention, Sotillo hesitated, glanced towards the doctor, who looked up and nodded,
then went on with a slight effort:

"Here, Señor Mitchell, is your watch. Learn how hasty and unjust has been your judgement of my patriotic soldiers."

Lying back in his seat, he extended his arm over the table and
pushed the watch away slightly. Captain Mitchell walked up with
undisguised eagerness, put it to his ear, then slipped it into his pocket
coolly.

Sotillo seemed to overcome an immense reluctance. Again he
looked aside at the doctor, who stared at him unwinkingly.

But as Captain Mitchell was turning away, without as much as a
nod or a glance, he hastened to say:

"You may go and wait downstairs for the Señor Doctor, whom I
am going to liberate, too. You foreigners are insignificant, to my
mind."

He forced a slight, discordant laugh out of himself, while Captain Mitchell, for the first time, looked at him with some interest.

"The law shall take note later on of your transgressions," Sotillo
hurried on. "But as for me, you can live free, unguarded, unobserved.
Do you hear, Señor Mitchell? You may depart to your affairs. You are

beneath my notice. My attention is claimed by matters of the very highest importance."

Captain Mitchell was very nearly provoked to an answer. It displeased him to be liberated insultingly; but want of sleep, prolonged anxieties, a profound disappointment with the fatal ending of the silver-saving business weighed upon his spirits. It was as much as he could do to conceal his uneasiness, not about himself perhaps, but about things in general. It occurred to him distinctly that something underhand was going on. As he went out he ignored the doctor pointedly.

"A brute!" said Sotillo, as the door shut.

Dr. Monygham slipped off the window-sill, and, thrusting his hands into the pockets of the long, grey dust coat he was wearing, made a few steps into the room.

Sotillo got up, too, and, putting himself in the way, examined him from head to foot.

"So your countrymen do not confide in you very much, Señor Doctor. They do not love you, eh? Why is that, I wonder?"

The doctor, lifting his head, answered by a long, lifeless stare and the words, "Perhaps because I have lived too long in Costaguana."

Sotillo had a gleam of white teeth under the black moustache.

"Aha! But you love yourself," he said, encouragingly.

"If you leave them alone," the doctor said, looking with the same lifeless stare at Sotillo's handsome face, "they will betray themselves very soon. Meantime, may I try to make Don Carlos speak?"

"Ah, Señor Doctor," said Sotillo, wagging his head, "you are a man of quick intelligence. We were made to understand each other." He turned away. He could bear no longer that expressionless and motionless stare, which seemed to have a sort of impenetrable emptiness like the black depth of an abyss.

Even in a man utterly devoid of moral sense there remains an appreciation of rascality which, being conventional, is perfectly clear. Sotillo thought that Dr. Monygham, so different from all Europeans, was ready to sell his countrymen and Charles Gould, his employer, for some share of the San Tomé silver. Sotillo did not despise him for that. The colonel's want of moral sense was of a profound and innocent character. It bordered upon stupidity, moral stupidity.

Nothing that served his ends could appear to him really reprehensible. Nevertheless, he despised Dr. Monygham. He had for him an immense and satisfactory contempt. He despised him with all his heart because he did not mean to let the doctor have any reward at all. He despised him, not as a man without faith and honour, but as a fool. Dr. Monygham's insight into his character had deceived Sotillo completely. Therefore he thought the doctor a fool.

Since his arrival in Sulaco the colonel's ideas had undergone some modification.

He no longer wished for a political career in Montero's administration. He had always doubted the safety of that course. Since he had learned from the chief engineer that at daylight most likely he would be confronted by Pedro Montero his misgivings on that point had considerably increased. The *guerrillero* brother of the general — the Pedrito of popular speech — had a reputation of his own. He wasn't safe to deal with. Sotillo had vaguely planned seizing not only the treasure but the town itself, and then negotiating at leisure. But in the face of facts learned from the chief engineer (who had frankly disclosed to him the whole situation) his audacity, never of a very dashing kind, had been replaced by a most cautious hesitation.

"An army — an army has crossed the mountains under Pedrito already," he had repeated, unable to hide his consternation. "If it had not been that I am given the news by a man of your position I would never have believed it. Astonishing!"

"An armed force," corrected the engineer, suavely.

His aim was attained. It was to keep Sulaco clear of any armed occupation for a few hours longer, to let those whom fear impelled leave the town. In the general dismay there were families hopeful enough to fly upon the road towards Los Hatos, which was left open by the withdrawal of the armed rabble under Señores Fuentes and Gamacho, to Rincón, with their enthusiastic welcome for Pedro Montero. It was a hasty and risky exodus, and it was said that Hernandez, occupying with his band the woods about Los Hatos, was receiving the fugitives. That a good many people he knew were contemplating such a flight had been well known to the chief engineer.

Father Corbelán's efforts in the cause of that most pious robber had not been altogether fruitless. The political chief of Sulaco had yielded at the last moment to the urgent entreaties of the priest, had signed a provisional nomination appointing Hernandez a general, and calling upon him officially in this new capacity to preserve order in the town. The fact is that the political chief, seeing the situation desperate, did not care what he signed. It was the last official document he signed before he left the palace of the Intendencia for the refuge of the O.S.N. Company's office. But even had he meant his act to be effective it was already too late. The riot which he feared and expected broke out in less than an hour after Father Corbelán had left him. Indeed, Father Corbelán, who had appointed a meeting with Nostromo in the Dominican Convent, where he had his residence in one of the cells, never managed to reach the place. From the Intendencia he had gone straight on to the Avellanos's house to tell his brother-in-law, and though he stayed there no more than half an hour he had found himself cut off from his ascetic abode. Nostromo, after waiting there for some time, watching uneasily the increasing uproar in the street, had made his way to the offices of the *Porvenir*, and stayed there till daylight, as Decoud had mentioned in the letter to his sister. Thus the Capataz, instead of riding towards the Los Hatos woods as bearer of Hernandez's nomination, had remained in town to save the life of the President-Dictator, to assist in repressing the outbreak of the mob, and at last to sail out with the silver of the mine.

But Father Corbelán, escaping to Hernandez, had the document in his pocket, a piece of official writing turning a bandit into a general in a memorable last official act of the Ribierist party, whose watchwords were honesty, peace, and progress. Probably neither the priest nor the bandit saw the irony of it. Father Corbelán must have found messengers to send into the town, for early on the second day of the disturbances there were rumors of Hernandez being on the road to Los Hatos ready to receive those who would put themselves under his protection. A strange-looking horseman, elderly and audacious, had appeared in the town, riding slowly while his eyes examined the fronts of the houses, as though he had never seen such high buildings before. Before the cathedral he had dismounted, and, kneeling in the middle of the Plaza, his bridle over his arm and his hat lying in front of him on the ground, had bowed his head, crossing himself and beating his breast for some little time. Remounting his horse, with a fearless but not unfriendly look round the little gathering formed about his public devotions, he had asked for the Casa Avellanos. A score of hands were extended in answer, with fingers pointing up the Calle de la Constitución.

The horseman had gone on with only a glance of casual curiosity upwards to the windows of the Amarilla Club at the corner. His stentorian voice shouted periodically in the empty street, "Which is the Casa Avellanos?" till an answer came from the scared porter, and he disappeared under the gate. The letter he was bringing, written by Father Corbelán with a pencil by the camp-fire of Hernandez, was addressed to Don José, of whose critical state the priest was not aware. Antonia read it, and, after consulting Charles Gould, sent it on for the information of the gentlemen garrisoning the Amarilla Club. For herself, her mind was made up; she would rejoin her uncle; she would entrust the last day—the last hours perhaps—of her father's life to the keeping of the bandit, whose existence was a protest against the irresponsible tyranny of all parties alike, against the moral darkness of the land. The gloom of Los Hatos woods was preferable; a life of hardships in the train of a robber band less debasing. Antonia embraced with all her soul her uncle's obstinate defiance of misfortune. It was grounded in the belief in the man whom she loved.

In his message the Vicar-General answered upon his head for Hernandez's fidelity. As to his power, he pointed out that he had remained unsubdued for so many years. In that letter Decoud's idea of the new Occidental State (whose flourishing and stable condition is a matter of common knowledge now) was for the first time made public and used as an argument. Hernandez, ex-bandit and the last general of Ribierist creation, was confident of being able to hold the tract of country between the woods of Los Hatos and the coast range till that devoted patriot, Don Martin Decoud, could bring General Barrios back to Sulaco for the reconquest of the town.

"Heaven itself wills it. Providence is on our side," wrote Father Corbelán; there was no time to reflect upon or to controvert his statement; and if the discussion started upon the reading of that letter in the Amarilla Club was violent, it was also short-lived. In the general bewilderment of the collapse some jumped at the idea with joyful astonishment as upon the amazing discovery of a new hope. Others became fascinated by the prospect of immediate personal safety for their women and children. The majority caught at it as a drowning man catches at a straw. Father Corbelán was unexpectedly offering them a refuge from Pedrito Montero with his *llaneros* allied to Señores Fuentes and Gamacho with their armed rabble.

All the latter part of the afternoon an animated discussion went on in the big rooms of the Amarilla Club. Even those members posted at the windows with rifles and carbines to guard the end of the street in case of an offensive return of the populace shouted their opinions and arguments over their shoulders. As dusk fell Don Juste Lopez, inviting those *caballeros* who were of his way of thinking to follow him, withdrew into the corridor, where at a little table in the light of two candles he busied himself in composing an address, or rather a solemn declaration to be presented to Pedrito Montero by a deputation of such members of Assembly as had elected to remain in town. His idea was to propitiate him in order to save the form at least of parliamentary institutions. Seated before a blank sheet of paper, a goose-quill in his hand, and surged upon from all sides, he turned to the right and to the left, repeating with solemn insistence:

"*Caballeros*, a moment of silence! A moment of silence! We ought to make it clear that we bow in all good faith to the accomplished facts."

The utterance of that phrase seemed to give him a melancholy satisfaction. The hubbub of voices round him was growing strained and hoarse. In the sudden pauses the excited grimacing of the faces would sink all at once into the stillness of profound dejection.

Meantime, the exodus had begun. Carretas full of ladies and children rolled swaying across the Plaza, with men walking or riding by their side; mounted parties followed on mules and horses; the poorest were setting out on foot, men and women carrying bundles, clasping babies in their arms, leading old people, dragging along the bigger children. When Charles Gould, after leaving the doctor and the engineer at the Casa Viola, entered the town by the harbour gate, all those that had meant to go were gone, and the others had barricaded themselves in their houses. In the whole dark street there was only one spot of flickering lights and moving figures, where the Señor Administrador recognized his wife's carriage waiting at the door of the Avellanos's house. He rode up, almost unnoticed, and looked on without a word while some of his own servants came out of the gate carrying Don José Avellanos, who, with closed eyes and motionless features, appeared perfectly lifeless. His wife and Antonia walked on each side of the improvised stretcher, which was put at once into the carriage. The two women embraced; while from the other side of the landau Father Corbelán's emissary, with his ragged beard all streaked with grey, and high, bronzed cheek-bones, stared, sitting upright in the saddle. Then Antonia, dry-eyed, got in by the side of the stretcher, and, after making the sign of the cross rapidly, lowered a thick veil upon her face. The servants and the three or four neighbours who had come to assist, stood back, uncovering their heads. On the box, Ignacio, resigned now to driving all night (and to having perhaps his throat cut before daylight) looked back surlily over his shoulder.

"Drive carefully," cried Mrs. Gould in a tremulous voice.

"*Sí*, carefully, *sí niña*," he mumbled, chewing his lips, his round leathery cheeks quivering. And the landau rolled slowly out of the light.

"I will see them as far as the ford," said Charles Gould to his wife. She stood on the edge of the sidewalk with her hands clasped lightly, and nodded to him as he followed after the carriage. And now the windows of the Amarilla Club were dark. The last spark of resistance had died out. Turning his head at the corner, Charles Gould saw his wife crossing over to their own gate in the lighted patch of the street. One of their neighbours, a well-known merchant and landowner of the province, followed at her elbow, talking with great gestures. As she passed in all the lights went out in the street, which remained dark and empty from end to end.

The houses of the vast Plaza were lost in the night. High up, like a star, there was a small gleam in one of the towers of the cathedral; and the equestrian statue gleamed pale against the black trees of the Alameda, like a ghost of royalty haunting the scenes of revolution. The rare prowlers they met ranged themselves against the wall. Beyond the last houses the carriage rolled noiselessly on the soft cushion of dust, and with a greater obscurity a feeling of freshness seemed to fall from the foliage of the trees bordering the country road. The emissary from Hernandez's camp pushed his horse close to Charles Gould.

"*Caballero*," he said in an interested voice, "you are he whom they call the King of Sulaco, the master of the mine? Is it not so?"

"Yes, I am the master of the mine," answered Charles Gould.

The man cantered for a time in silence, then said, "I have a brother, a *sereno* in your service in the San Tomé valley. You have proved yourself a just man. There had been no wrong done to anyone since you called upon the people to work in the mountains. My brother says that no official of the Government, no oppressor of the Campo, has been seen on your side of the stream. Your own officials do not oppress the people in the gorge. Doubtless they are afraid of your severity. You are a just man and a powerful one," he added.

He spoke in an abrupt, independent tone, but evidently he was communicative with a purpose. He told Charles Gould that he had been a *ranchero* in one of the lower valleys, far south, a neighbour of Hernandez in the old days, and godfather to his eldest boy; one of those who joined him in his resistance to the recruiting raid which was the beginning of all their misfortunes. It was he that, when his *compadre** had been carried off, had buried his wife and children, murdered by the soldiers.

"*Sí, señor*," he muttered, hoarsely, "I and two or three others, the lucky ones left at liberty, buried them all in one grave near the ashes of their ranch, under the tree that had shaded its roof."

It was to him, too, that Hernandez came after he had deserted, three years afterwards. He had still his uniform on with the sergeant's stripes on the sleeve, and the blood of his colonel upon his hands and breast. Three troopers followed him, of those who had started in pursuit but had ridden on for liberty. And he told Charles Gould how he and a few friends, seeing those soldiers, lay in ambush behind some rocks ready to pull the trigger on them, when he recognized his *compadre* and jumped up from cover, shouting his name, because he knew that Hernandez could not have been coming back on an errand of injustice and oppression. Those three soldiers, together with the party who lay behind the rocks, had formed the nucleus of the famous band and he, the narrator, had been the favourite lieutenant of Hernandez for many, many years. He

---

*Friend.

mentioned proudly that the officials had put a price upon his head, too; but it did not prevent it getting sprinkled with grey upon his shoulders. And now he had lived long enough to see his *compadre* made a general.

He had a burst of muffled laughter. "And now from robbers we have become soldiers. But look, *caballero*, all those who made us soldiers and him a general! Look at these people!"

Ignacio shouted. The light of the carriage lamps, running along the nopal* hedges that crowned the bank on each side, flashed upon the scared faces of people standing aside in the road, sunk deep, like an English country lane, into the soft soil of the Campo. They cowered; their eyes glistened very big for a second; and then the light, running on, fell upon the half-denuded roots of a big tree, on another stretch of nopal hedge, caught up another bunch of faces glaring back apprehensively. Three women—of whom one was carrying a child—and a couple of men in civilian dress—one armed with a sabre and another with a gun—were grouped about a donkey carrying two bundles tied up in blankets. Farther on Ignacio shouted again to pass a carreta, a long wooden box on two high wheels, with the door at the back swinging open. Some ladies in it must have recognized the white mules, because they screamed out, "Is it you, Doña Emilia?"

At the turn of the road the glare of a big fire filled the short stretch vaulted over by the branches meeting overhead. Near the ford of a shallow stream a roadside *rancho* of woven rushes and a roof of grass had been set on fire by accident, and the flames, roaring viciously, lit up an open space blocked with horses, mules, and a distracted, shouting crowd of people. When Ignacio pulled up, several ladies on foot assailed the carriage, begging Antonia for a seat. To their clamour she answered by pointing silently to her father.

"I must leave you here," said Charles Gould, in the uproar. The flames leaped up sky-high, and in the recoil from the scorching heat across the road the stream of fugitives pressed against the carriage. A middle-aged lady dressed in black silk, but with a coarse manta over

---

*Type of cactus found in Mexico and Central America; similar to a prickly pear cactus.

her head and a rough branch for a stick in her hand, staggered against the front wheel. Two young girls, frightened and silent, were clinging to her arms. Charles Gould knew her very well.

"*Misericordia!** We are getting terribly bruised in this crowd!" she exclaimed, smiling up courageously to him. "We have started on foot. All our servants ran away yesterday to join the democrats. We are going to put ourselves under the protection of Father Corbelán, of your sainted uncle, Antonia. He has wrought a miracle in the heart of a most merciless robber. A miracle!"

She raised her voice gradually up to a scream as she was borne along by the pressure of people getting out of the way of some carts coming up out of the ford at a gallop, with loud yells and cracking of whips. Great masses of sparks mingled with black smoke flew over the road; the bamboos of the walls detonated in the fire with the sound of an irregular fusillade. And then the bright blaze sank suddenly, leaving only a red dusk crowded with aimless dark shadows drifting in contrary directions; the noise of voices seemed to die away with the flame; and the tumult of heads, arms, quarrelling, and imprecations passed on fleeing into the darkness.

"I must leave you now," repeated Charles Gould to Antonia. She turned her head slowly and uncovered her face. The emissary and *compadre* of Hernandez spurred his horse close up.

"Has not the master of the mine any message to send to Hernandez, the master of the Campo?"

The truth of the comparison struck Charles Gould heavily. In his determined purpose he held the mine, and the indomitable bandit held the Campo by the same precarious tenure. They were equals before the lawlessness of the land. It was impossible to disentangle one's activity from its debasing contacts. A close-meshed net of crime and corruption lay upon the whole country. An immense and weary discouragement sealed his lips for a time.

"You are a just man," urged the emissary of Hernandez. "Look at those people who made my *compadre* a general and have turned us all into soldiers. Look at those oligarchs fleeing for life, with only the clothes on their backs. My *compadre* does not think of that, but

---

*Mercy!

our followers may be wondering greatly, and I would speak for them to you. Listen, *señor*! For many months now the Campo has been our own. We need ask no man for anything; but soldiers must have their pay to live honestly when the wars are over. It is believed that your soul is so just that a prayer from you would cure the sickness of every beast, like the orison of the upright judge. Let me have some words from your lips that would act like a charm upon the doubts of our *partida*, where all are men."

"Do you hear what he says?" Charles Gould said in English to Antonia.

"Forgive us our misery!" she exclaimed, hurriedly. "It is your character that is the inexhaustible treasure which may save us all yet; your character, Carlos, not your wealth. I entreat you to give this man your word that you will accept any arrangement my uncle may make with their chief. One word. He will want no more."

On the site of the roadside hut there remained nothing but an enormous heap of embers, throwing afar a darkening red glow, in which Antonia's face appeared deeply flushed with excitement. Charles Gould, with only a short hesitation, pronounced the required pledge. He was like a man who had ventured on a precipitous path with no room to turn, where the only chance of safety is to press forward. At that moment he understood it thoroughly as he looked down at Don José stretched out, hardly breathing, by the side of the erect Antonia, vanquished in a lifelong struggle with the powers of moral darkness, whose stagnant depths breed monstrous crimes and monstrous illusions. In a few words the emissary from Hernandez expressed his complete satisfaction. Stoically Antonia lowered her veil, resisting the longing to inquire about Decoud's escape. But Ignacio leered morosely over his shoulder.

"Take a good look at the mules, *mi amo*,"* he grumbled. "You shall never see them again!"

---

*Master.

CHAPTER 4

CHARLES GOULD TURNED TOWARDS the town. Before him jagged peaks of the Sierra came out all black in the clear dawn. Here and there a muffled *lepero* whisked round the corner of a grass-grown street before the ringing hoofs of his horse. Dogs barked behind the walls of the gardens; and with the colourless light the chill of the snows seemed to fall from the mountains upon the disjointed pavements and the shuttered houses with broken cornices and the plaster peeling in patches between the flat pilasters of the fronts. The daybreak struggled with the gloom under the arcades on the Plaza, with no signs of country people disposing their goods for the day's market, piles of fruit, bundles of vegetables ornamented with flowers, on low benches under enormous mat umbrellas; with no cheery early-morning bustle of villagers, women, children, and loaded donkeys. Only a few scattered knots of revolutionists stood in the vast space, looking all one way from under their slouched hats for some sign of news from Rincón. The largest of those groups turned about like one man as Charles Gould passed, and shouted, *"Viva la libertad!"* after him in a menacing tone.

Charles Gould rode on, and turned into the archway of his house. In the patio littered with straw, a *practicante*[16] one of Dr. Monygham's native assistants, sat on the ground with his back against the rim of the fountain, fingering a guitar discreetly, while two girls of the lower class, standing up before him, shuffled their feet a little and waved their arms, humming a popular dance tune. Most of the wounded during the two days of rioting had been taken away already by their friends and relations, but several figures could be seen sitting up balancing their bandaged heads in time to the music. Charles Gould dismounted. A sleepy *mozo* coming out of the bakery door took hold of the horse's bridle; the *practicante* endeavoured to conceal his guitar hastily; the girls, unabashed, stepped back smiling; and Charles Gould, on his way to the staircase, glanced into a dark corner of the patio at another group, a mortally wounded *cargador* with a woman kneeling by his side; she mumbled prayers rapidly, trying at the same time to force a piece of orange between the stiffening lips of the dying man.

The cruel futility of things stood unveiled in the levity and sufferings of that incorrigible people; the cruel futility of lives and of deaths thrown away in the vain endeavour to attain an enduring solution of the problem. Unlike Decoud, Charles Gould could not play lightly a part in a tragic farce. It was tragic enough for him in all conscience, but he could see no farcical element. He suffered too much under a conviction of irremediable folly. He was too severely practical and too idealistic to look upon its terrible humours with amusement, as Martin Decoud, the imaginative materialist, was able to do in the dry light of his scepticism. To him, as to all of us, the compromises with his conscience appeared uglier than ever in the light of failure. His taciturnity, assumed with a purpose, had prevented him from tampering openly with his thoughts; but the Gould Concession had insidiously corrupted his judgement. He might have known, he said to himself, leaning over the balustrade of the corridor, that Ribierism could never come to anything. The mine had corrupted his judgement by making him sick of bribing and intriguing merely to have his work left alone from day to day. Like his father, he did not like to be robbed. It exasperated him. He had persuaded himself that, apart from higher considerations, the backing up of Don José's hopes of reform was good business. He had gone forth into the senseless fray as his poor uncle, whose sword hung on the wall of his study, had gone forth — in the defence of the commonest decencies of organized society. Only his weapon was the wealth of the mine, more far-reaching and subtle than an honest blade of steel fitted into a simple brass guard.

More dangerous to the wielder, too, this weapon of wealth, double-edged with the cupidity and misery of mankind, steeped in all the vices of self-indulgence as in a concoction of poisonous roots, tainting the very cause for which it is drawn, always ready to turn awkwardly in the hand. There was nothing for it now but to go on using it. But he promised himself to see it shattered into small bits before he let it be wrenched from his grasp.

After all, with his English parentage and English upbringing, he perceived that he was an adventurer in Costaguana, the descendant of adventurers enlisted in a foreign legion, of men who had sought fortune in a revolutionary war, who had planned revolutions, who had believed in revolutions. For all the uprightness of his character, he had something of an adventurer's easy morality which takes count of personal risk in the ethical appraising of his action. He was prepared, if need be, to blow up the whole San Tomé mountain sky high out of the territory of the Republic. This resolution expressed the tenacity of his character, the remorse of that subtle conjugal infidelity through which his wife was no longer the sole mistress of his thoughts, something of his father's imaginative weakness, and something, too, of the spirit of a buccaneer throwing a lighted match into the magazine rather than surrender his ship.

Down below in the patio the wounded *cargador* had breathed his last. The woman cried out once, and her cry, unexpected and shrill, made all the wounded sit up. The *practicante* scrambled up to his feet, and, guitar in hand, gazed steadily in her direction with elevated eyebrows. The two girls—sitting now one on each side of their wounded relative, with their knees drawn up and long cigars between their lips—nodded at each other significantly.

Charles Gould, looking down over the balustrade, saw three men dressed ceremoniously in black frockcoats with white shirts, and wearing European round hats, enter the patio from the street. One of them, head and shoulders taller than the two others, advanced with marked gravity, leading the way. This was Don Juste Lopez, accompanied by two of his friends, members of Assembly, coming to call upon the Administrador of the San Tomé mine at this early hour. They saw him, too, waved their hands to him urgently, walking up the stairs as if in procession.

Don Juste, astonishingly changed by having shaved off altogether his damaged beard, had lost with it nine-tenths of his outward dignity. Even at that time of serious preoccupation Charles Gould could not help noting the revealed ineptitude in the aspect of the man. His companions looked crestfallen and sleepy. One kept on passing the tip of his tongue over his parched lips; the other's eyes strayed dully over the tiled floor of the corridor, while Don Juste,

standing a little in advance, harangued the Señor Administrador
of the San Tomé mine. It was his firm opinion that forms had to
be observed. A new governor is always visited by deputations from
the Cabildo, which is the Municipal Council, from the Consulado,
the Commercial Board, and it was proper that the Provincial Assembly should send a deputation, too, if only to assert the existence of
parliamentary institutions. Don Juste proposed that Don Carlos
Gould, as the most prominent citizen of the province, should join
the Assembly's deputation. His position was exceptional, his personality known through the length and breadth of the whole Republic.
Official courtesies must not be neglected, if they are gone through
with a bleeding heart. The acceptance of accomplished facts may
save yet the precious vestiges of parliamentary institutions. Don
Juste's eyes glowed dully; he believed in parliamentary institutions—
and the convinced drone of his voice lost itself in the stillness of the
house like the deep buzzing of some ponderous insect.

Charles Gould had turned round to listen patiently, leaning his
elbow on the balustrade. He shook his head a little, refusing, almost
touched by the anxious gaze of the President of the Provincial Assembly. It was not Charles Gould's policy to make the San Tomé
mine a party to any formal proceedings.

"My advice, *señores*, is that you should wait for your fate in your
houses. There is no necessity for you to give yourselves up formally
into Montero's hands. Submission to the inevitable, as Don Juste
calls it, is all very well, but when the inevitable is called Pedrito Montero there is no need to exhibit pointedly the whole extent of your surrender. The fault of this country is the want of measure in political
life. Flat acquiescence in illegality, followed by sanguinary reaction—
that, *señores*, is not the way to a stable and prosperous future."

Charles Gould stopped before the sad bewilderment of the faces,
the wondering, anxious glances of the eyes. The feeling of pity for
those men, putting all their trust into words of some sort, while
murder and rapine stalked over the land, had betrayed him into
what seemed empty loquacity. Don Juste murmured:

"You are abandoning us, Don Carlos. . . . And yet, parliamentary
institutions—"

He could not finish from grief. For a moment he put his hand
over his eyes. Charles Gould, in his fear of empty loquacity, made

no answer to the charge. He returned in silence their ceremonious bows. His taciturnity was his refuge. He understood that what they sought was to get the influence of the San Tomé mine on their side. They wanted to go on a conciliating errand to the victor under the wing of the Gould Concession. Other public bodies—the Cabildo, the Consulado—would be coming, too, presently, seeking the support of the most stable, the most effective force they had ever known to exist in their province.

The doctor, arriving with his sharp, jerky walk, found that the master had retired into his own room with orders not to be disturbed on any account. But Dr. Monygham was not anxious to see Charles Gould at once. He spent some time in a rapid examination of his wounded. He gazed down upon each in turn, rubbing his chin between his thumb and forefinger; his steady stare met without expression their silently inquisitive look. All these cases were doing well; but when he came to the dead *cargador* he stopped a little longer, surveying not the man who had ceased to suffer, but the woman kneeling in silent contemplation of the rigid face, with its pinched nostrils and a white gleam in the imperfectly closed eyes. She lifted her head slowly, and said in a dull voice:

"It is not long since he had become a *cargador*—only a few weeks. His worship the Capataz had accepted him after many entreaties."

"I am not responsible for the great Capataz," muttered the doctor, moving off.

Directing his course upstairs towards the door of Charles Gould's room, the doctor at the last moment hesitated; then, turning away from the handle with a shrug of his uneven shoulders, slunk off hastily along the corridor in search of Mrs. Gould's *camerista*.

Leonarda told him that the *señora* had not risen yet. The *señora* had given into her charge the girls belonging to that Italian *posadero*. She, Leonarda, had put them to bed in her own room. The fair girl had cried herself to sleep, but the dark one—the bigger—had not closed her eyes yet. She sat up in bed clutching the sheets right up under her chin and staring before her like a little witch. Leonarda did not approve of the Viola children being admitted to the house. She made this feeling clear by the indifferent tone in which she inquired whether their mother was dead yet. As to the *señora*, she must be asleep. Ever since she had gone into her room after seeing the departure of Doña Antonia with her dying father, there had been no sound behind her door.

The doctor, rousing himself out of profound reflection, told her abruptly to call her mistress at once. He hobbled off to wait for Mrs. Gould in the *sala*. He was very tired, but too excited to sit down. In this great drawing-room, now empty, in which his withered soul had been refreshed after many arid years and his outcast spirit had accepted silently the toleration of many side-glances, he wandered haphazardly amongst the chairs and tables till Mrs. Gould, enveloped in a morning wrapper, came in rapidly.

"You know that I never approved of the silver being sent away," the doctor began at once, as a preliminary to the narrative of his night's adventures in association with Captain Mitchell, the engineer-in-chief, and old Viola, at Sotillo's headquarters. To the doctor, with his special conception of this political crisis, the removal of the silver had seemed an irrational and ill-omened measure. It was as if a general were sending the best part of his troops away on the eve of battle upon some recondite pretext. The whole lot of ingots might have been concealed somewhere where they could have been got at for the purpose of staving off the dangers which were menacing the security of the Gould Concession. The Administrador had acted as if the immense and powerful prosperity of the mine had been founded on methods of probity, on the sense of usefulness. And it was nothing of the kind. The method followed had been the only one possible. The Gould Concession had ransomed its way through all those years. It was a nauseous process. He quite understood that Charles Gould had got sick of it and had left the old path to back up that hopeless attempt at reform. The doctor did not believe in the reform of Costaguana. And now the mine was back again in its old path, with the disadvantage that henceforth it had to deal not only with the greed provoked by its wealth, but with the resentment awakened by the attempt to free itself from its bondage to moral corruption. That was the penalty of failure. What made him uneasy was that Charles Gould seemed to him to have weakened at the decisive moment when a frank return to the old methods was the only chance. Listening to Decoud's wild scheme had been a weakness.

The doctor flung up his arms, exclaiming, "Decoud! Decoud!" He hobbled about the room with slight, angry laughs. Many years ago both his ankles had been seriously damaged in the course of a certain investigation conducted in the castle of Sta. Marta by a commission composed of military men. Their nomination had been signified to them unexpectedly at the dead of night, with scowling brow, flashing eyes, and in a tempestuous voice, by Guzman Bento. The old tyrant, maddened by one of his sudden accesses of suspicion, mingled spluttering appeals to their fidelity with imprecations and horrible menaces. The cells and casements of the castle on the hill had been already filled with prisoners. The commission was charged now with the task of discovering the iniquitous conspiracy against the Citizen-Saviour of his country.

The dread of the raving tyrant translated itself into a hasty ferocity of procedure. The Citizen-Saviour was not accustomed to wait. A conspiracy had to be discovered. The courtyards of the castle resounded with the clanking of leg-irons, sounds of blows, yells of pain; and the commission of high officers laboured feverishly, concealing their distress and apprehensions from each other, and especially from their secretary, Father Berón, an army chaplain, at that time very much in the confidence of the Citizen-Saviour. That priest was a big round-shouldered man, with an unclean-looking, overgrown tonsure on the top of his flat head, of a dingy, yellow complexion, softly fat, with greasy stains all down the front of his lieutenant's uniform, and a small cross embroidered in white cotton on his left breast. He had a heavy nose and a pendant lip. Dr. Monygham remembered him still. He remembered him against all the force of his will striving its utmost to forget. Father Berón had been adjoined to the commission by Guzman Bento expressly for the purpose that his enlightened zeal should assist them in their labours. Dr. Monygham could by no manner of means forget the zeal of Father Berón, or his face, or the pitiless, monotonous voice in which he pronounced the words, "Will you confess now?"

The memory did not make him shudder, but it had made of him what he was in the eyes of respectable people, a man careless of common decencies, something between a clever vagabond and a disreputable doctor. But not all respectable people would have had the necessary delicacy of sentiment to understand with what trouble of mind and accuracy of vision Dr. Monygham, medical officer of the San Tomé mine, remembered Father Berón, army chaplain, and once a secretary of a military commission. After all these years Dr. Monygham, in his rooms at the end of the hospital building in the San Tomé gorge, remembered Father Berón as distinctly as ever. He remembered that priest at night, sometimes, in his sleep. On such nights the doctor waited for daylight with a candle lighted, and walked the whole length of his rooms to and fro, staring down at his bare feet, his arms hugging his sides tightly. He would dream of Father Berón sitting at the end of a long black table, behind which, in a row, appeared the heads, shoulders, and epaulettes of the military members, nibbling the feather of a quill pen, and listening with weary and impatient scorn to the protestations of some prisoner calling heaven to witness of his innocence, till he burst out, "What's the use of wasting time over that miserable nonsense! Let me take him outside for a while." And Father Berón would go outside after the clanking prisoner, led away between two soldiers. Such interludes happened on many days, many times, with many prisoners. When the prisoner returned he was ready to make a full confession, Father Berón would declare, leaning forward with that dull, surfeited look which can be seen in the eyes of gluttonous persons after a heavy meal.

The priest's inquisitorial instincts suffered but little from the want of classical apparatus of the Inquisition. At no time of the world's history have men been at a loss how to inflict mental and bodily anguish upon their fellow-creatures. This aptitude came to them in the growing complexity of their passions and the early refinement of their ingenuity. But it may safely be said that primeval man did not go to the trouble of inventing tortures. He was indolent and pure of heart. He brained his neighbor ferociously with a stone axe from necessity and without malice. The stupidest mind may invent a rankling phrase or brand the innocent with a cruel aspersion. A piece of string and a ramrod; a few muskets in combination with a length of hide rope; or even a simple mallet of heavy, hard wood applied with a swing to human fingers or to the joints of a human body is enough for the infliction of the most exquisite torture. The doctor had been a very stubborn prisoner, and, as a natural consequence of that "bad disposition" (so Father Berón called it), his subjugation had been very crushing and very complete. That is why the limp in his walk, the twist of his shoulders, the scars on his cheeks were so pronounced. His confessions, when they came at last, were very complete, too. Sometimes on the nights when he walked the floor, he wondered, grinding his teeth with shame and rage, at the fertility of his imagination when stimulated by a sort of pain which makes truth, honour, self-respect, and life itself matters of little moment.

And he could not forget Father Berón with his monotonous phrase, "Will you confess now?" reaching him in an awful iteration and lucidity of meaning through the delirious incoherence of unbearable pain. He could not forget. But that was not the worst. Had he met Father Berón in the street after all these years Dr. Monygham was sure he would have quailed before him. This contingency was not to be feared now. Father Berón was dead; but the sickening certitude prevented Dr. Monygham from looking anybody in the face.

Dr. Monygham had become, in a manner, the slave of a ghost. It was obviously impossible to take his knowledge of Father Berón home to Europe. When making his extorted confessions to the Military Board, Dr. Monygham was not seeking to avoid death. He longed for it. Sitting half-naked for hours on the wet earth of his prison, and so motionless that the spiders, his companions, attached their webs to his matted hair, he consoled the misery of his soul with acute reasonings that he had confessed to crimes enough for a sentence of death—that they had gone too far with him to let him live to tell the tale.

But, as if by a refinement of cruelty, Dr. Monygham was left for months to decay slowly in the darkness of his grave-like prison. It was no doubt hoped that it would finish him off without the trouble of an execution; but Dr. Monygham had an iron constitution. It was Guzman Bento who died, not by the knife thrust of a conspirator, but from a stroke of apoplexy, and Dr. Monygham was liberated hastily. His fetters were struck off by the light of a candle, which, after months of gloom, hurt his eyes so much that he had to cover his face with his hands. He was raised up. His heart was beating violently with the fear of this liberty. When he tried to walk the extraordinary lightness of his feet made him giddy, and he fell down. Two sticks were thrust into his hands, and he was pushed out of the passage. It was dusk; candles glimmered already in the windows of the officers' quarters round the courtyard; but the twilight sky dazed

him by its enormous and overwhelming brilliance. A thin poncho
hung over his naked, bony shoulders; the rags of his trousers came
down no lower than his knees; an eighteen months' growth of hair
fell in dirty grey locks on each side of his sharp cheek-bones. As he
dragged himself past the guard-room door, one of the soldiers,
lolling outside, moved by some obscure impulse, leaped forward
with a strange laugh and rammed a broken old straw hat on his
head. And Dr. Monygham, after having tottered, continued on his
way. He advanced one stick, then one maimed foot, then the other
stick; the other foot followed only a very short distance along the
ground, toilfully, as though it were almost too heavy to be moved at
all; and yet his legs under the hanging angles of the poncho appeared no thicker than the two sticks in his hands. A ceaseless trembling agitated his bent body, all his wasted limbs, his bony head, the
conical ragged crown of the sombrero, whose ample flat rim rested
on his shoulders.

In such conditions of manner and attire did Dr. Monygham go
forth to take possession of his liberty. And these conditions seemed
to bind him indissolubly to the land of Costaguana like an awful
procedure of naturalization, involving him deep in the national
life, far deeper than any amount of success and honour could have
done. They did away with his Europeanism; for Dr. Monygham
had made himself an ideal conception of his disgrace. It was a conception eminently fit and proper for an officer and a gentleman.
Dr. Monygham, before he went out to Costaguana, had been sur-
geon in one of Her Majesty's regiments of foot. It was a conception
which took no account of physiological facts or reasonable arguments; but it was not stupid for all that. It was simple. A rule of conduct resting mainly on severe rejections is necessarily simple. Dr.
Monygham's view of what it behoved him to do was severe; it was
an ideal view, in so much that it was the imaginative exaggeration
of a correct feeling. It was also, in its force, influence, and persistency, the view of an eminently loyal nature.

There was a great fund of loyalty in Dr. Monygham's nature. He
had settled it all on Mrs. Gould's head. He believed her worthy of
every devotion. At the bottom of his heart he felt an angry uneasiness before the prosperity of the San Tomé mine, because its
growth was robbing her of all peace of mind. Costaguana was no

place for a woman of that kind. What could Charles Gould have been thinking of when he brought her out there! It was outrageous! And the doctor had watched the course of events with a grim and distant reserve which, he imagined, his lamentable history imposed upon him.

Loyalty to Mrs. Gould could not, however, leave out of account the safety of her husband. The doctor had contrived to be in town at the critical time because he mistrusted Charles Gould. He considered him hopelessly infected with the madness of revolutions. That is why he hobbled in distress in the drawing-room of the Casa Gould on that morning, exclaiming, "Decoud, Decoud!" in a tone of mournful irritation.

Mrs. Gould, her colour heightened, and with glistening eyes, looked straight before her at the sudden enormity of that disaster. The finger-tips on one hand rested lightly on a low little table by her side, and the arm trembled right up to the shoulder. The sun, which looks late upon Sulaco, issuing in all the fullness of its power high up on the sky from behind the dazzling snow-edge of Higuerota, had precipitated the delicate, smooth, pearly greyness of light, in which the town lies steeped during the early hours, into sharp-cut masses of black shade and spaces of hot, blinding glare. Three long rectangles of sunshine fell through the windows of the *sala*; while just across the street the front of the Avellanos's house appeared very sombre in its own shadow seen through the flood of light.

A voice said at the door, "What of Decoud?"

It was Charles Gould. They had not heard him coming along the corridor. His glance just glided over his wife and struck full at the doctor.

"You have brought some news, doctor?"

Dr. Monygham blurted it all at once, in the rough. For some time after he had done, the Administrador of the San Tomé mine remained looking at him without a word. Mrs. Gould sank into a low chair with her hands lying on her lap. A silence reigned between those three motionless persons. Then Charles Gould spoke:

"You must want some breakfast."

He stood aside to let his wife pass first. She caught up her husband's hand and pressed it as she went out, raising the handkerchief to her eyes. The sight of her husband had brought Antonia's position to her mind, and she could not contain her tears at the thought of the poor girl. When she rejoined the two men in the dining-room after having bathed her face, Charles Gould was saying to the doctor across the table:

"No, there does not seem any room for doubt."

And the doctor assented.

"No, I don't see myself how we could question that wretched Hirsch's tale. It's only too true, I fear."

She sat down desolately at the head of the table and looked from one to the other. The two men, without absolutely turning their heads away, tried to avoid her glance. The doctor even made a show of being hungry; he seized his knife and fork, and began to eat with emphasis, as if on the stage. Charles Gould made no pretence of the sort; with his elbows raised squarely, he twisted both ends of his flaming moustaches—they were so long that his hands were quite away from his face.

"I am not surprised," he muttered, abandoning his moustaches and throwing one arm over the back of his chair. His face was calm with that immobility of expression which betrays the intensity of a mental struggle. He felt that this accident had brought to a point all the consequences involved in his line of conduct, with its conscious and subconscious intentions. There must be an end now of this silent reserve, of that air of impenetrability behind which he had been safeguarding his dignity. It was the least ignoble form of dis-sembling forced upon him by that parody of civilized institutions which offended his intelligence, his uprightness, and his sense of right. He was like his father. He had no ironic eye. He was not amused at the absurdities that prevail in this world. They hurt him in his innate gravity. He felt that the miserable death of that poor Decoud took from him his inaccessible position of a force in the background. It committed him openly unless he wished to throw up the game—and that was impossible. The material interests re-quired from him the sacrifice of his aloofness—perhaps his own safety too. And he reflected that Decoud's separationist plan had not gone to the bottom with the lost silver.

The only thing that was not changed was his position towards Mr. Holroyd. The head of silver and steel interests had entered into Costaguana affairs with a sort of passion. Costaguana had become necessary to his existence; in the San Tomé mine he had found the imaginative satisfaction which other minds would get from drama, from art, or from a risky and fascinating sport. It was a special form of the great man's extravagance, sanctioned by a moral intention, big enough to flatter his vanity. Even in this aberration of his genius he served the progress of the world. Charles Gould felt sure of being understood with precision and judged with the indulgence of their common passion. Nothing now could surprise or startle this great man. And Charles Gould imagined himself writing a letter to San Francisco in some such words: ". . . The men at the head of the movement are dead or have fled; the civil organization of the province is at an end for the present; the Blanco party in Sulaco has collapsed inexcusably, but in the characteristic manner of this country. But Barrios, untouched in Cayta, remains still available. I am forced to take up openly the plan of a provincial revolution as the only way of placing the enormous material interests involved in the prosperity and peace of Sulaco in a position of permanent safety. . . ." That was clear. He saw these words as if written in letters of fire upon the wall at which he was gazing abstractedly.

Mrs. Gould watched his abstraction with dread. It was a domestic and frightful phenomenon that darkened and chilled the house for her like a thunder-cloud passing over the sun. Charles Gould's fits of abstraction depicted the energetic concentration of a will haunted by a fixed idea. A man haunted by a fixed idea is insane. He is dangerous even if that idea is an idea of justice; for may he not bring the heaven down pitilessly upon a loved head? The eyes of Mrs. Gould, watching her husband's profile, filled with tears again. And again she seemed to see the despair of the unfortunate Antonia.

"What would I have done if Charley had been drowned while we were engaged?" she exclaimed, mentally, with horror. Her heart turned to ice, while her cheeks flamed up as if scorched by the blaze of a funeral pyre consuming all her earthly affections. The tears burst out of her eyes.

"Antonia will kill herself!" she cried out.

This cry fell into the silence of the room with strangely little effect. Only the doctor, crumbling up a piece of bread, with his head inclined on one side, raised his face, and the few long hairs sticking out of his shaggy eyebrows stirred in a slight frown. Dr. Monygham thought quite sincerely that Decoud was a singularly unworthy object for any woman's affection. Then he lowered his head again, with a curl of his lip, and his heart full of tender admiration for Mrs. Gould.

"She thinks of that girl," he said to himself; "she thinks of the Viola children; she thinks of me; of the wounded; of the miners; she always thinks of everybody who is poor and miserable! But what will she do if Charles gets the worst of it in this infernal scrimmage those confounded Avellanos have drawn him into? No one seems to be thinking of her."

Charles Gould, staring at the wall, pursued his reflections subtly.

"I shall write to Holroyd that the San Tomé mine is big enough to take in hand the making of a new State. It'll please him. It'll reconcile him to the risk."

But was Barrios really available? Perhaps. But he was inaccessible. To send off a boat to Cayta was no longer possible, since Sotillo was master of the harbour, and had a steamer at his disposal. And now, with all the democrats in the province up, and every Campo township in a state of disturbance, where could he find a man who would make his way successfully overland to Cayta with a message, a ten days' ride at least; a man of courage and resolution, who would avoid arrest or murder, and if arrested would faithfully eat the paper? The Capataz de Cargadores would have been just such a man. But the Capataz of the Cargadores was no more.

And Charles Gould, withdrawing his eyes from the wall, said gently, "That Hirsch! What an extraordinary thing! Saved himself by clinging to the anchor, did he? I had no idea that he was still in Sulaco. I thought he had gone back overland to Esmeralda more than a week ago. He came here once to talk to me about his hide business and some other things. I made it clear to him that nothing could be done."

"He was afraid to start back on account of Hernandez being about," remarked the doctor.

"And but for him we might not have known anything of what has happened," marveled Charles Gould.

Mrs. Gould cried out:

"Antonia must not know! She must not be told. Not now."

"Nobody's likely to carry the news," remarked the doctor. "It's no one's interest. Moreover, the people here are afraid of Hernandez as

if he were the devil." He turned to Charles Gould. "It's even awk-
ward, because if you wanted to communicate with the refugees you
could find no messenger. When Hernandez was ranging hundreds
of miles away from here the Sulaco populace used to shudder at the
tales of him roasting his prisoners alive."

"Yes," murmured Charles Gould; "Captain Mitchell's Capataz
was the only man in the town who had seen Hernandez eye to eye.
Father Corbelán employed him. He opened the communications
first. It is a pity that—"

His voice was covered by the booming of the great bell of the
cathedral. Three single strokes, one after another, burst out explo-
sively, dying away in deep and mellow vibrations. And then all the
bells in the tower of every church, convent, or chapel in town, even
those that had remained shut up for years, pealed out together with
a crash. In this furious flood of metallic uproar there was a power
of suggesting images of strife and violence which blanched
Mrs. Gould's cheek. Basilio, who had been waiting at table, shrinking within himself, clung to the sideboard with chattering teeth. It
was impossible to hear yourself speak.

"Shut these windows!" Charles Gould yelled at him, angrily. All
the other servants, terrified at what they took for the signal of a general
massacre, had rushed upstairs, tumbling over each other, men and
women, the obscure and generally invisible population of the ground
floor on the four sides of the patio. The women, screaming *"Misericordia!"* ran right into the room, and, falling on their knees against
the walls, began to cross themselves convulsively. The staring heads
of men blocked the doorway in an instant—*mozos* from the stable,
gardeners, nondescript helpers living on the crumbs of the munificent
house—and Charles Gould beheld all the extent of his domestic establishment, even to the gatekeeper. This was a half-paralysed old
man, whose long white locks fell down to his shoulders: an heirloom
taken up by Charles Gould's familial piety. He could remember
Henry Gould, an Englishman and a Costaguanero of the second
generation, chief of the Sulaco province; he had been his personal
mozo years and years ago in peace and war; had been allowed to attend his master in prison; had, on the fatal morning, followed the
firing-squad; and, peeping from behind one of the cypresses growing
along the wall of the Franciscan Convent, had seen, with his eyes

starting out of his head, Don Enrique throw up his hands and fall
with his face in the dust. Charles Gould noted particularly the big
patriarchal head of that witness in the rear of the other servants. But
he was surprised to see a shriveled old hag or two, of whose existence
within the walls of his house he had not been aware. They must have
been the mothers, or even the grandmothers, of some of his people.
There were a few children, too, more or less naked, crying and clinging to the legs of their elders. He had never before noticed any sign of
a child in his patio. Even Leonarda, the *camerista*, came in a fright,
pushing through, with her spoiled, pouting face of a favourite maid,
leading the Viola girls by the hand. The crockery rattled on table and
sideboard, and the whole house seemed to sway in the deafening
wave of sound.

CHAPTER 5

DURING THE NIGHT THE expectant populace had taken possession of
all the belfries in the town in order to welcome Pedrito Montero,
who was making his entry after having slept the night in Rincón.
And first came straggling in through the land gate the armed mob
of all colours, complexions, types, and states of raggedness, calling
themselves the Sulaco National Guard, and commanded by Señor
Gamacho. Through the middle of the street streamed, like a torrent
of rubbish, a mass of straw hats, ponchos, gun-barrels, with an enormous green and yellow flag flapping in their midst, in a cloud of
dust, to the furious beating of drums. The spectators recoiled against
the walls of the houses shouting their *"Vivas!"* Behind the rabble
could be seen the lances of the cavalry, the "army" of Pedro Montero. He advanced between Señores Fuentes and Gamacho at the
head of his *llaneros*, who had accomplished the feat of crossing the
páramos of the Higuerota in a snow-storm. They rode four abreast,
mounted on confiscated Campo horses, clad in the heterogeneous
stock of roadside stores they had looted hurriedly in their rapid ride
through the northern part of the province; for Pedro Montero had
been in a great hurry to occupy Sulaco. The handkerchiefs knotted

loosely around their bare throats were glaringly new, and all the right sleeves of their cotton shirts had been cut off close to the shoulder for greater freedom in throwing the *lazo*. Emaciated greybeards rode by the side of lean dark youths, marked by all the hardships of campaigning, with strips of raw beef twined round the crowns of their hats, and huge iron spurs fastened to their naked heels. Those that in the passes of the mountain had lost their lances had provided themselves with the goads used by the Campo cattlemen: slender shafts of palm fully ten feet long, with a lot of loose rings jingling under the iron-shod point. They were armed with knives and revolvers. A haggard fearlessness characterized the expression of all these sun-blacked countenances; they glared down haughtily with their scorched eyes at the crowd, or, blinking upwards insolently, pointed out to each other some particular head amongst the women at the windows. When they had ridden into the Plaza and caught sight of the equestrian statue of the King dazzlingly white in the sunshine, towering enormous and motionless above the surges of the crowd, with its eternal gesture of saluting, a murmur of surprise ran through their ranks. "What is that saint in the big hat?" they asked each other.

They were a good sample of the cavalry of the plains with which Pedro Montero had helped so much the victorious career of his brother the general. The influence which that man, brought up in coast towns, acquired in a short time over the plainsmen of the Republic can be ascribed only to a genius for treachery of so effective a kind that it must have appeared to those violent men but little removed from a state of utter savagery, as the perfection of sagacity and virtue. The popular lore of all nations testified that duplicity and cunning, together with bodily strength, were looked upon, even more than courage, as heroic virtues by primitive mankind. To overcome your adversary was the great affair of life. Courage was taken for granted. But the use of intelligence awakened wonder and respect. Stratagems, providing they did not fail, were honourable; the easy massacre of an unsuspecting enemy evoked no feelings but those of gladness, pride, and admiration. Not perhaps that primitive men were more faithless than their descendants of today, but that they went straighter to their aim, and were more artless in their recognition of success as the only standard of morality.

We have changed since. The use of intelligence awakens little wonder and less respect. But the ignorant and barbarous plainsmen engaging in civil strife followed willingly a leader who often managed to deliver their enemies bound, as it were, into their hands. Pedro Montero had a talent for lulling his adversaries into a sense of security. And as men learn wisdom with extreme slowness, and are always ready to believe promises that flatter their secret hopes, Pedro Montero was successful time after time. Whether only a servant or some inferior official in the Costaguana Legation in Paris, he had rushed back to his country directly he heard that his brother had emerged from the obscurity of his frontier *comandancia.** He had managed to deceive by his gift of plausibility the chiefs of the Ribierist movement in his capital, and even the acute agent of the San Tomé mine had failed to understand him thoroughly. At once he had obtained an enormous influence over his brother. They were very much alike in appearance, both bald, with bunches of crisp hair above their ears, arguing the presence of some Negro blood. Only Pedro was smaller than the general, more delicate altogether, with an ape-like faculty for imitating all the outward signs of refinement and distinction, and with a parrot-like talent for languages. Both brothers had received some elementary instruction by the munificence of a great European traveller, to whom their father had been a body-servant during his journeys in the interior of the country. In General Montero's case it enabled him to rise from the ranks. Pedrito, the younger, incorrigibly lazy and slovenly, had drifted aimlessly from one coast town to another, hanging about counting-houses, attaching himself to strangers as a sort of *valet de place,*† picking up an easy and disreputable living. His ability to read did nothing for him but fill his head with absurd visions. His actions were usually determined by motives so improbable in themselves as to escape the penetration of a rational person.

Thus at first sight the agent of the Gould Concession in Sta. Marta had credited him with the possession of sane views, and even with a restraining power over the general's everlastingly discontented vanity. It could never have entered his head that Pedrito

---

*Command.
†Temporary servant (Fr.).

Montero, lackey or inferior scribe, lodged in the garrets of the various Parisian hotels where the Costaguana Legation used to shelter its diplomatic dignity, had been devouring the lighter sort of historical works in the French language, such, for instance, as the books of Imbert de Saint Amand upon the Second Empire. But Pedrito had been struck by the splendour of a brilliant court, and had conceived the idea of an existence for himself where, like the Duc de Morny, he would associate the command of every pleasure with the conduct of political affairs and enjoy power supremely in every way. Nobody could have guessed that. And yet this was one of the immediate causes of the Monterist Revolution. This will appear less incredible by the reflection that the fundamental causes were the same as ever, rooted in the political immaturity of the people, in the indolence of the upper classes and the mental darkness of the lower.

Pedrito Montero saw in the elevation of his brother the road wide open to his wildest imaginings. This was what made the Monterist *pronunciamiento* so unpreventable. The general himself probably could have been bought off, pacified with flatteries, dispatched on a diplomatic mission to Europe. It was his brother who had egged him on from first to last. He wanted to become the most brilliant statesman of South America. He did not desire supreme power. He would have been afraid of its labour and risk, in fact. Before all, Pedrito Montero, taught by his European experience, meant to acquire a serious fortune for himself. With this object in view he obtained from his brother, on the very morrow of the successful battle, the permission to push on over the mountains and take possession of Sulaco. Sulaco was the land of future prosperity, the chosen land of material progress, the only province in the Republic of interest to European capitalists. Pedrito Montero, following the example of the Duc de Morny, meant to have his share of this prosperity. This is what he meant literally. Now his brother was master of the country, whether as president, dictator, or even as Emperor — why not as an Emperor? — he meant to demand a share in every enterprise — in railways, in mines, in sugar estates, in cotton mills, in land companies, in each and every undertaking — as the price of his protection. The desire to be on the spot early was the real cause of the celebrated ride over the mountains with some two hundred *llaneros*, an enterprise of which the dangers had not appeared at first clearly to his impatience. Coming from a series of victories, it seemed to him that a Montero had only to appear to be master of the situation. This illusion had betrayed him into a rashness of which he was becoming aware. As he rode at the head of his *llaneros* he regretted that there were so few of them. The enthusiasm of the populace reassured him. They yelled *"Viva Montero! Viva Pedrito!"* In order to make them still more enthusiastic, and from the natural pleasure he had in dissembling, he dropped the reins on his horse's neck, and with a tremendous effect of familiarity and confidence slipped his hands under the arms of Señores Fuentes and Gamacho. In that posture, with a ragged town *mozo* holding his horse by the bridle, he rode triumphantly across the Plaza to the door of the Intendencia. Its old gloomy walls seemed to shake in the acclamations that rent the air and covered the crashing peals of the cathedral bells.

Pedro Montero, the brother of the general, dismounted into a shouting and perspiring throng of enthusiasts whom the ragged Nationals were pushing back fiercely. Ascending a few steps he surveyed the large crowd gaping at him and the bullet-speckled walls of the houses opposite lightly veiled by a sunny haze of dust. The word "PORVENIR" in immense black capitals, alternating with broken windows, stared at him across the vast space; and he thought with delight of the hour of vengeance, because he was very sure of laying his hands upon Decoud. On his left hand, Gamacho, big and hot, wiping his hairy wet face, uncovered a set of yellow fangs in a grin of stupid hilarity. On his right, Señor Fuentes, small and lean, looked on with compressed lips. The crowd stared literally open-mouthed, lost in eager stillness, as though they had expected the great *guerrillero*, the famous Pedrito, to begin scattering at once some sort of visible largesse. What he began was a speech. He began it with the shouted word "Citizens!" which reached even those in the middle of the Plaza. Afterwards the greater part of the citizens remained fascinated by the orator's action alone, his tip-toeing, the arms flung above his head with the fists clenched, a hand laid flat upon the heart, the silver gleam of rolling eyes, the sweeping, pointing, embracing gestures, a hand laid familiarly on Gamacho's shoulder; a hand waved formally towards the little black-coated person of Señor Fuentes, advocate and politician and a true friend of

The new Jefe Político* only jerked his head sideways, and took a puff at his cigarette in sign of his agreement with this method for ridding the town of Gamacho and his inconvenient rabble.

Pedrito Montero looked with disgust at the absolutely bare floor, and at the belt of heavy gilt picture-frames running round the room, out of which the remnants of torn and slashed canvases fluttered like dingy rags.

"We are not barbarians," he said.

This was what said his Excellency, the popular Pedrito, the *guer-rillero* skilled in the art of laying ambushes, charged by his brother at his own demand with the organization of Sulaco on democratic principles. The night before, during the consultation with his partisans, who had come out to meet him in Rincón, he had opened his intentions to Señor Fuentes:

"We shall organize a popular vote, by yes or no, confiding the destinies of our beloved country to the wisdom and valiance of my heroic brother, the invincible general. A plebiscite. Do you understand?"

And Señor Fuentes, puffing out his leathery cheeks, had inclined his head slightly to the left, letting a thin, bluish jet of smoke escape through his pursed lips. He had understood.

His Excellency was exasperated at the devastation. Not a single chair, table, sofa, *étagère*, or console had been left in the state rooms of the Intendencia. His Excellency, though twitching all over with rage, was restrained from bursting into violence by a sense of his remoteness and isolation. His heroic brother was very far away. Meantime, how was he going to take his siesta? He had expected to find comfort and luxury in the Intendencia after a year of hard camp life, ending with the hardships and privations of the daring dash upon Sulaco—upon the province which was worth more in wealth and influence than all the rest of the Republic's territory. He would get even with Gamacho by-and-by. And Señor Gamacho's oration, delectable to popular ears, went on in the heat and glare of the Plaza like the uncouth howlings of an inferior sort of devil cast into a white-hot furnace. Every moment he had to wipe his streaming face

---

*Political Boss.

the people. The *"Vivas!"* of those nearest to the orator bursting out suddenly propagated themselves irregularly to the confines of the crowd, like flames running over dry grass, and expired in the opening of the streets. In the intervals, over the swarming Plaza brooded a heavy silence, in which the mouth of the orator went on opening and shutting, and detached phrases—"The happiness of the people," "Sons of the country," "The entire world, *el mundo entiero"*—reached even the packed steps of the cathedral with a feeble clear ring, thin as the buzzing of a mosquito. But the orator struck his breast; he seemed to prance between his two supporters. It was the supreme effort of his peroration. Then the two smaller figures disappeared from the public gaze and the enormous Gamacho, left alone, advanced, raising his hat high above his head. Then he covered himself proudly and yelled out, *"Ciudadanos!"** A dull roar greeted Señor Gamacho, ex-pedlar of the Campo, Comandante of the National Guard.

Upstairs Pedrito Montero walked about rapidly from one wrecked room of the Intendencia to another, snarling incessantly:

"What stupidity! What destruction!"

Señor Fuentes, following, would relax his taciturn disposition to murmur:

"It is all the work of Gamacho and his Nationals"; and then, inclining his head on his left shoulder, would press together his lips so firmly that a little hollow would appear at each corner. He had his nomination for Political Chief of the town in his pocket, and was all impatience to enter upon his functions.

In the long audience-room, with its tall mirrors all starred by stones, the hangings torn down, and the canopy over the platform at the upper end pulled to pieces, the vast, deep muttering of the crowd and the howling voice of Gamacho speaking just below reached them through the shutters as they stood idly in dimness and desolation.

"The brute!" observed his Excellency Don Pedro Montero through clenched teeth. "We must contrive as quickly as possible to send him and his Nationals out there to fight Hernandez."

---

*Citizens!

with his bare forearm; he had flung off his coat, and had turned up the sleeves of his shirt high above the elbows; but he kept on his head the large cocked hat with white plumes. His ingenuousness cherished this sign of his rank as Comandante of the National Guard. Approving and grave murmurs greeted his periods. His opinion was that war should be declared at once against France, England, Germany, and the United States, who, by introducing railways, mining enterprises, colonization, and under such other shallow pretences, aimed at robbing poor people of their lands, and with the help of these Goths and paralytics, the aristocrats would convert them into toiling and miserable slaves. And the *leperos*, flinging about the corners of their dirty white mantas, yelled their approbation. General Montero, Gamacho howled with conviction, was the only man equal to the patriotic task. They assented to that, too.

The morning was wearing on; there were already signs of disruption, currents and eddies in the crowd. Some were seeking the shade of the walls and under the trees of the Alameda. Horsemen spurred through, shouting; groups of sombreros set level on heads against the vertical sun were drifting away into the streets, where the open doors of *pulperías* revealed an enticing gloom resounding with the gentle tinkling of guitars. The National Guards were thinking of siesta, and the eloquence of Gamacho, their chief, was exhausted. Later on, when, in the cooler hours of the afternoon, they tried to assemble again for further consideration of public affairs, detachments of Montero's cavalry camped on the Alameda charged them without parley, at speed, with long lances levelled at their flying backs as far as the ends of the streets. The National Guards of Sulaco were surprised by this proceeding. But they were not indignant. No Costaguanero had ever learned to question the eccentricities of a military force. They were part of the natural order of things. This must be, they concluded, some kind of administrative measure, no doubt. But the motive of it escaped their unaided intelligence, and their chief and orator, Gamacho, Comandante of the National Guard, was lying drunk and asleep in the bosom of his family. His bare feet were upturned in the shadows repulsively, in the manner of a corpse. His eloquent mouth had dropped open. His youngest daughter, scratching her head with one hand, with the other waved a green bough over his scorched and peeling face.

CHAPTER 6

THE DECLINING SUN HAD shifted the shadows from west to east amongst the houses of the town. It had shifted them upon the whole extent of the immense Campo, with the white walls of its *haciendas* on the knolls dominating the green distances; with its grass-thatched *ranchos* crouching in the folds of ground by the banks of streams; with the dark islands of clustered trees on a clear sea of grass, and the precipitous range of the Cordillera, immense and motionless, emerging from the billows of the lower forests like the barren coast of a land of giants. The sunset rays striking the snow-slope of Higuerota from afar gave it an air of rosy youth, while the serrated mass of distant peaks remained black, as if calcined in the fiery radiance. The undulating surface of the forests seemed powdered with pale gold dust; and away there, beyond Rincón, hidden from the town by two wooded spurs, the rocks of the San Tomé gorge, with the flat wall of the mountain itself crowned by gigantic ferns, took on warm tones of brown and yellow, with red rusty streaks, and the dark green clumps of bushes rooted in crevices. From the plain the stamp sheds and the houses of the mine appeared dark and small, high up, like the nests of birds clustered on the ledges of a cliff. The zigzag paths resembled faint tracings scratched on the wall of a cyclopean blockhouse. To the two *serenos* of the mine on patrol duty, strolling, carbine in hand, and watchful eyes, in the shade of the trees lining the stream near the bridge, Don Pepe, descending the path from the upper plateau, appeared no bigger than a large beetle.

With his air of aimless, insect-like going to and fro upon the face of the rock, Don Pepe's figure kept on descending steadily, and, when near the bottom, sank at last behind the roofs of storehouses, forges, and workshops. For a time the pair of *serenos* strolled back and forth before the bridge, on which they had stopped a horseman holding a large white envelope in his hand. Then Don Pepe, emerging in the village street from amongst the houses, not a stone's throw from the frontier bridge, approached, striding in wide dark trousers tucked into boots, a white linen jacket, sabre at his side, and revolver at his belt. In this disturbed time nothing could find the Señor Gobernador with his boots off, as the saying is.

At a slight nod from one of the *serenos*, the man, a messenger from the town, dismounted, and crossed the bridge, leading his horse by the bridle.

Don Pepe received the letter from his other hand, slapped his left side and his hips in succession, feeling for his spectacle case. After settling the heavy silver-mounted affair astride his nose, and adjusting it carefully behind his ears, he opened the envelope, holding it up at about a foot in front of his eyes. The paper he pulled out contained some three lines of writing. He looked at them for a long time. His grey moustache moved slightly up and down, and the wrinkles, radiating at the corners of his eyes, ran together. He nodded serenely. "*Bueno*," he said. "There is no answer."

Then, in his quiet, kindly way, he engaged in a cautious conversation with the man, who was willing to talk cheerily, as if something lucky had happened to him recently. He had seen from a distance Sotillo's infantry camped along the shore of the harbour on each side of the Custom House. They had done no damage to the buildings. The foreigners of the railway remained shut up within the yards. They were no longer anxious to shoot poor people. He cursed the foreigners; then he reported Montero's entry and the rumours of the town. The poor were going to be made rich now. That was very good. More he did not know, and, breaking into propitiatory smiles, he intimated that he was hungry and thirsty. The old major directed him to go to the *alcalde* of the first village. The man rode off, and Don Pepe, striding slowly in the direction of a little wooden belfry, looked over a hedge into a little garden, and saw Father Román sitting in a white hammock slung between two orange trees in front of the presbytery.

An enormous tamarind shaded with its dark foliage the whole white frame-house. A young Indian girl with long hair, big eyes, and small hands and feet, carried out a wooden chair, while a thin old woman, crabbed and vigilant, watched her all the time from the veranda.

Don Pepe sat down in the chair and lighted a cigar; the priest drew in an immense quantity of snuff out of the hollow of his palm. On his reddish-brown face, worn, hollowed as if crumbled, the eyes, fresh and candid, sparkled like two black diamonds.

Don Pepe, in a mild and humorous voice informed Father Román that Pedrito Montero, by the hand of Señor Fuentes, had asked him on what terms he would surrender the mine in proper working order to a legally constituted commission of patriotic citizens, escorted by a small military force. The priest cast his eyes up to heaven. However, Don Pepe continued, the *mozo* who brought the letter said that Don Carlos Gould was alive, and so far unmolested.

Father Román expressed in a few words his thankfulness at hearing of the Señor Administrador's safety.

The hour of oration had gone by in silvery ringing of a bell in the little belfry. The belt of forest closing the entrance of the valley stood like a screen between the low sun and the street of the village. At the other end of the rocky gorge, between the walls of basalt and granite, a forest-clad mountain, hiding all the range from the San Tomé dwellers, rose steeply, lighted up and leafy to the very top. Three small rosy clouds hung motionless overhead in the great depth of blue. Knots of people sat in the street between the wattled huts. Before the *casa* of the *alcalde*, the foremen of the nightshift, already assembled to lead their men, squatted on the ground in a circle of leather skull-caps, and, bowing their bronze backs, were passing round the gourd of maté. The *mozo* from the town, having fastened his horse to a wooden post before the door, was telling them the news of Sulaco as the blackened gourd of the decoction passed from hand to hand. The grave *alcalde* himself, in a white waist-cloth and a flowered chintz gown with sleeves, open wide upon his naked stout person with an effect of a gaudy bathing robe, stood by, wearing a rough beaver hat at the back of his head, and grasping a tall staff with a silver knob in his hand. These insignia of his dignity had been conferred upon him by the Administration of the mine, the fountain of honour, of prosperity, and peace. He had been one of the first immigrants into this valley; his sons and sons-in-law worked within the mountain which seemed with its treasures to pour down the thundering ore shoots of the upper *mesa*, the gifts of well-being, security, and justice upon the toilers. He listened to the news from the town with curiosity and indifference, as if concerning another world than his own. And it was true that they appeared to him so. In a very few years the sense of belonging to a powerful organization had been developed in these harassed, half-wild Indians. They were proud of, and attached to, the mine. It had secured their confidence and belief. They invested it with a protecting and invincible virtue as though it were a fetish made by their own hands, for they were ignorant, and in other respects did not differ appreciably from the rest of mankind which puts infinite trust in its own creations. It never entered the *alcalde's* head that the mine could fail in its protection and force. Politics were good enough for the people of the town and the Campo. His yellow, round face, with wide nostrils, and motionless in expression, resembled a fierce full moon. He listened to the excited vapourings of the *mozo* without misgivings, without surprise, without any active sentiment whatever.

Padre Román sat dejectedly balancing himself, his feet just touching the ground, his hands gripping the edge of the hammock. With less confidence, but as ignorant as his flock, he asked the major what did he think was going to happen now.

Don Pepe, bolt upright in the chair, folded his hands peacefully on the hilt of his sword, standing perpendicular between his thighs, and answered that he did not know. The mine could be defended against any force likely to be sent to take possession. On the other hand, from the arid character of the valley, when the regular supplies from the Campo had been cut off, the population of the three villages could be starved into submission. Don Pepe exposed these contingencies with serenity to Father Román, who, as an old campaigner, was able to understand the reasoning of a military man. They talked with simplicity and directness. Father Román was saddened at the idea of his flock being scattered or else enslaved. He had no illusions as to their fate, not from penetration, but from long experience of political atrocities, which seemed to him fatal and unavoidable in the life of a State. The working of the usual public institutions presented itself to him most distinctly as a series of calamities overtaking private individuals and flowing logically from each other through hate, revenge, folly, and rapacity, as though they had been part of a divine dispensation. Father Román's clearsightedness was served by an uninformed intelligence; but his heart, preserving its tenderness amongst scenes of carnage, spoliation, and violence, abhorred these calamities the more as his association with the victims was closer. He entertained towards the Indians of the valley feelings of paternal scorn. He had been marrying, baptizing, confessing, absolving, and burying the workers of the San Tomé mine with dignity and unction for five years or more; and he believed in the sacredness of these ministrations, which made them his own in a spiritual sense. They were dear to his sacerdotal supremacy. Mrs. Gould's earnest interest in the concerns of these people enhanced their importance in the priest's eyes, because it really augmented his own. When talking over with her the innumerable Marias and Brigidas of the villages, he felt his own humanity expand. Padre Román was incapable of fanaticism to an almost reprehensible degree. The English *señora* was evidently a heretic; but at the same time she seemed to him wonderful and angelic. Whenever that confused state of his feelings occurred to him, while strolling, for instance, his breviary under his arm, in the wide shade of the tamarind, he would stop short to inhale with a strong snuffling noise a large quantity of snuff, and shake his head profoundly. At the thought of what might befall the illustrious *señora* presently, he became gradually overcome with dismay. He voiced it in an agitated murmur. Even Don Pepe lost his serenity for a moment. He leaned forward stiffly.

"Listen, Padre. The very fact that those thieving *macaques* in Sulaco are trying to find out the price of my honour proves that Señor Don Carlos and all in the Casa Gould are safe. As to my honour, that also is safe, as every man, woman, and child knows. But the Negro liberals who have snatched the town by surprise do not know that. *Bueno.* Let them sit and wait. While they wait they can do no harm."

And he regained his composure. He regained it easily, because whatever happened his honour of an old officer of Paez was safe. He had promised Charles Gould that at the approach of an armed force he would defend the gorge just long enough to give himself time to destroy scientifically the whole plant, buildings, and workshops of the mine with heavy charges of dynamite; block with ruins the main tunnel, break down the pathways, blow up the dam of the water-power, shatter the famous Gould Concession into fragments, flying sky-high out of a horrified world. The mine had got hold of Charles Gould with a grip as deadly as ever it had laid upon his father. But this extreme resolution had seemed to Don Pepe the most natural thing in the world. His measures had been taken with judgement. Everything was prepared with a careful completeness. And Don Pepe folded his hands pacifically on his sword hilt, and nodded at the priest. In his excitement, Father Román had flung snuff in handfuls at his face, and, all besmeared with tobacco, round-eyed, and beside himself, had got out of the hammock to walk about, uttering exclamations.

Don Pepe stroked his grey and pendant moustache, whose fine ends hung far below the clean-cut line of his jaw, and spoke with conscious pride in his reputation.

"So, Padre, I don't know what will happen. But I know that as long as I am here Don Carlos can speak to that *macaque*, Pedrito Montero, and threaten the destruction of the mine with perfect assurance that he will be taken seriously. For people know me."

He began to turn the cigar in his lips a little nervously, and went on:

"But that is talk—good for the *políticos*. I am a military man. I do not know what may happen. But I know what ought to be done—the mine should march upon the town with guns, axes, knives tied up to sticks—*por Dios*. That is what should be done. Only—"

His folded hands twitched on the hilt. The cigar turned faster in the corner of his lips.

"And who should lead but I? Unfortunately—observe—I have given my word of honour to Don Carlos not to let the mine fall into the hands of these thieves. In war—you know this, Padre—the fate of battles is uncertain, and whom could I leave here to act for me in case of defeat? The explosives are ready. But it would require a man of high honour, of intelligence, of judgement, of courage, to carry out the prepared destruction. Somebody I can trust with my honour as I can trust myself. Another officer of Paez, for instance. Or—or—perhaps one of Paez's old chaplains would do."

He got up, long, lank, upright, hard, with his martial moustache and the bony structure of his face, from which the glance of the sunken eyes seemed to transfix the priest, who stood still, an empty wooden snuff-box held upside down in his hand, and glared back, speechless, at the governor of the mine.

CHAPTER 7

AT ABOUT THAT TIME, in the Intendencia of Sulaco, Charles Gould was assuring Pedrito Montero, who had sent a request for his presence there, that he would never let the mine pass out of his hands for the profit of a Government who had robbed him of it. The Gould Concession could not be resumed. His father had not desired it. The son would never surrender it. He would never surrender it alive. And once dead, where was the power capable of resuscitating such an enterprise in all its vigour and wealth out of the ashes and ruin of destruction? There was no such power in the country. And where was the skill and capital abroad that would condescend to touch such an ill-omened corpse? Charles Gould talked in the impassive tone which had for many years served to conceal his anger and contempt. He suffered. He was disgusted with what he had to say. It was too much like heroics. In him the strictly practical instinct was in profound discord with the almost mystic view he took of his right. The Gould Concession was symbolic of abstract justice. Let the heavens fall. But since the San Tomé mine had developed its world-wide fame his threat had enough force and effectiveness to reach the rudimentary intelligence of Pedro Montero, wrapped up as it was in the futilities of historical anecdotes. The Gould Concession was a serious asset in the country's finance, and, what was more, in the private budgets of many officials as well. It was traditional. It was known. It was said. It was credible. Every Minister of Interior drew a salary from the San Tomé mine. It was natural. And Pedrito intended to be Minister of the Interior and President of the Council in his brother's Government. The Duc de Morny had occupied those high posts during the Second French Empire with conspicuous advantage to himself.

A table, a chair, a wooden bedstead had been procured for His Excellency, who, after a short siesta, rendered absolutely necessary by the labours and the pomps of his entry into Sulaco, had been getting hold of the administrative machine by making appointments, giving orders, and signing proclamations. Alone with Charles Gould in the audience room, His Excellency managed with his well-known skill to conceal his annoyance and consternation. He had begun at first to talk loftily of confiscation, but the want of all proper feeling and mobility in the Señor Administrador's features ended by affecting adversely his power of masterful expression. Charles Gould had repeated: "The Government can certainly bring about the destruction of the Sam Tomé mine if it likes; but without me it can do nothing else." It was an alarming pronouncement, and well calculated to hurt the sensibilities of a politician whose mind is bent upon the spoils of victory. And Charles Gould said also that the destruction of the San Tomé mine would cause the ruin of other undertakings, the withdrawal of European capital, the withholding, most probably, of the last instalment of the foreign loan. That stony fiend of a man said all these things (which were accessible to His Excellency's intelligence) in a cold-blooded manner which made one shudder.

A long course of reading historical works, light and gossipy in tone, carried out in garrets of Parisian hotels, sprawling on an untidy bed, to the neglect of his duties, menial or otherwise, had affected the manners of Pedro Montero. Had he seen around him the splendour of the old Intendencia, the magnificent hangings, the gilt furniture ranged along the walls; had he stood upon a daïs on a noble square of red carpet, he would have probably been very dangerous from a sense of success and elevation. But in this sacked and devastated residence, with the three pieces of common furniture huddled up in the middle of the vast apartment, Pedrito's imagination was subdued by a feeling of insecurity and impermanence. That feeling and the firm attitude of Charles Gould who had not once, so far, pronounced the word "Excellency," diminished him in his own eyes. He assumed the tone of an enlightened man of the world, and begged Charles Gould to dismiss from his mind every cause for alarm. He was now conversing, he reminded him, with the brother of the master of the country, charged with a reorganizing mission. The trusted brother of the master of the country, he repeated. Nothing was farther from the thoughts of that wise and patriotic hero than ideas of destruction. "I entreat you, Don Carlos, not to give way to your antidemocratic prejudices," he cried, in a burst of condescending effusion.

Pedrito Montero surprised one at first sight by the vast development of his bald forehead, a shiny yellow expanse between the crinkly coal-black tufts of hair without any lustre, the engaging form of his mouth, and an unexpectedly cultivated voice. But his eyes, very glistening as if freshly painted on each side of his hooked nose, had a round, hopeless, birdlike stare when opened fully. Now, however, he narrowed them agreeably, throwing his square chin up and speaking with closed teeth slightly through the nose, with what he imagined to be the manner of a *grand seigneur.**

In that attitude, he declared suddenly that the highest expression of democracy was Caesarism: the imperial rule based upon the direct popular vote. Caesarism was conservative. It was strong. It recognized the legitimate needs of democracy which requires orders, titles, and distinctions. They would be showered upon deserving men. Caesarism was peace. It was progressive. It secured the prosperity of a country. Pedrito Montero was carried away. Look at what the Second Empire had done in France. It was a régime which delighted to honour men of Don Carlos's stamp. The Second Empire fell, but that was because its chief was devoid of that military genius which had raised General Montero to the pinnacle of fame and glory. Pedrito elevated his hand jerkily to help the idea of pinnacle, of fame. "We shall have many talks yet. We shall understand each other thoroughly, Don Carlos!" he cried in a tone of fellowship. Republicanism had done its work. Imperial democracy was the power of the future. Pedrito, the *guerrillero*, showing his hand, lowered his voice forcibly. A man singled out by his fellow-citizens for the honourable nickname of El Rey de Sulaco could not but receive a full recognition from an imperial democracy as a great captain of industry and a person of weighty counsel, whose popular designation would be soon replaced by a more solid title. "Eh, Don Carlos? No! What do you say? Conde de Sulaco—Eh?—or marquis. . . ."

He ceased. The air was cool on the Plaza, where a patrol of cavalry rode round and round without penetrating into the streets,

---

*Great lord (Fr.).

which resounded with shouts and the strumming of guitars issuing from the open doors of *pulperías*. The orders were not to interfere with the enjoyments of the people. And above the roofs, next to the perpendicular lines of the cathedral towers, the snowy curve of Higuerota blocked a large space of darkening blue sky before the windows of the Intendencia. After a time Pedrito Montero, thrusting his hand in the bosom of his coat, bowed his head with slow dignity. The audience was over.

Charles Gould on going out passed his hand over his forehead as if to disperse the mists of an oppressive dream, whose grotesque extravagance leaves behind a subtle sense of bodily danger and intellectual decay. In the passages and on the staircases of the old palace Montero's troopers lounged about insolently, smoking and making way for no one; the clanking of sabres and spurs resounded all over the building. Three silent groups of civilians in severe black waited in the main gallery, formal and helpless, a little huddled up, each keeping apart from the others, as if in the exercise of a public duty they had been overcome by a desire to shun the notice of every eye. These were the deputations waiting for their audience. The one from the Provincial Assembly, more restless and uneasy in its corporate expression, was overtopped by the big face of Don Juste Lopez, soft and white, with prominent eyelids and wreathed in impenetrable solemnity as if in a dense cloud. The President of the Provincial Assembly, coming bravely to save the last shred of parliamentary institutions (on the English model), averted his eyes from the Administrador of the San Tomé mine as a dignified rebuke of his little faith in that only saving principle.

The mournful severity of that reproof did not affect Charles Gould, but he was sensible to the glances of the others directed upon him without reproach, as if only to read their own fate upon his face. All of them had talked, shouted, and declaimed in the great *sala* of the Casa Gould. The feeling of compassion for those men, struck with a strange impotence in the toils of moral degradation, did not induce him to make a sign. He suffered from his fellowship in evil with them too much. He crossed the Plaza unmolested. The Amarilla Club was full of festive ragamuffins. Their frowsy heads protruded from every window, and from within came drunken shouts, the thumping of feet, and the twanging of harps. Broken bottles strewed the pavement below. Charles Gould found the doctor still in his house.

Dr. Monygham came away from the crack in the shutter through which he had been watching the street.

"Ah! You are back at last!" he said in a tone of relief. "I have been telling Mrs. Gould that you were perfectly safe, but I was not by any means certain that the fellow would have let you go."

"Neither was I," confessed Charles Gould, laying his hat on the table.

"You will have to take action."

The silence of Charles Gould seemed to admit that this was the only course. This was as far as Charles Gould was accustomed to go towards expressing his intentions.

"I hope you did not warn Montero of what you mean to do," the doctor said, anxiously.

"I tried to make him see that the existence of the mine was bound up with my personal safety," continued Charles Gould, looking away from the doctor, and fixing his eyes upon the water-colour sketch upon the wall.

"He believed you?" the doctor asked, eagerly.

"God knows!" said Charles Gould. "I owed it to my wife to say that much. He is well enough informed. He knows that I have Don Pepe there. Fuentes must have told him. They know that the old major is perfectly capable of blowing up the San Tomé mine without hesitation or compunction. Had it not been for that I don't think I'd have left the Intendencia a free man. He would blow everything up from loyalty and from hate—from hate of these Liberals, as they call themselves. Liberals! The words one knows so well have a nightmarish meaning in this country. Liberty, democracy, patriotism, government—all of them have a flavour of folly and murder. Haven't they, doctor? . . . I alone can restrain Don Pepe. If they were to—to do away with me, nothing could prevent him."

"They will try to tamper with him," the doctor suggested, thoughtfully.

"It is very possible," Charles Gould said very low, as if speaking to himself, and still gazing at the sketch of the San Tomé gorge upon the wall. "Yes, I expect they will try that." Charles Gould looked for the first time at the doctor. "It would give me time," he added.

"Exactly," said Dr. Monygham, suppressing his excitement. "Especially if Don Pepe behaves diplomatically. Why shouldn't he give them some hope of success? Eh? Otherwise you wouldn't gain so much time. Couldn't he be instructed to—"

Charles Gould, looking at the doctor steadily, shook his head, but the doctor continued with a certain amount of fire:

"Yes, to enter into negotiations for the surrender of the mine. It is a good notion. You would mature your plan. Of course, I don't ask what it is. I don't want to know. I would refuse to listen to you if you tried to tell me. I am not fit for confidences."

"What nonsense!" muttered Charles Gould, with displeasure.

He disapproved of the doctor's sensitiveness about that far-off episode of his life. So much memory shocked Charles Gould. It was like morbidness. And again he shook his head. He refused to tamper with the open rectitude of Don Pepe's conduct, both from taste and from policy. Instructions would have to be either verbal or in writing. In either case they ran the risk of being intercepted. It was by no means certain that a messenger could reach the mine; and, besides, there was no one to send. It was on the tip of Charles's tongue to say that only the late Capataz de Cargadores could have been employed with some chance of success and the certitude of discretion. But he did not say that. He pointed out to the doctor that it would have been bad policy. Directly Don Pepe let it be supposed that he could be bought over, the Administrador's personal safety and the safety of his friends would become endangered. For there would be then no reason for moderation. The incorruptibility of Don Pepe was the essential and restraining fact. The doctor hung his head and admitted that in a way it was so.

He couldn't deny to himself that the reasoning was sound enough. Don Pepe's usefulness consisted in his unstained character. As to his own usefulness, he reflected bitterly, it was also his own character. He declared to Charles Gould that he had the means of keeping Sotillo from joining his forces with Montero, at least for the present.

"If you had had all this silver here," the doctor said, "or even if it had been known to be at the mine, you could have bribed Sotillo to throw off his recent Monterism. You could have induced him either to go away in his steamer or even to join you."

"Certainly not that last," Charles Gould declared, firmly. "What could one do with a man like that, afterwards—tell me, doctor? The silver is gone, and I am glad of it. It would have been an immediate and strong temptation. The scramble for that visible plunder would have precipitated a disastrous ending. I would have had to defend it, too. I am glad we've removed it—even if it is lost. It would have been a danger and a curse."

"Perhaps he is right," the doctor, an hour later, said hurriedly to Mrs. Gould, whom he met in the corridor. "The thing is done, and the shadow of the treasure may do just as well as the substance. Let me try to serve you to the whole extent of my evil reputation. I am off now to play my game of betrayal with Sotillo, and keep him off the town."

She put out both her hands impulsively. "Dr. Monygham, you are running a terrible risk," she whispered, averting from his face her eyes, full of tears, for a short glance at the door of her husband's room. She pressed both his hands, and the doctor stood as if rooted to the spot, looking down at her, and trying to twist his lips into a smile.

"Oh, I know you will defend my memory," he uttered at last, and ran tottering down the stairs across the patio, and out of the house. In the street he kept up a great pace with his smart hobbling walk, a case of instruments under his arm. He was known for being *loco*. Nobody interfered with him. From under the seaward gate, across the dusty, arid plain, interspersed with low bushes, he saw, more than a mile away, the ugly enormity of the Custom House, and the two or three other buildings which at that time constituted the seaport of Sulaco. Far away to the south groves of palm trees edged the curve of the harbour shore. The distant peaks of the Cordillera had lost their identity of clear-cut shapes in the steadily deepening blue of the eastern sky. The doctor walked briskly. A darkling shadow seemed to fall upon him from the zenith. The sun had set. For a time the snows of Higuerota continued to glow with the reflected glory of the west. The doctor, holding a straight course for the Custom House, appeared lonely, hopping amongst the dark bushes like a tall bird with a broken wing.

Tints of purple, gold, and crimson were mirrored in the clear water of the harbour. A long tongue of land, straight as a wall, with the grass-grown ruins of the fort making a sort of rounded green mound, plainly visible from the inner shore, closed its circuit; while beyond the Placid Gulf repeated those splendours of colouring on a greater scale and with a more sombre magnificence. The great mass of cloud filling the head of the gulf had long red smears amongst its convoluted folds of grey and black, as of a floating mantle stained with blood. The three Isabels, overshadowed and clear cut in a great smoothness confounding the sea and sky, appeared suspended, purple-black, in the air. The little wavelets seemed to be tossing tiny red sparks upon the sandy beaches. The glassy bands of water along the horizon gave out a fiery red glow, as if fire and water had been mingled together in the vast bed of the ocean.

At last the conflagration of sea and sky, lying embraced and still in a flaming contact upon the edge of the world, went out. The red sparks in the water vanished together with the stains of blood in the black mantle draping the sombre head of the Placid Gulf; a sudden breeze sprang up and died out after rustling heavily the growth of bushes on the ruined earthwork of the fort. Nostromo woke up from a fourteen hours' sleep, and arose full length from his lair in the long grass. He stood knee deep amongst the whispering undulations of the green blades with the lost air of a man just born into the world. Handsome, robust, and supple, he threw back his head, flung his arms open, and stretched himself with a slow twist of the waist and a leisurely growling yawn of white teeth, as natural and free from evil in the moment of waking as a magnificent and unconscious wild beast. Then, in the suddenly steadied glance fixed upon nothing from under a thoughtful frown, appeared the man.

CHAPTER 8

AFTER LANDING FROM HIS swim Nostromo had scrambled up, all dripping, into the main quadrangle of the old fort; and there, amongst ruined bits of walls and rotting remnants of roofs and sheds, he had slept the day through. He had slept in the shadow of the mountains, in the white blaze of noon, in the stillness and solitude of that overgrown piece of land between the oval of the harbour and the spacious semi-circle of the gulf. He lay as if dead. A *rey zamuro*,* appearing like a tiny black speck in the blue, stooped, circling prudently with a stealthiness of flight startling in a bird of that great size. The shadow of his pearly-white body, of his black-tipped wings, fell on the grass no more silently than he alighted himself on a hillock of rubbish within three yards of that man, lying as still as a corpse. The bird stretched his bare neck, craned his bald head, loathsome in the brilliance of varied colouring, with an air of voracious anxiety towards the promising stillness of that prostrate body. Then, sinking his head deeply into his soft plumage, he settled himself to wait. The first thing upon which Nostromo's eyes fell on waking was this patient watcher for the signs of death and corruption. When the man got up the vulture hopped away in great, side-long, fluttering jumps. He lingered for a while, morose and reluctant, before he rose, circling noiselessly with a sinister droop of beak and claws.

Long after he had vanished, Nostromo, lifting his eyes up to the sky, muttered, "I am not dead yet."

The Capataz of the Sulaco Cargadores had lived in splendour and publicity up to the very moment, as it were, when he took charge of the lighter containing the treasure of silver ingots.

The last act he had performed in Sulaco was in complete harmony with his vanity, and as such perfectly genuine. He had given

---

*Carrion vulture.

his last dollar to an old woman moaning with the grief and fatigue of a dismal search under the arch of the ancient gate. Performed in obscurity and without witnesses, it had still the characteristics of splendour and publicity, and was in strict keeping with his reputation. But this awakening in solitude, except for the watchful vulture, amongst the ruins of the fort, had no such characteristics. His first confused feeling was exactly this—that it was not in keeping. It was more like the end of things. The necessity of living concealed somehow, for God knows how long, which assailed him on his return to consciousness, made everything that had gone before for years appear vain and foolish, like a flattering dream come suddenly to an end.

He climbed the crumbling slope of the rampart, and, putting aside the bushes, looked upon the harbour. He saw a couple of ships at anchor upon the sheet of water reflecting the last gleams of light, and Sotillo's steamer moored to the jetty. And behind the pale long front of the Custom House, there appeared the extent of the town like a grove of thick timber on the plain with a gateway in front, and the cupolas, towers, and miradors rising above the trees, all dark, as if surrendered already to the night. The thought that it was no longer open to him to ride through the streets, recognized by everyone, great and little, as he used to do every evening on his way to play *monte* in the *posada* of the Mexican Domingo; or to sit in the place of honour, listening to songs and looking at dances, made it appear to him as a town that had no existence.

For a long time he gazed on, then let the parted bushes spring back, and, crossing over to the other side of the fort, surveyed the vaster emptiness of the great gulf. The Isabels stood out heavily upon the narrowing long band of red in the west, which gleamed low between their black shapes, and the Capataz thought of Decoud alone there with the treasure. That man was the only one who cared whether he fell into the hands of the Monterists or not, the Capataz reflected bitterly. And that merely would be an anxiety for his own sake. As to the rest, they neither knew nor cared. What he had heard Giorgio Viola say once was very true. Kings, ministers, aristocrats, the rich in general, kept the people in poverty and subjection; they kept them as they kept dogs, to fight and hunt for their service.

The darkness of the sky had descended to the line of the horizon, enveloping the whole gulf, the islets, and the lover of Antonia alone

with the treasure on the Great Isabel. The Capataz, turning his
back on these things invisible and existing, sat down and took his
face between his fists. He felt the pinch of poverty for the first time
in his life. To find himself without money after a run of bad luck at
monte in the low, smoky room of Domingo's *posada*, where the fraternity of *cargadores* gambled, sang, and danced of an evening; to
remain with empty pockets after a burst of public generosity to
some *peyne d'oro* girl or other (for whom he did not care), had none
of the humiliation of destitution. He remained rich in glory and
reputation. But since it was no longer possible for him to parade the
streets of the town, and be hailed with respect in the usual haunts of
his leisure, this sailor felt himself destitute indeed.

His mouth was dry. It was dry with heavy sleep and extremely
anxious thinking, as it had never been dry before. It may be said
that Nostromo tasted the dust and ashes of the fruit of life into
which he had bitten deeply in his hunger for praise. Without re-
moving his head from between his fists, he tried to spit before
him — "Tfui" — and muttered a curse upon the selfishness of all the
rich people.

Since everything seemed lost in Sulaco (and that was the feeling
of his waking), the idea of leaving the country altogether had presented itself to Nostromo. At that thought he had seen, like the beginning of another dream, a vision of steep and tideless shores, with
dark pines on the heights and white houses low down near a very
blue sky. He saw the quays of a big port, where the coasting feluccas, with their lateen sails* outspread like motionless wings, enter
gliding silently between the end of long moles of squared blocks
that project angularly towards each other, hugging a cluster of shipping to the superb bosom of a hill covered with palaces. He remembered these sights not without some filial emotion, though he
had been habitually and severely beaten as a boy on one of these
feluccas by a short-necked, shaven Genoese, with a deliberate and
distrustful manner, who (he firmly believed) had cheated him out
of his orphan's inheritance. But it is mercifully decreed that the
evils of the past should appear but faintly in retrospect. Under the

---

*Triangular sails extended by a long spar slung to a low mast.

sense of loneliness, abandonment, and failure, the idea of return to
these things appeared tolerable. But, what? Return? With bare feet
and head, with one check shirt and a pair of cotton *calzoneros* for
all worldly possessions?

The renowned Capataz, his elbows on his knees and a fist dug
into each cheek, laughed with self-derision, as he had spat with disgust, straight out before him into the night. The confused and intimate impressions of universal dissolution which beset a subjective
nature at any strong check to its ruling passion had a bitterness approaching that of death itself. He was simple. He was as ready to become the prey of any belief, superstition, or desire as a child.

The facts of his situation he could appreciate like a man with a
distinct experience of the country. He saw them clearly. He was as if
sobered after a long bout of intoxication. His fidelity had been
taken advantage of. He had persuaded the body of cargadores to
side with the Blancos against the rest of the people; he had had in-
terviews with Don José; he had been made use of by Father Corbelán for negotiating with Hernandez; it was known that Don
Martin Decoud had admitted him to a sort of intimacy, so that he
had been free of the offices of the Porvenir. All these things had flattered him in the usual way. What did he care about their politics?
Nothing at all. And at the end of it all—Nostromo here and Nostromo there—where is Nostromo? Nostromo can do this and that—
work all day and ride all night—behold! he found himself a marked
Ribierist for any sort of vengeance Gamacho, for instance, would
choose to take, now the Montero party had, after all, mastered the
town. The Europeans had given up; the caballeros had given up.
Don Martin had indeed explained it was only temporary—that he
was going to bring Barrios to the rescue. Where was that now—with
Don Martin (whose ironic manner of talk had always made the Capataz feel vaguely uneasy) stranded on the Great Isabel? Everybody
had given up. Even Don Carlos had given up. The hurried removal
of the treasure out to sea meant nothing else than that. The Capataz de Cargadores, on a revulsion of subjectiveness, exasperated
almost to insanity, beheld all his world without faith and courage.
He had been betrayed!

With the boundless shadows of the sea behind him, out of his
silence and immobility, facing the lofty shapes of the lower peaks

crowded around the white, misty sheen of Higuerota, Nostromo laughed aloud again, sprang abruptly to his feet, and stood still. He must go. But where?

"There is no mistake. They keep us and encourage us as if we were dogs born to fight and hunt for them. The *vecchio* is right," he said, slowly and scathingly. He remembered old Giorgio taking his pipe out of his mouth to throw these words over his shoulder at the café, full of engine-drivers and fitters from the railway workshops. This image fixed his wavering purpose. He would try to find old Giorgio if he could. God knows what might have happened to him! He made a few steps, then stopped again and shook his head. To the left and right, in front and behind him, the scrubby bush rustled mysteriously in the darkness.

"Teresa was right, too," he added in a low tone touched with awe. He wondered whether she was dead in her anger with him or still alive. As if in answer to this thought, half of remorse and half of hope, with a soft flutter and oblique flight, a big owl, whose appalling cry: "Ya-acabo! Ya-acabo! — it is finished; it is finished" — announces calamity and death in the popular belief, drifted vaguely like a large dark ball across his path. In the downfall of all the realities that made his force, he was affected by the superstition, and shuddered slightly. Signora Teresa must have died, then. It could mean nothing else. The cry of the ill-omened bird, the first sound he was to hear on his return, was a fitting welcome for his betrayed individuality. The unseen powers which he had offended by refusing to bring a priest to a dying woman were lifting up their voice against him. She was dead. With admirable and human consistency he referred everything to himself. She had been a woman of good counsel always. And the bereaved old Giorgio remained stunned by his loss just as he was likely to require the advice of his sagacity. The blow would render the dreamy old man quite stupid for a time.

As to Captain Mitchell, Nostromo, after the manner of trusted subordinates, considered him as a person fitted by education perhaps to sign papers in an office and to give orders, but otherwise of no use whatever, and something of a fool. The necessity of winding round his little finger, almost daily, the pompous and testy self-importance of the old seaman had grown irksome with use to Nostromo. At first it had given him an inward satisfaction. But the necessity of overcoming small obstacles becomes wearisome to a self-confident personality as much by the certitude of success as by the monotony of effort. He mistrusted his superior's proneness to fussy action. That old Englishman had no judgement, he said to himself. It was useless to suppose that, acquainted with the true state of the case, he would keep it to himself. He would talk of doing impracticable things. Nostromo feared him as one would fear saddling one's self with some persistent worry. He had no discretion. He would betray the treasure. And Nostromo had made up his mind that the treasure should not be betrayed.

The word had fixed itself tenaciously in his intelligence. His imagination had seized upon the clear and simple notion of betrayal to account for the dazed feeling of enlightenment as to being done for, of having inadvertently gone out of his existence on an issue in which his personality had not been taken into account. A man betrayed is a man destroyed. Signora Teresa (may God have her soul!) had been right. He had never been taken into account. Destroyed! Her white form sitting up bowed in bed, the falling black hair, the wide-browed suffering face raised to him, the anger of her denunciations appeared to him now majestic with the awfulness of inspiration and of death. For it was not for nothing that the evil bird had uttered its lamentable shriek over his head. She was dead—may God have her soul!

Sharing in the anti-priestly freethought of the masses, his mind used the pious formula from the superficial force of habit, but with a deep-seated sincerity. The popular mind is incapable of scepticism; and that incapacity delivers their helpless strength to the wiles of swindlers and to the pitiless enthusiasms of leaders inspired by visions of a high destiny. She was dead. But would God consent to receive her soul? She had died without confession or absolution, because he had not been willing to spare her another moment of his time. His scorn of priests as priests remained; but after all, it was impossible to know whether what they affirmed was not true. Power, punishment, pardon are simple and credible notions. The magnificent Capataz de Cargadores, deprived of certain simple realities, such as the admiration of women, the adulation of men, the admired publicity of his life, was ready to feel the burden of sacrilegious guilt descend upon his shoulders.

Bareheaded, in a thin shirt and drawers, he felt the lingering warmth of the fine sand under the soles of his feet. The narrow strand gleamed far ahead in a long curve, defining the outline of this wild side of the harbour. He flitted along the shore like a pursued shadow between the sombre palm-groves and the sheet of water lying as still as death on his right hand. He strode with headlong haste in the silence and solitude as though he had forgotten all prudence and caution. But he knew that on this side of the water he ran no risk of discovery. The only inhabitant was a lonely, silent, apathetic Indian in charge of the *palmarías*,* who brought sometimes a load of coconuts to the town for sale. He lived without a woman in an open shed, with a perpetual fire of dry sticks smouldering near an old canoe lying bottom up on the beach. He could be easily avoided.

The barking of the dogs about that man's *ranche* was the first thing that checked his speed. He had forgotten the dogs. He swerved sharply, and plunged into the palm-grove, as into a wilderness of columns in an immense hall, whose dense obscurity seemed to whisper and rustle faintly high above his head. He traversed it, entered a ravine, climbed to the top of a steep ridge free of trees and bushes.

From there, open and vague in the starlight, he saw the plain between the town and the harbour. In the woods above some nightbird made a strange drumming noise. Below beyond the *palmaría* on the beach, the Indian's dogs continued to bark uproariously. He wondered what had upset them so much, and, peering down from his elevation, was surprised to detect accountable movements of the ground below, as if several oblong pieces of the plain had been in motion. Those dark, shifting patches, alternately catching and eluding the eye, altered their place always away from the harbour, with a suggestion of consecutive order and purpose. A light dawned upon him. It was a column of infantry on a night march towards the higher broken country at the foot of the hills. But he was too much in the dark about everything for wonder and speculation.

The plain had resumed its shadowy immobility. He descended the ridge and found himself in the open solitude, between the harbour and the town. Its spaciousness, extended indefinitely by an

---

*Palm groves.

effect of obscurity, rendered more sensible his profound isolation. His pace became slower. No one waited for him; no one thought of him; no one expected or wished his return. "Betrayed! Betrayed!" he muttered to himself. No one cared. He might have been drowned by this time. No one would have cared—unless, perhaps, the children, he thought to himself. But they were with the English *signora*, and not thinking of him at all.

He wavered in his purpose of making straight for the Casa Viola. To what end? What could he expect there? His life seemed to fail him in all its details, even to the scornful reproaches of Teresa. He was aware painfully of his reluctance. Was it that remorse which she had prophesied with, what he saw now, was her last breath?

Meantime, he had deviated from the straight course, inclining by a sort of instinct to the left, towards the jetty and the harbour, the scene of his daily labours. The great length of the Custom House loomed up all at once like the wall of a factory. Not a soul challenged his approach, and his curiosity became excited as he passed cautiously towards the front by the unexpected sight of two lighted windows.

They had the fascination of a lonely vigil kept by some mysterious watcher up there, those two windows shining dimly upon the harbour in the whole vast extent of the abandoned building. The solitude could almost be felt. A strong smell of wood smoke hung about in a thin haze, which was faintly perceptible to his raised eyes against the glitter of the stars. As he advanced in the profound silence, the shrilling of innumerable cicadas in the dry grass seemed positively deafening to his strained ears. Slowly, step by step, he found himself in the great hall, sombre and full of acrid smoke.

A fire built against the staircase had burnt down impotently to a low heap of embers. The hard wood had failed to catch; only a few steps at the bottom smouldered, with a creeping glow of sparks defining their charred edges. At the top he saw a streak of light from an open door. It fell upon the vast landing, all foggy with a slow drift of smoke. That was the room. He climbed the stairs, then checked himself, because he had seen within the shadow of a man cast upon one of the walls. It was a shapeless, high-shouldered shadow of somebody standing still, with lowered head, out of his line of sight. The Capataz, remembering that he was totally unarmed, stepped aside, and, effacing himself upright in a dark corner, waited with his eyes fixed on the door.

The whole enormous ruined barrack of a place, unfinished, without ceilings under its lofty roof, was pervaded by the smoke swaying to and fro in the faint cross-draughts playing in the obscurity of many lofty rooms and barnlike passages. Once one of the swinging shutters came against the wall with a single sharp crack, as if pushed by an impatient hand. A piece of paper scurried out from somewhere, rustling along the landing. The man, whoever he was, did not darken the lighted doorway. Twice the Capataz, advancing a couple of steps out of his corner, craned his neck in the hope of catching sight of what he could be at, so quietly, in there. But every time he saw only the distorted shadow of broad shoulders and bowed head. He was doing apparently nothing, and stirred not from the spot, as though he were meditating—or, perhaps, reading a paper. And not a sound issued from the room.

Once more the Capataz stepped back. He wondered who it was—some Monterist? But he dreaded to show himself. To discover his presence on shore, unless after many days, would, he believed, endanger the treasure. With his own knowledge possessing his whole soul, it seemed impossible that anybody in Sulaco should fail to jump at the right surmise. After a couple of weeks or so it would be different. Who could tell he had not returned overland from some port beyond the limits of the Republic? The existence of the treasure confused his thoughts with a peculiar sort of anxiety, as though his life had become bound up with it. It rendered him timorous for a moment before that enigmatic, lighted door. Devil take the fellow! He did not want to see him. There would be nothing to learn from his face, known or unknown. He was a fool to waste his time there in waiting.

Less than five minutes after entering the place the Capataz began his retreat. He got away down the stairs with perfect success, gave one upward look over his shoulder at the light on the landing, and ran stealthily across the hall. But at the very moment he was turning out of the great door, with his mind fixed upon escaping the notice of the man upstairs, somebody he had not heard coming briskly along the front ran full into him. Both muttered a stifled exclamation of surprise, and leaped back and stood still, each indistinct to the other.

Nostromo was silent. The other man spoke first, in an amazed and deadened tone.

"Who are you?"

Already Nostromo had seemed to recognize Dr. Monygham. He had no doubt now. He hesitated the space of a second. The idea of bolting without a word presented itself to his mind. No use! An inexplicable repugnance to pronounce the name by which he was known kept him silent a little longer. At last he said in a low voice:

"A *cargador*."

He walked up to the other. Dr. Monygham had received a shock. He flung his arms up and cried out his wonder aloud, forgetting himself before the marvel of this meeting. Nostromo angrily warned him to moderate his voice. The Custom House was not so deserted as it looked. There was somebody in the lighted room above.

There is no more evanescent quality in an accomplished fact than its wonderfulness. Solicited incessantly by the considerations affecting its fears and desires, the human mind turns naturally away from the marvellous side of events. And it was in the most natural way possible that the doctor asked this man whom only two minutes before he believed to have been drowned in the gulf:

"You have seen somebody up there? Have you?"

"No, I have not seen him."

"Then how do you know?"

"I was running away from his shadow when we met."

"His shadow?"

"Yes. His shadow in the lighted room," said Nostromo, in a contemptuous tone. Leaning back with folded arms at the foot of the immense building, he dropped his head, biting his lips slightly, and not looking at the doctor. "Now," he thought to himself, "he will begin asking me about the treasure."

But the doctor's thoughts were concerned with an event not as marvellous as Nostromo's appearance, but in itself much less clear. Why had Sotillo taken himself off with his whole command with this suddenness and secrecy? What did this move portend? However, it dawned upon the doctor that the man upstairs was one of the officers left behind by the disappointed colonel to communicate with him.

"I believe he is waiting for me," he said.

"It is possible."

"I must see. Do not go away yet, Capataz."

"Go away where?" muttered Nostromo.

Already the doctor had left him. He remained leaning against the wall, staring at the dark water of the harbour; the shrilling of cicadas filled his ears. An invincible vagueness coming over his thoughts took from them all power to determine his will.

"Capataz! Capataz!" the doctor's voice called urgently from above.

The sense of betrayal and ruin floated upon his sombre indifference as upon a sluggish sea of pitch. But he stepped out from under the wall, and, looking up, saw Dr. Monygham leaning out of a lighted window.

"Come up and see what Sotillo has done. You need not fear the man up here."

He answered by a slight, bitter laugh. Fear a man! The Capataz of the Sulaco Cargadores fear a man! It angered him that anybody should suggest such a thing. It angered him to be disarmed and skulking and in danger because of the accursed treasure, which was of so little account to the people who had tied it round his neck. He could not shake off the worry of it. To Nostromo the doctor represented all these people. . . . And he had never even asked after it. Not a word of inquiry about the most desperate undertaking of his life.

Thinking these thoughts, Nostromo passed again through the cavernous hall, where the smoke was considerably thinned, and went up the stairs, not so warm to his feet now, towards the streak of light at the top. The doctor appeared in it for a moment, agitated and impatient.

"Come up! Come up!"

At the moment of crossing the doorway the Capataz experienced a shock of surprise. The man had not moved. He saw his shadow in the same place. He started, then stepped in with a feeling of being about to solve a mystery.

It was very simple. For an infinitesimal fraction of a second, against the light of two flaring and guttering candles, through a blue, pungent, thin haze which made his eyes smart, he saw the man standing, as he had imagined him, with his back to the door, casting an enormous and distorted shadow upon the wall. Swifter than a flash of lightning followed the impression of his constrained, toppling attitude—the shoulders projecting forward, the head sunk low upon the breast. Then he distinguished the arms behind his back, and wrenched so terribly that the two clenched fists, lashed together, had been forced up higher than the shoulder-blades. From there his eyes traced in one instantaneous glance the hide rope going upwards from the tied wrists over a heavy beam and down to a staple in the wall. He did not want to look at the rigid legs, at the feet hanging down nervelessly, with their bare toes some six inches above the floor, to know that the man had been given the estrapade till he had swooned. His first impulse was to dash forward and sever the rope at one blow. He felt for his knife. He had no knife—not even a knife. He stood quivering, and the doctor, perched on the edge of the table, facing thoughtfully the cruel and lamentable sight, his chin in his hand, uttered, without stirring:

"Tortured—and shot dead through the breast—getting cold."

This information calmed the Capataz. One of the candles flickering in the socket went out. "Who did this?" he asked.

"Sotillo, I tell you. Who else? Tortured—of course. But why shot?" The doctor looked fixedly at Nostromo, who shrugged his shoulders slightly. "And mark, shot suddenly, on impulse. It is evident. I wish I had his secret."

Nostromo had advanced, and stooped slightly to look. "I seem to have seen that face somewhere," he muttered. "Who is he?"

The doctor turned his eyes upon him again. "I may yet come to envying his fate. What do you think of that, Capataz, eh?"

But Nostromo did not even hear these words. Seizing the remaining light, he thrust it under the drooping head. The doctor sat oblivious, with a lost gaze. Then the heavy iron candlestick, as if struck out of Nostromo's hand, clattered on the floor.

"Hullo!" exclaimed the doctor, looking up with a start. He could hear the Capataz stagger against the table and gasp. In the sudden extinction of the light within, the dead blackness sealing the window-frames became alive with stars to his sight.

"Of course, of course," the doctor muttered to himself in English. "Enough to make him jump out of his skin."

Nostromo's heart seemed to force itself into his throat. His head swam. Hirsch! The man was Hirsch! He held on tight to the edge of the table.

"But he was hiding in the lighter," he almost shouted. His voice fell. "In the lighter, and—and—"

"And Sotillo brought him in," said the doctor. "He is no more startling to you than you were to me. What I want to know is how he induced some compassionate soul to shoot him."

"So Sotillo knows—" began Nostromo, in a more equable voice.

"Everything!" interrupted the doctor.

The Capataz was heard striking the table with his fist. "Everything? What are you saying, there? Everything? Know everything? It is impossible! Everything?"

"Of course. What do you mean by impossible? I tell you I have heard this Hirsch questioned last night, here, in this very room. He knew your name, Decoud's name, and all about the loading of the silver. . . . The lighter was cut in two. He was grovelling in abject terror before Sotillo, but he remembered that much. What do you want more? He knew least about himself. They found him clinging to their anchor. He must have caught at it just as the lighter went to the bottom."

"Went to the bottom?" repeated Nostromo, slowly. "Sotillo believes that? *Bueno!*"

The doctor, a little impatiently, was unable to imagine what else anybody could believe. Yes, Sotillo believed that the lighter was sunk, and the Capataz de Cargadores, together with Martin Decoud and perhaps one or two other political fugitives, had been drowned.

"I told you well, Señor Doctor," remarked Nostromo at that point, "that Sotillo did not know everything."

"Eh? What do you mean?"

"He did not know I was not dead."

"Neither did we."

"And you did not care—none of you *caballeros* on the wharf— once you got off a man of flesh and blood like yourselves on a fool's business that could not end well."

"You forget, Capataz, I was not on the wharf. And I did not think well of the business. So you need not taunt me. I tell you what, personality—the only thing lost in that desperate affair. But the doctor, engrossed by a desperate adventure of his own, was terrible in the pursuit of his idea. He let an exclamation of regret escape him.

"I could almost wish you had shouted and shown a light."

This unexpected utterance astounded the Capataz by its character of cold-blooded atrocity. It was as much as to say, "I wish you had shown yourself a coward; I wish you had had your throat cut for your pains." Naturally he referred it to himself, whereas it related only to the silver, being uttered simply and with many mental reservations. Surprise and rage rendered him speechless, and the doctor pursued, practically unheard by Nostromo, whose stirred blood was beating violently in his ears.

"For I am convinced Sotillo in possession of the silver would have turned short round and made for some small port abroad. Economically it would have been wasteful, but still less wasteful than having it sunk. It was the next best thing to having it at hand in some safe place, and using part of it to buy up Sotillo. But I doubt whether Don Carlos would have ever made up his mind to it. He is not fit for Costaguana, and that is a fact, Capataz."

The Capataz had mastered the fury that was like a tempest in his ears in time to hear the name of Don Carlos. He seemed to have come out of it a changed man—a man who spoke thoughtfully in a soft and even voice.

"And would Don Carlos have been content if I had surrendered this treasure?"

"I should not wonder if they were all of that way of thinking now," the doctor said, grimly. "I was never consulted. Decoud had it his own way. Their eyes are opened by this time, I should think. I for one know that if that silver turned up this moment miraculously ashore I would give it to Sotillo. And, as things stand, I would be approved."

"Turned up miraculously," repeated the Capataz very low; then raised his voice. "That, *señor*, would be a greater miracle than any saint could perform."

"I believe you, Capataz," said the doctor, drily.

He went on to develop his view of Sotillo's dangerous influence upon the situation. And the Capataz, listening as if in a dream, felt himself of as little account as the indistinct, motionless shape of the man, we had but little leisure to think of the dead. Death stands near behind us all. You were gone."

"I went, indeed!" broke in Nostromo. "And for the sake of what—tell me?"

"Ah! that is your own affair," the doctor said, roughly. "Do not ask me."

Their flowing murmurs paused in the dark. Perched on the edge of the table with slightly averted faces, they felt their shoulders touch, and their eyes remained directed towards an upright shape nearly lost in the obscurity of the inner part of the room, that with projecting head and shoulders, in ghastly immobility, seemed intent on catching every word.

"*Muy bien!*" Nostromo muttered at last. "So be it. Teresa was right. It is my own affair."

"Teresa is dead," remarked the doctor, absently, while his mind followed a new line of thought suggested by what might have been called Nostromo's return to life. "She died, the poor woman."

"Without a priest?" the Capataz asked, anxiously.

"What a question! Who could have got a priest for her last night?"

"May God keep her soul!" ejaculated Nostromo, with a gloomy and hopeless fervour which had no time to surprise Dr. Monygham, before, reverting to the previous conversation, he continued in a sinister tone, "*Sí*, Señor Doctor. As you were saying, it is my own affair. A very desperate affair."

"There are no two men in this part of the world that could have saved themselves by swimming as you have done," the doctor said, admiringly.

And again there was silence between those two men. They were both reflecting, and the diversity of their natures made their thoughts born from their meeting swing afar from each other. The doctor, impelled to risky action by his loyalty to the Goulds, wondered with thankfulness at the chain of accident which had brought that man back where he would be of the greatest use in the work of saving the San Tomé mine. The doctor was loyal to the mine. It presented itself to his fifty-years-old eyes in the shape of a little woman in a soft dress with a long train, with a head attractively overweighted by a great mass of fair hair and the delicate preciousness of her inner worth, partaking of a gem and a flower, revealed in every attitude of her person.

As the dangers thickened round the San Tomé mine this illusion acquired force, permanency, and authority. It claimed him at last! This
claim, exalted by a spiritual detachment from the usual sanctions of
hope and reward, made Dr. Monygham's thinking, acting, individuality, extremely dangerous to himself and to others, all his scruples
vanishing in the proud feeling that his devotion was the only thing
that stood between an admirable woman and a frightful disaster.

It was a sort of intoxication which made him utterly indifferent
to Decoud's fate, but left his wits perfectly clear for the appreciation
of Decoud's political idea. It was a good idea—and Barrios was the
only instrument of its realization. The doctor's soul, withered and
shrunk by the shame of moral disgrace, became implacable in the
expansion of its tenderness. Nostromo's return was providential. He
did not think of him humanely, as of a fellow-creature just escaped
from the jaws of death. The Capataz for him was the only possible
messenger to Cayta. The very man. The doctor's misanthropic mistrust of mankind (the bitterer because based on personal failure)
did not lift him sufficiently above common weaknesses. He was under the spell of an established reputation. Trumpeted by Captain
Mitchell, grown in repetition, and fixed in general assent, Nostromo's faithfulness had never been questioned by Dr. Monygham
as a fact. It was not likely to be questioned now he stood in desperate need of it himself. Dr. Monygham was human; he accepted the
popular conception of the Capataz's incorruptibility simply because no word or fact had ever contradicted a mere affirmation. It
seemed to be a part of the man, like his whiskers or his teeth. It was
impossible to conceive him otherwise. The question was whether
he would consent to go on such a dangerous and desperate errand.
The doctor was observant enough to have become aware from the
first of something peculiar in the man's temper. He was no doubt
sore about the loss of the silver.

"It will be necessary to take him into my fullest confidence," he
said to himself, with a certain acuteness of insight into the nature he
had to deal with.

On Nostromo's side the silence had been full of black irresolution, anger, and mistrust. He was the first to break it, however.

"The swimming was no great matter," he said. "It is what went
before—and what comes after that—"

He did not quite finish what he meant to say, breaking
as though his thought had butted against a solid obstacle.
tor's mind pursued its own schemes with Machiavellian
He said as sympathetically as he was able:

"It is unfortunate, Capataz. But no one would think of
you. Very unfortunate. To begin with, the treasure ought
have left the mountain. But it was Decoud who—howeve
dead. There is no need to talk of him."

"No," assented Nostromo, as the doctor paused, "there is n
to talk of dead men. But I am not dead yet."

"You are all right. Only a man of your intrepidity coul
saved himself."

In this Dr. Monygham was sincere. He esteemed highly
trepidity of that man, whom he valued but little, being disillu
as to mankind in general, because of the particular instan
which his own manhood had failed. Having had to enco
single-handed during his period of eclipse many physical da
he was well aware of the most dangerous element common to
all: of the crushing, paralysing sense of human littleness, wh
what really defeats a man struggling with natural forces, alon
from the eyes of his fellows. He was eminently fit to appreciat
mental image he made for himself of the Capataz, after hou
tension and anxiety, precipitated suddenly into an abyss of w
and darkness, without earth or sky, and confronting it not only
an undismayed mind, but with sensible success. Of course,
man was an incomparable swimmer, that was known, but the
tor judged that this instance testified to a still greater intrepidit
spirit. It was pleasing to him; he augured well from it for the suc
of the arduous mission with which he meant to entrust the Capa
so marvellously restored to usefulness. And in a tone vaguely gr
fied, he observed:

"It must have been terribly dark!"

"It was the worst darkness of the Golfo," the Capataz assent
briefly. He was mollified by what seemed a sign of some faint int
est in such things as had befallen him, and dropped a few descr
tive phrases with an affected and curt nonchalance. At that mome
he felt communicative. He expected the continuance of that intere
which, whether accepted or rejected, would have restored to him h

dead man whom he saw upright under the beam, with his air of listening also, disregarded, forgotten like a terrible example of neglect.

"Is it for an unconsidered and foolish whim that they came to me, then?" he interrupted, suddenly. "Had I not done enough for them to be of some account, *por Dios?* Is it that the *hombres finos*—the gentlemen—need not think as long as there is a man of the people ready to risk his body and soul? Or, perhaps, we have no souls—like dogs?"

"There was Decoud, too, with his plan," the doctor reminded him again.

"*Sí!* And the rich man in San Francisco who had something to do with that treasure, too—what do I know? No! I have heard too many things. It seems to me that everything is permitted to the rich."

"I understand, Capataz," the doctor began.

"What Capataz?" broke in Nostromo, in a forcible but even voice. "The Capataz is undone, destroyed. There is no Capataz. Oh, no! You will find the Capataz no more."

"Come, this is childish!" remonstrated the doctor; and the other calmed down suddenly.

"I have been indeed like a little child," he muttered.

And as his eyes met again the shape of the murdered man suspended in his awful immobility, which seemed the uncomplaining immobility of attention, he asked, wondering gently:

"Why did Sotillo give the estrapade to this pitiful wretch? Do you know? No torture could have been worse than his fear. Killing I can understand. His anguish was intolerable to behold. But why should he torment him like this? He could tell no more."

"No; he could tell nothing more. Any sane man would have seen that. He had told him everything. But I tell you what it is, Capataz. Sotillo would not believe what he was told. Not everything."

"What is it he would not believe? I cannot understand."

"I can, because I have seen the man. He refuses to believe that the treasure is lost."

"What?" the Capataz cried out in a discomposed tone.

"That startles you—eh?"

"Am I to understand, *señor,*" Nostromo went on in a deliberate and, as it were, watchful tone, "that Sotillo thinks the treasure has been saved by some means?"

"No! no! That would be impossible," said the doctor, with conviction; and Nostromo emitted a grunt in the dark. "That would be impossible. He thinks that the silver was no longer in the lighter when she was sunk. He has convinced himself that the whole show of getting it away to sea is a mere sham got up to deceive Gamacho and his Nationals, Pedrito Montero, Señor Fuentes, our new Jefe Político, and himself, too. Only, he says, he is no such fool."

"But he is devoid of sense. He is the greatest imbecile that ever called himself a colonel in this country of evil," growled Nostromo.

"He is no more unreasonable than many sensible men," said the doctor. "He has convinced himself that the treasure can be found because he desires passionately to possess himself of it. And he is also afraid of his officers turning upon him and going over to Pedrito, whom he has not the courage either to fight or trust. Do you see that, Capataz? He need fear no desertion as long as some hope remains of that enormous plunder turning up. I have made it my business to keep this very hope up."

"You have!" the Capataz de Cargadores repeated cautiously. "Well, that is wonderful. And how long do you think you are going to keep it up?"

"As long as I can."

"What does that mean?"

"I can tell you exactly. As long as I live," the doctor retorted in a stubborn voice. Then, in a few words, he described the story of his arrest and the circumstances of his release. "I was going back to that silly scoundrel when we met," he concluded.

Nostromo had listened with profound attention. "You have made up your mind, then, to a speedy death," he muttered through his clenched teeth.

"Perhaps, my illustrious Capataz," the doctor said, testily. "You are not the only one here who can look an ugly death in the face."

"No doubt," mumbled Nostromo, loud enough to be overheard. "There may be even more than two fools in this place. Who knows?"

"And that is my affair," said the doctor, curtly.

"As taking out the accursed silver to sea was my affair," retorted Nostromo. "I see. *Bueno*. Each of us has his reasons. But you were the last man I conversed with before I started, and you talked to me as if I were a fool."

Nostromo had a great distaste for the doctor's sardonic treatment of his great reputation. Decoud's faintly ironic recognition used to make him uneasy; but the familiarity of a man like Don Martin was flattering, whereas the doctor was a nobody. He could remember him a penniless outcast, slinking about the streets of Sulaco, without a single friend or acquaintance, till Don Carlos Gould took him into the service of the mine.

"You may be very wise," he went on, thoughtfully, staring into the obscurity of the room, pervaded by the gruesome enigma of the tortured and murdered Hirsch. "But I am not such a fool as when I started. I have learned one thing since, and that is that you are a dangerous man."

Dr. Monygham was too startled to do more than exclaim:

"What is it you say?"

"If he could speak he would say the same thing," pursued Nostromo, with a nod of his shadowy head silhouetted against the star-lit window.

"I do not understand you," said Dr. Monygham faintly.

"No? Perhaps, if you had not confirmed Sotillo in his madness, he would have been in no haste to give the estrapade to that miserable Hirsch."

The doctor started at the suggestion. But his devotion, absorbing all his sensibilities, had left his heart steeled against remorse and pity. Still, for complete relief, he felt the necessity of repelling it loudly and contemptuously.

"Bah! You dare to tell me that, with a man like Sotillo. I confess I did not give a thought to Hirsch. If I had it would have been useless. Anybody can see that the luckless wretch was doomed from the moment he caught hold of the anchor. He was doomed, I tell you! Just as I myself am doomed—most probably."

This is what Dr. Monygham said in answer to Nostromo's remark, which was plausible enough to prick his conscience. He was not a callous man. But the necessity, the magnitude, the importance of the task he had taken upon himself dwarfed all merely humane considerations. He had undertaken it in a fanatical spirit. He did not like it. To lie, to deceive, to circumvent even the basest of mankind was odious to him. It was odious to him by training, instinct, and tradition. To do these things in the character of a traitor was abhorrent to his nature and terrible to his feelings. He had made that sacrifice in a spirit of abasement. He had said to himself bitterly, "I am the only one fit for that dirty work." And he believed this. He was not subtle. His simplicity was such that, though he had no sort of heroic idea of seeking death, the risk, deadly enough, to which he exposed himself, had a sustaining and comforting effect. To that spiritual state the fate of Hirsch presented itself as part of the general atrocity of things. He considered that episode practically. What did it mean? Was it a sign of some dangerous change in Sotillo's delusion? That the man should have been killed like this was what the doctor could not understand.

"Yes. But why shot?" he murmured to himself.

Nostromo kept very still.

CHAPTER 9

DISTRACTED BETWEEN DOUBTS AND hopes, dismayed by the sound of bells pealing out the arrival of Pedrito Montero, Sotillo had spent the morning in battling with his thoughts; a contest to which he was unequal, from the vacuity of his mind and the violence of his passions. Disappointment, greed, anger, and fear made a tumult in the colonel's breast louder than the din of bells in the town. Nothing he had planned had come to pass. Neither Sulaco nor the silver of the mine had fallen into his hands. He had performed no military exploit to secure his position, and had obtained no enormous booty to make off with. Pedrito Montero, either as friend or foe, filled him with dread. The sound of bells maddened him.

Imagining at first that he might be attacked at once, he had made his battalion stand to arms on the shore. He walked to and fro all the length of the room, stopping sometimes to gnaw the finger-tips of his right hand with a lurid sideways glare fixed on the floor; then, with a sullen, repelling glance all round, he would resume his tramping in savage aloofness. His hat, horsewhip, sword, and revolver were lying on the table. His officers, crowding the window giving the view of the town gate, disputed amongst themselves the use of his field-glass bought last year on long credit from Anzani. It passed from hand to hand, and the possessor for the time being was besieged by anxious inquiries.

"There is nothing; there is nothing to see!" he would repeat, impatiently.

There was nothing. And when the picket in the bushes near the Casa Viola had been ordered to fall back upon the main body, no stir of life appeared on the stretch of dusty and arid land between the town and the waters of the port. But late in the afternoon a horseman issuing from the gate was made out riding up fearlessly. It was an emissary from Señor Fuentes. Being all alone he was allowed to come on. Dismounting at the great door he greeted the silent bystanders with cheery impudence, and begged to be taken up at once to the *"muy valiente"** colonel.

Señor Fuentes, on entering upon his functions of Jefe Político, had turned his diplomatic abilities to getting hold of the harbour as well as of the mine. The man he pitched upon to negotiate with Sotillo was a Notary Public, whom the revolution had found languishing in the common jail on a charge of forging documents. Liberated by the mob along with the other "victims of Blanco tyranny," he had hastened to offer his services to the new Government.

He set out determined to display much zeal and eloquence in trying to induce Sotillo to come into town alone for a conference with Pedrito Montero. Nothing was farther from the colonel's intentions. The mere fleeting idea of trusting himself into the famous Pedrito's hands had made him feel unwell several times. It was out of the question—it was madness. And to put himself in open hostility was madness, too. It would render impossible a systematic search for that treasure, for that wealth of silver which he seemed to feel somewhere about, to scent somewhere near.

But where? Where? Heavens! Where? Oh! why had he allowed that doctor to go! Imbecile that he was. But no! It was the only right course, he reflected distractedly, while the messenger waited downstairs chatting agreeably to the officers. It was in that scoundrelly doctor's true interest to return with positive information. But what if

---

*Very valiant.

anything stopped him? A general prohibition to leave the town, for instance! There would be patrols!

The colonel, seizing his head in his hands, turned in his tracks as if struck with vertigo. A flash of craven inspiration suggested to him an expedient not unknown to European statesmen when they wish to delay a difficult negotiation. Booted and spurred, he scrambled into the hammock with undignified haste. His handsome face had turned yellow with the strain of weighty cares. The ridge of his shapely nose had grown sharp; the audacious nostrils appeared mean and pinched. The velvety, caressing glance of his fine eyes seemed dead and even decomposed; for these almond-shaped, languishing orbs had become inappropriately bloodshot with much sinister sleeplessness. He addressed the surprised envoy of Señor Fuentes in a deadened, exhausted voice. It came pathetically feeble from under a pile of ponchos, which buried his elegant person right up to the black moustaches, uncurled, pendant, in sign of bodily prostration and mental incapacity. Fever, fever—a heavy fever had overtaken the *"muy valiente"* colonel. A wavering wildness of expression, caused by the passing spasms of a slight colic which had declared itself suddenly, and the rattling teeth of repressed panic, had a genuineness which impressed the envoy. It was a cold fit. The colonel explained that he was unable to think, to listen, to speak. With an appearance of superhuman effort the colonel gasped out that he was not in a state to return a suitable reply or to execute any of his Excellency's orders. But tomorrow! Tomorrow! Ah! tomorrow! Let his Excellency Don Pedro be without uneasiness. The brave Esmeralda Regiment held the harbour, held— And closing his eyes, he rolled his aching head like a half-delirious invalid under the inquisitive stare of the envoy, who was obliged to bend down over the hammock in order to catch the painful and broken accents. Meantime, Colonel Sotillo trusted that his Excellency's humanity would permit the doctor, the English doctor, to come out of town with his case of foreign remedies to attend upon him. He begged anxiously his worship the *caballero* now present for the grace of looking in as he passed the Casa Gould, and informing the English doctor, who was probably there, that his services were immediately required by Colonel Sotillo, lying ill of fever in the Custom House. Immediately. Most urgently required. Awaited with extreme impatience. A thousand thanks. He closed his eyes wearily and would not open them again, lying perfectly still, deaf, dumb, insensible, overcome, vanquished, crushed, annihilated by the fell disease.

But as soon as the other had shut after him the door of the landing, the colonel leaped out with a fling of both feet in an avalanche of woollen coverings. His spurs having become entangled in a perfect welter of ponchos he nearly pitched on his head, and did not recover his balance till the middle of the room. Concealed behind the half-closed jalousies he listened to what went on below.

The envoy had already mounted, and turning to the morose officers occupying the great doorway, took off his hat formally.

"*Caballeros*," he said, in a very loud tone, "allow me to recommend you to take great care of your colonel. It has done me much honour and gratification to have seen you all, a fine body of men exercising the soldierly virtue of patience in this exposed situation, where there is much sun, and no water to speak of, while a town full of wine and feminine charms is ready to embrace you for the brave men you are. *Caballeros*, I have the honour to salute you. There will be much dancing tonight in Sulaco. Good-bye!"

But he reined in his horse and inclined his head sideways on seeing the old major step out, very tall and meagre, in a straight narrow coat coming down to his ankles as if it were the casing of the regimental colours rolled round their staff.

The intelligent old warrior, after enunciating in a dogmatic tone the general proposition that the "world was full of traitors," went on pronouncing deliberately a panegyric upon Sotillo. He ascribed to him with leisurely emphasis every virtue under heaven, summing it all up in an absurd colloquialism current amongst the lower class of Occidentals (especially about Esmeralda). "And," he concluded, with a sudden rise in the voice, "a man of many teeth — '*hombre de muchos dientes.*' *Sí, señor.* As to us," he pursued, portentous and impressive, "your worship is beholding the finest body of officers in the Republic, men unequalled for valour and sagacity, '*y hombres de muchos dientes.*'"

"What? All of them?" inquired the disreputable envoy of Señor Fuentes, with a faint, derisive smile.

"*Todos. Sí, señor,*" the major affirmed, gravely, with conviction. "Men of many teeth."

The other wheeled his horse to face the portal resembling the high gate of a dismal barn. He raised himself in his stirrups, extended one arm. He was a facetious scoundrel, entertaining for these stupid Occidentals a feeling of great scorn natural in a native from the central provinces. The folly of Esmeraldians especially aroused his amused contempt. He began an oration upon Pedro Montero, keeping a solemn countenance. He flourished his hand as if introducing him to their notice. And when he saw every face set, all the eyes fixed upon his lips, he began to shout a sort of catalogue of perfections: "Generous, valorous, affable, profound"—he snatched off his hat enthusiastically—"a statesman, an invincible chief of partisans—" He dropped his voice startlingly to a deep, hollow note—"and a dentist."

He was off instantly at a smart walk; the rigid straddle of his legs, the turned-out feet, the stiff back, the rakish slant of the sombrero above the square, motionless set of the shoulders expressing an infinite, awe-inspiring impudence.

Upstairs, behind the jalousies, Sotillo did not move for a long time. The audacity of the fellow appalled him. What were his officers saying below? They were saying nothing. Complete silence. He quaked. It was not thus that he had imagined himself at that stage of the expedition. He had seen himself triumphant, unquestioned, appeased, the idol of the soldiers, weighing in secret complacency the agreeable alternatives of power and wealth open to his choice. Alas! How different! Distracted, restless, supine, burning with fury, or frozen with terror, he felt a dread as fathomless as the sea creep upon him from every side. That rogue of a doctor had to come out with his information. That was clear. It would be of no use to him—alone. He could do nothing with it. Malediction! The doctor would never come out. He was probably under arrest already, shut up together with Don Carlos. He laughed aloud insanely. Ha! ha! ha! ha! It was Pedrito Montero who would get the information. Ha! ha! ha! ha!—and the silver. Ha!

All at once, in the midst of the laugh, he became motionless and silent as if turned into stone. He, too, had a prisoner. A prisoner who must, must know the real truth. He would have to be made to speak.

And Sotillo, who all that time had not quite forgotten Hirsch, felt an inexplicable reluctance at the notion of proceeding to extremities.

He felt a reluctance—part of that unfathomable dread that crept on all sides upon him. He remembered reluctantly, too, the dilated eyes of the hide merchant, his contortions, his loud sobs and protestations. It was not compassion or even mere nervous sensibility. The fact was that though Sotillo did never for a moment believe his story—he could not believe it; nobody could believe such nonsense—yet those accents of despairing truth impressed him disagreeably. They made him feel sick. And he suspected also that the man might have gone mad with fear. A lunatic is a hopeless subject. Bah! A pretence. Nothing but a pretence. He would know how to deal with that.

He was working himself up to the right pitch of ferocity. His fine eyes squinted slightly; he clapped his hands; a bare-footed orderly appeared noiselessly; a corporal, with his bayonet hanging on his thigh and a stick in his hand.

The colonel gave his orders, and presently the miserable Hirsch, pushed in by several soldiers, found him frowning awfully in a broad armchair, hat on head, knees wide apart, arms akimbo, masterful, imposing, irresistible, haughty, sublime, terrible.

Hirsch, with his arms tied behind his back, had been bundled violently into one of the smaller rooms. For many hours he remained apparently forgotten, stretched lifelessly on the floor. From that solitude, full of despair and terror, he was torn out brutally, with kicks and blows, passive, sunk in hebetude.* He listened to threats and admonitions, and afterwards made his usual answers to questions, with his chin sunk on his breast, his hands tied behind his back, swaying a little in front of Sotillo, and never looking up. When he was forced to hold up his head, by means of a bayonet-point prodding him under the chin, his eyes had a vacant, trance-like stare, and drops of perspiration as big as peas were seen hailing down the dirt, bruises, and scratches of his white face. Then they stopped suddenly.

Sotillo looked at him in silence. "Will you depart from your obstinacy, you rogue?" he asked. Already a rope, whose one end was

---

*Lethargy, dullness.

fastened to Señor Hirsch's wrists, had been thrown over a beam, and three soldiers held the other end, waiting. He made no answer. His heavy lower lip hung stupidly. Sotillo made a sign. Hirsch was jerked up off his feet, and a yell of despair and agony burst out in the room, filled the passages of the great building, rent the air outside, caused every soldier of the camp along the shore to look up at the windows, started some of the officers in the hall babbling excitedly, with shining eyes; others, setting their lips, looked gloomily at the floor.

Sotillo, followed by the soldiers, had left the room. The sentry on the landing presented arms. Hirsch went on screaming all alone behind the half-closed jalousies while the sunshine, reflected from the water of the harbour, made an ever-running ripple of light high up on the wall. He screamed with uplifted eyebrows and a wide-open mouth—incredibly wide, black, enormous, full of teeth—comical.

In the still burning air of the windless afternoon he made the waves of his agony travel as far as the O.S.N. Company's offices. Captain Mitchell on the balcony, trying to make out what went on generally, had heard him faintly but distinctly, and the feeble and appalling sound lingered in his ears after he had retreated indoors with blanched cheeks. He had been driven off the balcony several times during that afternoon.

Sotillo, irritable, moody, walked restlessly about, held consultations with his officers, gave contradictory orders in this shrill clamour pervading the whole empty edifice. Sometimes there would be long and awful silences. Several times he had entered the torture-chamber where his sword, horsewhip, revolver, and field-glass were lying on the table, to ask with forced calmness, "Will you speak the truth now? No? I can wait." But he could not afford to wait much longer. That was just it. Every time he went in and came out with a slam of the door, the sentry on the landing presented arms, and got in return a black, venomous, unsteady glance, which, in reality, saw nothing at all, being merely the reflection of the soul within—a soul of gloomy hatred, irresolution, avarice, and fury.

The sun had set when he went in once more. A soldier carried in two lighted candles and slunk out, shutting the door without noise.

"Speak, thou Jewish child of the devil! The silver! The silver, I say? Where is it? Where have you foreign rogues hidden it? Confess or—"

A slight quiver passed up the taut rope from the racked limbs, but the body of Señor Hirsch, enterprising businessman from Esmeralda, hung under the heavy beam perpendicular and silent, facing the colonel awfully. The inflow of the night air, cooled by the snows of the Sierra, spread gradually a delicious freshness through the close heat of the room.

"Speak—thief—scoundrel—*pícaro*—or—"

Sotillo had seized the riding-whip, and stood with his arm lifted up. For a word, for one little word, he felt he would have kneeled, cringed, grovelled on the floor before the drowsy, conscious stare of those fixed eyeballs starting out of the grimy, dishevelled head that drooped very still with its mouth closed askew. The colonel ground his teeth with rage and struck. The rope vibrated leisurely to the blow, like the long string of a pendulum starting from a rest. But no swinging motion was imparted to the body of Señor Hirsch, the well-known hide merchant on the coast. With a convulsive effort of the twisted arms it leaped up a few inches, curling upon itself like a fish on the end of a line. Señor Hirsch's head was flung back on his straining throat; his chin trembled. For a moment the rattle of his chattering teeth pervaded the vast, shadowy room, where the candles made a patch of light round the two flames burning side by side. And as Sotillo, staying his raised hand, waited for him to speak, with the sudden flash of a grin and a straining forward of the wrenched shoulders, he spat violently into his face.

The uplifted whip fell, and the colonel sprang back with a low cry of dismay, as if aspersed by a jet of deadly venom. Quick as thought he snatched up his revolver, and fired twice. The report and the concussion of the shots seemed to throw him at once from ungovernable rage into idiotic stupor. He stood with drooping jaw and stony eyes. What had he done, *sangre de Dios!** What had he done? He was basely appalled at his impulsive act, sealing for ever these lips from which so much was to be extorted. What could he say? How could he explain? Ideas of headlong flight somewhere, anywhere, passed through his mind; even the craven and absurd notion of hiding under the table occurred to his cowardice. It was

---

*Blood of God!

too late; his officers had rushed in tumultuously, in a great clatter of scabbards, clamouring, with astonishment and wonder. But since they did not immediately proceed to plunge their swords into his breast, the brazen side of his character asserted itself. Passing the sleeve of his uniform over his face he pulled himself together. His truculent glance turned slowly here and there, checked the noise where it fell; and the stiff body of the late Señor Hirsch, merchant, after swaying imperceptibly, made a half turn, and came to a rest in the midst of awed murmurs and uneasy shuffling.

A voice remarked loudly, "Behold a man who will never speak again." And another, from the back row of faces, timid and pressing, cried out:

"Why did you kill him, *mi coronel?*"

"Because he has confessed everything," answered Sotillo, with the hardihood of desperation. He felt himself cornered. He brazened it out on the strength of his reputation with very fair success. His hearers thought him very capable of such an act. They were disposed to believe his flattering tale. There is no credulity so eager and blind as the credulity of covetousness, which, in its universal extent, measures the moral misery and the intellectual destitution of mankind. Ah! he had confessed everything, this fractious Jew, this *bribón*. Good! Then he was no longer wanted. A sudden dense guffaw was heard from the senior captain—a bigheaded man, with little round eyes and monstrously fat cheeks which never moved. The old major, tall and fantastically ragged like a scarecrow, walked round the body of the late Señor Hirsch, muttering to himself with ineffable complacency that like this there was no need to guard against any future treacheries of that scoundrel. The others stared, shifting from foot to foot, and whispering short remarks to each other.

Sotillo buckled on his sword and gave curt, peremptory orders to hasten the retirement decided upon in the afternoon. Sinister, impressive, his sombrero pulled right down upon his eyebrows, he marched first through the door in such disorder of mind that he forgot utterly to provide for Dr. Monygham's possible return. As the officers trooped out after him, one or two looked back hastily at the late Señor Hirsch, merchant from Esmeralda, left swinging rigidly at rest, alone with the two burning candles. In the emptiness of the room the burly shadow of head and shoulders on the wall had an air of life.

Below, the troops fell in silently and moved off by companies without drum or trumpet. The old scarecrow major commanded the rearguard; but the party he left behind with orders to fire the Custom House (and "burn the carcass of the treacherous Jew where it hung') failed somehow in their haste to set the staircase properly alight. The body of the late Señor Hirsch dwelt alone for a time in the dismal solitude of the unfinished building, resounding weirdly with sudden slams and clicks of doors and latches, with rustling scurries of torn papers, and the tremulous sighs that at each gust of wind passed under the high roof. The light of the two candles burning before the perpendicular and breathless immobility of the late Señor Hirsch threw a gleam afar over land and water, like a signal in the night. He remained to startle Nostromo by his presence, and to puzzle Dr. Monygham by the mystery of his atrocious end.

"But why shot?" the doctor again asked himself, audibly. This time he was answered by a dry laugh from Nostromo.

"You seem much concerned at a very natural thing, Señor Doctor. I wonder why? It is very likely that before long we shall all get shot one after another, if not by Sotillo, then by Pedrito, or Fuentes, or Gamacho. And we may even get the estrapade, too, or worse—*quién sabe?*—with your pretty tale of the silver you put into Sotillo's head."

"It was in his head already," the doctor protested. "I only—"

"Yes. And you only nailed it there so that the devil himself—"

"That is precisely what I meant to do," caught up the doctor.

"That is what you meant to do. *Bueno.* It is as I say. You are a dangerous man."

Their voices, which without rising had been growing quarrelsome, ceased suddenly. The late Señor Hirsch, erect and shadowy against the stars, seemed to be waiting attentive, in impartial silence.

But Dr. Monygham had no mind to quarrel with Nostromo. At this supremely critical point of Sulaco's fortunes it was borne upon him at last that this man was really indispensable, more indispensable than ever the infatuation of Captain Mitchell, his proud discoverer, could conceive; far beyond what Decoud's best dry raillery about "my illustrious friend, the unique Capataz de Cargadores," had ever intended. The fellow was unique. He was not "one in a thousand." He was absolutely the only one. The doctor surrendered.

There was something in the genius of that Genoese seaman which dominated in the destinies of great enterprises and of many people, the fortunes of Charles Gould, the fate of an admirable woman. At this last thought the doctor had to clear his throat before he could speak.

In a completely changed tone he pointed out to the Capataz that, to begin with, he personally ran no great risk. As far as everybody knew he was dead. It was an enormous advantage. He had only to keep out of sight in the Casa Viola, where the old Garibaldino was known to be alone—with his dead wife. The servants had all run away. No one would think of searching for him there, or anywhere else on earth, for that matter.

"That would be very true," Nostromo spoke up, bitterly, "if I had not met you."

For a time the doctor kept silent. "Do you mean to say that you think I may give you away?" he asked in an unsteady voice. "Why? Why should I do that?"

"What do I know? Why not? To gain a day perhaps. It would take Sotillo a day to give me the estrapade, and try some other things perhaps, before he puts a bullet through my heart—as he did to that poor wretch here. Why not?"

The doctor swallowed with difficulty. His throat had gone dry in a moment. It was not from indignation. The doctor, pathetically enough, believed that he had forfeited the right to be indignant with anyone—for anything. It was simple dread. Had the fellow heard his story by some chance? If so, there was an end of his usefulness in that direction. The indispensable man escaped his influence, because of that indelible blot which made him fit for dirty work. A feeling as of sickness came upon the doctor. He would have given anything to know, but he dared not clear up the point. The fanaticism of his devotion, fed on the sense of his abasement, hardened his heart in sadness and scorn.

"Why not, indeed?" he re-echoed, sardonically. "Then the safe thing for you is to kill me on the spot. I would defend myself. But you may just as well know I am going about unarmed."

"*Por Dios!*" said the Capataz, passionately. "You fine people are all alike. All dangerous. All betrayers of the poor who are your dogs."

"You do not understand," began the doctor, slowly.

"I understand you all!" cried the other with a violent movement, as shadowy to the doctor's eyes as the persistent immobility of the late Señor Hirsch. "A poor man amongst you has got to look after himself. I say that you do not care for those that serve you. Look at me! After all these years, suddenly, here I find myself like one of these curs that bark outside the walls—without a kennel or a dry bone for my teeth. *Caramba!*" But he relented with a contemptuous fairness. "Of course," he went on, quietly, "I do not suppose that you would hasten to give me up to Sotillo, for example. It is not that. It is that I am nothing! Suddenly—" He swung his arm downwards. "Nothing to anyone," he repeated.

The doctor breathed freely. "Listen, Capataz," he said, stretching out his arm almost affectionately towards Nostromo's shoulder. "I am going to tell you a very simple thing. You are safe because you are needed. I would not give you away for any conceivable reason, because I want you."

In the dark Nostromo bit his lip. He had heard enough of that. He knew what that meant. No more of that for him. But he had to look after himself now, he thought. And he thought, too, that it would not be prudent to part in anger from his companion. The doctor, admitted to be a great healer, had, amongst the populace of Sulaco, the reputation of being an evil sort of man. It was based solidly on his personal appearance, which was strange, and on his rough ironic manner—proofs visible, sensible, and incontrovertible of the doctor's malevolent disposition. And Nostromo was of the people. So he only grunted incredulously.

"You, to speak plainly, are the only man," the doctor pursued. "It is in your power to save this town and . . . everybody from the destructive rapacity of men who—"

"No, *señor*," said Nostromo, sullenly. "It is not in my power to get the treasure back for you to give up to Sotillo, or Pedrito, or Gamacho. What do I know?"

"Nobody expects the impossible," was the answer.

"You have said it yourself—nobody," muttered Nostromo, in a gloomy, threatening tone.

But Dr. Monygham, full of hope, disregarded the enigmatic words and the threatening tone. To their eyes, accustomed to obscurity, the late Señor Hirsch, growing more distinct, seemed to have come nearer. And the doctor lowered his voice in exposing his scheme as though afraid of being overheard.

He was taking the indispensable man into his fullest confidence. Its implied flattery and suggestion of great risks came with a familiar sound to the Capataz. His mind, floating in irresolution and discontent, recognized it with bitterness. He understood well that the doctor was anxious to save the San Tomé mine from annihilation. He would be nothing without it. It was his interest. Just as it had been the interest of Señor Decoud, of the Blancos, and of the Europeans to get his Cargadores on their side. His thoughts became arrested upon Decoud. What would happen to him?

Nostromo's prolonged silence made the doctor uneasy. He pointed out, quite unnecessarily, that though for the present he was safe, he could not live concealed for ever. The choice was between accepting the mission to Barrios, with all its dangers and difficulties, and leaving Sulaco by stealth, ingloriously, in poverty.

"None of your friends could reward you and protect you just now, Capataz. Not even Don Carlos himself."

"I would have none of your protection and none of your rewards. I only wish I could trust your courage and your sense. When I return in triumph, as you say, with Barrios, I may find you all destroyed. You have the knife at your throat now."

It was the doctor's turn to remain silent in the contemplation of horrible contingencies.

"Well, we would trust your courage and your sense. And you, too, have a knife at your throat."

"Ah! And whom am I to thank for that? What are your politics and your mines to me—your silver and your constitutions—your Don Carlos this, and Don José that—"

"I don't know," burst out the exasperated doctor. "There are innocent people in danger whose little finger is worth more than you or I and all the Ribierists together. I don't know. You should have asked yourself before you allowed Decoud to lead you into all this. It was your place to think like a man; but if you did not think, then try to act like a man now. Did you imagine Decoud cared very much for what would happen to you?"

"No more than you care for what will happen to me," muttered the other.

"No; I care for what will happen to you as little as I care for what will happen to myself."

"And all this because you are such a devoted Ribierist?" Nostromo said in an incredulous tone.

"All this because I am such a devoted Ribierist," repeated Dr. Monygham, grimly.

Again Nostromo, gazing abstractedly at the body of the late Señor Hirsch, remained silent, thinking that the doctor was a dangerous person in more than one sense. It was impossible to trust him.

"Do you speak in the name of Don Carlos?" he asked at last.

"Yes. I do," the doctor said, loudly, without hesitation. "He must come forward now. He must," he added in a mutter, which Nostromo did not catch.

"What did you say, *señor*?"

The doctor started. "I say that you must be true to yourself, Capataz. It would be worse than folly to fail now."

"True to myself," repeated Nostromo. "How do you know that I would not be true to myself if I told you to go to the devil with your propositions?"

"I do not know. Maybe you would," the doctor said, with a roughness of tone intended to hide the sinking of his heart and the faltering of his voice. "All I know is that you had better get away from here. Some of Sotillo's men may turn up here looking for me."

He slipped off the table, listened intently. The Capataz, too, stood up.

"Suppose I went to Cayta, what would you do meantime?" he asked.

"I would go to Sotillo directly you had left—in the way I am thinking of."

"A very good way—if only that engineer-in-chief consents. Remind him, *señor*, that I looked after the old rich Englishman who pays for the railway, and that I saved the lives of some of his people that time when a gang of thieves came from the south to wreck one of his pay-trains. It was I who discovered it all at the risk of my life, by pretending to enter into their plans. Just as you are doing with Sotillo."

"Yes. Yes, of course. But I can offer him better arguments," the doctor said, hastily. "Leave it to me."

"Ah, yes! True. I am nothing."

"Not at all. You are everything."

They moved a few paces towards the door. Behind them the late Señor Hirsch preserved the immobility of a disregarded man.

"That will be all right. I know what to say to the engineer," pursued the doctor, in a low tone. "My difficulty will be with Sotillo."

And Dr. Monygham stopped short in the doorway as if intimidated by the difficulty. He had made the sacrifice of his life. He considered this a fitting opportunity. But he did not want to throw his life away too soon. In his quality of betrayer of Don Carlos's confidence, he would have ultimately to indicate the hiding-place of the treasure. That would be the end of his deception, and the end of himself as well, at the hands of the infuriated colonel. He wanted to delay him to the very last moment; and he had been racking his brains to invent some place of concealment at once plausible and difficult of access.

He imparted his trouble to Nostromo, and concluded:

"Do you know what, Capataz? I think that when the time comes and some information must be given, I shall indicate the Great Isabel. That is the best place I can think of. What is the matter?"

A low exclamation had escaped Nostromo. The doctor waited, surprised, and after a moment of profound silence, heard a thick voice stammer out "Utter folly," and stop with a gasp.

"Why folly?"

"Ah! You do not see it," began Nostromo, scathingly, gathering scorn as he went on. "Three men in half an hour would see that no ground had been disturbed anywhere on that island. Do you think that such a treasure can be buried without leaving traces of the work—eh! Señor Doctor? Why, you would not gain half a day more before having your throat cut by Sotillo. The Isabel! What stupidity! What miserable invention! Ah! you are all alike, you fine men of intelligence. All you are fit for is to betray men of the people into undertaking deadly risks for objects that you are not even sure about. If it comes off you get the benefit. If not, then it does not matter. He is only a dog. Ah! *Madre de Dios,** I would—" He shook his fists above his head.

---

*Mother of God.

The doctor was overwhelmed at first by this fierce, hissing vehemence.

"Well! It seems to me on your own showing that the men of the people are no mean fools, too," he said, sullenly. "No, but come. You are so clever. Have you a better place?"

Nostromo had calmed down as quickly as he had flared up.

"I am clever enough for that," he said, quietly, almost with indifference. "You want to tell him of a hiding-place big enough to take days in ransacking—a place where a treasure of silver ingots can be buried without leaving a sign on the surface."

"And close at hand," the doctor put in.

"Just so, *señor.* Tell him it is sunk."

"This has the merit of being the truth," the doctor said, contemptuously. "He will not believe it."

"You tell him that it is sunk where he may hope to lay his hands on it, and he will believe you quick enough. Tell him it has been sunk in the harbour in order to be recovered afterwards by divers. Tell him you found out that I had orders from Don Carlos Gould to lower the cases quietly overboard somewhere in a line between the end of the jetty and the entrance. The depth is not too great there. He has no divers, but he has a ship, boats, ropes, chains, sailors—of a sort. Let him fish for the silver. Let him set his fools to drag backwards and forwards and crossways while he sits and watches till his eyes drop out of his head."

"Really, this is an admirable idea," muttered the doctor.

"*Sí.* You tell him that, and see whether he will not believe you! He will spend days in rage and torment—and still he will believe. He will have no thought for anything else. He will not give up till he is driven off—why, he may even forget to kill you. He will neither eat nor sleep. He—"

"The very thing! The very thing!" the doctor repeated in an excited whisper. "Capataz, I begin to believe that you are a great genius in your way."

Nostromo had paused; then began again in a changed tone, sombre, speaking to himself as though he had forgotten the doctor's existence.

"There is something in a treasure that fastens upon a man's mind. He will pray and blaspheme and still persevere, and will curse the day he ever heard of it, and will let his last hour come upon him unawares, still believing that he missed it only by a foot. He will see it every time he closes his eyes. He will never forget it till he is dead—and even then—Doctor, did you ever hear of the miserable *gringos* on Azuera, that cannot die? Ha! ha! Sailors like myself. There is no getting away from a treasure that once fastens upon your mind."

"You are a devil of a man, Capataz. It is the most plausible thing." Nostromo pressed his arm.

"It will be worse for him than thirst at sea or hunger in a town full of people. Do you know what that is? He shall suffer greater torments than he inflicted upon that terrified wretch who had no invention. None! none! Not like me. I could have told Sotillo a deadly tale for very little pain."

He laughed wildly and turned in the doorway towards the body of the late Señor Hirsch, an opaque long blotch in the semi-transparent obscurity of the room between the two tall parallelograms of the windows full of stars.

"You man of fear!" he cried. "You shall be avenged by me—Nostromo. Out of my way, doctor! Stand aside—or, by the suffering soul of a woman dead without confession, I will strangle you with my two hands."

He bounded downstairs into the black, smoky hall. With a grunt of astonishment, Dr. Monygham threw himself recklessly into the pursuit. At the bottom of the charred stairs he had a fall, pitching forward on his face with a force that would have stunned a spirit less intent upon a task of love and devotion. He was up in a moment, jarred, shaken, with a queer impression of the terrestrial globe having been flung at his head in the dark. But it wanted more than that to stop Dr. Monygham's body, possessed by the exaltation of self-sacrifice; a reasonable exaltation, determined not to lose whatever advantage chance put into its way. He ran with headlong, tottering swiftness, his arms going like a windmill in his effort to keep his balance on his crippled feet. He lost his hat; the tails of his open gaberdine flew behind him. He had no mind to lose sight of the indispensable man. But it was a long time, and a long way from the Custom House, before he managed to seize his arm from behind, roughly, out of breath.

"Stop! Are you mad?"

Already Nostromo was walking slowly, his head dropping, as if checked in his pace by the weariness of irresolution.

"What is that to you? Ah! I forgot you want me for something. Always. *Siempre Nostromo.*"

"What do you mean by talking of strangling me?" panted the doctor.

"What do I mean? I mean that the king of the devils himself has sent you out of this town of cowards and talkers to meet me tonight of all the nights of my life."

Under the starry sky the Albergo d'Italia Una emerged, black and low, breaking the dark level of the plain. Nostromo stopped altogether.

"The priests say he is a tempter, do they not?" he added, through his clenched teeth.

"My good man, you drivel. The devil has nothing to do with this. Neither has the town, which you may call by what name you please. But Don Carlos Gould is neither a coward nor an empty talker. You will admit that?" He waited. "Well?"

"Could I see Don Carlos?"

"Great heavens! No! Why? What for?" exclaimed the doctor in agitation. "I tell you it is madness. I will not let you go into the town for anything."

"I must."

"You must not!" hissed the doctor, fiercely, almost beside himself with the fear of the man doing away with his usefulness for an imbecile whim of some sort. "I tell you you shall not. I would rather—"

He stopped at a loss for words, feeling fagged out, powerless, holding on to Nostromo's sleeve, absolutely for support after his run.

"I am betrayed!" muttered the Capataz to himself; and the doctor, who overheard the last word, made an effort to speak calmly.

"That is exactly what would happen to you. You would be betrayed."

He thought with a sickening dread that the man was so well known that he could not escape recognition. The house of the Señor Administrador was beset by spies, no doubt. And even the very servants of the *casa* were not to be trusted. "Reflect, Capataz," he said, impressively . . . "What are you laughing at?"

"I am laughing to think that if somebody that did not approve of my presence in town, for instance—you understand, *señor doctor*— if somebody were to give me up to Pedrito, it would not be beyond my power to make friends even with him. It is true. What do you think of that?"

"You are a man of infinite resource, Capataz," said Dr. Monygham, dismally. "I recognize that. But the town is full of talk about you; and those few *cargadores* that are not in hiding with the railway people have been shouting '*Viva Montero!*' on the Plaza all day."

"My poor *cargadores!*" muttered Nostromo. "Betrayed! Betrayed!"

"I understand that on the wharf you were pretty free in laying about you with a stick amongst your poor *cargadores*," the doctor said in a grim tone, which showed that he was recovering from his exertions. "Make no mistake. Pedrito is furious at Señor Ribiera's rescue, and at having lost the pleasure of shooting Decoud. Already there are rumours in the town of the treasure having been spirited away. To have missed that does not please Pedrito either; but let me tell you that if you had all the silver in your hand for your ransom it would not save you."

Turning swiftly, and catching the doctor by the shoulders, Nostromo thrust his face close to his.

"*Maladetta!** You follow me speaking of the treasure. You have sworn my ruin. You were the last man who looked upon me before I went out with it. And Sidoni the engine-driver says you have an evil eye."

"He ought to know. I saved his broken leg for him last year," the doctor said, stoically. He felt on his shoulders the weight of these hands famed amongst the populace for snapping thick ropes and bending horseshoes. "And to you I offer the best means of saving yourself—let me go—and of retrieving your great reputation. You boasted of making the Capataz de Cargadores famous from one end of America to the other about this wretched silver. But I bring you a better opportunity—let me go, *hombre!*"

Nostromo released him abruptly, and the doctor feared that the indispensable man would run off again. But he did not. He walked

---

*Badly said! (It.).

on slowly. The doctor hobbled by his side till, within a stone's throw from the Casa Viola, Nostromo stopped again.

Silent in inhospitable darkness, the Casa Viola seemed to have changed its nature; his home appeared to repel him with an air of hopeless and inimical mystery. The doctor said:

"You will be safe there. Go in, Capataz."

"How can I go in?" Nostromo seemed to ask himself in a low, inward tone. "She cannot unsay what she said, and I cannot undo what I have done."

"I tell you it is all right. Viola is all alone in there. I looked in as I came out of the town. You will be perfectly safe in that house till you leave it to make your name famous on the Campo. I am going now to arrange for your departure with the engineer-in-chief, and I shall bring you news here long before daybreak."

Dr. Monygham, disregarding, or perhaps fearing to penetrate the meaning of Nostromo's silence, clapped him lightly on the shoulder, and starting off with his smart, lame walk, vanished utterly at the third or fourth hop in the direction of the railway track. Arrested between the two wooden posts for people to fasten their horses to, Nostromo did not move, as if he, too, had been planted solidly in the ground. At the end of half an hour he lifted his head to the deep baying of the dogs at the railway yards, which had burst out suddenly, tumultuous and deadened as if coming out from under the plain. That lame doctor with the evil eye had got there pretty fast.

Step by step Nostromo approached the Albergo d'Italia Una, which he had never known so lightless, so silent, before. The door, all black in the pale wall, stood open as he had left it twenty-four hours before, when he had nothing to hide from the world. He remained before it, irresolute, like a fugitive, like a man betrayed. Poverty, misery, starvation! Where had he heard these words? The anger of a dying woman had prophesied that fate for his folly. It looked as if it would come true very quickly. And the *leperos* would laugh—she had said. Yes, they would laugh if they knew that the Capataz de Cargadores was at the mercy of the mad doctor whom they could remember, only a few years ago, buying cooked food from a stall on the Plaza for a copper coin—like one of themselves.

At that moment the notion of seeking Captain Mitchell passed through his mind. He glanced in the direction of the jetty and saw a small gleam of light in the O.S.N. Company's building. The thought of lighted windows was not attractive. Two lighted windows had decoyed him into the empty Custom House, only to fall into the clutches of that doctor. No! He would not go near lighted windows again on that night. Captain Mitchell was there. And what could he be told? That doctor would worm it all out of him as if he were a child.

On the threshold he called out "Giorgio!" in an undertone. Nobody answered. He stepped in. "*Olá! viejo!** Are you there? . . ." In the impenetrable darkness his head swam with the illusion that the obscurity of the kitchen was as vast as the Placid Gulf, and that the floor dipped forward like a sinking lighter. "*Ola! viejo!*" he repeated, falteringly, swaying where he stood. His hand, extended to steady himself, fell upon the table. Moving a step forward, he shifted it, and felt a box of matches under his fingers. He fancied he had heard a quiet sigh. He listened for a moment, holding his breath; then, with trembling hands, tried to strike a light.

The tiny piece of wood flamed up quite blindingly at the end of his fingers, raised above his blinking eyes. A concentrated glare fell upon the leonine white head of old Giorgio against the black fireplace—showed him leaning forward in a chair in staring immobility, surrounded, overhung, by great masses of shadow, his legs crossed, his cheek in his hand, and empty pipe in the corner of his mouth. It seemed hours before he attempted to turn his face; at the very moment the match went out, and he disappeared, overwhelmed by the shadows, as if the walls and roof of the desolate house had collapsed upon his white head in ghostly silence.

Nostromo heard him stir and utter dispassionately the words:

"It may have been a vision."

"No," he said, softly. "It is no vision, old man."

A strong chest voice asked in the dark:

"Is that you I hear, Giovann' Battista?"

"*Sí, viejo*. Steady. Not so loud."

After his release by Sotillo, Giorgio Viola, attended to the very door by the good-natured engineer-in-chief, had re-entered his

---

*Hello! old man!

house, which he had been made to leave almost at the very moment of his wife's death. All was still. The lamp above was burning. He nearly called out to her by name; and the thought that no call from him would ever again evoke the answer of her voice, made him drop heavily into the chair with a loud groan, wrung out by the pain as of a keen blade piercing his breast.

The rest of the night he made no sound. The darkness turned to grey, and on the colourless, clear, glassy dawn the jagged sierra stood out flat and opaque, as if cut out of paper.

The enthusiastic and severe soul of Giorgio Viola, sailor, champion of oppressed humanity, enemy of kings, and, by the grace of Mrs. Gould, hotel-keeper of the Sulaco harbour, had descended into the open abyss of desolation amongst the shattered vestiges of his past. He remembered his wooing between two campaigns a single short week in the season of gathering olives. Nothing approached the grave passion of that time but the deep, passionate sense of his bereavement. He discovered all the extent of his dependence upon the silenced voice of that woman. It was her voice that he missed. Abstracted, busy, lost in inward contemplation, he seldom looked at his wife in those later years. The thought of his girls was a matter of concern, not of consolation. It was her voice that he would miss. And he remembered the other child—the little boy who died at sea. Ah! a man would have been something to lean upon. And, alas! even Gian' Battista—he of whom, and of Linda, his wife had spoken to him so anxiously before she dropped off into her last sleep on earth, he on whom she had called aloud to save the children, just before she died—even he was dead!

And the old man, bent forward, his head in his hand, sat through the day in immobility and solitude. He never heard the brazen roar of the bells in town. When it ceased the earthenware filter in the corner of the kitchen kept on its swift musical drip, drip into the great porous jar below.

Towards sunset he got up, and with slow movements disappeared up the narrow staircase. His bulk filled it; and the rubbing of his shoulders made a small noise as of a mouse running behind the plaster of a wall. While he remained up there the house was as dumb as a grave. Then, with the same faint rubbing noise, he descended. He had to catch at the chairs and tables to regain his seat. He seized his pipe off the high mantel of the fireplace—but made no attempt to reach the tobacco—thrust it empty into the corner of his mouth, and sat down again in the same staring pose. The sun of Pedrito's entry into Sulaco, the last sun of Señor Hirsch's life, the first of Decoud's solitude on the Great Isabel, passed over the Albergo d'Italia Una on its way to the west. The tinkling drip, drip of the filter had ceased, the lamp upstairs had burnt itself out, and the night beset Giorgio Viola and his dead wife with its obscurity and silence that seemed invincible till the Capataz de Cargadores, returning from the dead, put them to flight with the splutter and flare of a match.

"Sí, viejo. It is me. Wait."

Nostromo, after barricading the door and closing the shutters carefully, groped upon a shelf for a candle, and lit it.

Old Viola had risen. He followed with his eyes in the dark the sounds made by Nostromo. The light disclosed him standing without support, as if the mere presence of that man who was loyal, brave, incorruptible, who was all his son would have been, were enough for the support of his decaying strength.

He extended his hand grasping the briar-wood pipe, whose bowl was charred on the edge, and knitted his bushy eyebrows heavily at the light.

"You have returned," he said, with shaky dignity. "Ah! Very well! I—"

He broke off. Nostromo, leaning back against the table, his arms folded on his breast, nodded at him slightly.

"You thought I was drowned! No! The best dog of the rich, of the aristocrats, of these fine men who can only talk and betray the people, is not dead yet."

The Garibaldino, motionless, seemed to drink in the sound of the well-known voice. His head moved slightly once as if in sign of approval; but Nostromo saw clearly that the old man understood nothing of the words. There was no one to understand; no one he could take into the confidence of Decoud's fate, of his own, into the secret of the silver. That doctor was an enemy of the people—a tempter. . . .

Old Giorgio's heavy frame shook from head to foot with the effort to overcome his emotion at the sight of that man, who had shared the intimacies of his domestic life as though he had been a grown-up son.

"She believed you would return," he said, solemnly.

Nostromo raised his head.

"She was a wise woman. How could I fail to come back—?"

He finished the thought mentally: "Since she has prophesied for me an end of poverty, misery, and starvation." These words of Teresa's anger, from the circumstances in which they had been uttered, like the cry of a soul prevented from making its peace with God, stirred the obscure superstition of personal fortune from which even the greatest genius amongst men of adventure and action is seldom free. They reigned over Nostromo's mind with the force of a potent malediction. And what a curse it was that which her words had laid upon him! He had been orphaned so young that he could remember no other woman whom he called mother. Henceforth there would be no enterprise in which he would not fail. The spell was working already. Death itself would elude him now. . . . He said violently:

"Come, *viejo*! Get me something to eat. I am hungry! *Sangre de Dios!* The emptiness of my belly makes me lightheaded."

With his chin dropped again upon his bare breast above his folded arms, barefooted, watching from under a gloomy brow the movements of old Viola foraging amongst the cupboards, he seemed as if indeed fallen under a curse—a ruined and sinister Capataz.

Old Viola walked out of a dark corner, and, without a word, emptied upon the table out of his hollowed palms a few dry crusts of bread and half a raw onion.

While the Capataz began to devour his beggar's fare, taking up with stony-eyed voracity piece after piece lying by his side, the Garibaldino went off, and squatting down in another corner filled an earthenware mug with red wine out of a wicker-covered demijohn. With a familiar gesture, as when serving customers in the café, he had thrust his pipe between his teeth to have his hands free.

The Capataz drank greedily. A slight flush deepened the bronze of his cheek. Before him, Viola, with a turn of his white and massive head towards the staircase, took his empty pipe out of his mouth, and pronounced slowly:

"After the shot was fired down here, which killed her as surely as if the bullet had struck her oppressed heart, she called upon you to save the children. Upon you, Gian' Battista."

The Capataz looked up.

"Did she do that, Padrone? To save the children! They are with the English *señora*, their rich benefactress. Hey! old man of the people. Thy benefactress. . . ."

"I am old," muttered Giorgio Viola. "An Englishwoman was allowed to give a bed to Garibaldi lying wounded in prison. The greatest man that ever lived. A man of the people, too—a sailor. I may let another keep a roof over my head. *Sí* . . . I am old. I may let her. Life lasts too long sometimes."

"And she herself may not have a roof over her head before many days are out, unless I. . . . What do you say? Am I to keep a roof over her head? Am I to try—and save all the Blancos together with her?"

"You shall do it," said old Viola in a strong voice. "You shall do it as my son would have. . . ."

"Thy son, *viejo*! . . . There never has been a man like thy son. Ha, I must try. . . . But what if it were only a part of the curse to lure me on? . . . And so she called upon me to save—and then—?"

"She spoke no more." The heroic follower of Garibaldi, at the thought of the eternal stillness and silence fallen upon the shrouded form stretched out on the bed upstairs, averted his face and raised his hand to his furrowed brow. "She was dead before I could seize her hands," he stammered out, pitifully.

Before the wide eyes of the Capataz, staring at the doorway of the dark staircase, floated the shape of the Great Isabel, like a strange ship in distress, freighted with enormous wealth and the solitary life of a man. It was impossible for him to do anything. He could only hold his tongue, since there was no one to trust. The treasure would be lost, probably—unless Decoud. . . . And his thought came abruptly to an end. He perceived that he could not imagine in the least what Decoud was likely to do.

Old Viola had not stirred. And the motionless Capataz dropped his long, soft eyelashes, which gave to the upper part of his fierce, black-whiskered face a touch of feminine ingenuousness. The silence had lasted for a long time.

"God rest her soul!" he murmured, gloomily.

sound of pipes and cymbals, green flags flying, a wild mass of men in white ponchos and green hats, on foot, on mules, on donkeys. Such a sight, sir, will never be seen again. The miners, sir, had marched upon the town, Don Pepe leading on his black horse, and their very wives in the rear on _burros_, screaming encouragement, sir, and beating tambourines. I remember one of these women had a green parrot seated on her shoulder, as calm as a bird of stone. They had just saved their Señor Administrador; for Barrios, though he ordered the assault at once, at night, too, would have been too late. Pedrito Montero had Don Carlos led out to be shot—like his uncle many years ago—and then, as Barrios said afterwards, "Sulaco would not have been worth fighting for." Sulaco without the Concession was nothing; and there were tons and tons of dynamite distributed all over the mountain with detonators arranged, and an old priest, Father Román, standing by to annihilate the San Tomé mine at the first news of failure. Don Carlos had made up his mind not to leave it behind, and he had the right men to see to it, too."

Thus Captain Mitchell would talk in the middle of the Plaza, holding over his head a white umbrella with a green lining; but inside the cathedral, in the dim light, with a faint scent of incense floating in the cool atmosphere, and here and there a kneeling female figure, black or all white, with a veiled head, his lowered voice became solemn and impressive.

"Here," he would say, pointing to a niche in the wall of the dusky aisle, "you see the bust of Don José Avellanos, 'Patriot and Statesman,' as the inscription says, 'Minister to Courts of England and Spain, etc., etc., died in the woods of Los Hatos worn out with his life-long struggle for Right and Justice at the dawn of the New Era.' A fair likeness. Parrochetti's work from some old photographs and a pencil sketch by Mrs. Gould. I was well acquainted with that distinguished Spanish-American of the old school, a true _hidalgo_, beloved by everybody who knew him. The marble medallion in the wall, in the antique style, representing a veiled woman seated with her hands clasped loosely over her knees, commemorates that unfortunate young gentleman who sailed out with Nostromo on that fatal night, sir. See, 'To the memory of Martin Decoud, his betrothed Antonia Avellanos.' Frank, simple, noble. There you have that lady, sir, as she is. An exceptional woman. Those who thought

CHAPTER 10

THE NEXT DAY WAS quiet in the morning, except for the faint sound of firing to the northward, in the direction of Los Hatos. Captain Mitchell had listened to it from his balcony anxiously. The phrase, "In my delicate position as the only consular agent then in the port, everything, sir, everything was a just cause for anxiety," had its place in the more or less stereotyped relation of the "historical events" which for the next few years was at the service of distinguished strangers visiting Sulaco. The mention of the dignity and neutrality of the flag, so difficult to preserve in his position, "right in the thick of these events between the lawlessness of that piratical villain Sotillo and the more regularly established but scarcely less atrocious tyranny of his Excellency Don Pedro Montero," came next in order. Captain Mitchell was not the man to enlarge upon mere dangers much. But he insisted that it was a memorable day. On that day, towards dusk, he had seen "that poor fellow of mine—Nostromo. The sailor whom I discovered, and, I may say, made, sir. The man of the famous ride to Cayta, sir. An historical event, sir!"

Regarded by the O.S.N. Company as an old and faithful servant, Captain Mitchell was allowed to attain the term of his usefulness in ease and dignity at the head of the enormously extended service. The augmentation of the establishment, with its crowds of clerks, an office in town, the old office in the harbour, the division into departments—passenger, cargo, lighterage, and so on—secured a greater leisure for his last years in the regenerated Sulaco, the capital of the Occidental Republic. Liked by the natives for his good nature and the formality of his manner, self-important and simple, known for years as a "friend of our country," he felt himself a personality of mark in the town. Getting up early for a turn in the marketplace while the gigantic shadow of Higuerota was still lying upon the fruit and flower stalls piled up with masses of gorgeous colouring, attending easily to current affairs, welcomed in houses, greeted by ladies on the Alameda, with his entry into all the clubs and a footing in the Casa Gould, he led his privileged old bachelor, man-about-town existence with great comfort and solemnity. But on mail-boat days he was down at the Harbour Office at an early hour, with his own gig, manned by a smart crew in white and blue, ready to dash off and board the ship directly she showed her bows between the harbour heads.

It would be into the Harbour Office that he would lead some privileged passenger he had brought off in his own boat, and invite him to take a seat for a moment while he signed a few papers. And Captain Mitchell, seating himself at his desk, would keep on talking hospitably:

"There isn't much time if you are to see everything in a day. We shall be off in a moment. We'll have lunch at the Amarilla Club—though I belong also to the Anglo-American—mining engineers and businessmen, don't you know—and to the Mirliflores as well, a new club—English, French, Italians, all sorts—lively young fellows mostly, who wanted to pay a compliment to an old resident, sir. But we'll lunch at the Amarilla. Interest you, I fancy. Real thing of the country. Men of the first families. The President of the Occidental Republic himself belongs to it, sir. Fine old bishop with a broken nose in the patio. Remarkable piece of statuary, I believe. Cavaliere Parrochetti—you know Parrochetti, the famous Italian sculptor—was working here for two years—thought very highly of our old bishop. . . . There! I am very much at your service now."

Proud of his experience, penetrated by the sense of historical importance of men, events, and buildings, he talked pompously in jerky periods, with slight sweeps of his short, thick arm, letting nothing "escape the attention" of his privileged captive.

"Lot of building going on, as you observe. Before the Separation it was a plain of burnt grass smothered in clouds of dust, with an ox-cart track to our Jetty. Nothing more. This is the Harbour Gate. Picturesque, is it not? Formerly the town stopped short there. We enter now the Calle de la Constitución. Observe the old Spanish houses. Great dignity. Eh? I suppose it's just as it was in the time of the Viceroys, except for the pavement. Wood blocks now. Sulaco National Bank there, with the sentry boxes each side of the gate. Casa Avellanos this side, with all the ground-floor windows shuttered. A

wonderful woman lives there—Miss Avellanos—the beautiful Antonia. A character, sir! A historical woman! Opposite—Casa Gould. Noble gateway. Yes, *the* Goulds of the original Gould Concession, that all the world knows of now. I hold seventeen of the thousand-dollar shares in the Consolidated San Tomé mines. All the poor savings of my lifetime, sir, and it will be enough to keep me in comfort to the end of my days at home when I retire. I got in on the ground floor, you see. Don Carlos, great friend of mine. Seventeen shares—quite a little fortune to leave behind one, too. I have a niece—married a parson—most worthy man, incumbent of a small parish in Sussex; no end of children. I was never married myself. A sailor should exercise self-denial. Standing under that very gateway, sir, with some young engineer-fellows, ready to defend that house where we had received so much kindness and hospitality, I saw the first and last charge of Pedrito's horsemen upon Barrios's troops, who had just taken the Harbour Gate. They could not stand the new rifles brought out by that poor Decoud. It was a murderous fire. In a moment the street became blocked with a mass of dead men and horses. They never came on again."

And all day Captain Mitchell would talk like this to his more or less willing victim:

"The Plaza. I call it magnificent. Twice the area of Trafalgar Square."

From the very centre, in the blazing sunshine, he pointed out the buildings:

"The Intendencia, now President's Palace—Cabildo, where the Lower Chamber of Parliament sits. You notice the new houses on that side of the Plaza? Compañía Anzani, a great general store, like those cooperative things at home. Old Anzani was murdered by the National Guards in front of his safe. It was even for that specific crime that the deputy Gamacho, commanding the Nationals, a bloodthirsty and savage brute, was executed publicly by garrotte upon the sentence of a court-martial ordered by Barrios. Anzani's nephews converted the business into a company. All that side of the Plaza had been burnt; used to be colonnaded before. A terrible fire, by the light of which I saw the last of the fighting, the *llaneros* flying, the Nationals throwing their arms down, and the miners of San Tomé, all Indians from the Sierra, rolling by like a torrent to

she would give way to despair were mistaken, sir. She has been blamed in many quarters for not having taken the veil. It was expected of her. But Doña Antonia is not the stuff they make nuns of. Bishop Corbelán, her uncle, lives with her in the Corbelán town house. He is a fierce sort of priest, everlastingly worrying the Government about the old Church lands and convents. I believe they think a lot of him in Rome. Now let us go to the Amarilla Club, just across the Plaza, to get some lunch."

Directly outside the cathedral on the very top of the noble flight of steps, his voice rose pompously, his arm found again its sweeping gesture.

"*Porvenir*, over there on that first floor, above those French plate-glass shop-fronts; our biggest daily. Conservative, or, rather, I should say, Parliamentary. We have the Parliamentary party here of which the actual Chief of the State, Don Juste Lopez, is the head; a very sagacious man, I think. A first-rate intellect, sir. The Democratic party in opposition rests mostly, I am sorry to say, on these socialist Italians, sir, with their secret societies, *camorras** and such-like. There are lots of Italians settled here on the railway lands, dismissed navvies, mechanics, and so on, all along the trunk line. There are whole villages of Italians on the Campo. And the natives, too, are being drawn into these ways. . . . American bar? Yes. And over there you can see another. New Yorkers mostly frequent that one—Here we are at the Amarilla. Observe the bishop at the foot of the stairs to the right as we go in."

And the lunch would begin and terminate its lavish and leisurely course at a little table in the gallery, Captain Mitchell nodding, bowing, getting up to speak for a moment to different officials in black clothes, merchants in jackets, officers in uniform, middle-aged *caballeros* from the Campo—sallow, little, nervous men, and fat, placid, swarthy men, and Europeans or North Americans of superior standing, whose faces looked very white amongst the majority of dark complexions and black, glistening eyes.

Captain Mitchell would lie back in the chair, casting around looks of satisfaction, and tender over the table a case full of thick cigars.

---

*Fights, wrangles.

"Try a weed with your coffee. Local tobacco. The black coffee you get at the Amarilla, sir, you don't meet anywhere in the world. We get the bean from a famous cafeteria in the foot-hills, whose owner sends three sacks every year as a present to his fellow members in remembrance of the fight against Gamacho's Nationals, carried on from these very windows by the *caballeros*. He was in town at the time, and took part, sir, to the bitter end. It arrives on three mules—not in the common way, by rail; no fear!—right into the patio, escorted by mounted peons, in charge of the Mayoral of his estate, who walks upstairs, booted and spurred, and delivers it to our committee formally with the words, 'For the sake of those fallen the third of May.' We call it 'Tres de Mayo' coffee. Taste it."

Captain Mitchell, with an expression as though making ready to hear a sermon in a church, would lift the tiny cup to his lips. And the nectar would be sipped to the bottom during a restful silence in a cloud of cigar smoke.

"Look at this man in black just going out," he would begin, leaning forward hastily. "This is the famous Hernandez, Minister of War. The *Times*'s special correspondent, who wrote that striking series of letters calling the Occidental Republic the 'Treasure House of the World,' gave a whole article to him and the force he has organized—the renowned Carabineers of the Campo."

Captain Mitchell's guest, staring curiously, would see a figure in a long-tailed black coat walking gravely, with downcast eyelids in a long, composed face, a brow furrowed horizontally, a pointed head, whose grey hair, thin at the top, combed down carefully on all sides and rolled at the ends, fell low on the neck and shoulders. This, then, was the famous bandit of whom Europe had heard with interest. He put on a high-crowned sombrero with a wide flat brim; a rosary of wooden beads was twisted about his right wrist. And Captain Mitchell would proceed:

"The protector of the Sulaco refugees from the rage of Pedrito. As general of cavalry with Barrios he distinguished himself at the storming of Tonoro, where Señor Fuentes was killed with the last remnant of the Monterists. He is the friend and humble servant of Bishop Corbelán. Hears three Masses every day. I bet you he will step into the cathedral to say a prayer or two on his way home to his siesta."

He took several puffs at his cigar in silence; then, in his best important manner, pronounced:

"The Spanish race, sir, is prolific of remarkable characters in every rank of life. . . . I propose we go now into the billiard-room, which is cool, for a quiet chat. There's never anybody there till after five. I could tell you episodes of the Separationist revolution that would astonish you. When the great heat's over, we'll take a turn on the Alameda."

The programme went on relentlessly, like a law of Nature. The turn on the Alameda was taken with slow steps and stately remarks.

"All the great world of Sulaco here, sir." Captain Mitchell bowed right and left with no end of formality; then with animation, "Doña Emilia, Mrs. Gould's carriage. Look. Always white mules. The kindest, most gracious woman the sun ever shone upon. A great position, sir. A great position. First lady in Sulaco—far before the President's wife. And worthy of it." He took off his hat; then, with a studied change of tone, added, negligently, that the man in black by her side, with a high white collar and a scarred, snarly face, was Dr. Monygham, Inspector of State Hospitals, chief medical officer of the Consolidated San Tomé mines. "A familiar of the house. Everlastingly there. No wonder. The Goulds made him. Very clever man and all that, but I never liked him. Nobody does. I can recollect him limping about the streets in a check shirt and native sandals with a watermelon under his arm—all he would get to eat for the day. A big-wig now, sir, and as nasty as ever. However. . . . There's no doubt he played his part fairly well at the time. He saved us all from the deadly incubus of Sotillo, where a more particular man might have failed—"

His arm went up.

"The equestrial statue that used to stand on the pedestal over there has been removed. It was an anachronism," Captain Mitchell commented, obscurely. "There is some talk of replacing it by a marble shaft commemorative of Separation, with angels of peace at the four corners, and bronze Justice holding an even balance, all gilt, on the top. Cavaliere Parrochetti was asked to make a design, which you can see framed under glass in the Municipal Sala. Names are to be engraved all round the base. Well! They could do no better than begin with the name of Nostromo. He has done for Separation as much as anybody else, and," added Captain Mitchell, "has got less

than many others by it—when it comes to that." He dropped on to
a stone seat under a tree, and tapped invitingly at the place by his
side. "He carried to Barrios the letters from Sulaco which decided
the General to abandon Cayta for a time, and come back to our
help here by sea. The transports were still in harbour fortunately.
Sir, I did not even know that my Capataz de Cargadores was alive. I
had no idea. It was Dr. Monygham who came upon him, by
chance, in the Custom House, evacuated an hour or two before by
the wretched Sotillo. I was never told; never given a hint, nothing—
as if I were unworthy of confidence. Monygham arranged it all. He
went to the railway yards, and got admission to the engineer-in-
chief, who, for the sake of the Goulds as much as for anything else,
consented to let an engine make a dash down the line, one hundred and eighty miles, with Nostromo aboard. It was the only way to
get him off. In the Construction Camp at the rail-head, he obtained
a horse, arms, some clothing, and started alone on that marvellous
ride—four hundred miles in six days, through a disturbed country,
ending by the feat of passing through the Monterist lines outside
Cayta. The history of that ride, sir, would make a most exciting
book. He carried all our lives in his pocket. Devotion, courage, fidelity, intelligence were not enough. Of course, he was perfectly
fearless and incorruptible. But a man was wanted that would know
how to succeed. He was that man, sir. On the fifth of May, being
practically a prisoner in the Harbour Office of my Company, I suddenly heard the whistle of an engine in the railway yards, a quarter
of a mile away. I could not believe my ears. I made one jump on to
the balcony, and beheld a locomotive under a great head of steam
run out of the yard gates, screeching like mad, enveloped in a white
cloud, and then, just abreast of old Viola's inn, check almost to a
standstill. I made out, sir, a man—I couldn't tell who—dash out of
the Albergo d'Italia Una, climb into the cab, and then, sir, that engine seemed positively to leap clear of the house, and was gone in
the twinkling of an eye. As you blow a candle out, sir! There was a
first-rate driver on the foot-plate, sir, I can tell you. They were fired
heavily upon by the National Guards in Rincón and one other
place. Fortunately the line had not been torn up. In four hours they
reached the Construction Camp. Nostromo had his start. . . . The
rest you know. You've got only to look round you. There are people

on this Alameda that ride in their carriages, or even are alive at all today, because years ago I engaged a runaway Italian sailor for a foreman of our wharf simply on the strength of his looks. And that's a fact. You can't get over it, sir. On the seventeenth of May, just twelve days after I saw the man from the Casa Viola get on the engine, and wondered what it meant, Barrios's transports were entering this harbour, and the 'Treasure House of the World,' as *The Times* man calls Sulaco in his book, was saved intact for civilization—for a great future, sir. Pedrito, with Hernandez on the west, and the San Tomé miners pressing on the land gate, was not able to oppose the landing. He had been sending messages to Sotillo for a week to join him. Had Sotillo done so there would have been massacres and proscription that would have left no man or woman of position alive. But that's where Dr. Monygham comes in. Sotillo, blind and deaf to everything, stuck on board his steamer watching the dragging for silver, which he believed to be sunk at the bottom of the harbour. They say that for the last three days he was out of his mind raving and foaming with disappointment at getting nothing, flying about the deck, and yelling curses at the boats with the drags, ordering them in, and then suddenly stamping his foot and crying out, 'And yet it is there! I see it! I feel it!'

"He was preparing to hang Dr. Monygham (whom he had on board) at the end of the after-derrick, when the first of Barrios's transports, one of our own ships at that, steamed right in, and ranging close alongside opened a small-arm fire without as much preliminaries as a hail. It was the completest surprise in the world, sir. They were too astounded at first to bolt below. Men were falling right and left like ninepins. It's a miracle that Monygham, standing on the after-hatch with the rope already round his neck, escaped being riddled through and through like a sieve. He told me since that he had given himself up for lost, and kept on yelling with all the strength of his lungs: 'Hoist a white flag! Hoist a white flag!' Suddenly an old major of the Esmeralda regiment, standing by, unsheathed his sword with a shriek: 'Die, perjured traitor!' and ran Sotillo clean through the body, just before he fell himself shot through the head."

Captain Mitchell stopped for a while.

"Begad, sir! I could spin you a yarn for hours. But it's time we started off to Rincón. It would not do for you to pass through

Sulaco and not see the lights of the San Tomé mine, a whole mountain ablaze like a lighted palace above the dark Campo. It's a fashionable drive. . . . But let me tell you one little anecdote, sir; just to show you. A fortnight or more later, when Barrios, declared Generalissimo, was gone in pursuit of Pedrito away south, when the Provisional Junta, with Don Juste Lopez at its head, had promulgated the new Constitution, and our Don Carlos Gould was packing up his trunk bound on a mission to San Francisco and Washington (the United States, sir, were the first great power to recognize the Occidental Republic)—a fortnight later, I say, when we were beginning to feel that our heads were safe on our shoulders, if I may express myself so, a prominent man, a large shipper by our line, came to see me on business, and, says he, the first thing: 'I say, Captain Mitchell, is that fellow' (meaning Nostromo) 'still the Capataz of your *cargadores* or not?' 'What's the matter?' says I. 'Because, if he is, then I don't mind; I send and receive a good lot of cargo by your ships; but I have observed him several days loafing about the wharf, and just now he stopped me as cool as you please with a request for a cigar. Now, you know, my cigars are rather special, and I can't get them so easily as all that.' 'I hope you stretched a point,' I said, very gently. 'Why, yes. But it's a confounded nuisance. The fellow's everlastingly cadging for smokes.' Sir, I turned my eyes away, and then asked, 'Weren't you one of the prisoners in the *cabildo*?'* 'You know very well I was, and in chains, too,' says he. 'And under a fine of fifteen thousand dollars?' He coloured, sir, because it got about that he fainted from fright when they came to arrest him, and then behaved before Fuentes in a manner to make the very *policianos*,† who had dragged him there by the hair of his head, smile at his cringing. 'Yes,' he says, in a sort of shy way. 'Why?' 'Oh, nothing. You stood to lose a tidy bit,' says I, 'even if you saved your life. . . . But what can I do for you?' He never even saw the point. Not he. And that's how the world wags, sir."

He rose a little stiffly, and the drive to Rincón would be taken with only one philosophical remark, uttered by the merciless

---

*Council hall.
†Police guards.

cicerone,* with his eyes fixed upon the lights of San Tomé, that seemed suspended in the dark night between earth and heaven.

"A great power, this, for good and evil, sir. A great power."

And the dinner of the Mirliflores would be eaten, excellent as to cooking, and leaving upon the traveller's mind an impression that there were in Sulaco many pleasant, able young men with salaries apparently too large for their discretion, and amongst them a few, mostly Anglo-Saxon, skilled in the art of, as the saying is, "taking a rise" out of his kind host.

With a rapid, jingling drive to the harbour in a two-wheeled machine (which Captain Mitchell called a curricle) behind a fleet and scraggy mule beaten all the time by an obviously Neapolitan driver, the cycle would be nearly closed before the lighted-up offices of the O.S.N. Company, remaining open so late because of the steamer. Nearly—but not quite.

"Ten o'clock. Your ship won't be ready to leave till half past twelve, if by then. Come in for a brandy-and-soda and one more cigar."

And in the superintendent's private room the privileged passenger by the *Ceres,* or *Juno,* or *Pallas,* stunned and as it were annihilated mentally by a sudden surfeit of sights, sounds, names, facts, and complicated information imperfectly apprehended, would listen like a tired child to a fairy tale; would hear a voice, familiar and surprising in its pompousness, tell him, as if from another world, how there was "in this very harbour" an international naval demonstration, which put an end to the Costaguana-Sulaco War. How the United States cruiser, *Powhattan,* was the first to salute the Occidental flag—white, with a wreath of green laurel in the middle encircling a yellow amarilla flower. Would hear how General Montero, in less than a month after proclaiming himself Emperor of Costaguana, was shot dead (during a solemn and public distribution of orders and crosses) by a young artillery officer, the brother of his then mistress.

"The abominable Pedrito, sir, fled the country," the voice would say. And it would continue: "A captain of one of our ships told me lately that he recognized Pedrito the Guerrillero, arrayed in purple

---

*Guide (It.).

slippers and a velvet smoking-cap with a gold tassel, keeping a disorderly house in one of the southern ports."

"Abominable Pedrito! Who the devil was he?" would wonder the distinguished bird of passage hovering on the confines of waking and sleep with resolutely open eyes and a faint but amiable curl upon his lips, from between which stuck out the eighteenth or twentieth cigar of that memorable day.

"He appeared to me in this very room like a haunting ghost, sir"— Captain Mitchell was talking of his Nostromo with true warmth of feeling and a touch of wistful pride. "You may imagine, sir, what an effect it produced on me. He had come round by sea with Barrios, of course. And the first thing he told me after I became fit to hear him was that he had picked up the lighter's boat floating in the gulf! He seemed quite overcome by the circumstance. And a remarkable enough circumstance it was, when you remember that it was then sixteen days since the sinking of the silver. At once I could see he was another man. He stared at the wall, sir, as if there had been a spider or something running about there. The loss of the silver preyed on his mind. The first thing he asked me about was whether Doña Antonia had heard yet of Decoud's death. His voice trembled. I had to tell him that Doña Antonia, as a matter of fact, was not then back in town yet. Poor girl! And just as I was making ready to ask him a thousand questions, with a sudden, 'Pardon me, *señor*,' he cleared out of the office altogether. I did not see him again for three days. I was terribly busy, you know. It seems that he wandered about in and out of the town, and on two nights he turned up to sleep in the baracoons* of the railway people. He seemed absolutely indifferent to what went on. I asked him on the wharf, 'When are you going to take hold again, Nostromo? There will be plenty of work for the *cargadores* presently.'

" '*Señor*,' says he, looking at me in a slow, inquisitive manner, 'would it surprise you to hear that I am too tired to work just yet? And what work could I do now? How can I look my *cargadores* in the face after losing a lighter?'

---

*Or barracoons, here meaning dormitories; the term can also refer to structures used for the temporary confinement of convicts.

"I begged him not to think any more about the silver, and he smiled. A smile that went to my heart, sir. 'It was no mistake,' I told him. 'It was a fatality. A thing that could not be helped.' '*Sí, sí!*' he said, and turned away. I thought it best to leave him alone for a bit to get over it. Sir, it took him years really, to get over it. I was present at his interview with Don Carlos. I must say that Gould is rather a cold man. He had to keep a tight hand on his feelings, dealing with thieves and rascals, in constant danger of ruin for himself and wife for so many years, that it had become a second nature. They looked at each other for a long time. Don Carlos asked what he could do for him, in his quiet, reserved way.

"'My name is known from one end of Sulaco to the other,' he said, as quiet as the other. 'What more can you do for me?' That was all that passed on that occasion. Later, however, there was a very fine coasting schooner for sale, and Mrs. Gould and I put our heads together to get her bought and presented to him. It was done, but he paid all the price back within the next three years. Business was booming all along this seaboard, sir. Moreover, that man always succeeded in everything except in saving the silver. Poor Doña Antonia, fresh from her terrible experiences in the woods of Los Hatos, had an interview with him, too. Wanted to hear about Decoud: what they said, what they did, what they thought up to the last on that fatal night. Mrs. Gould told me his manner was perfect for quietness and sympathy. Miss Avellanos burst into tears only when he told her how Decoud had happened to say that his plan would be a glorious success. . . . And there's no doubt, sir, that it is. It is a success."

The cycle was about to close at last. And while the privileged passenger, shivering with the pleasant anticipations of his berth, forgot to ask himself what on earth Decoud's plan could be, Captain Mitchell was saying, "Sorry we must part so soon. Your intelligent interest made this a pleasant day to me. I shall see you now on board. You had a glimpse of the 'Treasure House of the World.' A very good name that." And the coxswain's voice at the door, announcing that the gig was ready, closed the cycle.

Nostromo had, indeed, found the lighter's boat, which he had left on the Great Isabel with Decoud, floating empty far out in the gulf. He was then on the bridge of the first of Barrios's transports, and within an hour's steaming from Sulaco. Barrios, always de-lighted with a feat of daring and a good judge of courage, had taken a great liking to the Capataz. During the passage round the coast the General kept Nostromo near his person, addressing him fre-quently in that abrupt and boisterous manner which was the sign of his high favour.

Nostromo's eyes were the first to catch, broad on the bow, the tiny, elusive dark speck, which, alone with the forms of the Three Isabels right ahead, appeared on the flat, shimmering emptiness of the gulf. There are times when no fact should be neglected as in-significant; a small boat so far from the land might have had some meaning worth finding out. At a nod of consent from Barrios the transport swept out of her course, passing near enough to ascertain that no one manned the little cockle-shell. It was merely a common small boat gone adrift with her oars in her. But Nostromo, to whose mind Decoud had been insistently present for days, had long be-fore recognized with excitement the dinghy of the lighter.

There could be no question of stopping to pick up that thing. Every minute of time was momentous with the lives and futures of a whole town. The head of the leading ship, with the General on board, fell off to her course. Behind her, the fleet of transports, scat-tered haphazard over a mile or so in the offing, like the finish of an ocean race, pressed on, all black and smoking on the western sky.

"*Mi General*," Nostromo's voice rang out loud, but quiet, from behind a group of officers, "I should like to save that little boat. *Por Dios*, I know her. She belongs to my Company."

"And, *por Dios*," guffawed Barrios, in a noisy, good-humoured voice, "you belong to me. I am going to make you a captain of cav-alry directly we get within sight of a horse again."

"I can swim far better than I can ride, *mi General*," cried Nos-tromo, pushing through to the rail with a set stare in his eyes. "Let me—"

"Let you? What a conceited fellow that is," bantered the Gen-eral, jovially, without even looking at him. "Let him go! Ha! ha! ha! He wants me to admit that we cannot take Sulaco without him! Ha! ha! ha! Would you like to swim off to her, my son?"

A tremendous shout from one end of the ship to the other stopped his guffaw. Nostromo had leaped overboard; and his black head bobbed up far away already from the ship. The General muttered an appalled *"Cielo!** Sinner that I am!" in a thunderstuck tone. One anxious glance was enough to show him that Nostromo was swimming with perfect ease; and then he thundered terribly, "No! no! We shall not stop to pick up this impertinent fellow. Let him drown—that mad Capataz."

Nothing short of main force would have kept Nostromo from leaping overboard. That empty boat, coming out to meet him mysteriously, as if rowed by an invisible spectre, exercised the fascination of some sign, of some warning, seemed to answer in a startling and enigmatic way the persistent thought of a treasure and of a man's fate. He would have leaped if there had been death in that half mile of water. It was as smooth as a pond, and for some reason sharks are unknown in the Placid Gulf, though on the other side of the Punta Mala the coastline swarms with them.

The Capataz seized hold of the stern and blew with force. A queer, faint feeling had come over him while he swam. He had got rid of his boots and coat in the water. He hung on for a time, regaining his breath. In the distance the transports, more in a bunch now, held on straight for Sulaco, with their air of friendly contest, of nautical sport, of a regatta; and the united smoke of their funnels drove like a thin, sulphurous fogbank right over his head. It was his daring, his courage, his act that had set these ships in motion upon the sea, hurrying on to save the lives and fortunes of the Blancos, the taskmasters of the people; to save the San Tomé mine; to save the children.

With a vigourous and skilful effort he clambered over the stern. The very boat! No doubt of it; no doubt whatever. It was the dinghy of the lighter No. 3—the dinghy left with Martin Decoud on the Great Isabel so that he should have some means to help himself if nothing could be done for him from the shore. And here she had come out to meet him empty and inexplicable. What had become of Decoud? The Capataz made a minute examination. He looked for some scratch, for some mark, for some sign. All he discovered was a brown stain on the gunwale abreast of the thwart. He bent his face

---

*Heaven!

over it and rubbed hard with his finger. Then he sat down in the
stern sheets, passive, with his knees close together and legs aslant.

Streaming from head to foot, with his hair and whiskers hanging
lank and dripping and a lustreless stare fixed upon the bottom
boards, the Capataz of the Sulaco Cargadores resembled a drowned
corpse come up from the bottom to idle away the sunset hour in a
small boat. The excitement of his adventurous ride, the excitement
of the return in time, of achievement, of success, all these excite-
ments centred round the associated ideas of the great treasure and of
the only other man who knew of its existence, had departed from
him. To the very last moment he had been cudgelling his brains as
to how he could manage to visit the Great Isabel without loss of time
and undetected. For the idea of secrecy had come to be connected
with the treasure so closely that even to Barrios himself he had re-
frained from mentioning the existence of Decoud and of the silver
on the island. The letters he carried to the General, however, made
brief mention of the loss of the lighter, as having its bearing upon the
situation in Sulaco. In the circumstances, the one-eyed tiger-slayer,
scenting battle from afar, had not wasted his time in making inquiries from the messenger. In fact, Barrios, talking with Nostromo,
assumed that both Don Martin Decoud and the ingots of San Tomé
were lost together, and Nostromo, not questioned directly, had kept
silent, under the influence of some indefinable form of resentment
and distrust. Let Don Martin speak of everything with his own lips—
was what he told himself mentally.

And now, with the means of gaining the Great Isabel thrown
thus in his way at the earliest possible moment, his excitement had
departed, as when the soul takes flight leaving the body inert upon
an earth it knows no more. Nostromo did not seem to know the gulf.
For a long time even his eyelids did not flutter once upon the glazed
emptiness of his stare. Then slowly, without a limb having stirred,
without a twitch of muscle or quiver of an eyelash, an expression, a
living expression came upon the still features, deep thought crept
into the empty stare—as if an outcast soul, a quiet, brooding soul,
finding that untenanted body in its way, had come in stealthily to
take possession.

The Capataz frowned: and in the immense stillness of sea, islands, and coast, of cloud-forms on the sky and trails of light upon

the water, the knitting of that brow had the emphasis of a powerful gesture. Nothing else budged for a long time; then the Capataz shook his head and again surrendered himself to the universal repose of all visible things. Suddenly he seized the oars, and with one movement made the dinghy spin round, head-on to the Great Isabel. But before he began to pull he bent once more over the brown stain on the gunwale.

"I know that thing," he muttered to himself, with a sagacious jerk of the head. "That's blood."

His stroke was long, vigourous, and steady. Now and then he looked over his shoulder at the Great Isabel, presenting its low cliff to his anxious gaze like an impenetrable face. At last the stem touched the strand. He flung rather than dragged the boat up the little beach. At once, turning his back upon the sunset, he plunged with long strides into the ravine, making the water of the stream spurt and fly upwards at every step, as if spurning its shallow, clear, murmuring spirit with his feet. He wanted to save every moment of daylight.

A mass of earth, grass, and smashed bushes had fallen down very naturally from above upon the cavity under the leaning tree. Decoud had attended to the concealment of the silver as instructed, using the spade with some intelligence. But Nostromo's half-smile of approval changed into a scornful curl of the lip by the sight of the spade itself flung there in full view, as if in utter carelessness or sudden panic, giving away the whole thing. Ah! They were all alike in their folly, these *hombres finos* that invented laws and governments and barren tasks for the people.

The Capataz picked up the spade, and with the feel of the handle in his palm the desire to have a look at the horse-hide boxes of treasure came upon him suddenly. In a very few strokes he uncovered the edges and corners of several; then, clearing away more earth, became aware that one of them had been slashed with a knife.

He exclaimed at that discovery in a stifled voice, and dropped on his knees with a look of irrational apprehension over one shoulder, then over the other. The stiff hide had closed, and he hesitated before he pushed his hand through the long slit and felt the ingots inside. There they were. One, two, three. Yes, four gone. Taken away. Four ingots. But who? Decoud? Nobody else. And why? For what purpose? For what cursed fancy? Let him explain. Four ingots carried off in a boat, and—blood!

In the face of the open gulf, the sun, clear, unclouded, unaltered, plunged into the waters in a grave and untroubled mystery of self-immolation consummated far from all mortal eyes, with an infinite majesty of silence and peace. Four ingots short!—and blood!

The Capataz got up slowly.

"He might simply have cut his hand," he muttered. "But, then—"

He sat down on the soft earth, unresisting, as if he had been chained to the treasure, his drawn-up legs clasped in his hands with an air of hopeless submission, like a slave set on guard. Once only he lifted his head smartly: the rattle of hot musketry fire had reached his ears, like pouring from on high a stream of dry peas upon a drum. After listening for a while, he said, half aloud:

"He will never come back to explain."

And he lowered his head again.

"Impossible!" he muttered gloomily.

The sounds of firing died out. The loom of a great conflagration in Sulaco flashed up red above the coast, played on the clouds at the head of the gulf, seemed to touch with a ruddy and sinister reflection the forms of the Three Isabels. He never saw it, though he raised his head.

"But, then, I cannot know," he pronounced, distinctly, and remained silent and staring for hours.

He could not know. Nobody was to know. As might have been supposed, the end of Don Martin Decoud never became a subject of speculation for anyone except Nostromo. Had the truth of the facts been known, there would always have remained the question, Why? Whereas the version of his death at the sinking of the lighter had no uncertainty of motive. The young apostle of Separation had died striving for his idea by an ever-lamented accident. But the truth was that he died from solitude, the enemy known but to few on this earth, and whom only the simplest of us are fit to withstand. The brilliant Costaguanero of the boulevards had died from solitude and want of faith in himself and others.

For some good and valid reasons beyond mere human comprehension, the sea-birds of the gulf shun the Isabels. The rocky head of Azuera is their haunt, whose stony levels and chasms resound with their wild and tumultuous clamour as if they were for ever quarrelling over the legendary treasure.

At the end of his first day on the Great Isabel, Decoud, turning in his lair of coarse grass, under the shade of a tree, said to himself:

"I have not seen as much as one single bird all day."

And he had not heard a sound, either, all day but that one now of his own muttering voice. It had been a day of absolute silence — the first he had known in his life. And he had not slept a wink. Not for all these wakeful nights and the days of fighting, planning, talking; not for all that last night of danger and hard physical toil upon the gulf, had he been able to close his eyes for a moment. And yet from sunrise to sunset he had been lying prone on the ground, either on his back or on his face.

He stretched himself, and with slow steps descended into the gully to spend the night by the side of the silver. If Nostromo returned — as he might have done at any moment — it was there that he would look first; and night would, of course, be the proper time for an attempt to communicate. He remembered with profound indifference that he had not eaten anything yet since he had been left alone on the island.

He spent the night open-eyed, and when the day broke he ate something with the same indifference. The brilliant "Son Decoud," the spoiled darling of the family, the lover of Antonia and journalist of Sulaco, was not fit to grapple with himself single-handed. Solitude from mere outward condition of existence becomes very swiftly a state of soul in which the affectations of irony and scepticism have no place. It takes possession of the mind, and drives forth the thought into the exile of utter unbelief. After three days of waiting for the sight of some human face, Decoud caught himself entertaining a doubt of his own individuality. It had merged into the world of cloud and water, of natural forces and forms of nature. In our activity alone do we find the sustaining illusion of an independent existence as against the whole scheme of things of which we form a helpless part. Decoud lost all belief in the reality of his action past and to come. On the fifth day an immense melancholy descended upon him palpably. He resolved not to give himself up to these people in Sulaco, who had beset him, unreal and terrible, like jibbering and obscene spectres. He saw himself struggling feebly in their midst, and Antonia, gigantic and lovely like an allegorical statue, looking on with scornful eyes at his weakness.

Not a living being, not a speck of distant sail, appeared within the range of his vision; and, as if to escape from this solitude, he absorbed himself in his melancholy. The vague consciousness of a misdirected life given up to impulses whose memory left a bitter taste in his mouth was the first moral sentiment of his manhood. But at the same time he felt no remorse. What should he regret? He had recognized no other virtue than intelligence, and had erected passions into duties. Both his intelligence and his passion were swallowed up easily in this great unbroken solitude of waiting without faith. Sleeplessness had robbed his will of all energy, for he had not slept seven hours in the seven days. His sadness was the sadness of a sceptical mind. He beheld the universe as a succession of incomprehensible images. Nostromo was dead. Everything had failed ignominiously. He no longer dared to think of Antonia. She had not survived. But if she survived he could not face her. And all exertion seemed senseless.

On the tenth day, after a night spent without even dozing off once (it had occurred to him that Antonia could not possibly have ever loved a being so impalpable as himself), the solitude appeared like a great void, and the silence of the gulf like a tense, thin cord to which he hung suspended by both hands, without fear, without surprise, without any sort of emotion whatever. Only towards the evening, in the comparative relief of coolness, he began to wish that this cord would snap. He imagined it snapping with a report as of a pistol—a sharp, full crack. And that would be the end of him. He contemplated that eventuality with pleasure, because he dreaded the sleepless nights in which the silence, remaining unbroken in the shape of a cord to which he hung with both hands, vibrated with senseless phrases, always the same but utterly incomprehensible, about Nostromo, Antonia, Barrios, and proclamations mingled into an ironical and senseless buzzing. In the daytime he could look at the silence like a still cord stretched to breaking-point, with his life, his vain life, suspended from it like a weight.

"I wonder whether I would hear it snap before I fell," he asked himself.

The sun was two hours above the horizon when he got up, gaunt, dirty, white-faced, and looked at it with his red-rimmed eyes. His limbs obeyed him slowly, as if full of lead, yet without tremor; and the effect of that physical condition gave to his movements an un-hesitating, deliberate dignity. He acted as if accomplishing some sort of rite. He descended into the gully; for the fascination of all that sil-ver, with its potential power, survived alone outside of himself. He picked up the belt with the revolver, that was lying there, and buck-led it round his waist. The cord of silence could never snap on the is-land. It must let him fall and sink into the sea, he thought. And sink! He was looking at the loose earth covering the treasure. In the sea! His aspect was that of a somnambulist. He lowered himself down on his knees slowly and went on grubbing with his fingers with in-dustrious patience till he uncovered one of the boxes. Without a pause, as if doing some work done many times before, he slit it open and took four ingots, which he put in his pockets. He covered up the exposed box again and step by step came out of the gully. The bushes closed after him with a swish.

It was on the third day of his solitude that he had dragged the dinghy near the water with an idea of rowing away somewhere, but had desisted partly at the whisper of lingering hope that Nostromo would return, partly from conviction of utter uselessness of all effort. Now she wanted only a slight shove to be set afloat. He had eaten a little every day after the first, and had some muscular strength left yet. Taking up the oars slowly, he pulled away from the cliff of the Great Isabel, that stood behind him warm with sunshine, as if with the heat of life bathed in a rich light from head to foot as if in a radi-ance of hope and joy. He pulled straight towards the setting sun. When the gulf had grown dark, he ceased rowing and flung the sculls in. The hollow clatter they made in falling was the loudest noise he had ever heard in his life. It was a revelation. It seemed to recall him from far away. Actually the thought, "Perhaps I may sleep tonight," passed through his mind. But he did not believe it. He be-lieved in nothing; and he remained sitting on the thwart.

The dawn from behind the mountains put a gleam into his un-winking eyes. After a clear daybreak the sun appeared splendidly above the peaks of the range. The great gulf burst into a glitter all around the boat; and in this glory of merciless solitude the silence appeared again before him, stretched taut like a dark, thin string.

His eyes looked at it while, without haste, he shifted his seat from the thwart to the gunwhale. They looked at it fixedly, while his hand, feeling about his waist, unbuttoned the flap of the leather case, drew the revolver, cocked it, brought it forward pointing at his breast, pulled the trigger, and, with convulsive force, sent the still-smoking weapon hurtling through the air. His eyes looked at it while he fell forward and hung with his breast on the gunwhale and the fingers of his right hand hooked under the thwart. They looked—

"It is done," he stammered out, in a sudden flow of blood. His last thought was: "I wonder how that Capataz died." The stiffness of the fingers relaxed, and the lover of Antonia Avellanos rolled overboard without having heard the cord of silence snap in the solitude of the Placid Gulf, whose glittering surface remained untroubled by the fall of his body.

A victim of the disillusioned weariness which is the retribution meted out to intellectual audacity, the brilliant Don Martin Decoud, weighted by the bars of San Tomé silver, disappeared without a trace, swallowed up in the immense indifference of things. His sleepless, crouching figure was gone from the side of the San Tomé silver; and for a time the spirits of good and evil that hover near every concealed treasure of the earth might have thought that this one had been forgotten by all mankind. Then, after a few days, another form appeared striding away from the setting sun to sit motionless and awake in the narrow black gully all through the night, in nearly the same pose, in the same place in which had sat that other sleepless man who had gone away for ever so quietly in a small boat, about the time of sunset. And the spirits of good and evil that hover about a forbidden treasure understood well that the silver of San Tomé was provided now with a faithful and lifelong slave.

The magnificent Capataz de Cargadores, victim of the disenchanted vanity which is the reward of audacious action, sat in the weary pose of a hunted outcast through a night of sleeplessness as tormenting as any known to Decoud, his companion in the most desperate affair of his life. And he wondered how Decoud had died. But he knew the part he had played himself. First a woman, then a man, abandoned each in their last extremity, for the sake of this accursed treasure. It was paid for by a soul lost and by a vanished life. The blank stillness of awe was succeeded by a gust of immense pride. There was no one in the world but Gian' Battista Fidanza, Capataz de Cargadores, the incorruptible and faithful Nostromo, to pay such a price.

He had made up his mind that nothing should be allowed now to rob him of his bargain. Nothing. Decoud had died. But how? That he was dead he had not a shadow of a doubt. But four ingots? . . . What for? Did he mean to come for more—some other time?

The treasure was putting forth its latent power. It troubled the clear mind of the man who had paid the price. He was sure that Decoud was dead. The island seemed full of that whisper. Dead? Gone! And he caught himself listening for the swish of bushes and the splash of footfalls in the bed of the brook. Dead! The talker, the *novio* of Doña Antonia!

"Ha!" he murmured, with his head on his knees, under the livid clouded dawn breaking over the liberated Sulaco and upon the gulf as grey as ashes. "It is to her that he will fly. To her that he will fly!"

And four ingots! Did he take them in revenge, to cast a spell, like the angry woman who had prophesied remorse and failure, and yet had laid upon him the task of saving the children? Well, he had saved the children. He had defeated the spell of poverty and starvation. He had done it all alone—or perhaps helped by the devil. Who cared? He had done it, betrayed as he was, and saving by the same stroke the San Tomé mine, which appeared to him hateful and immense, lording it by its vast wealth over the valour, the toil, the fidelity of the poor, over war and peace, over the labours of the town, the sea, and the Campo.

The sun lit up the sky behind the peaks of the Cordillera. The Capataz looked down for a time upon the fall of loose earth, stones, and smashed bushes, concealing the hiding-place of the silver.

"I must grow rich very slowly," he meditated, aloud.

CHAPTER 11

Sᴜʟᴀᴄᴏ ᴏᴜᴛsᴛʀɪᴘᴘᴇᴅ Nᴏsᴛʀᴏᴍᴏ's ᴘʀᴜᴅᴇɴᴄᴇ, growing rich swiftly on the hidden treasures of the earth, hovered over by the anxious spirits of good and evil, torn out by the labouring hands of the people. It was like a second youth, like a new life, full of promise, of unrest, of toil, scattering lavishly its wealth to the four corners of an excited world. Material changes swept along in the train of material interests. And other changes more subtle, outwardly unmarked, affected the minds and hearts of the workers. Captain Mitchell had gone home to live on his savings invested in the San Tomé mine; and Dr. Monygham had grown older, with his head steel-grey and the unchanged expression of his face, living on the inexhaustible treasure of his devotion drawn upon in the secret of his heart like a store of unlawful wealth.

The Inspector-General of State Hospitals (whose maintenance is a charge upon the Gould Concession), Official Adviser on Sanitation to the Municipality, Chief Medical Officer of the San Tomé Consolidated Mines (whose territory, containing gold, silver, copper, lead, cobalt, extends for miles along the foothills of the Cordillera), had felt poverty-stricken, miserable, and starved during the prolonged, second visit the Goulds paid to Europe and the United States of America. Intimate of the *casa*, proved friend, a bachelor without ties and without establishment (except of the professional sort), he had been asked to take up his quarters in the Gould house. In the eleven months of their absence the familiar rooms, recalling at every glance the woman to whom he had given all his loyalty, had grown intolerable. As the day approached for the arrival of the mail boat *Hermes* (the latest addition to the O.S.N. Company's splendid fleet), the doctor hobbled about more vivaciously, snapped more sardonically at simple and gentle out of sheer nervousness.

He packed up his modest trunk with speed, with fury, with enthusiasm, and saw it carried out past the old porter at the gate of the

Casa Gould with delight, with intoxication; then, as the hour approached, sitting alone in the great landau behind the white mules,
a little sideways, his drawn-in face positively venomous with effort
of self-control, and holding a pair of new gloves in his left hand, he
drove to the harbour.

His heart dilated within him so, when he saw the Goulds on the
deck of the *Hermes*, that his greetings were reduced to a casual mutter. Driving back to town, all three were silent. And in the patio the
doctor, in a more natural manner, said:

"I'll leave you now to yourselves. I'll call tomorrow if I may?"

"Come to lunch, dear Dr. Monygham, and come early," said
Mrs. Gould, in her travelling dress and her veil down, turning to
look at him at the foot of the stairs; while at the top of the flight the
Madonna, in blue robes and the Child on her arm, seemed to welcome her with an aspect of pitying tenderness.

"Don't expect to find me at home," Charles Gould warned him.
"I'll be off early to the mine."

After lunch, Doña Emilia and the Señor Doctor came slowly
through the inner gateway of the patio. The large gardens of the
Casa Gould, surrounded by high walls, and the red-tile slopes of
neighbouring roofs, lay open before them, with masses of shade
under the trees and level surfaces of sunlight upon the lawns. A
triple row of old orange trees surrounded the whole. Bare-footed,
brown gardeners, in snowy white shirts and wide *calzoneras*, dotted the grounds, squatting over flowerbeds, passing between the
trees, dragging slender india-rubber tubes across the gravel of the
paths; and the fine jets of water crossed each other in graceful
curves, sparkling in the sunshine with a slight pattering noise
upon the bushes, and an effect of showered diamonds upon the
grass.

Doña Emilia, holding up the train of a clear dress, walked by the
side of Dr. Monygham, in a longish black coat and severe black
bow on an immaculate shirt-front. Under a shady clump of trees,
where stood scattered little tables and wicker easy-chairs, Mrs. Gould
sat down in a low and ample seat.

"Don't go yet," she said to Dr. Monygham, who was unable to
tear himself away from the spot. His chin nestling within the points
of his collar, he devoured her stealthily with his eyes, which, luckily,

were round and hard like clouded marbles, and incapable of disclosing his sentiments. His pitying emotion at the marks of time
upon the face of that woman, the air of frailty and weary fatigue that
had settled upon the eyes and temples of the "Never-tired Señora"
(as Don Pepe years ago used to call her with admiration), touched
him almost to tears. "Don't go yet. Today is all my own," Mrs. Gould
urged, gently. "We are not back yet officially. No one will come. It's
only tomorrow that the windows of the Casa Gould are to be lit up
for a reception."

The doctor dropped into a chair.

"Giving a *tertulia?*"* he said, with a detached air.

"A simple greeting for all the kind friends who care to come."

"And only tomorrow?"

"Yes. Charles would be tired out after a day at the mine, and so
I— It would be good to have him to myself for one evening on our
return to this house I love. It has seen all my life."

"Ah, yes!" snarled the doctor, suddenly. "Women count time
from the marriage feast. Didn't you live a little before?"

"Yes; but what is there to remember? There were no cares."

Mrs. Gould sighed. And as two friends, after a long separation,
will revert to the most agitated period of their lives, they began to
talk of the Sulaco Revolution. It seemed strange to Mrs. Gould that
people who had taken part in it seemed to forget its memory and its
lesson.

"And yet," struck in the doctor, "we who played our part in it had
our reward. Don Pepe, though superannuated, still can sit a horse.
Barrios is drinking himself to death in jovial company away somewhere on his *fundación* beyond the Bolson de Tonoro. And the
heroic Father Román—I imagine the old padre blowing up system-
atically the San Tomé mine, uttering a pious exclamation at every
bang, and taking handfuls of snuff between the explosions—the
heroic Padre Román says that he is not afraid of the harm Holroyd's
missionaries can do to his flock, as long as *he* is alive."

Mrs. Gould shuddered a little at the allusion to the destruction
that had come so near to the San Tomé mine.

---

*Party.

"Ah, but you, dear friend?"

"I did the work I was fit for."

"You faced the most cruel dangers of all. Something more than death."

"No, Mrs. Gould! Only death — by hanging. And I am rewarded beyond my deserts."

Noticing Mrs. Gould's gaze fixed upon him, he dropped his eyes.

"I've made my career — as you see," said the Inspector-General of State Hospitals, taking up lightly the lapels of his superfine black coat. The doctor's self-respect, marked inwardly by the almost complete disappearance from his dreams of Father Berón, appeared visibly in what, by contrast with former carelessness, seemed an immoderate cult of personal appearance. Carried out within severe limits of form and colour, and in perpetual freshness, this change of apparel gave to Dr. Monygham an air at the same time professional and festive; while his gait and the unchanged crabbed character of his face acquired from it a startling force of incongruity.

"Yes," he went on. "We all had our rewards — the engineer-in-chief, Captain Mitchell —"

"We saw him," interrupted Mrs. Gould, in her charming voice. "The poor dear man came up from the country on purpose to call on us in our hotel in London. He comported himself with great dignity, but I fancy he regrets Sulaco. He rambled feebly about 'historical events' till I felt I could have a cry."

"H'm," grunted the doctor; "getting old, I suppose. Even Nostromo is getting older — though he is not changed. And, speaking of that fellow, I wanted to tell you something —"

For some time the house had been full of murmurs, of agitation. Suddenly the two gardeners, busy with rose trees at the side of the garden arch, fell upon their knees with bowed heads on the passage of Antonia Avellanos, who appeared walking beside her uncle.

Invested with the red hat after a short visit to Rome, where he had been invited by the Propaganda, Father Corbelán, missionary to the wild Indians, conspirator, friend and patron of Hernandez the robber, advanced with big, slow strides, gaunt and leaning forward, with his powerful hands clasped behind his back. The first Cardinal-Archbishop of Sulaco had preserved his fanatical and morose air; the aspect of a chaplain of bandits. It was believed that his unexpected elevation to the purple was a counter-move to the Protestant invasion of Sulaco organized by the Holroyd Missionary Fund. Antonia, the beauty of her face as if a little blurred, her figure slightly fuller, advanced with her light walk and her high serenity, smiling from a distance at Mrs. Gould. She had brought her uncle over to see dear Emilia, without ceremony, just for a moment before the siesta.

When all were seated again, Dr. Monygham, who had come to dislike heartily everybody who approached Mrs. Gould with any intimacy, kept aside, pretending to be lost in profound meditation. A louder phrase of Antonia made him lift his head.

"How can we abandon, groaning under oppression, those who have been our countrymen only a few years ago, who *are* our countrymen now?" Miss Avellanos was saying. "How can we remain blind, and deaf without pity to the cruel wrongs suffered by our brothers? There is a remedy."

"Annex the rest of Costaguana to the order and prosperity of Sulaco," snapped the doctor. "There is no other remedy."

"I am convinced, Señor Doctor," Antonia said, with the earnest calm of invincible resolution, "that this was from the first poor Martin's intention."

"Yes, but the material interests will not let you jeopardize their development for a mere idea of pity and justice," the doctor muttered, grumpily. "And it is just as well perhaps."

The Cardinal-Archbishop straightened up his gaunt, bony frame.

"We have worked for them; we have made them, these material interests of the foreigners," the last of the Corbeláns uttered in a deep, denunciatory tone.

"And without them you are nothing," cried the doctor from the distance. "They will not let you."

"Let them beware, then, lest the people, prevented from their aspirations, should rise and claim their share of the wealth and their share of the power," the popular Cardinal-Archbishop of Sulaco declared, significantly, menacingly.

A silence ensued, during which his Eminence stared, frowning at the ground, and Antonia, graceful and rigid in her chair, breathed calmly in the strength of her convictions. Then the conversation took a social turn, touching on the visit of the Goulds to Europe. The Cardinal-Archbishop, when in Rome, had suffered from neuralgia in the head all the time. It was the climate—the bad air.

When uncle and niece had gone away, with the servants again falling on their knees, and the old porter, who had known Henry Gould, almost totally blind and impotent now, creeping up to kiss his Eminence's extended hand, Dr. Monygham, looking after them, pronounced the one word:

"Incorrigible!"

Mrs. Gould, with a look upwards, dropped wearily on her lap her white hands flashing with the gold and stones of many rings.

"Conspiring. Yes!" said the doctor. "The last of the Avellanos and the last of the Corbeláns are conspiring with the refugees from Sta. Marta that flock here after every revolution. The Café Lambroso at the corner of the Plaza is full of them; you can hear their chatter across the street like the noise of a parrot-house. They are conspiring for the invasion of Costaguana. And do you know where they go for strength, for the necessary force? To the secret societies amongst immigrants and natives, where Nostromo—I should say Captain Fidanza—is the great man. What gives him that position? Who can say? Genius? He has genius. He is greater with the populace than ever he was before. It was as if he had some secret power; some mysterious means to keep up his influence. He holds conferences with the Archbishop, as in those old days which you and I remember. Barrios is useless. But for a military head they have the pious Hernandez. And they may raise the country with the new cry of wealth for the people."

"Will there be never any peace? Will there be no rest?" Mrs. Gould whispered. "I thought that we—"

"No!" interrupted the doctor. "There is no peace and no rest in the development of material interests. They have their law, and their justice. But it is founded on expediency, and is inhuman; it is without rectitude, without the continuity and the force that can be found only in a moral principle. Mrs. Gould, the time approaches when all that the Gould Concession stands for shall weigh as heavily upon the people as the barbarism, cruelty, and misrule of a few years back."

"How can you say that, Dr. Monygham?" she cried out, as if hurt in the most sensitive place of her soul.

"I can say that is true," the doctor insisted, obstinately. "It'll weigh as heavily, and provoke resentment, bloodshed, and vengeance, because the men have grown different. Do you think that now the mine would march upon the town to save their Señor Administrador? Do you think that?"

She pressed the backs of her entwined hands on her eyes and murmured hopelessly:

"Is it this we have worked for, then?"

The doctor lowered his head. He could follow her silent thought. Was it for this that her life had been robbed of all the intimate felicities of daily affection which her tenderness needed as the human body needs air to breathe? And the doctor, indignant with Charles Gould's blindness, hastened to change the conversation.

"It is about Nostromo that I wanted to talk to you. Ah! that fellow has some continuity and force. Nothing will put an end to him. But never mind that. There's something inexplicable going on—or perhaps only too easy to explain. You know, Linda is practically the lighthouse keeper of the Great Isabel light. The Garibaldino is too old now. His part is to clean the lamps and to cook in the house; but he can't get up the stairs any longer. The black-eyed Linda sleeps all day and watches the light all night. Not all day, though. She is up towards five in the afternoon, when our Nostromo, whenever he is in harbour with his schooner, comes out on his courting visit, pulling in a small boat."

"Aren't they married yet?" Mrs. Gould asked. "The mother wished it, as far as I can understand, while Linda was yet quite a child. When I had the girls with me for a year or so during the War of Separation, that extraordinary Linda used to declare quite simply that she was going to be Gian' Battista's wife."

"They are not married yet," said the doctor, curtly. "I have looked after them a little."

"Thank you, dear Dr. Monygham," said Mrs. Gould; and under the shade of the big trees her little, even teeth gleamed in a youthful smile of her gentle malice. "People don't know how really good you are. You will not let them know, as if on purpose to annoy me, who have put my faith in your good heart long ago."

The doctor, with a lifting up of his upper lip, as though he were longing to bite, bowed stiffly in his chair. With the utter absorption of a man to whom love comes late, not as the most splendid of illusions, but like an enlightening and priceless misfortune, the sight of that woman (of whom he had been deprived for nearly a year) suggested ideas of adoration, of kissing the hem of her robe. And this excess of feeling translated itself naturally into an augmented grimness of speech.

"I am afraid of being overwhelmed by too much gratitude. However, these people interest me. I went out several times to the Great Isabel light to look after old Giorgio."

He did not tell Mrs. Gould that it was because he found there, in her absence, the relief of an atmosphere of congenial sentiment in old Giorgio's austere admiration for the "English signora—the benefactress"; in black-eyed Linda's voluble, torrential, passionate affection for "our Doña Emilia—that angel"; in the white-throated, fair Giselle's adoring upward turn of the eyes, which then glided towards him with a sidelong, half-arch, half-candid glance, which made the doctor exclaim to himself mentally, "If I weren't what I am, old and ugly, I would think the minx is making eyes at me. And perhaps she is. I dare say she would make eyes at anybody." Dr. Monygham said nothing of this to Mrs. Gould, the providence of the Viola family, but reverted to what he called "our great Nostromo."

"What I wanted to tell you is this: Our great Nostromo did not take much notice of the old man and the children for some years. It's true, too, that he was away on his coasting voyages certainly ten months out of the twelve. He was making his fortune, as he told Captain Mitchell once. He seems to have done uncommonly well. It was only to be expected. He is a man full of resource, full of confidence in himself, ready to take chances and risks of every sort. I remember being in Mitchell's office one day, when he came in with that calm, grave air he always carries everywhere. He had been away trading in the Gulf of California, he said, looking straight past us at the wall, as his manner is, and was glad to see on his return that a lighthouse was being built on the cliff of the Great Isabel. Very glad, he repeated. Mitchell explained that it was the O.S.N. Company who were building it, for the convenience of the mail service, on his own advice. Captain Fidanza was good enough to say that it was excellent advice.

I remember him twisting up his moustaches and looking all round the cornice of the room before he proposed that old Giorgio should be made the keeper of that light."

"I heard of this. I was consulted at the time," Mrs. Gould said. "I doubted whether it would be good for these girls to be shut up on that island as if in a prison."

"The proposal fell in with the Garibaldino's humour. As to Linda, any place was lovely and delightful enough for her as long as it was Nostromo's suggestion. She could wait for her Gian' Battista's good pleasure there as well as anywhere else. My opinion is that she was always in love with that incorruptible Capataz. Moreover, both father and sister were anxious to get Giselle away from the attentions of a certain Ramirez."

"Ah!" said Mrs. Gould, interested. "Ramirez? What sort of man is that?"

"Just a *mozo* of the town. His father was a *cargador*. As a lanky boy he ran about the wharf in rags, till Nostromo took him up and made a man of him. When he got a little older, he put him into a lighter and very soon gave him charge of the No. 3 boat—the boat which took the silver away, Mrs. Gould. Nostromo selected that lighter for the work because she was the best sailing and the strongest boat of all the Company's fleet. Young Ramirez was one of the five *cargadores* entrusted with the removal of the treasure from the Custom House on that famous night. As the boat he had charge of was sunk, Nostromo, on leaving the Company's service, recommended him to Captain Mitchell for his successor. He had trained him in the routine of work perfectly, and thus Mr. Ramirez, from a starving waif, becomes a man and the Capataz of the Sulaco *cargadores*."

"Thanks to Nostromo," said Mrs. Gould, with warm approval.

"Thanks to Nostromo," repeated Dr. Monygham. "Upon my word, the fellow's power frightens me when I think of it. That our poor old Mitchell was only too glad to appoint somebody trained to work, who saved him trouble, is not surprising. What is wonderful is the fact that the Sulaco *cargadores* accepted Ramirez for their chief, simply because such was Nostromo's good pleasure. Of course, he is not a second Nostromo, as he fondly imagined he would be; but still, the position was brilliant enough. It emboldened him to make reappear with the child seated on his shoulder. He passed through the gateway between the garden and the patio with measured steps, careful of his light burden.

The doctor, with his back to Mrs. Gould, contemplated a flower-bed away in the sunshine. People believed him scornful and soured. The truth of his nature consisted in his capacity for passion and in the sensitiveness of his temperament. What he lacked was the polished callousness of men of the world, the callousness from which springs an easy tolerance for oneself and others; the tolerance wide as poles asunder from true sympathy and human compassion. This want of callousness accounted for his sardonic turn of mind and his biting speeches.

In profound silence, and glaring viciously at the brilliant flower-bed, Dr. Monygham poured mental imprecations on Charles Gould's head. Behind him the immobility of Mrs. Gould added to the grace of her seated figure the charm of art, of an attitude caught and interpreted for ever. Turning abruptly, the doctor took his leave.

Mrs. Gould leaned back in the shade of the big trees planted in a circle. She leaned back with her eyes closed and her white hands lying idle on the arms of her seat. The half-light under the thick mass of leaves brought out the youthful prettiness of her face; made the clear, light fabrics and white lace of her dress appear luminous. Small and dainty, as if radiating a light of her own in the deep shade of the interlaced boughs, she resembled a good fairy, weary with a long career of well-doing, touched by the withering suspicion of the uselessness of her labours, the powerlessness of her magic.

Had anybody asked her of what she was thinking, alone in the garden of the *casa*, with her husband at the mine and the house closed to the street like an empty dwelling, her frankness would have had to evade the question. It had come into her mind that for life to be large and full, it must contain the care of the past and of the future in every passing moment of the present. Our daily work must be done to the glory of the dead, and for the good of those who come after. She thought that, and sighed without opening her eyes—without moving at all. Mrs. Gould's face became set and rigid for a second, as if to receive, without flinching, a great wave of loneliness that swept over her head. And it came into her mind, too, that no one would ever ask her with solicitude what she was thinking of. No one.

up to Giselle Viola, who, you know, is the recognized beauty of the town. The old Garibaldino, however, took a violent dislike to him. I don't know why. Perhaps because he was not a model of perfection like his Gian' Battista, the incarnation of the courage, the fidelity, the honour of 'the people.' Signor Viola does not think much of Sulaco natives. Both of them, the old Spartan and that white-faced Linda, with her red mouth and coal-black eyes, were looking rather fiercely after the fair one. Ramirez was warned off. Father Viola, I am told, threatened him with his gun once."

"But what of Giselle herself?" asked Mrs. Gould.

"She's a bit of a flirt, I believe," said the doctor. "I don't think she cared much one way or another. Of course she likes men's attentions. Ramirez was not the only one, let me tell you, Mrs. Gould. There was one engineer, at least, on the railway staff who got warned off with a gun, too. Old Viola does not allow any trifling with his honour. He has grown uneasy and suspicious since his wife died. He was very pleased to remove his youngest girl away from the town. But look what happens, Mrs. Gould. Ramirez, the honest, lovelorn swain, is forbidden the island. Very well. He respects the prohibition, but naturally turns his eyes frequently towards the Great Isabel. It seems as though he had been in the habit of gazing late at night upon the light. And during these sentimental vigils he discovers that Nostromo, Captain Fidanza that is, returns very late from his visits to the Violas. As late as midnight at times."

The doctor paused and stared meaningly at Mrs. Gould.

"Yes. But I don't understand," she began, looking puzzled.

"Now comes the strange part," went on Dr. Monygham. "Viola, who is king on his island, will allow no visitor on it after dark. Even Captain Fidanza has got to leave after sunset, when Linda has gone up to tend the light. And Nostromo goes away obediently. But what happens afterwards? What does he do in the gulf between half past six and midnight? He has been seen more than once at that late hour pulling quietly into the harbour. Ramirez is devoured by jealousy. He dare not approach old Viola; but he plucked up courage to rail Linda about it on Sunday morning as she came on the mainland to hear Mass and visit her mother's grave. There was a scene on the wharf, which, as a matter of fact, I witnessed. It was early morning. He must have been waiting for her on purpose. I was there by the merest chance, having been called to an urgent consultation by the doctor of the German gunboat in the harbour. She poured wrath, scorn, and flame upon Ramirez, who seemed out of his mind. It was a strange sight, Mrs. Gould: the long jetty, with this raving *cargador* in his crimson sash and the girl all in black, at the end; the early Sunday-morning quiet of the harbour in the shade of the mountains; nothing but a canoe or two moving between the ships at anchor, and the German gunboat's gig coming to take me off. Linda passed me within a foot. I noticed her wild eyes. I called out to her. She never heard me. She never saw me. But I looked at her face. It was awful in its anger and wretchedness."

Mrs. Gould sat up, opening her eyes wide.

"What do you mean, Dr. Monygham? Do you mean to say that you suspect the younger sister?"

"*Quién sabe!* Who can tell?" said the doctor, shrugging his shoulders like a born Costaguanero. "Ramirez came up to me on the wharf. He reeled—he looked insane. He took his head into his hands. He had to talk to someone—simply had to. Of course for all his mad state he recognized me. People know me well here. I have lived too long amongst them to be anything else but the evil-eyed doctor, who can cure all the ills of the flesh, and bring bad luck by a glance. He came up to me. He tried to be calm. He tried to make it out that he wanted merely to warn me against Nostromo. It seems that Captain Fidanza at some secret meeting or other had mentioned me as the worst despiser of all the poor—of the people. It's very possible. He honours me with his undying dislike. And a word from the great Fidanza may be quite enough to send some fool's knife into my back. The Sanitary Commission I preside over is not in favour with the populace. 'Beware of him, Señor Doctor. Destroy him, Señor Doctor,' Ramirez hissed right into my face. And then he broke out. 'That man,' he spluttered, 'has cast a spell upon both these girls.' As to himself, he had said too much. He must run away now—run away and hide somewhere. He moaned tenderly about Giselle, and then called her names that cannot be repeated. If he thought she could be made to love him by any means, he would carry her off from the island. Off into the woods. But it was no good. . . . He strode away, flourishing his arms above his head. Then I noticed an old Negro, who had been sitting behind a pile of

cases, fishing from the wharf. He wound up his lines and slu[n] away at once. But he must have heard something, and must ha[ve] talked, too, because some of the old Garibaldino's railway friends[,] suppose, warned him against Ramirez. At any rate, the father ha[s] been warned. But Ramirez has disappeared from the town."

"I feel I have a duty towards these girls," said Mrs. Gould, u[n]easily. "Is Nostromo in Sulaco now?"

"He is, since last Sunday."

"He ought to be spoken to—at once."

"Who will dare speak to him? Even the love-mad Ramirez ru[n] away from the mere shadow of Captain Fidanza."

"I can. I will," Mrs. Gould declared. "A word will be enough fo[r] a man like Nostromo."

The doctor smiled sourly.

"He must end this situation which lends itself to— I can't be[-]lieve it of that child," pursued Mrs. Gould.

"He's very attractive," muttered the doctor, gloomily.

"He'll see it, I am sure. He must put an end to all this by marry[-]ing Linda at once," pronounced the first lady of Sulaco with im[-]mense decision.

Through the garden gate emerged Basilio, grown fat and slee[k] with an elderly hairless face, wrinkles at the corners of his eyes, an[d] his jet-black, coarse hair plastered down smoothly. Stooping careful[ly] behind an ornamental clump of bushes, he put down with preca[u-]tion a small child he had been carrying on his shoulder—his o[wn] and Leonarda's last born. The pouting, spoiled *camerista* and [the] head *mozo* of the Casa Gould had been married for some years n[ow.]

He remained squatting on his heels for a time, gazing fondl[y] his offspring, which returned his stare with imperturbable grav[ity;] then, solemn and respectable, walked down the path.

"What is it, Basilio?" asked Mrs. Gould.

"A telephone call came through from the office of the mine. [The] master remains to sleep at the mountain tonight."

Dr. Monygham had got up and stood looking away. A prof[ound] silence reigned for a time under the shade of the biggest trees [of the] lovely gardens of the Casa Gould.

"Very well, Basilio," said Mrs. Gould. She watched hi[m] away along the path, step aside behind the flowering bus[h]

No one, but perhaps the man who had just gone away. No; no one who could be answered with careless sincerity in the ideal perfection of confidence.

The word "incorrigible"—a word lately pronounced by Dr. Monygham—floated into her still and sad immobility. Incorrigible in his devotion to the great silver mine was the Señor Administrador! Incorrigible in his hard, determined service of the material interests to which he had pinned his faith in the triumph of order and justice. Poor boy! She had a clear vision of the great hairs on his temples. He was perfect—perfect. What more could she have expected? It was a colossal and lasting success; and love was only a short moment of forgetfulness, a short intoxication, whose delight one remembered with a sense of sadness, as if it had been a deep grief lived through. There was something inherent in the necessities of successful action which carried with it the moral degradation of the idea. She saw the San Tomé mountain hanging over the Campo, over the whole land, feared, hated, wealthy; more soulless than any tyrant, more pitiless and autocratic than the worst Government; ready to crush innumerable lives in the expansion of its greatness. He did not see it. He could not see it. It was not his fault. He was perfect. Perfect; but she would never have him to herself. Never; not for one short hour altogether to herself in this old Spanish house she loved so well! Incorrigible, the last of the Corbeláns, the last of the Avellanos, the doctor had said; but she saw clearly the San Tomé mine possessing, consuming, burning up the life of the last of the Costaguana Goulds; mastering the energetic spirit of the son as it had mastered the lamentable weakness of the father. A terrible success for the last of the Goulds. The last! She had hoped for a long, long time that perhaps— But no! There were to be no more. An immense desolation, the dread of her own continued life, descended upon the first lady of Sulaco. With a prophetic vision she saw herself surviving alone the degradation of her young ideal life, of love, of work—all alone in the Treasure House of the World. The profound, blind, suffering expression of a painful dream settled on her face with its closed eyes. In the indistinct voice of an unlucky sleeper, lying passive in the grip of a merciless nightmare, she stammered out aimlessly the words:

"Material interest."

CHAPTER 12

NOSTROMO HAD BEEN GROWING rich very slowly. It was an effect of his prudence. He could command himself even when thrown off his balance. And to become the slave of a treasure with full self-knowledge is an occurrence rare and mentally disturbing. But it was also in a great part because of the difficulty of converting it into a form in which it could become available. The mere act of getting it away from the island piecemeal, little by little, was surrounded by difficulties, by the dangers of imminent detection. He had to visit the Great Isabel in secret, between his voyages along the coast, which were the ostensible source of his fortune. The crew of his own schooner were to be feared as if they had been spies upon their dreaded captain. He did not dare stay too long in port. When his coaster was unloaded, he hurried away on another trip, for he feared arousing suspicion even by a day's delay. Sometimes during a week's stay, or more, he could only manage one visit to the treasure. And that was all. A couple of ingots. He suffered through his fears as much as through his prudence. To do things by stealth humiliated him. And he suffered most from the concentration of his thought upon the treasure.

A transgression, a crime, entering a man's existence, eats it up like a malignant growth, consumes it like a fever. Nostromo had lost his peace; the genuineness of all his qualities was destroyed. He felt it himself, and often cursed the silver of San Tomé. His courage, his magnificence, his leisure, his work, everything was as before, only everything was a sham. But the treasure was real. He clung to it with a more tenacious, mental grip. But he hated the feel of the ingots. Sometimes, after putting away a couple of them in his cabin—the fruit of a secret night expedition to the Great Isabel—he would look fixedly at his fingers, as if surprised they had left no stain on his skin.

He had found means of disposing of the silver bars in distant ports. The necessity to go far afield made his coasting voyages long, and caused his visits to the Viola household to be rare and far between. He was fated to have his wife from there. He had said so once to Giorgio himself. But the Garibaldino had put the subject aside with a majestic wave of his hand, clutching a smouldering black briar-root pipe. There was plenty of time; he was not the man to force his girls upon anybody.

As time went on, Nostromo discovered his preference for the younger of the two. They had some profound similarities of nature, which must exist for complete confidence and understanding, no matter what outward differences of temperament there may be to exercise their own fascination of contrast. His wife would have to know his secret or else life would be impossible. He was attracted by Giselle, with her candid gaze and white throat, pliable, silent, fond of excitement under her quiet indolence; whereas Linda, with her intense, passionately pale face, energetic, all fire and words, touched with gloom and scorn, a chip off the old block, true daughter of the austere republican, but with Teresa's voice, inspired him with a deep-seated mistrust. Moreover, the poor girl could not conceal her love for Gian' Battista. He could see it would be violent, exacting, suspicious, uncompromising—like her soul. Giselle, by her fair but warm beauty, by the surface placidity of her nature holding a promise of submissiveness, by the charm of her girlish mysteriousness, excited his passion and allayed his fears as to the future.

His absences from Sulaco were long. On returning from the longest of them, he made out lighters loaded with blocks of stone lying under the cliff of the Great Isabel; cranes and scaffolding above; workmen's figures moving about, and a small lighthouse already rising from its foundations on the edge of the cliff.

At this unexpected, undreamt-of, startling sight, he thought himself lost irretrievably. What could save him from detection now? Nothing! He was struck with amazed dread at this turn of chance, that would kindle a far-reaching light upon the only secret spot of his life; that life whose very essence, value, reality, consisted in its reflection from the admiring eyes of men. All of it but that thing which was beyond common comprehension; which stood between him and the power that hears and gives effect to the evil intention of curses. It was dark. Not every man had such a darkness. And they were going to put a light there. A light! He saw it shining upon disgrace, poverty, contempt. Somebody was sure to. . . . Perhaps somebody had already. . . .

The incomparable Nostromo, the Capataz, the respected and feared Captain Fidanza, the unquestioned patron of secret societies, a republican like old Giorgio, and a revolutionist at heart (but in another manner), was on the point of jumping overboard from the deck of his own schooner. That man, subjective almost to insanity, looked suicide deliberately in the face. But he never lost his head. He was checked by the thought that this was no escape. He imagined himself dead, and the disgrace, the shame going on. Or, rather, properly speaking, he could not imagine himself dead. He was possessed too strongly by the sense of his own existence, a thing of infinite duration in its changes, to grasp the notion of finality. The earth goes on for ever.

And he was courageous. It was a corrupt courage, but it was as good for his purposes as the other kind. He sailed close to the cliff of the Great Isabel, throwing a penetrating glance from the deck at the mouth of the ravine, tangled in an undisturbed growth of bushes. He sailed close enough to exchange hails with the workmen, shading their eyes on the edge of the sheer drop of the cliff overhung by the jib-head of a powerful crane. He perceived that none of them had any occasion even to approach the ravine where the silver lay hidden; let alone to enter it. In the harbour he learned that no one slept on the island. The labouring gangs returned to port every evening, singing chorus songs in the empty lighters towed by a harbour tug. For the moment he had nothing to fear.

But afterwards? he asked himself. Later, when a keeper came to live in the cottage that was being built some hundred and fifty yards back from the low light-tower, and four hundred or so from the dark, shaded, jungly ravine, containing the secret of his safety, of his influence, of his magnificence, of his power over the future, of his defiance of ill-luck, of every possible betrayal from rich and poor alike—what then? He could never shake off the treasure. His audacity, greater than that of other men, had welded that vein of silver into his life. And the feeling of fearful and ardent subjection, the feeling of his slavery—so irremediable and profound that often, in his thoughts, he compared himself to the legendary *gringos*, neither dead nor alive, bound down to their conquest of unlawful wealth on Azuera—weighted heavily on the independent Captain Fidanza, owner and master of a coasting schooner, whose smart appearance (and fabulous good luck in trading) were so well known along the western seaboard of a vast continent.

Fiercely whiskered and grave, a shade less supple in his walk, the vigour and symmetry of his powerful limbs lost in the vulgarity of a brown tweed suit, made by Jews in the slums of London, and sold by the clothing department of the Compañía Anzani, Captain Fidanza was seen in the streets of Sulaco attending to his business, as usual, that trip. And, as usual, he allowed it to get about that he had made a great profit on his cargo. It was a cargo of salt fish, and Lent was approaching. He was seen in tramcars going to and fro between the town and the harbour; he talked with people in a café or two in his measured, steady voice. Captain Fidanza was *seen*. The generation that would know nothing of the famous ride to Cayta was not born yet.

Nostromo, the miscalled Capataz de Cargadores, had made for himself, under his rightful name, another public existence, but modified by the new conditions, less picturesque, more difficult to keep up in the increased size and varied population of Sulaco, the progressive capital of the Occidental Republic.

Captain Fidanza, unpicturesque, but always a little mysterious, was recognized quite sufficiently under the lofty glass and iron roof of the Sulaco railway station. He took a local train, and got out in Rincón, where he visited the widow of the *cargador* who had died of his wounds (at the dawn of the New Era, like Don José Avellanos) in the patio of the Casa Gould. He consented to sit down and drink a glass of cool lemonade in the hut, while the woman, standing up, poured a perfect torrent of words to which he did not listen. He left some money with her, as usual. The orphaned children, growing up and well schooled, calling him uncle, clamoured for his blessing. He gave that, too; and in the doorway paused for a moment to look at the flat face of the San Tomé mountain with a faint frown. This slight contraction of his bronzed brow casting a marked tinge of severity upon his usual unbending expression, was observed at the Lodge which he attended—but went away before the banquet. He wore it at the meeting of some good comrades, Italians and

Occidentals, assembled in his honour under the presidency of an indigent, sickly, somewhat hunchbacked little photographer, with a white face and a magnanimous soul dyed crimson by a bloodthirsty hate of all capitalists, oppressors of the two hemispheres. The heroic Giorgio Viola, old revolutionist, would have understood nothing of his opening speech; and Captain Fidanza, lavishly generous as usual to some poor comrades, made no speech at all. He had listened, frowning with his mind far away, and walked off unapproachable, silent, like a man full of cares.

His frown deepened as, in the early morning, he watched the stone-masons go off to the Great Isabel, in lighters loaded with squared blocks of stone, enough to add another course to the squat light-tower. That was the rate of the work. One course per day.

And Captain Fidanza meditated. The presence of strangers on the island would cut him off completely from the treasure. It had been difficult and dangerous enough before. He was afraid, and he was angry. He thought with the resolution of a master and the cunning of a cowed slave. Then he went ashore.

He was a man of resource and ingenuity; and, as usual, the expedient he found at a critical moment was effective enough to alter the situation radically. He had the gift of evolving safety out of the very danger, this incomparable Nostromo, this "fellow in a thousand." With Giorgio established on the Great Isabel, there would be no need for concealment. He would be able to go openly, in daylight, to see his daughters—one of his daughters—and stay late talking to the old Garibaldino. Then in the dark. . . . Night after night. . . . He would dare to grow rich quicker now. He yearned to clasp, embrace, absorb, subjugate in unquestioned possession this treasure, whose tyranny had weighed upon his mind, his actions, his very sleep.

He went to see his friend Captain Mitchell—and the thing was done as Dr. Monygham had related to Mrs. Gould. When the project was mooted to the Garibaldino, something like the faint reflection, the dim ghost of a very ancient smile, stole under the white and enormous moustaches of the old hater of kings and ministers. His daughters were the object of his anxious care. The younger, especially. Linda, with her mother's voice, had taken more her mother's place. Her deep, vibrating "Eh, Padre?" seemed, but for the change of the word, the very echo of the impassioned, remonstrating "Eh, Giorgio?" of poor Signora Teresa. It was his fixed opinion that the town was no proper place for his girls. The infatuated but guileless Ramirez was the object of his profound aversion, as resuming the sins of the country whose people were blind, vile *esclavos*.

On his return from his next voyage, Captain Fidanza found the Violas settled in the light-keeper's cottage. His knowledge of Giorgio's idiosyncrasies had not played him false. The Garibaldino had refused to entertain the idea of any companion whatever, except his girls. And Captain Mitchell, anxious to please his poor Nostromo, with that felicity of inspiration which only true affection can give, had formally appointed Linda Viola as underkeeper of Isabel's Light.

"The light is private property," he used to explain. "It belongs to my Company. I've the power to nominate whom I like, and Viola it shall be. It's about the only thing Nostromo—a man worth his weight in gold, mind you—has ever asked me to do for him."

Directly his schooner was anchored opposite the New Custom House, with its sham air of a Greek temple, flat-roofed, with a colonnade, Captain Fidanza went pulling his small boat out of the harbour, bound for the Great Isabel, openly in the light of a declining day, before all men's eyes, with a sense of having mastered the fates. He must establish a regular position. He would ask him for his daughter now. He thought of Giselle as he pulled. Linda loved him, perhaps, but the old man would be glad to keep the eldest, who had his wife's voice.

He did not pull for the narrow strand where he had landed with Decoud, and afterwards alone on his first visit to the treasure. He made for the beach at the other end, and walked up the regular and gentle slope of the wedge-shaped island. Giorgio Viola, whom he saw from afar, sitting on a bench under the front wall of the cottage, lifted his arm slightly to his loud hail. He walked up. Neither of the girls appeared.

"It is good here," said the old man, in his austere, far-away manner. Nostromo nodded; then, after a short silence:

"You saw my schooner pass in not two hours ago? Do you know why I am here before, so to speak, my anchor has fairly bitten into the ground of this port of Sulaco?"

"You are welcome like a son," the old man declared, quietly, staring away upon the sea.

"Ah! thy son. I know. I am what thy son would have been. It is well, *viejo*. It is a very good welcome. Listen, I have come to ask you for—"

A sudden dread came upon the fearless and incorruptible Nostromo. He dared not utter the name in his mind. The slight pause only imparted a marked weight and solemnity to the changed end of the phrase.

"For my wife!" . . . His heart was beating fast. "It is time you—"

The Garibaldino arrested him with an extended arm. "That was left for you to judge."

He got up slowly. His beard, unclipped since Teresa's death, thick, snow-white, covered his powerful chest. He turned his head to the door, and called out in his strong voice:

"Linda."

Her answer came sharp and faint from within; and the appalled Nostromo stood up, too, but remained mute, gazing at the door. He was afraid. He was not afraid of being refused the girl he loved—no mere refusal could stand between him and a woman he desired—but the shining spectre of the treasure rose before him, claiming his allegiance in a silence that could not be gainsaid. He was afraid, because, neither dead nor alive, like the *gringos* on Azuera, he belonged body and soul to the unlawfulness of his audacity. He was afraid of being forbidden the island. He was afraid, and said nothing.

Seeing the two men standing up side by side to await her, Linda stopped in the doorway. Nothing could alter the passionate dead whiteness of her face; but the black eyes seemed to catch and concentrate all the light of the low sun in a flaming spark within the black depths, covered at once by the slow descent of heavy eyelids.

"Behold thy husband, master, and benefactor." Old Viola's voice resounded with a force that seemed to fill the whole gulf.

She stepped forward with her eyes nearly closed, like a sleepwalker in a beatific dream.

Nostromo made a superhuman effort. "It is time, Linda, we two were betrothed," he said, steadily, in his level, careless, unbending tone.

She put her hand into his offered palm, lowering her head, dark with bronze glints, upon which her father's hand rested for a moment.

"And so the soul of the dead is satisfied."

This came from Giorgio Viola, who went on talking for a while of his dead wife; while the two, sitting side by side, never looked at each other. Then the old man ceased; and Linda, motionless, began to speak.

"Ever since I felt I lived in the world, I have lived for you alone, Gian' Battista. And that you knew! You knew it . . . Battistino."

She pronounced the name exactly with her mother's intonation. A gloom as of the grave covered Nostromo's heart.

"Yes. I knew," he said.

The heroic Garibaldino sat on the same bench bowing his hoary head, his old soul dwelling alone with its memories, tender and violent, terrible and dreary—solitary on the earth full of men.

And Linda, his best-loved daughter, was saying, "I was yours ever since I can remember. I had only to think of you for the earth to become empty to my eyes. When you were there, I could see no one else. I was yours. Nothing is changed. The world belongs to you, and you let me live in it. . . ." She dropped her low, vibrating voice to a still lower note, and found other things to say—torturing for the man at her side. Her murmur ran on ardent and voluble. She did not seem to see her sister, who came out with an altar-cloth she was embroidering in her hands, and passed in front of them, silent, fresh, fair, with a quick glance and a faint smile, to sit a little away on the other side of Nostromo.

The evening was still. The sun sank almost to the edge of a purple ocean; and the white lighthouse, livid against the background of clouds filling the head of the gulf, bore the lantern red and glowing, like a live ember kindled by the fire of the sky. Giselle, indolent and demure, raised the altar-cloth from time to time to hide nervous yawns, as of a young panther.

Suddenly Linda rushed at her sister, and, seizing her head, covered her face with kisses. Nostromo's brain reeled. When she left her, as if stunned by the violent caresses, with her hands lying in her lap, the slave of the treasure felt as if he could shoot that woman. Old Giorgio lifted his leonine head.

"Where are you going, Linda?"

"To the light, *padre mio*."*

"*Sí, sí*—to your duty."

He got up, too, looked after his eldest daughter; then, in a tone whose festive note seemed the echo of a mood lost in the night of ages:

"I am going in to cook something. Aha! Son! The old man knows where to find a bottle of wine, too."

He turned to Giselle, with a change to austere tenderness.

"And you, little one, pray not to the God of priests and slaves, but to the God of orphans, of the oppressed, of the poor, of little children, to give thee a man like this one for a husband."

His hand rested heavily for a moment on Nostromo's shoulder; then he went in. The hopeless slave of the San Tomé silver felt at these words the venomous fangs of jealousy biting deep into his heart. He was appalled by the novelty of the experience, by its force, by its physical intimacy. A husband! A husband for her! And yet it was natural that Giselle should have a husband at some time or other. He had never realized that before. In discovering that her beauty could belong to another he felt as though he could kill this one of old Giorgio's daughters also. He muttered moodily:

"They say you love Ramirez."

She shook her head without looking at him. Coppery glints rippled to and fro on the wealth of her gold hair. Her smooth forehead had the soft, pure sheen of a priceless pearl in the splendour of the sunset, mingling the gloom of starry spaces, the purple of the sea, and the crimson of the sky in a magnificent stillness.

"No," she said, slowly. "I never loved him. I think I never. . . . He loves me—perhaps."

The seduction of her slow voice died out of the air, and her raised eyes remained fixed on nothing, as if indifferent and without thought.

"Ramirez told you he loved you?" asked Nostromo, restraining himself.

"Ah! once—one evening. . . ."

"The miserable. . . . Ha!"

---

*My father.

He had jumped up as if stung by a gad-fly, and stood before her mute with anger.

"*Misericordia Divina!** You, too, Gian' Battista! Poor wretch that I am!" she lamented in ingenuous tones. "I told Linda, and she scolded—she scolded. Am I to live blind, dumb, and deaf in this world? And she told father, who took down his gun and cleaned it. Poor Ramirez! Then you came, and she told you."

He looked at her. He fastened his eyes upon the hollow of her white throat, which had the invincible charm of things young, palpitating, delicate, and alive. Was this the child he had known? Was it possible? It dawned upon him that in these last years he had really seen very little—nothing—of her. Nothing. She had come into the world like a thing unknown. She had come upon him unawares. She was a danger. A frightful danger. The instinctive mood of fierce determination that had never failed him before the perils of this life added its steady force to the violence of his passion. She, in a voice that recalled to him the song of running water, the tinkling of a silver bell, continued:

"And between you three you have brought me here into this captivity to the sky and water. Nothing else. Sky and water. Oh, *Santissima Madre.*† My hair shall turn grey on this tedious island. I could hate you, Gian' Battista!"

He laughed loudly. Her voice enveloped him like a caress. She bemoaned her fate, spreading unconsciously, like a flower its perfume in the coolness of the evening, the indefinable seduction of her person. Was it her fault that nobody ever had admired Linda? Even when they were little, going out with their mother to Mass, she remembered that people took no notice of Linda, who was fearless, and chose instead to frighten her, who was timid, with their attention. It was her hair like gold, she supposed.

He broke out:

"Your hair like gold, and your eyes like violets, and your lips like the rose; your round arms, your white throat. . . ."

Imperturbable in the indolence of her pose, she blushed deeply all over to the roots of her hair. She was not conceited. She was no

---

*Divine Mercy!
†Most Holy Mother!

more self-conscious than a flower. But she was pleased. And perhaps even a flower loves to hear itself praised. He glanced down, and added, impetuously:

"Your little feet!"

Leaning back against the rough stone wall of the cottage, she seemed to bask languidly in the warmth of the rosy flush. Only her lowered eyes glanced at her little feet.

"And so you are going at last to marry our Linda. She is terrible. Ah! now she will understand better since you have told her you love her. She will not be so fierce."

"*Chica!*"* said Nostromo, "I have not told her anything."

"Then make haste. Come tomorrow. Come and tell her, so that I may have some peace from her scolding and—perhaps—who knows. . . ."

"Be allowed to listen to your Ramirez, eh? Is that it? You. . . ."

"Mercy of God! How violent you are, Giovanni," she said, unmoved. "Who is Ramirez . . . Ramirez. . . . Who is he?" she repeated, dreamily, in the dusk and gloom of the clouded gulf, with a low red streak in the west like a hot bar of glowing iron laid across the entrance of a world sombre as a cavern, where the magnificent Capataz de Cargadores had hidden his conquests of love and wealth.

"Listen, Giselle," he said, in measured tones; "I will tell no word of love to your sister. Do you want to know why?"

"Alas! I could not understand perhaps, Giovanni. Father says you are not like other men; that no one has ever understood you properly; that the rich will be surprised yet. . . . Oh! saints in heaven! I am weary."

She raised her embroidery to conceal the lower part of her face, then let it fall on her lap. The lantern was shaded on the land side, but slanting away from the dark column of the lighthouse they could see the long shaft of light, kindled by Linda, go out to strike the expiring glow in a horizon of purple and red.

Giselle Viola, with her head resting against the wall of the house, her eyes half closed, and her little feet, in white stockings and black slippers, crossed over each other, seemed to surrender

---

*Girl!

already by their folly and their betrayal. For he had been betrayed—he said—deceived, tempted. She believed him. . . . He had kept the treasure for purposes of revenge; but now he cared nothing for it. He cared only for her. He would put her beauty in a palace on a hill crowned with olive trees—a white palace above a blue sea. He would keep her there like a jewel in a casket. He would get land for her—her own land fertile with vines and corn—to set her little feet upon. He kissed them. . . . He had already paid for it all with the soul of a woman and the life of a man. . . . The Capataz de Cargadores tasted the supreme intoxication of his generosity. He flung the mastered treasure superbly at her feet in the impenetrable darkness of the gulf, in the darkness defying—as men said—the knowledge of God and the wit of the devil. But she must let him grow rich first—he warned her.

She listened as if in a trance. Her finger stirred in his hair. He got up from his knees reeling, weak, empty, as though he had flung his soul away.

"Make haste, then," she said. "Make haste, Giovanni, my lover, my master, for I will give thee up to no one but God. And I am afraid of Linda."

He guessed at her shudder, and swore to do his best. He trusted the courage of her love. She promised to be brave in order to be loved always—far away in a white palace upon a hill above a blue sea. Then with a timid, tentative eagerness she murmured:

"Where is it? Where? Tell me that, Giovanni."

He opened his mouth and remained silent—thunderstruck.

"Not that! Not that!" he gasped out, appalled at the spell of secrecy that had kept him dumb before so many people falling upon his lips again with unimpaired force. Not even to her. Not even to her. It was too dangerous. "I forbid thee to ask," he cried at her, deadening cautiously the anger of his voice.

He had not regained his freedom. The spectre of the unlawful treasure arose, standing by her side like a figure of silver, pitiless and secret, with a finger on its pale lips. His soul died within him at the vision of himself creeping in presently along the ravine, with the smell of earth, of damp foliage in his nostrils—creeping in, determined in a purpose that numbed his breast, and creeping out again loaded with silver, with his ears alert to every sound. It must be done on this very night—that work of a craven slave!

herself, tranquil and fatal, to the gathering dusk. The charm of her body, the promising mysteriousness of her indolence, went out into the night of the Placid Gulf like a fresh and intoxicating fragrance spreading out in the shadows, impregnating the air. The incorruptible Nostromo breathed her ambient seduction in the tumultuous heaving of his breast. Before leaving the harbour he had thrown off the store clothing of Captain Fidanza, for greater ease in the long pull out to the islands. He stood before her in the red sash and check shirt as he used to appear on the Company's wharf—a Mediterranean sailor come ashore to try his luck in Costaguana. The dusk of purple and red enveloped him, too—close, soft, profound, as no more than fifty yards from that spot it had gathered evening after evening about the self-destructive passion of Don Martin Decoud's utter scepticism, flaming up to death in solitude.

"You have got to hear," he began at last, with perfect self-control. "I shall say no word of love to your sister, to whom I am betrothed from this evening, because it is you that I love. It is you! . . ."

The dusk let him see yet the tender and voluptuous smile that came instinctively upon her lips shaped for love and kisses, freeze hard in the drawn, haggard lines of terror. He could not restrain himself any longer. While she shrank from his approach, her arms went out to him, abandoned and regal in the dignity of her languid surrender. He held her head in his two hands, and showered rapid kisses upon the upturned face that gleamed in the purple dusk. Masterful and tender, he was entering slowly upon the fullness of his possession. And he perceived that she was crying. Then the incomparable Capataz, the man of careless loves, became gentle and caressing, like a woman to the grief of a child. He murmured to her fondly. He sat down by her and nursed her fair head on his breast. He called her his star and his little flower.

It had grown dark. From the living-room of the light-keeper's cottage, where Giorgio, one of the Immortal Thousand, was bending his leonine and heroic head over a charcoal fire, there came the sound of sizzling and the aroma of an artistic *frittura*.*

---

*Fry-up.

In the obscure disarray of that thing, happening like a cataclysm, it was in her feminine head that some gleam of reason survived. He was lost to the world in their embraced stillness. But she said, whispering into his ear:

"God of mercy! What will become of me—here—now—between this sky and this water I hate? Linda, Linda—I see her! . . ." She tried to get out of his arms, suddenly relaxed at the sound of that name. But there was no one approaching their black shapes, enlaced and struggling on the white background of the wall. "Linda! Poor Linda! I tremble! I shall die of fear before my poor sister Linda, betrothed today to Giovanni—my lover! Giovanni, you must have been mad! I cannot understand you! You are not like other men! I will not give you up—never—only to God himself! But why have you done this blind, mad, cruel, frightful thing?"

Released, she hung her head, let fall her hands. The altar-cloth, as if tossed by a great wind, lay far away from them, gleaming white on the black ground.

"From fear of losing my hope of you," said Nostromo.

"You knew that you had my soul! You know everything! It was made for you! But what could stand between you and me? What? Tell me!" she repeated, without impatience, in superb assurance.

"Your dead mother," he said, very low.

"Ah! . . . Poor mother! She has always. . . . She is a saint in heaven now, and I cannot give you up to her. No, Giovanni. Only to God alone. You were mad—but it is done. Oh! what have you done? Giovanni, my beloved, my life, my master, do not leave me here in this grave of clouds. You cannot leave me now. You must take me away—at once—this instant—in the little boat. Giovanni, carry me off tonight, from my fear of Linda's eyes, before I have to look at her again."

She nestled closer to him. The slave of the San Tomé silver felt the weight as of chains upon his limbs, a pressure as of a cold hand upon his lips. He struggled against the spell.

"I cannot," he said. "Not yet. There is something that stands between us and the freedom of the world."

She pressed her form closer to his side with a subtle and naïve instinct of seduction.

"You rave, Giovanni—my lover!" she whispered, engagingly. "What can there be? Carry me off—in thy very hands—to Doña Emilia—away from here. I am not very heavy."

It seemed as though she expected him to lift her up at once in his two palms. She had lost the notion of all impossibility. Anything could happen on this night of wonder. As he made no movement, she almost cried aloud:

"I tell you I am afraid of Linda!" And still he did not move. She became quiet and wily. "What can there be?" she asked, coaxingly.

He felt her warm, breathing, alive, quivering in the hollow of his arm. In the exulting consciousness of his strength, and the triumphant excitement of his mind, he struck out for his freedom.

"A treasure," he said. All was still. She did not understand. "A treasure. A treasure of silver to buy a gold crown for thy brow."

"A treasure?" she repeated in a faint voice, as if from the depths of a dream. "What is it you say?"

She disengaged herself gently. He got up and looked down at her, aware of her face, of her hair, her lips, the dimples on her cheeks—seeing the fascination of her person in the night of the gulf as if in the blaze of noonday. Her nonchalant and seductive voice trembled with the excitement of admiring awe and ungovernable curiosity.

"A treasure of silver!" she stammered out. Then pressed on faster: "What? Where? How did you get it, Giovanni?"

He wrestled with the spell of captivity. It was as if striking a heroic blow that he burst out:

"Like a thief!"

The densest blackness of the Placid Gulf seemed to fall upon his head. He could not see her now. She had vanished into a long, obscure, abysmal silence, whence her voice came back to him after a time with a faint glimmer, which was her face.

"I love you! I love you!"

These words gave him an unwonted sense of freedom; they cast a spell stronger than the accursed spell of the treasure; they changed his weary subjection to that dead thing into an exulting conviction of his power. He would cherish her, he said, in a splendour as great as Doña Emilia's. The rich lived on wealth stolen from the people, but he had taken from the rich nothing—nothing that was not lost to the

He stooped low, pressed the hem of her skirt to his lips, with a muttered command:

"Tell him I would not stay," and was gone suddenly from her, silent, without as much as a footfall in the dark night.

She sat still, her head resting indolently against the wall, and her little feet in white stockings and black slippers crossed over each other. Old Giorgio, coming out, did not seem to be surprised at the intelligence as much as she had vaguely feared. For she was full of inexplicable fear now—fear of everything and everybody except of her Giovanni and his treasure. But that was incredible.

The heroic Garibaldino accepted Nostromo's abrupt departure with a sagacious indulgence. He remembered his own feelings, and exhibited a masculine penetration of the true state of the case.

"*Va bene.* Let him go. Ha! ha! No matter how fair the woman, it galls a little. Liberty, liberty. There's more than one kind! He has said the great word, and son Gian' Battista is not tame." He seemed to be instructing the motionless and scared Giselle. . . . "A man should not be tame," he added, dogmatically out of the doorway. Her stillness and silence seemed to displease him. "Do not give way to the enviousness of your sister's lot," he admonished her, very grave, in his deep voice.

Presently he had to come to the door again to call in his younger daughter. It was late. He shouted her name three times before she even moved her head. Left alone, she had become the helpless prey of astonishment. She walked into the bedroom she shared with Linda like a person profoundly asleep. That aspect was so marked that even old Giorgio, spectacled, raising his eyes from the Bible, shook his head as she shut the door behind her.

She walked right across the room without looking at anything, and sat down at once by the open window. Linda, stealing down from the tower in the exuberance of her happiness, found her with a lighted candle at her back, facing the black night full of sighing gusts of wind and the sound of distant showers—a true night of the gulf, too dense for the eye of God and the wiles of the devil. She did not turn her head at the opening of the door.

There was something in that immobility which reached Linda in the depths of her paradise. The elder sister guessed angrily: the child is thinking of that wretched Ramirez. Linda longed to talk.

She said in her arbitrary voice, "Giselle!" and was not answered by the slightest movement.

The girl that was going to live in a palace and walk on ground of her own was ready to die with terror. Not for anything in the world would she have turned her head to face her sister. Her heart was beating madly. She said with subdued haste:

"Do not speak to me. I am praying."

Linda, disappointed, went out quietly; and Giselle sat on, unbelieving, lost, dazed, patient, as if waiting for the confirmation of the incredible. The hopeless blackness of the clouds seemed part of a dream, too. She waited.

She did not wait in vain. The man whose soul was dead within him, creeping out of the ravine, weighted with silver, had seen the gleam of the lighted window, and could not help retracing his steps from the beach.

On that impenetrable background, obliterating the lofty mountains by the seaboard, she saw the slave of the San Tomé silver, as if by an extraordinary power of a miracle. She accepted his return as if henceforth the world could hold no surprise for all eternity.

She rose, compelled and rigid, and began to speak long before the light from within fell upon the face of the approaching man.

"You have come back to carry me off. It is well! Open thy arms, Giovanni, my lover. I am corning."

His prudent footsteps stopped, and with his eyes glistening wildly, he spoke in a harsh voice:

"Not yet. I must grow rich slowly." . . . A threatening note came into his tone. "Do not forget that you have a thief for your lover."

"Yes! Yes!" she whispered, hastily. "Come nearer! Listen! Do not give me up, Giovanni! Never, never! . . . I will be patient! . . ."

Her form drooped consolingly over the low casement towards the slave of the unlawful treasure. The light in the room went out, and weighted with silver, the magnificent Capataz clasped her round her white neck in the darkness of the gulf as a drowning man clutches at a straw.

CHAPTER 13

ON THE DAY MRS. GOULD was going, in Dr. Monygham's words, to "give a *tertulia*," Captain Fidanza went down the side of his schooner lying in Sulaco harbour, calm, unbending, deliberate in the way he sat down in his dinghy and took up his sculls. He was later than usual. The afternoon was well advanced before he landed on the beach of the Great Isabel, and with a steady pace climbed the slope of the island.

From a distance he made out Giselle sitting in a chair tilted back against the end of the house, under the window of the girl's room. She had her embroidery in her hands, and held it well up to her eyes. The tranquillity of that girlish figure exasperated the feeling of perpetual struggle and strife he carried in his breast. He became angry. It seemed to him that she ought to hear the clanking of his fetters—his silver fetters, from afar. And while ashore that day, he had met the doctor with the evil eye, who had looked at him very hard.

The raising of her eyes mollified him. They smiled in their flower-like freshness straight upon his heart. Then she frowned. It was a warning to be cautious. He stopped some distance away, and in a loud, indifferent tone, said:

"Good day, Giselle. Is Linda up yet?"

"Yes. She is in the big room with father."

He approached then, and, looking through the window into the bedroom for fear of being detected by Linda returning there for some reason, he said, moving only his lips:

"You love me?"

"More than my life." She went on with her embroidery under his contemplating gaze and continued to speak, looking at her work, "Or I could not live. I could not, Giovanni. For this life is like death. Oh, Giovanni, I shall perish if you do not take me away."

He smiled carelessly. "I will come to the window when it's dark," he said.

429

"No, don't, Giovanni. Not tonight. Linda and father have been talking together for a long time today."

"What about?"

"Ramirez, I fancy I heard. I do not know. I am afraid. I am always afraid. It is like dying a thousand times a day. Your love is to me like your treasure to you. It is there, but I can never get enough of it."

He looked at her very still. She was beautiful. His desire had grown within him. He had two mastes now. But she was incapable of sustained emotion. She was sincere in what she said, but she slept placidly at night. When she saw him she flamed up always. Then only an increased taciturnity marked the change in her. She was afraid of betraying herself. She was afraid of pain, of bodily harm, of sharp words, of facing anger, and witnessing violence. For her soul was light and tender with a pagan sincerity in its impulses. She murmured:

"Give up the palazzo, Giovanni, and the vineyards on the hills, for which we are starving our love."

She ceased, seeing Linda standing silent at the corner of the house.

Nostromo turned to his affianced wife with a greeting, and was amazed at her sunken eyes, at her hollow cheeks, at the air of illness and anguish in her face.

"Have you been ill?" he asked, trying to put some concern into this question.

Her black eyes blazed at him. "Am I thinner?" she asked.

"Yes—perhaps—a little."

"And older?"

"Every day counts—for all of us."

"I shall go grey, I fear, before the ring is on my finger," she said, slowly, keeping her gaze fastened upon him.

She waited for what he would say, rolling down her turned-up sleeves.

"No fear of that," he said, absently.

She turned away as if it had been something final, and busied herself with household cares while Nostromo talked with her father. Conversation with the old Garibaldino was not easy. Age had left his faculties unimpaired, only they seemed to have withdrawn somewhere deep within him. His answers were slow in coming, with an effect of august gravity. But that day he was more animated, quicker; there seemed to be more life in the old lion. He was uneasy for the integrity of his honour. He believed in Sidoni's warning as to Ramirez's designs upon his younger daughter. And he did not trust her. She was flighty. He said nothing of his cares to "Son Gian' Battista." It was a touch of senile vanity. He wanted to show that he was equal yet to the task of guarding alone the honour of his house.

Nostromo went away early. As soon as he had disappeared, walking towards the beach, Linda stepped over the threshold and, with a haggard smile, sat down by the side of her father.

Ever since that Sunday, when the infatuated and desperate Ramirez had waited for her on the wharf, she had no doubts whatever. The jealous ravings of that man were no revelation. They had only fixed with precision, as with a nail driven into her heart, that sense of unreality and deception which, instead of bliss and security, she had found in her intercourse with her promised husband. She had passed on, pouring indignation and scorn upon Ramirez; but, that Sunday, she nearly died of wretchedness and shame, lying on the carved and lettered stone of Teresa's grave, subscribed for by the engine-drivers and the fitters of the railway workshops, in sign of their respect for the hero of Italian Unity. Old Viola had not been able to carry out his desire of burying his wife in the sea; and Linda wept upon the stone.

The gratuitous outrage appalled her. If he wished to break her heart—well and good. Everything was permitted to Gian' Battista. But why trample upon the pieces; why seek to humiliate her spirit? Aha! He could not break that. She dried her tears. And Giselle! Giselle! The little one that, ever since she could toddle, had always clung to her skirt for protection. What duplicity! But she could not help it probably. When there was a man in the case the poor featherheaded wretch could not help herself.

Linda had a good share of the Viola stoicism. She resolved to say nothing. But woman-like she put passion into her stoicism. Giselle's short answers, prompted by fearful caution, drove her beside herself by their curtness that resembled disdain. One day she flung herself upon the chair in which her indolent sister was lying and impressed the mark of her teeth at the base of the whitest neck in Sulaco. Giselle cried out. But she had her share of the Viola heroism. Ready to faint with terror, she only said, in a lazy voice, "*Madre de Dios!*

Are you going to eat me alive, Linda?" And this outburst passed off leaving no trace upon the situation. "She knows nothing. She cannot know anything," reflected Giselle. "Perhaps it is not true. It cannot be true," Linda tried to persuade herself.

But when she saw Captain Fidanza for the first time after her meeting with the distracted Ramirez, the certitude of her misfortune returned. She watched him from the doorway go away to his boat, asking herself stoically, "Will they meet tonight?" She made up her mind not to leave the tower for a second. When he had disappeared she came out and sat down by her father.

The venerable Garibaldino felt, in his own words, "a young man yet." In one way or another a good deal of talk about Ramirez had reached him of late; and his contempt and dislike of that man who obviously was not what his son would have been, had made him restless. He slept very little now; but for several nights past instead of reading—or only sitting, with Mrs. Gould's silver spectacles on his nose, before the open Bible—he had been prowling actively all about the island with his old gun, on watch over his honour.

Linda, laying her thin brown hand on his knee, tried to soothe his excitement. Ramirez was not in Sulaco. Nobody knew where he was. He was gone. His talk of what he would do meant nothing.

"No," the old man interrupted. "But son Gian' Battista told me—quite of himself—that the cowardly *esclavo* was drinking and gambling with the rascals of Zapiga, over there on the north side of the gulf. He may get some of the worst scoundrels of that scoundrelly town of Negroes to help him in his attempt upon the little one. . . . But I am not so old. No!"

She argued earnestly against the probability of any attempt being made; and at last the old man fell silent, chewing his white moustache. Women had their obstinate notions which must be humoured—his poor wife was like that, and Linda resembled her mother. It was not seemly for a man to argue. "Maybe. Maybe," he mumbled.

She was by no means easy in her mind. She loved Nostromo. She turned her eyes upon Giselle, sitting at a distance, with something of maternal tenderness, and the jealous anguish of a rival outraged in her defeat. Then she rose and walked over to her.

"Listen—you," she said, roughly.

The invincible candour of the gaze, raised up all violet and dew, excited her rage and admiration. She had beautiful eyes—the *chica*—this vile thing of white flesh and black deception. She did not know whether she wanted to tear them out with shouts of vengeance or cover up their mysterious and shameless innocence with kisses of pity and love. And suddenly they became empty, gazing blankly at her, except for a little fear not quite buried deep enough with all the other emotions in Giselle's heart.

Linda said, "Ramirez is boasting in town that he will carry you off from the island."

"What folly!" answered the other, and in a perversity born of long restraint, she added: "He is not a man," in a jesting tone with a resembling audacity.

"No?" said Linda, through her clenched teeth. "Is he not? Well, then, look to it; because father has been walking about with a loaded gun at night."

"It is not good for him. You must tell him not to, Linda. He will not listen to me."

"I shall say nothing—never any more—to anybody," cried Linda, passionately.

This could not last, thought Giselle. Giovanni must take her away soon—the very next time he came. She would not suffer these terrors for ever so much silver. To speak with her sister made her ill. But she was not uneasy at her father's watchfulness. She had begged Nostromo not to come to the window that night. He had promised to keep away for this once. And she did not know, could not guess or imagine, that he had another reason for coming on the island.

Linda had gone straight to the tower. It was time to light up. She unlocked the little door, and went heavily up the spiral staircase, carrying her love for the magnificent Capataz de Cargadores like an ever-increasing load of shameful fetters. No; she could not throw it off. No; let Heaven dispose of these two. And moving about the lantern, filled with twilight and the sheen of the moon, with careful movements she lighted the lamp. Then her arms fell along her body.

"And with our mother looking on," she murmured. "My own sister—the *chica*!"

The whole refracting apparatus, with its brass fittings and rings of prisms, glittered and sparkled like a dome-shaped shrine of diamonds, containing not a lamp, but some sacred flame, dominating the sea. And Linda, the keeper, in black, with a pale face, drooped low in a wooden chair, alone with her jealousy, far above the shames and passions of the earth. A strange, dragging pain, as if somebody were pulling her about brutally by her dark hair with bronze glints, made her put her hands up to her temples. They would meet. They would meet. And she knew where, too. At the window. The sweat of torture fell in drops on her cheeks, while the moonlight in the offing closed as if with a colossal bar of silver the entrance of the Placid Gulf—the sombre cavern of clouds and stillness in the surf-fretted seaboard.

Linda Viola stood up suddenly with a finger on her lip. He loved neither her nor her sister. The whole thing seemed so objectless as to frighten her, and also give her some hope. Why did he not carry her off? What prevented him? He was incomprehensible. What were they waiting for? For what end were these two lying and deceiving? Not for the ends of their love. There was no such thing. The hope of regaining him for herself made her break her vow of not leaving the tower that night. She must talk at once to her father, who was wise, and would understand. She ran down the spiral stairs. At the moment of opening the door at the bottom she heard the sound of the first shot ever fired on the Great Isabel.

She felt a shock, as though the bullet had struck her breast. She ran on without pausing. The cottage was dark. She cried at the door, "Giselle! Giselle!" then dashed round the corner and screamed her sister's name at the open window, without getting an answer; but as she was rushing, distracted, round the house, Giselle came out of the door, and darted past her, running silently, her hair loose, and her eyes staring straight ahead. She seemed to skim along the grass as if on tiptoe, and vanished.

Linda walked on slowly, with her arms stretched out before her. All was still on the island; she did not know where she was going. The tree under which Martin Decoud spent his last days, beholding a life like a succession of senseless images, threw a large blotch of black shade upon the grass. Suddenly she saw her father, standing quietly all alone in the moonlight.

The Garibaldino—big, erect, with his snow-white hair and beard—had a monumental repose in his immobility, leaning upon a rifle. She put her hand upon his arm lightly. He never stirred.

"What have you done?" she asked, in her ordinary voice.

"I have shot Ramirez—*infame!*"* he answered, with his eyes directed to where the shade was blackest. "Like a thief he came, and like a thief he fell. The child had to be protected."

He did not offer to move an inch, to advance a single step. He stood there, rugged and unstirring, like a statue of an old man guarding the honour of his house. Linda removed her trembling hand from his arm, firm and steady like an arm of stone, and, without a word, entered the blackness of the shade. She saw a stir of formless shapes on the ground, and stopped short. A murmur of despair and tears grew louder to her strained hearing.

"I entreated you not to come tonight. Oh, my Giovanni! And you promised. Oh! Why—why did you come, Giovanni?"

It was her sister's voice. It broke on a heartrending sob. And the voice of the resourceful Capataz de Cargadores, master and slave of the San Tomé treasure, who had been caught unawares by old Giorgio while stealing across the open towards the ravine to get some more silver, answered careless and cool, but sounding startlingly weak from the ground.

"It seemed as though I could not live through the night without seeing thee once more—my star, my little flower."

The brilliant *tertulia* was just over, the last guests had departed, and the Señor Administrador had gone to his room already, when Dr. Monygham, who had been expected in the evening but had not turned up, arrived driving along the wood-block pavement under the electric-lamps of the deserted Calle de la Constitución, and found the great gateway of the *casa* still open.

He limped in, stumped up the stairs, and found the fat and sleek Basilio on the point of turning off the lights in the *sala*. The prosperous majordomo remained open-mouthed at this late invasion.

"Don't put out the lights," commanded the doctor. "I want to see the *señora*."

---

*Villain! (It.).

"The *señora* is in the Señora Administrador's *cancillaría*,"* said Basilio, in an unctuous voice. "The Señor Administrador starts for the mountain in an hour. There is some trouble with the workmen to be feared, it appears. A shameless people without reason and decency. And idle, *señor*. Idle."

"You are shamelessly lazy and imbecile yourself," said the doctor, with that faculty for exasperation which made him so generally beloved. "Don't put the lights out."

Basilio retired with dignity. Dr. Monygham, waiting in the brilliantly lighted *sala*, heard presently a door close at the farther end of the house. A jingle of spurs died out. The Señor Administrador was off to the mountain.

With a measured swish of her long train, flashing with jewels and the shimmer of silk, her delicate head bowed as if under the weight of a mass of fair hair, in which the silver threads were lost, the "first lady of Sulaco," as Captain Mitchell used to describe her, moved along the lighted corridor, wealthy beyond great dreams of wealth, considered, loved, respected, honoured, and as solitary as any human being had ever been, perhaps, on this earth.

The doctor's "Mrs. Gould! One minute!" stopped her with a start at the door of the lighted and empty *sala*. From the similarity of mood and circumstance, the sight of the doctor, standing there all alone amongst the groups of furniture, recalled to her emotional memory her unexpected meeting with Martin Decoud; she seemed to hear in the silence the voice of that man, dead miserably so many years ago, pronounce the words, "Antonia left her fan here." But it was the doctor's voice that spoke, a little altered by his excitement. She remarked his shining eyes.

"Mrs. Gould, you are wanted. Do you know what has happened? You remember what I told you yesterday about Nostromo. Well, it seems that a *lancha*, a decked boat, coming from Zapiga, with four Negroes in her, passing close to the Great Isabel, was hailed from the cliff by a woman's voice—Linda's, as a matter of fact—commanding them (it's a moonlight night) to go round to the beach and take up

---

*Or *cancillería*; chancellery.

a wounded man to the town. The *patron** (from whom I've heard all this), of course, did so at once. He told me that when they got round to the low side of the Great Isabel, they found Linda Viola waiting for them. They followed her: she led them under a tree not far from the cottage. There they found Nostromo lying on the ground with his head in the younger girl's lap, and father Viola standing some distance off leaning on his gun. Under Linda's direction they got a table out of the cottage for a stretcher, after breaking off the legs. They are here, Mrs. Gould. I mean Nostromo and—and Giselle. The Negroes brought him in to the first-aid hospital near the harbour. He made the attendant send for me. But it is not me he wanted to see—it was you, Mrs. Gould! It was you."

"Me?" whispered Mrs. Gould, shrinking a little.

"Yes, you!" the doctor burst out. "He begged me—his enemy, as he thinks—to bring you to him at once. It seems he has something to say to you alone."

"Impossible!" murmured Mrs. Gould.

"He said to me, 'Remind her that I have done something to keep a roof over her head.' . . . Mrs. Gould," the doctor pursued, in the greatest excitement. "Do you remember the silver? The silver in the lighter—that was lost!"

Mrs. Gould remembered. But she did not say she hated the mere mention of that silver. Frankness personified, she remembered with an exaggerated horror that for the first and last time of her life she had concealed the truth from her husband about that very silver. She had been corrupted by her fears at that time, and she had never forgiven herself. Moreover, that silver, which would never have come down if her husband had been made acquainted with the news brought by Decoud, had been in a roundabout way nearly the cause of Dr. Monygham's death. And these things appeared to her very dreadful.

"Was it lost, though?" the doctor exclaimed. "I've always felt that there was a mystery about our Nostromo ever since. I do believe he wants now, at the point of death—"

---

*Skipper.

"The point of death," repeated Mrs. Gould.

"Yes. Yes. . . . He wants perhaps to tell you something concerning that silver which—"

"Oh, no! No!" exclaimed Mrs. Gould, in a low voice. "Isn't it lost and done with? Isn't there enough treasure without it to make everybody in the world miserable?"

The doctor remained still, in a submissive, disappointed silence. At last he ventured, very low:

"And there is that Viola girl, Giselle. What are we to do? it looks as though father and sister had—"

Mrs. Gould admitted that she felt in duty bound to do her best for these girls.

"I have a *volante** here," the doctor said. "If you don't mind getting into that—"

He waited, all impatience, till Mrs. Gould reappeared, having thrown over her dress a grey cloak with a deep hood.

It was thus that, cloaked and monastically hooded over her evening costume, this woman, full of endurance and compassion, stood by the side of the bed on which the splendid Capataz de Cargadores lay stretched out motionless on his back. The whiteness of sheets and pillows gave a sombre and energetic relief to his bronzed face, to the dark, nervous hands, so good on a tiller, upon a bridle, and on a trigger, lying open and idle upon a white coverlet.

"She is innocent," the Capataz was saying in a deep and level voice, as though afraid that a louder word would break the slender hold his spirit still kept upon his body. "She is innocent. It is I alone. But no matter. For these things I would answer to no man or woman alive."

He paused. Mrs. Gould's face, very white within the shadow of the hood, bent over him with an invincible and dreary sadness. And the low sobs of Giselle Viola, kneeling at the end of the bed, her gold hair with coppery gleams loose and scattered over the Capataz's feet, hardly troubled the silence of the room.

"Ha! Old Giorgio—the guardian of thine honour! Fancy the Vecchio coming upon me so light of foot, so steady of aim. I myself

---

*Horse-drawn carriage with long shafts.

could have done no better. But the price of a charge of powder might have been saved. The honour was safe. . . . *Señora*, she would have followed to the end of the world Nostromo the thief. . . . I have said the word. The spell is broken!"

A low moan from the girl made him cast his eyes down.

"I cannot see her. . . . No matter," he went on, with the shadow of the old magnificent carelessness in his voice. "One kiss is enough, if there is no time for more. An airy soul, *señora*! Bright and warm, like sunshine—soon clouded, and soon serene. They would crush it there between them. *Señora*, cast on her the eye of your compassion, as famed from one end of the land to the other as the courage and daring of the man who speaks to you. She will console herself in time. And even Ramirez is not a bad fellow. I am not angry. No! It is not Ramirez who overcame the Capataz of the Sulaco Cargadores." He paused, made an effort, and in a louder voice, a little wildly, declared:

"I die betrayed—betrayed by—"

But he did not say by whom or by what he was dying betrayed.

"She would not have betrayed me," he began again, opening eyes very wide. "She was faithful. We were going very far—very soon. I could have torn myself away from that accursed treasure for her. For that child I would have left boxes and boxes of it—full. And Decoud took four. Four ingots. Why? *Picardía*! To betray me? How could I give back the treasure with four ingots missing? They would have said I had purloined them. The doctor would have said that. Alas! It holds me yet!"

Mrs. Gould bent low, fascinated—cold with apprehension.

"What became of Don Martin on that night, Nostromo?"

"Who knows! I wondered what would become of me. Now I know. Death was to come upon me unawares. He went away! He betrayed me. And you think I have killed him! You are all alike, you fine people. The silver has killed me. It has held me. It holds me yet. Nobody knows where it is. But you are the wife of Don Carlos, who put it into my hands and said, 'Save it on your life.' And when I returned, and you all thought it was lost, what do I hear? It was nothing of importance. Let it go. Up, Nostromo, the faithful, and ride away to save us, for dear life!"

"Nostromo!" Mrs. Gould whispered, bending very low. "I, too, have hated the idea of that silver from the bottom of my heart."

"Marvellous!—that one of you should hate the wealth that you know so well how to take from the hands of the poor. The world rests upon the poor, as old Giorgio says. You have been always good to the poor. But there is something accursed in wealth. *Señora*, shall I tell you where the treasure is? To you alone. . . . Shining! Incorruptible!"

A pained, involuntary reluctance lingered in his tone, in his eyes, plain to the woman with the genius of sympathetic intuition. She averted her glance from the miserable subjection of the dying man, appalled, wishing to hear no more of the silver.

"No, Capataz," she said. "No one misses it now. Let it be lost for ever."

After hearing these words, Nostromo closed his eyes, uttered no word, made no movement. Outside the door of the sickroom Dr. Monygham, excited to the highest pitch, his eyes shining with eagerness, came up to the two women.

"Now, Mrs. Gould," he said, almost brutally in his impatience, "tell me, was I right? There is a mystery. You have got the word of it, have you not? He told you—"

"He told me nothing," said Mrs. Gould, steadily.

The light of his temperamental enmity to Nostromo went out of Dr. Monygham's eyes. He stepped back submissively. He did not believe Mrs. Gould. But her word was law. He accepted her denial like an inexplicable fatality affirming the victory of Nostromo's genius over his own. Even before that woman, whom he loved with secret devotion, he had been defeated by the magnificent Capataz de Cargadores, the man who had lived his own life on the assumption of unbroken fidelity, rectitude, and courage!

"Pray send at once somebody for my carriage," spoke Mrs. Gould from within her hood. Then, turning to Giselle Viola, "Come nearer me, child; come closer. We will wait here."

Giselle Viola, heartbroken and childlike, her face veiled in her falling hair, crept up to her side. Mrs. Gould slipped her hand through the arm of the unworthy daughter of old Viola, the immaculate republican, the hero without a stain. Slowly, gradually, as a withered flower droops, the head of the girl, who would have followed a thief to the end of the world, rested on the shoulder of Doña Emilia, the first lady of Sulaco, the wife of the Señor Administrador of the San Tomé mine. And Mrs. Gould, feeling her suppressed sobbing, nervous and excited, had the first and only moments of bitterness in her life. It was worthy of Dr. Monygham himself.

"Console yourself, child. Very soon he would have forgotten you for his treasure."

"*Señora*, he loved me. He loved me," Giselle whispered, despairingly. "He loved me as no one had ever been loved before."

"I have been loved, too," Mrs. Gould said in a severe tone.

Giselle clung to her convulsively. "Oh, *señora*, but you shall live adored to the end of your life," she sobbed out.

Mrs. Gould kept an unbroken silence till the carriage arrived. She helped in the half-fainting girl. After the doctor had shut the door of the landau, she leaned over to him.

"You can do nothing?" she whispered.

"No, Mrs. Gould. Moreover, he won't let us touch him. It does not matter. I just had one look. . . . Useless."

But he promised to see old Viola and the other girl that very night. He could get the police-boat to take him off to the island. He remained in the street, looking after the landau rolling away slowly behind the white mules.

The rumour of some accident—an accident to Captain Fidanza— had been spreading along the new quays with their rows of lamps and the dark shapes of towering cranes. A knot of night-prowlers— the poorest of the poor—hung about the door of the first-aid hospital, whispering in the moonlight of the empty street.

There was no one with the wounded man but the pale photographer, small, frail, bloodthirsty, the hater of capitalists, perched on a high stool near the head of the bed with his knees up and his chin in his hands. He had been fetched by a comrade who, working late on the wharf, had heard from a Negro belonging to a *lancha* that Captain Fidanza had been brought ashore mortally wounded.

"Have you any dispositions to make, comrade?" he asked, anxiously. "Do not forget that we want money for our work. The rich must be fought with their own weapons."

Nostromo made no answer. The other did not insist, remaining huddled up on the stool, shock-headed, wildly hairy, like a hunchbacked monkey. Then, after a long silence:

"Comrade Fidanza," he began, solemnly, "you have refused all aid from that doctor. Is he really a dangerous enemy of the people?"

In the dimly lit room Nostromo rolled his head slowly on the pillow and opened his eyes, directing at the weird figure perched by his bedside a glance of enigmatic and profound inquiry. Then his head rolled back, his eyelids fell, and the Capataz de Cargadores died without a word or moan after an hour of immobility, broken by short shudders testifying to the most atrocious sufferings.

Dr. Monygham, going out in the police-galley to the islands, beheld the glitter of the moon upon the gulf and the high black shape of the Great Isabel sending a shaft of light afar, from under the canopy of clouds.

"Pull easy," he said, wondering what he would find there. He tried to imagine Linda and her father, and discovered a strange reluctance within himself. "Pull easy," he repeated.

From the moment he fired at the thief of his honour, Giorgio Viola had not stirred from the spot. He stood, his old gun grounded, his hand grasping the barrel near the muzzle. After the *lancha* carrying off Nostromo for ever from her had left the shore, Linda, coming up, stopped before him. He did not seem to be aware of her presence, but when, losing her forced calmness, she cried out: "Do you know whom you have killed?" he answered: "Ramirez the vagabond."

White, and staring insanely at her father, Linda laughed in his face. After a time he joined her faintly in a deep-toned and distant echo of her peals. Then she stopped, and the old man spoke as if startled:

"He cried out in son Gian' Battista's voice."

The gun fell from his opened hand, but the arm remained extended for a moment as if still supported. Linda seized it roughly.

"You are too old to understand. Come into the house."

He let her lead him. On the threshold he stumbled heavily, nearly coming to the ground together with his daughter. His excitement, his activity of the last few days, had been like the flare of a dying lamp. He caught the back of his chair.

"In son Gian' Battista's voice," he repeated in a severe tone. "I heard him—Ramirez—the miserable—"

Linda helped him into the chair, and, bending low, hissed into his ear:

"You have killed Gian' Battista."

The old man smiled under his thick moustache. Women had strange fancies.

"Where is the child?" he asked, surprised at the penetrating chilliness of the air and the unwonted dimness of the lamp by which he used to sit up half the night with the open Bible before him.

Linda hesitated a moment, then averted her eyes.

"She is asleep," she said. "We shall talk of her tomorrow."

She could not bear to look at him. He filled her with terror and with an almost unbearable feeling of pity. She had observed the change that came over him. He would never understand what he had done; and even to her the whole thing remained incomprehensible. He said with difficulty:

"Give me the book."

Linda laid on the table the closed volume in its worn leather cover, the Bible given him ages ago by an Englishman in Palermo.

"The child had to be protected," he said, in a strange, mournful voice.

Behind his chair Linda wrung her hands, crying without noise. Suddenly she started for the door. He heard her move.

"Where are you going?" he asked.

"To the light," she answered, turning round to look at him balefully.

"The light! Sí—duty."

Very upright, white-haired, leonine, heroic in his absorbed quietness, he felt in the pocket of his red shirt for the spectacles given him by Doña Emilia. He put them on. After a long period of immobility he opened the book, and from on high looked through the glasses at the small print in double columns. A rigid, stern expression settled upon his features with a slight frown, as if in response to some gloomy thought or unpleasant sensation. But he never detached his eyes from the book while he swayed forward, gently, gradually, till his snow-white head rested upon the open pages. A wooden clock ticked methodically on the white-washed wall, and growing slowly cold the Garibaldino lay alone, rugged, undecayed, like an old oak uprooted by a treacherous gust of wind.

The light of the Great Isabel burned unfailing above the lost treasure of the San Tomé mine. Into the bluish sheen of a night without stars the lantern sent out a yellow beam towards the far horizon. Like a black speck upon the shining panes, Linda, crouching in the outer gallery, rested her head on the rail. The moon, drooping in the western board, looked at her radiantly.

Below, at the foot of the cliff, the regular splash of oars from a passing boat ceased, and Dr. Monygham stood up in the stern sheets.

"Linda!" he shouted, throwing back his head. "Linda!"

Linda stood up. She had recognized the voice.

"Is he dead?" she cried, bending over.

"Yes, my poor girl. I am coming round," the doctor answered from below. "Pull to the beach," he said to the rowers.

Linda's black figure detached itself upright on the light of the lantern with her arms raised above her head as though she were going to throw herself over.

"It is I who loved you," she whispered, with a face as set and white as marble in the moonlight. "I! Only I! She will forget thee, killed miserably for her pretty face. I cannot understand. I cannot understand. But I shall never forget thee. Never!"

She stood silent and still, collecting her strength to throw all her fidelity, her pain, bewilderment, and despair into one great cry.

"Never! Gian' Battista!"

Dr. Monygham, pulling round in the police-galley, heard the name pass over his head. It was another of Nostromo's triumphs, the greatest, the most enviable, the most sinister of all. In that true cry of undying passion that seemed to ring aloud from Punta Mala to Azuera and away to the bright line of the horizon, overhung by a big white cloud shining like a mass of solid silver, the genius of the magnificent Capataz de Cargadores dominated the dark gulf containing his conquests of treasure and love.

ENDNOTES

1. (p. 35) *the great man who had led him in a glorious struggle where, under the walls of Gaeta, tyranny would have expired for ever had it not been for that accursed Piedmontese race of kings and ministers. . . . Cavour—the arch intriguer . . . liberty that traitor had strangled:* "The great man" is a reference to Italian nationalist leader Giuseppe Garibaldi (1807–1882), who led his volunteer army, known as the "Thousand Redshirts," to a resounding victory over Francis II, king of the Two Sicilies (the kingdoms of Sicily and Naples) on the River Volturno in October 1860, thereby conquering Sicily and Naples. Francis II retreated to his fortress at Gaeta, near Naples. Through the scheming of the Count Camillo Benso di Cavour (1810–1861), a leading Piedmontese politician, Garibaldi ceded control of southern Italy to Victor Emmanuel II, king of Sardinia and the Piedmont. In 1861 Victor Emmanuel was proclaimed king of a unified Italy. Here Viola is portrayed as a Republican Redshirt, still bitter at the "arch intriguer" Cavour.

2. (p. 39) *the navy of Montevideo, then under the command of Garibaldi:* Garibaldi (see note 1) was in South America between 1834 and 1848. He became famous for leading the defense of Montevideo, the capital of Uruguay, against invading forces from Argentina.

3. (p. 39) *the fatal day of Aspromonte:* In August 1862, Garibaldi (see note 1) attempted to take control of Rome, which was then a papal state protected by the French. He was wounded in the foot, captured, and imprisoned at Aspromonte. The new kingdom of Italy, founded in 1861 (see note 1), was able to claim Rome in October 1870.

4. (p. 40) *Samuel . . . commanded a Negro company under Garibaldi, during the famous siege of Montevideo, and died heroically with his Negroes at the fording of the Boyana:* The reference is to an Englishman who fought with Garibaldi at the siege of Montevideo, leading approximately fifty men, all of whom were killed in action. Garibaldi said of Samuel that he "never saw a braver man."

5. (p. 52) *fought . . . under Bolívar, in that famous English legion which on the battlefield of Carabobo had been saluted by the great Liberator as Saviours of his country:* The "great Liberator" is South American revolutionary leader Simón Bolívar (1783–1830). Bolívar's victory in

445

the battle of Carabobo was the turning point in the struggle over Venezuela in 1821, marking the end of royalist domination.

6. (p. 59) *it took to his mind the form of the Old Man of the Sea fastened upon his shoulders:* This is an allusion to the fifth voyage of Sinbad the Sailor in *The Arabian Nights*, in which the Old Man of the Sea sits on Sinbad's back, refusing to get off; Sinbad finally throws the old man off after getting him drunk. In other words, the Old Man of the Sea represents a burden or imposition that one can only escape through extraordinary cunning—or outright trickery.

7. (p. 74) *"the Atacama nitrate fields. . . . War came of it"*: This is an allusion to the Chilean-Peruvian War of 1879–1882, also called the War of the Pacific, fought between Chile and the allied nations Peru and Bolivia over nitrate mines in the Atacama Desert. Chile won the war and acquired Atacama, Bolivia's only coastal territory.

8. (p. 85) *"Lucia di Lammermoor!":* The reference is to the popular opera by Gaetano Donizetti (1797–1848), the story of which is drawn from Sir Walter Scott's 1818 novel *The Bride of Lamermoor*. Conrad, a well-known lover of opera, praises *Lucia* in his memoir *A Personal Record* (1912).

9. (p. 120) *an old flag of Cortés:* The flag recalls Spanish conquistador Hernanado Cortés (1485–1547), who imposed his rule on Mexico.

10. (p. 126) *Nestor-inspirer:* In the epic poems the *Iliad* and the *Odyssey*, attributed to the ancient Greek poet Homer, Nestor is the king of Pylos, and the most experienced and crafty of the strategists of the battle of Troy.

11. (p. 131) *become a poet like that other foreigner of Spanish blood, José Maria Heredia:* José Maria de Herédia (1842–1905) was a French poet, born in Cuba, who lived in France, Mexico, and the United States; he wrote in French and was a key figure in the Parnassian movement of French poets, which stressed metrical form and precision over the emotionalism of the Romantics. His best-known book of poems is *Les Trophées* (1893).

12. (p. 139) *fought against the French by the side . . . of Juarez:* Mexican revolutionary and statesman Benito Pablo Juárez (1806–1872) served several terms as president of Mexico. The reference here is to his defeat of the French in their attempt to establish a Mexican empire (1864–1867).

13. (p. 153) *"you were a very terrible person, a sort of Charlotte Corday. . . . I suppose you would have stuck a knife into Guzman Bento?":* French patriot Charlotte Corday (1768–1793) sympathized with the moderate Girondists during the French Revolution. On July 13, 1793, she assassinated Jacobin leader Jean-Paul Marat by stabbing him while he was in his bath. She was executed at the guillotine.

14. (p. 154) *"with the inscription, 'Intrada de la Sombra'"*: At bullfights, the Intrada de la Sombra lets spectators into the shady side of the arena, while the Intrada del Sol leads to the less expensive seats under the sun.

15. (p. 196) *his ambition seemed to be to become a sort of Duc de Morny to a sort of Napoleon:* The Duc de Morny (1811–1865), a French nobleman and politician, was the half-brother and a key supporter of Louis-Napoléon (Napoléon III).

16. (p. 293) *In the patio littered with straw, a* practicante: A *practicante* is a medical assistant who may be a trained apothecary or a male nurse. In South America in the late nineteenth and early twentieth centuries, many indigenous *practicantes* worked under European doctors.

COMMENTS & QUESTIONS

In this section, we aim to provide the reader with an array of perspectives on the text, as well as questions that challenge those perspectives. The commentary has been culled from sources as diverse as reviews contemporaneous with the work, letters written by the author, literary criticism of later generations, and appreciations written throughout the work's history. Following the commentary, a series of questions seeks to filter Joseph Conrad's Nostromo *through a variety of points of view and bring about a richer understanding of this enduring work.*

Comments

WILLIAM L. ALDEN

Mr. Conrad's new novel, "Nostromo" has just been published. It is his most ambitious attempt. Hitherto his books have been painted on a small canvas. They have dealt with a few characters and have been virtually short stories expanded. But "Nostromo" is a full-grown novel. It aims apparently at two things—to give us a complete picture of life in a Central American republic and a study of the character "Nostromo," the hero of the book. There is a vast deal in the book, and in nearly every way it compels our admiration; but as a whole I fancy that most of Mr. Conrad's admirers will find it tiresome. Had he made of it a story of, say, thirty thousand words, dealing wholly with "Nostromo" as "Lord Jim" deals wholly with its hero, he would have given us a book with which no fault could be found. As it is, his portrayal of Nostromo is a wonderful piece of work, as perfect in its way as the best that Mr. Conrad has yet given us. There are other men and women in the book who are thoroughly alive and as thoroughly consistent with themselves as is Nostromo. But the general verdict will probably be that Mr. Conrad has given us far too much of the [San Tomé mine] and far too much of the politics of Costaguana. Frankly, "Nostromo" is to me, who yields to no one in admiration of Mr. Conrad's genius, a disappointment. There are superb things in the book, but they do not redeem it from the fault of tediousness. At least this is the unwilling conclusion to which I have been obliged to come, but very possibly others will come to a different conclusion, and will find the book thoroughly interesting from beginning to end.

—*New York Times* (October 29, 1904)

NEW YORK TIMES

Apart from its truth and comprehensiveness as a picture of conditions in the South American republics, "Nostromo" was undoubtedly meant by its author to be read as a parable upon modern conditions the world over, and it is this deeper and finer significance of Mr. Conrad's story that so many seem to have missed or misunderstood. The events that in the story lead up to and follow the Costaguana Revolution are simply a parable upon the prevalent and erroneous belief that industrial prosperity and peace, and the opportunity to earn in safety individual livings, are any guarantee of the ultimate contentment and progress of a people.

—December 31, 1904

JOSEPH CONRAD

Mainly Nostromo is what he is because I received the inspiration for him in my early days from a Mediterranean sailor. Those who have read [*The Mirror and the Sea*] will see at once what I mean when I say that Dominic, the *padrone* of the *Tremolino*, might under given circumstances have been a Nostromo. At any rate Dominic would have understood the younger man perfectly—if scornfully. He and I were engaged together in a rather absurd adventure, but the absurdity does not matter. It is a real satisfaction to think that in my very young days there must, after all, have been something in me worthy to command that man's half-bitter fidelity, his half-ironic devotion. Many of Nostromo's speeches I have heard first in Dominic's voice. His hand on the tiller and his fearless eyes roaming the horizon from within the monkish hood shadowing his face, he would utter the usual exordium of his remorseless wisdom: '*Vous autres gentilshommes!*' in a caustic tone that hangs on my ear yet. Like Nostromo! 'You *hombres finos!*' Very much like Nostromo.

But Dominic the Corsican nursed a certain pride of ancestry from which my Nostromo is free; for Nostromo's lineage had to be more ancient still. He is a man with the weight of countless generations behind him and no parentage to boast of. . . . Like the People.

—from his preface to *Nostromo* (1917)

EDWARD GARNETT

In "Nostromo," a tale of the seaboard of Central America, Mr. Conrad has achieved something which it is not in the power of any English contemporary novelist to touch. His genius, that rose to the consummate art of "The Heart of Darkness" and the beauty of "Youth," has in "Nostromo" descended a step or two to a lower plane to weave the more orthodox, structured novel, with a plot and *dénouement*. For we cannot disguise that the weak point of the ordinary novel is the conventionalized plan of its structure. Happily, however, Mr. Conrad's gifts have triumphed over the regular form prescribed for the public's consumption: "Nostromo" is not particularly orthodox in its structure, and the larger canvas Mr. Conrad has chosen on this occasion gives him more elbow room to show the working unity and harmonious balance of his gifts. . . .

This great gift of Mr. Conrad's, his special sense of *the psychology of scene*, that he shares with certain of the great poets and the great artists who have developed it each on his own chosen lines, it is that marks him out for pre-eminence among the novelists. His method of poetic realism is, indeed, intimately akin to that of the great Russian novelists, but Mr. Conrad, often inferior in the psychology of character, has outstripped them in his magical power of creating the whole mirage of Nature.

—from *Friday Nights: Literary Criticisms and Appreciations* (1922)

Questions

1. Can you identify any class or political group in *Nostromo* that has the author's complete sympathy? Does any of them escape his irony?

2. Decoud's skepticism ultimately destroys him. But is Decoud's skepticism any greater than Conrad's? What do you think about Decoud's capability for falling in love? Is it plausible? Is Conrad making a point about how intelligence loses out to emotion?

3. *Nostromo* was written at the beginning of the twentieth century. Is it still relevant? Does it seem still to comment on large events taking place in the world?

4. In a number of Conrad's novels—*The Secret Agent, Lord Jim,* and *Nostromo* among them—a kind of foster father kills his foster son. Can this motif be understood as a comment on how the dead hand of the past holds back the future? Does advancing mean getting over this? According to Freud, for a male to grow up, he has to get past the psychological equivalent of parricide. Is Conrad's idea the same?

5. Is *Nostromo* the right title for this novel? If not, what would be a better title for it?

FOR FURTHER READING

Other Works by Joseph Conrad

Almayer's Folly (1895)
An Outcast of the Islands (1896)
The Nigger of the "Narcissus" (1897)
Tales of Unrest (1898)
Heart of Darkness (1899)
Lord Jim (1900)
The Inheritors, with Ford Madox Ford (1901)
Youth: A Narrative; and Two Other Stories (1902)
Romance, with Ford Madox Ford (1903)
Typhoon and Other Stories (1903)
The Mirror of the Sea, with Ford Madox Ford (1906)
The Secret Agent (1907)
Under Western Eyes (1911)
'Twixt Land and Sea (1912)
Chance (1914)
Victory (1915)
The Shadow-Line (1917)
The Rescue (1920)

Biographies and Related Materials

Baines, Jocelyn. *Joseph Conrad: A Critical Biography.* London: Weidenfeld and Nicolson, 1960.

Berthoud, Jacques. *Joseph Conrad: The Major Phase.* Cambridge and New York: Cambridge University Press, 1978.

Ford, Ford Madox. *Joseph Conrad: A Personal Remembrance.* London: Duckworth, 1924.

Karl, Frederick R. *Joseph Conrad: The Three Lives—A Biography*. New York: Farrar, Straus and Giroux, 1979.

Meyers, Jeffrey. *Joseph Conrad: A Biography*. New York: Charles Scribner's Sons, 1991.

Morf, Gustav. *The Polish Heritage of Joseph Conrad*. London: S. Low, Marston and Co., 1930.

Najder, Zdzislaw. *Joseph Conrad: A Chronicle*. Cambridge: Cambridge University Press, 1983.

Sherry, Norman. *Conrad and His World*. London: Thames and Hudson, 1972.

Watts, Cedric. *Joseph Conrad: A Literary Life*. Basingstoke, UK: Macmillan, 1989.

Selected Critical Studies

Bloom, Harold, ed. *Joseph Conrad's Nostromo*. New York: Chelsea House, 1987.

Guerard, Albert J. *Conrad the Novelist*. Cambridge, MA: Harvard University Press, 1958.

Jameson, Fredric. *The Political Unconscious: Narrative as a Socially Symbolic Act*. Ithaca, NY: Cornell University Press, 1981.

Leavis, F. R. *The Great Tradition: George Eliot, Henry James, Joseph Conrad*. London: Chatto and Windus, 1948.

Said, Edward W. *Beginnings: Intention and Method*. 1975. Reprint: New York: Columbia University Press, 1985.

Sherry, Norman. *Conrad's Western World*. Cambridge: Cambridge University Press, 1971.

——, ed. *Conrad: The Critical Heritage*. London and Boston: Routledge and Kegan Paul, 1973.

Watt, Ian. *Conrad in the Nineteenth Century*. Berkeley: University of California Press, 1979.

——. *Joseph Conrad: Nostromo*. New York: Cambridge University Press, 1988.

Watts, Cedric. *A Preface to Conrad*. Second edition: London and New York: Longman, 1993.

——. *Joseph Conrad: "Nostromo."* London: Penguin, 1990.

Other Works Cited in the Introduction

Conrad, Joseph. "Books." In *Notes on Life and Letters*. 1921. Reprint: Garden City, NY: Doubleday, 1924.

———. *A Personal Record*. 1912. Reprint: Garden City, NY: Doubleday, 1924.

———. *The Mirror of the Sea*. 1906. Reprint: Garden City, NY: Doubleday, 1924.

———. *The Collected Letters of Joseph Conrad*. Vol. 2: 1898–1902. Edited by Frederick R. Karl and Laurence Davies. Cambridge and New York: Cambridge University Press, 1986.

———. *The Collected Letters of Joseph Conrad*. Vol. 3: 1903–1907. Edited by Frederick R. Karl and Laurence Davies. Cambridge and New York: Cambridge University Press, 1988.

———. *The Collected Letters of Joseph Conrad*. Vol. 5: 1912–1916. Edited by Frederick R. Karl and Laurence Davies. Cambridge and New York: Cambridge University Press, 1996.

———. *The Collected Letters of Joseph Conrad*. Vol. 6: 1917–1919. Edited by Laurence Davies, Frederick R. Karl, and Owen Knowles. Cambridge and New York: Cambridge University Press, 2002.

Kirschner, Paul. *Conrad: The Psychologist as Artist*. Edinburgh: Oliver and Boyd, 1968.

Norman, Sherry. "Introduction" to Joseph Conrad. *Nostromo*. London: Dent/Everyman's Library, 1972.

Warren, Robert Penn. "Introduction" to Joseph Conrad. *Nostromo*. New York: Modern Library, 1951.

Woolf, Virginia. "Mr. Conrad's Crisis." *Times Literary Supplement* (March 14, 1918). Collected in *The Essays of Virginia Woolf*. Vol. 2: 1912–1918, edited by Andrew McNeillie. San Diego, CA: Harcourt Brace Jovanovich, 1987.